FIGHTING DESIRE

I fought Gideon. I had to fight him. I struck out with hard fists at his head and shoulders, pounded them into his back as he caught me and dragged me forward against his chest. I did everything, in fact, but the one thing that *would* have stopped him, this simple calling out to my maid for help. His mouth hurt mine, his tongue parting my lips was an invasion, his teeth sinking into my tongue seemed to draw blood, his hands, taking in possession of whatever they could, maddened me. I fought him and the lasting truth is—oh yes, and I was well aware of it—that I was fighting not to make him stop but because the battle itself was exciting, splendid, a rich and rare feast in itself for my starved senses.

I wanted Gideon—and I feared him. . . .

An
Independent Woman

Great Reading from SIGNET

An Independent Woman

by
Brenda Jagger

Ⓞ

A SIGNET BOOK

NEW AMERICAN LIBRARY

TIMES MIRROR

Publisher's Note

This novel is a work of fiction. Names, characters, places, and incidents either are the product of the author's imagination or are used fictitiously, and any resemblance to actual persons, living or dead, events, or locales is entirely coincidental.

Copyright © 1982 by Brenda Jagger

Published in Great Britain under the title THE SLEEPING SWORD

 SIGNET TRADEMARK REG. U.S. PAT. OFF. AND FOREIGN COUNTRIES
REGISTERED TRADEMARK—MARCA REGISTRADA
HECHO EN CHICAGO, U.S.A.

SIGNET, SIGNET CLASSIC, MENTOR, PLUME, MERIDIAN AND NAL BOOKS are published by The New American Library, Inc., 1633 Broadway, New York, New York 10019

First Signet Printing, December, 1983

1 2 3 4 5 6 7 8 9

PRINTED IN THE UNITED STATES OF AMERICA

To Marjory
who was with me every step of the way.

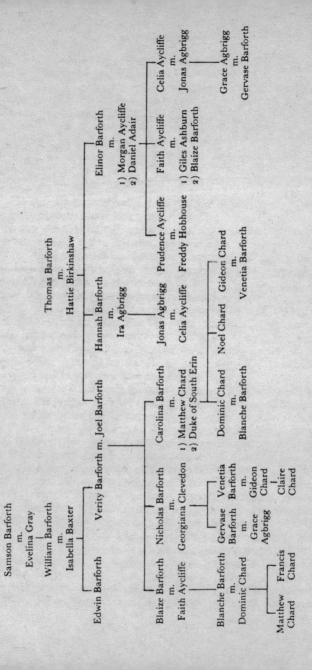

I

IT WOULD HAVE BEEN EASIER, perhaps, had my father's wife been a truly wicked woman, in which case I could have detested her with a whole heart and a clear conscience. But her villainy was of a mild enough variety, the result, mainly, of her desire to be my father's wife rather than the mother of his child. And, in all fairness, it must be said that I made no great effort to be lovable.

Her name, when we first knew her, was Mrs. Tessa Delaney and she was a handsome woman of large proportions, very smooth and wise and persuasive; not virtuous, of course, in any conventional sense since she had first taken up residence in our thriving factory city under the protection of one of its most distinguished aldermen, the elderly, childless and reputedly self-indulgent worsted-spinner, Mr. Matthew Oldroyd of Fieldhead Mills. Yet their affair had been so discreetly conducted that even the Oldroyd relatives came to regard it on the whole as a good thing, the keeping of so sensible a mistress being preferable in their eyes and working out much cheaper than the greedy sixteen year olds to which his aging fancy had hitherto been prone.

Indeed, the Oldroyd nephews and nieces who certainly expected to inherit his money would have been much inclined to offer Mrs. Delaney some material token of their gratitude at the end—allowed her to keep his watch or even the lease on the house he had taken for her—had not his last will and testament revealed that for the twelve secretive and shameful months before he died she had been no mistress at all but Mr. Matthew Oldroyd's second and decidedly legal wife.

Clandestine marriages, needed it be said, did not suit the taste of our plain-spoken, strait-laced town of Cullingford in the County of Yorkshire, and there had been immediate talk of breaking the Oldroyd will. And even when the Oldroyd lawyer, my father Mr. Jonas Agbrigg, declared himself unable to place any legal obstacle in the lady's way when she proceeded to move into the mill-house at Fieldhead, it was felt that she would not reign there long. After all, she had cheated the Oldroyd nephews—Cullingford men every one—out of their rightful inheritance and if the Law as represented by Mr. Jonas Agbrigg could not touch her then surely a Greater Law might be relied on to prevail? Surely—and Cullingford men were deeply moved by this—Fate could not allow any female so rapacious, so cunning, to actually *enjoy* her ill-gotten gains?

But the proud, easy carriage, the clear skin and excellent white teeth we had seen in Mrs. Delaney continued to flourish in the new Mrs. Oldroyd to such a degree that my father, who had won a reputation for shrewdness rather than kindness of heart—although he was always kindness itself to me—married her as soon as he was able, thus making himself absolute master of her fortune and creating a scandal of a magnitude rarely seen in the cautious, conventional Law Valley.

No one thought any the worse of a man who married for money, since most men did so, and a widower with an eleven year old daughter to raise and whose ambitions had always been larger than his pocket, could not afford to be too romantic when it came to matrimony. But my father's hasty union with Mrs. Delaney marked him not merely as a fortune-hunter but as a conspirator. And Cullingford had a thing or two to say about that.

He had been Matthew Oldroyd's lawyer, after all, and Cullingford well remembered how completely Mr. Oldroyd had trusted him. He had certainly been aware of the secret ceremony which had transformed Mr. Oldroyd from Mrs. Delaney's lover, who might have left her a few hundred a year, to a doting husband who had bequeathed her everything. Even more certainly he had been aware of Mr. Oldroyd's new will, signed in my father's office on that furtive wedding morning, when the decaying bridegroom had virtually disinherited every one of his relations, his first wife's family it was true, not his own blood kin, but decent Yorkshire folk just the same who had deserved better of him than that. And afterwards my father had moved quietly through Cullingford's dining-rooms and drawing-rooms, a close-mouthed man accustomed to secrets, listening as the Oldroyd nephews hinted at their plans for Fieldhead Mills, for the railway shares and brewery shares, the coal deposits and bank deposits of which Mr. Oldroyd had been so amply possessed.

He had listened without comment, without encouragement,

but when the awful truth burst upon them the mere fact that he had listened at all was enough to condemn him. He was marrying the whore Delaney not for her money but for *theirs;* for the fortune which he, with his lawyer's cunning, had helped her to steal from a bemused and senile man. They had conspired together—*of course* they had—Mr. Jonas Agbrigg and Mrs. Tessa Delaney, the cool, fastidious man of the law, the mature and sensible Jezebel, and Cullingford did not intend to countenance treachery such as that. No Cullingford woman of any standing would ever receive the new Mrs. Agbrigg, at least so they said and probably believed, while Cullingford men would be interested to see what use the Cambridge educated Jonas Agbrigg might make of his Latin and his Greek in the spinning-sheds at Fieldhead.

My father's own mother, my outspoken and unbending Grandmother Agbrigg and my grandfather, who had several times been mayor of Cullingford, would not attend the wedding and retired soon afterwards to Scarborough unable to tolerate their son's disgrace. My mother's mother, my dainty and sentimental Grandmamma Elinor, could not bring herself to attend either and she too, with a rapidity I could not help associating with these painful nuptials, soon lost her taste for Cullingford, exchanging her house in imposing but narrow-minded Blenheim Lane for a villa in the South of France. Only my mother's sister, Aunt Faith, was present in the Parish Church on my father's wedding day among the Fieldhead managers and their wives—proving they knew on which side their bread was buttered—and a handful of others, Mr. Septimus Rawnsley of the Cullingford Commercial Bank, Mr. Outhwaite, a local architect who could not afford to ignore the rumours of repairs and extensions at Fieldhead; a few ecclesiastical gentlemen who believed in the forgiveness of sinners, a few commercial gentlemen for whom the only real sin was poverty and who could detect no trace of it in the regal bearing of my father's bride. While I, banished to the seaside for the duration of the honeymoon, felt my solid, reliable world turn suddenly to an uncertain angle and then start to slip away—as my grandparents, my home, my father's good name, our shared and precious affection had slipped away—between my hands.

My memories of my mother at that time were recent and uneasy for she had died only a year before my father's second marriage and it was a matter of great concern to me that I did not really miss her. She had been an invalid since my birth, tense and timid and often very low in spirits, the tumult of her nerves demanding drawn curtains, hushed voices, a great walking-on-tiptoe on my part through her sufferings which oppressed me, sometimes annoyed me and then instantly filled me with guilt. And I knew two things about her relationship with my father; that he was not happy with her and that he had been lucky to get her.

My father was the academically brilliant son of a man who had risen from great poverty to become a mill-manager, a rise quite astonishing in itself although never quite enough to satisfy the social ambitions of Grandmother Agbrigg who had decided very early to make at least a cabinet minister out of her son. And since a mill-manager can earn so much and no more and political careers are notoriously expensive, it had been essential for my father to marry well, his choice falling on my mother—Miss Celia Aycliffe—I suspect because she had been very young, exceedingly innocent, and so crammed full of romantic notions that she had been ready to fall in love with the first person who asked.

She had brought him a substantial dowry for her father had been a master-builder, responsible for the erection of most of Cullingford and its environs, and he had left his widow—my pert little Grandmamma Elinor—and his daughters very well provided. But the dowry had been sufficient only for the purchase of a suitable house and a partnership with a local solicitor, my mother's interests had all been domestic, her disposition retiring—not at all the stuff that cabinet ministers' wives are made of—and they had not been content together.

Perhaps he felt she had given him less than he deserved. No doubt, in her view, he had received more than any man in his position could reasonably expect, for, money apart, she had brought him family connections worth their weight in gold. Her own family, the Aycliffes, were themselves people of enormous local consequence. Their cousins, the Barforths, were the most powerful industrialists the Law Valley had ever known, the Barforth brothers, Nicholas and Blaize—who had married Aunt Faith, my mother's sister—appearing to own outright or to have a controlling interest in everything of value in Cullingford. While the Barforth sister, my Aunt Caroline, being unable to compete on the battleground of commerce on account of her sex, had chosen to devote her quite formidable energies to the pursuit of social advancement, becoming Lady Chard of Listonby Park, thus widening our horizons by allying us to the landed gentry.

With connections such as these my mother was at a loss to

know what else she could offer her husband. She concluded it should be a son, miscarried eight times to produce a daughter and devoted herself thereafter to the supervision of her servants—by no means so numerous as those of her sister, Aunt Faith—fretting over specks of dust, smears on silver, stains on linen, wearing out her nerves and my father's patience until the day she died. And exactly one year later her well-dusted, well-polished house was sold to strangers, the daughter whose birth had cost her her health believed herself to be unwanted and lonely, while her husband was a poor relation of the mighty Barforths no longer but the master of Fieldhead.

Fieldhead mill-house was a square, sombre pile built at the start of the Oldroyd fortunes, large, high-ceilinged rooms, functional and plain, a vast, stone-flagged kitchen equipped with a strict eye to efficiency, no eye at all to comfort, not even a rocking chair by the hearth on the day I was invited to inspect this new setting for my life. "A very handsome house" the Law Valley called it yet the only concession I could see to beauty was the profusion of polished wood, each room oak-panelled, fragrant with bees-wax and the winter hyacinths set out everywhere in copper bowls, a combination of odours which even now returns me to the afternoon I first stood there, tall for a girl of not quite twelve, long legs, thin shoulders that were too wide, dark brown hair Aunt Faith had brushed and plaited for the approval of my father's wife, although for my part I could not see the necessity for that approval, feeling, I believe, that she should have been anxious to gain mine. And had I been old enough to cope with the hostility she at once aroused in me—for he was my father, *mine*, and not even my own mother had expected him to love her better than me—perhaps I would have admired her.

They had called her the whore Delaney and now—Aunt Faith had explained to me—in order to be considered respectable at all she would have to be very respectable indeed. Her housekeeping, if it was barely to satisfy her ill-wishers, would have to be superb, her manners altogether beyond anyone's reproach. She had far more important things to do, in fact, than cater to the whims of a green and awkward girl, having made up her mind to take the entire fortress of polite Cullingford society by storm. And when she received me that first time in the Fieldhead drawing-room she had not only the air of a woman born to these surroundings but of one at whose christening all the virtues—honesty, chastity, industry and the rest—had attended. She wore a dark silk dress, jet beads, narrow gold chains, her black hair smoothly parted at the centre and drawn down in two modest wings to frame a countenance of placid dignity. She walked erect and very slow, sat straight-backed, her large brown hands quietly folded. She spoke words of authority, her voice low, gentle, inescapable. She had presence and power and she was very handsome. I detested her and for the five years that remained to me before childhood officially ended and my upswept hair and long skirts proclaimed me a young lady my life was marred constantly and foolishly by our mutual resentment, the thoughtless cruelty of my youth, the anxious cruelty of her middle-age, which caused us to struggle for the same not always happy man.

At no time did it occur to me that he might be fond of her. He had married her for money, *only* for money, I insisted upon that, and although privately I did not think it worthy of him I justified it all on the grounds of his frustrated brilliance, the long bitterness I knew he had felt on seeing other men succeed—the Barforth men, for instance—not because they surpassed him in intelligence or energy—who, I wondered, could surpass him in that?—but because they had been born to fathers who could pay. And although my faith in him had wavered I soon learned to be proud of him again. He had come late to the spinning trade, a soft-skinned lawyer in middle life, and the thoroughness with which he mastered each technical process, the determination which took him to the mill-yard at the grim morning hour of five o'clock and kept him there, often enough, until midnight won him not only my regard but the grudging respect of many who had firmly intended to despise him. Cullingford might never again consider him a good man. He was beyond question a fortune-hunter. He may even have tipped Mr. Oldroyd's scales a little in the direction of matrimony and that scandalous will. But, very soon, he was *making a profit* and after a year or two it became the considered opinion of the Piece Hall and the Wool Exchange that much could be forgiven a man who did that.

The new Mrs. Agbrigg, who had been the new Mrs. Oldroyd, who had been the whore Delaney, had won her battle and all might have been peace and contentment at Fieldhead had I not been there to question her slightest command, to pick disdainful holes in her explanations, to neglect no opportunity of letting her know that the bond between father and daughter—or at least between *this* father and daughter—was of a far higher order than anything that might exist between a man and his second wife.

"You see it all through such young eyes," Aunt Faith murmured once or twice, attempting—as my mother's sister and therefore my closest female relation—to console and advise me. But youth is not compassionate and at fourteen, fifteen, even at sixteen when I found my eyes on a level with hers, I could see nothing in the new Mrs. Agbrigg to arouse my pity. She had wanted wealth and security. They were hers. She had desired, from the colourful remains of Tessa Delaney, to create a new woman of intense, heavy-textured respectability. She had achieved that too. Yet this same woman who assembled her servants each morning for prayers, who served tea and charity to this clergyman and that each tedious afternoon, had also retained a weapon I had not yet learned to call sensuality. Her sombre dignity, her suave piety stifled me, but the sight of her hand on my father's arm at dinner time, the voluptuous curve of neck and shoulder she offered him through the lamplight aroused in me a prickly senation I recognized as shame.

"Jonas darling, it is late," and to avoid the hush that fell around them whenever she spoke those simple words I became an almost professional guest in the other people's houses, lingering with Aunt Faith and her daughter Blanche from Christmas to Easter, spending easy, if well-chaperoned summers at the sea with my other Barforth cousin, Venetia. A guest, a close friend, not quite a member of any family not even my own, so that growing sharp-eyed, self-contained, careful of how and where I might tread, it was no hardship to me to go abroad to Italy and Switzerland, to acquire the accomplishments thought appropriate to the heiress—no less—of Fieldhead.

I was as tall as my father when he came to Lucerne to fetch me home, my hair piled high and swept back in a cascade of curls, my skirts most fashionably tight in front, most fashionably and intricately draped behind over a bustle I had learned to manage with style, having acquired by studious practice the art of kicking my train aside in order to turn smartly around, the equally precise art of sitting down. And as I demonstrated my knowledge of Italian and French and German Swiss, of painting and sculpture and as much philosophy as they had thought safe for a young lady—my flair for mathematics being considered quite unladylike—I found him far less exacting, an easier or perhaps just an older man than I remembered. I had gained not only an understanding of art and science but of humanity—or so I imagined—and now that my father was no longer the centre of my universe, now that I was the polished Miss Grace Agbrigg whose experiences had ranged far beyond the confines of Cullingford, I believed I could be at peace with him.

"You see it all through such young eyes," Aunt Faith had said, but my eyes were kinder now—I thought, I hoped—while my tongue might even school itself, in the interests of domestic harmony, to call my father's wife "mamma."

She was on the carriage drive to greet us, smooth, impassive, her gown of chocolate coloured silk drawn into a modest bustle, nothing but a fall of lace at neck and hem to relieve its housekeeper's plainness. But the fabric itself was very rich, the cross at her throat was of massive gold, there were rings of great value on her patiently folded, housekeeper's hands, her voice speaking its soft welcome, her eyes going beyond me to my father, wryly conveying to him, "So she's home again. Ah well—we must make the best of it, you and I." And everything was the same, exactly as it had always been and as I had known it would be.

There were great things astir in Cullingford. My cousin Blanche was to be richly married, which was the destiny Blanche Barforth had always envisaged. My other Barforth cousin, Venetia, was believed not for the first time to have involved herself with an unsuitable man. While as to myself, for all my new found philosophy and compassion, it was very clear to me from the hour of my return that the only way I could ever restore harmony to my father's house was by leaving it.

2

My COUSIN, BLANCHE BARFORTH, WAS married on a sparkling summer morning, her veil of gauze embroideries mistily revealing the silver and ivory tints of her hair and skin, her long, quiet hands clasping their bouquet of apricot carnations and white roses. She looked fragile and mysterious, passive as a lily, the prize men seek for their valour and expect for their cunning. A most perfect bride.

She was not, of course, in love nor did she wish to be. She was merely following to its logical conclusion her personal and undeniably excellent strategy of doing the right thing at the right time and doing it magnificently. In the manner of Queen Victoria and Prince Albert she was marrying her first cousin and in true imperial fashion appeared to believe that her own role in the proceedings was simply to be looked at.

For the past six months she had been ''the fiancée'' offering herself up tranquilly to the world's admiration and envy while her harassed mother and her Aunt Caroline, who was soon to be her mother-in-law, arranged her wedding around her. Today she was ''the bride,'' offering herself once again with that air of cool serenity to a bridegroom who, by the untimely death of his father on the hunting field, had recently been transformed from a supercilious and, in my view, not entirely good-tempered young man into an extremely eligible if no better-humoured Sir Dominic Chard of Listonby.

Without his lands and titles it would not have occurred to Blanche to marry him. Had she been obtainable to him in any other way he would not have married her, since a gentleman of only twenty-four summers with health and wealth and boundless opportunity on his side rarely feels the need to limit himself in matrimony so soon. But pale, silvery Blanche *had* her loveliness and her calm, infinitely challenging purity. Dominic *had* his baronetcy, his three thousand ancestral acres, his beautiful, quite famous ancestral mansion. There was no more to be said.

"I am to be married," Blanche had written to me in Switzerland. "I am to be Lady Chard of Listonby, just like Aunt Caroline—except, of course, that I am taking her title from her. You are to come home and be my bridesmaid." And so, feeling the moment opportune, I returned to Cullingford to divide my time, as I had so often done, between my Barforth cousins, Blanche who was to be splendidly married and Venetia who would quite like to be married but would much rather fall intensely, no matter how unwisely, in love.

I had, of course, envied Blanche from time to time as most people did, not only for her looks, her composure and her placid, sometimes comic, belief that she could always get her way, but for the possession of so affectionate a mother as Aunt Faith, so generous a father as Uncle Blaize who was not, perhaps, the richer of the two Barforth brothers but certainly the more agreeable.

"That child is the image of her mother," they had been saying in Cullingford ever since the days when a fragile, fairy-tale Blanche had first taken her daily airings in the Barforth landau, her gown a miniature copy of Aunt Faith's, each silver ringlet bound up with silver ribbon, exhibiting even then a certain cool graciousness far beyond her years which came, perhaps, from an inbred knowledge that her abundant pale silk hair and startling blue-green eyes would be quite enough to open any door *she* might be likely to choose in life.

And what she chose at the tender age of seventeen was to be Lady Chard of Listonby Park, a decision which had disappointed her mother who believed ardently in love and was saddened to see that her only daughter did not, and which had infuriated the existing, dowager Lady Chard—Aunt Caroline—who, having been the absolute ruler of Listonby Park for the past twenty-five years did not feel at all inclined to abdicate her authority, her keys, her place at the head of the baronial table to lovely, lazy, self-indulgent Blanche.

So strongly, in fact, did Aunt Caroline Chard feel that, at the merest hint of an engagement she had despatched her son Dominic to London, hoping at worst that he would find distraction, at best the earl's or the cabinet minister's daughter she believed *his* breeding and *her* ambition deserved. For although Lady Caroline Chard had once, long ago, been Miss Caroline Barforth, a mill-master's daughter just like Blanche, she had shed that commercial identity and very nearly forgotten it. Barforth money, indeed, had enabled her to shine at Listonby, her own share of Barforth energy, tenacity, the urge all the Barforths felt to pursue success had enabled her to place it among the most luxurious and hospitable houses of the North. The Barforth in her had caused her to break down, trample underfoot, or simply to ignore all obstacles in her path, but that same Barforth driving force, even as it had swept her on from triumph to social triumph, had, by some strange act of metamorphosis, converted her entirely into a Chard. And in her heart of hearts she did not believe that Blanche Barforth, who was beautiful and rich and her own brother's daughter, could really be good enough for her eldest son.

But Dominic had always been stubborn. Blanche had made up both his mind and her own, and here they were, an exquisite bride, a handsome groom, with myself and Venetia standing behind them in our bridesmaids finery of apricot silk, thinking, I suppose, that next time—quite soon—eventually—we would be brides and wives and mothers ourselves.

Venetia was the daughter of the second Barforth brother, Mr. Nicholas Barforth, a gentleman whose restless ambition and overwhelming shrewdness had not allowed him to be content with the fortune his father had left him and which he and his brother had divided between them. Blanche's father, Uncle Blaize, had taken good care of his money, making absolutely certain that it amply sufficed for the very pleasant life he enjoyed with Aunt Faith. But Venetia's father had set himself, with a singleness of purpose rare even in the Law Valley, to increase his inheritance, had extended and diversified it to become the owner not only of the original Barforth mills of Lawcroft Fold and Low Cross where worsteds of the very finest quality continued to be woven, but of such gigantic undertakings as the Law Valley Woolcombers, the Law Valley Dyers and Finishers, and, more recently, a brand new structure of Italianate design built on the site of an old mill at Nethercoats where the weaving of silk and velvet was making Mr. Nicholas Barforth's fortune for the second, the third, or even for the fourth time.

Yet his acute judgment in the field of commerce had not extended to his private life and even his well-wishers—relatively few, it seemed, in number—were forced to admit that none of his personal relationships had prospered. He had quarrelled violently and unforgiveably with his brother and no hostess in Cullingford would have dared invite both Blaize and Nicholas Barfoth to her table at the same time. He had quarrelled with all his mill-managers in turn, making no secret that although he paid high wages a man needed nerves of steel and the stamina of an ox to earn them. He was known to live in a state of bitter discord with his son, to have little time for Venetia, his daughter, while his relationship with his wife had been a source of gossip and speculation in Cullingford for many a long day.

Unlike his brother who had chosen Aunt Faith from the manufacturing middle-classes, Mr. Nicholas Barforth, following his sister Caroline's lead perhaps, had married into the landed gentry. But while Caroline Barforth's marriage had brought her Listonby Park and the title that went with it, Nicholas Barforth had received nothing but a fine-boned, high-bred, quite penniless lady and—it was rumoured—a great deal of trouble. For once, long ago in Venetia's early childhood, her mother had run away from her father and had been brought back again—or so we believed—a mystery Cullingford had never solved to its satisfaction, the gentleman in the story being unapproachable, the lady well-nigh invisible.

"How is your dear mamma?" Cullingford's matrons, unwilling to be cheated of so promising a scandal, were fond of asking Venetia.

"Very well indeed," was her only reply. But the fact that her mother lived almost exclusively at her house in the country, the ancient estate of Galton Abbey with its few hundred scrubby acres and its decaying mansion—a far cry from Listonby Park—which had been in Mrs. Barforth's family for generations, while her father resided permanently at *his* house in Cullingford, troubled Venetia deeply. And this pall of scandal hovering around her parents—for if they *were* separated then there must have been a mighty scandal indeed—had drawn us together; Venetia about whose mother strange things were whispered, nothing proved, and myself, Grace Agbrigg, motherless daughter of a man who, by his marriage to a rich and disreputable woman, had invited scandal and for most of the time managed to ignore it.

Venetia was not beautiful like Blanche, her figure being of an extreme quite boyish slenderness, something sudden and brittle about her movements, an air—every now and then—that was both vulnerable and eager; for whereas Blanche had always known what she wanted from life Venetia quite simply wanted everything life had to offer, its joys and sorrows, triumphs and disasters, as soon as she could lay her hands on them and in double measure. She had a thin, fine-textured face, a delicate skin, eyebrows that flew away at a wide angle, hair the rich colour of a woodland fox, her pointed auburn looks owing nothing to her tough-grained Barforth father but coming entirely from her mother, the lady who had been the subject, or the cause, of scandal. And although Venetia herself had done nothing of a scandalous nature Cullingford believed, on the whole, in the saying "like mother like daughter" and many would have advised Mr. Nicholas Barforth, had they dared, to get his daughter married while he was able.

But today, standing meekly behind immaculate, triumphant Blanche, we were shielded from past gossip, being simply "the bridesmaids," anonymous girls in pretty dresses provided like the icing on the cake, the lace frills around the bridal posies, simply to decorate. It was, of course, a lovely wedding, somewhat to the surprise of the bridegroom's mother, Aunt Caroline, who, with her vast enthusiasm for entertaining, her twenty-five years experience of balls and dinners, house parties, hunting parties, parties of all shapes and sizes at Listonby had found it hard to leave to Aunt Faith the planning of so vital an event as the wedding of Listonby's eldest son. But, despite her predictions that Aunt Faith would forget this and neglect that, nothing had been overlooked, nothing left to chance.

The horses which brought the bridal procession to church were all high-stepping, glossy with good health and good grooming and—as Aunt Caroline had insisted was essential for a wedding—all perfectly, correctly grey. The carriages were lined with white satin, the church transformed into a flower-garden of white and apricot blossoms, the aristocratic Chards on one side of the aisle, a sprinkling of baronets and Members of Parliament, at least three bishops, half a dozen generals and one real duke among them; the manufacturing Barforths on the other side, millmasters, ironmasters, bankers, builders, although the differences between them were less marked than they had once been. A commercial gentleman of a generation ago might have felt a sense of achievement, of having breached a stronghold hitherto impregnable to men of his station had he succeeded in bestowing his daughter on a High Church, High Tory squire. But now, although all three of those Chard bishops still preached the doctrine that God, having called all men to the position he had selected for them in life wished them to stay there, the Barforths knew better than that, my manufacturing Uncle Blaize escorting his daughter to her noble bridegroom with grace and good humour, perfectly at ease among the "ruling classes," especially nowadays when, in many cases, their power to go on ruling depended on the co-operation of his—and his brother's—money.

A lovely wedding. There was a flood of golden sunshine as we left the church, a cloudless summer sky, no need at all for the huge marquee spread like the palace of an Arabian prince on the lawns of Aunt Faith's home in suburban Elderleigh. There were bowls of pale roses on every table, in accordance with Aunt Caroline's oft repeated suggestion that in Aunt Faith's place she would be *lavish* with the flowers. The menu-cards—printed in silver and in French—had the additional extravagance of silver lace borders. The cake, which Aunt Caroline had feared would never be big enough to conform to Chard standards of size and grandeur, was immense, intricate, surrounded by sprays of the same white roses and apricot carnations which made up the bridal bouquet and which would be distributed later to each female guest.

There was champagne, violins concealed romantically by the swaying summer trees, curiosity, a little mild envy, a few sentimental tears. "A handsome couple" everyone was saying and so they were, Blanche looking more fragile than ever among the dark, large-boned Chards, her bridegroom and his two brothers with whom I was not well acquainted, for unlike the young commercial gentlemen I knew who had all been educated at our local grammar school, the Chard boys had gone away to school at an early age, returning at midsummer and Christmastime when I had found their loud, drawling voices irritating, their manners condescending. And they had looked so much alike—Dominic, Noel, Gideon—that they had seemed to me to be quite interchangeable; self-opinionated boys who would grow to be haughty men of the kind one encountered on the hunting field, in fashionable regiments and fashionable London clubs or half asleep on the benches of the House of Commons.

Dominic's future, of course, had been mapped out for him at birth for he was the eldest, the heir to his father's lands and titles, Squire of Listonby, Master of Foxhounds, Chairman of the Bench of Magistrates, while his twin brother Noel—born ten vital minutes too late to claim the inheritance—and Gideon, 18 months younger still, were simply the extra sons who—unless some tragic fate should befall the heir—would be obliged to make their own way in the world, their father having no secondary titles, no spare estates to bestow on them. Following the family tradition of service Noel—it had been decided as Aunt Caroline first looked into his cradle—would go into the army, Gideon into the church where, having completed the preliminaries of promotion their mother saw no reason why they should not join the prosperous ranks of Chard generals, Chard bishops and make advantageous marriages while they were about it. And Aunt Caroline had expressed these aims so often, with such total certainty, that in my half-attending mind they had become aims no longer but realities. Noel *was* a general, Gideon *was* a bishop so that I had been mildly surprised on my return from Switzerland to meet a very gallant Lieutenant Noel Chard and to hear some very strange rumours indeed in respect to Gideon.

"I suppose one can feel for Aunt Caroline," Blanche had informed me airily. "For she has never liked her plans to be upset, and first there was Dominic who was supposed to be a bachelor until his fifties, or so she hoped, so she could go on queening it at Listonby. And now there is Gideon."

And when I had expressed a degree of interest I did not feel, she went on, "Yes, indeed. Poor Aunt Caroline. She had set her heart on making Gideon a bishop and he has turned her down flat. He says there is no money in religion, which surprises me since all the clergymen we know seem to live very well—except that I think Gideon means a *lot* of money and spending it on things clergymen don't have, or shouldn't have. I expect you are dying to hear what it is he means to do?"

"I expect you are dying to tell me."

"He says he will go where the money is—heavens, I can picture Aunt Caroline's face when he said that—and so he has made an approach to my Uncle Nicholas Barforth with a view to joining him in his mills. Yes, you may stare, indeed you may, for I stared too. A Chard in trade! Whatever next? The Barforth blood coming out, I suppose, and Aunt Caroline cannot bear to mention it—not to her London friends and her foxhunting friends at any rate. But since we all know the trouble Uncle Nicholas Barforth has with Cousin Gervase—although Venetia, of course, will not hear a word against her brother—well, I think he may be glad of Gideon. Poor Aunt Caroline, indeed. For if Gideon does well with Uncle Nicholas he will surely try to marry Venetia. Well, of course he will, Grace. In fact he *must* marry her in order to secure his position, for if he does not then someone else surely will. And that 'someone,' if he has the sense he was born with, will be bound to cut Gideon out of the business. It absolutely stands to reason."

So it did, and remembering it now on Blanche's own wedding day, I shivered, for I was an heiress too—like Venetia, like Blanche—who might be so easily married not for the pleasure of my company but because marriage to me brought with it the eventual ownership of Fieldhead Mills. Naturally my father would take care in his selection, would look for a bridegroom who was sound in business, high of principle, even kind-hearted. But I knew that the dread of it, the sheer humiliation of being courted for anything other than myself, had made me aloof and suspicious of men since I first understood the size of my fortune and its implications. I could not accept it. I did not think Venetia could accept it either and, watching Blanche for whom it all seemed perfectly natural, who considered her money a fair enough exchange for Dominic's title, I shivered once again.

Aunt Faith received her guests with enormous tact and skill, necessary accomplishments in a family gathering such as ours where the Chards were uncompromisingly Tory and High Church to a man, the Barforths Liberal in politics and Noncomformist in religion, where it was vital that my father's wife and my father's mother should be kept apart; where my father himself must not be allowed to stray into the company of anyone connected at all closely with the Oldroyd nephews; where Mr. Nicholas Barforth, the uncle of the bride, had not spoken a civil word to his brother, the bride's father, in twenty years; where Mr. Nicholas Barforth's wife, if she came at all, would only come under suffrance, to "keep up appearances" and must be sheltered from the curiosity of Cullingford's ladies, the occasionally ribald speculation of our gentlemen.

On Aunt Faith's instructions my Grandmother Agbrigg was at once surrounded by a screen of elderly ladies, my Stepmother Agbrigg just as swiftly introduced to one of the Chard bishops—since what in the world could convey more respectability than that?—and to a merry little gentleman who happened to be the Duke of South Erin, neither particularly rich nor particularly important but a *duke* just the same, and a frequent visitor of Aunt Caroline Chard's at Listonby. But no skill of Aunt Faith's could halt the sudden whispering, the turning of heads, the eyes that pretended not to look and the eyes that looked openly, avidly, when Mr. Nicholas Barforth's carriage was seen on the drive, a lady in a tall green hat beside him, for this was no local scandal, no simple tale of prickly middle-class morality but was of interest to everyone. Mrs. Tessa Delaney had been notorious in Cullingford. Mrs. Agbrigg was still somewhat suspect there. But the whole County of Yorkshire, or the sporting, landed portion of it, was acquainted with Mrs. Georgiana Barforth who was usually to be found not under her husband's imposing roof but in her decaying manor house at Galton Abbey. All three of the

Chard bishops knew her. The Chard generals and colonels had served in the same regiment or played cards at the same clubs as her father; the Duke of South Erin had shot grouse over her moor at Galton many a time. And if these gentlemen were inclined to take a broader, easier view than Cullingford, she remained nevertheless a woman who did not appear to lead a regular life, who might be socially very dangerous, or very interesting, to know; who could, in fact, be approached with a familiarity and with an intent no man would permit himself with a lady who was *known* to reside safely in her matrimonial home.

And, of course, it was the uncertainty which everyone found so intriguing and so maddening. Were the Nicholas Barforths separated or were they not? Did she live in the country for her health, as had once or twice been hinted, or was that just a part of the charade they were playing to make things *look* right; so that their conflict might not damage their unmarried and consequently very vulnerable daughter? Had Mr. Nicholas Barforth banished his wife from his hearth and home unable to support her aristocratic freedom of manner, which had never been greatly to the liking of Cullingford in any case? Or had she fled away from him in protest at his money-grubbing, middle-class ways? Had there been misconduct, which in Cullingford could be taken to mean adultery, and if so whose adultery, when, with whom?

Mrs. Rawnsley of Rawnsley's Bank felt certain that there had been cruelty and adultery on the gentleman's part which the lady had probably deserved. Mrs. Sheldon, the devoted wife of Mr. Thomas Sheldon MP tended, without actually saying so, to take the deserted husband's part since the wife, as a woman, had no vote and could therefore be no serious loss to Mr. Sheldon at election time. Miss Fielding, the spinster daughter of our other now very elderly MP condemned no one, such an attitude being contrary to her Christian principles, although having done her own duty unstintingly all her life she was bound to feel that Mrs. Georgiana Barforth, by this desertion of her husband and her home, had lamentably failed in hers. And the rest of Cullingford, sifting through these divers views, concluded that, like everything else of importance in the Law Valley, it had simply been a matter of money.

Mrs. Barforth had been well-bred but extremely poor. Mr. Nicholas Barforth had been common, as Cullingford itself was common beneath its prosperous veneer, but extremely rich. "She got what she came for and then she left," Cullingford gleefully pronounced, finding it pleasantly ironic that Mr. Nicholas Barforth who used his money so ruthlessly to manipulate others should have been so blatantly married for it.

Yet whatever the true facts of the matter, Mr. Barforth had retained the power to call his elusive lady to his side whenever it suited him, producing her annually at the Christmas concerts in the Memorial Hall, escorting her, always splendidly dressed, to the anniversary dinner of Cullingford's Charter, the gala opening of a new hotel, a fashionable wedding, so that no one, however inventive or malicious, could ever be sure.

But to Venetia's frank and eager nature these parental deceits were insupportable and I heard the sharp intake of her breath, saw how painfully she bit her lip, as she watched her mother get down from the Barforth carriage and take her father's arm.

"I told her not to come," she whispered, "for she cannot bear to see these Cullingford hens cackling and staring whenever she shows herself. I told her *I* wouldn't come, in her place. She just smiled and said that at my age she wouldn't have come either. And I can't tell you how much that startled me—to think she was once like me and has lost her nerve. How terrible."

She came slowly across the grass, her hand still on her husband's arm, trailing her elaborately draped skirts behind her with a regal disregard for the frailty or the cost of apple green satin and Brussels lace. Her hair, which had the same auburn sheen as Venetia's, was fashionably curled, her fine-etched, pointed face fashionably gay, a quick smile flitting on and off her lips in automatic greeting, her green eyes unwavering, nothing in her manner to indicate how much she had dreaded coming here, except that everyone knew it and many were hoping she would finally reach the end of her aristocratic tether and let it show.

But there was an added flavour to the spectacle today since Mr. Nicholas Barforth was not merely parading his wife to a hostile public but was on uncertain ground himself, having last entered this house over ten years ago with a legal document in his hand terminating his association with Blaize Barforth, his brother. And I heard, behind me, a collective sigh of anticipation as these two powerful men at last came face to face.

Cullingford, quite naturally had hoped for emotion. But such hopes were instantly dashed.

"Nicholas," said Blaize Barforth with a crisp, quite impersonal nod.

"Blaize," Nicholas Barforth replied in kind.

Clearly there was no more that could be usefully said.

We took our places at table soon afterwards, partook of rich food and old wines, laughed and applauded the witty, easy speech of the bride's father, admired the few well-chosen words of the groom—chosen, one could not doubt, by his mother Aunt Caroline. We drank toasts as we were bid, grew sentimental, or languid, or even a trifle bored. And when Blanche had floated away upstairs to change into the travelling dress Monsieur Worth had made for her in Paris, I watched my father's wife, Mrs. Agbrigg, rise from her place and skillfully reclaim her bishop, saw my father join the group of serious gentlemen who, on the paved terrace, were discussing wool prices, share prices, wondering when trade with France would be likely to pick up again now that so free-spending an emperor as the third Napoleon had been chased off his throne. I saw Mrs. Georgiana Barforth get up too and launch herself into the crowd like a blind swimmer, her progress impeded at every step by an ingratiating Cullingford smile, an inquisitive Cullingford eye, her own eyes constantly darting to her husband seeking his reassurance that she was saying the things he had brought her here to say, playing the part he had designed for her in the manner he had intended. I saw Aunt Caroline—the *Dowager* Lady Chard now—grimace in an unguarded moment with visible pain, her eyes on the chair Blanche had just vacated, her mind certainly dwelling on the beauty and prosperity of Listonby which she, who had created it, must now relinquish to a careless seventeen-year-old girl.

But the weather-beaten little Duke of South Erin moved quickly to Aunt Caroline's side. Venetia's brother, Gervase, came strolling around the corner of the house, glass in hand, to join the mother he so resembled, a wild young man who was far more at home, one heard, among the aristocratic pleasures of the hunting field and the gaming table than in his father's counting-house. The day was almost over. The Blaize Barforths had creditably married their daughter. Lady Caroline Chard had lost her life's work at Listonby as well as her son. The Nicholas Barforths had demonstrated that they were, in a manner of speaking, sufficiently united to stifle the worst of the rumours which might wreck the matrimonial prospects of *their* daughter, Venetia. Mrs. Agbrigg, my father's wife, had made the acquaintance of a bishop.

I had gained nothing, lost nothing. But remembering that tomorrow morning and the morning after I would be obliged to sit in Mrs. Agbrigg's drawing-room and dine at her table, I got up too and began to move aimlessly through the throng, recognizing myself to be as complete a captive as Mrs. Georgiana

Barforth and for the same reasons. We were women. We had no
money of our own and no means of earning or otherwise obtain-
ing any. We were dependent, luxuriously but completely, and
had the freedom of choice, it seemed to me, merely between the
authority of a father or of a husband.

I found Venetia as I had expected surrounded by her admirers,
swaying slightly towards this one and that, almost taking flight
in her eagerness to offer them her quick gestures and quick
smiles, her swift ripple of laughter, giving a little of herself to
each one and then, I soon noticed, turning back—for approval,
for pleasure, to make sure he was still watching her—to the same
man. No one, of course, of whom her father could possibly
approve but a certain Mr. Liam Adair, a relative of mine by
marriage, who had long been classified matrimonially as a bad
risk.

I had not consciously thought of Liam Adair for a long time
but watching him now, the dark, heavy-featured face I remembered,
the merry almost insolent black eyes, I was not surprised. He
was the son of an exceedingly witty and resourceful gentleman,
now deceased, who had had the great and good fortune in middle
life to marry his employer's widow, my pretty little Grandmamma Elinor. But my late grandfather had tied his money up in
so shrewd a fashion that no predatory second husband could
touch it and Liam Adair had been required to make his own way
in the world, an erratic way I'd heard which no lady could be
asked to share. He had travelled, gambled, taken chances which,
more often than not, he had lost and although for the past year or
two he had been employed by Venetia's father to sell worsted
cloth abroad I had heard no rumour that he had settled down.
And that alone, coupled with his height, his breadth, his swagger,
would be more than enough for Venetia. Was this, then, the
"unsuitable involvement" my step-mother's tea-time ladies had
hinted at? Yet Venetia had spoken to me of Liam Adair only a
few days ago warmly but too easily as a "dear friend" and
perhaps I hoped—since it would have been far better that way—
that it was the presence of Gideon Chard that was making her so
excitable and flirtatious.

I did not feel my best in the pretty apricot silk which had been
Blanche's choice, but I looked well enough I suppose and there
were a few among Venetia's following who, rating their chances
of her favour very low and considering my fortune to be every
bit as interesting as hers, began at once to pay me attention, a
young member of Rawnsley's Bank saying all that was needful

about my stay in Switzerland, the nephew of Mr. Sheldon MP requesting my opinion of Venice and listening, quite intently, while I gave it.

"Bit of a pest hole, Venice, if you ask me," drawled Gideon Chard from the fringes of the crowd, and although I had not asked him and would have done better to ignore him entirely, the self-assurance of his manner, that accumulation of three hundred years of Chard authority and Chard arrogance at Listonby stung me badly, stirring a certain arrogance of my own that came from another source entirely. For if his ancestors had been privileged and powerful mine had been tough-fibred and long-suffering, had fought hard for their prosperity not tamely inherited it, releasing themselves from the trap of poverty by their own stubborn refusal to stay there. And in actual terms he was only the third son of a baronet while I was the heiress to the whole of Fieldhead.

He had not changed greatly in the two years I had been away unless it was that he had simply become the man I had always expected of him. He was the youngest of the Chards for whom the estate could make no provision and who would not be needed by that estate for the purposes of procreation or management unless accident or disease—which seemed unlikely—should carry off both his brothers. And perhaps it was because he had been so carefully taught to respect the claims of primogeniture and to acknowledge the superior rights of those brothers that he had turned out to be a slightly better shot, a keener horseman, a rather more perfect example of his creed, his public school, his class, than either. Yet despite his pedigree, his expensive education, his exquisite manners, his air—and his conviction—of enormous superiority, he was every bit as much an opportunist and a fortune-hunter as Liam Adair, the kind of young gentleman—I was absolutely sure of it—that I had always dreaded, who believed that middle-class heiresses like myself and Venetia were not only fair game and ripe for the plucking but should be glad to pay for the privilege of marrying his noble name. And instantly he inspired me with a great antagonism, a most irrational desire to topple him from his aristocratic height into a puddle of real, industrial, Cullingford mud.

"Venice did not meet with your approval then, Gideon?"

"I can't say that it did."

"Poor Venice."

But, nevertheless, a moment later and without knowing exactly how I had submitted to it, I found myself strolling beside him among Aunt Faith's roses, Venetia and Liam Adair a few paces ahead of us, my humour worsening by the moment since I knew I had been "managed," as Mrs. Agbrigg sometimes "managed" me, and I did not like it.

"What a lovely day."

I agreed that it was.

"In fact a very fine summer altogether."

I was not disposed to quarrel with that. But there was no doubt that I wanted to quarrel with him about something, being eager to let him know that there was at least one Cullingford heiress who had "seen through him," who could never be flattered and consequently never deceived by him.

"How well Venetia is looking," I said, indicating as clearly as good manners allowed that she was much admired—for *herself* not for those Barforth millions—and that even with her father's backing he would have his work cut out to get her. But the sight of her vivid face upturned to Liam Adair could be of no consequence to a Chard—since Liam would not be allowed to have her in any case—and, disliking him the more for not being jealous, I transferred my attack to his self-esteem.

"So you are going into the mill, Gideon."

And I believed—hoped—that few things could be more galling to even the third son of a baronet than the necessity for that.

"Am I?" he said, toying with the remark and all too obviously amused by it. "Is that what you call it? I rather imagined I was joining my uncle's business—or might be doing so."

"Which happens to be a mill, or rather several of them."

"So it does. With room for several more, I imagine, if this boom lasts."

"My word, Gideon, I have never thought of you as a commercial man."

"Ah—then you *have* thought of me, Grace?"

"Have I? I imagine I must have done, at one time or another."

"But not as a millmaster?"

"Hardly."

"How then?"

"As a Chard, I expect, among Chards."

"And you have quite forgotten that my 'other grandfather' as my brother Dominic calls him—my mother's father—was Sir Joel Barforth, that prince of commerce?"

"Well, I have hardly thought of you in such detail as that, Gideon. But, of course, if you are modelling yourself on a prince."

"It would seem a reasonable place to begin, would it not," he said, smiling with a dry humour, "for a Chard?"

But instead of laughing with him as I should have done I felt my own humour desert me entirely to be replaced by a quite absurd notion that I must be on my guard, must not—absolutely *must* not—allow this man to win me over.

"I take it, then, that you are an expert on the worsted trade?"

"No—no—I cannot pretend to that. I have an appreciation, merely, of how things are bought and sold and some skill with mathematics. I imagine my Grandfather Barforth would have made his fortune equally well with whatever came to hand. The product might have varied but his methods, and his results, would have been the same."

"Yes, and the necessity of working eighteen hours a day in the dust and heat and the quite abominable racket of the weaving sheds—*every* day, of course, even in the fine weather—even in the middle of the hunting season . . . That would have remained the same too."

"Of course."

"And you would have enjoyed that, Gideon?"

"I wonder. Fortunately I shall be spared the necessity of finding out since my Grandfather Barforth was kind enough to put in all the spadework somewhat before my time."

"You think hard work to have gone out of fashion, then?"

But if I had believed him cornered, or had hoped to expose his weakness—to find him lazy, which was a considerable crime in Cullingford, rather than just greedy which was not—I was disappointed.

"Did I say so? Surely not. My grandfather did everything himself because there was no one else to do it, or no one else who could do it. The machine age was in its infancy then and one had simply to manage as best one could. It is not so today. We have progressed to an age of experts, you see. And nowadays not even a man like my Grandfather Barforth, nor even my Uncle Nicholas Barforth, could maintain and repair his own very complex engines, design his own cloth, oversee its production, go out into the world and sell it, as the old millmasters used to do. We have professional engineers and designers, salesmen, accountants, a whole tribe of specialists."

"I do have some knowledge, Gideon, of—"

"Do you really?"

"Of course I do. My father, after all, is master of Fieldhead." He smiled, giving me a slight bow which reduced the knowledge I had claimed to the level of knitting needles and embroidery frames, pressed flowers and charcoal sketches, the trivial occupations of femininity.

"Why yes, of course he is. I had not forgotten. And so you will know better than to underestimate the value of the man who decides what policy those specialists should pursue—since he takes the risk and the responsibility."

"He takes the risk," I snapped, "because he invests the money."

"Quite so."

And because even in the blackest of my rages I was still far too well brought up to hurl at him, "And you are preparing to sell that aristocratic profile of yours for the money to invest," I increased my pace to catch up with Venetia.

She had come to a halt some way ahead of me, waiting with an unusual quality of motionlessness about her as her mother and father, her brother and several others came walking towards us. And as our groups met and mingled displaying the polite veneer of our intricate civilization, I felt suddenly overcrowded, hemmed in by an array of quite separate hostilities; ambitious, cool-eyed Gideon seeking the means, through Venetia, to support in appropriate style his aristocratic birth and breeding; Venetia's moody, unmanageable brother who might despise his rich inheritance but would surely not give it away so tamely to Gideon; Venetia's admirer, Liam Adair, who had neither inheritance nor breeding, an even more typical adventurer than Gideon Chard except that his heart, I thought, might be rather warmer. And Venetia herself, eager, vivid, hopeful, standing on the rose-strewn pathway looking once again poised for flight, ready to soar upwards and magnificently, cleanly, away from the ambitions, the greeds, the conflicting pressures around her as she smiled a very private welcome to a young man I had never seen before.

"Grace," she said so very quietly, imparting to me a precious, still fragile secret. "You are not acquainted with Charles Heron. Charles, this is my cousin, Grace Agbrigg—my dear friend." And it was all there in her voice, her radiance, that quality of stillness so new to her which now formed an aura of light and air around her, separating her and this pleasant yet for all I could see unremarkable young man from the rest of us, the commonplace herd of humanity who were not in love.

3

HE WAS, SO SHE TOLD me the next morning, the son of a clergyman whose religion was both harsh and self-indulgent, the very kind she most despised, a man who preached the virtues of poverty and self-restraint with a glass of vintage port in his hand, so that she had understood from the first moment why Charles had found the parental vicarage unendurable. He had run away from its cloying hypocrisy at a tender age and had kept on running until he grew too old to be apprehended and fetched home; and now—since without paternal assistance few young men can prosper—he was a teacher of Greek and Latin at a local school where the Spartan regime, the narrow belief that the mechanics of language counted for more than its poetry, were deeply offensive to him. They had first met at Listonby where Mr. Heron, who was perfectly well born, was sometimes invited to dine, and since then they had seen one another, oh—here and there, a concert at the Morgan Aycliffe Hall, Aunt Caroline's hunt ball, a shooting party at Galton Abbey where his lack of expertise with a gun, his preference for absorbing the scents and shades of the autumn moors rather than slaughtering its winged residents— which was so favourite a pastime of her mother and brother—had not displeased her. And if she had flirted a little with Liam Adair—and of course she *had* flirted with him—it had been absolutely necessary, to conceal just for a short while the direction her interest was really taking; and Laim, who was worldly and extremely flirtatious in any case, would not mind.

"I have always known what I was looking for," she told me simply, quietly, still enveloped in her unnatural stillness. "I have always wanted to *feel*, not at all in moderation but so strongly that it tests me and stretches me, *demands* my utmost of me. And now I do."

But love, now that she had encountered him, had proved

frailer than she had supposed, no bold and adventurous wayfarer
like Liam Adair but a young man of sensitivity whose spirit
bruised more easily than her own. And she was herself astonished and a little afraid at the depth of her desire not only to love
him but to protect him, the sudden and acute need of her body
not only to be touched by him but to shield him from harm.

He had no money, but what could that matter when she would
have so much and when his needs, and hers, were very simple?
She required from her father no more than the means to open a
school of their own where Charles could put into practice his
theory that young people should be taught first of all to enjoy
learning rather than have it beaten into them, as nowadays
seemed to be the case. While Charles himself would be unwilling
to accept even that much.

"He does not approve of large fortunes," she told me, wrinkling her nose. "He believes they cannot have been made honestly or without great exploitation of others."

"Well, he is quite right. But he had better not say so to your
father."

"Lord, no!—but there is far worse, for he will have nothing to
do with religion and he is something very like a republican . . ."

"Perhaps your father will not mind so much about that."

"No, but others will mind. He was dismissed from his last
school, in Sussex, because the parents objected to his advanced
views, and he came north because he thought people would be
less hidebound up here. But they are not. At least, the ones who
can afford the fees at St. Walburga's School are not, and he will
not bring himself to compromise."

"In fact he is even more honest and straightforward than you
are, Venetia."

She laughed, tossed her head in a gesture designed to banish
anxiety.

"So he is. Well, never mind, for if my father should cut me
off without a shilling there will be that much more for Gervase. I
will come to see you again, Grace, tomorrow—the next day—"

But there remained the question of Gideon Chard, of family
convenience—for the more I thought of it, the more convinced I
became that Mr. Nicholas Barforth would find it convenient.
And although as yet this marriage could be no more than a
possibility, depending very largely on how well Gideon might
adapt himself to the manufacturing life, I felt absurdly threatened
by it, being so much aware of the frailty behind Venetia's rash
courage, of how easily hurt she really was and how very slow,

once hurt, to heal, that when she did not appear on the tenth day I borrowed Mrs. Agbrigg's carriage, altogether by stealth, and went to Tarn Edge to find her.

I should not, of course, have paid this visit, since Mrs. Agbrigg had forbidden it, and should certainly not have gone alone, but the old Barforth house in its several acres of elaborate, impersonal gardens, had no mistress nowadays who might be offended by my impropriety and there would be no other callers, no Mrs. Rawnsley or Miss Fielding to carry tales to my stepmamma, no Mrs. Thomas Sheldon MP to smother me in sweet and serious tones with her advice. There would be no one, indeed, but a housekeeper, her courtesy largely reserved for Mr. Nicholas Barforth, who paid her wages; an indifferent butler who did not encourage callers; and hopefully there would be Venetia.

The house, built by the founder of the Barforth fortunes, Sir Joel Barforth, at the pinnacle of his success, was many times larger than Fieldhead, its Gothic façade a marvel of carved stone, its walls rising to ornamental turrets and spires, with a stained-glass window on the South side that would not have disgraced a cathedral. When Sir Joel and his wife—my mother's Aunt Verity—had lived here, no house in the Law Valley had contained such luxuries nor entertained its guests so royally. But Sir Joel had died, Lady Verity had moved away, and only the Nicholas Barforths had remained at Tarn Edge.

For a while, I suppose, nothing had appeared changed, Lady Verity's well-paid and competent servants continuing to function in the old ways without need of supervision. But the new mistress—who had been Miss Georgiana Clevedon of Galton Abbey, a squire's daughter—had not cared for manufacturers' houses, new houses built with new money, and inevitably her lack of interest in Tarn Edge had infected her staff so that the work became slipshod or was not done at all; a careless mistress being carelessly served until the day she went away.

A series of housekeepers had followed her, none of them staying long, for Mr. Barforth was exacting and quick-tempered, his son, Gervase, exremely troublesome, while it had not occurred to Venetia, as it would probably have occurred to Blanche, certainly to me, that she was old enough now to take things in hand. But Aunt Faith, I think, was grieved by the neglect, enquiring whenever I visited there as to the progress of a decay she was unable either to witness or prevent. Was it true that the bronze stag which had guarded the hall since her early childhood had lost an antler after a party, a most unruly gathering she'd heard, held in his father's absence by Gervase? Had someone really chipped the tiles of the drawing-room fireplace which her Aunt Verity had had specially sent over from Italy, and scorched the priceless rug where, every Christmas of her youth, Sir Joel Barforth had stood to drink his family's health? No; the stag, I discovered, was intact, larger than life, magnificent, the drawing-room too perfect if anything, a cool air of disuse about it, the Aubusson rug Aunt Faith had described no longer there, its disappearance casually explained by Venetia: "Oh *that*—oh yes, Gervase set fire to it one night, I don't know how and he can't remember. Threw his cigar into the fire, I expect, and missed." And so the house, when I first knew it, had acquired the air of an expensive but somewhat mismanaged hotel.

Venetia and her brother were still at breakfast when I arrived at a little after eleven o'clock that morning, a circumstance less shocking in her case than in his, and as I entered the small breakfast-parlour—no servant troubling either to warn them of my arrival or to show me the way—I saw that they were quarrelling and had no intention, for my sake, of concealing it.

The room was small only by Tarn Edge standards, a table in the centre which could have comfortably seated two dozen, sideboards on two walls, one of them presenting a bare, none too well polished surface, the other set out with a princely array of hot dishes—princely, that is, in the massively embossed silver of the dishes themselves, since not one of them was more than a quarter full, being too large for the family they now served, and no one, very clearly, having thought of buying new. There was a large silver coffee-pot at Venetia's elbow, a stain on the damask cloth beside it where she too had aimed badly—today? yesterday? —the odd blending of luxury and neglect one came to expect in that house and for which Venetia, had she noticed it, would have felt no need to apologize. For after all what did a torn napkin, a chipped saucer *really* matter when there was a vast, sparkling sky above her windows, living green earth beneath. When there was Charles Heron.

"Darling Grace," she said, pushing a cup and saucer towards me with scant ceremony, "we are having a little tiff, Gervase and I. Do come and join us."

"Do you think I should? Is it safe?"

"You mean is it proper? Oh heavens, yes—don't turn out to be like Blanche who can do nothing unless it *looks* right. Gervase is being selfish, not for the first time, and thinking he can get away with it because he is a man—thinking *I* should take the consequences because females don't amount to much. Why on earth should you be shy, Grace? It's only Gervase."

"Thank you," he said, his quite voice light yet rather hoarse, his eyes narrowing as if the quite muted daylight hurt him. "But perhaps—before we go on—surely one ought to say how very nice to see you, Grace, after all this time. May one hope you had a pleasant journey home?"

"Yes I did, thank you. Very pleasant."

"And you are very well?"

"Yes, I am. And you?"

"Absolutely splendid!"

"No he's not," Venetia said, wishing to be cool and cutting, but biting back a chuckle. "He drove his cabriolet off the path last night and ploughed up about half an acre of father's roses. Yes, yes, I saw it all, Gervase, from my window, and how you stopped from overturning I shall never know. I felt quite proud of you, or would have done if you had not been drunk—since getting drunk is so shameful and silly—like that time you went steeplechasing after dinner at Listonby with a broken arm. I suppose that was silly too."

"I suppose it was—except that I won."

"Yes—I know," and rippling with her sudden laughter she brushed her hand lightly against his, a swift reminder of shared affection, unconditional support, two of them against the world, an attitude I envied since in my case there had only ever been one.

Gervase Barforth closely resembled his sister, the pointed, auburn looks of his mother's family, which in him had an extra leanness, green eyes that were almost always narrowed as if against strong sunlight, a thin, hard mouth tilted by a not altogether compassionate humour. And although I had known him, at a distance, all my life, I understood no more of him than the plain facts which were available to anyone.

He was twenty-four years old and so far as I knew had never performed what anyone in Cullingford would consider a hard day's work in his life. He had an office at Nethercoats Mill, a desk, a portrait of his mother on the wall, but what he actually did there no one in Cullingford could rightly say. He was neither physically lazy nor mentally slow as rich men's sons sometimes seem to be, possessing on the contrary a restlessness which made him uneasy company. Yet even his queerness of temper, his ability to touch raw nerves in others, would have been tolerated had he bothered to conceal his contempt for the values which had made Cullingford—and his father—great.

"Reckons himself too fine a gentleman for the textile trade, yon lad," Cullingford had decided, secretly pleased that Mr. Nicholas Barforth, who had succeeded in everything else, should have failed so dismally with his wife and son.

"Takes after his mother, young Master Gervase." And so perhaps he did, not merely in those finespun, auburn looks but in his disgust for factory cities, his intolerance of the middle classes into which he, unlike his Clevedon mother, had been born.

"The young squire" they called him at the Barforth mills, and indeed he rode to hounds, shot grouse and pheasant in season, drank brandy and claret, played cards in low company, associated, I suppose, with low women, pastimes by no means unusual among the squirearchy but which in Cullingford—where manufacturers required their sons to devote a fair amount of their time to the processes of manufacturing—were considered to be not so much sinful as unprofitable, definitely not to be encouraged. And since he had been christened Gervase *Clevedon* Barforth and was the last male survivor of that proud line it was generally believed that he might one day drop the name of Barforth altogether, that like his mother before him he was simply awaiting his share of the Barforth fortune in order to turn his back on Cullingford and the manufacturing side of his ancestry altogether.

If there was more than that to Gervase, then I had not discovered it; and would be unlikely to do so now, I thought, for as Venetia, having reassured him of her affection, began not so much to quarrel with him as to urge him to action, he gave a faint shudder and closed his eyes, conveying the impression that his constitution this morning was exceedingly fragile, his head painful and his stomach sour, his sympathy with his sister's troubles at a low ebb.

"*Must* it be now, Venetia?"

"Of course it must, for I am obliged to deal with you when I can catch you, and unless we have this out now you will be off again. Do pay attention—and there is no need for you to look so pained about it. You may put your head in the sand as often as you please, Gervase, but—I warn you—*I* will not go away."

And in a rush of words and gestures and exclamations she presented him with her impression of the visit she had made the day before, the two or three rooms at Galton Abbey kept open by her mother, the stone-flagged hall with its array of family portraits and ancient weaponry, the small sitting-room with its rag rugs and tapestry chairs, a long, low-ceilinged kitchen, its door standing open to wind and weather, the air that came spiced and sharp from the moor, the movement of a clear, fast-running stream.

It had been an enchanting day of sun and wind and glorious liberty, nothing in her mother's manner to indicate discontent, except that Venetia *knew* she was discontented; no hint of frustration, except that Venetia could sense it as clearly as one can sometimes divine the presence of hidden water. And indeed the life of a woman living apart from her husband was both sad and strange, for although she was deprived—albeit at her own choosing—of his status and his protection, she was still as subject by law to his control as if she had never set foot outside the matrimonial front door. Mrs. Barforth may well have retired to her family estate but in fact that estate, which had come to her in her grandfather's will, did not really belong to her at all but to her husband. Separated or not separated, she remained his wife and as such could own no property apart from him. What she possessed he possessed. What he possessed was his absolutely. He could claim Galton as his own, could sell it or knock it down as he chose, without her consent, and there was no authority to which she could realistically complain. A married woman, we all knew, assumed her husband's name and was absorbed into his identity. A separated woman appeared to have no identity at all, and no protection, being obliged to depend financially, legally and every other way on the whim of the man who was still her legal guardian. If Mrs. Barforth had tried to run away, she had not gone very far, her bolt for freedom—if such it had been—ending in a fresh captivity which, however irksome it might or might not be to herself, was the cause of much honest indignation to her daughter.

"They should be together or they should be separate—one thing or the other," was Venetia's deeply held opinion. "And she should stand up to him and tell him so, for he is not so terrible and she is brave enough in other ways. *I* would tell him . . ."

Her mother, in fact, despite her outer layer of cheerfulness, had reminded Venetia of nothing so much as a woodland creature tethered in its natural habitat on a very long chain which, while permitting an illusion of freedom, could be drawn tight at any moment to suit the purposes of its master. And although she knew her father's hand was on that chain, she believed the cause of it—at least partly—to be Gervase. Left to her own devices, her mother—Venetia was sure of it—would have evaded all restraint long ago and flown away. But she remained; and since daughters, in the Clevedon tradition, had never counted for much, the reason for her enforced docility could only be her son.

"Ah yes," he said, outwardly very languid now. "Do blame me—do follow the fashion."

"So I will, because she is sitting on that land guarding it for you—you know she is."

"And rightly so, since I am the last of the Clevedons."

"And do you know that every time father tells her to do something she does it, however much she loathes it, because she's afraid he'd sell the estate if she disobeyed him?"

"Yes, Venetia. I am a little older than you, if you remember, and none of this is news to me. But she cares about the land, Venetia—she *wants* to be there."

"Exactly. But do you?"

"I beg your pardon?"

"You know what I mean. She wants the land—yes, more than anything—but she doesn't see the estate as hers. It was her grandfather's and her father's; it was going to be her brother's. And when he was killed she started to think of it as yours. But I don't know, Gervase—really I don't. You used to run off to Galton when we were children, and she'd keep you there when you should have been at school, until father came to drag you back. And now sometimes you can't bear to keep away—you run off there now when you should be at the mills—but there are times when mother hardly sees you at all. And when she does you're not always sweet."

He paused, smiled, moved one very weary hand towards the coffee-pot and smiled again, evidently deciding that, since neither of us showed signs of coming to his assistance, the effort of picking up the pot and pouring would be too much for him.

"Oddly enough," he said, still smiling, "there's really no need to be sweet with mother. That's the great thing about her, you know. She actually likes the kind of man I am. In fact, I'll go further than that, and say she rather thinks that's the way men *ought* to be."

For a moment there was a heavy silence, Venetia leaning forward perplexed and frowning, while Gervase, his eyes half-closed again, seemed very far away.

"Do you want that estate?" she suddenly flung at him. "Are you going to let her down? I'm not so sure."

He got up and crossed to the sideboard, glancing with dislike at the overcooked sausages cowering in a corner of their dish, the congealed eggs and bacon, and then, helping himself rather gingerly, came back to the table.

"I feel I should eat something," he said. "In fact I absolutely must . . . So you don't think I'm cut out to be squire of Galton, Venetia?"

"I didn't say that. I said I'm not always sure you want it."

"Mother's sure."

"I know."

"So we'll consider it settled, shall we—since if you imagine I'm cut out to run those mills, then you haven't been listening to father. And is it really all my fault, Venetia? We know why mother keeps up the illusion—to protect Galton for me. I'll grant you that. But why does father do it? What does *he* want out of it? He wants you safely married and off his hands, Venetia— that's what he wants—before the illusion cracks and the gossip starts. So if your heart is really bleeding for mother, then use that to bargain with. Tell him you'll get married and he can pick the groom."

"That's terrible—" she began, her mind on Charles Heron, her face as pale as if she were already a captive bride. But almost at once, with the lightning shifts of mood common to them both, her colour came flooding back, he smiled.

"Idiot!" she said, her own mouth trembling into unwilling mirth. "They'd have to drag me down the aisle—"

"No, no—no need for that. I'd shoot you if it came to it— much kinder." And when their father came into the room a moment later they were still laughing, reconciled, joining themselves instinctively together in mutual defense against him.

He was a very large man, as dark and solid as they were light and fine, a man of substance and presence who had been very handsome once and would have been handsome still, perhaps, had he been less morose. A silent man, accustomed to issuing orders rather than holding conversations, who did nothing without a purpose or the expectation of a profit, and who in my father's informed opinion was the hardest and shrewdest of the very many shrewd and far from tender-hearted gentlemen in our Law Valley.

"Sir?" Gervase murmured by way of greeting, a slight question in his voice.

"Oh—" said Venetia, biting her lip, a child caught in a guilty act, although there was no reason why she, at least, should not be breakfasting at this late hour.

But Mr. Barforth ignored both his children and, turning to me, said quietly: "Good morning, Grace."

"Good morning, Mr. Barforth. May I apologize for calling so early?"

"I wouldn't call it early," he said, his eyes straying to Gervase, implying, I knew, that he and the greater part of Cullingford had been at their work for some hours already. "And you are always welcome. You could give me some coffee, miss."

And although this last remark was certainly addressed to Venetia, she had become so strangely downcast—remembering, no doubt, that this awesome parent would never appreciate Charles Heron—that I took the pot myself, ascertained Mr. Barforth's requirements as to cream and sugar, and handed him his cup quite steadily, feeling that if I had managed to contend with Mrs Agbrigg all these years I should not be intimidated by him.

He smiled, drank deep as men do after an hour or so in the weaving-sheds, and without really looking at Gervase, said, "You're back, I see. It occurred to me as I was shaving this morning that I hadn't seen you for a day or two—five or six, I reckon. But then on my way out I noticed a certain amount of destruction that told me you might have come home to roost again."

"Well yes, sir—bad penny and all that."

"Quite so. It's the end of the month, isn't it? And you'll be overspent."

"That's about it, sir."

And what surprised me was not the hostility of their relationship but the lack of it, the absence, almost, of any relationship at all, which was not often seen in an area like ours, where mill masters thought nothing of chasing their sons to the factory yard with a horse-whip if necessary and of keeping them permanently short of money to make sure they stayed there. It had been the boast of Sir Joel Barforth that he could usually make his first thousand pounds of the morning while his competitors were still cooling their porridge. Mr. Nichols Barforth, his son, whose business was even larger, could probably do better than that. Gervase Barforth had never by his own ingenuity made a single penny, and would not be asked to try, it seemed to me, because Mr. Barforth quite simply, quite coldly, did not think this difficult, almost alien son of his to be worth the trouble. He had written him off, I thought, as he would have done a bad debt, dealing with the consequences, resigning himself to the loss, and it did not escape me that Gervase—who from the moment of his father's arrival had become more languid, more dissipated and trivial than ever—was fully aware of it.

"Badly overspent, Gervase?" Mr. Barforth asked, naming in an astoundingly casual manner an offence any other Cullingford father would have dealt with as a major crime. To which his son, still lounging at ease—although he seemed to have turned rather pale—replied in like manner, presenting so complete a picture of an expensive, useless young gentleman that I glanced at him keenly, finding his portrayal too perfect and wondering if he was attempting, as I often did with Mrs. Agbrigg, to see just how far he could go.

"Much the same as usual."

"And is there a chance this month, do you think, of my getting a return on my money?"

"It rather depends what sort of return you had in mind, sir."

"Oh, nothing much—I wouldn't ask much."

"That's good of you, sir."

And now the atmosphere between them, although I could still not have called it anger, chilled me, warning me that, whatever name they gave to it, it was tortuous and hurtful and unpleasant.

"I want somebody to go down to London and take a man out to dinner. You could manage that, I reckon?"

"Well, yes, I could," agreed Gervase, his drawling accent belonging so accurately to the public school he had never attended that once again I glanced at him, recognizing his intention to provoke, to enrage, to demonstrate that his father's opinion of him was if anything not bad enough. And what hurt him and strained him—as I had so often been hurt and strained in my combat with Mrs. Agbrigg—was that his father would not be provoked, had no need to be enraged, being possessed absolutely of the power and the authority that would ensure him, every time, an easy victory.

"I know where London is, sir—there'd be no trouble about that. But this man you want me to meet—does he understand the wool trade?"

"No," Mr. Barforth said, smiling grimly, "he does not. He understands horses and guns—the American variety of both—and I reckon you'll find other things in common. You could take him to a tailor and a music-hall—and a few other places of entertainment I expect you'll know about—if you feel up to the responsibility, that is."

"One tends to rise to the occasion."

"Good. Tomorrow, then. The morning train. I'd planned to send Liam Adair but he's needed."

"How very nice for him," Gervase said sweetly, "to be needed."

And now at last there was anger, just a moment that contained the possibility of a bellow of rage, a box on the ear, the easy, healthy curses which any other father would already have been hurling at any other son. But—since anger implies a degree of caring, or hoping, and is a warm thing in any case—the moment froze, or withered, and with a casual "I'll make my arrangements, then," Gervase got up and walked away, brushing a hand lightly against Venetia's shoulder as he passed.

"Doesn't it occur to you, papa," she said, staring down at her hands, folded tightly before her on the table, "that one day perhaps he won't come back? In his place I don't think I'd come back—not every time."

But her father chose neither to hear nor to reply, asking me instead for more coffee, which he accepted with a smile of amazing charm, his grim contempt giving way to an altogether unexpected cordiality.

"I hear you did very well in Switzerland, Grace."

"As well as I could, Mr. Barforth."

"Aye—which put you so far at the head of your class as to set your father wishing you'd been born a boy. He reckons you could run Fieldhead mill, if you were the right gender, without much trouble."

"I am very pleased he should think so."

And offering me once again that astonishing smile he submitted me to a moment's scrutiny, examining me as carefully as if he had never seen me before, a keen mind assessing not only my appearance, my character, but the uses to which they might be put, as if—like Gideon Chard—I had come to him for employment.

"Didn't you know," Venetia said when he had left the room, "how charming he can be?"

"Why, yes—I suppose I did."

"I suppose you did not, because he has never taken the trouble to be nice to you before. Lord, he even charms me sometimes! Well, Grace, you had better watch out, because he must want something from you, or from your father. I wonder what it can be? Perhaps he wants to send me abroad, out of harm's way, and thinks you'd be the one to keep an eye on me. Or perhaps he's just picked you out as the right wife for Gervase. Heavens! I didn't mean to say that—"

"Then please don't say it again."

"I won't, for there's no hope of it. Gervase won't get married for ages yet. He's enjoying himself too much. And when he does he'll go to one of the foxhunting set—Diana Flood, I suppose, if she keeps on making eyes at him in that odious fashion."

"I gather you don't care much for Diana Flood."

She shrugged, her mind probing beyond Miss Flood, who was known to me only as the niece of Sir Julian Flood whose family had held the manor of Cullingford as long as there had been Chards at Listonby and Clevedons at Galton Abbey; a gentleman, in fact, who intrigued me rather more than the equestrienne Diana, since it had long been rumoured that if Venetia's mother had ever had a lover, then most assuredly it had been—might still be—the impecunious, unsteady, yet undeniably well-bred Sir Julian. Yet if these rumours had reached Venetia she made light of them now, displaying no more than a mild irritation towards the girl who might well become her sister-in-law, a young lady whose aristocratic notions and athletic habits must surely appeal both to Gervase Barforth and to his Clevedon mother.

"Oh, there's no harm in her—at least, if she'd leave Gervase alone she'd be as bearable as the rest of them, with their eternal hunting stories."

"You go hunting yourself, Venetia."

"So I do. But that's not all I do. It's not all I think about. It's not all Gervase thinks about either—except that when he spends too much time with the Floods and the Chards and the rest he becomes so like them that really one can hardly tell the difference."

"Do you see much of the Chards?" I asked cautiously, hoping against all the odds that she might blush, turn coy, make some fond reference to Gideon which would reassure me that Charles Heron had not really absorbed the whole of her heart and her mind. But she only shrugged again, her gesture tossing the very substantial Chards quite easily away.

"From time to time. Dominic and Noel never come to town, but Gideon is here sometimes, talking textiles to father and talking down to Gervase. He doesn't talk to me."

"Don't you like him?"

"Gideon? He's well enough. Clever, of course, and very good-looking, and my word doesn't he just know it! But all the Chards are like that. I believe I envy them. It must be very pleasant to have such a good opinion of oneself."

"Ah—I see. You have a poor opinion of Venetia Barforth, do you?"

She laughed and shook her head. "I suppose not. It's just that sometimes I'm not too sure who Venetia Barforth really is—or Gervase. It has never been easy, you know, with a father who is so very much a Barforth and a mother so much a Clevedon that all our lives what has been right for her has been wrong for him. And because we could never please them both, we were always in a state somehow of having to choose. Well, I suppose for me those days are over. I'm a female and females don't inherit. No one is going to make me squire of Galton or master of the Barforth mills. Gervase is the one who has to make that decision. I just hope he lives long enough."

"Now what on earth does that mean?" She smiled, shook herself a little.

"Oh, well—the Clevedon males tend to burn themselves out rather soon, you know, or they get themselves killed. The grave-yard at Galton is full of them, most of them cut down or shot down in battle, but others not— My mother's father fell an early victim to the brandy bottle and there was her brother, of course, our Uncle Perry, who took one fence too many and broke his neck. The wild red Clevedons—you must have heard the country people call us that? It appeals mightily to Gervase, until he remembers his name is actually Barforth."

"And then?"

"Yes—then he takes a higher fence or a wider ditch. Whatever the Floods or the Chards or the Wintertons can do, he can do it better or more of it. He can, too—so far."

"And you, Venetia?"

"Yes," she said, her face softening, richly glowing as always at any reminder of Charles Heron. "I have my own fences to jump too, do I not? I am not naive, Grace. I know my father will never consent to Charles. It makes no difference at all to the way I feel. I think Gervase could fall in love too—I really think so."

"And you wouldn't like it to be with Diana Flood?"

"No," she said, frowning, concentrating hard, as if, quite slowly, she was working something out, reaching a long-suspected conclusion. "No, I wouldn't. I know mother wouldn't agree with me, because Diana likes all the things mother likes and can do all the things mother can do, and of course she'd make a splendid new mistress for Galton—and that matters tremendously to mother. But Galton is made of stone and he's not. What I'm saying is—oh dear!—"

"That you don't want to lose your brother to the foxhunting set?"

"Oh, that's part of it—a big part. But there are two sides to him, you know, and whatever he says, and whatever mother says, I'm not sure the Clevedon side is the strongest. He's a Barforth, after all, and what's wrong with that? Why shouldn't he be a Barforth? Oh Grace, I don't know why I never thought of this before, and of course I shouldn't say it and I know it won't happen—nothing so marvellous *could* happen. But if I could have a wish—just one—since I already have Charles, then I'd—"

"Venetia, if it's what I think it is, then please—"

"Then please just let me say it, just once, in case a good fairy should be listening. If I could have that solitary wish, then I'd wish for Gervase to marry you."

4

"MR. GERVASE BARFORTH," MRS. AGBRIGG remarked sweetly the following morning across the breakfast table, "is a young man of a most unreliable disposition. It is a connection I do not wish to encourage and must ask you to co-operate."

"He will be very rich, Mrs. Agbrigg."

"And very spendthrift. On the other hand, Mr. Gideon Chard has a most pleasing manner . . ."

"And nothing much to be spendthrift with, Mrs. Agbrigg, I imagine, since he is only a third son."

"But of such an excellent mother," she said, still very sweetly smiling, demolishing my insolence by ignoring it.

"So we are to encourage the Chard connection?"

"If we have the sense we were born with, dear Grace, we must endeavour to do so."

"You have not heard the rumour then, that he is being held in reserve for Venetia?"

"I have," she said, stately, imperturbable. "But rumour is often at fault. An ambitious man requires a woman of sense to partner him—which Venetia is not. A man who enjoys material possessions rather than philosophical concepts—and I believe Gideon Chard to be that kind of man—needs a wife of a practical rather than a whimsical turn of mind. Venetia may be fascinating and affectionate, but a young man with his way to make in the world might not feel safe with her, no matter what promises were made to him by her father."

"Heavens, Mrs. Agbrigg, how dull you make me sound! Am I really so safe and sensible and thrifty?"

"Sensible enough," she said quietly, "to get yourself creditably married. Tell me, dear, do you see any particular reason for delay?"

I did not expect either Gideon or Gervase to pay me any

further attention, for Gideon's best interests were certainly with Venetia, while Gervase, who despised commerce, could hardly wish to ally himself to one of its daughters. But Mrs. Agbrigg's next "at home" day brought first one and then the other, Gervase accompanied by his father, who may, for all I knew, have dragged him to that stuffy gathering of teacups and bread and butter by the scruff of his neck. The two young men came separately and did not meet each other, remaining no longer than the correct quarter of an hour, Gervase replying very languidly, almost without opening his lips, to the few remarks which Mrs. Agbrigg, aware of his father's powerful eye upon her, addressed to him.

"Yes, ma'am."

"As you say, ma'am."

And when her back was turned he gave me an almost imperceptible wink, an exaggerated grimace of dismay which inclined me—for the first time in that hushed and hallowed drawing-room—to giggle.

But Gideon Chard was received with an enthusiasm I found distasteful, an eagerness to display our worldly goods to him and hint at the existence of more which covered me with shame.

"Pleasant house you have here, Mrs. Agbrigg," he told her, rather, it seemed to me, as if he owned it and was thinking of increasing her rent.

"Pleasant enough, Mr. Chard—only a mill-house, of course, although I do my best with it. I have had my little notions of moving into the country, but my husband—as yet—cannot bear to be separated from his mill."

And there, in those few words, she had placed it all before him, had sown a tempting seed to convince him that the Agbrigg daughter had not only good sense, a safe disposition and a prosperous business to offer her husband, but the possibility of a country estate, which would be regarded as a most enticing bonus by the sporting Mr. Gideon Chard.

"No, I cannot persuade my husband to leave the view of the mill we have from this window."

"Indeed?" he said, striding to the window she indicated and staring keen-eyed down the slope of lawn and flower-beds and over the hedge to the mill-yard. "An excellent view—and a splendid building, if I may say so."

"How kind! Should industrial architecture be of interest to you, my husband would be delighted to show you around."

"I should be very much obliged to him."

"Then please consider it settled."

"It is not so large," I said, my mouth very dry, "as any one of the Barforth mills."

But, involved with their own thoughts and with one another, they ignored me.

"Shall we say the day after tomorrow at three o'clock? I will tell my husband to expect you, and if you should care to walk up here afterwards and take tea . . . ?"

"I should like that enormously."

I did not like it at all.

"What an exceedingly fine vase," he said, his landlord's eye carefully assessing our treasures. "Meissen, I think?"

"Oh goodness!" Mrs. Agbrigg fluttered. "I am always confused by the porcelain. Grace will tell you."

"Meissen," I said shortly, rudely, receiving a raised eyebrow from the lady, a slight bow from the gentleman.

"We will see you the day after tomorrow then, Mr. Chard."

"With the greatest of pleasure."

He came, inspected the mill from top to bottom as if he had the means to make an offer for it, fired sharp, pertinent questions at my father and then sat for a full hour at ease in the drawing-room—too much at ease for my liking—and paid court not to me but to Mrs. Agbrigg, recognizing her at once as the source of authority.

"What a charming young man, Grace!"

"He's a fortune-hunter, Mrs. Agbrigg."

"Well, of course he is, dear. All men are hunting for something or other. It is in their natures—and when one has a fortune, what else can one expect? The great thing about it, my dear, is that a fortune, if placed in the right hands—unlike youth and beauty—has no tendency to fade but can even be made to grow."

But Gideon Chard did nothing to commit himself, biding his time in true commercial fashion until the climate of the marriage-market should be exactly right. And when later that month it was made known to us that he had become an official Barforth employee, I believed Mrs. Agbrigg's game to be lost. He would try to marry Venetia now, I was sure of it, and would probably do anything to get her, since he could hardly enjoy the prospect of investing his time and energy in the Barforth business to let half of it go with Venetia to someone else.

He was often to be seen in Cullingford accompanying his uncle on his daily round of the mills—splendid Lawcroft, smaller but thriving Low Cross, brand-new, awe-inspiring Nethercoats and the rest—or at the Piece Hall, the platform for the London train, the Wool Exchange; sometimes with Gervase in attendance and sometimes not. But it was not generally expected that he would long endure the discipline, the sheer physical discomfort of the textile trade; the factory hooter which every morning shrieked out a demand for punctuality which he, like the meanest operative, would be expected to obey; the heat, the dust, the grinding, monotonous toil of the sheds. "Come the first taste of autumn," they said, "and he'll be off, riding down some poor farmer's crops to catch those blasted foxes. They're not *steady*, the gentry. They're only glorified farmers themselves, after all, used to following the seasons instead of the clock. And if Nick Barforth can't handle his own lad, what chance has he got with Lady Caroline's?"

But it was Gervase, as I had known it would be, who disappeared in mid-August, called to Galton Abbey by the early grouse, while Gideon could still be seen strolling towards the Piece Hall on market-day and afterwards in the bar parlour of one of our new commercial hotels where deals were often finalized, a most perfect man of business in his black frock coat and light grey trousers, plain grey silk waistcoat and immaculate linen, only the pearl in his neck-cloth and his own very superior manner marking him as the son of a baronet, albeit the third.

"My father is very pleased with him," Venetia offered, too deep in her dream of Charles Heron to take the effect this might have on her own life in any way seriously. "Although I believe our managers dislike him, which is not to be wondered at, for they have been expecting an easy time of it under Gervase when father retires. And although Gideon cannot yet be sure of himself and has so much to learn, they can see that he means to be *hard*. No, they really don't like him at all but I doubt he cares a fig for that, since he has not come to us for affection, simply to get rich."

"Venetia—" I said, wanting to say more, but she shook her head in the coltish movement that was so impatient of restraint, and smiled.

"Oh yes, I am not such a goose as you seem to think. I know they are all expecting him to marry me. But that is all nonsense, you know. It is just my father and Aunt Caroline thinking that everything must be arranged their way. And in any case I believe I have seen Gideon looking at you."

I replied very calmly that I had not noticed it, but her remark

sent me out into the garden when she left me, needing solitude in
which to ponder the growing trouble of my mind and my body,
which had both endured the restraints of total dependence, of the
"young-lady-at-home," for too long.

I had returned from Switzerland feeling myself to be a woman,
my chaperonage abroad having consisted of governesses and paid
companions, who although by no means careless of my reputation had been for the most part reasonable. And while I had done
nothing disgraceful nor even particularly adventurous, I had at
least been allowed the dignity of choice.

In short I had been trusted, my own judgement of what I could
or could not do, with whom I might or might not associate, had
been respected. And since I had not abused that trust I had not
anticipated its withdrawal. But from the day of my return Mrs.
Agbrigg had shown a determination to keep me as cloistered as a
flighty fifteen-year-old, not, I suspected, out of any concern for
my virtue or my safety, but quite simply to drive me away.

I had made a scene the first time she asked to read a letter of
mine, had thrown it at her feet and vowed to take up her excess
of zeal—her excess of spite—with my father. But he had come
home late from the mill that night, weary and dispirited and
coughing, a pain in his chest, a pain in his head, glad of the
mulled wine she had ready, his chair with the cushions placed
just so, the warm sympathy of *her* voice, not the shrill protest of
mine; and watching her smooth the tensions out of him, I had
found nothing to say.

The immediate solution, of course, would be to go abroad
again, to Paris, perhaps, now that the war with Prussia was over.
It would be interesting, I thought, to watch the new republic
emerge from its troubled infancy, to hear at first hand those
elusive, tantalizing ideals of liberty and fraternity which had
been born in France a century ago. It would be fascinating to
watch and to hope that this time, after so many years of bloodshed,
so much pain and sacrifice, they had been able to get their
formula right. But in the end I would be obliged to come home
again, to find these same conflicts waiting for me unresolved,
and catching sight of the mill below me, a charcoal sketch of
rooftops around it, a damp, grey sky above, I knew that no
matter how long or how frequent my journeyings I would always
wish to return.

I had seen splendid cities, the heart-rending, crumbling elegance of Venice, imperial Rome, the opulence of Vienna, sparkling Lucerne. I had seen towering blue-white mountains, the

extravagant massing of southern flowers, the rich profusion of the summer vine. I had seen the outpouring of artistic genius in paint and in marble, the jewelled and silken interiors of churches and ducal palaces. And Cullingford had none of these. But there was something in these narrow, grimy streets climbing so tenaciously up hill and down which moved me; some force of energy and resolution, a blunt refusal to submit to blind authority, or blind fate, of which I felt myself to be a part.

I knew there was injustice here, and oppression, knew that my father's sheds were full of women who, labouring the ten hours a day which the law allowed, returned each night to hovels built back to back in dingy rows and the further drudgery of an everlasting maternity; I knew that in all the streets around Fieldhead, around Lawcroft and Low Cross and every other mill in our town, small children were turned out of doors in flocks and left to roam unattended from early morning until the murky evening hour when the factory gates were unlocked to release their mothers.

Yet I was a part of that too, for if my Grandfather Aycliffe had made his fortune by building these hovels, my other grandfather, known to us all as Mayor Agbrigg, had lived in such places himself; my father had been born there, and the memory perhaps had been bred in me. Mayor Agbrigg had been a pauper brat, sent north by the overseer of a poorhouse at so young an age that he had no recollection even of his proper name, being called "Agbrigg"—since, like a dog, it was necessary to give him a name of some sort to answer to—by an overlooker of the mill where my grandfather had slaved for seventeen hours a day until he turned twenty-one, eating and sleeping on a pile of waste in the corner of a weaving-shed. Yet this remarkable grandparent of mine, who might never have reached that ripe old age of twenty-one, had not only survived but had prospered, had risen by the dogged endurance I so ardently admired to a position of authority, to be Mayor of Cullingford and to send a son to Cambridge. And he had survived, not bitterly and harshly, but with the compassion of true courage, a conviction that all men—and all women—were entitled to basic human dignities.

Grandfather Agbrigg was a plain man, hard-handed, grey-visaged, blunt-spoken like Cullingford itself, yet his strength, to me, was magnificent and at the same time quite familiar in our steep, cobbled streets where so many of our men—our patient, labouring women—also possessed it. He had suffered and overcome, as not everyone could do, but I believed that Cullingford itself, which he seemed so accurately to personify, could overcome its blights, its cruelties, its greeds, could—now that the first mad fever of industrial expansion was over—grow graciously, kindly, with care for all. And that was the challenge—not the agony of the Paris barricades—in which I felt entitled to participate.

Yet my participation, as I well knew, was hampered by three things: my sex, my single status, and by Mrs. Agbrigg. I had never set foot in the clamorous sheds of Fieldhead, prevented by my female gender from concerning myself as to the means by which my family fortune, my dowry and my inheritance were made. But watching the mill-girls file into the yard on many a cold morning wrapped in their blankets, clogs surrounding painfully on the frozen cobbles, I knew that, had my grandfather failed in his endeavours, I might well have been among them; knew that, had I been a boy, I would already have been set above them as the "young master" of Fieldhead.

My father's son would have been in no way subject to the interference of his stepmamma, escaping daily from her cloying world of manners and morals to the realities of work and responsibility, the challenges to which my father's daughter felt equally suited to respond. My father's son would have had his own horses by now and his own carriage, would have taken the train to Leeds or London when in his own judgement his circumstances required it. My father's son would have had opinions, commitments, obligations, aims, would have taken risks and made decisions, would have suffered, perhaps, a diversity of blows and failures, but would have been equipped at all times with the glorious weapon of freedom.

My father's daughter, who may not have differed greatly from her unborn brother in temperament and ability, had but one obligation, to be virtuous and obedient; while the only real choice open to her was simply to be married or not to be married. And sitting in my father's garden that day, the hushed, well-polished house behind me, the sprawling, unpolished town below, I rather thought I would be married.

I cannot say that I was consciously looking for love, for although a barely acknowledged part of myself might have gone eagerly towards it, the side of my nature with which I was most familiar had acquired a cautious view of emotion. As a child, made solitary and serious by an invalid mother, I had adored my father, and although in his view he had not failed me—having given me riches, which in Cullingford were looked on as the very warp and weft of happiness—I had known desolate moments since his marriage, a loneliness far colder than my childhood solitude, which did not incline me to build my life once again around another person. Certainly I did not wish to make a marriage of convenience, but while I could appreciate, could almost envy, the rapture which was the breath of life to Venetia, it seemed to me so dangerous that I had small inclination to hazard myself in that direction at all.

A marriage, then, neither of convenience nor of passion, but of mutual trust and liking, an ideal arrangement which in a recess of my mind I was forced to colour with gratitude since it offered me escape both from Mrs. Agbrigg and the limitations of spinsterhood. And if no suitable gentleman should immediately present himself, then I would not be foolish—or so I imagined—but would endeavour, within those iron bands surrounding a "young-lady-at-home," to find some congenial occupation. For my father's daughter was Agbrigg enough to detest failure, and what could be more humiliating, more destructive, more inescapable than a bad marriage?

Not that I could have named, offhand, more than one or two that I envied. Mrs. Rawnsley, I knew, had married for the simple reason that at the age of twenty-three she had no longer been able to support the shame of remaining Miss Milner. Mrs. Agbrigg had married for respectability, Mrs. Sheldon from a desire not so much for the person of Mr. Thomas Sheldon MP as for his political standing. The girls I had met at school appeared with few exceptions to be scrambling into matrimony just as soon as they were able, some of them honestly finding domesticity and motherhood alluring, some of them because "what else was there to do?," others quite simply to get away from "papa."

Yet, on the other hand, I saw nothing in the lives of the maiden ladies I knew best to inspire me with enthusiasm, being frankly irritated by the self-effacing Miss Fielding—daughter of our senior MP—whose fluttering devotion was given not really to God but to his servant, our vicar, whose willing slave she had become; while only the example of Miss Rebecca Mandelbaum offered me a little hope, a little entertainment.

Miss Mandelbaum was unusual for a number of reasons, not least among them her talent as a pianist, which could have taken her to the concert stage had not her parents—for what seemed to them the best of reasons—opposed it. Following the deaths of those parents some years ago, she had taken up residence alone in the no longer fashionable but still very genteel neighbourhood of Blenheim Lane, her independence made possible by her mature years, a substantial inheritance and the understanding of her brother, who as head of the family might well have preferred to keep her at home.

She was a rounded, stately woman who passed her days talking to friends on such thoughtful topics as art, music and philosophy, the nature of truth and justice. Miss Mandelbaum did not care in the least for the triumphs and heartbreaks of an Assembly Rooms Ball; nor, I suspect, did the inadequate drainage of large areas of Cullingford enter her mind other than rarely. But the respective merits of Botticelli and Andrea del Sarto could arouse her to excitement, a Beethoven sonata could leave her mesmerized, while the National Society for Women's Suffrage inspired her, quite rightly, with passion.

"Forgive me, Miss Agbrigg," she had murmured to me on my third or fourth visit to her quiet house, "I do not care to speak of personal matters, but I wonder if you have considered how very wealthy you might be one day?"

And when I had assured her that I had, she still seemed compelled to apologize. "I mention it merely because I am myself very adequately provided for. And do you know, Miss Agbrigg, it has often seemed strange to me that the man from whom I purchase my groceries, any man, in fact, who can, however meagrely, be called a householder, is entitled to his vote at election time. Whereas I, who own this house and another by the sea and a street or two of rented property in Cullingford, am allowed no vote at all. Is it any wonder that so many of the laws of our land are unjust to women, or simply take no account of women at all, when no woman has had a hand in their making?"

"You are a suffragist then, Miss Mandelbaum?"

"My dear, I believe I am, for I made the acquaintance on a recent visit to Manchester of Miss Lydia Becker, a founder of the Society for Women's Suffrage. Should I succeed in persuading her to visit me and speak a few words, perhaps you would care to attend?"

Miss Becker, as it turned out, was unable to oblige but sent instead her lieutenant, a dry and rather angry Miss Tighe, who explained to our select gathering certain matters which seemed to me so obvious and so right that I understood—with the force of a revelation—that I had been born believing them.

I knew—as who did not—that the Reform Bill of 1832 had

given the vote to all middle class gentlemen, a privilege which had hitherto belonged exclusively to the aristocracy and any others who possessed property and connections enough to number themselves among the "ruling classes." The Reform Bill of 1867—considerably overdue—had fallen far short of the universal male suffrage which had been demanded, but had granted "household suffrage," a phrase, Miss Tighe told us, in which a loophole had been spotted, nearly four thousand women in Manchester alone—Miss Tighe among them—who owned houses and income far above the minimum property qualification the bill required, having attempted to place their names on the electoral register.

Miss Tighe had taken her claim to court, where it had been defended by the dedicated and philanthropic barrister Dr. Richard Marsden Pankhurst, a man so devoted to the many facets of social justice that he had declared his intention of remaining unmarried the better to pursue them. But the law had declared Miss Tighe's claim to be invalid, maintaining in effect that although the right to vote depended on the amount of property one possessed, that right—like most others—was automatically rendered null and void by the sorry accident of having been born a woman.

Miss Tighe had been present in 1868, immediately after the passing of the Second Reform Bill, at the first public meeting of the newly formed Manchester National Society for Women's Suffrage in Manchester's Free Trade Hall, and had since then associated herself closely with Miss Lydia Becker and those male champions of the suffragist cause, the Quaker politician Mr. Jacob Bright and the lawyer Dr. Pankhurst. Nor had they contented themselves with public meetings, having agreed—in the very appropriate setting of the Free Trade Hall—to adopt the tactics of the Anti-Corn Law League which a quarter of a century ago had done successful battle against import controls and had given us Free Trade.

It was the aim of the National Society for Women's Suffrage, Miss Tighe went on, to attract attention to the female cause by presenting regular petitions to Parliament as the Anti-Corn Law League had done, Miss Lydia Becker herself having produced a pamphlet entitled "Directions for Preparing a Petition to the House of Commons" which Miss Tighe would be glad to distribute among us. In 1869 alone, she said, without once referring to any notes or figures, two hundred and fifty-five petitions, requesting the vote for women on the same terms as it had been granted to men, had been presented. The flow of these petitions would continue, the flow of Private Members' Bills must be encouraged to flow with it. Mr. Jacob Bright having introduced such a bill two years ago which had passed its second reading in the House before being annihilated by that great enemy of the Women's Cause, the leader of the Liberal Party, Mr. Gladstone, who like numerous others believed female suffrage to be a serious threat to family life.

Mr. Gladstone, it was very clear, believed in the concept of woman as domestic angel, his reluctance to burden her with electoral responsibilities stemming from his oft-expressed fear that her fine and gentle nature might be damaged, the delicate structure of her mind distracted from her rightful worship of hearth and home. And if it had occurred to him that the population of England numbered rather more women than men, which would—if enfranchised—make the female a mighty power to be reckoned with, he had not said so.

But the Women's Cause had few other champions in high places. The Conservative leader, Mr. Benjamin Disraeli, had expressed cautious sympathy in his younger days when speeches on controversial issues had been very much his style. But once he had taken office and had no need of controversy to get himself noticed, little more had been heard from him on the matter. Nor could the movement rely overmuch on the support of famous women, the great Florence Nightingale having heartily condemned her own sex as being narrow-minded, uncooperative and unsympathetic, while it was no secret that Queen Victoria, although a reigning monarch, enjoyed nothing better than the domination of the male, having always insisted in private—during her husband's lifetime—on regarding herself as his "little wife." And so strongly was she opposed to the notion of women's rights that she believed any lady—titled or otherwise—who spoke openly in their favour deserved a good whipping, presumably by a dominating male hand.

Women, in Miss Florence Nightingale's opinion, were too feeble. In Queen Victoria's view they could not be feeble enough. What did Miss Mandelbaum think, or Miss Fielding and Miss Agbrigg, Miss Tighe wanted to know?

"You might care to consider getting up a petition of your own," she said, her keen eyes passing speculatively, a little scornfully, from Miss Mandelbaum's enthusiastic but somewhat flustered expression to Miss Fielding who, as the daughter of a Liberal M P, had not liked the reference to Mr. Gladstone, and who furthermore had suspected from the start that the Church, with its creed of submission, could not possibly approve of this. And then her sharp, rather stony gaze resting on me, Miss Tighe smiled.

"The future of the movement—perhaps the fruits of it—must belong to you," she told me, coming to sit beside me as we partook of Miss Mandelbaum's scented tea and ratafia cakes. "Why not pay a visit to Manchester, Miss Agbrigg, and make the acquaintance of Miss Lydia Becker and Dr. Pankhurst? I could ask my friends the Gouldens to invite you—a perfectly respectable manufacturing family whose daughter Emmeline must be about your age."

And even had I been less convinced by her explanation of the Women's Cause, the mere fact that I wanted badly to accept her invitation and knew I would not be allowed to do so would have converted me.

Mr. Nicholas Barforth invited us to dine that autumn, a circumstance astonishing enough in itself, since for a very long time his entertaining had been done expensively but impersonally in hotels, a necessary if tedious part of his business which he delegated whenever possible to Liam Adair or to Gervase. But his invitation now was most specific and most correct, gilt-edged, gilt-lettered, designed to fill Mrs. Agbrigg's heart with joy had she not been too well aware of his intentions.

Mr. Nicholas Barforth, it seemed, had decided to take a hand in his son's affairs, to give him, perhaps, one final opportunity. For after all, blood was notoriously thicker than water, and knowing that Gervase would one day have to stand alone against the ambitions of men like his cousin Gideon, Mr. Barforth would certainly bring him up to the mark if he could.

"Steady yourself down," I could imagine him saying, "and get a steady woman to help you—a sensible lass with money of her own behind her." And it could be no secret that I was the "good catch," the strong-minded, steady Law Valley woman of his choice.

"I see," my father said, the invitation in his hands.

"Precisely," Mrs. Agbrigg answered him. "I have been dreading this approach, for with the best will in the world I cannot discover one shred of evidence to alter my opinion of that young man. And considering the irregular position of his mother, the rumours by which she is surrounded, I wonder—well, perhaps Grace might have a convenient headache that evening and find herself indisposed?"

But the knowledge—conveyed by Venetia—that Gideon Chard would be among the guests confused Mrs. Agbrigg's tactics to a point where, on the evening in question, she failed to make the objections I had been expecting to the rather scanty bodice of my peach-coloured silk, nor to the skirt cut very straight in front and very full behind, the folds of the bustle and the train studded with black velvet bows. She was herself in cinnamon brown, a shade much darker but not unrelated to the tint of her skin, my father narrow and correct in his evening clothes, his face wise and sad as he helped me from the carriage, his own opinion of this almost-proposed marriage—his desire to dispose of me or his fear of losing me—remaining unspoken.

"A historic occasion," he said as the huge, carved oak door of Tarn Edge was opened to us by the indifferent Barforth butler, who announced our names and abandoned us to a considerably amused Venetia who, having never played hostess before, could not bring herself to treat it as anything but a game.

There was a huge fire in the marble fireplace, costly treasures of Sèvres and Meissen on the mantelshelf, a clock sprouting Cupids and acanthus leaves of a metal which appeared to be gold. The Aubusson rug—repaired, one presumed—was back in its place by the hearth, Mr. Barforth standing firmly upon it, his back to the flames, Mr. Gideon Chard standing, too, at the corner of the fender, his feet not yet on the precious rug but not too far away, while Gervase, lounging in a red velvet armchair, took a moment to rise, as if his body, after an arduous day of pleasure, required care.

"We have just ridden in from Galton," Venetia said, as vibrant with energy as her brother was listless. "Or, at least, no more than an hour ago, so if I am not immaculately enough turned out for you, you will know the reason why. We were out with the Lawdale at five o'clock this morning, when even the foxes were sleepy."

"Too sleepy," put in Gervase, his eyelids drooping. "There's no sense—and I'll keep on saying it—in disturbing a night-feeder at that hour, when he's still too full of his dinner to run. An afternoon fox, that's the thing—not that Noel Chard would take notice of it."

"I expect Noel knows what he's doing," said Gideon, drawling out the words as if none of them could matter less, although we understood quite well that he would allow no criticism of his brother's mastership of the Lawdale Hunt, an office which his family had held for generations.

"You must miss your sport, Mr. Chard, in this fine weather," murmured Mrs. Agbrigg artfully offering him an opportunity to demonstrate his worth—since he *was* a sportsman by birth and breeding and *had*, unlike Gervase, spent this glorious afternoon at the mill.

"I miss it enormously," he said, his voice suave and serious. "But then, one is obliged to put first things first, after all."

"Oh lord!" Venetia exclaimed. "Do you know, Gideon, when you talk like that I wonder if you might have done better as a bishop."

To which Mr. Gideon Chard, without the slightest hint of ill-humour, gave her a slight bow, and smiled.

We ate gamebirds, as I remember, as was appropriate to the season, and various over-cooked vegetables unworthy of their massive silver dishes. The crystal was magnificent, the wine highly satisfactory to the gentlemen, who all drank a great deal, the chocolate cream a decided failure, being of a most uneven consistency and far too sweet. Nor was the conversation more evenly blended, my father and Mr. Barforth talking warp and weft, profit and loss, Gervase refusing deliberately and impudently to speak one word that was not connected with foxhunting, while Gideon Chard maintained an attentive and rather careful silence, appalled, I imagine, by the food, which would never have been permitted to leave the kitchens at Listonby, and by the haphazard service, which as his mother's son must have amazed him.

I was silent too, feeling stiff and awkward and false, and it was a relief to me when, the meal over, Venetia finally remembered her duty and escorted her female guests back to the drawing-room and installed us in deep armchairs by the fireside, Mrs. Agbrigg placidly partaking of coffee and cakes while Venetia, her cheeks flushed with wine and firelight, lost herself at once in an apparently blissful dream.

There was a long silence, Mrs. Agbrigg and I having nothing to say to each other, Venetia and I nothing that could be said in Mrs. Agbrigg's hearing, and noting her sharp eyes seeking out the flaw in the Aubusson rug, her satisfied smile when she found it, I was reminded of her objections to Venetia as a friend, to Gervase as a husband, and felt my colour rise.

He was not, of course, attracted to me, I felt absolutely certain of that. But should sufficient pressure be brought to bear I thought he might well find it easier, safer, to succumb; might shrug those lean, mischievous shoulders and say "Why

not?'' thus making me mistress of this grand, neglected house
and sister to Venetia. And because Venetia, already, was closer
to me than any sister, I allowed that imaginary future to ease
itself into my mind, my fancy restoring Tarn Edge to its former
splendour, my voice speaking sharply to that supercilious butler,
that disastrous cook; taking my breakfast with Venetia in the
back parlour, declaring myself ''not at home'' when Mrs. Agbrigg
came to call; and then I found myself smiling, because in this
pleasant, schoolroom fantasy of marriage I had entirely forgotten
the husband—Gervase.

One could not, of course, forget Gideon Chard. He would take
and maintain his place anywhere, in fact or in fantasy, by his
simple refusal ever to be overlooked. But I had no reason to
believe he had ever thought of me with anything warmer than
self-interest. Mr. Nicholas Barforth was the wealthiest man in
the Law Valley and Venetia's share of his fortune would be
considerable, but her inheritance was encumbered by the existence of a brother who *might*—how could one ever be sure?
—discover within himself a sudden interest in commerce. Whereas
I, although I did not know the exact terms of my father's will,
could expect my share of his worldly goods eventually to consist
of the whole. And I had no brother to stand between my husband
and complete possession of Fieldhead.

Yet Fieldhead itself suddenly oppressed me—Mrs. Agbrigg's
house, never mine—and I knew with a fierce and persistent
certainty that I must marry a man with the means to take me
away from there. No husband of mine must ever depend entirely
on Agbrigg favour, reducing me from the sorry position of
''daughter-at-home'' to the even more unbearable level of
''married-daughter-at-home,'' the young mistress forever subservient to the old. I must have an establishment of my own, must
have some measure of authority and freedom; and no fortune-
hunter, however noble or shrewd or desirable, could give me
that.

''You seem very comfortable,'' Mr. Barforth told us from the
doorway, crossing the room to stand on the hearthrug again, his
son and his nephew and my father following behind.

''Sit down by your wife, Jonas,'' he said, and my father, with
his sad, wry smile, obediently sat. ''Venetia, you can give us
our coffee. Gideon, sit there. Gervase—there.'' It was done.

He had arranged us to his own satisfaction and for as long as it
suited him, for life perhaps, Venetia, still in her blissful dream
of Charles Heron, inattentive and uncaring, but sitting neverthe-

less by Gideon Chard; Gervase, his mother's son, sitting just the same by me; Mr. Barforth himself still planted on the hearthrug, dominating the room, his wide back absorbing the warmth of the fire, his keen eyes well satisfied. He had arranged us, and knowing his disposition to be both autocratic and vindictive, I wondered how he would bear his disappointment, so certain was I that it could never be.

5

It was an autumn of petty and intense frustrations, of officious supervision and an unremitting, heavy-handed control. Aunt Faith's sister, Mrs. Frederick Hobhouse—my Aunt Prudence—the owner of a flourishing school for girls in Ambleside, invited me to stay with her and was told, with scant courtesy, that I was too young to travel in such wild country alone. Miss Tighe sent a correct little letter from Manchester wondering if Mrs. Agbrigg could "spare" me for a week or two and was refused in terms which humiliated me, although Miss Tighe, when I met her again, seemed amused by them.

"Poor lamb," she said, her shrewd, hard eyes atwinkle. "You are bound hand and foot, I know it. And although the bonds, if you examine them well, are made of nothing but convention, we have been so thoroughly trained, have we not, to obey mamma and papa, that it seems impossible to break free. Yes, dear, a strong-minded mamma can be a great burden. You may find a husband somewhat easier to manage."

And I was in no doubt that, day by day, Mrs. Agbrigg was forcing me towards that same conclusion.

My cousin Blanche returned home at the start of the winter, looking as lovely and—one could not avoid noticing it—as virginal as ever, and immediately Aunt Caroline, who had been living quietly since the wedding, awoke to her accustomed activity, organizing an ambitious programme of winter events which one could only assume to be her swan-song. The house once more was full of guests, foxhunting gentlemen from London availing themselves of the well-stocked Listonby stables, ladies with double-barrelled names and flat, high-bred voices who sat about all day—like Blanche—in the Great Hall, where tea and muffins, hot chocolate and gingerbread, chilled white or hot, spiced wine were in constant supply, served by footmen in Listonby's blue

and gold livery who seemed possessed of the ability to material-
ize from thin air.

"Wonderful, is it not," Blanche asked me, stifling a contented yawn, "how it all happens, as if by magic?"

But the magician—as Blanche well knew—had been up since
dawn setting these luxurious wheels in motion and would not
retire that night until the last of her guests had been escorted
ceremoniously to bed.

"Aunt Caroline must work extremely hard," I suggested, but
Blanche only smiled.

"She loves it, Grace—simply thrives on it. She wouldn't be
without it for the world. And as for me—well, I haven't the least
notion of depriving her. It would be too unkind."

Yet, although Blanche seemed content to remain a pampered
guest in her own home for ever, there would be times, surely,
when Sir Dominic's wife must take precedence over his widowed
mother? And I wondered, with some amusement and a certain
sympathy, how Aunt Caroline would come to terms with that.

There was a change of guests that first fine November Saturday,
one house-party being carefully conveyed to the station to catch
the morning train, the next one not due until Monday, making
dinner that night a family occasion in the small, early Georgian
saloon, an apartment the colour of musk roses where Aunt
Caroline—who had "improved" so much else at Listonby—had
retained the original century old Baroque mouldings, the elegant,
satin-covered Regency chairs, the impression of great age and
the gradual, heart-searching decay of great beauty.

"How nice to be *en famille*," she said, smiling very brightly
as Blanche sat down at the head of the table opposite her
bridegroom, not troubling in the least as to where anyone else
should sit; claiming, in fact, the privileges of the lady of the
manor while not even appearing to notice the responsibilities.
But the Duke of South Erin, very much *en famille* at Listonby,
automatically took the place of honour to the right of Blanche,
Aunt Caroline to the right of Dominic, Gideon Chard and Venetia
finding themselves side by side, an indication, one supposed,
that Aunt Caroline had abandoned her hopes of an earl's daughter and decided to "see reason"; while Noel Chard, not receiving any instructions, hesitated, his eyes on the empty chair
beside Blanche, wondering perhaps if he should be paying attention to me until his mother deposited me to the left of Dominic
and released him.

Unlike Tarn Edge, the food was superb, the service miraculous, the conversation dull, I thought, but without strain, Sir Dominic and the weather-beaten little duke confining themselves to hunting and shooting stories of a technicality which rendered them incomprehensible to me, although Gideon and even Venetia from time to time joined in, having all of them in their day jumped a wider ditch in pursuit of a craftier fox, confirming my belief, as the brandied oranges and champagne syllabubs were brought in, that a sportsman will discuss his sport with the same fervour as an invalid listing his symptoms, and to the same stultifying effect.

Noel Chard, who had served as master of the Lawdale Hunt during Sir Dominic's absence, made small contribution to these equine enthusiasms, his attention absorbed by Blanche, his solicitude arousing in her an even greater helplessness than usual, a total inability to manage her napkin or reach her glass which clearly convinced Noel—if few others—of her frailty and her need, at all times, to be handled with care. Aunt Caroline too was silent, not really listening to the strident voices of her sons, not even calling them to order when one of them let slip an audible "damn," a sure indication that her thoughts were very much occupied.

"When does Aunt Faith return from France?" she asked me, although Blanche had mentioned the date not an hour before, and when I said that it would be the week after Christmas, she sighed and muttered: "How inconvenient, since they could join us—" without specifying who or where.

The dessert over, there was a pause, my eyes and Venetia's going automatically to Aunt Caroline for our signal to withdraw, Dominic too glancing sharply at his mother, who had never before kept the ladies in the dining-room so long, depriving the squire of his port and cigars and the freedom to say "damn" and worse than that if he had a mind.

"Mamma?" he said, puzzled and rather put out, revealing himself already as a gentleman who not only expected to get his own way but to get it at once, the very moment—as any fool could see—that he desired it.

"Yes, Dominic?" she replied.

"Shouldn't you—?"

"No," she said. "Not I, dear—not now."

And even then there was a moment before Blanche, catching her husband's irritable eye, exclaimed, "Oh goodness! Are you waiting for *me*?" and started to her feet, her movement clearly

requiring the assistance of Noel Chard if it was to be successfully completed.

But Aunt Caroline, having scored her point and proved her
daughter-in-law to be incompetent, shook her head, turning
imperious again.

"In a moment, dear. First there is a word to be said, and a
toast to be drunk, I think."

"Oh yes," Blanche agreed, sliding back into her chair, assuming the toast was to be "long life and happiness to the bride," so
that she was unprepared and completely vulnerable when Aunt
Caroline announced: "Dominic, as the head of the family, already knows what I have to say. I have his approval and am in
no doubt of yours. The Duke of South Erin has asked me to be his
wife—and I have agreed to it, which should surprise no one."

And through the sudden scraping back of chairs, the exclamations and the laughter as the little duke was shaken by the hand
and the tall duchess kissed in turn by each of her tall sons—all
three of them keenly alive to the advantages of a ducal step-
papa—I heard Venetia's clear voice say "Lord, what a lark!
You've always been a duchess, Aunt Caroline," while Blanche,
feeling the weight of Listonby already on her shoulders, howled
out her dismay. "You didn't *tell* me, Dominic."

The match, of course, was altogether splendid, for while
South Erin was not a great political duke, his family no older
than the Clevedons and the Chards themselves, he was of the
nobility, not the simple landed gentry as they were, and even Sir
Dominic, whose view of his own worth must have been a great
comfort to him, was impressed.

There would be a tall, somewhat dilapidated house in Belgravia
for Aunt Caroline to renovate, an estate in Devonshire for her to
"improve" in her unique fashion, a presentation at Court, for
although our Queen did not approve of second marriages, considering that the heart of any decent widow should belong, like her
own, in her husband's grave, she could hardly refuse audience to
the new Duchess of South Erin.

Aunt Caroline, in fact, had done far better than anyone had
expected for the second time in her life, and there was no doubt
that her sons—Dominic already contemplating a flirtation with
politics, Noel eager for military promotion, Gideon ready to pick
up power and influence wherever he found it—were very pleased
with her. They remained a long time in the dining-room with the
pleasant, nut-brown little duke, to tell him so; and finding
Blanche's indignation hard to bear—having no answer to her

"How am I to manage this great barracks of a place when everyone knows I have no head for figures and cannot remember names—when I just want to be peaceful and *comfortable*"—I soon made my escape.

From the painted, panelled staircase rising out of the Great Hall one reached the ballroom, the darkness of a winter evening not really hiding its gilt and crystal splendour, and beyond it came the Long Gallery, lined on both sides with massively framed Chards, their stern faces registering no surprise, in this cheapjack modern world, that a tradesman's daughter had first married one of their descendants and had now snared herself a duke.

But I had seen these portraits too many times before to play the old game of deciding which ones reminded me most of Dominic, or Noel, or Gideon, and walking briskly from end to end, it seemed to me that in Blanche's shoes I would have welcomed this marriage. In Blanche's shoes I would have resented so powerful a mother-in-law as Aunt Caroline, would already have acquainted myself with every linen cupboard and china cupboard at Listonby, with the guest book and the menu book, with the staff and the tenants, with the formidable expertise of my predecessor, so that hopefully and in time I might do even better. But Blanche's shoes—alas—included the sporting, self-centred Sir Dominic, and smiling as I realized how little I desired to acquaint myself with him—how little, indeed, there was in him with which to be acquainted—I turned to retrace my steps and encountered Gideon, amazing myself by the lurch my stomach gave at the suspicion—I would not call it the hope—that he had come here not by chance but to look for me.

Amazed. And then, because it was absolutely necessary to be cool, I said coolly, lightly, "What exciting news!" deliberately setting a tone of insipid and safe formality.

"Yes indeed—although Blanche does not seem to think so."

"Oh well, there is no need to worry about Blanche. She will find someone else to look after her."

"I daresay—except that my brother Noel will be obliged to rejoin his regiment in the New Year."

And not wishing to answer this, finding it too personal, too apt to lead to other things, although I could not have named them, I turned back to the portraits, chancing on the one gentleman in that gallery who was not a Chard, a saturnine and undoubtedly handsome face reminding me strongly of Mr. Nicholas Barforth, although it was Sir Joel Barforth, his and Aunt Caroline's father.

"My manufacturing grandfather," Gideon said, half-smiling. "Do you know, I believe Dominic will take that picture down when mamma has gone to South Erin. We were made to suffer, somewhat, at school because father had married into 'trade.' "

"But Dominic has done the same."

"Yes. But Blanche is a generation away from the more sordid side of it. And she *is* very beautiful."

"Yes."

"And very spoiled."

"Yes. And I am very fond of her."

"So are we all, for there is nothing of the heavy woollen district about her. One could take her just about anywhere. And, of course, she has such a lot of money."

I should have been very angry with him then. He had spoken, I think, with that intention. But there was something behind his words which caught and distracted my temper, something directed against himself which, instead of the sharp retort I could have made, caused me most astonishingly to enquire, "Is Dominic—displeased—that you have gone into trade yourself? Does he feel—?"

"What? That I am a traitor to my class? Very likely."

"Well—I am sorry for that."

"How kind. But there is no need. He may well call me a money-grubbing tradesman the next time we quarrel, but if anyone else dared to do so you can be sure my brother Dominic would knock him down."

"And you would do the same for Dominic, naturally."

"Naturally."

"Gideon—" and I did not at all wish to ask him this question, did not wish to offer him what he would see as sympathy—which *was* sympathy. "Gideon—have you found it very difficult—I mean, in the Piece Hall and the Wool Exchange?"

"Oh yes," he said, very nonchalant, negligent almost. "To tell the truth, I find Cullingford difficult altogether. But then, difficulties exist to be overcome, don't you know?"

"Yes, I do know."

"I rather thought you might."

And having no answer ready—because he should not have been thinking of me at all and I should not have been so very pleased, so cat-in-the-cream-pot smug to know he had—I looked up into his face and for what seemed a long time could not look away again, held by something I was unable to name but which my body recognized as desire. And not his desire alone, not merely the narrowing of his eyes in sudden concentration, the faint air of surprise about him, his attitude of listening to his own body, the quickening of his own pulse-beat, the stirrings of heat and hunger. Not that alone but my own response to it, the feeling of new blood being somehow released inside me and flowing vigorously, rhythmically, towards an awareness not only of my own body but of the dark, hard, beautiful body of Gideon Chard, rushing me headlong towards the recognition, the *expectation* of physical pleasure.

I had grown accustomed to thinking of myself as a young woman of sense and moderation, but what had awakened in me now—and how could I doubt it had always been there?—was a most immoderate sensuality. And although I had known of the existence of this phenomenon—natural, I had been led to believe, in men but wanton in women—I was unprepared for the sheer force of it, the enormity, this tempestuous arousal not of the feminine side of my nature but of the *female*; the deep-rooted, primitive urge to submit. How glorious! How appalling! How total the self-betrayal! How complete the self-fulfilment! How perilous! Yet that spice of fear was in itself desirable, and nothing in my glowing, expanding limbs nor in my dizzy head held me away from it. He had only to touch me—only that. I could not resist him, no matter what it cost me—*could* not—until the moment I did so and said in a quick, cool little voice: "It is very dark in here and rather chilly."

"Yes," he said, "so it is," his voice telling me nothing, a man not without experience of women, who knew when his moment had passed.

It was over. I had come to no harm. But as I walked back down the painted staircase I was as careful on my feet as an invalid, aware that I had escaped not by my own resolution alone, for if he *had* touched me, if— And my thought could extend no further, cut out, veered aside, refusing, like a fractious horse at a ditch, to hazard itself.

We were to drive to Galton Abbey the next morning, Blanche's satisfaction in being a married woman who could now act as chaperone to Venetia and myself altogether swamped by her gloom at Aunt Caroline's desertion. And as we negotiated the bare November lanes she had much to say on the subject of her mother-in-law's ambition and duplicity.

"She does not care a fig about the poor little man himself, you can be very sure of that. All she sees is a ducal coronet and being a society hostess in Belgravia. Not that she will even stay in London once she gets there. Oh no, she will be forever coming back to Listonby to satisfy herself that things were better in her day. And it is not my fault, for if she intended running off like this—as I am sure she did—then she should have *said* so. Dominic thinks it a small matter. Just carry on, he tells me, as mother does. Well—Dominic Chard has not the faintest idea of how those stupendous meals arrive on his table four times every day, and neither have I.''

Nor much intention, I thought, of finding out, since by the end of the first mile she was considering how a secretary, a companion, and her cousin Grace Agbrigg, might be pressed into her service.

"You could come over every Friday to Monday and stay on until Tuesday, or not go home at all. You would be glad to get away from Mrs. Agbrigg, and I would be glad of you."

But Venetia, dismissing this suggestion out of hand, made her own designs on my future very clear by declaring, "Nonsense, Blanche, you must manage your own life as best you can, for Grace—if she would like it—could soon have a life of her own."

The house at Galton was quite small and very old, older indeed than the date of its construction, the first Clevedon having come here as a conqueror, a supporter of King Henry's breach with papal authority which had allowed him, an English Protestant, to pull the Roman Catholic abbey down and use its ancient stones to build himself a manor. I had been here only once before in childhood, when the house had seemed dark and eerie, an emptiness about it of which I could not be sure, which did not seem, somehow, to be empty at all, so that I had spent a night of terror in a low-ceilinged chamber, a heavily curtained bed, plagued by the creaking of old wood and the unaccustomed noises of the open countryside, convinced that the room was dangerous, yet not daring to venture into the passage outside, that airless, pitch-black tunnel which might have taken me anywhere.

But today, although the house was certainly low, its colour a shade darker than the November sky, its situation, on what in another season would be a leafy bend of the river, was very beautiful; the parlour where Mrs. Barforth awaited us furnished with over-stuffed chintz, a good fire burning, an ageing dog and cat lying on the rug in pleasing harmony.

It was not a tidy room, the pewter jugs on the mantelshelf

brimming over with odds and ends of letters and bills, a buttonhook, a scrap of leather, a pair of riding gloves thrown down on the sofa, the sofa itself showing traces of animal hair. Nor was Mrs. Barforth a tidy woman, having come indoors, I thought, when our carriage wheels had reminded her she was expecting guests, leaving herself no time and probably no inclination to change her riding-habit for a morning gown.

"Darling," she said, giving Venetia's cheek a companionable kiss, "and Lady Chard—good heavens, Blanche, how very grand that sounds! Is it not altogether too heavy for you? And Miss Agbrigg—"

And although her smile and her swift, light green gaze were as frank as Venetia's her handclasp firm and honest, my suspicion that her husband must have told her to consider me as a possible bride for Gervase stiffened my manner and my tongue, making me formal and cold.

"What an interesting house, Mrs. Barforth."

"Oh, do you think so? Then allow me to show it to you." And while Blanche dozed by the fire, displaying the same purring delight in her creature comforts as the cat, I was taken on a tour of the house which meant far more to Mrs. Georgiana Barforth than any riches the Barforth mills could provide, for which she had been prepared to sacrifice her liberty and her peace of mind—one supposed—so that she might pass on this noble heritage of the Clevedons to her Clevedon–Barforth son.

There was a Great Hall here too, minute when compared to Listonby, being only twenty feet square, a bare, stone floor, a few battered oak chests, a long oak table set out with bowls and tankards of dented pewter. There was a high stone fireplace, weaponry and family portraits on the walls, stone steps leading to the upper floor where that creaking rabbit-warren of passages awaited, those low, stone-flagged bedchambers with their tiny mullioned windows, their impression of peopled emptiness which comes from great age.

"That," Venetia said, indicating a picture of a narrow-gowned Georgian lady, "was my Great-grandmamma Venetia, who was an earl's daughter no less, although I have heard that the noble earl was not pleased to be connected with us, mamma."

"He was not," Mrs. Barforth cheerfully agreed. "So little pleased that he disinherited her, or would have done so had there been anything to inherit. She was very poor, alas, like the rest of us—"

"Are we poor, mamma? I had not noticed it."

"Ah," Mrs. Barforth said, smiling, meeting Venetia's clear, slightly accusing eyes without flinching, "I believe I was speaking of the past, when we were truly poor, my brother and I and Sir Julian and everyone else we knew, and one forgets— Miss Agbrigg, do tell me what you think of this picture over here."

It was a large canvas, prominently displayed above the hearth, showing a young man the same age as Gervase, the same sporting jacket and flamboyant neck-tie Gervase often wore, the same nervous, whipcord energy that could just as easily ebb or flow, the pale pointed face and auburn hair that for some reason she wished me to mistake for Gervase, although I knew it could not be he.

"It is my Uncle Peregrine," Venetia said flatly, denying her mother this small satisfaction. "You were supposed to take him for Gervase. Everyone else does. But it is the famous Perry Clevedon who could bring down eighty grouse with eighty shots any day of the week—"

"My brother," Mrs. Barforth said, smiling at her daughter sadly, although she was offering the explanation to me, "died some years ago, unmarried. We were very closely united, for we had been brought up here together without any other company and needing none. We were, I believe, perfectly happy. A dangerous gift, I admit, for any child, such happiness, since one tended to think the whole of life would be like that, and learned only slowly otherwise. His death was not only a great and lasting grief to me but it left Galton, for the first time in three hundred years, without a direct male heir. I wonder, Miss Agbrigg, if you realize how much that matters to people like us?"

"Very likely I do not, Mrs. Barforth. I know the name of my great-grandparents but beyond that I am uncertain as to just who, or what, my family may have been."

"Yes—forgive me, Miss Agbrigg, but I believe the word 'inheritance' as used in the cities tends to imply money, or property which can be readily converted into money . . .? With us it is not quite like that. What this estate of Galton means is not profit, not material gain of any kind, but a tradition of service to the land that has supported us these three hundred years, service to the tenants who farm it, and to the village communities settled upon it. It is a very hard life, Miss Agbrigg, a very dedicated, specialized existence—not so much an inheritance, I think, as a *trust* with which the men of my family have always kept faith."

And being in no doubt at all that, albeit gently and with

considerable embarrassment, she was nevertheless warning me
that my middle-class values could accord neither with Galton nor
with her son, I made some non-committal answer and moved
away from the fire to the narrow mullioned window, seeking a
distraction and instantly finding it in the sight of horsemen
approaching at speed down the hillside.

They came splashing across the stream and into the courtyard,
Gervase Barforth and all three Chards, mud-spattered, wet through,
and quite magnificent, shaking off the physical discomforts of
November wind and weather with a lordly nonchalance proper to
the squirearchy. And instantly Mrs. Barforth, whose house had
seemed ill-equipped for the serving of tea to ladies, broke free
from the restraints my presence had imposed upon her, her face
glowing with the uncomplicated joy of being among her "own
people" as she served them strong ale and mulled wine, standing
companionably among them as they crowded to the fire and
drank deep, their coats steaming. And while Noel Chard did
briefly say to her "You may have heard that mamma is to be a
duchess," to which she replied "Oh yes—I have a maid who
talks to the maids at Listonby . . ." her attention was not
diverted from these young men who in their insolent, unruly
splendour were a thousand miles away from Cullingford.

Yet they were not a contented band, having found no sport
that morning, so little prospect of it that afternoon that in disgust
they had decided to ride home, the scarcity of foxes inclining Sir
Dominic to believe that some villainous gang of farmers, in
order to protect their miserable chicken-runs, had been shooting
the beasts or poisoning them, instead of leaving them to be
properly slaughtered by gentlemen.

"Not on my land they haven't," said Gervase.

"What land is that?" enquired Sir Dominic who, as a first-
born son, liked to be precise in matters of inheritance.

"This land."

"Oh—I beg your pardon. I thought *this* land belonged to your
father."

Perhaps no real slight had been intended, Sir Dominic feeling
quite simply a little peevish and knowing no reason why others
should not suffer for it. But for an instant there was an ugly
flaring of tempers, Gervase tensing himself like an angry, wary
cat, the Chards closing ranks, three hounds, I thought, of high
and disdainful pedigree who would turn as one and rend to
pieces all who threatened them. But it was Blanche, or rather her
voice drifting lazily from the doorway, which put out this spark

of combat, drawing all eyes towards her as she came into the room and simply stood there, allowing herself to be looked at, rosy and a little dishevelled from her sleep, her whole body languorous, still purring with the pleasures of idleness.

Noel Chard succumbed at once, wanting nothing now but to gaze at her.

"Heavens," she said, "such a racket!—I thought we had been invaded." And now it was Gideon who, grinning suddenly, relaxed and gave her a slight bow.

"I had forgotten you would be here," said Sir Dominic, a man who rarely remembered his wife until bedtime in any case. But looking at her now, the silvery and ivory of her, the dreamy, slumberous quality which was not sensuality but which he perhaps had mistaken for sensuality, I saw him swallow hard, his quarrel with Gervase, his irritation with his gamekeepers and with the foxes shrinking to a proper childishness before the instinctive, eternal wisdom of a beautiful woman.

"I have been asleep," she said, her manner, her tone, everything about her conveying that this simple remark of hers—if one really listened to it—was not only of great importance but exceedingly profound.

Noel Chard smiled at her fondly; Gideon Chard smiled too, not fondly but with amusement and speculation, and Gervase smiled with him. Dominic Chard, her husband, continued to look at her with the same acute concentration I had seen the night before in Gideon, calculating the extent of his desire.

"There now," she said, stretching herself a little. "I believe I am awake." And with none of the book-learning Venetia and I had so diligently acquired at school, she had disarmed them all.

A simple country luncheon was set out on the hall table, bread and cheese and pickles, jugs of milk and mugs of ale, a huge plum cake, sweet red apples. And afterwards, the sun having made up its mind to shine, the gentlemen strolled outside, having drunk themselves through their ill-humour and back again, to an even greater restlessness.

"I shall go back to the parlour, Aunt Georgiana, if I may," said Blanche, "for they will be making wagers ere long, and doing foolish things—one can read the signs. You had better stay with me, Grace, and keep warm." But half an hour of renewed complaining about her mother-in-law wearied me and as soon as her eyelids began to close I took my cloak and went outdoors, responding gladly to the onslaught of the raw, damp wind, delighted by the very greyness of the sky, the sweep of the bare brown land.

Venetia and her mother were standing by the dry-stone wall of a nearby field, both women watching intently as Gervase came cantering across the rough grass and took his horse cleanly over a long pole supported between two posts which had been cut quite roughly so that the jump could be lowered or, as seemed the present intention, made higher still.

There had, quite naturally, been a wager, Gervase having declared his chestnut mare capable of jumping higher than Dominic's roan or the two sleek Listonby bays of Noel and Gideon. And since he had offered twenty Barforth guineas to back his claim—a sum which Noel, at least, would find hard to raise from his army pay, or Gideon from whatever salary Mr. Barforth paid him—they had set up the practice fence which, as apparently all Galton and Listonby knew, the legendary Perry Clevedon had jumped regularly, drunk or sober, day or night, to a height of seven feet.

I could see no real danger except to someone's pride or someone's pocket, for I was no horsewoman and had nothing but imagination to tell me of the terrors and exhilarations, the cool nerve and fine judgement that propelled each animal in turn into that fierce-arched leaping and safely to the wet, uneven ground again.

"Higher?" said Gervase.

And since Mrs. Barforth's two elderly grooms had enough to do elsewhere without catering to the whims of gentlemen, Noel Chard and Gervase were obliged to lift the pole from its groove and slot it into the one above, Sir Dominic disdaining so menial a task, Gideon quite simply ignoring it.

Noel, predictably, was the first to go; a moment of insufficient determination, or the habit perhaps of never taking first place, which caused his horse to pull up short in stubborn refusal, sending Noel over the animal's head and into the mud from which he emerged smiling, a good sport and a good loser.

"Higher?" said Gervase.

And a quarter of an hour later it was Sir Dominic who hit the ground, demonstrating, as he got up, that although he was furious and had *expected* to win—felt that a man in his position *ought* to win—he had the good manners not to say so.

"Well, Gideon—" he ordered curtly, not wishing to make too much of it, but implying, just the same, that the honour of Listonby was now at stake and must not be sacrificed to this mongrel Clevedon–Barforth. And Gideon, responding to the appeal of family loyalty—although he may also have been thinking of those twenty guineas—rode his tall bay horse forward at the gallop and lifting himself in the saddle cleared what amounted to the height of a man with apparent ease.

"Well done," said Noel.

"Not bad," said Sir Dominic.

"Higher?" said Gervase.

"Oh lord!" called out Venetia, "do we have to stand here all day?" But she did not move, her eyes fixed on her brother with an intensity which forced me to look at him too, and after a long scrutiny to see what Venetia may always have seen in him and which their mother—the sister of Peregrine Clevedon—might not care to contemplate.

There had from the start been something in his manner which I felt certain I had remarked in him before, and it took time—more time than was readily available—to understand the similarity between this lithe, keen-eyed rider and the young gentleman who at eleven o'clock one morning had lounged at the breakfast-table playing a languid but very dangerous game with his father's temper.

That young gentleman had been malicious, provocative, foolhardy. He had also been afraid. And his fear had not only been of his father—who was a frightening man—but of his own compulsion to put himself so continuously to the test. He had deliberately and skilfully aroused his father's wrath that morning. *This* morning it had been Gervase, not the Chards, who had flung down the challenge, Gervase who seemed determined to see it through to a possibly bitter end. And watching his lean figure astride that fretful, difficult horse, his resemblance to his uncle, Perry Clevedon, now so marked that the portrait in the hall might have come to life, I knew, with a great, complex pang of surprise and sympathy and irritation, that he was afraid of this too. And I had no need of Venetia's frowning anxiety to tell me that if his nerve should suddenly snap—as it might, as eventually, I supposed, it *must*—then he would grievously hurt himself.

"Higher?" he said.

"As high as you please," answered Gideon. And with a spitefulness quite alien to my nature I concluded that Gideon—that country gentleman of impeccable pedigree who believed he might find the way to pick up a manufacturer's fortune without soiling his hands—lacked the imagination to be afraid.

At their first attempt both horses refused, snorting and wild of eye, steaming with effort. But at the second try both Gideon and Gervase cleared the seven-foot pole by an inch apiece, which should, I thought, have been more than enough.

"We could leave it there," said Noel. "What about it, Dominic?" But before the baronet could pass judgement, Gervase, demonstrating that he was not subject to the laws of Listonby, shook his head.

"We need a clear decision, don't we—if you're up to it, Gideon?"

Gideon Chard shrugged his wide shoulders, nodded his head, and once again, with far less than an inch to spare this time, he got his sweating mount over the jump, inelegantly I thought, with more force about it than finesse, demanding more from the horse than it had wanted to give and offering only a casual pat on the neck as a reward.

But he was clear for the second time. He had completed his course and whatever happened now he had made his profit.

With every breath in my body I wanted Gervase to win. My muscles strained for him, my own city-bred spirit flinched with him as his horse began to churn up the mud again, the smell of steaming horseflesh and the animal's laboured breathing remaining in my memory long after; a remnant of it lodging there still.

I never understood the technicalities of what occurred. I thought for a moment that he had jumped clear, but the pole was knocked loose and the horse—they told me afterwards—came down hard upon it with a front hoof. I think I heard the crack of splintering bone—perhaps not; certainly I heard that terrible screaming and the crash as they fell to earth together, horse and rider and that murderous wooden structure; the thud of feet and the short, bitten-off curses as the Chards flung themselves from their own saddles and came running.

"Dear God!" I heard Mrs. Barforth mutter as they dragged Gervase clear of the lovely, ruined chestnut body which made no attempt to rise with him.

"No—" said Venetia, pushing some invisible menace away with a clenched hand. "Gervase—"

But although he stood erect for a moment, his neck, his spine, his legs unbroken, having escaped once again the fate of his uncle Peregrine, he suddenly sank down on one knee and remained there, his face lowered and hidden, his hand on the neck of the horse which lay quivering and, even to my inexpert eye, dying on the muddy ground.

Get up, I thought, Gervase get up, for although it would have seemed natural enough to me—and touchingly human—had he flung his arms around the horse's head and wept, I knew the Chards would not find it so. For there were rules now, of custom, of breeding, of good manners, which must be obeyed. The horse was dying and must be put out of its misery. And since it belonged to Gervase and he was to blame for the position in which it found itself, then what—three pairs of disdainful Chard eyes wanted to know—was he doing kneeling beside it, his head bowed as if he were praying over it, instead of stirring himself to do the decent thing?

"You should go and fetch a gun, shouldn't you," said Gideon, not really asking a question.

"And you'd best be quick about it," ordered Sir Dominic, "for that animal is suffering. Good God, *Gervase*—"

"Should I—?" began Noel, and was instantly quelled by the baronet who believed, quite rightly, that the disposal of a man's horse was no one's business but his own.

They were, of course, quite right about everything. The horse must be shot. That dreadful, quivering agony must be ended, and quickly, by the man who had caused it, or the whole of the county would hear of it—and condemn it—by tomorrow morning.

But Gervase did not lift his head, could not expose whatever it was he might be feeling to anyone. And realizing that neither Venetia nor his mother—who certainly would have gone to fetch that gun by now—knew how to help him, I took a step forward, looked without seeing at the mess on the ground, and said, very tart and prim and city-bred: "Well, whatever is to happen, I can see no reason why we should all stand around and watch. I have never owned a horse, but I can well imagine that its loss must be a private matter. In any case, I am cold and would like to go indoors to that glorious fire of yours, Mrs. Barforth, if I may? I told Blanche I would only be a moment and she might be growing concerned."

"Yes—yes, of course," Mrs. Barforth answered absently, her face very white, and then suddenly understanding. *"Of course—* let's all go in, shall we? I had quite forgotten Blanche."

And so we talked of Blanche as we made our way back to the house, the men leading their horses, my voice continuing to exclaim about the cold weather, the hope that my cousin had not ventured outdoors and lost her way, any commonplace remark my tongue could find to speak, while at some tunnel at the end of my mind I watched that kneeling figure made smaller by distance and by solitude; a man griefing for what? Because he was not Peregrine Clevedon, nor even Nicholas Barforth? Because the conflict around him and within him did not allow him a true identity at all? Because he wanted, and did not want, the same things at the same time? I couldn't know. It was not my concern. It would be better, I thought, to leave the conclusion to Venetia, or to Miss Diana Flood.

6

WE HEARD THE SHOT AS we sat drinking tea in the chintzy, firelit parlour, and although Venetia winced and Mrs. Barforth looked as if she badly wanted to rush outdoors, she sat down again while Blanche continued to pour and to murmur "Sugar and cream?" as if nothing had happened at all.

"The afternoon is drawing in," she said brightly, "we must soon be on our way. I have had such a pleasant afternoon, Aunt Georgiana."

"I am so glad, dear."

But Venetia, as always, disdained these social posturings.

"I must see Gervase before I leave," she declared and, since the Chards had already gone, I soon found myself pressed into her service.

"He will not be in the house. I will look in the stables, Grace, while you look in the cloister." And when I began to protest that I would not know what to say to him and should one not respect his evident wish to be alone, she stamped her foot and almost flew at me. "Heavens, Grace, how stubborn you are! All you need say is that I want to see him, and I am sure he will not bite you for that."

"But Venetia—the cloister?"

"Lord—what is there in the cloister to bother you? I don't ask you to go to the stables because I know you are nervous of the horses and ladylike about the muck. But there is nothing in the cloister except, one hopes, Gervase—and even that is not likely."

And so, trusting her, I hurried to the little side dōor she indicated and the short covered walk which took me to the cloister, the only part of the original abbey to remain intact, a hushed and airless place, too old for comfort, where I found Gervase—as she had known I would—leaning against one blank wall and staring at another.

There was no point in prolonging a silence that could only be awkward and, realizing he had seen me, I called out at once, "Gervase, I am sorry but we are leaving now, and Venetia is looking for you."

"Is she?" he said, his voice, to my great relief, perfectly under control, the lounging, drawling young squire again, hard and insensitive, although still rather pale. "I imagine she knows where to find me."

"Well—she has gone to the stables."

"Then that means she wanted *you* to find me."

"Oh—well then, since I have found you, shall I go and find Venetia and tell her so?"

"How very busy that sounds. Have you nothing to ask me about the horse?"

"What should I wish to know?"

"There must be something—if only how I am to raise the twenty guineas I have lost to the Chards."

"You are not short of money, surely?"

"No," he said, a ripple of nervous laughter running through him. "I surely am not. Twenty guineas might have been a problem to Gideon Chard, but hardly to me. You think me a coward, I suppose."

"You might be."

"How kind—"

"But not because you disliked shooting a horse. It would have upset me greatly."

"Ah yes, but in your case, you see, you would have been allowed your emotions. It would even have been expected of you. It was not expected of me."

"Does it really matter, since you did it in the end?"

"Did I?"

"I heard the gun."

"Which proves what? Only that a gun was fired. But did I fire it? Or, once the coast was clear—once you had cleared it for me—did I fetch one of the grooms to do the dirty deed in my place?"

"Gervase, does *that* matter either?"

There was a pause, the silence of the ancient walls closing in on us, creating a strange distortion of time and distance, a little space, perhaps, where time overlapped and we stepped forward, without knowing it, to a moment which might never come to pass, a threshold of familiarity we might never actually cross, but which enabled us somehow to speak freely.

"It matters to me," he said. "One thinks of oneself as a certain type of man, and it is rather galling to prove oneself so wrong. The Chards would not have behaved as I did. Whatever they may have felt, they would have concealed it admirably, as old Etonions have been trained to do, so that no one need have been embarrassed by it. Our great public schools specialize in the building of 'character,' you see. After today the Chards will feel entitled to say that I—as a mere product of Cullingford Grammar School—have none."

"Do you care?"

"Yes. I care. Feeble of me, perhaps, but I care both for their opinion and for my own estimate of myself."

"You mean, I suppose, that if you are not the man you thought you were, then who are you?"

"Is that what I mean? How very profound of me!"

"I also think you did shoot that horse."

"Do you indeed?"

"Yes, I do. And the Chards will think so too—because they lack the imagination to think otherwise."

He bowed very slightly, hardly easing his body away from the wall, and meeting his gaze—because it has always seemed best to me to look people straight in the eye at awkward moments—I found his eyes so light a green that they seemed quite transparent, the fine skin around them crinkled by his habit of keeping them half-closed, something in his regard which was not open and frank like Venetia's but which—for just a moment—seemed every bit as vulnerable.

"What do you think of this place?" he said abruptly, settling his back once more against the old stone, making contact with it, I thought, or possessing it.

"Of Galton? Well, I—"

"You may speak the truth."

"I shall. When I came here as a child it scared me. I expected to see a ghost at every bend of the stair. When we arrived today I thought it—austere. And so it is, but I am beginning to think it *should* be like that."

He nodded very lightly, his eyes skimming along the passage, the pale grey walls, the fan-vaulted arch of the ceiling, before coming back to me.

"Yes, it has something about it, this place—some power . . . My mother once tried to leave my father, you know—really leave him—and it was Galton that held her back. She really thought she could do it, I suppose, but when it came down to it, when he actually told her 'Do as I say or the estate goes under the hammer,' she couldn't let it happen.''

"Gervase, should you be telling me—"

"Yes," he said, his eyes showing that bitter, transparent green again, his thin mouth very tight. "There's no 'should' or 'should not' about it. I'm a spoiled and vicious young man, everybody knows it, and it's what I *want*, not what I *ought*, that counts. If Uncle Peregrine had lived, it would have been different. The estate would have passed to him and he—well, he'd have been in his fifties by now, just about ready to take a fifteen-year-old wife and get himself an heir, so there'd have been no need for me. My mother could have left my father if she'd wanted, or she might have settled down with him and given Uncle Perry her pin-money every month, which is what she used to do when he was alive. But Uncle Perry broke his neck—"

"Doing what you were doing this afternoon."

"Quite so—or something very like it. And instead of leaving the estate in trust for me, as he could have done, my mother's grandfather left it to her—which, as Miss Grace Agbrigg will be sure to know, was the same as leaving it to my father.''

"And your father wished to sell it.''

"No—*threatened* to sell it—used it as a lever, a weapon, whatever seemed useful to him at the time. One day, according to their agreement, it comes to me. But until that day dawns— and it will be of his choosing—he has her and can hold her fast. For if he sells Galton—well, Grace Agbrigg, there are three hundred years of Clevedons in the graveyard over there. How can we let him dispose of that?''

He paused, from indignation or pity or the sheer weight of that three-hundred-year-old burden I couldn't tell, although it gave me time to ask the question that was uppermost in my mind.

"Your father is very determined to keep your mother by him. Why is that?''

"My dear girl!'' he threw up a hand in mock astonishment. "You cannot be suggesting he should allow her to leave him? Women are very grateful to the men who marry them—or ought to be. Certainly they fight hard enough to get a man to the altar. And having endowed a woman with all his worldly goods, and rescued her from the shame of being a spinster to boot, it must be embarrassing—wouldn't you say?—if she throws it all back at him. People would talk, Miss Agbrigg. They would say he must have been very wicked, or very peculiar, for a woman to give up all that.''

"Gervase, I asked you a serious question."

"I answered it. I answered it. I don't really know. Venetia has something to do with it, I suppose. He *is* her father, after all, and he can't wish her to be involved in an open scandal. No one could accuse him of doting on her, but he's never been one for shirking his responsibilities. The Barforths are like that."

"So am I."

"Yes, I believe you are. So he may want to avoid a scandal for Venetia's sake. He may even want to protect my mother from herself—or from Julian Flood. He's not likely to tell me. We don't stand on such friendly terms as that. Gideon Chard may know, of course—perhaps you'd care to ask him?"

But I was unwilling to be distracted.

"If those really should be his motives, then I don't think you could call him either wicked or peculiar—really, I don't."

He grinned, the first real amusement I had seen in him.

"You approve of my father then, do you, Grace Agbrigg?"

"I am not in the habit of making judgements—"

"Are you not? I thought quite otherwise. You seem so very determined and so positive to me. And I would know, wouldn't I—being so negative myself."

"Being so full of self-pity, you mean."

"You don't pity me? I rather thought you might. After all, you were very efficient and very prompt just now, out in the long meadow—taking them all away in case I couldn't manage to pull myself together and they should begin to laugh at me."

"Gervase—was it only the horse?"

"My word, are you a philosopher too, besides all the other marvels I hear of you? No—since you ask—not only the horse. I was—tired. There are times when I do tire rather easily—rather suddenly. A little instability of temperament, perhaps, which you might find interesting?"

"I don't believe so. In fact I am beginning to find this whole conversation quite pointless."

"Then you shouldn't linger, should you, Grace, in lonely places with strange men."

"You are not a strange man."

"Am I not?" He threw back his head and laughed, as delighted as any other far less complicated man would have been with the trap he had set for me and into which I had fallen. "Well—at least in one respect I am not strange. I can prove it, if you like—in fact I really think I ought—"

"You'll do no such thing."

But as he moved away from the wall and took a step towards me, I was not afraid of him as I had been afraid of Gideon Chard. It had nothing to do with weight or size, for although Gervase was lighter and smaller, he was strong enough to hurt me and more likely, I thought, to offer me violence than Gideon, who would not see the need for it. It was simply that nothing in Gervase's lean, overwrought body menaced me as Gideon's had done, the very absence of fear—which I had too little knowledge to recognize as the absence of desire—unchaining my curiosity, my eagerness to participate, to experience, to grow; for with Blanche already married and Venetia so rapturously in love, it was irksome to me that, at eighteen, I had still to receive my first kiss.

And having made up my mind to it, I remember quite distinctly willing him to stop talking and to *get on,* surprised, when his hand brushed my cheek and slid to my neck, to find his touch so cautious and so cold, having expected a deliberate courseness in this wild young squire, a mouth which demanded or took by force instead of asking so hesitant a question. I made no response, no answer, simply allowing his lips to touch mine, his tongue to part them, remaining calm and still, no pulse-beat leaping inside me but no awkwardness, a rather pleasing consciousness at the back of my mind that, although this was very pleasant and rather daring, I was still very much in control.

"Grace Agbrigg," he said, his mouth against my ear, his quick, nervous laughter making my spine tingle. "I have misjudged you. I thought you a schoolroom innocent, and now I am bound to ask myself what did they teach you in Switzerland?"

To which I replied, with studied composure, "Good heavens! Gervase, at eighteen years old I am not likely to swoon on account of a kiss."

When he rode over to Listonby the next morning and asked me to marry him, my first reaction, quite simply, was to wonder why, so that my answer, far from being romantic, sounded even in my own ears like a scold.

"Really, Gervase, if it is because of what happened in the cloister, I can tell you that I do not feel in any way compromised. If you have come out of a sense of obligation or because you imagined yourself committed—"

But he would not allow me to continue, his odd, light eyes slitted with anger. "So—I kissed you in the cloister and what of it, Grace Agbrigg? I'd not be here, asking this, unless I wanted it, even if I'd done far worse than that to you."

And when he was calm enough to accept my refusal and went away, I was obliged to endure, an hour later, the recriminations of his sister, whose heart, she insisted, I had also broken.

"There is no question of broken hearts, Venetia. Gervase is not in love with me."

"How do you know?"

"Because I know. And anyway, he didn't say so—"

"Of course he didn't. He wouldn't know how. But what *I* know—absolutely and beyond question—is that it was not done because father told him to. That in itself would be enough to make him *not* ask you. And the fact that he *did* ask means he wants you—and I want you—and father wants you. And the reason I know how much he wants you is because mother doesn't—simply doesn't at all—and he hardly ever goes against her. You could do so much for him, Grace."

"And what could he do for me?"

She smiled and tucked her hand into mine.

"Well—first of all he could make you my sister. And then, of course, he's very rich. And don't you think he's rather beautiful?"

"I suppose I must say he is, since he looks like you."

"Thank you, darling. And will you say yes when he asks you again?"

There was no danger of that, I decided. It had been a whim on his part, no more, some quirk of his complicated nature which had picked up my sympathy that day at Galton and converted it into something which had briefly attracted him. Certainly he would not ask again, would be more inclined, I thought, to thank me for my good sense in refusing him, and if he still felt the need of a wife would already be gravitating towards Diana Flood. Yet it was Miss Flood herself who showed me my mistake, for when I met her a day or so later, having extended my visit to Listonby at Blanche's request, her manner was taut and miserable and she had no more to say to me than a forced "Are you well, Miss Agbrigg?"

Miss Flood herself clearly was not well, and I felt myself wince slightly at Venetia's casual, "Oh—Diana. Well, she'll just have to find herself a real squire, won't she—the genuine, beefy variety—and make the best of him."

I returned to Fieldhead and to the centre of a storm, a glacial Mrs. Agbrigg losing no time in enquiring why I was so little to be trusted, for Gervase, it seemed, had not only informed his mother and possibly Miss Flood of his intentions, but had ridden home to Tarn Edge that same day and for the first time in years, perhaps the first time ever, had asked his father's help. Mr. Barforth had driven at once to Fieldhead and made his proposition to my father. I was the girl he wanted for Tarn Edge. My father might have some reservations about Gervase but the marriage-contract could be as tight as my father liked. I could have, in the way of pin-money and housekeeping money, anything I desired. Mr. Barforth was ready to be generous, and although he would expect my father to be the same, he made it clear that my welfare would be his personal concern. Gervase Barforth, in fact, would make me happy or would answer to Nicholas Barforth for it. And feeling the need to finalize the matter in case Gervase should change his mind, he went next to Galton and warned his wife—to my everlasting regret—that she would be well advised to be pleased about it too.

"You should not have told your father," I reproached him when next we met.

"I know that. But a desperate man will stoop to anything."

"I wish you would not describe yourself as desperate. It sounds very foolish."

"My father seems highly delighted with the state I am in. And I can't quite get over how natural it seemed to turn to him."

"Perhaps you should make a habit of it."

"Do you think so?"

"I think you would be happier if you could."

"I'd like to. I need you to show me the way."

"What nonsense, Gervase—"

"No," he said, his eyes turning that wild transparent green again: "No—not nonsense at all, I'm afraid. Grace, you won't stop me from coming to see you? I'll be calm. I'll behave—"

The only ally I found was, of all people, my father's wife.

"This is all quite ridiculous," she said. "Jonas—you must put a stop to it."

"It is for Grace to decide," my father told her sadly. "I will neither force her nor persuade her in any direction. This is the most important decision of her life—perhaps the only real decision she will be called upon to make. I cannot interfere with her right to make it."

But although I declared firmly and frequently that I had already decided, that I had refused him once and would do so again, no one appeared to believe me, being too involved with their own desires to notice mine.

I should be sent abroad again, Mrs. Agbrigg decreed. I would be gone soon enough, my father replied, and for the first time since his marriage stepped firmly between us and ordered her to leave me alone. I was not to be rushed, Mr. Barforth agreed. I was young and it was a big step to take. I could take it, thought Mr. Barforth, in my own good time, provided I made haste, saw reason, bowed—as a woman should—to the highly convenient workings of Fate. And quite soon, each time I opened my mouth to say no, there was no step to take, I couldn't marry him, I had a nightmare sensation that no one heard me, that I was voiceless or that my words were somehow being converted into a foreign tongue.

"An excellent match," wrote my Grandmother Agbrigg from her home in Scarborough, for she had been a Miss Hannah Barforth herself and liked the idea of the Barforth money remaining in the family.

"I said you would be our next bride," Grandmamma Elinor wrote enthusiastically from her winter retreat in Cannes, for she too had been a Barforth, a pretty, dimpled Miss Elinor who had married once for money and once for love, and was still exceedingly romantic.

"You would be very rich," said Blanche, "with more pin-money, I daresay, than I have, since Listonby seems to cost a great deal and Westminster—now that Dominic seems set on having a go at politics—will cost even more."

But Mr. Nicholas Barforth, taking my measure more accurately, sent Venetia to assure me that the position awaiting me at Tarn Edge would not be without its element of authority and freedom.

"I know you hate the whole idea," she told me, dropping down beside me on my bedroom sofa, "and will probably end up hating me for talking about it. But my father says—if you come to us—that you should pay no heed to me at all. I am just the daughter-at-home who has nothing to say to anything, and since mamma is never there you would be as much the mistress of Tarn Edge as if it already belonged to Gervase. Father says you could engage servants or discharge them as you wanted and make changes to suit your fancy—the house is so badly run, he says, that *any* change must be for the better. And Mrs. Agbrigg, you know, would never, absolutely never, be able to get past father. We just wondered if you realized that no one at all would stand in your way—"

I had not wished to realize it, suspecting how much it would tempt me. And now, being tempted, I was forced to consider it, my desire for a free and independent existence stirring me to a considerable discomfort. It would not, of course, be total freedom,

for at the end of every road I would have a husband and a
father-in-law to answer to. But within the confines of four very
splendid walls I would have as much authority, as much liberty,
as any woman could expect; more of it, perhaps, than I would
ever be likely to find elsewhere. And, my mind leaping from one
idea to the next, as Mr. Nicholas Barforth may have known it
would, I was quick to see the scope of what he was offering, its
potential and its extent; quick to realize that, since marriage was
the only career open to me, I would be unlikely to find one more
advantageous than this.

Of course I had no intention of marrying Gervase, since there
was far more to be considered—far more—than advantage. But
just supposing I did marry him, then I saw no reason why the
two sides of his nature, his double inheritance, could not be
reconciled. I saw no reason, in fact, why he could not enjoy both
the sporting estate of Galton, the Barforth mills, and Fieldhead
besides.

Someone, in fact, must take care of Tarn Edge, for Mr.
Barforth eventually would grow old and Venetia, I was sure of
it, would not marry Gideon Chard nor anyone else of whom her
father would be likely to approve. Her choice would be idealistic,
soft-spoken, sweet-natured, a dreamer like Charles Heron who
would fare no better in the mills than Gervase. When the time
came someone would have to be there with a level head and a
practical disposition, someone who knew how those mills had
risen from the ground and did not want to see them sink back
again.

Naturally, it would not be Grace Agbrigg, but Grace Agbrigg
could do it if she wanted to, could make a life for herself at Tarn
Edge and for some others, could provide herself with that commodity so rarely available to females of her station: some *real*
work to do. And although these pressures, these enticements,
would not in themselves have swayed my resolution, they moved
me, step by slow-moving step, in their chosen direction to a
point where the challenge of Tarn Edge seemed matched by the
challenge of Gervase's complex nature; to a point where I began
to ask myself, with a decided loss of composure, why he wanted
me.

It was not money, as with many men—perhaps with most
men—it would have been; and I was ready now to admit how
much the dread of being courted for my fortune, used and
subsequently set aside, had haunted me. Perhaps I was even
ready—although I am not sure of this—to admit a certain disap-

pointment at the rapidity with which Gideon Chard had with-drawn from me, having made up his mind, I supposed, that if he obstructed Mr. Barforth's plans on my account he ran the risk of losing his employment and his chance of Venetia with it.

No, Gervase Barforth did not want my money. What then?

"Darling, you're beautiful," cried Venetia.

"Nonsense—utter nonsense!"

"Oh, yes, you are. I've always envied you that mass of dark hair and those blue-grey eyes, you know I have—and you have *presence,* Grace, simply heaps of it. When you come into a room people look at you, and when you talk they listen. And in any case, none of that really matters. You're beautiful because I love you."

"Gervase doesn't know me well enough to love me."

"Now that," Venetia declared, "really is nonsense. Lord! it took me all of half an hour to fall in love with Charles, and now—only look at me—I love him more and more by the minute. And it's *good* for me. I actually think it makes my hair curl and even Princess Blanche, who never notices other women, asked me the other day what I was using to give my skin such a glow. Not a jar *she's* likely to dip into, I can tell you, or perhaps I should tell poor Noel. But, Grace—don't you want to be loved?"

Yes. Yes, of course. For even studious little girls who grow to be sensible, efficient young women have indulged in a little romantic dreaming, especially when, as in my case, childhood had been cool in terms of affection, girlhood sometimes quite barren.

"My dear," murmured Mrs. Rawnsley, who badly wanted to be the first to know, "that poor young man is so smitten that, really, one would need a heart of iron not to pity him. And when one remembers how wild he was—my dear, you have scored a triumph."

"He loves you," Venetia told me again. "Don't ask why, just be glad of it. What else in the world can compare with *that*?"

And quite soon it came about that, although I still maintained I had no emotion to give him, I was fascinated by his.

He did not give me the easy assurance of "I love you, I cannot live without you," but, pacing Mrs. Agbrigg's drawing-room with the taut, nervous step of a caged feline, carrying from one corner to another his chagrin that once again I had turned him down, he told me: "I'll wait. I was too hasty before. Don't say anything now, Grace—please don't say a word. Just consider—*Please*."

"I *have* considered. I think you are mistaken in me, Gervase. I believe your mother cannot approve of this—"

"She will forgive me. She will see that, with you, I will be steadier and easier—because I will be happier. She will see that everything will turn out to her satisfaction just the same. Grace, they are equally my parents. Is there any reason in the world why I shouldn't please them both?"

"I think it can be done."

"I believe you. I thought it altogether impossible, but now I believe you. I have to have you, Grace."

And so, due to the highly organized communications system of Mr. Nicholas Barforth, it became known in Cullingford and in Scarborough, in certain areas of London and the South of France, that in fact he did have me; that I had become the exclusive property of the Barforths upon which any other aspiring male would be ill-advised to trespass.

Annoying, of course, when the other young men I knew kept their distance, or when Miss Mandelbaum murmured to me softly: "My dear, it seems you are to be congratulated, although I fear Miss Tighe will be disappointed. She was relying on you to organize our petition for woman suffrage and you will have no time now, of course—and no inclination." Annoying to feel myself manipulated by the powerful Mr. Barforth, yet exhilarating too, sometimes, to realize that his approval was not easily won and to wonder if I had the skill to retain it.

And increasingly, almost daily, there was Gervase, *present* in my life, absorbing more and more of my time and my attention, confusing and exasperating me, making me smile, warming me, sometimes touching me, sometimes making me cruel and sometimes kind—but present.

"What a nuisance you are, Gervase!"

"So I am."

So he was, casting me those looks of mute reproach across everybody's drawing-room; but if, the next day, he did not come to find me, did not appear in some doorway just a little dishevelled, a little pale, that transparent look in his eyes, quite soon I began to wonder why, to watch for him, to expect him, to miss him.

There was an evening of acute misery, an Assembly Rooms Ball, when, in a low-cut dress of white lace draped up over black silk roses, I danced with a flattering variety of young men, aware at every step—when I had been so determined not to notice it—of a silent, suffering Gervase leaning like a spectre in the buffet corner, his face drawn and strained by his inexplicable burden of wanting me. And when we did dance together I could feel no flesh on his hands, simply the bones crushing my fingers, wanting to hurt me.

"You have no right to be jealous, Gervase—no right to be so miserable."

"There is nothing you can do about it, Grace. I am jealous. I am miserable."

I made up my mind, with great firmness, that I would not be influenced by his misery. I would be pleasant and reasonable but cool, until this strange emotion of his, which had risen, like fretful summer fires, from nowhere, should burn itself out. But when he strode from the ballroom, leaving me, as he said, to my pleasures, I worried, wanted him back again, not because I actually wanted *him*—of course not that—but because he had looked so pale, so reckless, so very likely to bring down his horse on the cobbles or get into a fight, and already I was beginning to feel responsible.

There was a sparkling December afternoon of hard frost and brilliant sunshine when he escorted Mrs. Agbrigg and myself on a tour of the new mill at Nethercoats, an occasion when every possible attention was paid to us, beginning with glasses of sherry served by Mr. Nicholas Barforth himself and ending with an inspection, not of the whole mill, which since it extended over a full six acres would have been too exhausting, but of the finer points of it, the elaborate Italianate façade, the chimney stack, two hundred and fifty feet high, the suite of offices with their opulent oak-panelling, the extensive warehousing, six floors in all, where Barforth expertise was storing away the silks and velvets and all the other soft, luxurious fabrics which had come into demand since fashion had abandoned the crinoline.

"You have a stupendous inheritance awaiting you, Mr. Barfoth," said Mrs. Agbrigg as Gervase assisted us to our carriage. And, almost a stranger in his dark coat and trousers, his plain white linen, he glanced swiftly around the bustling mill-yard, the enormous chimney directly behind him, four other factory chimneys, very nearly as huge, dominating every corner of Cullingford's horizon, each one forming part of that stupendous, that crushing birthright.

"So I have, Mrs. Agbrigg," he said very quietly. "And unfortunately I have no natural aptitude for it. I must simply do the best I can. Grace—may I come and see you tomorrow?"

"Yes—tomorrow."

And instinctively, because it seemed the right thing to do—the only thing to do—I held out my hand and ignored Mrs. Agbrigg's sharply drawn breath when he kissed it.

Lady Caroline Chard became the Duchess of South Erin in the small village church at Listonby, two days before Christmas, in the presence of her mother, Lady Verity Barforth, who had come over specially from the South of France; her brothers, Mr. Nicholas Barforth and Sir Blaize; their wives, Mrs. Georgiana Barforth resplendent in the emerald and diamond finery she kept for these occasions, Aunt Faith her sweet and lovely self in soft shades of amber and aquamarine; and a few other carefully selected guests.

Sir Dominic gave his mother away, Blanche drifting forlornly into the church to take her place between Gideon and Noel, who looked extremely handsome in the full dress uniform of a hussar, while I sat with Mrs. Agbrigg on one side of me, Gervase and Venetia on the other, Gervase taut and silent, Venetia flushed with a triumphant ecstasy since she had somehow procured an invitation for Charles Heron.

She had, I knew, seen a great deal of him lately, her father, intent on arranging his son's affairs, having accepted her explanations of afternoons with her mother or with me when in fact she had seized any opportunity, rushed any distance, to spend an hour with Charles.

"I am in the process," she told me gaily, "of losing my reputation." Yet I knew, quite definitely, that nothing improper had occurred. She may, in the first rapture of meeting, have rushed into his arms—very likely she had—and, indeed, the mere fact of being alone with a young man by assignation was quite enough to condemn her. But Venetia was too deeply and too idealistically in love for impropriety, her embrace offering trust rather than sensuality, conveying to him no tale of urgent passion but a slow and lovely building of her hopes for the future, the strength and devotion of her whole life.

I hardly knew him; a fair, sensitive face, a quiet, hesitant manner of speaking, although his habitual themes of social justice, atheism and republicanism were strident enough. Yet he had abandoned God, I thought, because he had confused him with his own harsh father, while his revolutionary principles, when compared to some I had heard abroad, seemed relatively mild. He believed in one man one vote, with which I heartily agreed, and he had not flinched when I suggested "one vote one woman." He believed in education for both sexes, and although he seemed to know more about knocking things down—like churches and royal palaces—than building things up again, there seemed every likelihood that in time he would settle down to be a responsible and, apart from his blue eyes and enchanting fair curls, quite unremarkable schoolmaster.

Charles Heron's republicanism—inspired mainly by the refusal of our sad little Queen to show herself in public—would probably go the same way as his disregard for money, his unrealistic, if undoubtedly Christian view, that the world's bounty should be equally shared. I smiled, knowing word for word how Mr. Nicholas Barforth would reply to that, and then in great confusion turned my head away, for in trying to locate Charles Heron at the back of the church I had found instead the dark, dissolute face of Sir Julian Flood and the tightly controlled misery of his niece Diana.

The new duchess and her merry little duke were not disposed to linger, having a mountain of Christmas engagements awaiting them in London. There was a lavish but by Listonby standards hurried wedding-breakfast, a great deal of champagne, the Duchess looking resolute and triumphant, Blanche rather smug since she had discovered a way of avoiding the social and domestic responsibilities of Listonby and of rather overshadowing her mother-in-law by announcing, the night before, that she was pregnant.

The Duchess put on her sable-trimmed coat and feathered hat, the Duke distributed handshakes and kisses as if they had been medals. There was a sudden scramble for carriages as the bridal party left for the London train, Blanche melting gracefully into tears, Venetia—glimpsed through a window-pane—holding out her narrow, boyish hand to Charles Heron, her face suffused with a joy that caused me a sharp stab of pain; and then there was Gervase, taking me out into the fine, frosty weather, to a pink winter sky above charcoal trees, a bare, empty sweep of parkland.

He had nothing to say, striding out in the sharp air at a speed somewhat beyond the capacity of my elaborate skirt and dainty shoes, his humour frowning and grim.

"Gervase, I am quite breathless."

"Yes, I see."

"Then do you mind—?"

"Yes," he said, "yes—I do." And coming to a halt by a

screening circle of evergreens, he took me by the shoulders with hard, horseman's hands and kissed me more with his teeth than his lips, a painful embrace from which I quickly broke free.

"I think that's quite enough—"

"I can't wait any longer, Grace."

"Then don't wait. I told you before—"

But once again he took me in that spiked embrace, except that this time, although he hurt me, I felt pain in him and a response in my own female body which had been conditioned through the generations to offer itself, in love and in healing, on all occasions such as these.

There was an ornate iron bench close to the hedge and we sat down, his shoulders hunched, his head bowed, hiding his face as I had seen him do before, the tension in his lean body so great that it vibrated through the air between us as sharp as needles. And remembering him kneeling in the field at Galton—that treacherous memory of him weak and vulnerable—I put my hand on his shoulder, startled by the tremor that went through him, by the wild, hurt face that looked up at me, the thin mouth spitting out the words: "I need you, Grace. God dammit, can't you see that? Grace—*please*."

And still I thought, why me? But I was breathless now, not only from walking, and a little dizzy, feeling that I could just as easily laugh or cry; and I had no resistance when he took both my hands, rather more gently, and kissed me again.

"I need you, Grace."

I shook my head. But I was expecting his kiss this time, leaned forward a little to meet it, the coolness and the lightness of him pleasing me, nothing at all to fear in his hard, hurt body as I put my arms around it and held him, the scent of lavender and of lemons rising to me from his skin, delighting my nostrils as the texture of the skin itself, so paper-fine across his cheek bones, delighted my lips.

We got up and walked back to the house without saying anything of importance, and wherever there was a tree or a shelter of any kind, we paused and I stood as if mesmerized while he kissed me, lifting my face towards him more readily each time, growing more and more obedient to the impulses of my body, those sweet, yielding sensations which pressed me ever more closely into his arms, holding me there longer, so that before we reached the prying windows of the house, I was kissing him too with curiosity and with a freedom from restraint which enchanted me. It was as if I had shaken my hair loose from its pins, kicked off the confining weight of petticoats and bustle and my long, trailing gown, and was basking for the first time in fresh air and sunshine. It was, I suppose, very wanton and I did not care.

I had not agreed to marry him. Nothing had been decided. But as we entered the house there were several people still drinking champagne in the hall who, seeing us, fell silent without meaning to, as people do when they have been told of "something in the air." And as we came forward to join them, walking a respectable distance apart, my hair no more dishevelled than could be accounted for by the wind, Gervase deliberately caught his father's eye and then, very slowly and firmly, reached out and took my hand.

"Good lad," Mr. Barforth said. It was done.

7

WE SPENT THE FIRST WEEKS of our married life in Cumbria, in a low-beamed slate-roofed cottage not far from the village of Grasmere, overlooking Rydal Water, relieved, I think, quite simply to be married and that the fuss was over.

There had been no open opposition, Mrs. Agbrigg being so glad to be rid of me that she was soon reconciled, while if Mrs. Georgiana Barforth reproached her son for what she must have seen as a class-betrayal, she reproached him privately and made nothing but polite murmurings to me.

Yet this alliance between two important commercial houses could not take place without its share of pomp and splendour. On such an occasion money—like justice and the sad little face of our Queen—must not only be spent but must be *seen*, very copiously, in the spending. The self-respect of both the Barforths and the Agbriggs required it, the same mountain of bridal trivia I had seen around Blanche piling up so rapidly at Fieldhead that the ceremony itself began to appear more than ever as a release from bondage.

The night before the wedding my father, in his capacity as a lawyer, called me into his study to explain what my new status as a married woman would be, in fact no status at all since when I left the parish church the next morning I would no longer exist, my identity absorbed entirely into the identity of my husband. There had been a Grace Cecilia Agbrigg, but the law would not recognize a Grace Cecilia Barforth, merely a Mrs. Gervase Barforth who could not, in any legal sense involving matters of finance, contract, or inheritance, be distinguished from the man whose name she bore. Mrs. Gervase Barforth, being the property of her husband, could not own property herself. Her dowry, her body, and in due course her children were all irrevocably his. She would be as absolutely dependent on his judgement and his authority, in fact, as if she had herself been his child; indeed, rather more so, since a son, on his majority, could claim his independence, a daughter, on marriage, would be transferred to the control of another man.

The Married Women's Property Act of 1870—now entering its third year—had not amounted to much, my father thought, its provisions going no further than to allow a married woman to retain her earnings. Useful, perhaps, in the case of some famous literary figure or of some fabulously talented prima donna or prima ballerina, of which there could not be many. Less appropriate in what could be seen as the real world, where women of even moderate means did not *earn* money, and could not earn it, since there was no paid work for them to do, the services of women being required at home by their men, who would reward them with food and shelter and, in fortunate circumstances, with love.

Nor, my father declared, had the Act of 1870 made any difference to the class below our own, where from early childhood both men and women were obliged to go out and scratch a living wherever they could, no labouring man in the poorer areas of Cullingford disputing the right of his wife to keep her earnings when every penny was needed for the purchase of their daily bread.

But, my father told me, none of this need greatly concern me, since the law—which had been made by men of property to serve the interests of property—provided, in cases such as mine, for the drawing up of a marriage contract, a settlement which by allowing me a most generous and untouchable allowance, and by a complicated series of trusts and restrictions imposed upon the property which would one day be mine, made it certain that I would never be in want.

My father, in addition, had obliged Mr. Barforth to be specific in the matter of Gervase's salary and in the provision he intended to make for Venetia and any husband and children she might acquire. My father, as my legal guardian, had felt entitled to know where I stood. Mr. Barforth had been most obliging, the financial position of my future husband no longer depending entirely on the whim of his father but on certain firm guarantees. However—and my father thought it wise to tell me this—when Mrs. Barforth had attempted to take advantage of her husband's good humour by suggesting to him that the time had come to make over to Gervase the ownership of the Galton estate, Mr. Barforth had merely replied, "Not yet."

When the explanations were over, my father took from a drawer of his desk a small, flat case and placed it gently before me, my throat instantly tight since I knew this was my mother's jewellery and I was not certain—if my father should become emotional—that I could bear it.

"You may not care for these," he said coolly, opening the lid and indicating a strand or two of gold and coral, a locket, a cameo, coral and turquoise ear-rings, a brooch of blue enamel. "Trinkets merely—not valuable. I was not a rich man in those days, you see, and your mother was not—not much given to display. There is no reason why you should wear these things, but perhaps you would like to have them—indeed, I can think of no one else to whom they could go."

"Thank you, papa." And as he gave me the case I caught his hand and held it, my throat aching now, longing to ask him, "Father, are you happy?" despairing because I could not say to him, "Father, I love you," although I was brimming over with love.

I had wanted us to be quite alone on our honeymoon night, no grand hotels, no complicated menus, no after-dinner conversations with knowing strangers, and the house at Grasmere, which belonged to my father—a book-lined, leafy retreat, a cottage garden, a discreet housekeeper—offered the warmest, most perfect solitude.

I had imagined, too, that we might use this quiet time to tell our secrets, to talk of his mother, the conflicts we had both known in childhood, our hopes now for the future which we could map out together. In fact we hardly talked at all. We made love, which I had not realized could be a conversation until he brought the lamp to our bedside that first evening and, with an almost idle hand, touched me, just touched me from the curve of my eyebrows to my breasts, to the hollows of my ankles, and then touched me again, his hand whispering gently into my skin, his body trembling so that he seemed once more to be vulnerable. And although I knew he had done this before with other women and should not have been uncertain, he was uncertain until I touched him too and heard, with astonished delight, the harmony of my hands and his fine-boned, fine-textured leanness, the lovely auburn skin that had so delicate a bloom as my mouth tasted it.

An hour, perhaps, of bemused caresses, a few moments to dispose of my virginity, no anxious questions afterwards as to if he had hurt me, but his head on my shoulder, his body sinking in my arms into his fretful sleep which rarely lasted, I was to learn, for more than two hours, so that at some far reach of the night I was kissed to a dreamy half-waking and being totally relaxed took his body into mine this time without pain.

We walked the lake path the next morning and paused every step or two to touch hand to hand, cheek to cheek, forehead to forehead, simply to touch, and there was nothing else we wished to do but that, to savour this communication of the senses, his need arousing mine until, at some imperceptible moment, the pleasure of being loved flowed into the pleasure of loving and became one with it, the same. I love him, I thought, and it took me by surprise. He needs me. How wonderful that he needs me. And it was but a breath away from confessing that I, too, needed him.

We made love or we looked at each other and imagined it. We dreamed of it, sighed out our longing for it, we did not speak of it. Our bodies said all that was needful, and very soon I did not wait—as a woman should wait to be loved—but, when I desired him, reached out and took him, to his delight and to my eventual, slow-building but quite devastating rapture.

"I need you, Grace."

"You have me."

With his hands upon me I was entirely his, unwilling, during that fragile spring, to stray a yard from his side, parched with the thirst of any half hour in which he had not caressed me; while he—I knew it—had delivered himself to me body and soul. It was a peak of intensity I had never expected to discover. I did not know how long such exaltation could be expected to last and perhaps I would have been fearful even then had I realized that Gervase desired it to continue, unabated, forever.

"I don't want to go home," he said, sounding so much like a child at the end of a party that I laughed and kissed him.

"I mean it, Grace. We could go down to London—why couldn't we?—and I could buy you a diamond."

"I have a diamond."

"Should you object to another?"

But we returned to Cullingford because, without being aware of exerting pressure upon him, it was what I wished to do, arriving on an afternoon of rain which could have accounted for his ill-humour, although once in our huge, luxurious yet not quite immaculate bedroom at Tarn Edge, he seized me as the dinner gong was sounding and made love to me as if it had been an act of defiance.

He went to the mill at a reasonable hour the next morning, not quite so early as his father or mine, but early enough, considering his past performances, to please Mr. Barforth, leaving me to what I recognized with apprehension and a little pride as my first day as mistress of Tarn Edge.

But before I could make myself known to my staff, I spent an hour with Venetia who, having welcomed me rapturously the night before, had nevertheless warned me that great things were afoot, and that all would be revealed, in true sisterly fashion, the very moment we could be alone at breakfast-time.

"You need not be alarmed," she told me, perching on the edge of her chair and wrinkling her nose, "for I shall not ask you for the details of the 'great wedded mystery.' I have spent too many hours in the stables at Galton to be entirely ignorant and I can see that you have taken to it in any case. Darling, I *knew* you would love each other and I am so happy, or would be if such positive disaster had not struck me—"

Yet this disaster, however positive, did not appear to have broken her for, leaning both elbows on the table, her pointed chin resting upon them, she spent a moment smiling and shaking her head, perhaps at her own folly, but by no means in despair. Like her mother, it seemed, she had hoped to take advantage of her father's unusual good humour and had introduced him to Charles Heron. The occasion had not been a success, Mr. Barforth finding a schoolmaster of radical opinions not at all to his liking, while Mr. Heron had been so overcome with shyness that her father, scorning the excuse of sensitivity, had declared him to be—in addition to everything else—a half-wit.

It was not Mr. Heron's poverty in itself to which my father-in-law objected, for, in certain circumstances, a poor man would have been very acceptable to him, someone like Gideon Chard who was shrewd and ambitious, or even Liam Adair who might not be quite respectable, but who knew how to put in a hard day's work for his pay. But Charles Heron had ideals in place of ambition, and Mr. Barforth, knowing of no market where ideals would be likely to fetch a profit, had simply declared: "That young man will not do." And when Venetia seemed disposed to argue he had threatened to pack her boxes and ship her off to her grandmother in the South of France.

"And so now," she wailed, "I am forbidden to see Charles

and—of all things—Gideon Chard is courting me, which is quite ridiculous.''

"Not really. Everyone expected it when he took employment with your father. You are not so innocent as all that, Venetia."

"Lord, yes, of course I knew people would say it, for it would have fitted in so neatly. But Grace, we are talking about *life*—the only life I shall ever have—my only chance to get it right. And *Gideon*, my goodness! Grace, ten years from now you will not be able to tell him from my father, except that he will be grander than father and more self-indulgent. Mark my words, he will make his fortune, Gideon Chard, and he will let it *show*. He will live like a king and you must know very well that I am in no way cut out to be a queen."

I asked them to clear the breakfast-table a little earlier, I think, than was usual at Tarn Edge and—armed with the knowledge I had acquired in Switzerland and my observations of that immaculate housekeeper, my father's wife—I spent the rest of the morning interviewing the upper servants one by one in the drawing-room, a procedure I deemed necessary in order to banish any notions that, because I was young and the wife of the son of the house not its master, I could easily be disregarded. This career of marriage, after all, now that I had embarked upon it, was of vital importance to me and I intended, with the full force of my Agbrigg nature, to make of it an immense success.

Mrs. Winch, the housekeeper, I had marked down as a careless woman, but once it was established that I had my own ideas as to how things should be done and that, of the two of us, my will was the stronger, I believed I would soon get on with her. She was in her mid-fifties, at an age when she would prefer to keep an old situation rather than hazard herself in the marketplace for a new, and seeing many more useful years in her yet, I was inclined to be hopeful, although her reaction to my first command was less co-operative than I might have wished.

"The serving dishes in use at present are far too large, Mrs. Winch, and I would like you to put them away. Have you nothing smaller?"

"Nothing at all, madam. I believe Sir Joel and Lady Barforth were accustomed to do things on a large scale, and with so many splendid dishes in every cupboard new purchases seemed unjustified—"

"They seem quite justified to me. There is nothing more unappetizing at breakfast than to see three sausages cowering in the corner of a dish a yard square. And a smaller coffee-pot would avoid the disposal of a pint of cold coffee each morning, and would thus pay for itself, quite soon I believe, by the saving of coffee beans."

"Very good, madam," she said, straightening her shoulders, and went away I believe not too unhappily.

I fared less well with the butler, Chillingworth, who had, I imagine, found life very easy in what had become a masculine household; an occasional rumpus, perhaps, in the smoking-room, glasses and cigar butts and a drunken young man or two to clear away, but no ladies with their "at homes," their constant de-mands for fires and fresh tea, their callers and dinners, their endless comings and goings. But now, instead of accepting the fact that my presence would make all these annoying duties inevitable, he made an ill-advised attempt to treat me like a starry-eyed child, hoping to intimidate me with his imposing male presence as a clever manservant can sometimes do with an inexperienced young mistress or a timid old one.

And thinking it wise to let him know right from the start that I was not timid and although inexperienced would be quick to learn, I gave him a detailed list of my intentions. The door-bell, I made it clear, would be increasingly demanding from now on and must be answered not merely promptly but at once. There would be the possibility of callers, as in all households where the mistress goes out into society, from Monday to Saturday at any hour between mid-morning and four o'clock in the afternoon. There would, every day of the week, be five o'clock tea, a meal not much partaken of by gentlemen but to which I had always been accustomed and which would delay the serving of dinner to a more fashionable if—for Chillingworth—more inconvenient hour. And since I had a large number of relatives and friends who would invite me to dine and must be invited in return, there would be formal dinners with a great deal of elaborate table-setting, a great polishing of silver and crystal, deft carving and serving of complicated dishes; every opportunity in the world for an enterprising butler to shine.

"Yes, madam," he murmured with the utmost deference, wishing me, I imagined, at the farthest corner of Far Cathay; and I was not certain whether or not I could rely on his goodwill.

I liked, at once, the head parlourmaid, a wholesome, capable-looking girl, assured in her movements and her manner without putting herself too much forward, although it seemed that the cook, Mrs. Loman, would be a thorn in my side for many a day. Like Chillingworth she had done very much as she pleased in the service of a family where no one seemed greatly interested in food, Mr. Barforth not caring what was on his plate so long as it was hot and plentiful, both he and Gervase being away a great deal in any case, while Venetia would have been happy enough on a diet of apples and cheese. The ample, rather peevish Mrs. Loman, I imagined, had fed herself rather better than the Barforths, dishing up a slight variation of the same thing day after day, and was not pleased to know that I would require her attendance in the back parlour every morning, as was quite usual, so that she and I could discuss the day's menus together.

"When Mrs. Nicholas Barforth was here she always left it up to me, madam."

"I daresay. But new brooms sweep clean, you know, Mrs. Loman. I feel sure you will be able to rise to the occasion."

But remembering the disastrous chocolate cream she had once served to me in this house, I was not convinced of it.

I had brought my own maid from Fieldhead, cheerful, pretty Sally, who was used to me, and I thought it best merely to assemble the others, chambermaids, kitchen-maids, assorted menservants, in the hall and say a few words of introduction, not wishing to usurp the duties of Mrs. Winch, Mrs. Loman and Chillingworth, there being no point in calling a woman a housekeeper and paying her a housekeeper's wages unless she can control her maids, no point in keeping a cook or a butler and then concerning oneself with the daily routines of footmen and bootboys or kitchen skivvies.

And having done all that, thinking that at least I had made a start, I awarded myself the supreme satisfaction of ordering the carriage and paying on Mrs. Agbrigg my first call as a married woman.

All had gone well so far—very well indeed. I was busy, happy, more pleased than otherwise to receive a note from Lawcroft Mills to the effect that my father-in-law could not dine at home that evening, having been called to Leeds, since his presence would be bound to impose restraint. But by dinner time Gervase had not come home either and, having delayed as long as I decently could, I was at last compelled by pride and the sheer indifference of Venetia, to eat without him.

"Could he be working late?"

"Oh lord, I doubt it. He's never worked late before—father thought himself lucky if he could get him to work at all."

"Could he have gone to Leeds with your father?"

"Did father's note say so?"

"No."

"Then he hasn't."

We had coffee together in the drawing-room, a smaller pot I noticed, the pleasure I should have felt unable to break through my anxiety, and leaning towards me Venetia chuckled knowingly, her eyes bright with mischief.

"Grace Agbrigg—I beg your pardon. Grace Barforth—admit now that I was right. You thought you didn't want him and now look at you—unable to spare him for an evening."

"Venetia, for heaven's sake!—it's not that."

"What then?"

"I should have thought it obvious. I am worried about him."

For a moment she quite simply did not understand.

"Worried? Oh, lord! you think he's dead in a ditch, do you? Be easy. He's no such thing. If you ask me, he could have gone to see mother—"

"Without letting me know?"

"Oh dear! Yes, Grace, he *could* have forgotten about that."

We sat an hour longer, Venetia's mind floating away somewhere with Charles, mine angry sometimes—because if he had gone off to Galton or anywhere else without the easy courtesy of a message then I believed I had a right to be angry—and then, at other times, for most of the time, frightened, remembering that he drove too fast, that there was rain again and no moon, wanting only—or so I thought—to know that he was safe.

I heard the door and froze as Chillingworth moved sedately across the hall to answer it, willing him to hurry, restraining myself from leaping to my feet as the double doors were smoothly opened—Chillingworth putting himself through his paces—and Liam Adair came into the room, with no air of tragedy about him, having come to deliver some documents to Mr. Barforth, which—since he must have known Mr. Barforth would not be here—meant that he had come to see Venetia.

She received him with open friendship, warmly jumping up from her chair and tripping to his side, her narrow, outstretched hands disappearing into his, looking very slight and fair beside him.

"Liam, do come and cheer us up for we are both in our miseries."

"We can't have that now, can we," he said, his voice still touched with that faint green memory of Ireland, his smile as roguish as I had ever seen it and his eyes as merry, although he must have known quite well that if she was suffering it was not for him. But Liam was the oldest of our generation, a man approaching thirty now, who before his father's marriage to my Grandmamma Elinor had lived precariously and afterwards had seen and survived so many changes of fortune that perhaps Charles Heron did not seem so great a threat to him.

"So what is this misery then?"

"Oh, I am being bullied, as usual, by papa and Grace is afraid Gervase may have run away—No, of course she is not and I didn't mean to say it. It is just that he did not come home for dinner and sent no word. Have you seen him today, Liam?"

"I have indeed—or rather the dust he was making along the top road—It struck me at the time that he'd be on his way to Galton."

"Well," said Venetia flatly, "I can think of nowhere else he'd get to on that road."

"So that's one misery settled," murmured Liam, knowing it was no such thing. "But what I *did* want to tell you, Grace, is that I've had the oddest little letter from Cannes from Grandmamma Elinor, and it wouldn't surprise me to hear by the next post that she's in love again."

And so, easily, mercifully, we discussed the whims and undeniably the fancies of that enchanting little lady, now entering her sixty-third year, and her generosity to Liam when his father died, although the Aycliffe money—unfortunately for Liam, fortunately, perhaps, for me—had been tied up so well that Grandmamma Elinor could not dispose of too much of it. And he had been glad, he said, to go on the road and sell cloth for Mr. Nicholas Barforth. It was the steadiest job he had ever had and it suited him. Far better, he thought, selling the high quality finished product which could be easily carried in his sample-case than shearing the raw wool off the sheep's back, as he'd once been obliged to do for a spell some years ago in Australia.

"Australia," breathed Venetia, her eyes shining, and immediately his rich, lilting voice took her there, showing her the parched, brash, perilous, thrilling country she wished to see, making her gasp with excitement and shake with incredulous, wholehearted laughter.

"Liam Adair, you never did that. Never."

"Now would I lie to you?"

"Yes. And I don't care—just go on telling me—*do* go on."

She was still laughing when he kissed her hand to say goodbye, having stayed far longer than her father would have allowed, and saying my own careful good-night, I went upstairs for the first time in a month alone, finding the bed huge and cold, while sleep, without the restless tossings and turnings of Gervase, was quite impossible.

I did not expect him to return that night and, even had I done so, I would not have waited up for him. I had made no provision for his return. I had not asked that a light should be left burning or a door unlocked, or that any servant be given the task of admitting him. Nor did I intend to spend the night straining my ears in the hope of his arrival, although lying in that chilly bed I soon realized that my determination not to listen only made me listen the harder, my mouth going dry when I at last heard a carriage, which proved to be my father-in-law.

Obviously he had gone to see his mother and there was nothing surprising in that. I had gone to see my father that afternoon and Mrs. Barforth was every bit as entitled to a visit from her son. Yet suddenly, in the cold and sinister night, the whole of the Galton estate, the wild moorland tangle of it, the thin, rapid waters rushing down its stony hillsides, the dark house built from those ancient stones, loomed large in my mind, recognizing me—since those weathered stones must surely know how to see and feel—as an enemy and an alien. And, having detected my animosity, how could I doubt their ability to defend themselves?

But there was nothing new in this, nothing I had not pondered a dozen times. And in marrying me, surely, the conflict of his double inheritance had been resolved? Certainly his father thought so. But his temperament, like Venetia's was mercurial, a summer's morning abruptly changing to a winter midnight, and supposing— supposing—he already regretted it? Supposing, having hated his day of confinement in the mill, he had taken his habitual, lifelong escape, not to me who believed men should be so confined, but to his mother who did not?

I had started to love him for the vain and selfish reason that he loved me, but now I had gone far beyond that. Now I needed him to love me. I had grown accustomed to it, to depend upon it, and would not easily let it go. And although I was possessive, certainly, I was more than ready to give him what I thought he had asked for, to keep the vows I had made him, since I would not have made them otherwise. I was brim-full of good faith and good intentions, and I wanted him here now, with me, to take advantage of them. I was hurt and unhappy, which had happened to me before. Most of all I was afraid, for I had not expected it to happen again.

I fell asleep at last, as one always sleeps in the end, and woke to find him in the room pulling a wet shirt over his head and letting it fall to the ground where his other garments already lay. It was around three o'clock in the morning, rain lashing against the window, a high wind blowing.

"Lovely driving weather," he said, stripped now and shivering.

"Is it really? I was sleeping."

"Ah—so I wasted my time, did I, driving through the storm just to get to your side?"

"I didn't expect you. I assumed you were at Galton and would stay there."

"So did I. I could have gone from there to the mill in the morning, but my mother said no, it wouldn't do, it was my duty to come home—and the Clevedons are very particular when it comes to duty. I told her she was probably sending me to my death but she reckoned a spot of rain wouldn't melt me, and if I went into the ditch—well, I've done that before."

It was the Gervase I had known in other days, Venetia's difficult brother, a stranger in my bed, keeping his distance so that it was to his naked back that I delivered my crisp reproach.

"You should have sent me a message."

"Saying what?"

"That you would not be home."

"Yes," he said. "I know I should."

And rising to the provocation, wanting it settled once and for all, I snapped: "Then why didn't you?"

He sighed and, turning, lay on his back for a moment.

"You do realize, don't you, Grace Barforth, that nothing obliges me to answer."

"You can suit yourself."

"Exactly. I didn't send a message because until I was on the road for Galton I wasn't sure I was going there."

"I see."

"I very much doubt it. I expect you had a splendid day, Grace, putting the house in order, making old Chillingworth mend his manners—my word, he was even polite to *me* just now when he let me in."

There had been tears clenched very tight in my throat from the moment of waking and now, horrified to feel them stinging my eyelids, I sat up, knowing merely that since I was being attacked it was necessary to defend, to let him know once and for all that I would not be downtrodden. But what had I done to deserve this cool hostility? What had I done that he had not expected me to

do, had not known I would do? I was exactly the same as I had
been in Grasmere, exactly as he had said he wanted me to be.
Nothing in me had altered except the depth of my love for him
and surely he could not be displeased with that? I was bewildered and hurt but determined—in order that it could be put
right—to know why. And because there were still a great many
tears in me which I was firmly resolved not to shed, my voice,
straining to hold them back, sounded cold when I asked: "How
is your mother?"

"Splendid—absolutely first-rate. Busy with her hound pups
just now, of course—sends you her very best."

"Gervase, I think it is high time I asked you this, and I think
you should answer. Your mother was not pleased, was she,
about our marriage?"

"No, Grace. My mother was not pleased about our marriage.
Good-night, Grace."

"That is no answer. Will she be reconciled?"

"I believe so. My father pointed out to her that, whatever
happens now, even if he should throw me out of Tarn Edge by
the scruff of my ungrateful neck, there will still be money
enough—your money, that is—for Galton. How can she quarrel
with that?"

I had not thought it possible that he could so wound me. He
had said "my father pointed out to her," not "I married you for
your dowry and your expectations," the very fate, in fact, which
I had so dreaded. But it made no difference. He had intended to
hurt me. He had done so. And for a long time, while he
appeared to sleep, I lay winded from the blow. If he had beaten
me with his fists I could not have felt more shocked, more
bruised, more completely bewildered, and in fact would have
coped better with physical violence, being strong enough and
determined enough to strike back very hard. But against his
spite—whether he meant it or not—I had no defence and was
obliged, quite simply and in a strangled silence, to endure.

I knew I could not fall asleep again but I slept, waking as I
had done in Grasmere to find his arms around me, his desire
already far advanced, and in that first moment I pushed him
roughly away, revolted at the thought of being so used, refusing,
no matter what the cost, to be an object of pleasure without
identity, a wife who was required by law and by custom to
submit. But his face, in the light of early morning, was pale and
tense as I had seen it in the garden at Listonby, his body
trembling as it had done on our first night together, nuzzling and

thrusting against me with the hurt and puzzled intensity of a child to which my own body responded, opened, enfolded him and held him long after his brief pleasure, until the trembling had ceased.

"Darling, what is it?"

"God knows—just hold me—and don't blame me too much. Just hold me."

So fluent in other ways he had no words for tenderness, the sighing relaxation of his body as he settled his head on my shoulder was my sole indication that, whether he was sorry or not for having hurt me, he appeared to love me again. And I believed I could be content with that.

8

BLANCHE HAD HER BABY THAT July, giving birth as effortlessly and as correctly as she did everything else, the confinement being without drama and the child a boy, the new heir of Listonby.

"So you have got it right first time," said Venetia when we called to congratulate her, to which Blanche serenely replied: "So I have—which means, with a little contriving, that I shall not be obliged to do it again."

"How feeble of you," Venetia told her. "I believe I should like a dozen." But Blanche, draped in white lace, surrounded by lace pillows and pink roses, smiled her infinite superiority and shook her head. "You know nothing about it, my dear. I would advise you to have *one* and see how you get on with it before making plans for a dozen. And in any case it is considered— well—a little over-enthusiastic to have such large families."

"The Queen has had nine children."

"Yes, but then the Queen, of course, is so very enthusiastic."

"Of course," said Venetia, winking at me behind Blanche's exquisite, indolent back, for Blanche—since her mother-in-law had become a duchess—had started to assume a familiarity with Court circles which both irritated and amused us. Not that Aunt Caroline had succeeded in penetrating the seclusion of so ostentatious a widow as our Queen who, having chosen to spend the rest of her life in mourning, expected others to do the same. But there was, in London, a gregarious Prince of Wales and his beautiful princess, the Danish Alexandra, a lady who, although her own temperament was placid and domestic, seemed prepared to understand that a prince—especially when his mother refuses to give him employment—must be amused. And to this prince Aunt Caroline had been drawn as a moth to a flame, being ready to declare to anyone who cared to listen that for all the scandals and half-scandals that surrounded him Victoria had no one but herself to blame.

It was taught, after all, in every charity school, board school and Sunday school in the land that "the devil finds work for idle hands to do," and in consequence it was most unwise of Victoria to exclude her son from all responsibility. And, having done so, it was more than unwise, it was downright foolish to set up such a caterwauling when, from sheer boredom, he got into mischief.

But the Queen, alas, could not trust a young man who reminded her far more of her uncles, the dissolute sons of King George III, than of her saintly Albert, who—it was widely believed—having gone virgin to his own bridal bed, had been heart-broken when it became clear to him that his son could not do the same. The Prince was now a man of thirty-two who wanted to work, all his efforts to obtain work having been frustrated by his mother's conviction that he was not fit for it. What, then, did the Queen expect? But Blanche, repeating to us Aunt Caroline's question, was not really interested in the answer—not much interested, I thought, in the new-born Matthew Chard—her fancy having been taken by the recent engagement of the Queen's second son, Prince Alfred, Duke of Edinburgh, to the Tsar of Russia's daughter, and the fuss it had created.

"Imagine," she said, very obviously quoting the Duchess of South Erin, "the Tsar has refused to send the girl over to Balmoral for the Queen to have a look at before the wedding, as was done even with Princess Alexandra. And then, to top it all, they are asking that their Grand Duchess Marie, who will only be the Duchess of Edinburgh after all, should take precedence over the Princess of Wales and all our Queen's daughters, even the one who is Crown Princess of Prussia."

"How very interesting," said Venetia, stifling a deliberate yawn.

"I think so," replied Blanche, settling down among her lace pillows, the baby luxuriously but quite definitely neglected at her side, no clouds now on her horizon since it had already occurred to her that by dividing her time between Aunt Caroline's house in Belgravia and country house visits in the southern shires, returning to Listonby only when Sir Dominic's sporting activities demanded it, she could enjoy the pleasures of high society with almost no effort at all.

"So much for Blanche," Venetia said as we drove home. "She will be off to London before that poor little mite is weaned, and she will leave him behind, just mark my words, with nursery-maid and nanny, until he is old enough to be sent away to school. If a mill woman treated her baby like that they would say she had abandoned him. But when Lady Blanche does it—well—that is the way things are *done* in good society. I see no point in having children if one means to leave them to strangers. In her place I'd want to curl up with him and snuffle him like a cat in a basket of kittens.''

"Venetia, I didn't know you were so fond of babies."

"Neither did I, because I'd never been close to one before. But when I held that little scrap just now I felt so—so—lord, I don't know what I felt except that I was bursting with it. And if I can feel so strongly about him—because, after all, he's half Blanche and half Dominic and I'm not wildly enthusiastic about either—then how would I feel about a child of my own, half me and half—well—some special, lovely man? Grace, can you even *imagine* the bliss? Don't you just long for it?''

I was not quite sure about that. It would happen, I supposed, in its own good time, since I knew of no way either to hasten or to prevent it. But for the moment Gervase occupied my ingenuity, demanded my attention and my time as fully as any child, and indeed I could not really imagine him a father.

We had been married for almost half a year now and I believed we were happy, were succeeding, little by little, in consolidating our uncertain foundations. I was the stronger, the steadier, the more determined—we both knew it. Perhaps that alone had first attracted him to me and there were still times when it was all he wanted. He had knelt in a field at Galton that winter's day, an injured horse beside him, unable either to administer the swift *coup de grâce* a gentleman's training and tradition demanded or to contain the remorse and pity which even his mother and sister would have seen as weakness. He had felt at that moment a dreadful alienation from his chosen surroundings, his chosen role in life, from his uncle, Peregrine Clevedon, whose physical likeness he bore and whose nature he had desired to stamp upon his own. But I—a city-bred girl from the other half of himself—had spoken out, offered help which he had taken grudgingly, then gladly. That had been our beginning, and it seemed as sure as any other. He had seen in me something he wanted and I had not deceived him. He had seen my true likeness and now, being sure of it, could draw strength and comfort from it as he chose, or could sometimes—not too often—strike out a fretful, a teasing, always a glancing blow, to test me or to assert himself.

"I can't tell you what a comfort it is, Grace, to know you are always right. So very pleasant, don't you see, no longer to be burdened by decisions."

"My dear wife, if you say I must then I must. Unless, of course, you would care to force me? In fact—yes—*do* force me—"

But it was said with his arms around me, his mouth nibbling at my shoulders and the nape of my neck, his body—in the act of love—stronger and more knowledgeable than mine. It was light, pleasant, erotic, part of our love-play which, if resentment was there even in some small measure—and I must have known it was there—love would be sure to cancel out.

He went to the mill every day—or very nearly—but when I enquired as to what he did there and the degree of his success he would merely reply: "Oh, I am not much use, you know, for I have no head for machines and mathematics. The only percentage I can arrive at with any certainty is ten, and I will readily admit that many things which appear quite obvious to my father and to Gideon are not at all obvious to me. But do persevere, Grace. You may make a business man out of me yet, one day."

"Do you get on with Gideon?" I carefully enquired.

"Is it necessary," he said coolly, "to 'get on' with one's employees?" And I was to reproach myself bitterly—most bitterly—for not heeding the warning contained in his reply.

Yet he continued to get up—most mornings—and make his appearance at the mill, which so pleased his father, who was anxious at this stage merely that he should *try*, that he willingly allowed him a week's shooting at Galton that autumn and a further week with the Lawdale, a concession which was either not extended to Gideon Chard or of which he did not take advantage, since he continued, throughout the fine, sporting weather, to attend to his labours. And gradually our lives fell into shape, or so it seemed, a pattern of my own designing which was therefore bound—if nothing else—to satisfy me.

The housekeeper, Mrs. Winch, and I were soon on terms of understanding, and to my surprise and pleasure the butler, Chillingworth, chose to accept the sensible view that, if I was a shade too exacting for my years, I was neither mean nor capricious and might be worth serving after all. Unfortunately Mrs. Loman continued to send in dubious sauces and soggy vegetables, talked down to me at our morning interviews—knowing that I had never with my own hands so much as boiled an egg—so that finally, when apple tart had appeared at dinner five nights in succession, I went to Manchester and found myself a Mrs. Kincaid who brought her own kitchen-maids with her, thus putting an end to Mrs. Loman.

"Poor soul," said Venetia, reminded of Mrs. Loman by the excellence of Mrs. Kincaid's soufflé. "I daresay she has ten starving children somewhere and a husband who takes all her wages for drink."

"Nonsense. No husband at all and one child, fat as a pig, who lives with her sister in Huddersfield."

"Venetia," said Gervase in mock reproach. "You should have realized that Grace would *know*."

The house became warm again and reliable. There were fires laid every morning in rooms where fires should be, hot water in constant supply, warm towels, maids who, because they were told what was expected of them, did it at the appointed hour and for the most part did it well. No one waited now at the front door of Tarn Edge while Chillingworth read the sporting papers he should have been ironing for Gervase. Callers were admitted promptly and then most carefully looked after. Meals were served punctually and then most beautifully, beds were well aired, linen immaculately pressed. I had set the wheels in motion as I had seen Aunt Faith and Mrs. Agbrigg do, and if Venetia scarcely noticed and Gervase did not seem particularly to care, I knew my father-in-law was pleased with me.

I had been apprehensive at the thought of sharing a home with him, knowing his nature to be both exacting and domineering, but it was soon clear to me that Mr. Barforth's main interest in life—perhaps the only true one—was work. He worked, certainly for money and for the authority it gave him, but he worked also for the sheer pleasure of the work itself, which like tobacco had become essential to him. He rose early, returned just in time for dinner and would then disappear to his library to be visited by one or other of his managers, his lawyer, his architect, by Liam Adair or Gideon Chard, sometimes by my father, when business would be discussed and a great deal of brandy consumed. On three or four nights a week he went out, going, one supposed, to drink brandy in some other man's library, and from time to time he would spend a night or two away, making a point of letting me know when he expected to return and notifying me, usually through Liam Adair, of any change of plan. He was uncommunicative but considerate, at least where I was concerned, so that when I realized how much his children and his wife were afraid of him I could not really see the reason why.

"Wait," Venetia said. "So far he has been kind to you, amazingly kind for him. But just wait until you want something and he doesn't want you to have it, and then you'll know. Because nothing can move him, believe me—nothing. Most people give in eventually. They get tired, or frightened, or it stops being important. Not father. He never gives way. And when you realize that, when you feel it, it wears you down. I think that's why Gervase used to run off so much. He knew if he stayed near father he'd give in to him, no matter what it cost him, because a moment comes—*believe* me—when you'll do anything just to end it. So Gervase used to run. Not that it did any good because father would only bring him back again."

"And you?"

"I can't stand up to him either, Grace," she said very seriously and sadly. "No one can."

And before I could ask her about Charles Heron she shook her head and raised a finger to her lips, hushing me.

"Grace, what you don't know can't grieve you—can it, darling? I won't burden you now with my secrets—it simply wouldn't be fair."

Mr. Barforth had issued no precise commands with regard to Charles Heron other than that his presence at Tarn Edge would be unwelcome, his aspirations with regard to Venetia unthinkable. If there was to be a chosen suitor, then, unless Venetia could provide someone of like calibre, Mr. Barforth decreed that it should be Gideon Chard. And perhaps it was her docile acceptance of that decree which stopped him from forbidding her to see Charles Heron elsewhere. Venetia, we all knew, had had her fancies before. Charles Heron could well be as fleeting as the rest, and I think Mr. Barforth would have been more alarmed by a man like Liam Adair, whose attractions—being more similar to his own—he could more easily understand, than this gentle young revolutionary, so different from himself in every way.

But, whatever his reasons, he did not issue the general prohibition which would have barred Charles Heron from any house where Venetia was likely to be a guest, so that when he scraped acquaintance with Aunt Faith she had no reason to send him away should Venetia happen to call nor any reason to warn Mr. Barforth—even if she had been on good terms with him—that they had spent half an hour in her shrubbery, within sight of her drawing-room windows, but technically alone.

Yet when Gideon Chard was mentioned, when the man himself strode into the house to smoke cigars and drink brandy with

her father, Venetia greeted him cheerfully, even pertly, as she
had always done.

"My word, Gideon, I never thought to see you so industrious."

"When something is worth working for, one does one's best."

"But such a pillar of virtue you have become."

"Hardly that, Venetia."

"Oh, absolutely, for you have been out with the Lawdale no
more than twice this season and I am constantly besieged by
young ladies asking your whereabouts."

"And what do you tell them?"

"Oh—that you have taken up residence in my father's counting-house and will not emerge until you have made yourself a
millionaire."

But when at my father-in-law's suggestion I tried out the paces
of my new cook by giving my first dinner party, she placidly
accepted Gideon as her partner for the evening, offering him the
sudden ripple of her laughter in exchange for whatever it was he
whispered to her at table, while Dominic, no longer interested in
flirtation, pronounced the *suprêmes de volaille* rather better than
he had expected, the chestnut purée interesting, the Chateau
Yquem altogether to his liking, paying no attention to Blanche as
she regaled us with the preparations for the Duke of Edinburgh's
Russian wedding at which, if one had not known better, one
would have assumed she was to be a guest.

"Well done," Mr. Barforth told me, and I was inclined to
agree with him. I was, on the whole very happy. My marriage
would not be perfect, but who has ever heard of a perfect
marriage? Who could even imagine or sustain such perfection?
Yet, quite soon, when simple freedom of movement, the right to
come and go as I pleased, no longer seemed so miraculous and
when Tarn Edge no longer required my constant presence to
keep it from falling down, I felt the need of other things to fill
my days. There was a by-election to be fought that year, due to
the collapse of Mr. Fielding from a congestion of the lungs, in
which Miss Mandelbaum and her suffragist group took a strong
interest, the new Liberal candidate having declared himself sympathetic to the female cause. Yet when I accepted Miss
Mandelbaum's invitation to meet him—although I had already
dined in his company both at Tarn Edge and at Fieldhead where
he had gone to assure himself of the Agbrigg and Barforth
vote—I found that my own position as a suffragist had greatly
altered.

The candidate, Mr. Colclough, and his colleague Mr. Sheldon

both made themselves very pleasant, enquiring most attentively as to the health of my husband, my father, my father-in-law, my grandfather Mayor Agbrigg, my grandmother's stepson Liam Adair, and any other male relative of mine who might be likely to vote for them. But the possibility of my own vote, which had never been great had now, I was given to understand, been rendered null and void by the simple act of matrimony.

"My dear," Miss Mandelbaum said nervously, glancing at Miss Tighe, who had lately taken up residence in Cullingford, "we have only ever asked for the vote for widows and spinsters— never for married women."

"And why is that?"

"If you had given serious thought to the matter, Mrs. Barforth," said Miss Tighe, "you would have found it obvious. At our first public meeting in Manchester, six years ago, a resolution was passed asking for the vote on the same terms as it had been, or would be, granted to men. It is the view of most of us, I believe—certainly it is the view of Miss Lydia Becker and her many supporters, including myself—that this resolution should not be tampered with."

"Why, Miss Tighe?"

"Because, Mrs. Barforth, the vote—the Government itself—is about property, not individual personalities."

"I do understand that, Miss Tighe."

"Then you will also understand that although some men have holdings large enough to entitle them to two votes, or more, there are others—something approaching half the male population of this country, my dear—who have so little property that they are not entitled to vote at all."

"And you think that right?"

"I have not said so. I am simply stating the facts. The vote concerns property, Mrs. Barforth, and since a married woman's property, on marriage, passes to her husband, what claim can she make—what justification—to the vote? A married woman has her husband to speak for her. To allow her to vote would be to allow the same piece of property to be represented twice."

"And does the whole of the Manchester Suffragist Society share your view, Miss Tighe?"

"No," she said tartly. "One does not expect any view to be universally accepted. There is an element of dissent. There have always been those who have advocated the extreme doctrine of one man one vote for which—however attractive—I cannot believe we are ready. Presumably these same extremists would offer the vote, if they had it, to married women. Our own Dr. Pankhurst and Mr. Bright, I believe, are among them. Ah well, I imagine Mr. Bright must have his own wife to answer to, although I am at a loss to comprehend what Dr. Pankhurst's motives may be in this.''

"And you, Mr. Colclough?" I asked the new candidate. "How do you stand?" But if I had hoped to embarrass him I was disappointed, Mr. Colclough possessing, like Mr. Sheldon, and Mr. Fielding before him, the career politician's ability to produce an opinion to suit every occasion, a quick glance around the room assuring him that he would do better tonight to support Miss Tighe, who knew more people and could do me more harm than I.

"Mrs. Barforth," he said with great solemnity, going through the motions of taking me seriously, just in case, by some Act of God or revolution, I should one day be enfranchised. "It is a many-sided question of enormous complexity. Perhaps I can do no better than quote the view of our leader, Mr. Gladstone, whose regard for women and the sanctity of marriage is such that he fears the vote would weaken the female situation rather than strengthen it. You are not burdened by the necessity of earning a living, Mrs. Barforth, as we men are. You are free to serve in many positions of influence, school boards and the like, where by making your views known you could bring in many votes. And by accepting such posts, which are unsalaried, you would enable the men who now hold them to take up paid appointments, thus easing their financial anxieties and liberating their energies for the benefit of *our* Party. When a woman can do all this, Mrs. Barforth, without losing one shred of her femininity or exposing herself to the slightest embarrassment—by remaining a *woman*— then one wonders why the vote should be at all necessary to her? I know Mr. Gladstone takes this view. While the Queen, you know, is most uncomfortable at the idea of women hazarding themselves in politics. No place for a woman, she declares, and one must admit she is in a position to know. Have I answered your question, Mrs. Barforth?''

"I believe so, Mr. Colclough."

And it was Venetia, who had seemed content to drink Miss Mandelbaum's tea in silence, who put an end to it, her low chuckle dispersing my gloom and making me smile.

"This is really no place for you at all," she told me. "You had best leave the government to Mr. Sheldon, Mr. Colclough, Miss Tighe and myself. Run home, Grace Barforth, to your husband and get on with your knitting!"

* * *

My first Christmas as a wife was spent at Listonby in a gathering of the whole family except for Mr. Nicholas Barforth, who remained at Tarn Edge, and his wife, who remained at Galton, although Gervase, Venetia and I spent a day with her. The Duke and Duchess of South Erin came up from London; *Captain* Noel Chard had leave from his regiment to celebrate his promotion; my father and Mrs. Agbrigg came over for the ball on Christmas Eve; while Blanche put herself and her son attractively on display and then sulked an hour or two when her father told her he was taking Aunt Faith abroad in the New Year and would therefore be unable to have the infant Matthew at Elderleigh while Blanche went to London.

Gervase gave me diamond ear-rings, galloped off on Boxing Day morning with the Lawdale and was back before noon, alone, his horse having gone lame, he said, although it looked sound enough to me, and we spent a glorious afternoon of winter sunshine in Listonby Woods, watching the squirrels frenziedly searching for the nuts they had hoarded in such careful hiding places, now forgotten.

I was happy. I believe Gervase was happy too, to the extent his complicated nature allowed. Blanche, I felt, was rapidly arranging matters to her entire satisfaction. And although Venetia burst into a characteristic blend of tears and laughter on Christmas Eve when the toasts were drunk, thinking, I supposed, of Charles Heron sampling the sparse festivities of nearby St. Walburga's School, she flirted most obligingly throughout the holiday with any young man who offered, including Gideon, allowing him to kiss her under the mistletoe in a way not entirely pleasing to his mother, who since her elevation to the peerage had started to wonder, once again, if she might do a little better than a manufacturer's daughter for her handsome younger son.

There was a charity ball at the Assembly Rooms in Cullingford in the New Year, an ambitious affair which I had helped to organize and which Gervase, at the last moment, was unable to attend, having been sent on a little tour of Barforth interests in the home counties which—although disappointed about the ball—I could only feel to be a step in the right direction. And wishing to believe what I wanted most to believe—as we all do—wanting Gervase to improve his commercial capacities and his father to trust him, it did not occur to me that, as the one person likely to resent the Chard connection, he had been deliberately sent out of the way.

But from the day of his departure Gideon was a much more frequent visitor to the house, calling regularly in the evenings to see Mr. Barforth, who instead of taking him into the library would casually invite him to stay to dinner—"I reckon Grace can manage another one"—and afterwards would contrive, if only for ten minutes, to leave Gideon and Venetia alone.

Mr. Barforth, in fact, had made up his mind with regard to his daughter's future and expected her to prove every bit as amenable—as biddable—as had his son. Yet Venetia herself, who should have been rebellious, furious, contemptuous, remained suspiciously untroubled.

"Do you mean to refuse him?" I asked her bluntly.

"No, for he will not ask."

"Venetia, he *will*—believe me."

"No, he will not, you can believe *me*."

And I heard her singing to herself as she went tripping around the house, her dreaming face enraptured.

Gideon Chard dined with us on the night of the charity ball, very handsome in the stark black and white of his evening clothes, the jacket fitting without a wrinkle across his wide shoulders, his shirt elaborately tucked and pleated, a heavy gold ring on his hand; a fastidious young man who took far more care of his appearance than either his millionaire uncle or his own elder brother, the baronet. And even then I did not realize what his marriage to Venetia might mean to me, and to Gervase, because I did not believe—and Gervase did not believe—that she would marry him.

She kept us waiting after dinner while she went upstairs to make some adjustment to her dress, leaving me to carry on the kind of stilted conversation with Gideon that people make when they know the carriage is at the door, their cloaks are being held ready in the hall, and the hour is late.

"I'll go up and fetch her, shall I?"

But then there she was, hovering in the doorway, her gauzy skirts floating around her like the wings of a green butterfly, that air of blissful expectancy about her, of an immense, secret joy she could not quite suppress.

"Venetia—you're beautiful," Gideon said, as if he was both surprised and rather pleased about it.

"Am I really? I'm so glad."

And as he held out a hand to her, she came with little dancing steps to meet him, her own hand outstretched, and then stopped abruptly, her hand falling to her side, her attitude one of almost comic regret.

"This is all nonsense, you know, Gideon."

"What is nonsense, Venetia?"

"All this—all this—you know what I mean, for you do not want me at all, and you know quite well that I very badly want somebody else."

"Ah," he said, and, his eyes never leaving her face, he smiled. "Shall we leave it—for now—at that?"

But Venetia, having wound herself up to this pitch, could not endure even a moment's silence and, clasping her hands together, began dancing a few more little steps up and down, jerky ones this time, which took her nowhere.

"Gideon—please believe me. I *do* want someone else."

"Venetia, I *do* believe you. But these things happen, we all know that, and we are not talking about wanting, my dear. We are talking about marrying." And perhaps because it seemed best to him, he was still tolerantly, easily smiling.

"It is the same thing, Gideon—for me it is the same."

"Then there is only one thing to be done. I shall have to see to it that you do want me."

"Gideon," she said, half exasperated, half shocked, unable, as she met his eye, to hold back her laughter. "Such an idea—really!"

"Yes—really! And you will do well enough with me, you know. I am not so terrible."

"Indeed you are not, not terrible at all. In fact if you did not remind me so much of my father I would very likely find you fascinating. And if he were not my father, I do believe I would find him fascinating, too. But you do see, Gideon, don't you, that all this is *his* idea, because you are doing so well at the mills? And *your* idea because if you marry me he will probably make you a partner, and when he dies half of everything will belong to you—and because if you don't marry me somebody else will get what you have started to think of as *your* share. I perfectly understand all that, and in your place I could even see the sense to it. But it would not *do*, you know. I would be a terrible wife to you, Gideon, without meaning you any harm, simply because I am not at all the kind of wife you *should* marry. And you are not at all in love with me. I am so glad of that, for if you cared—"

"I *do* care, Venetia."

"Oh," she said, considerably taken aback. "No, you do not. I made sure of that, for otherwise I would not have given you the slightest encouragement . . ."

But he shook his head, allowing her voice to peter out before he smiled again.

"Then you have been in error. I do care for you, Venetia. Who would not? You are thoroughly exasperating—everyone says so."

"Do they really?"

"Yes, indeed. And I absolutely agree. But you are just as thoroughly amusing."

"How very nice!"

"I think so. You are very nice altogether, Venetia."

"Gideon, I could almost believe you."

"You *do* believe me. Shall we go now and dance at Grace's ball?"

She smiled, offering yet another glimpse of that lovely, inner joy.

"Yes," she said. "I'll dance with you, Gideon." And reaching herself towards us, she slipped an arm through mine, the other through his, and went out with us into the frosty night.

9

I SLEPT LATE THE NEXT DAY, very late, Gervase not being there to disturb me with his tossing and turning, and it did not surprise me when I reached the breakfast parlour to find myself alone. It was a dull, February morning, a low grey sky over the chimney-stacks, damp clinging air, an occasional peevish handful of rain, a day to make up the fire and doze, perhaps, like Blanche, over a book, a cup of chocolate, a day when I could almost agree with Mr. Colclough and Mr. Sheldon that it was pleasant to be spared the burden of earning a living.

And thus idling my time away it was not until luncheon, when I sent up a tray for Venetia, that I learned she was gone.

Yet, gone where? She had staggered to her bed at four o'clock that morning and had told her maid she would probably sleep "for ever." No one had disturbed her. If Miss Venetia wanted breakfast she would ring for it. Her bed appeared to have been slept in, her gauzy dress placed over a chair, awaiting attention, since she had torn the hem. Could she possibly—and I prayed for it to be true—have got herself up and dressed and gone out for a breath of air? No, of course she could not. Or, at least, not once the servants were awake. Far more likely that she had allowed her maid to undress her, had sent the girl away, had waited until Chillingworth had made all secure for what remained of the night, and then, putting on a travelling dress and a warm, dark cloak, had let herself out through the side door Gervase had used for his night-prowlings and had run off somewhere to meet Charles Heron.

I knew it and would not believe it, worked hard to convince myself otherwise—for this was not the unique destiny I had imagined for her and I would miss her terribly—until her maid picked up her ball gown, thinking she might as well get on with her mending, and from its green gauze skirts fluttered Venetia's letter to me.

"Darling, you did not think this of me, did you? And believe me, I would have preferred the parish church and all the family, and father to give me away. But you must know he would never allow it and I have told you I cannot stand up to him. Darling, I wanted to tell you. I even wanted to tell Gideon last night and to apologize to him because I have used him rather, to throw sand in father's eyes—not that Gideon will care for that. Gervase will understand that this is right for me, that I don't mind about the money should father decide to disown me. Dear Grace, I told you once before that this is the only life I have, my one chance to get it right. And this *is* right. Please tell Gervase and learn to be happy for me."

I sat down on her bed and let a long time go by while I prayed, fervently yet without too much conviction: "Venetia, I do hope so"; then more time while I indulged myself in a few tears and a great deal of slow, brooding anxiety. And then I wrote a note to my father-in-law stressing how urgently I required to see him and had them take it to the mill.

I had no idea what I could say to him and, in fact, said nothing, simply handing him the note and waiting, not daring to look at him, while he read it. But no thunder bolts came crashing over my head, just a curt voice saying to me: "The man's name?"

"Charles Heron."

"The schoolmaster?"

"Yes."

"And where do you suppose they have run off to?"

"To Scotland, surely—to be married?"

He glanced down at the letter, tapped it against his hand and then slid it into his pocket.

"Scotland? Yes, that would seem a possibility. Grace, would you kindly send to Lawcroft Mills and ask Liam Adair to come here?"

I heard, of course, only later and very gradually the details of what next occurred, piecing together from the varying accounts of those most closely concerned a picture which seemed to be exact. A lesser man than Mr. Barforth, a warmer man, would, I imagine, have set off post haste for Gretna Green, where Scottish law so obligingly allowed runaways to be married. It was the obvious place to go, too obvious to Mr. Nicholas Barforth, who all his commercial life had sat straight-faced and keen-eyed while men far shrewder than Charles Heron and far more devious than Venetia had tried to hoodwink him.

"Ah, Liam," he said, greeting him in the hall with a brief handshake, "a word in your ear, and then a little job for you"; and twenty minutes later, while Mr. Barforth remained smoking a cigar in his library, Liam rode off to St. Walburga's School, where with the inbred charm of the Irish he acquired enough snippets of information to conclude that Charles Heron had probably not taken Venetia north to a speedy and foregone conclusion, but south where the implications were less obvious and rather more sinister.

North was a declaration of certain intent, marriage at any price, a race to the altar after which the irate father might do his worst. North shouted out loud: "Disinherit us if you must. All that matters to us is being together." North was where idealistic Charles and headstrong Venetia *should* have gone, for once the matrimonial knot was tied, what could her father do to her except stop her money? And she had declared often enough how little she cared for that.

South was not quite so outspoken. South, in fact, might just be the direction in which a man might take a girl to be seduced rather than married, knowing that, since there is no place in the marriage-market for damaged goods, the father of a girl so damaged must be glad to take any man—even her seducer—as her husband, at a price the husband will feel entitled to dictate. Except, of course, that Charles Heron was not that kind of man.

"Well, Liam," said Mr. Barforth, having ideas of his own on that score, and very soon the carriage stood at the door to take them to the train, Mr. Barforth stern and quiet, Liam serious and concerned but with a flash of excitement in him too, for if a husband should be required for Venetia in a hurry this might be his golden opportunity.

They experienced no difficulty in finding Charles Heron's father, since vicars are not notably anonymous, and the reverend gentleman proving susceptible to the temptation of golden guineas and rather intimidated in any case by the generous muscular endowment of Liam Adair, they were soon apprised of all that was needful. And less than an hour later they had located the runaways sharing the one upper room of a singularly unattractive inn, Venetia's eyes terrified, not, Liam thought, of her father but of her own disillusion. For this was not what she had expected. This was not right. She had trusted Charles Heron implicitly, feeling him so much a part of herself that it would have been impossible not to trust him. To go north, he had said, would be too great a risk. North was the direction in which her father would first look with an excellent chance of finding her before the ceremony had taken place. And so she had put her hand in his and kept it there as they headed south, to that sure hiding place which had turned out to be a meagre inn, a narrow bed where he, two nights ago now, had asked her with tears to prove her love.

She had been most reluctant to comply, having cherished for a long time a dream of her wedding night which was very far removed from this. But the loss of her virginity, being the key to Charles Heron's whole plan, could not be delayed, and using the strength of her emotions as his best weapon he had somehow made her feel that to refuse him her body would be the same as withdrawing her love. And since he couldn't live without her love, she would be killing him.

Yet, having longed for months for his embraces, she found that she could not now enjoy them, her distaste being so apparent that she felt compelled to apologize for it and was persuaded by his show of hurt feelings to go through the sorry performance again. It was to have been a magical experience, a slow progression towards perfect physical harmony. It was, in fact, quick and clumsy, as half-baked as his revolutionary theories had really been, a mere stumbling along a road that had Charles Heron's orgasm at the end of it; and when, on the second night, he pressed his hand against her stomach and said: "Only think— you have very likely got my son in there by now," she turned away from him and wept.

She had expected him to cower with fright when they saw her father striding across the inn yard and up the stairs, but he had remained perfectly calm, his composure—or so she thought later— increasing her suspicions that he had wanted to be discovered.

"Mr. Barforth," he said.

"Mr. Heron," my father-in-law answered him. "And would this, by any chance, be Mrs. Heron?"

"You might think it desirable that she should be. Perhaps we could step downstairs to discuss how best it might be contrived?"

"No need for that, young man. It's straightforward enough, I reckon. You've seduced my daughter, by the look of her, and I'd like to know how much you think that ought to cost me. I assume you have the figure in mind?"

"If we could step downstairs, sir," said Charles, somewhat

embarrassed. "I see no reason for Venetia to be obliged to listen to this."

But although Mr. Barforth had never doubted his ability to find his daughter and bring her home, it was no part of his plan to have her spend the next few months of her life pining for a scoundrel and he shook his head.

"I see every reason for Venetia to listen. And because it won't be pleasant for her and she's looking out of sorts, I'll make it short. There's no money, Mr. Charles Heron. Marry her, if she'll have you. But there's no money."

"I can't believe that, sir."

"Believe it. She thinks you can live on love. I reckon you know different. There's no money."

A braver man than Charles Heron might just have taken the gamble. Cullingford was a small town, thirsty for gossip, where a scandal of this magnitude could never be lived down. Surely Mr. Barforth could not run the risk of taking her back there as if nothing had occurred? Charles Heron had been brought up to believe in female virginity, in the enormity of its value, the tragedy of its loss. So had I. So had we all. He knew that a girl who lost it would—unless her seducer consented to marry her—be better off dead. He knew that an unmarried girl who became pregnant had no real alternative but to die, and apparently always did so, since none of us had ever encountered such a person. But Mr. Nicholas Barforth seemed unaware of his own desperate situation, ignorant of the disgrace, and would do nothing but repeat, "Marry her, if you like. But there's no money"; while Venetia herself, instead of falling at his feet and begging him to save her from ruin—as she *ought* to have done—simply turned her face to the wall and said not a word.

"Marry her, if she'll have you." And glancing at her taut, poker-straight back, Charles Heron was no longer sure she would. And when he muttered something to the effect that his heart was broken, Mr. Barforth, in order that Venetia should be in no doubt at all as to her lover's true character, offered to compensate him for any damage to that organ with the sum of a thousand pounds. That, Charles Heron declared, was paltry, ridiculous. Possibly, Mr. Barforth agreed, but nevertheless his offer would hold good until three o'clock that afternoon, at which hour it would be reduced by half. And since the time was then approaching five minutes to three, Charles Heron, so as not to come away empty-handed, took his thousand.

"Don't think I didn't love you," he said to Venetia's blind

back. "Don't think that. I never pretended to be strong. And you don't know—you just can't even imagine what it's like to be poor."

"Perhaps now you'd care to step downstairs with my friend here," said Mr. Barforth, "who will explain to you exactly what I want for my money—which is exactly nothing, no words, no letters, no boasting one night when you've had a glass or two—nothing, Mr. Heron. Mr. Adair will make it plain to you."

And whether or not it was done on Mr. Barforth's instructions, Charles Heron tripped and fell down those inn stairs with Liam Adair's boot behind him and was kicked out into the inn yard to be paid off and sent, slightly bleeding, about his business.

"Come on, love," Mr. Barforth said to Venetia, "let's go home"; and that was all he said to her, leaving Liam to distract her as best he could throughout the difficult journey, which passed for her in a confused haze.

She had been wrong about everything. She had believed completely in Charles and, having lost faith in him, she had lost faith in herself. The world had moved, somehow, out of focus, distorting her vision so that objects she had thought solid became thin air between her fingers, objects she had thought soft and yielding seemed suddenly possessed of the power to scratch and burn her hands. Yet her loss of faith had not, to her unbearable distress, brought with it a loss of love, for the clumsy stranger of the last two days had not really been her Charles Heron. She had lost *her* Charles and certainly would never find him again—since he had never really existed—but she had loved him with her whole heart and now, totally disassociating him from the commonplace fortune-hunter, the commonplace trap into which she had fallen, she grieved for him. She could see no hope for herself, and had her father proposed some convenient, undramatic way of self-destruction she would have been glad of it.

She could not face me when they finally brought her back to Tarn Edge, hiding her face in her father's shoulder when I came running out to the carriage-drive, clinging to him with such desperate, drowning hands that I kept my distance as he lifted her up like the child she had suddenly become and carried her upstairs.

"Liam?"

"She'll be all right," he said. "She'll mend." And we went together into the drawing-room, Liam answering my questions absently, listening for Mr. Barforth's return so that the first steps on the landing took him out into the hall again.

"Ah, Liam—" said Mr. Barforth, descending the stairs slowly, a vigorous, healthy man who even in the fiftieth year of his age made nothing of a sleepless night or two in a train. And Liam Adair answered him, "Yes, sir?" his whole body alert, excited yet cautious, knowing that his own future, which lay in the hand of this powerful man, had already been decided.

"I believe I'm in debt to you, Liam."

"There's no debt, sir."

"That's what I thought you'd say. Good lad, Liam. But I've made myself free with your time. You'll be wanting to get home now."

"Is there—nothing else I can do for you, Mr. Barforth?"

"That's very civil of you, Liam. If there should be anything I'll let you know."

"I'll be off then, sir."

"Yes—take the carriage."

And as Liam accepted his dismissal and turned to leave, Mr. Barforth said: "Chillingworth, have this note sent round to my nephew, Mr. Chard."

Once again my father-in-law had not only made up his mind, but had succeeded against all the odds in getting his way. Yet I wondered, as I went meekly back to the drawing-room, if he would find Gideon as biddable, as grateful, perhaps as greedy as he clearly expected. The seriousness of Venetia's position required immediate marriage. Everyone would agree on that. Liam Adair would have taken her with nothing but promises for his future and the present security of her dowry. Three days ago, Gideon Chard might have done the same. But now, with these new cards in his hands, he would drive a harder bargain and Mr. Barforth would probably think him a fool if he did not. He was being asked, after all, not only to avert a scandal with the power of his noble name but, just possibly, to give that name to another man's child. And, to that end, surely, important financial concessions would be required, specific guarantees which, as I contemplated their possible nature, gave me a sharp reminder of my duty to Gervase.

I heard Gideon's step in the hall, Mr. Barforth walking firmly to meet it. I let them talk an hour, the half of another, and then, realizing with some surprise that it was still only four o'clock in the afternoon, I went upstairs for my hat and gloves and ordered the carriage. Until now I had thought only of Venetia, but Gervase was even more entitled to my loyalty, entitled, most definitely, to know what plans were being made for his sister's future, which must affect our own. And since he was not here to enquire and Mr. Barforth would be unlikely to explain himself to me, I would go to my father and ask him to take whatever steps seemed necessary on Gervase's behalf.

But Mr. Barforth, who could not have heard the carriage from his library, had evidently instructed someone to keep an eye on me, for I had barely set foot on the drive when he appeared, the inevitable cigar in his hand.

"Grace, may I have a word with you?"

"Of course."

And putting an arm around me he walked me a little way down the garden, leading me gently yet very decidedly away from the carriage.

He had never touched me before, but now the very bulk of him, which had often seemed so menacing, comforted me, that wide chest wreathed in cigar smoke, the square, brown hands with their powerful, competent fingers, the habit of authority. And I had hardly slept for three nights. I was anxious and uncertain and very tired.

"Where were you off to, Grace?"

"I thought I should see my father."

"Quite right. But I'd be obliged if you'd put it off until morning. If it's Gervase you're thinking of, then think carefully, Grace. We'd do well to keep him out of this, you know. If he found out about it too soon, before we get it properly settled, then I reckon there's a chance he might just go and take a shot at that young scoundrel. That's what Venetia's afraid of at any rate and it wouldn't help matters. Duelling has been against the law for some while now, you know. They call it 'murder' these days, not 'honour.' And in any case it wouldn't help. Talk to Venetia about it when you see her presently—I reckon she might be asking for you ere long."

We walked back to the house and I saw that the carriage had gone and my resolution with it, for how could I go to Fieldhead when Venetia needed me, how could I take the risk that my father might telegraph to Gervase and that he might then go looking for Charles Heron with a gun, as Peregrine Clevedon would have been sure to do? Mr. Barforth, no doubt, had manipulated me—I quite saw that—but it seemed to be not only to his own advantage but to mine and Venetia's. It seemed right.

"Will you be dining?" I asked, taking off my gloves.

"Possibly."

And it was then that I caught a glimpse of Gideon Chard as

the library door opened and swiftly closed to admit a servant with a tray in his hand.

"Yes, Gideon is still here," Mr. Barforth said. "And I reckon he'll stay just where he is for some time yet, since he has a little problem to solve. Should he enquire for me, I shall be upstairs with my daughter. Have them fetch me down."

And I turned and hurried away, my skin suddenly cold, for there had been nothing at all in Gideon's scowling, brooding countenance, nor in the fastidious, almost pained set of his jaw to indicate a happy bridegroom.

The engagement was announced the next morning and caused no sensation, a great many people—knowing that Mr. Barforth wanted it—being mildly surprised, if anything, that it had not happened sooner. Venetia came herself to tell me of it, very early, sitting on the edge of my bed, her eyes dark-shadowed, her manner that of a quiet and docile stranger. She had no wish to speak of the past. It would be better, indeed, never to speak of it again. She simply wanted me to know that she was to marry Gideon. "And it is good of him," she said, "very good—you must never forget that. One would have expected him to find me distasteful—lord knows I am distasteful to myself. But he says not—silly merely. *Silly.* Good heavens, such a little word! I have been a silly little girl, but that is not how I feel. Poor Gideon, I don't know how he can bring himself to do it—even for the money. He must hate being poor, in his degree, every bit as much as Charles. Grace, will you do something for me?"

"Of course I will."

"Promise?"

"What is it?" And, naturally, it could not have been too much.

"Just this. Don't tell Gervase. *Please.* Grace, I am so ashamed. I don't want him to be ashamed of me too. Just let him think that Gideon asked me and I said yes—just that. Father says I am to tell myself over and over that it did happen like that, until I believe it—that I *must* believe it, for Gideon's sake, since I owe him so much. Grace, please let me keep my brother's good opinion."

"You would not lose it. He is not so narrow as that."

"But I have been such an idiot, you see. I have been mistaken in everything. I thought Charles right and my father wrong, yet my father has been so kind. I thought he would murder me if he caught me and instead of that he was kind—*kind*—and *right*. I am not fit to decide anything any more. I don't want to decide anything. The whole world seems upside-down to me and strange—and I am the strangest thing in it. But please, Grace, you know how little it takes for Gervase to quarrel with father, and I couldn't stand it—not now. After all, marriage is for life, and since it is the only thing women are supposed to do, then somehow or other I must manage to do it properly—I must work hard and be good at it. That is what father says.''

They were married very splendidly and very quickly, using a forthcoming business trip to America and the well-known impetuousness of youth to account for their haste, for although she had discovered by now that she was not expecting Charles Heron's child, she was still most touchingly anxious to carry out her father's wishes, having abdicated her will, it seemed, entirely to his. She was still docile, listless, easily tired, her attention apt to wander, so that one had to ask her the same question several times and even then she could not always answer. "Did I order the carriage? Heavens! I must have done. Do I want to drive to town? I don't think so. Surely—isn't there something I ought to be doing?'' She had become obedient, as she had never been in childhood, wanting to be guided, wanting to please, a little girl again who could escape from the world and all its ills by hiding her face in her father's broad chest and murmuring "Yes, papa.'' She looked very small that morning in the parish church, overwhelmed by a sumptuous bridal gown of white satin stitched all over with clusters of seed pearls and crystal, the skirt extending to a train of imperial proportions, decorated not with the common orange blossom but with orchids, her father's wedding gift of diamonds in her ears, a strand of them around her throat. She carried orchids in one lean, boyish hand, the other hand, bearing a diamond of great size and ostentatious value, resting on the arm of her large, handsome father as she entered the church, and of her large, handsome cousin as she left it.

"What is that lace on her sleeves?'' whispered Blanche. "It looks like Valenciennes. Heavens! what does that cost per yard, Grace, and I declare there are yards of it—and those diamonds! Mamma said diamonds were too old for me on my wedding day, but only *look* at that solitaire. Lord—if this is her trousseau, one wonders what the dowry may be.''

"She looks very pale,'' said Aunt Faith. "I suppose it is the excitement.''

"She was always excitable,'' the Duchess of South Erin replied, no better pleased with Venetia as a daughter-in-law, no matter what the size of the dowry, than she had been with Blanche.

The wedding-breakfast was not unduly prolonged, the bride and groom wishing to take an early London train, and when it was done I returned with Mrs. Barforth and Gervase to Galton where we were to spend the night, Mrs. Barforth changing for dinner that evening somewhat in reverse, discarding her emerald green satin—her Barforth clothes—as soon as she could for a dress of brown foulard that had no particular style about it, her hair brushed out of its elaborate Barforth ringlets and coiled none too securely on the nape of her neck. "There now," her manner seemed to say, her ringless hands happily greeting her dogs. "I am *myself* again."

The meal was served in the stone-flagged hall, candlelight and firelight leaving their crowded shadows in every corner, a sudden burst of flame showing me the ancient weaponry on the walls and that host of gold-framed Clevedons, sharp-etched and light-boned like Gervase and his mother, like Venetia, a fine vein of recklessness, a free adventurous spirit extending down the years from one to another, with a flaw in it somewhere—surely—which caused them in times of crisis to droop, sometimes to give way; their courage blazing out like that brightly crackling fire yet lacking the dogged persistence of the Barforths or the Agbriggs, the undramatic heroism of every day.

"Well, mother," said Gervase, filling his glass from the claret jug at his elbow and holding it up to the light. "You have married your daughter to a Chard. Do I raise my glass to celebrate or to commiserate?"

And with a gesture that appeared to salute the portrait of Peregrine Clevedon hanging directly above him, he tossed down the wine and reached out for the claret jug again.

"Well, mother, what do you make of it? And what does Grace make of it, I wonder? I should dearly like to know."

And feeling his eyes upon me, I said hastily, unwisely, in answer to the question he had not asked and which I ought not to have understood, "There is no reason at all—*none*—why Gideon should not adore her."

"Which means, Grace dear, that you know perfectly well that he does not adore her, that he has taken her for her money and for as much of mine as he can lay his hands on."

"Then you must make sure he doesn't lay his hands on it, or on anything else that is yours."

"Ah yes," he said, once again taking up the claret jug, his lean face turning away from me to his mother. "You see how concise Grace is, mamma—how very certain. You can imagine her, can

you not, standing her ground when the Chards begin to advance
and commanding 'Hands off'—or the ladylike equivalent?''

"Gervase, is it necessary?'' she said, leaning towards him,
their similarity of face and feature, texture and colour excluding
me. "You have a most decent income already. Is the rest even
important?''

"There is a great deal of it, mamma.''

"Oh yes, a mountain of it. A mountain of gold—I know.''

"And why should I leave it all to Gideon Chard?''

"It would not come to that. Your father has given certain
guarantees which would enable you to—''

"To what, mamma? To live here like a gentleman?''

"Only if you want to, Gervase—although I have always believed you did want that.''

He got up, the claret jug in his hand, and stood with one foot
on the hearth directly below the portrait of his uncle, two sharp-
etched profiles, two pairs of light green eyes that seemed permanently narrowed from days on horseback in strong sunlight,
nights among the smoke and wine-fumes of the gaming tables,
two lean, light bodies stretched to their limits of nerve and
muscle and endurance. And I knew neither one of them.

"Shall we set wanting aside for the moment, mamma,'' he
said, his hooded gaze on the flames. "Yes, father has made
certain guarantees, but do you imagine that Gideon will abide by
them a moment longer than necessary? Will he really be content
to work seven days a week as father does and then pay out half
his profits to me? If he can find a way to force me out, or cheat
me out—even to buy me out—do you think he will not take it?
Yes—there is a mountain of gold, mamma. There are times
when I grow very jealous of my share of it.''

She stood up too, arrow straight, her hands palm down on the
table, the firelight deepening the red of her hair, shading the
years from her pointed face so that she could have been Venetia.

"I wanted it for myself once,'' she said, "for Galton and for
my brother—I saw it as nourishment for our soil, prosperity for
our tenants, an extension of our land to what it used to be. I saw
it as ease for my grandfather in his old age, and security for
Peregrine and the children he should have had. I saw it as a
bright future for all of us, and not even the whole mountain, not
even the half. I was not greedy and would have taken nothing
that could not be spared. It did no good. Give it up, Gervase, for
it belongs to *them*. Don't burden yourself with it as I have done.
Dear God, if I could only be free of it—''

And now, in that treacherous firelight, she *became* Venetia, crying out to me down the years to come, her bright, eager hopes long vanished, their shadow absorbed into this single yearning—that had neither hope nor brightness—for liberty.

"Oh dear," she said, pressing both her hands to her cheeks. "Oh dear! I am being very frail and foolish—quite unforgivable. Whatever will Grace think of me?"

"She will forgive you, mamma."

"Yes, of course she will. I must just go and tidy my hair and then, perhaps, I will say good-night."

She hurried away, giving me a quick apologetic smile, and we sat for rather too long in silence, Gervase continuing to brood by the fireside—continuing to drink—while I, with some amusement, some small annoyance, tried to decide whether or not she had wished to offend me. For the income she had spoken of was my income, those guarantees had been made on my behalf, the future of her estate—very evidently—was to be secured at my expense, and she had not even consulted my wishes, had simply assumed that, as a woman, I existed to serve the best interests of my men. She had assumed, in fact, that my marriage would purchase Galton for Gervase as hers had not succeeded in purchasing it for Peregrine. How dare she? Yet my indignation lasted no more than the moment it took me to realize that she was not so much unfeeling as disappointed, not hardhearted but simply a woman of her class and her time, obedient in all things to her training.

Once, in a previous generation, she would have been sent out to win political connections for Galton, to settle—with her hand in marriage—a disputed boundary; her purpose, as the daughter of one noble house, being not to inherit but rather to breed heirs for another. But in her day it had been hard cash—the substance her grandfather had thought demeaning to carry on his person—which had been lacking and with that inbred, female impulse of self-sacrifice she had attempted to provide it. She had accepted the inferior status of womankind and had sold herself, not for her own profit, but for the benefit of her grandfather, of her brother, and of Gervase. And how terrible now if he—her son, *my* husband—should declare her sacrifice to have been in vain. How terrible for *her*. But I, with my own future to consider, did not feel so greatly inclined for sacrifice. Nor, having escaped one captivity, was I anxious to enter another, and although her cry for freedom had moved me I did not feel called upon to give up my own. After all, she had not sacrificed herself for me but for pale, auburn Peregrine, and I was not yet certain that Gervase wished, or felt able to accept, her complex and weighty bequest. But one thing I knew beyond the slightest question. If he decided to come here, then I would be obliged to accompany him, as all women are obliged to follow their husbands, but I would come not as a mild-mannered daughter-in-law but as mistress. If my money was to be spent here, then one way or another I would have my say in the spending.

He came back to the table and dropped irritably into his chair, pouring out the last drop of wine and then pushing the jug away from him so that it slid perilously along the polished surface, to be retrieved just in time by my careful, commercial hand.

"It's empty," he said unnecessarily.

"Yes."

"And I've not had enough. What do you suggest I do?"

"I suggest that you've had enough."

He began to rise rather unsteadily, gave me an exaggerated bow and fell back into his chair again.

"Then of course you must be right, since that's what you're good at, Grace—being right."

"If I have done something to offend you, Gervase, then you had better say so."

"Good heavens, no—the very idea! How could one be offended by perfection?"

"It appears *one* has managed it. Obviously you intend to quarrel with me. May I know why?"

"I don't know why. Perhaps I'm just bad-tempered. Perhaps I didn't enjoy seeing my sister walking down the aisle today wearing those diamonds as if they were shackles."

"Gervase—"

"Perhaps I wondered why it needed quite so many diamonds as that to dazzle Gideon Chard."

"I don't know what you mean."

"I hope not, Grace—I hope there is no meaning. I hope, as I said, that I'm just bad-tempered."

"Then I won't be the whipping-post for it. Either I have done something to displease you or I haven't. If I have, then say so. But I won't bear the brunt of your temper unless I have caused it."

"Bravo," he said, his face sharp and spiteful. "Perfect—and absolute rubbish, my dear. You have done nothing to displease me. I wouldn't dare be displeased."

"What nonsense—"

"No, Grace, the living truth. You have your feet so precisely on the ground. Wherever we happen to be going, you know how to get there. I don't."

"So—is it my fault if you are a spoiled—"

"What? A spoiled child? So you make me feel."

"How can you say that?"

"Easily. Shall I say it again?"

"I don't care what you say. If you behave like a spoiled child, you must expect to be treated like one."

He got up and stood by the fireplace again, his face no longer spiteful but sombre and brooding, his body, even with the table between us, so taut that I could feel the strain of it.

"No one has ever really spoiled me, Grace, you know—except you."

"Obviously I have done wrong."

"No—no. Perhaps you are just too good for me."

"That is a dreadful thing to say."

"Yes. I suppose it is."

But as I got up, to run for cover, I think, before the tears started, he spun round and threw words, like stones, across the room to me. "That's not the same as saying I don't want you."

I stopped, my breath laboured as if I had been running, tears clasped so tight, held so fiercely in check that I feared they would choke me.

"Grace—for God's sake!" And he reached me with a rapid stride, to throw hard, urgent arms around me.

"I have been drinking all day, Grace, you know—all day and last night—and it turns me sour sometimes. This business of Venetia—and *Gideon*. Christ, I have to see him as it is every day at the mill. I don't want to live with him."

"Surely there is no need for that? *Surely* they must want a home of their own?"

"Not a bit of it. Venetia has no care for such things. And Gideon will not move from Tarn Edge, mark my words, until he can afford to build himself something better. He will take care never to come down in the world, Cousin Gideon, you may be very sure."

"Then we can move away."

"Where? Here?"

"There are other houses, Gervase."

"Are there?"

And when I had made a movement of impatience, having already started to lay the foundations of some elegant new villa in my mind, his arms tightened their grip, his cheek pressing hard against mine, his body whispering to me, coaxing me, talking to me as his voice alone could never do.

"I have to get this house settled first, Grace. And if I do and if it seems right to live here—will you live here with me?"

"If it seems right—yes." But even then I believe I qualified that promise, in my mind, to "Yes—if it seems right to *me*."

"I really am quite drunk, you know," he said into my ear, his familiar scent of citrus and lavender reaching me through the wine.

"Yes, I do know."

"And I have been a brute?"

"Yes."

"And a bore?"

"Very boring."

But the pain and the man who had inflicted it were both gone, the man in my arms continuing to make a direct apology with his body to mine, his forgiveness being quickly granted.

"Did I hurt you, Grace?"

"Yes—you did."

"One strikes out, I suppose, at one's nearest and dearest. I'll be very good to you from now on."

"Every day?"

"Well—that's a tall order, but I'll do my damndest. I need you, Grace."

"You most certainly do, if you are to get up those stairs without breaking your neck."

"I'm forgiven then?"

"It would appear so."

"Thank God for that!" he said fervently, and as we began to negotiate the stone stairs, his arms around me, laughing and easy and expecting to make love—my husband now far more than her son—I glanced down into the hall, at the portrait above the hearth, and thought, "To hell with you, Perry Clevedon. Go to hell!"

10

THE HONEYMOON WAS NOT A success, for although Venetia was
still docile and grateful, humble in a way which broke my heart,
she was quite simply unable at certain precise and crucial moments to believe that she was married at all.

For months past she had felt herself to be Charles Heron's
wife in every aspect, which to her had seemed essential. With
Gideon she had submitted to the rites of religion and sensuality
and the law, but she could not during those tense honeymoon
nights convince herself that all this had really made him her
husband. Try as she might, and she tried very hard, he remained
her supercilious Chard cousin whose naked presence in her bed
horribly embarrassed her.

They spent their first few days in an expensive London hotel,
indulging Gideon's appetite for complex food and fine champagne,
his manner towards her indulgent, teasing, not unaffectionate.
But when he began to make love to her, all she could really see
was the stranger with Charles Heron's face who in that squalid
bed had hurt and humiliated her, her body becoming so rigid that
her husband's lovemaking deteriorated into a mere act of
possession, after which, to his unconcealed disgust, she had been
unable to stifle her tears.

The next morning he was curt and businesslike, inclining to
sarcasm as the day progressed, but he took her to the theatre that
evening and to a rather famous restaurant afterwards, and later,
her body full of guilt and champagne, she threw herself into his
arms and *endured* as best she could, pushing the ghost of Charles
Heron away until it was done. He made love to her every night
after that, being a man whose temperament required it and
having been brought up to believe, like the rest of us, that
honeymoons were intended solely for that purpose; but his satisfaction could only be quick and solitary, and although Venetia,

far from refusing him, was almost too anxious to please, she knew that it would not suffice. By the time they returned to Cullingford she had read his nature accurately enough to know he would probably make up the deficiency elsewhere and felt she had no right to blame him if he did.

Gervase displayed all the delicate watchfulness of a cat on the day of their return, smiling at the bridegroom's insistence, before his bags had been carried upstairs, on going off to the mill.

"It's all right, Gideon," he said soothingly, maliciously. "It's all right—we managed to put the fire out."

He was very quiet at dinner-time, not even appearing to listen as his father and Gideon discussed market trends, the growth of foreign competition, the demand, nowadays, for "soft" goods of silk, velvet, plush, the constant need to develop new products and designs now that the demise of the crinoline had put an end to the manufacture of heavy lustre cloths, causing severe embarrassment to such Cullingford manufacturers who had not moved with the times. Neither Gideon nor Mr. Barforth so much as glanced aside as Venetia and I withdrew, and when they eventually joined us for coffee Gervase was not with them. Nor, it seemed, had they noticed him leave. He came back long after everyone else had gone to bed, reverting to his old nocturnal habits of slipping in by the side door, having drunk himself to a pleasant state of unreason in which my reproaches, like lustre cloths and percentages and Peregrine Clevedon's wild horses, could only amuse him. But I made no reproaches. "I'm cold," he said and I threw back the covers, put my arms around him, warmed him and indulged him, made up my mind that now, in these altered circumstances, I must be watchful too.

Gideon left for America three weeks later with Liam Adair—a trip I thought Gervase should have taken—and although the journey was a commercial success Liam came back with the same cautious air about him I had seen in Gervase and almost immediately presented Mr. Barforth with his resignation.

"So much for Liam Adair," Gervase said, far too quietly.

"But he resigned, Gervase—surely—no one asked him to go."

"I absolutely agree. No one asked him to go. But 'someone' may have made it clear to him—on that long transatlantic crossing, perhaps—that he had no reason to stay."

Liam called to see me on the day he cleared out his desk at Nethercoats, his step as jaunty, his manner as carefree as ever as he told me that he had just bought a small printing firm which had cost—I assumed—just about every penny he had.

"What do you know about printing, Liam?" and he smiled broadly, not in the least dismayed.

"Nothing. That's the beauty of it. I couldn't shear sheep or drive a goods wagon or sell textiles until I tried."

"You could lose everything, you know."

"So I could. But then 'everything' in my case doesn't amount to all that much, Grace. And I could just as well end up a millionaire." But when it also became known that he had heavily involved himself and his printing presses in the production of the ailing *Cullingford Star*, I doubted it.

For as long as I could remember, the only newspaper of any significance in Cullingford had been Mr. Roundwood's *Courier & Review*, Mr. Roundwood himself being a frequent dinner guest at Fieldhead, where throughout my girlhood I had heard him express the same Liberal and Methodistical views as his editorials. The *Courier*, in fact, was designed to please the commercial gentlemen who purchased it, approving what they approved, demanding or condemning whatever the Barforths, Agbriggs, Mandelbaums and Rawnsleys demanded or condemned. To the Liberal leader, Mr. Gladstone, it gave unlimited praise and maximum coverage, extending only a cautious hand to his opposite number, the flamboyant Mr. Disraeli, whose heart, the *Courier* would have us believe, was in the keeping of our natural enemy the squirearchy. The *Courier* reported no royal scandals, informing us instead of the success of our own charity balls, the weddings and christenings and glowing obituaries of our neighbours and friends, considering a concert of sacred music at the Morgan Aycliffe Hall of far greater social significance than the glittering receptions of the Prince of Wales at Marlborough House, the war between France and Prussia interesting only for its effect on the worsted trade, rumours of coming conflict between ourselves and Russia for control of the East noteworthy for the amount of uniform cloth likely to be required.

Such violence as we had in Cullingford was not to be found in its pages, Mr. Roundwood having no interest and assuming us to have none in the rough and tumble of our back alleys on Friday nights. The *Courier*, in fact, was a publication which a gentleman might safely leave on his hall table, the picture of solid well-being and conventional values it presented being more likely to bore his wife and children, should it fall into their hands, than corrupt them. The *Courier* acknowledged virtue, ignored vice, in the hope perhaps that it would go away. It spoke to prosperous people about prosperity—assuring us that we were rich because

we were industrious, that the poor had only themselves to blame
for their poverty—while the *Star*, on the other hand, spoke to
very few people at all, operating from a ramshackle first floor
and basement in unkempt Gower Street, its circulation, which
had never been robust, limping now to a halt.

It had been founded in the "bad old days," almost fifty years
ago now, by a group of radical intellectuals, a member of my
own family, my mother's half-brother, Mr. Crispin Aycliffe,
among them, who had wished to shatter Mr. Roundwood's
complacent middle-class dream. The *Star* had not ignored vice,
although it had located it in places far removed from our gin-
shops and our unlit, unpaved alleys. It had reported violence in
our streets but also in our weaving-sheds, where, before the
legislation the *Courier* so abhorred, five-year-old children had
been regularly beaten to keep them awake at their labours. It had
reported the filthy conditions of our working classes, and pointed
out the unpalatable fact that they were unwashed largely because
they had no water; ignorant because education was either not
available or beyond their means; of inferior physique because
their employers, the readers of the *Courier & Review*, were in
the habit of keeping wages so low that they did not always get
enough to eat.

But the readership of this volatile little publication, which now
appeared only once or twice each week, had always been small,
the excessive stamp duty on newspapers in its early days putting
it beyond the purchase of the working man for whom it had been
intended. And now, although it was cheap enough to be within
anyone's reach and it was estimated that at least half of
Cullingford's population could read, it had somehow not "caught
on," deteriorating from its crusading fervour to mere peevishness,
one of its main obstacles being the odd but undoubted ambition
of a large proportion of the working classes to be middle class,
and consequently to take the *Courier & Review*.

"What do you know about newspapers, Liam?" I asked him.

"Nothing," he cheerfully replied to that as well.

"And can you tell me just who reads the *Star*."

"Well now, Grace, I reckon *you* might if I started to advocate
votes for women."

"Do you believe in woman suffrage, Liam?"

"I don't see why I shouldn't. It never crossed my mind to
give it a thought before. But now I do think of it—well, I can't
say that I *believed* in Barforth cloth, when it comes down to it.
But that never stopped me from selling it—thousands and thou-

sands of miles of it, all over the world. So I think it might pay me to drink a pot of tea one of these days with Miss Mandelbaum and Miss Tighe.''

"It seems to me you'll need more than Miss Tighe.''

"It seems to me you're right. I'll need—well, there's our mutual relative, Grandmamma Elinor, and her good friend Lady Verity Barforth. I've never known either of them refuse to support a worthy cause. And then there's Grace Barforth, of course, my stepmamma's granddaughter, who might care to invest her pin-money.''

"Liam Adair, you are preying on women.''

"I wouldn't put it quite like that. But if I should be, then at least I'll make sure they get some enjoyment out of it.''

"Liam—do you regret leaving the mill?''

"Well now, whatever your reason for asking me that question, Grace, I reckon you'll know my reason for thinking it was time I moved on. And I expect you'll have your hands full now, won't you, Grace, with an extra appetite to feed—and a fine, fierce appetite at that.''

It had entered no one's head, with the possible exception of mine, that Gideon and Venetia should look for a home of their own. Tarn Edge was an enormous house. It suited Mr. Barforth's convenience to have Gideon in it. There was no more to be said. A large front bedroom was prepared for them and an adjoining dressing-room with a bath-tub in a tiled recess. I had the wide, canopied bed aired and scented with herbs and lavender. I put daffodils on the broad window-sill, a bowl of fragrant pot pourri on the toilet table. I had the brass fender polished, a small fire laid in the grate, and wondered, not for the first time, about the inevitable tensions of a house with two mistresses and two—possibly three—masters.

But Venetia had so little interest in domesticity that my suggestion of shared responsibility positively amazed her. She could have responded to the challenge of keeping house for Charles Heron on a limited income, the sheer novelty of scrimping and saving, the satisfaction of seeing each economy, each effort, as a brick in the building of their life together. But Tarn Edge—her father's house—held neither challene nor novelty and had always functioned adequately with no effort of hers.

"Heavens! Grace, I don't mean to interfere. You do it all so beautifully and we all know I can do nothing right in any case.'' And she sank back quickly, perhaps gratefully, into her position of "daughter-at-home,'' shedding her garments and leaving them where they lay, ordering her tea without the slightest notion of how it was purchased or prepared, littering the hall table as she had always done with her riding gloves and crop, her tall shiny hat, coming and going with no explanation and no regard for either the weather or the hour, the only real change in her circumstances being that now she went to bed every night with a man.

But—as I had known, as I had feared—the house could not absorb Gideon's presence so lightly, for his nature, like his mother's nature, was definite and precise in its requirements, his temperament exacting. When he entered a room one became instantly aware of him, the tone and temper of one's conversation altered to accommodate him, one realized—at once—that he was not a person who could be taken for granted, the more so since the past eighteen months spent in his uncle's employment had not been easy for him.

He had come late to the textile trade from a world where trade itself was held in contempt, so that he had encountered prejudice from all directions, from his old schoolfriends and hunting friends who were puzzled and a little embarrassed by him; from the Barforth managers who thought he was getting too much too soon and too easily; from the weavers who laughed at his accent and made jokes about his masculinity, since no *man* ought to talk like that. And although his brother the baronet and his mother the duchess both loved him and would have defended him to the death, they had made it plain that when he was a visitor at Listonby or South Erin or Mayfair they would prefer him not to be too explicit about what he did for a living.

It was a difficult time for him. I knew it and although I thought him mercenary and predatory and kept a sharp look out at all times for the dagger I believed him capable of stabbing into my husband's back, I could sympathize too, knowing that in his place, had I been ambitious and poor and a man, I might have fought just as hungrily and with as little scruple. He had told me that he had no particular knowledge of textiles, merely some appreciation of how things were bought and sold. Mr. Barforth had insisted from the start that he should learn—as Gervase had never been made to learn—every process of cloth manufacture, scouring, combing, spinning, weaving, dyeing and finishing, not merely by observation but by his own toil, his own sweat, so that he would know the skills, the snags, the tricks involved, without relying on the explanations of mill-managers who might know a trick or two of their own.

"If they tell you it can't be done and you want it done, then you've got to know how," Mr. Barforth decreed. "*I* know how. My brother Blaize only thinks he knows. That's why he's got one mill and I've got half a dozen. He can sell cloth. I can spin it and weave it, mend my own looms if I have to, and then I can sell it too. Nobody can cheat you, lad, if you know their job better than they do."

Alien notions these, perhaps, to a Chard of Listonby Park, who would not dream of enquiring into his tenants' affairs so long as the rent was paid, nor his gamekeeper's so long as the grouse and the pheasant were plentiful. But Gideon, nevertheless, applied himself with stern calculation and unflagging energy to this task for which, after all, he had been hired, enduring his employer's often unreasonable demands and tempers, enduring the sheer discomfort a man brought up in the open air was bound to feel for those close-confined weaving-sheds, the screech of machinery, the heat, the dust, the stench of raw wool and engine grease—enduring the painful hesitations of a wife who, despite all her efforts, could not love him—enduring the whole of it not patiently, not meekly, but with a deliberate purpose, since he had long recognized Mr. Barforth as a grand master of his chosen craft: that of becoming and remaining a wealthy man.

Long working hours, frequent absences from home in those early months, relieved or delayed the tension I had feared between him and Gervase, yet Gideon, who might never be the owner of Tarn Edge, knew exactly how he and everyone else ought to be served within it, and I was soon to feel the strain of his demands.

He had survived the harsh discipline of his public school, had been obliged to wash every morning of the winter term in cold water at a stand-pipe in the school-yard, had been flogged and bullied and humiliated, the better to force his character into the sparse, unyielding mould of an empire-builder. He had followed the hunt since he was five years old, and when he took a tumble had learned to bother no one with such trivialities as cuts and bruises and a cracked ankle. He had learned to control both his lusts and his emotions, to appreciate the importance of good taste and good manners, the underplaying of anything from a spear-thrust in his side to a broken heart. But his mother's drawing-room and the drawing-rooms of her friends were all luxurious, their tables superb. At Listonby he was accustomed not only to the highest quality but to the utmost variety, no dish appearing twice among the hundreds Aunt Caroline presented every month, no wine ever leaving her cellars that was not merely old but venerable, unusual; her cuisine a delight both to the palate and to the eyes. These were his standards. He had not expected to lower them, and although he made no complaints, being far too well-mannered for that, he had a way of toying with the food when it displeased or bored him, prodding it gingerly with a fork in a disdainful manner that once or twice caused Gervase to look up sharply and say, "What is it, Gideon? The food not to your liking?"

"The food?" Gideon replied, the faint question in his voice so clearly implying "Food? Good God! is *that* what it is?" that I winced, while Gervase's eyes—as always in moments of suppressed emotion—lost their colour. And determined that there should be no conflict if I could help it, my interviews with my cook, Mrs. Kincaid, became every morning more difficult.

"No, no, Mrs. Kincaid, not haddock and certainly not cod—nothing so commonplace as that."

"Turbot then, madam?"

"Oh yes—turbot is very well, I suppose. But since we had it twice last week it will have to be done in some other fashion than a lobster sauce."

"Salmon then, Mrs. Barforth."

"Yes—but how might it be served?"

"Oh—with mushrooms and truffles in béchamel sauce."

"Why yes, Mrs. Kincaid—how clever!"

"And as to the haddock, madam, I could make it into a mousseline and wrap it in slices of smoked salmon."

"Excellent, Mrs. Kincaid. Please do that."

"Yes, madam, but hardly for luncheon since—as you will know—a mousseline takes time."

"Oh, not for luncheon, Mrs. Kincaid. Mr. Chard will not be here for luncheon. You may please yourself as to luncheon."

"Thank you, madam."

"So we have settled on the salmon with mushrooms and truffles, and the sauté of lamb in *sauce chasseur*, and a really good rich *crème Chantilly* for dessert, do you think? And a strawberry syllabub? No, perhaps not, since they are too much alike in consistency—both creamy."

"Pears marinated in brandy, madam. Or a *mille-feuilles* with strawberries and whatever else is available and of good quality?"

"Yes, Mrs. Kincaid—the *crème Chantilly*, and the pears—and yes, the *mille-feuilles* too—all three to be on the safe side."

"Very good. And the soup, Mrs. Barforth? Will you leave that to me?"

"Oh yes, but something *different*. Or at least something that cannot be easily identified."

The wines, of course, were beyond my province, Mr. Barforth stocking his cellars to suit his own preference for the heavier clarets, a taste which Gideon shared but not exclusively, Gervase quickly seizing the opportunity to express his wonder at the extreme sensitivity of the Chard palate and the amount of titillation it required. There was trouble too about Gideon's linen, the pressing of his trousers, the polishing of his boots, trouble not violently but fastidiously expressed, his attitude reminding me rather of the Englishman abroad who, with the best will in the world, cannot always quite understand the natives.

"Is it possible to have something done about this?" he enquired, indicating with that faint, infuriating curl of distaste what looked like a perfectly respectable shirt.

"Lord! I don't know," answered Venetia. "Ask Grace."

"I wouldn't dream of troubling her."

Yet he did trouble me, his insistence on being well served, well valeted, well nourished, on observing what he considered to be not the luxuries of life but its common decencies, offering me both a challenge and a practical method of keeping the peace.

"Are you protecting him against me, Grace, or is it the other way round?" Gervase wanted to know.

"I am trying to be a peacemaker so that I might inherit the earth."

"Ah—if we are talking of inheritance and if you are doing all this to watch over mine, then I suppose I cannot complain."

Yet his own behaviour, quite soon, became less watchful and perhaps—although who can say?—had I spent less time fretting over lobster sauces and cambric shirt-frills I might have noticed it, might even have understood it in time.

Every morning Mr. Barforth and Gideon left early for the mill, Gervase sometimes accompanying them, sometimes not. They returned late and separately each evening, dined and retired to Mr. Barforth's library, where Gideon would invariably stay the course and Gervase would more often than not slip away to drink his brandy in the bar parlour of the Station Hotel or the Old Swan. And because he would have the appealing air of a naughty schoolboy on his return—and perhaps because his very absence had made the evening glide by much smoother—I made no greater fuss than could be turned to other purposes when he had persuaded me to forgive him.

"I know its past midnight, Grace—an hour or two past, I daresay. But look at it like this—if I never did anything wrong then you couldn't scold me and I couldn't coax you into granting me a pardon. And you do enjoy that, you know. Don't you?"

Yes, I enjoyed it, particularly at the end of a tense evening when the beef had been too rare, Venetia too flippant, when I had just—and only just—managed to keep Gideon and Gervase apart. I enjoyed his comic but slightly anxious apologies, my own grudging forgiveness quickly turning to laughter, his head nuzzling into my shoulder, those teasing, tender, enraptured conversations, his body still held with mine. I enjoyed it, even the taste and smell of the barroom about him not displeasing me, bringing me a glimpse of a wicked, masculine world which—like many an indulgent, affectionate woman before me—I could not feel to be as wicked as all that.

He came back to me, we made love, and when he took himself off to Galton without warning and his father complained of it, I defended him, insisting I knew his whereabouts—for my own pride's sake, perhaps—when I did not.

"Well, then, Grace, since he keeps you so perfectly informed perhaps you can inform *me* when I'm likely to see him again?"

"Tomorrow morning, at the mill."

"Can you guarantee it?"

"Oh—"

"Good girl, Grace Barforth. Goes against your commercial instincts, doesn't it, my lass, to give guarantees when there aren't any. I'm glad to see you understand that."

Yet his absences, even in that first year, grew longer, and an evening soon came when he strode into the house white with anger, his father a menacing step behind him, their quarrel locked in the library for half an hour before I heard the door slam, Gervase's step in the hall, and ten minutes later the sounds of a carriage going fast and precariously down the drive.

"It would appear that your husband will not be dining," Mr. Barforth told me, looking like a thunder cloud at the drawing-room door, his massive body still so full of rage that an outlet was clearly required.

"Oh? Why is that?"

"Because your husband, by his incompetence, has lost me a certain sum of money. Not a great deal—not by his standards at any rate—but that is not the point, is it?"

"I suppose not."

"No, because money lost is money lost, and worse than that, for it involves an order, a contract—God dammit it involves a reputation. Because your husband was not where he should have been *when* he should have been, a certain gentleman who has done business with me for years has placed his order—his trifling little order—elsewhere. And if he gets good service and good quality he may do likewise with the next one—which may not be so trifling. Do you follow me?"

"I do."

"Apparently your husband—my son—did not."

"Where has he gone?"

"Gone? To his mother, I suppose. To his bolt-hole in that damned abbey cloister. He can stay there—believe me—for as long as he pleases."

"Then perhaps I had better join him."

"I beg your pardon?"

"If he is to be at Galton for any length of time, I should go there too. I will set off in the morning."

He crossed the room, lit a cigar and stood for a while with his back to the fire, frowning, the anger that had been spilling out of him in almost visible sparks subsiding now, the eyes he eventually turned on me losing their ferocity.

"He has a treasure in you, Grace. I hope he appreciates it."

"Oh—as to that—" And then, approaching him carefully, for even in this softer mood he was still a very awesome gentleman, I said quite hesitantly: "Father-in-law, he has no natural aptitude for business as you have, as Gideon has. It is not easy for him—perhaps sometimes he needs to get away. And he has tried. Until recently I think he tried very hard."

He listened as my voice, lacking the resolution at the last moment to complain of Gideon, trailed away. And then, drawing deeply on his cigar, he smiled at me with his rare, astonishing charm.

"Until recently? You mean until Gideon came? Yes, I know he doesn't like Gideon being here. He was never intended to like it. He has to learn to compete, Grace, if he hopes to succeed. You know that. And if he can't learn—if he can't cope—then at least he has to make up his mind. Had he convinced me he was ready to take on the management of his mother's estate, I might have released certain sums of money which have been set aside for him. He has not convinced me. Has he convinced you?"

I shook my head and, his own head wreathed in smoke, he

leaned towards me and gave what in any other man I would have called a grin.

"There is a lot of money, you see, Grace. And if he parted company with me now, who knows where I might leave it? In his place I'd be inclined to wait for me to die. But if that's his purpose, you'd oblige me by telling him this—he can't have it all ways. Sooner or later he has to make up his mind, and if I were you, Grace—since I know you don't want to live at Galton—I'd set about making it up for him. I reckon you'll know the way."

Perhaps I still believed that I could and so—short-sighted if not entirely blinded by self-confidence, by faith in my own future—it was Venetia, under my eyes all day and every day, who worried me more than Gervase.

Her docility had survived her honeymoon and had changed, very gradually, to a passivity I could not like. She had been eager and vivid. Now she seemed always half asleep and very far away. In her swirling apple-green silks she had been quite lovely. In her tall shiny hat and the mannish cut of her riding-habit she had been an enchanting madcap, worthy of any man's admiring eye. But her charm had stemmed from her fierce joy in living, her tumultuous eagerness for the future, and now, with that joy removed, her future irrevocably decided, she seemed unlit and empty.

She had no interest in the wedding-gifts which, her father's commercial reputation being world wide, continued to arrive by every train.

"Heavens! what use are they? The cupboards here are full of such things."

Nor could she be persuaded to apply herself to the writing of letters of thanks.

"Venetia, I can't do it for you."

"Of course not. I'll make a start tomorrow."

"Why not now? Here is your pen, Venetia, and paper."

But although she sat down with a good will, I found her an hour later fast asleep at the table, the one letter she had started crumpled in her hand.

"Oh dear! I just couldn't *concentrate,* I don't know why. And then this wave of absolute weariness came over me."

It was a wave which swamped her very frequently, washing her away to some hidden, comfortable shore each evening after dinner, so that even when our menfolk joined us in the drawing-room she would remain curled up in her chair, dozing and yawning and rubbing her eyes.

"I'm so *sleepy.*"

"Then go to bed," her father told her.

"Oh—" and her eyes would dart nervously to Gideon like a little girl who was asking "May I?"

She was still so pathetically anxious to please him that her very eagerness became a source of irritation, and ere long there were tenser moments, for Gideon's notions of how a wife should conduct herself were as exact as his notions of *haute cuisine*, whereas Venetia on both these issues had no precise notions at all, believing the sole purpose of food to be the keeping of body and soul together, the sole purpose of marriage to be love.

"Venetia, I happened to see Mr. Rawnsley today and he happened to mention that his wife had been expecting you to tea and was—shall we say puzzled?—at your non-appearance."

"Lord!—oh lord!—next week, surely?"

"No, Venetia. This week. Yesterday, in fact."

"Gideon, I am so sorry. And one day is so much like another."

"I daresay. Mrs. Rawnsley, however, had gone to some trouble, I believe. She had other guests—not local people—who were expected to meet you and who must have taken offence. Naturally you will be able to put matters right, won't you?"

"I shouldn't bother," said Gervase from the depth of an armchair, barely lifting his eyes from their perusal of the sporting press.

"Wouldn't you?" enquired Gideon, his jaw tightening.

"I reckon not. Mrs. Rawnsley don't rate so high in my book, nor in my sister's either, for that matter. And as for those other guests who were not local people, don't trouble about *them*, Venetia. Businessmen's wives from Manchester, stout old bodies whose husbands might be of interest to Gideon, I grant you, since he's rather new, after all, to this sort of thing. But we've met them all before, Venetia, you and I, and we've never cared for them."

"Oh—" She said quite helplessly, sensing, as I did, the snap of Gideon's temper, which we had not yet seen but assumed to be monumental. And for a moment my own voice speaking against his pent-up anger—against the pent-up resentment of Gervase—sounded hollow and false.

"I don't think much harm was done. I met Amelia Rawnsley this afternoon and she seemed happy enough with my invitation to dinner. If we step in to see her for a moment or two tomorrow,

Venetia, and admire the silver she worked so hard to inherit from that great aunt of hers, then—''

''Please *do* that, Venetia,'' snapped Gideon Chard to his wife and strode out of the room.

''Well done!'' drawled Gervase Barforth to *his* wife, withdrawing himself from the scene as effectively as Gideon by closing his eyes.

We made our peace with Amelia Rawnsley the next morning, Venetia becoming very quiet on the homeward journey, very listless as she drifted into the hall at Tarn Edge, totally disinclined for the task of sorting out the drawers of her writing-desk as she had promised, in case other forgotten invitations should be hidden there.

''I believe I will go to bed for an hour before luncheon.''

But a great many notes and cards had been delivered to her of late, many of them, I suspected, unread, and since it was easier to give in to me than resist me, we went together into the back parlour where both our writing-tables had been placed and set to work.

''Venetia, how can you find anything in such a muddle?''

''I can't. That seems to be the problem.''

''Good heavens! there is a note here from Miss Mandelbaum asking you to bring Gideon to meet Miss Tighe. Did you ever reply to it?''

''I don't think so.''

''And this letter from the Sheldons has not even been opened.''

''Tom Sheldon is a pompous ass.''

''I know, but a talkative one, and a Member of Parliament— which always has its uses. Why do you think we contribute so heavily to his campaign funds? Obviously there are things we want him to do. And this note could be about anything.''

She shrugged her shoulders.

''Don't you even mean to open it and find out?''

Again she made that odd, jerky movement of the shoulders, her head turned abruptly away, and then, quite shockingly, two fierce hands swept the desk clear of all it contained, scattering pen and ink and sealing-wax, letters opened and unopened, all of them unanswered, to the floor while she threw herself across the desk top in a storm of grief, beating her forehead and her fists against the wood in a deliberate search for pain. And when at last it subsided, all she could say, her face drained and pinched and horrified, was: ''What happens to me next, Grace? What next?''

But she knew the answer, and getting up unsteadily she began to pat her face and her hair, making an effort to be as brave and sensible as her father had told her to be, and as she had truly intended. She had been in a state of shock and terror from which now she was most painfully emerging. Her speedy marriage, designed to screen a pregnancy which had not occurred, had removed the terror. And now the shock which had numbed her and cushioned her from reality was receding too, opening her eyes fully to her exact condition and the knowledge that it could never change. She had herself told me, many times, that she had one life and but one chance to get it right. The chance had come and gone and she had neither taken it nor refused it. Others had decided for her, manipulated her, moved her this way and that, and having submitted she had no choice now but to submit again.

"Nothing else will happen to me," she said. "I see that. This is all there is." And I could have told no one how deeply her words and her calm, sorrowing figure moved me.

"Venetia—?"

"Yes, I see that. And I shall manage, I suppose."

"Do you care nothing at all for Gideon?"

"Lord, yes! He is very clever and tries to be patient, and I fail him in everything. He will end by detesting me."

"I cannot believe that."

"Oh, but you may as well believe it for it is the exact truth. Poor man—he has a man's needs after all, and I cannot— Grace, let me tell you this for it is eating me away."

"Yes, of course."

"It will shock you, I know."

"That doesn't matter."

"Grace—when he touches me—in the dark—oh lord! what a state I am in, for sometimes he becomes Charles Heron, which I suppose is natural enough, but sometimes—and this is horrible— sometimes it seems to be my father lying there."

"Venetia—oh, Venetia, how dreadful!"

"Yes. Quite dreadful. It makes my skin crawl. It freezes me. And how can I explain to him? How can I tell him why I have to turn away—how can I ever tell him that? And then I forget invitations from his friends and don't trouble to read their letters. Poor man! He has a sorry wife in me."

"Darling, it will pass, surely?"

"Do you think so?"

"I do." And struck suddenly by her air of contrition and

apathy, I found myself urging her: "Venetia, there is no reason to be so humble. He is not perfect."

"Heavens no! But I—"

"*Venetia*, don't put so little value on yourself."

"Oh darling, what real value have I?"

"Enormous value. Indeed you have. You are generous and kind and quite lovely when you are in good spirits."

"Oh no—not now."

"Yes. Now as much as ever. And in any case he did not take you from charity—*never* think that. He wanted to marry you, Venetia, right from the start. And whatever your shortcomings—and they will not last—he has done well enough in other ways. He *wanted* you, Venetia. You should not forget it."

She smiled. "Oh Grace, we know very well what he wanted and I do hope it will content him. Because—as you say—he was no gallant knight, was he, galloping to my rescue? On no, *that* was Liam Adair. And do you know, I still wonder how he could bring himself to take me—a Chard of Listonby condescending to such a prodigal, such a poor little drab as I was then. Liam would have done it for my sake alone, which would have been noble, you know. But it was not noble of Gideon, I quite see that, nor even compassionate. It was just for the money. And when one looks at it like that, then perhaps we have both got as much—or as little—as we deserve."

She was a little more wide-awake at dinner that night, talking mainly to Gervase but at least saying something. She wrote a few letters the next day, had her hair done differently, began to smile rather often and in a new, perhaps brittle way that was at least better than her vague, disquieting stare. She was just possibly mending, or, if she remained unhappy, had begun to learn—as so many women must—the futility of letting it show.

A year passed and the half of another. I was purposeful, successful, had established myself as the mistress of an impressive household, as a hostess and as a wife. I had achieved, within the limits of my sex and my class, my cherished measure of authority and freedom. My father and my father-in-law were pleased with me. My mother, had she been alive, could have held me up as an example to other women's daughters. And how can I say just when it was, in those busy, commonplace months, that I lost Gervase?

11

I SAW LESS AND LESS OF Blanche. She had returned to London shortly after Venetia's marriage to participate in the festivities occasioned by the arrival of a number of Russian "Imperials," a state visit which had a distinctly family flavour about it, Queen Victoria's second son, Prince Alfred, having recently married the Tsar's only daughter, Marie, whose brother, the Tsarevitch, heir to the Russian throne, was the husband of Princess Dagmar, sister of our own Princess Alexandra of Wales.

There was, of course, the possibility that we would have to fight Russia ere long to safeguard our interests in India, but the next Russian tsar would be the brother-in-law of our future king, the tsar after him would be our king's nephew, and until hostilities broke out—if they ever did—London was prepared to be very gay.

The Duchess of South Erin served caviar that season, discovered a balaleika player to serenade her guests and procured invitations to a costume ball at Marlborough House, where the bare-shouldered, enticing but altogether untouchable Blanche had been noticed by no less a person than the Prince of Wales. Had she been of a warmer or more adventurous disposition, the degree of his interest was such that she might well have become a royal mistress as famous as Mrs. Langtry, Lady Brooke or Mrs. Keppel. Perhaps the offer was made and Blanche, in her cool, vague fashion, pretended not to understand it. Perhaps—and this seems rather more likely—the Prince was far too experienced in the ways of women to look for passion where quite clearly there was none to be found. But, just the same, my cousin pleased his eye, and when it was realized that he would be far more likely to accept a dinner invitation if Blanche was invited too, then her place not only in society but in her mother-in-law's heart was irrevocably secure.

With no greater effort than the dressing of her silver-blond hair, the displaying of her magnificent bosom and her sleepy smile, Blanche had filled Aunt Caroline's drawing-room with the world's élite, and transformed herself in the process from the little manufacturing niece who had not been quite good enough for Dominic to the Duchess of South Erin's pride and joy. There could be no question now of those arduous domestic duties at Listonby, no question of playing the hostess, the chatelaine, or even the mother, when all these matters could be delegated to others, leaving Blanche free to practice her supreme art of attracting the rakish heir to Victoria's throne.

But in the October of 1875 the Prince set off on a six months visit to India, and the Chards, whether by mutual agreement or separate inclination, decided to use this time as profitably as they could by making a more prolonged autumn visit than usual to Listonby, where Sir Dominic could attend to his stock and his estate, the Duchess to her son's house and his larder, and where Blanche could produce another child, preferably male, no gentleman being able to feel himself secure with only one heir to his name.

There was, of course, a dance, the ballroom having been redecorated in white and gold for the occasion, the chairs in the Long Gallery re-covered in oyster satin, every chandelier in the house dismantled for cleaning, every item of plate, linen and china got out for the inspection of Aunt Caroline, while Blanche, installed by the fire in the Great Hall, took it upon herself to acquaint me with the details of upper-class adultery which she seemed to find not so much immoral as unnecessary.

"Naturally," she said, "Aunt Caroline would not hear of it in this house, nor at South Erin, and she appears not to notice it in the other houses we visit. But in fact there is a great deal of it about. No one seems to mind so long as one obeys the rules."

"And what are the rules, Blanche—in case I should ever need to know?"

"Oh, quite simple really. If Lord A and Lady B decide to fall in love, all may go swimmingly unless his wife, or her husband, should decide to make a fuss, in which case one cancels immediately, since it would be embarrassing to do otherwise. After all, one could hardly expose one's friends to jealous scenes or oneself to the Divorce Court."

"I should think not."

"Exactly. Which is why the Prince and Princess of Wales get on so famously. When he takes a fancy to someone or other,

Alexandra simply looks the other way. She keeps herself busy with her knitting and her children and leaves him quite free to please himself.''

"How convenient!"

Blanche pouted and shrugged. "For those who care for it, I suppose it is. You have seen the new skirts, have you, Grace? Very tight in front with almost no bustle. They will suit you this winter far better than they will suit me, for I am already three months in the family way, although I am determined to have it over and done with by March. Yes, a boy in March, April and May to recover, and back to London in June. I feel I shall have earned that.''

But I was no more confident of my ability to wear the new tight skirts than Blanche, having experienced, these past few weeks, the symptoms of a pregnancy I could not quite bring myself to admit. I knew of no contraceptive practices in those days and had not sought to discover any. I belonged to a society where women were expected to bear children. I was a woman. I would probably bear children. It should have been as simple as that. Indeed, being already in the third year of marriage, I should have been glad of it, and only too anxious to rid myself of the stigma of sterility. But every morning since the start of my suspicions I had awoken not only to nausea but to a burden of unease which grew heavier throughout the day.

I was neither physically afraid nor emotionally ill-equipped. Women died in childbirth in their thousands, I well knew it, but I did not expect to be among them, nor to shirk in any way this supreme responsibility. I knew exactly how a nursery should be staffed and furnished and had my own notions as to the care of the young. I would be a good and conscientious mother. I had quite made up my mind to it. Yet somehow, for all my good intentions, I could not contemplate my condition without panic, and quite soon could hardly contemplate it at all.

Three times I drove to Elderleigh to tell Aunt Faith. Three times I failed. A hundred times, with stiff lips and a tight, dry throat, I began to tell Gervase who had, after all, a right to know. A hundred times I heard my voice inform him instead that the night was fine, that dinner would be late or early, that it would probably rain by morning, and on the night of the Listonby ball he was still—perhaps happily—unaware of his approaching fatherhood.

It was from the start a difficult evening, Gervase arriving

home late and in an odd humour, out of sorts and disinclined for company.

"Do we have to go, Grace?"

"Of course we do."

"Why? Because Princess Blanche is expecting us? Listen—take off that ball gown and come to bed with me. And then pack a bag and we'll go off to Grasmere until Monday. You'd like that, wouldn't you?"

"Yes, I would. And you know quite well it can't be done—not tonight."

"I know quite well *you* can't do it tonight, Grace. That's not the same thing."

And when I had told him how unreasonable he was, that he should have taken me to Grasmere two weeks ago when *I* had suggested it, instead of going off with the Lawdale, that in any case one simply could not please oneself in these matters when it involved letting other people down; when I had said all that and he had grudgingly, sourly, got into his evening clothes, it was Venetia who delayed us, losing first an ear-ring and then a glove, dashing upstairs again when the carriage was already at the door, to put another comb in her hair, so that Gideon's impatience, never well concealed, became black enough to feel.

"We shall be very late, Venetia."

"Lord, yes! But does it matter? After all, it is only kings who are obliged to be punctual—or queens. And Aunt Caroline is hardly that."

"Quite so. But she is my mother, to whom courtesy—I should have thought—is due."

"And Listonby, after all, is where you belong, Gideon, wouldn't you say so," drawled Gervase, leaning against the mantelpiece as if he had all the time in the world at *his* disposal.

And for a moment, before he gave his answer, Gideon stood and measured us all with an angry but careful eye, accepting both the challenge of Gervase's hostility and the reasons for it, calculating with a swift glance that, although he was outnumbered, he might just as well take up that challenge now as later.

"I might say that," he agreed looking directly at Gervase. "I was born at Listonby, which has to mean something. But I believe a man belongs where he decides to belong—where he can carve out a place for himself."

"Or take somebody else's place?"

"Yours?"

"If you like."

"Are you making me an offer, Gervase—or a gift?"

"I might be stating a fact."

"That's very civil of you, Gervase. If I had a place ready carved out for me, I doubt I'd let another man step into it."

"Then you've no need to worry, have you, Gideon, since there's not much competition in the world to be the third son of a baronet."

It was the moment I had dreaded, the confrontation I had made up my mind must not take place, but which now, when I needed to be strong, touched my already uneasy stomach to nausea, reminding me of my condition—my frailty—precisely when I could not afford it.

"Oh lord—" Venetia said, her hands clasped tight together, her voice trailing off into a faint, nervous breath of laughter. And then—because it was the very best I could do—I said tartly: "Well, if it's to be pistols at dawn perhaps you'd have the good manners to wait until dawn. There's no sense in spilling blood on the drawing-room carpet."

"I beg your pardon," said Gideon, bowing stiffly.

"Ah," said Gervase, "it goes against your commercial instincts, does it, Grace?" And although he had said much the same thing to me often enough before with the wry, teasing humour of our love-games, I heard the insult in him now—the distance—the deliberate separation of his values from mine, and turned cold.

He did not speak to me throughout the drive, did not help me to get down from the carriage, walking ahead of me into the house where he tossed his hat and cloak irritably down. But he made his greetings pleasantly enough, kissed Aunt Caroline on her hand, Aunt Faith on the cheek, Blanche, to her great distaste, on the corner of her mouth, a procedure designed, I thought, not only to upset Blanche but her brother-in-law, Captain Noel Chard, who during his frequent leaves of absence from his regiment rarely strayed from her side.

"Gervase—really!" she said, pushing him away. "Why must men carry on so?"

"Men are made that way, Blanche, don't you know? Or *don't* you know?"

I walked quickly into the ballroom, making a point of not looking behind me to see if he was following, simply assuming—hoping—that he would, although, as a husband of three years' standing, no one could expect him to remain long at my side. He would go to the billiard room or the smoking-room, I supposed, as soon as he could, where, in his present childish humour, he would drink too much, play cards for stakes I thought scandalous, wasteful, and lose, which would sour his temper tomorrow when we had been invited to Galton, thus increasing the difficulties of what I expected to be a difficult visit. What a nuisance he could be, how irresponsible!

"Gervase—" I commanded.

"Yes," he said, "I know. You are telling me to behave."

"I am asking you, since we are here, to make the best of it. And as to what happened between you and Gideon—well, it wasn't the moment."

"My word!" he said. "Can I believe my ears? Are you actually apologizing to me for not leaping to my defence?"

"Gervase, that is nonsense—"

But he was gone.

All around me were faces I recognized, my everyday neighbours transformed by those mirrored walls, those rivers of candle-lit crystal, into glamorous creatures of silk and satin who, just the same, would chat very cosily to me. And although as a young matron I did not expect to dance, since it was neither the duty nor particularly to the advantage of any gentleman to dance with me, there was a great deal to observe, and a decided pleasure in the company of Aunt Faith, who so long as the Barforth family feud endured could not visit me at Tarn Edge. And so for a pleasant hour or two we talked quietly together of Blanche, who was so serenely content, and of Venetia, who was perhaps not made for contentment, although she seemed better that night, dancing a wild polka with some London stranger, than I had seen her since her marriage.

"She is recovering her glow," Aunt Faith murmured, "and her madcap spirits. Just look at her now, with her skirts flying—what a pity we married ladies are not supposed to enjoy ourselves quite so much as that. I fear her mother-in-law is about to call her to order."

And sure enough Aunt Caroline, appearing purposefully on the edge of the dance-floor, extracted her third son's wife from that frenzied polka with a single wave of her hand.

"Venetia, you are *breathless*."

"Lord, yes! Aunt Caroline—and loving it."

But Aunt Caroline, for whom a ballroom was no place for enjoyment but for the serious business of social advancement, shook her head.

"No, dear. Sit down *there*, by Grace and Aunt Faith, and compose yourself. We have certain 'politicals' here this evening who could be useful to Dominic and may wish to speak a word to his brother's wife. A *word*, dear, no more—and should they enquire as to the extent of your father's commercial reputation, all that need concern them is that it is *vast*.''

"And my brother's part in it?''

"Really, my dear!'' Aunt Caroline said vaguely, drifting off, her nonchalance telling us very clearly that, so far as Dominic's political friends were concerned, Venetia had no brother, the whole of Mr. Nicholas Barforth's commercial empire being destined—they had been given to understand—for Gideon, who in true feudal fashion would not hesitate to place it at his brother's political disposal.

"So Dominic is to be Prime Minister is he?'' Venetia enquired pertly of Aunt Caroline's retreating back.

"Hush, dear,'' murmured Aunt Faith, "for the sad thing, you know, is that Aunt Caroline would do the job of Prime Minister far better herself.''

I did not expect to see Gervase in the ballroom again and it was not until my generous Uncle Blaize offered to dance with me that I glimpsed his reflection in the long mirrored wall, lounging beside a chair that contained Diana Flood. There was nothing in the sight to disturb me. I was very definite about that. She had been married a year ago to a military, rather older cousin, thus changing her status but not her name, and I had attended her wedding without any particular feeling of involvement. She had been a thin, excitable girl who three years ago had wanted to marry Gervase. Instead he had married me, Diana had married her Major Compton Flood and had increased neither in weight nor in composure, retaining the nervous but not unattractive restlessness I had often remarked in her thoroughbred uncle. There was no more to it than that, no reason at all why Gervase should not be sitting with her and her foxhunting friends—*his* friends until the demands of commerce and matrimony had made such friendships inappropriate. And in acknowledgement of the rightness and naturalness of it all, I smiled at her very civilly as I danced by, receiving in exchange a startled movement of her head, a trill of nervous laughter which told me I had been the subject of their conversation. They had been whispering together, intimately, unkindly, enjoying their own high-bred malice, their own wit; and I had been the subject of it. I stared for a moment aghast, recoiled, and then, taking a deep breath, drew myself together with an almost cruel resolve, my back very straight, my head high.

I had received my first lesson in the defence I was to practise so skilfully and for so long; the proud but painful art of pretending not to care.

I went down to supper with Uncle Blaize and Aunt Faith, keeping up a flow of reminiscences and observations to which they calmly and easily replied. I ate what it was proper for me to eat and in the right quantity, refusing to notice that my husband, in a corner of the same room, was entertaining another woman; refusing to wince at the consistent, high-pitched note of her laughter; refusing, absolutely, to wonder how much of that giggling was directed at me. And to make my performance complete, when her mirth became too persistent to ignore, I turned and smiled indulgently in her direction, letting it be clearly seen that what did not alarm me need trouble no one.

Pride? Very possibly. But there was bewilderment underneath it too, the numbing sensation of a blow not really felt because I could not quite believe in it. And perhaps my fresh awareness of physical unease, an ache at the small of my back, the return of nausea, was a relief to me.

A few hours before and I would simply have found Gervase, told him I was unwell and gone to bed. Now I could not. Nor could I get up and take my leave without loss of self-esteem. If I did so then he would think me jealous. *She* would think me jealous. There was nothing to be done but sit and chat and smile—nothing at all—and it was not until the ballroom crowd was growing thin and I had seen Sir Julian Flood take his niece away that I accepted Aunt Faith's advice and went to bed. And then, half-way up the stairs, it struck me most unpleasantly that I had perhaps erred in the opposite direction, exposing the jealousy I resolutely *would* not feel by lingering too long.

But as I entered one of Listonby's spacious, rose-pink bedrooms a fresh assault of nausea erased such considerations from my mind, and when it became necessary to ring for assistance and two worried maids had brought me a clean water jug and basin and installed me gingerly between clean sheets, I was too weak for anything but a few self-indulgent tears.

I drifted into a shallow sleep, my head filled with racing, half-coherent thoughts, my body still unreliable, and I was too feverish and confused on waking to find it strange that Gervase should not be there. And when I understood, a while later, that it was very strange indeed, I was too weary, too sick and too unaccustomed to sickness to feel any real alarm. I fell asleep again, beyond anxiety, waking this time to panic, for he had still not come to bed, would surely not come now, and what could I do about it? Was there, in fact, anything that should be done? Of course not. *Of course* not. He could quite simply have fallen asleep in the smoking room, a brandy glass at his elbow, as happened to some gentleman or other at every party. And, failing that, there would certainly be a card game in progress somewhere in this house tonight and no reason why Gervase should not be involved in it. He played cards. He drank brandy. He also rode fast and ill-tempered horses over dark fields, high hedges, to settle some stupid wager. And as a pang of terror twisted my stomach—for he could be lying dead somewhere in a ditch, there was no doubt about it—I swung myself out of bed and was sick again, as neatly as I could contrive, in the basin.

I took the quilt from the bed and spent what little remained of the night in an armchair by the window, shivering and sweating in turn, yet not trusting myself to lie down or close my eyes; crushed, in that crowded house, by an appalling isolation, my world shrunk to the dimensions of the jug and basin, regulated by the heaving of my tormented belly. And it was when I was empty, my energy and my will all spent, that I thought of him with Diana Flood and burst into a storm of hot and exceedingly foolish tears.

I had seen her hands on him, plucking at his sleeve as they sat in the supper room. I had seen her fingers touching his as he gave her her glass. I had seen her thin figure swaying closer to him than was proper and then withdrawing, laughing, swaying forward again. I had seen hundreds of women—hundreds of them—go through the same flirtatious performance with hundreds of men. And what did it signify? Who remembered it, even, in the morning? But supposing, when her uncle came to fetch her, she had called out to Gervase: "Why don't you ride home with us? What a lark!" would he have refused? Could he, in fact, have answered: "Let's ride to Galton on the way and drink champagne in the cloister." Of course he could, for there had been champagne parties often enough in the cloister in the days when I had been warned against him, and she was no virgin now but a married woman who went about without her husband.

Yes, quite definitely they could be together, for he had been angry enough to hurt me, had started the whole shabby nonsense on purpose to hurt me, and it would be like him to carry it on too far. And once again that persistent wave of nausea made it impossible for me to decide in any detail what ought to be done, what *could* be done.

I was resolute enough by breakfast-time and, determined not to be the first downstairs, entered the crowded dining-room with a smile, although the smell of so much fried food revolted me, and there was still that gnawing ache at the bottom of my back. I had toast and coffee, spoke a few words to strangers—Blanche and Aunt Faith being still in bed, Venetia, it seemed, in the billiard room, where no lady had any business to be, the Chards and other kindred spirits out long ago with the hunt. Could Gervase be with them? And the realization that I could not possibly enquire jolted my tired brain a fraction away from reality to a confused, nightmare sensation of frantic hurry, of constantly opening wrong doors.

"My dear," a London lady told me, "you are looking very pale."

"Yes, I think I need a breath of air."

And it was then that I found him, coming across the grass with half a dozen others, young bloods still in their evening clothes, moving with the careful step of men who, emerging from their drunken oblivion, are finding the world a very loud and very garish place.

"Good morning, Gervase."

"Good morning, Grace." And he would have walked on had I not put out a hand as imperious as Aunt Caroline's and detained him, seeing no reason to wait a moment longer for an explanation.

"Later, Grace—"

"Now."

"Grace—I'm not up to it."

But seeing the set of my jaw he sighed, shrugged, and turning to his waiting friends—all strangers to me—he made a grimace that said, "Good God!—women—"

I was too hurt to speak. My throat seemed stiff and all my terrible anxiety—my dread of finding him with his neck broken like his uncle Perry Clevedon—seemed converted, now that he was safe, into a fierce anger. And striding forward around the corner of the house, my whole body trembling, so hurt—so hurt—that I had to find release, I spun round intending to be glacial, dignified, to insult him certainly, but with propriety, and hit him instead, hard, across his cheek.

Perhaps I expected him to hit me back. Perhaps I wanted him to hit me, was ready for it, needed his savagery to match and encourage my own, but my blow seemed to have taken the malice out of him, stunning him so that he could do nothing for a long moment but stand and stare.

"Christ!" he said at last, "Oh, Christ!" and even with my vision blurred by outrage, I could see he had not the least idea how to cope with me. "Grace, for God's sake! Whatever you may have been thinking, it wasn't all that bad, you know—"

But nothing he could have said just then, no apology, no threat, would have made any difference, since I could not bear to listen to it. Nor could I bear to look at him or stand beside him, and having fretted over his absence for so many tortured hours, all I now desired was for him to go away again. And since he seemed unwilling to move, I set off myself, still trembling, going anywhere so long as it was far away.

"Grace—"

"Just leave me alone."

"Good God—!"

"Leave me alone! Don't follow me. Just leave me."

"All right," he shouted after me. "All right. If that's what you want—I will."

But one does not carry one's personal conflicts into the homes even of one's closest relations and when we met at luncheon I was outwardly very calm. Nor did I feel able to cancel that long-arranged visit to Galton Abbey, my relationship with my mother-in-law being too delicate to risk a misunderstanding, and I set off as arranged in the early autumn afternoon, the small portion of roast chicken and *crème caramel* I had managed to swallow pressing like a dead weight against my stomach.

I made the journey in one of the Listonby victorias, Gervase on horseback very far ahead. Although we had only five miles to go, they were all uphill and then, quite sickeningly, down again, narrow lanes and jolting, rutted tracks that jarred my back as they descended, through a sharp, spiteful little wind, the slope that led to Galton. And although I knew, because everyone had told me so, that it was a glorious day, a vivid blue sky streaked with hurrying cloud above the deep reds and golds of October, I was too intent on ignoring the reminder of that *crème caramel*, that infuriating ache in my back, and did not notice.

"What a glorious day!" my mother-in-law called out, lifting her pointed face with keen enjoyment into the spicy, smoky air. And because there were other horses standing beside Gervase's bay on the drive, I kept the smile on my lips as I walked through the hall and into the untidy, chintzy parlour where Diana Flood, pushing a cat from her knee, got up and held out to me a well-bred, ill-manicured hand.

Her uncle, Sir Julian, was with her, and another man, somewhat younger but very much like him, thin and dark and nervous like all the Floods.

"Mrs. Barforth, you will remember my husband?"

"Yes indeed—Major Flood, how do you do?"

"What a glorious day!" he told me.

"Yes—very fine."

"Downright criminal, I call it, to stay indoors on a day like this."

"Oh, yes—yes, indeed."

"Oh, come now!" Diana Flood cut in. "Mrs. Gervase Barforth is being polite, darling, for she does not care for the countryside. Is that not so, Mrs. Barforth?"

But all I cared for just then was to sit down, somewhat speedily, before the weakness of my legs became apparent, and my only answer was what she may have taken for a frosty smile.

Tea was served, for no one's benefit but mine, the gentlemen seeing the appearance of the tea-kettle as a signal for escape into that glorious outdoors, Diana Flood and my mother-in-law remaining only because it would have been ill-mannered to leave me alone. But conversation was stilted, quite painful, constantly broken by such exclamations as "Oh, listen! I believe they have brought out the new black mare—I would know that whinny in a thousand," so that when no second cup was offered and Mrs. Barforth suggested "A breath of air? Shall we walk to the bridge?" I got up at once, declaring myself very willing.

"I fear Mrs. Gervase Barforth is not dressed for walking," remarked Diana Flood, glancing at her own stout riding-boots, "real walking, that is." But I could think of nothing worth saying to that and went outside again into the crisp, amber day, unable to suppress a shiver as the wind, coming fresh from the moor, struck me its first blow.

"Exhilarating," said Diana Flood.

"Yes—quite so."

But as we walked to the unsteady wooden bridge spanning the little stream, her faint contempt meant nothing to me compared with the enormous effort of moving and continuing to move one leg after the other, of keeping that aching back erect, of forcing that taut, uneasy stomach to obey my commandment that, come what may, I would not—absolutely *would* not—vomit in a public place.

"Oh, yes! Look! There is Gervase on the mare. My word, Aunt Georgiana, she is absolutely first-rate!"

"Is she not? And brave and willing into the bargain. Grace,

dear, come off the bridge or you will get rather wet as they ride across.''

We had been all three on the ramshackle bridge together, looking down at the stony river-bed and the clear, rushing water. They had moved away and I had barely noticed it. I followed them meekly, stood beside them, their conversation, which seemed mainly to be of hocks and withers, defeating me; and clenching my teeth to conceal a sudden, brief pain—a gesture they may have mistaken for sullenness or bad temper—I watched as Gervase and the two Floods rode their horses into the stream and up the bank beside us.

I no longer knew if I had forgiven him. I could not even judge how much or exactly what there had been to forgive, so urgently did I now require to concentrate on the basic function of keeping on my feet. And when he swung out of his saddle, his beautiful black mare—just a *horse* to me—momentarily screening us from the others, his evident ill-humour seemed far less menacing to me than the claw which had embedded itself somehow at the base of my spine.

"Is it necessary to look so peevish?" he hissed from the corner of his mouth. "Whatever it is I am supposed to have done to you does not concern my mother. You will oblige me by not making her pay your price for it."

But I couldn't answer him.

The black mare was now the object of their most minute attention. They looked at it loudly, ecstatically, touched it, picked up its hooves and examined its eyes and teeth, arguing at length which one of its many qualities should be counted the best. And when that was done, all that remained was for them to put it through its paces, to match their own mounts against it somewhere where the hedges were high enough, the ditches wide and deep, where there was sufficient flat ground for a good gallop.

"Stargate Meadows," announced Major Compton Flood, naming a stretch of land belonging to Sir Julian, not far from the Flood manor, and as Diana waited for her own horse to be brought she smiled at my mother-in-law and said: "Aunt Georgiana, won't you come with us?" knowing full well that only my presence prevented it.

"Hardly, dear—''

"Please," I said quickly. "If you would like to go, please do. I shall be perfectly comfortable.''

But the Clevedon code did not permit the abandoning of one's guests, even such tiresome city-bred creatures as myself who—in this glorious weather—did not ride.

"No—no, dear. We shall be very comfortable together."

"Goodbye, mamma!" called out Gervase, leaning down from the saddle to kiss her cheek. But if he made a deliberate attempt to slight me—and of course he had—then his effort was wasted, for I was incapable by then of resentment or jealousy or any human emotion at all. All that concerned me was that something inside my body appeared to be breaking and I needed peace and solitude, a corner in which to hide, and if possible to mend myself.

They rode off. I turned, moved, went inside, my mother-in-law's voice behind me still murmuring of the fine weather. And then the stone fireplace in the Great Hall which had seemed quite far away came suddenly towards me, or I to it, so that I put out both hands to push myself clear of it and encountered nothing at all against my fingers.

"Oh, my dear!" Mrs. Barforth whispered urgently. "My poor dear!" And as her strong, horsewoman's hands took hold of me, I felt myself to be bleeding and understood I had started to lose my child.

12

PERHAPS I HAD EXPECTED HER to be efficient, for she was accustomed to mares in foal, to hound bitches and their litters, and had none of the squeamishness of the city-bred. I had even expected her to be kind, or to go through the motions of kindness, since she had always tried to like me and had done her best to behave as if she did. I had not expected to believe in her kindness, to need it, had not thought I could cling to her in that desperate fashion, nor find such reassurance in her lean, firm hands. I had not expected to be so afraid, but in the half-hour before the doctor came I was terrified of death, assaulted by the rushing memories of all those thousands of women who every year must bleed away their lives in this fashion. I couldn't end like this. Until not so very long ago I had believed I could never end at all. That illusion had faded, but even so I could not bear it to be like this, not now; and as the futility of it, the waste of it, reduced me to helplessness, she put her arms around me and held me gently but in a manner which conveyed her very definite intention of not letting me go.

I suppose there was nothing the doctor could really do, and being accustomed to a country practice where there were no great fees to be earned, he said so quite bluntly, assuring me that nature, which had put me in this predicament in the first place, would now take its course. He would make me as comfortable as he could, and after that there would be some days in bed, how many he was not yet prepared to specify, and with proper rest and food I would soon be up and about again.

"Beef tea," he said. "Herb tea. Red wine and raw eggs. Anything you like. If you believe it's doing you good, then it probably will be. No reason to make a fuss. It happens every day."

And I was calmer after that.

"My dear," Mrs. Barforth said, bringing me the hot milk and cinnamon I had requested. "I really didn't know—"

"I hardly knew myself."

"Gervase?"

"No. I didn't tell him. I wish there was no need to tell him now."

"Dearest, how can we avoid it?"

"We can't. Where is he?"

"I imagine he must be at the Floods' by now, for they will surely have invited him to dine. I have sent word."

But she must have known as well as I did that he would not come soon. She had also sent word to Listonby, for, not long after, I heard a carriage and there was my maid with my hairbrushes, my bottles of toilet water, my clean linen, a note from Blanche saying all that was needful, promising she would come when she could, telling me that Venetia, who would have come then and there, had returned to Cullingford directly after luncheon with Gideon. And unaware until that moment of how much I had been longing for Venetia, I was ashamed of the tears in my eyes and considerably annoyed by this strange new tendency to weep.

I no longer felt any pain. I was simply weary to my very bones, drowning in the weight of it, the effort of saying "No, thank you" to offers of food and drink and nursing becoming so tremendous that I closed my eyes, not to sleep but to escape. And I supposed it to be far into the night when I heard the sound of hooves below me and Mrs. Barforth, hastily rising from her chair, hurried downstairs to meet Gervase who only later—*much* later I thought—appeared in the doorway, looking at me and trying not to see me with an expression I vaguely recognized.

"Are you—all right?"

"Yes. Quite all right."

"You should have told me—shouldn't you?"

"I wasn't really sure. Do come in."

He came, gingerly, treading like a cat unsure of its ground, ready, I think, to avert his gaze from the many things around me and within me which he thought might alarm or disgust him. And abruptly I remembered when I had seen him like this before and pressed my eyelids together to shut away yet another onslaught of those feeble, irritating tears.

"When did it start?"

"Does it matter?"

"No, I suppose not. I—I'm sorry."

"Yes."

And I knew that, whether or not he wanted to take my hand, he would not take it, that he was as helpless now, faced with my pain, as on the day he had knelt beside an injured horse in the paddock just beyond this bedroom window, holding himself responsible for those injuries as now he was accepting the blame for mine. He was suffering and I knew it. Yet I was suffering too and his anguish, in my present weakness, did not console me.

"They say you should rest."

"Yes—as much as I can."

"So—do I disturb you?"

I shook my head.

"Grace—?"

"Yes?"

But, whatever it was that he wished to say, it could not be said. It may have been some expression of tenderness or self-reproach, the things one hopes a lover might say at such a moment. "I could not bear to lose you" or quite simply "I love you." Very likely it *was* something like that, and anything would have sufficed. But it was beyond him. He swallowed hard, took a nervous step up and down the room, said nothing, and was very glad, I suppose, when he glanced at me, to find I had apparently fallen asleep.

He came to see me the next morning very early, hovering once again in my doorway.

"They say you had a good night."

"Yes."

"Grace—you don't need me for anything, do you?"

"No."

"Then—look here—the thing is I'm supposed to be at the mill this morning."

"Then you'd better hurry."

"If you'd rather—?"

"I'm *all right*. Your mother can look after me."

"Of course."

He crossed the room, possibly disliking the part of himself that could barely wait to be off; disliking too, the effort it cost him to brush the back of his hand against my cheek. And because I was stung afresh by the memory of that dying horse and was yet again close to tears, I said tartly: "You'd do well not to keep your father waiting."

I heard his voice and his mother's in the yard below and then, when my breakfast tray had been brought and Mrs. Barforth, coming in behind it, had persuaded me to a cup of hot, fragrant chocolate, she sat down beside me and sent the maid away.

"You do know, my dear, that Gervase feels terribly to blame?"

"I know."

"Is he to blame? He says you quarrelled at Listonby and that he was—difficult. But he did not realize—I did not realize—yesterday afternoon, that you were ill. We thought—"

"You thought I was in a sulk."

"Oh, dear! And if you had been in a sulk I wonder if I should be surprised at it, knowing how difficult Gervase can be? But to have inflicted that drive on you—and that walk to the bridge—"

"I inflicted all that on myself, Mrs. Barforth."

"I wonder if you can convince Gervase of that?"

"Should he ever ask me, I will try."

The doctor came soon after, expressing himself well satisfied, and then there came a note from Mrs. Agbrigg murmuring her regret both at my misfortune and my father's absence in Manchester. But she would visit me herself that afternoon. Blanche too, I thought, might well stir herself to drive those few miles from Listonby and would perhaps bring Noel Chard with her. But I soon became aware, as the slow, sickroom hours passed, that I was simply waiting for Venetia.

Gervase, I calculated, would have reached Cullingford by eight o'clock, and even if he had gone straight to the mill, he or his father would have sent a note which could bring her here by mid-morning. Gervase would know I wanted to see her. She would know it. She would drop everything—naturally she would—and come. But one always recognizes the final moment when if something does not happen *now,* it will never happen at all. And struggling with a disappointment enlarged by physical weakness, I failed to notice the change in the weather and was surprised when Mrs. Barforth murmured: "I cannot think anyone will have set out from Cullingford today. The sky has been black in that direction since luncheon, and Blanche will not risk herself even from Listonby in this rain. I fear there is a storm coming."

"She could have been here by now."

"Who, darling? Mrs. Agbrigg? I doubt it, for if she set off at all she may have thought better of it, since she will wish to get home again."

"No—no—Venetia—"

"My dear—oh heavens! is it Venetia you have been pining for?"

"Of course it is."

Light and quick in all her movements, she got up from the window-seat and slipped her narrow hand into mine.

"Dearest, I am so sorry. Naturally I should have sent a message to Tarn Edge first of all, I suppose. But I did not. She cannot have heard, unless Mrs. Agbrigg—which seems unlikely."

"But she *must* have heard. Gervase will have let her know."

"Gervase?"

"Of course. He went to the mill this morning and must have arrived in time to—he may even have gone by Tarn Edge, surely? And his father, or Gideon—or Mrs. Winch—"

And as my voice trailed off into those damnable, ridiculous tears, my mother-in-law looked, for just a moment, as if she might weep with me.

"He did go to the mill, didn't he, Mrs. Barforth?"

"Oh, my dear, he may have done. That is what he *said*. Grace, if it eases you to cry, there is no shame, you know—no shame at all. I will not look, and I will never tell."

I slept for perhaps an hour, waking to a late afternoon sky black with rain, a wind, risen from the moor, howling in cold anger about the roof tiles. Mrs. Barforth was not there, my maid, Sally, sitting alone as close to the fire as she could, and for a long time I lay without speaking, staring at the small mullioned window and the desolate prospect it offered me of dark sky and naked, wind-raked trees.

I was alive and would apparently remain so. My personal danger was over, and with its passing there was now room inside me for the despair I had so far held at bay, the terrible realization that what had oozed so painfully out of me yesterday afternoon and evening had been a human life, an individual, unrepeatable being, deprived by me of the future.

Gervase might well blame himself for the distress he had caused me. I might blame him too. But I—who had known of my condition as he had not—had taken no care of it. I had attended the Listonby ball and had stayed up half the night, my body clamouring for rest, in order to demonstrate to Gervase that he had not succeeded in making me jealous. I had followed him here the next day in that bitter wind, enduring those bone-shaking miles, for the same reason. I had obeyed the demands of my pride and my self-respect, and in so doing had violated the most basic and most profound instinct of the bearing female. I had failed to protect my child. And grief for that child so overwhelmed me that I turned my face into the pillow and sobbed helplessly, dreadfully, releasing now the tears I had suppressed from all the other griefs of my life.

But my maid Sally was accustomed to finding me rational and calm, and had so little idea of how to manage me in this extremity that her alarm in itself restored my composure.

"Oh, my!" she said, round-eyed with fright, "and Mrs. Barforth not here—"

"Where is she, Sally?"

"Oh—gone to Tarn Edge for Miss Venetia—or Mrs. Chard, as I suppose we must call her, although it never sounds right."

"Sally. She has gone to Tarn Edge *herself*—in this weather?"

"So she has, ma'am, the weather being the cause of it, since nobody else could handle her horses in a storm, or should be asked to. That's what she said, ma'am. She'll be back before nightfall although its been night all day today, I reckon. Chicken broth she said you were to have for dinner. Shall I fetch it, ma'am?"

I heard the storm break half an hour later, a great crack of thunder that shook the lamps and set the candles flickering, and then a great lashing of rain as if some floodgate had been opened directly above us.

"Here it comes, ma'am." And there it was, the lightning flash that could induce panic in horses far less nervous and flighty than my mother-in-law's, the wind, the blinding rain, the pitch dark, the rutted, pock-marked roads. I had not liked her and had believed she disliked me. Perhaps she did. But it no longer mattered. She had seen my need, had understood that Gervase had not supplied it, and so, recklessly but quite suddenly, she had gone herself. I was terrified for her, proud of her, more than ever ashamed of my tears.

She would—or so I hoped—have reached Tarn Edge before the storm. Naturally she would not set out again but would spend the night there and return with Venetia in the morning. Even if she was foolhardy enough—magnificent enough—to make the attempt tonight, neither Mr. Barforth nor Gideon would allow it. And knowing full well that both mother and daughter were magnificent enough—mad enough—I prayed that my father-in-law had indeed been there to prevent them, straining my ears at the same time for the sound of their carriage.

"She is gone in the cabriolet, ma'am."

Dear God! such a light, flimsy equipage, a young man's carriage stripped down for sport and speed.

"They are saying in the kitchen, ma'am, that there is a tree struck by lightning on the Cullingford road—quite blocking the way, ma'am."

"They seem very well informed, in the kitchen."

"And if the river rises, ma'am, as it usually does, there will be no way to get across and every chance of her wheels bogged down in the mud."

"Sally, I don't really care to know what the kitchenmaids are saying."

"Will you take chicken broth, ma'am?"

"Yes—and I would like anybody who is able-bodied in that kitchen to go out with lanterns to make sure she is not bogged down by the river."

But there was no need for it. I heard the horses, the burst of welcoming laughter, the gruff voice of her groom trying to hide his thankfulness, those tears again—which I had determined to control—welling up behind my eyelids as the door flew open and the room came alive with the exuberance of Venetia, soaked to the skin and frozen to the marrow, but glowing once again with the simple, joyful excitement of being alive.

"Darling, I am too wet to kiss you, for there is no sense in coming all this way just to give you pneumonia—and how lovely you look! That *must* be the wrong thing to say, but it is quite true. Oh dear, Grace—how terrible! How sad! The poor little baby! But I have come to cheer you, not depress you. Thank goodness father was not home from the mill when mamma came to tell me—nor Gideon. Well, now that I am here they may be angry with me for coming through the storm, but I am *here* and they can hardly fetch me back again. I shall stay, of course, until you are well."

And, knowing the answer, I did not ask her when she had last seen Gervase.

There were more visitors the next few days than Galton had seen in years, my father the most frequent among them, although his visits were less satisfactory than I had hoped. My mother had miscarried, I remembered, several times before my birth and several times after, undermining her health in her determination to give him the son he had not particularly desired, and it troubled him so much to see me like this that he could hardly contain his distress. Yet, since Jonas Agbrigg had believed all his life in the rigid control of emotion, he did contain it, permitting himself to do no more than press my hand and say quite tonelessly: "There is no hurry, you know. You are still young enough, and for my part I cannot subscribe to the theory that a woman's worth is measured by her fertility. And as to this instinct of maternal devotion we hear so much about, I imagine a woman may lavish that kind of thing equally well on a dog."

And because I knew he was really saying "I love you, Grace. For my sake, don't put yourself in danger again," I smiled and murmured "Yes, papa."

Aunt Faith came often; Uncle Blaize, pleading the excuse of business, although in truth he was ill at ease at Galton, which was, after all, his brother's house, sent me out-of-season flowers obtained, I knew, at great effort and expense. Grandmamma Elinor, being in the South of France, was not informed, but my grandmother Agbrigg sent me pages of good advice, while my grandfather, the Mayor, came himself from Scarborough and spent a day at my bedside, entertaining me in his broad, West Riding accents with reminiscences of his younger days. Mrs. Agbrigg, whose visit I had not welcomed, came once, assured herself with her usual, smooth efficiency that everything was being properly done and thereafter, with unexpected tact, allowed my father to come alone, sending with him some nourishing and invariably delicious concoction she had made herself. Blanche came, accompanied by both Dominic and Noel, although her husband, who was easily bored, soon rode off on business of his own, leaving his brother—his natural second in command—to take Blanche home.

Aunt Caroline and her husband spent an hour with me, the Duchess jollying me along, telling me, in effect, to take my disappointment like a man; the Duke, with embarrassed kindliness, wishing me better luck next time. Mr. Nicholas Barforth looked in and instructed me in the curt tones which made his managers tremble to take care of myself. I felt surrounded by friendship and affection and was grateful—once again with those absurd tears—that my welfare should be of concern to so many. I ate up my broth, drank my chocolate and the red wine my mother-in-law insisted was good for me, and promised them all—when they required it of me—that I would get well.

Gervase, of course, came too, but contrived adroitly never to be alone with me for very long. I never learned where he had spent the day of the storm, except that it was neither at the mill nor at the Floods', as became clear when they called to pay me their respects. He offered no explanations. I did not enquire, which was in itself a sure sign of danger and decay. Once—just a week or so ago—when I had believed he loved me and needed me, when there had been trust between us, I would have demanded to know his exact whereabouts and expected a quick and convincing answer. But now, when the trust had gone, I did not ask. For now—until I was stronger—I could not risk the truth. I was still too weak to quarrel, too weak to make demands or decisions and it seemed safer—while the weakness lasted—just to be polite.

I got out of bed after five days or so and into a chair, a feat considered unworthy of admiration by my village doctor, who informed me that a peasant woman or a mill woman would have been back in the fields or at her loom long ago. But soon graduated to the parlour sofa and almost immediately became available to the ministrations, the sympathy, the curiosity of Cullingford's ladies—Miss Mandelbaum, Miss Tighe, Mrs. Sheldon and the rest—who had felt unable to visit me while I remained upstairs. And, when all this feminine gentility began to cloy, there was Liam Adair, dividing his attention so neatly between Venetia and myself that not even the lady's husband—had he condescended to notice it—could have complained.

Liam had not, of course, grown prosperous, his flirtation with the *Cullingford Star* satisfying his instincts as an adventurer and winning him a certain notoriety which he frankly enjoyed, but by no means filling his pockets. The *Star*, for all his efforts, remained a shoddy and irregular publication, its continued existence depending largely on money borrowed from my Grandmamma Elinor, Liam having made the journey to the villa she shared with Lady Verity Barforth near Cannes on purpose to acquire her championship of his cause.

"I coax what I can out of her," he frankly confessed, "and she enjoys it. Better me, I reckon, than the casino or that black-eyed violin player she had about her the last time I was there. And when I printed that piece about the houses her first husband built being unfit for pigs to live in, she near died laughing. In fact she offered to put her own name to it to give it an extra dash of spice. I tell you—she enjoys it."

I believed him, for if the air he brought into my sickroom was not precisely fresh, being too heavily laced with tobacco and

Irish whisky for that, it was at least bracing and had a far greater chance of stimulating my still-flagging energies than Miss Fielding's gentle committees for the relief of the not-too-wicked poor, Mrs. Rawnsley's obsession with her neighbours' social and sexual peccadilloes, even Miss Tighe's oft-repeated conviction that the vote should only be given to women of property and militant virginity like herself.

Liam Adair was not much interested in the Prince of Wales's visit to India nor in the recent atrocities in far off Bulgaria, being more concerned with atrocities in the poorer areas of Cullingford, in those dingy streets and verminous dwellings which had made my Grandmamma Elinor's first husband his fortune. The Turkish empire, no doubt, *was* crumbling. The Russians, equally without doubt, *would* take advantage of it to strengthen their position—and weaken ours—in the East unless we sent a few timely gunboats to prevent it. But Liam, nonchalantly dismissing those gunboats as something designed to please the readers of the *Courier & Review*, was far more impressed by the astuteness of our admittedly very astute Prime Minister Mr. Disraeli in purchasing, before the ruin of the Turkish empire came about, a majority shareholding—177,000 shares out of 400,000—in the Suez Canal company, thus ensuring without bloodshed our passage to India no matter which empire—Turkish, Russian or British—should gain effective control of Egypt.

"I believe Mr. Disraeli to have great influence with the Queen," murmured Miss Fielding, who was uncomfortable with share manipulations but perfectly at ease with royal widows. And indeed the artful Mr. Disraeli appeared to show the same skill at coaxing the Queen little by little from her seclusion as Liam himself when it came to increasing his allowance from Grandmamma Elinor, although there were few in Liberal Cullingford with a good word to say for this exotic, imaginative Tory whose greatest claim on the affections of Liam Adair lay in his legislation to control the purity of our daily bread and of the butter with which—if we could afford it—it was spread.

The practice of increasing the bulk, improving the appearance or simply reducing the price of foodstuffs by the addition of odd and in some cases downright lethal substances was as long-established as the poverty of those who purchased them, and their need to fill the mouths of hungry children with anything that was cheap and could be made to "go round." All my life I had been hearing whispers of brick-dust in cocoa, sand in sugar, flour whitened with chalk, red lead used to colour the rind of cheese. I had heard of brewers who added green vitriol or sulphate of iron to put the froth on their beer and improve, with deadly results, its flavour, while as a child I had been warned never to accept sweets from strangers, since these tempting little confections might well be coloured with copper and lead. One learned to purchase one's tea with care, for the green China variety *could* have been doctored with verdigris, the black Indian variety with black lead. All the world knew that water was frequently added to milk and no one expected a cow-shed to be clean.

But the *Cullingford Star*, from its squalid little offices in Gower Street, expected it, and availing himself of the services of a chemist—paid for, one supposed, by Grandmamma Elinor— Liam Adair had purchased loaves from every baker in Cullingford and its environs, sent them for analysis and published his results, naming the place of origin of all bread in which traces of chalk or alum or any other dubious ingredient had been found.

The ground-floor windows of the *Star* had been broken a night or two later, and for the sake of expediency had been roughly boarded up again, since the following week he had printed a tale of dried ash leaves added as a makeweight to someone's tea, and mentioned the sour welcome he had received in certain ale-houses, which had caused him to suspect that their landlords had *something* to hide.

He had, of course, increased the circulation of his paper and thoroughly enjoyed himself, but Liam, while not for one moment forgetting either his profits or his pleasures, had the Irishman's instinctive sympathy for the oppressed, and Disraeli's Act to control the sale of food and drugs had pleased him at a more personal level than he cared to admit. He had no real conviction that it would be adequately enforced, no real convictions about anything, or so he insisted; but sitting at ease in my mother-in-law's parlour, his long legs stretched out to the fire, he could easily be persuaded to tell us, with a chuckle, about the shop-keepers who put up their shutters rather than sell him a pound of tea or coffee, and of the landlady who, as the sister of a local baker, had felt obliged to ask him to return the keys of his lodgings and move on.

"What next, Liam?" breathed Venetia.

"Oh, something will turn up. There's always a crusade."

"A crusade? I hadn't thought of that. Now *I* would have gone

on a real crusade, Liam—sold all my possessions and set off
without even a map to rescue the Holy Land. But not you.''

"No, not I. I'd get myself a map all right, which would make
me a useful man to meet in the desert. Because one has to get
back, you know.''

But Venetia laughed and shook her head. "Oh no, Liam, if
one thought about getting back safe and sound that wouldn't be a
crusade, don't you see—just an expedition. The whole point of a
crusade, surely, is that one gives everything—one just goes
forward and does what must be done, without a thought for what
happens after? *That* is what I call a crusade. Had I been a knight
in the Middle Ages—yes, do you know, I would have been very
comfortable with that. I would have been right for it—don't you
think so?''

I did, and for just a moment I felt a prickle of unease, a
premonition, perhaps, which began to take shape and was then
scattered by her frank, wholehearted laughter. She had been
constrained and silent with Liam for a long time after her marriage.
She had been constrained and silent with everyone, but now, in
her mother's house, it was a delight to see the return of her
vivacity.

I asked her no questions, for the facts of her life remained the
same. She, who had believed so ardently in love, had married
for convenience, and it would have been too much to expect that
Life, or Destiny or whatever one might choose to call it, should
now arrange by way of compensation for her to fall in love with
her husband. But human nature finds its own compensations,
acquires the good sense to compromise—at least *my* nature
intended to do so—and perhaps she too was learning now to live
with herself and with Gideon. I hoped so, and was dismayed to
be so soon proved wrong.

There was a day of strong sunshine and sparkling frost, glorious holiday weather which had Venetia and her mother out of
doors by early morning, so that I was alone when Gideon came,
his arrival producing in me a condition I could only describe as
flustered, an enormous reluctance to admit, even in the veiled
phrases of good society, the physical and sexual nature of my
malady. At Tarn Edge I concerned myself with his dinner,
ordered his carriage to take him to the station, kept his bed well
aired for his return, and was as remote from him as the owner of
a good hotel is remote from her guests. But here, where we were
both guests together, it was not the same. Here I was obliged to

meet him, not as a brother-in-law or a second cousin, but as a man whose presence, for reasons I saw no sense in examining too closely, embarrassed me so much that I was glad when the excited yelping of a dog advised us of the approach of Venetia.

She had been heaven knew where, following the wind and weather like a gypsy, her arms full of heather gathered for good luck, the tangy fragrance of the moorland all about her; unkempt perhaps—for the hem of her dress was splashed and stained, and her hands clutching the purple heather were not clean—but enchanting, a woman, surely, who was like no other?

"Good God, what have we here?" said Gideon, by no means displeased with her, looking, on the contrary, as if this gypsy charm could please him enormously, could please her too if she would allow him to show her the way. But it was not to be.

She had not seen him for ten days and now—taken completely unawares—she stared at him aghast, as if she had forgotten his very existence and was now most painfully remembering, her vivacity draining from her and leaving her no longer a captivating woodland nymph but a rather awkward young lady who no longer knew what to do with that armful of heather.

She put it down on the table and spent a moment retrieving the sprigs which fell to the ground, the dog which had come in with her yapping around her heels in shrill excitement, leaping on and off the chintz-covered armchairs, treating us all to the antics of a half-trained, muddy and extremely boisterous pup until Gideon, who was no longer smiling, said coldly, "Should that dog be allowed in the house?"

And when, looking as flustered as I had felt ten minutes before, she failed to retrieve the playful little hound, he eventually took it by the scruff of its neck and dropped it none too gently through the parlour window.

"Until a dog can behave, it should stay outdoors."

"I suppose it should."

"There are no dogs allowed inside, ever, at Listonby."

"Well, you country people don't really care for animals. You eat them, or ride them, or train them to retrieve your game-birds for you—*work* for you, in fact—but you don't *like* them."

"Really?"

"Yes, really. And of course you kill them too. But never mind. Have you been here long, Gideon?"

"No," he snapped. "Not long. And I cannot stay long either. I thought you might care to come home with me now, since Grace comes back tomorrow."

"Yes, of course," she said, because those were the words assigned to the role she had been given to play in life. "That seems a good idea. I will tell them to pack my things. How long before we must leave?"

"An hour."

"Yes."

And smiling, she turned dutifully away, her manner telling me that there had been no compromise, no adjustment, that these ten happy days had been, quite simply, a reprieve which now was over.

13

I REMEMBER NO PRECISE MOMENT, no single event, no threshold between the condition of a woman who, having once been happy and loved, believed she could be so again and a woman in true emotional disarray, whose marriage—like so many others—was no more than a financial and physical convenience, a hollow but indissoluble sham. The two conditions, it seemed, had blended together, had perhaps always simultaneously existed, the condition of failure gradually becoming the stronger until it had absorbed the other.

I had allowed the silence to fall between us because I had been too weak to break it and when I regained my strength I could think of nothing to say. Gervase brought me home from Galton. He enquired carefully as to the progress of my health, ate his dinner more often than not at my table, slept in my bed. He gave me his escort and his company when the social niceties required it. He behaved, in public, as a husband and I as a wife, and in private we remained polite.

We even became lovers again, or rather he reclaimed his conjugal rights, since I could not glorify what passed between us by the name of love-making; his body, which had turned its fastidious back to me all night, being drawn to mine sometimes in the moment of half-waking, a performance part duty, part need, which any nameless female could have satisfied and during which I lay quite still, as nameless females do, despising myself for this submission, despising him for accepting it. But the law, which called me his wife, forced me to give him free use of my body whenever he required it. He was not even obliged to ask, simply to take, and gradually, as the rift widened, I learned how to insult him with my passivity as his hurried satisfactions insulted me. And when we had reached that dismal stage I was no worse, perhaps, than those many thousands of other women for whom this side of marriage had always been a burden, or those many thousands of others who prided themselves on their skill in avoiding it altogether; except that it had not always been so with us.

Nor could I recall any single moment when I became certain of his infidelity. I merely anticipated it, so that by the time I became aware of it I understood that it had already been taking place for some time; and although I suffered I was not surprised. He was not, at the start, unfaithful to me with Diana Flood, as I might have expected, nor with anyone else I could identify. I simply knew that there was someone, and then someone else, learning with a delicate species of self-torture to read the signs, an indefinable but to me quite unmistakable air about him that fluctuated from wariness to nervous gaiety, from a brooding self-disgust to a bruised and satiated fatigue, his humour varying with the woman who—for the days or the hours these affairs lasted—had tempted him, amused him, consoled him, briefly delighted him, left him only half satisfied, or who had revealed, in a few cases, some new aspect of his carnal nature which in the clear daylight appalled him.

And I did nothing.

Even on the summer night when, strolling into the cloister at Galton, I saw him at the far end of the tunnel kissing the bare shoulders of a woman I vaguely took to be one of Blanche's London friends, I did nothing. I simply turned and hurried away, thankful he had not seen me, hoping the woman had not seen me either. I did nothing because I was proud, and afraid, and for the stark and simple reason that I could think of nothing to do. I was a betrayed wife. So were hundreds of thousands of others. Woman was, by nature and by necessity, a faithful animal. Man was not. Brood mares stayed peacefully with the herd. Stallions ran wild. "My dear," I could imagine a dozen female voices murmuring to me, "men are simply made that way. You must forgive and understand." And above the other voices would be Mrs. Rawnsley's shrill, smug whisper: "Make him buy you something, Grace, to apologize—something really expensive. I always do."

I could not tolerate those whispers.

There was, of course, the time-honoured and possibly effective method of running home to my father. But I could not do that either, knowing as I did what my happiness meant to him. He had had few joys in his life. His main concern now was that I should have joy in mine, and I was determined above all not to let him down. He desired to see me happy. He *would* see me happy. He *did* see me happy. It was the least I could do for the man who had done so much for me. And even had I been tempted to weaken—and I was not tempted—I could never have contemplated the possibility of sharing a home with Mrs. Agbrigg again.

But even so, had I retained just a small measure of hope, I might not have been so scrupulous. Had I believed it possible to be truly reconciled, I might have turned to anyone, resorted to anything which might have brought it about. But I well knew that Gervase's neglect of me and his infidelity were in themselves only symptoms of the disease. The real tragedy—and so I named it—lay in the one simple fact that my husband, who had thought he loved me, no longer did so, no longer found me desirable nor even interesting. And how could I, or anyone, remedy that?

There had been no physical violence, no public humiliation, no tangible insult with which his father or mine could grapple. He was not, after all, keeping a mistress in style and leaving me to starve. Nor did he flaunt himself and his women in local places of entertainment as Mr. Rawnsley had been known to do. He had never subjected me to any unnatural form of lust, nor infected me with any form of disease. He "pleased himself," as Cullingford put it, rather too often, but so did plenty of others, and although it was all very regrettable no one would really have thanked me for making a fuss.

I did not make a fuss, for my own and for my father's sake. I had chosen to marry a difficult man and those who had warned me against him—Mrs. Agbrigg the chief among them—had been right. I had believed in his love and it had not lasted. And I preferred to suffer the lack of it than make any attempt to force him or shame him into some feeble pretence.

The love and the need, then, were both over, but the marriage would last for the rest of our lives. The shell remained. I could leave it empty or I could fill it with venom, but either way I became obsessed with my determination to keep that shell intact. No one must know. And when I realized the impossibility of this—since the women who received Gervase's attentions knew, and their friends, and their maids—I once again adopted the shameful device of pretending not to care.

What did not trouble me need trouble no one else—I had learned that on the night of the Listonby ball and had lost my baby—and I became an expert at the indulgent smile, implying,

"Heavens! of *course* men are made that way, the poor darlings. What can it signify?"; expert too at the unruffled greeting, making no more and no less of the suspected mistress, the current fancy, than of anyone else, introducing Gervase's name into my conversation no more and no less than I had always done and keeping myself busy—busy—busy, so that it could be said "Dear Grace, she is so occupied with her organizing and her entertaining that it is hardly surprising she does not notice—" or "Grace Barforth—good heavens! of *course* she notices. What of it? She has that mansion to live in, hasn't she, and what does she care for the man so long as she can have the spending of his money?" And if the rumours climbed the hill to Fieldhead, then I knew that Mrs. Agbrigg—who could not be eager to share her home with me either—would have the good sense and the skill to keep them from my father.

Naturally I suffered—naturally and abominably—for these decisions which sound so cool were not taken coolly, and although logic was certainly employed I was often obliged to wring it out of myself through layers of heartache. There were times when I ordered the carriage to go to Fieldhead and could not complete the journey, telling my coachman to take me anywhere, out of the city streets and the prosperous suburbs to a country lane where no one knew me or pitied me or thought I had got as much as I deserved; where no kind soul was anxious to tell me—in case I didn't already know it—that my husband had been in dubious company in Manchester last Friday night; where I was not obliged to be bright and busy and brittle, but could indulge myself with silence.

There were times when my own suppressed emotions threatened to break free and the urge to throw myself weeping against Gervase's lean, fastidious chest—or to put a knife into it—became almost too great to resist. I resisted it. My nature was constructed and moulded in such a way that I could do no other than resist, although these urges, turning inward, caused me much solitary grieving and bitterness.

There was jealousy too—how could there not have been?—of women I barely knew, acquaintances of the Chards who, visiting Listonby for a Friday-to-Monday might never come again; and of women I did not know at all, strangers from Bradford and Leeds and the Theatre Royal who briefly aroused not so much his appetite, since he was not prone to enormous sexual hungers, but his curiosity, the need of a man who does not know what he is searching for to try everything. And although logically it was wrong to hate these women, since it was Gervase, not they, who was doing me harm, I could not always be logical. There were times when I murdered them all, quite horribly, in my imagination and was sickened afterwards by the violence I had done only to myself.

But all this took place, as I have said, little by little, and on my return from Galton that autumn of my miscarriage, Venetia's affairs appeared more urgent than mine. She had had her period of mourning, her period of humbleness and gratitude. She had endured fear and shame and a kind of despairing lethargy. She had regained her physical strength and with it a portion of her self-esteem. What now? And because she had not found the answer, because she suspected there was no answer—and because the role of good, obedient, contrite little girl no longer sufficed—she grew subject to abrupt swings of mood that winter, troughs of despair and peaks of nervous elation which made her as unpredictable and often as difficult as Gervase.

"Grace, I absolutely must *do* something. I really don't want to waste another day. There must be something—something important—that has to be done?"

But none of the activities I discovered or invented for my own diversion could hold her attention for long, her initial frenzy of enthusiasm soon giving way to a shrug, a sigh, a sudden drooping of her spirits.

"Oh lord!—what's the use of it? What is it really good for?"

And the dinner-party invitations I had asked her to write would not be finished, the recipes of a famous French chef I had found in a borrowed magazine would remain uncopied, the flowers she had been arranging with a flair I did not myself possess would be left half done and wilting.

"What's the good of it? When I die will they put on my tombstone that I wrote an excellent copper-plate and could arrange a very pretty vase of carnations? Why trouble to be alive for *that*?"

And one day, after an hour of restless silence, she startled me badly by saying without any warning, "I wonder if it would be possible to discover what has become of Charles Heron?"

"Possible, I suppose. But it could hardly be wise."

She gave a short, rueful laugh, and jumping to her feet began pacing up and down the room, picking up small objects as she passed and setting them down again.

"There is no need for you to look so sour, Grace. I am not in the least in love with him now, you know."

"Then why should you care what has happened to him?"

"Because—" she paused, shrugged her fine-boned shoulders, her pointed face taking on a dreaming, very disturbing quality as her eyes became focused on the past. "Because—oh, yes—because to tell you the truth I believe I am in love with—yes—with myself as I was in those days."

And because it had been a bad day for me, because Gervase had done me some small, stinging injury and she resembled him, I said tartly, "You would do better to fall in love with Gideon."

She came to a halt, not angrily but rather as if the mere sound of his name acted as a brake, or a weight which slowed her down.

"How very tidy that would be."

"Venetia, I am sorry to have mentioned it, but since I have, then—really—I would be very glad if you could grow to love him."

"Do you know, Grace—so would I. Very glad indeed."

"Then, surely—?"

"What? You think wanting is half-way there?"

"Yes. I do think so."

"Then you are quite wrong."

She moved again, just a step or two, almost sedately, with a composure and a certainty I had not seen in her before.

"Gideon would have to want it too," she said. "And he does not."

"Oh Venetia—surely? He *must.*"

"There is no must about it. You should know quite well, Grace, that one does not tell Gideon what he *must* do. He doesn't want me to love him. He wants me to be his wife."

"I should have thought the two might easily go together."

She shrugged.

"Not in our case. And, of course, the sad thing is that perhaps I could love him if he would allow it. I realize now that love is not so very exclusive as I thought. It simply exists in the body and one needs to release it. One even needs to feel loyalty and devotion and sacrifice—to go on crusade a little—at least I do. I suppose there are dozens—hundreds—of men I could love and be faithful unto death should I happen to meet them, so why not Gideon?"

"Yes—why not?"

"Because it is not what he wants. Does Dominic want Blanche to love him? I doubt if it has even crossed his mind and never will so long as she is in his bed when he desires her and at the head of his table when it suits him or flatters him or is to his advantage to have other men desire her. Gideon would like the same from me—exactly that—and no, it is not too much, don't you see? The terrible thing is that it is not enough. If he'd ask something more of me—something real and that I could see the sense of—then I'd try. I'd respond to the *challenge* of him, because after all he's good to look at and the very circumstances of our marriage are a challenge in themselves. It would be *magnificent* to make something lovely and lasting out of our appalling start, to get to know each other and forgive each other, and then to be friends, and lovers. Just think of the range of emotion one would need for all that.''

"You have the range, Venetia."

She smiled, her eyes twinkling with a rueful humour, laughing not without affection at herself.

"I know. It's the one thing about myself that I'm sure of and that rather pleases me. I'd be very good at nursing him through some near-fatal illness, you know, and if he lost his money I'd manage to be brave about it. If there should ever be a riot at the mill I'd be more inclined to stand by him than not. And should he ever be disgraced and sent to prison I'd be rather splendid about waiting for him and doing my utmost to clear his name— can't you just imagine it? I don't even require quite so much drama as that. I'd be perfectly willing just to rejoice with him whenever he scored a triumph, or help him to overcome his disappointments if he'd just let me know what his triumphs and his disappointments are. But I have no talent for sitting about the dining-room in a low-cut dress so his colleagues can see what a lucky fellow he is, and wearing his jewels so they'll all know he's doing well at the mill. And as for the other thing—as for the desire—well, I don't mind it now as I used to, but one can hardly build one's life around it—at least, I can't."

"Venetia, are you really sure?"

"About Gideon? Of course I am. Wives are for drawing-rooms and bedrooms, my dear, and by that reckoning I rate very low. After all, I suppose a wife can only measure her success by the effect she has on her husband, which definitely places me among the failures. It's women like Blanche, I find, who do best. She knows what's expected of her. She even likes what's expected of her. She understands the rules and knows how to get her way without breaking a single one of them. She was a silly girl, I always thought, but she's a clever woman. And I suppose I'm the ninny now."

But she was not always so humble, nor so inclined to measure herself on the yardstick of Gideon's estimation, the docility to which she had accustomed him giving way quite often now to bursts of nonchalance, amusement, and the beginnings of defiance.

"Lord, Gideon, does it matter whether we go or not? It is only to Miss Mandelbaum's."

"Miss Mandelbaum's brother, Mr. Jacob Mandelbaum, is a wool merchant—as you may know—who does a great deal of business with me."

"The Mandelbaums have always done business with *us*, of course I know. Is that a reason to spend this lovely evening listening to Rebecca Mandelbaum thumping her piano?"

"Your father may think so."

"I daresay. But I see he does not feel obliged to go himself."

"Why should he?" Gideon said with a tight, sarcastic smile. "He has me to do it for him. If Gervase should ever be available, perhaps I might be excused. But until then you will have to accompany me."

"Take Grace. She understands about Mozart."

"You will not be required to understand Mozart, Venetia, merely to behave as if you do."

"Oh, I see. In that case you had better take Blanche."

They went together to Miss Mandelbaum's recital, returning in a state of mutual irritation which quickly, as Gideon slammed down his hat and gloves on the hall table, flared into their first open quarrel. Neither, it seemed, had appreciated a note of the music, Gideon being more concerned in making the acquaintance of a gentleman from Hamburg who had some importance in the wool trade and of a merchant banker from Berlin, instinctively obeying the rules his mother had taught him that these personal contacts, if carefully nourished, were often worth their weight in gold.

"May I present you to my wife," he had said, but his wife, instead of assuming a graceful pose and allowing herself to be looked at, as Blanche would have done, or of asking a few safe if uninspired questions about the German landscape which might have been my solution, ignored these worthy gentlemen altogether, devoting herself entirely to the praise of Miss Mandelbaum's performance, her enthusiasm increasing in proportion to the guilt she felt at not having really listened to it.

"Miss Mandelbaum, I have heard nothing better on the concert stage."

"My dear, as a girl that is where I longed to be."

"Then why did you not—?"

"Oh, naturally, my parents would not allow it."

"What nonsense. You should have defied them, you know—for your art's sake."

"Oh no, dear. That would have been impossible."

"Not a bit of it. We must stand up for ourselves, Miss Mandelbaum, indeed we must. Miss Tighe would say the same."

And Venetia, in a spirit part mischief and part genuine compassion for these wasted talents, began to urge a considerably startled Miss Mandelbaum to abandon her gentle, comfortable life in Cullingford and to adopt the vagabond and—Venetia insisted—thrilling status of an artiste.

"Just think how gloriously free! Goodness, it makes me wish I had learned the piano myself, or at least the violin."

The two foreign gentlemen may well have been amused. Their wives were not. Venetia—it was abundantly clear—would not be remembered kindly in the commercial circles of Hamburg and Berlin, and neither Frau Grassmann nor Frau Goldsmith would be likely to resist the temptation of conveying the poor impression she had created to their numerous cousins in every business centre of Europe.

Gideon, who had been with the firm of Nicholas Barforth for over four years now, was by no means content either with his progress or with his lot. He was determined, as his mother the Duchess of South Erin would have been determined, to carve out for himself an international reputation and take his place eventually among Europe's industrial élite. Far from assisting him, Venetia by her frivolous behaviour had antagonized two well-established members of that élite, thus casting doubt on the sound judgement of the man who had married her.

"Lord!" she now declared. "What a pair they were, those two foreign women—one of them like a dressed up stick and the other with a moustache—you can believe me, Grace—beneath her ringlets."

"Mrs. Goldsmith," said Gideon coldly, "is an extremely intelligent woman. She speaks five or six languages fluently, I believe."

"And what is the use of that if she has nothing interesting to say?"

"Venetia, did it not occur to you that Goldsmith could be very useful to me?"

"No," she said very clearly, looking directly up at him. "It

did not. I am not accustomed to judging people by their usefulness,
nor by the profit I might expect to make from their acquaintance.''

"Then you are very naive.''

"Naive? Or honest—don't you think so?''

"Naive. Or stupid—that might come a little nearer.''

"Ah,'' she said, making the sound insolent, provocative, and
then swiftly repenting. "Heavens, Gideon, and just what damage
have I done? This is not Listonby or Mayfair or South Erin, you
know, where everything depends on being invited to dinner by
the right people and having the right calling-cards on one's hall
table. This is Cullingford. If you have something to sell and your
price is right and the other person wants it, or needs it, then he
buys. It can make no difference whether or not I am on good
terms with his wife.''

He stood by the fire, on the centre of the hearthrug as her
father often did, looking at her with a fine-drawn, entirely Chard
disdain that seemed, despite its muted quality, to fill the room.

"I am indebted to you,'' he said, "for the information. But
the world has grown somewhat larger, I fear, since your grandfather founded these mills—larger and faster and infinitely more
complicated. Your grandfather had very little competition from
other manufacturers—since there was no more than a handful of
them able to compete—and he could sell undisturbed in any
market he liked. The markets are still there, but the manufacturers have increased a hundredfold. And what is a man to do—Mr.
Goldsmith, for example?—if he encounters a dozen, or a hundred manufacturers whose prices and whose delivery dates are
equally convenient? I imagine he would turn to the manufacturer
he knows best, whose character he judges to be sound—a manufacturer whose personal standards are high and whose wife can
be trusted to behave. Don you think he might do that? And one's
horizons need not necessarily be bound by Cullingford—at least,
mine need not.''

I saw her chin quiver very slightly, her eyes cast down as she
murmured, "Does it matter? There is so much money already—
more than one could ever spend. Why this fever for more of the
same thing. *Why*?''

But her answer was the slam of the door as he strode from the
room, his patience at an end, leaving her to bite her lip for a
moment, half afraid of her defiance, for Gideon in his anger had
looked more than ever like her father.

The Goldsmiths, the Grassmanns, Rebecca and Jacob Mandelbaum dined with us some days later, my efforts to convey the

impression that Venetia was their hostess being defeated by
Venetia herself who, as each course was brought in, made some
remark of delighted but tell-tale surprise. Yet she made herself
very pleasant to the shrill, Mrs. Goldsmith, sitting beside her in
the drawing-room after the meal and listening with an almost
mesmerized attentiveness—in fact the daze of a crushing
boredom—to that lady's particular theories on the culinary and
domestic arts, agreeing with eager nods of her auburn head each
time Mrs. Goldsmith paused for breath or demanded "Is that not
so?"

Miss Mandelbaum played and sang for us, Mr. Jacob Mandelbaum, a cultured and worldly man, talked music and landscape,
and managed, with a fine discretion, to prevent his sister from
asking me why my husband was not present, since it must have
been clear from the odd number at my table that he had been
expected.

The gentlemen from Hamburg and Berlin remained in the
drawing-room for a very long time with Gideon, smoking cigars
and discussing, almost with love, the intricacies of finance at an
exalted level where money was not for spending but for
manipulation, a world-wide chess game which Gideon, with the
Barforth fortune behind him and his own fierce ambitions driving
him towards the making of another, might one day be invited to
play.

"When you are next in Berlin—" Mr. Goldsmith said, taking
Gideon's hand in both of his at parting.

"You will find much in Hamburg to interest you," said Mr.
Grassmann.

"Lord!" said Venetia when they were all safely gone. "Do
tell me—am I not heroic?"

And meeting Gideon's cool eyes, the lift of his eyebrows that
plainly said, "Heroic? Just barely adequate, I'd call it," I saw
her own brows come together in a frown, her pointed face flush
with a rare loss of temper.

"All right," she said, squaring her slight shoulders, her back
very straight. "You have no need to tell me. I have not been
heroic. I have simply been a hypocrite. Is that what you want
from me?"

She had never allowed herself to be really angry with him
before, had been too quick, if anything, to agree with his every
opinion, to accommodate his least desire, but now, after a slight
start of surprise, he merely sighed as one does when dealing with
a troublesome child.

"Venetia, must you be so enthusiastic?" And we were in no doubt that he had used the word in its Listonby and Mayfair sense of "brash," "melodramatic," "middle-class."

"Oh, don't play the squire with me, Gideon," she told him, "although truly it is what you are."

"Is this necessary, Venetia?"

"Indeed it is, for I wish to know if I have pleased you. I have spent the evening flattering a woman I dislike and who dislikes me, for the purpose—if I understand aright—of procuring you an invitation to her house in Berlin. Not because you care two straws for her or for her husband, but because he might be of *use* to you. Is that what I have been doing?"

"Is it? I rather thought you had been giving a dinner-party, or that Grace had been giving one on your behalf. Why all this fuss, Venetia?"

"Because I want to know if I have done well. Have you got your invitation? Is this what you want from me?"

And for what seemed to me a very long time, during which I longed to leave the room and frankly dared not desert her, he did not reply.

"Ah well," he said at last and taking a cigar lit it, inhaled with calm enjoyment, his attention apparently caught by the gracefully curving spiral of tobacco. But the silence was too much for Venetia—as he had intended—and taking a deep breath she raised herself on tiptoe, attempting, I suppose, to match his height and suddenly threw at him, "Damnation—yes, I mean *damnation!* Do you know, Gideon, I believe I would think better of you if you wanted to make love to that woman, if you found her desirable instead of just a stepping stone to her husband's good graces. Yes, if you desired her, I could understand it. You see—you wrinkle your nose at the thought of it, don't you, which means you don't like her either."

"It means I am appalled by your manners, or lack of them."

"No, it does not. It means I have made you look at her and admit she is an old harpy—for so she is. But I ask myself, does that matter to you: Would it matter if—" And I could hear on the tip of her tongue—as he could surely hear them—the words that must never be spoken: "If you had to make love to her, Gideon, to get what you want, would you go so far? Would it be no more and no less a hardship to you than making love to me?"

No one, of course, in the complexity of human relationships can ever be entirely right or wholly wrong. Gideon was a hard, ambitious man—qualities much valued in Cullingford who expected no more than he had been brought up to expect from a wife. He had seen his mother devote the whole of her formidable energies to creating at Listonby an atmosphere which attracted influential men like bees to clover; men, need it be said, who could be of service, not to Aunt Caroline herself, but to her husband and to her sons. He had seen Aunt Faith drop everything at the sight of a telegram from Uncle Blaize and, not caring what engagements she cancelled nor whom she offended, set off on the hundred- or thousand-mile journey to join him. He had seen Mrs. Sheldon force herself, entirely against her nature, to make public speeches in her husband's praise, giving up her own friends and her own occupation as a landscape painter to devote herself to the humdrum work of the constituency in order that Thomas Sheldon MP might be at liberty to bask in the delights of Westminster. He knew that Mrs. Rawnsley, who was neither particularly kind nor particularly clever, would nevertheless defend in any drawing-room or at any tea-table the interests of Mr. Septimus Rawnsley, her not particularly faithful husband, and had sense enough to make herself very pleasant to all those who transacted their business through Rawnsley's Bank. And these ladies were not making sacrifices. They were simply doing what they *ought* to be doing. They were keeping their marriage vows.

In the beginning he had been surprisingly patient and even now, when patience was growing fragile at its borders, remained conscious of his responsibilities. He would, I believe, have been ready to give Venetia every conceivable luxury, would have enjoyed seeing her swathed in sables and dripping diamonds, not so much as evidence of his generosity but of the fact that he—the third son of a baronet—could afford them. He would have allowed her to travel too, as often as she had a mind, since he lacked the middle-class notion that husband and wife should never be apart. He would not have objected too strenuously had she acquired her mother's passion for the hunt, so long as she hunted with "decent" people and took care always to be well mounted and well dressed. He would have turned a blind or an indulgent eye to the occasional card-party, since useful acquaintances can be made at a fashionable whist-table, providing she took the trouble to wear an expensive gown and did not lose too much. She could have stayed in bed all morning, like Blanche, while he went to the mill to earn their daily portion of caviar and champagne, had he been able to rely on finding her, vivacious and hospitable, at his dinner-table at night.

But Gideon's ambitions, while not incomprehensible to Venetia, irritated her, increasing her feeling of alienation. She understood money and knew there was plenty of it. Why, then, should she devote her one, precarious, already blemished life to the task of making it grow? What concerned her was the *quality* of life, not its luxury. What she most desired was an intense and demanding relationship which would test her ingenuity and stretch her resources to the full, an emotional crusade requiring the investment of her whole heart. And she could see no similarity between these fierce longings and the driving force of Gideon's ambition which could not be content with the fortune his uncle and his wife had brought him, which goaded him into a crusade of his own.

Grand in his ideas, lavish in his tastes, it pleased his vanity—that touchiness of a younger son for whom no provision has been made—to consider the splendid Barforth mills as no more than a starting point. He had not been born a manufacturer. The rules of primogeniture had forced him to it and from the first he had determined to conduct himself with style, to lift himself by his own efforts from the confines of grubby, middle-class Cullingford to a plane where business was conducted by gentlemen. After all, it had been a Rothschild—a prince not of the blood but of commerce—who had enabled the British government to purchase its controlling interest in the Suez Canal, and although Gideon had no interest in politics himself, his brother Sir Dominic was soon to take his seat in the House of Commons behind the flamboyant Mr. Disraeli, and there was no reason why the Chards, if the game was played aright, should not attain influence in the land. Blanche would play her part in that game, Aunt Caroline would glory in it. But if Venetia could be brought to understand it at all, she would be very likely to enquire, "What's the good of it? What does it matter? It's not even *real*."

She may well have been right. I did not set myself to judge, merely to perform, each day, the tasks I found to hand, the building of a façade which screened us all but which only Gideon seemed to appreciate.

"That menu was exceedingly well chosen, Grace."

"Thank you, Gideon."

"Tell me—how did you get on with Frank Brewster's wife over coffee?"

"Famously. She believes she will never survive the journey to New York next week."

"So they are going to New York, are they? Now why—I wonder—did Brewster forget to mention that?"

"Well—they are staying with the Ellison-Turnbulls."

"Are they, by God? Thank you, Grace."

And so it continued.

I became, that year and the year after, an obsessive house-keeper and hostess, a great compiler of lists and designer of domestic routines. I kept files in date order of my menus and my invitations, so that no dish was ever served to the same guest twice over. I kept files on the guests themselves, their gastronomic and personal preferences, the names of their children, their enemies and their friends. I made it my business to know which notable would be arriving in Cullingford, having found a reliable informant at the Station Hotel, and if Gideon wished to meet them I never failed to find the correct approach, or to make the impression he desired. It became a challenge, finally a compulsion, my pride in discovering the favourite wine of a total stranger, his wife's favourite flower, and having both in plentiful supply when they came to dine, outweighing by far its object.

My aims had reduced themselves perhaps—in fact, they were much reduced—but were altogether "in keeping" with my status, a perfect dinner-party, the organization of a charity ball at which I walked roughshod over any lady who dared to question my authority taking on the importance of the Balkan Crisis, not because I cared about charity balls but because this—unlike my relationship with Gervase—was a matter in which I could be certain of success. The reality of my marriage was a hollow sham. The illusion it created was still very widely admired. It was the illusion which, of necessity, counted.

I sat at my dinner-table one summer evening, enjoying the rose-scented air through the open windows, knowing that everything in this huge, ornate house that should be polished had been polished most thoroughly, that every item of linen requiring starch was starched to perfection, every inch of upholstery meticulously brushed. I knew my larder shelves were full, my drawers and cupboards scented with sweet herbs and lavender, my staff respectful and respectable, even the beds where the kitchenmaids slept supplied with good mattresses and warm blankets.

I was surrounded by order and efficiency, I was at the centre of a beehive of ongoing tasks which I knew would be well done. And if the running of this house was a small matter compared to the running of the Barforth and Agbrigg mills—to the affairs of the real world outside—then at least no one, I believed, could have done it better. I was making a constructive effort of my life—as some others were not—and whenever it troubled me that the effort was really very small, that Grace Agbrigg, surely, with her flair for mathematics and languages, had been capable of far more than this, it seemed wiser and safer to belittle that flair, to shrink my capabilities, to narrow myself down to fit the reality of my situation; and be content.

There was no conversation at table that night, Venetia staring listlessly at the white brocade wall, Gideon's mind on facts and figures, Gervase leaning back in his chair, eating little, saying not a word. And when their silence oppressed me I began to tell them whatever came into my mind, Aunt Faith's return from Paris, a dinner at Mrs. Rawnsley's the night before, when her parlourmaid had spilled a decanter of wine on a brand-new carpet.

"What rotten luck!" said Gideon whose training as a gentleman always enabled him to produce some sort of reply.

"Mmmmmmm," said Venetia.

"Yes, terrible luck, for the carpet is pale green and the wine, as you might imagine, was red. I am not at all sure the stain can be removed."

Gervase leaned towards me, his face very pale in the twilight, his eyes carefully narrowed, his mouth touched by a smile that deceived me, since he was not much given to smiling these days.

"Grace," he said very distinctly, "what a bore you are."

To which I coolly and to no one in particular replied, "Do you know, I believe this sauce is much improved by that dash of tarragon. I must remember to tell cook."

14

ONE NIGHT THE FOLLOWING AUTUMN, my maid, Sally Grimshaw, who had been given permission to attend a wedding, did not return, her absence being only grudgingly explained to me by Mrs. Winch, my housekeeper, who did not seem to think it my concern. The girl, while walking back to Tarn Edge alone at what could not be called a respectable hour of the night, had been "set upon" by some unknown male, and as a result of her injuries had been taken by a constable to the Infirmary. The constable had then been kind enough to inform Mrs. Winch, who for her part saw no reason to trouble me. Sally would be missed, of course, but either Mary-Ann or Martha-Jane would be able to do my hair and mend my linen and should they not give satisfaction Mrs. Winch knew an agency which could be trusted to supply a proper lady's maid at short notice.

What injuries? Not serious. Shock, mainly, thought Mrs. Winch, and the cuts and bruises one would expect after such an affray. But I must remember that she had been "set upon," after all, by a man she said she had not recognized, although there was no way to be sure of that.

"You mean she has been raped?"

"Yes, madam, I do."

And she was very angry with me, I could tell, for using the word, even angrier when I ordered my carriage and went off to see for myself.

Cullingford's Infirmary, at the top of steep, cobbled Sheepgate, was an old and inconvenient building, clean enough since Miss Florence Nightingale had taught us that, if hospitals could not always cure the sick, they should not by their filth and squalor actually do them harm. But it was equipped as sparsely as a workhouse, black iron bedsteads pushed close together against a stark white wall, cheerless, not intended for the affluent who would be nursed at home, but for the poor, the vagrant, the disgraced, who for one reason or another were homeless. And what disturbed me most about Sally was not the evidence of a brutal beating but her fear.

I was interviewed with barely adequate courtesy by the physician in charge, an elderly, ill-tempered, possibly overworked man who, like Mrs. Winch, did not really know what I was doing here and had no time and certainly no patience with my indignation. There was in his view no need to make a fuss. After all, these things occurred with enormous, in fact with tedious regularity and he had seen worse—far worse—than Sally, who had broken no bones and lost no teeth.

"My dear lady," he said finally, his tolerance at an end, "one must take a rational view. Your sympathy does you credit, but the young woman *was* alone in a questionable area of the city at an advanced hour of the night. In such circumstances any woman must expect to be molested. Her assailant no doubt mistook her for a prostitute."

"I see. It is permissible, then, to rape a prostitute?"

He raised a dry, somewhat disgusted eyebrow.

"Madam—I would consider it to be something of an impossibility."

"I cannot agree."

"Indeed? It astonishes me, Mrs. Barforth, that you—as a gentlewoman—should have any views on the matter at all. And I will give you a further piece of advice. You would do well not to trouble our constabulary with a sorry episode such as this, for if that young woman's assailant was really unknown to her, she cannot name him; and if he was not the stranger she claims, then she *will* not name him. These incidents are best left to settle themselves. Good-day to you, Mrs. Barforth."

I took Sally back to Tarn Edge in the victoria, Mrs. Winch greeting me with tight-lipped disapproval. Did I realize, she wondered, the extra work involved, the trays to be carried upstairs, the hot water, the bed linen? And when I reminded her that we had had sick maids before who had not been turned outdoors like stray kittens, she folded her hands, drew a deep breath and compressed her lips even further.

"I wonder, madam, if you have considered the effect of this on—well—the others?"

"Why should there be any effect at all, Mrs. Winch?"

"Because she is not suffering from influenza, madam, or a

sprained ankle. In fact we cannot be sure what she *is* suffering from.''

''Mrs. Winch, what do you mean by that?''

''I will tell you, madam. I keep these girls well under control. I think you will agree with that, and it is essential they should be controlled. But most of them are naturally flighty, and a thing like this can only arouse their curiosity. They will be around her bed, mark my words, like bees round honey, asking their silly questions, letting it all go to their heads and neglecting their work. And we have menservants too, Mrs. Barforth, please do not forget that. It is difficult enough, at the best of times, to preserve the decencies in these large households, and one cannot expect these young footmen to treat a girl who has—well, they will not treat her as they treat the others, you may take my word for it. I cannot think it right to take her back and I believe you will find the girl herself does not wish to stay.''

''If she is treated as something between a leper and a Jezebel, then most likely she will not.''

But Mrs. Winch, armoured by her self-righteousness, did not lack courage and, quite calmly, had something more to say.

''Mrs. Barforth, that girl should be discharged at once for the sake of your own peace of mind. She may well be pregnant, Mrs. Barforth, and since you would *have* to discharge her then, it is better to do it now, when no one can be sure. That way she will have time to make her arrangements and your conscience will be clear. I was forced to dismiss a pregnant thirteen-year-old in my last place, madam, and it was most distressing. Sally Grimshaw is older, has more sense, and she will be far better off now with her mother.''

I had never thought of Sally in terms of a mother, family, or in any terms whatsoever that did not involve the dressing of my hair, the laying out of my clothes, the cleaning of my brushes. She had been present, the plump, pink and white face glimpsed behind me in the mirror, the quick, capable hands wielding a button-hook, her cheerful gossip of disaster on the night I had lost a child of my own. I was neither fond of her nor otherwise. I was simply used to her. But I was appalled, now, by the callousness her plight had aroused in the normally well-meaning Mrs. Winch, and made it my concern that very afternoon to go and see her mother.

I had come with sad tidings and expected them to cause distress, an honest show of indignation, a desire for revenge, and I was badly shaken by the indifference with which the gaunt, grey woman who was Sally's mother lifted her shoulders, displaying a body which I at first thought to be misshapen by accident or disease but which was in fact pregnant.

The house was as small and dark as I had expected, one room downstairs and one above, a bare floor and a kitchen chair or two, mattresses rolled up and stacked in corners, a flat stone sink, a steep, littered staircase leading to the upper floor, stone steps leading down to a dank, open cellar. All this I had expected to see, but even Liam Adair's fluent denunciations in the pages of the *Star* had not prepared me for the smell of damp and poor drainage, of the overflowing privy a yard or two from the door, the sweat and the urine soaked into those splintering floorboards, a smell which, at this our first encounter, stung my eyelids and took my breath away.

"It happens. She'll get over it. She'll have to," said Mrs. Grimshaw, one hand on her swollen belly, another child no more than two years old straddling her hip. "And she knows not to expect anything from me."

Mrs. Grimshaw, I discovered, was the mother of seventeen children, a large family she was ready to admit but not unusually so in a district where the men were mostly unemployed and, as she put it, "had nothing else to do." She herself worked in the weaving-sheds—anybody's weaving-sheds—when her health permitted, and when it didn't she took in washing for anybody who could afford to pay her a penny or two, since her husband was not, she said, "reliable." She had married at sixteen, when she had already given birth to her first child, and had been recovering from one pregnancy or starting another very nearly ever since. And she had alleviated the squalor of nineteen persons in two dingy rooms by the simple procedure of pushing each child out of the nest as soon as, or even a shade before, they had started to fly. The boys were welcome to stay as long as they were earning and could bring something in, although two had gone to sea, another into the Army, and unless trade picked up she supposed the rest would follow. But her one prize possession was a sister who had done well in the service of a clerical gentleman at Elderleigh, and, as each of her daughters approached the age of eleven or twelve, this sister had never yet failed to place them as kitchenmaids, maids of all work, skivvies; after which Mrs. Grimshaw rarely saw them again. They moved on, or, if they succeeded and became parlourmaids or lady's maids like Sally, they grew proud. Her eldest girl had taken employment so far away that Mrs. Grimshaw had been unable to attend her death-bed and, far from complaining, had simply been relieved that the girl's employer had agreed to bury her.

"I'd stopped her funeral club payments, you see," she told me in her flat, monotonous voice. "And it would have been awkward having to borrow. Because they won't put a nail in the coffin unless you can pay cash down." And as for Sally, she had given her the best start in life she could and had not received so much as a shilling from her ever since. Nothing, on either side, was owing. And there was nothing to spare.

She shrugged her shoulders again, her hollow eyes asking me, "What can I do? I feed them, and clothe them after a fashion, until they're big enough to see to themselves. And after that I have to think of the babies—the babies—until this wretched body of mine is too old for babies."

I knew from that first meeting—although indeed I never met her again, merely hundreds like her—that I could not judge her, and leaving behind the few coins I had on me, ashamed at this easy gift of money and her lethargic acceptance, I went home with the smell of her so deep in my memory that my bath-tub of scented water, carried upstairs by girls who could have been her daughters, gave me no comfort. And even when I had explained to Sally that she need not be afraid, that in any eventuality she would be looked after, I saw that neither her fear nor my discomfort had subsided.

She was a victim, but I seemed the only one able to believe it. She had been forced to the ground and held there as dogs hold bitches, her whole life possibly ruined to satisfy a drunken caprice, a fit of madness, a "poor fellow's mistake." A woman alone after dark must expect to be molested, they had told me, and I could not accept it. He mistook her for a prostitute, the doctor had said, considering this sufficient justification. I could not accept that either.

"My dear, the girl probably knew him and led him on," murmured Mrs. Rawnsley, who had been something of a "tease" in her younger days.

"If it should come to the worst," Mrs. Sheldon told me in her sweet and serious manner, "I may be able to arrange for the adoption of the child."

"She did not feel the disgrace as we should," Miss Tighe insisted stoutly. "They have their own morality, these girls, you know, and a mishap of this nature can make little difference. She will find somebody ready to marry her, I expect—especially if

you should feel called upon to make her a decent wedding
present—and all will be forgiven.''

"Lord! What does it matter?" said Venetia. "She's only a
woman, and what's a woman for, after all?"

But Sally had done nothing wrong. A crime had been committed against her by a man for whom these ladies, with their talk of
"leading on," the eternal, discreetly whispered "My dear, men
are made that way," seemed ready to supply with excuses. "It is
always the woman who suffers," they said, finding this state of
affairs if not precisely desirable then at least quite natural. And
of all my acquaintance only Liam Adair seemed able to comprehend my indignation.

"Aye, these women are the very devil," he told me cheerfully,
"especially when it comes to tearing another woman to pieces.
Fear, I reckon, in this case, because some of them dread it
happening to them and some of them are plain terrified they
might like it. So if they can blame the girl it makes them feel
safer and better. Grace—I know there are men who do these
things, but we're not all the same. Come now, you don't really
think I'd force my attentions on some poor helpless soul, do
you?"

"Oh, you wouldn't have to, Liam. With your famous charm
how could it ever be necessary? Quite the other way round,
sometimes, I'd say."

But, just the same, the spectre of male violence clung to me,
giving me a wariness of the men I knew, an unwillingness to
take my coachman's muscular arm when he came to assist me at
the carriage-step, a positive discomfort in the presence of Gideon
Chard, for although he was a gentleman to his fingertips, fastidious in his tastes and his manners, I knew that in the most private
areas of his life he did not need the refinement of affection. And
from there it was an easy step to ask myself what remained of
affection in the few early morning encounters that had become
my own marriage? Why did I submit to it? To what degree of
compulsion was I myself subjected? Or was I in fact playing the
prostitute to secure my way of life, to keep the peace, in simple
obedience to the way society—but not my nature—had fashioned
me? I was not certain, but the next time Gervase touched me my
body could not endure the insult and turned rigid with disgust.

"I beg your pardon," he said coldly, and although I had
probably given him the excuse he needed, I had salvaged some
minute part of my self-esteem.

It was not merely Sally but her mother who haunted me, and I was grateful to Liam Adair for including in his paper an article on the brutalizing effects of poverty and constant childbearing, describing as if it had happened to himself, my interview with that apathetic and defeated mother of seventeen.

"You did well by me there, Grace," he told me, "for she'd never have talked so freely to a man. Why don't you pay the *Star* a visit one of these days and see how it's done?"

And perhaps my own need for diversion and my even more pressing need to divert Venetia inclined me to accept.

"What does it matter?" she still sometimes enquired, but increasingly her phrase would be "I don't care whether it matters or not," or, even more positively than that, "I don't give a damn. Yes—I mean a *damn*." And no doubt it was to provoke Gideon, to see how far she could go, that, on her way back from Galton with Gervase a week or so later, she stopped on the outskirts of town to attend—of all things—a cock-fight.

It had been very nearly criminal of Gervase to take her there. I knew it and could not defend him, for, impropriety apart, she had been in real danger among such rough company. I was shocked and furious, yet just the same profoundly grateful that he was not in the house the following evening when Gideon strode into the drawing-room and spat out the one word "Why?"

I had never seen him so angry, had never felt such a boiling of wrath in any man, but Venetia, instead of shrivelling in the heat of it, jumped to her feet and flew at once to the attack.

"To see how men pass their time—to see what pleases them."

"Have you any idea who saw you there?"

"Oh, I don't care about that, although I know *you* care. And whoever saw me must have been there himself, so what does it signify? If *he* could be there, why shouldn't I? Have you never been there yourself, Gideon?"

"Yes," he said. "Oh yes, I've been cock-fighting many a time, Venetia, with the whores and the thieves—the rabble—yes."

"And did you enjoy it, Gideon?"

"I may have done—once. What's more to the point is did you enjoy it, Venetia?"

"I hated it," she shrieked at him, her control snapping. "It was cruel and degrading and disgusting. I loathed it and I loathed *them* for enjoying it—even Gervase. It was foul. But don't take that to mean I won't go again—or that I won't do something else men do, just to find out why they do it, and why they tell me I must not. That is—if I feel inclined. You follow your inclinations, don't you, Gideon, so why should I not follow mine?"

If she had planned to take his breath away I think she had succeeded, for he seemed momentarily unable to speak, an incoherence which, had he not quickly mastered it, would probably have led him to strike her. And watching as she swayed a little towards him, her pointed face trying hard to be insolent, I saw that she wanted him to strike her and thought—perhaps—that it might be a good thing if he did. But what he gave her was not the hot flaring of anger which must have contained some spice of emotion, but his silence, his back turned towards her in a gesture of cool and fastidious dismissal. A bitter thing for them both.

We visited Liam Adair the morning after, Venetia and I, my coachman showing serious displeasure when I gave him the address of the *Star*, not, I imagine, out of any consideration for me but because it was not a neighbourhood in which he cared to venture his horses. And so from the start it was an adventure, the broad paved thoroughfares we knew giving way first to warehouses and old, half-used mills sagging listlessly by the canal bank, and then to the dingy row of lodging-houses, ale houses and cheap shops that was Gower Street.

The lower windows of the *Star* were still boarded over following Liam's dispute with the baking trade, there being no sense, he thought, in replacing the glass when he would surely offend somebody else ere long, and had we not glimpsed his printing presses on our way upstairs I suppose we could have been in the office of some small and slightly shady lawyer, a vast quantity of papers, documents, odds and ends, covering the surface of two battered desks, spilling from half-open drawers and spread in haphazard piles all over the floor; an air of comfortable confusion, a smell of cigar smoke, beer from the pot-house next door, dung from the street, and gas.

"How very thrilling!" said Venetia, meaning it, needing quite badly to be thrilled, so that I glanced sharply at Liam, who had once been in love with her and who would surely not be unmoved today by her straight, fine-boned little body in its sheath of amber silk, her upturned face vivid with curiosity. Liam would have married her in place of Gideon. I wished he had. But her father had chosen otherwise, and catching my eye—reading my thought—Liam nodded to me as if in agreement, then shrugged and smiled.

"Aye, so thrilling in fact that when the landlord comes knocking at the door I'm obliged to pass the hat round to pay the rent."

"Oh Liam, I fear you'll never get rich."

"Why should he wish to?" enquired a voice from the corner of the room, a head which had been bent—decidedly "at work"—since the moment of our arrival looking up now to reveal a dark, by no means handsome face, thin and intense, and at first acquaintance without humour.

"Why not?" Venetia said, startled, having taken the man for a clerk, a menial, and being clearly taken off guard to hear an accent as pure and privileged as Gideon's.

"Because we are not in the business of getting rich, Mrs. Chard. We are in the business of giving information or education or such assistance as we can—of giving. Naturally there is no money in that."

"Lord!" she said, rippling—as I had not seen her do for a long time—with laughter. "And just who are you? A saint?"

"He's Robin Ashby," Liam said easily. "My assistant—my conscience. He doesn't believe in money."

He stood up, revealing an angular, slightly awkward body, and we shook hands, telling each other we were "delighted" although he was clearly not pleased at this interruption to his work.

"I was at school with your husband, Mrs. Chard," he said coldly. "No, he will not remember me, although I believe he is acquainted with my cousin, Lord Macclesworth."

"Good heavens!" said Venetia, as we drove home, having spent the rest of our visit dutifully examining Liam's presses. "Lord Macclesworth's cousin, and did you see his threadbare coat and the state of his shirt collar? And his bones all sticking through as if he had not eaten for a week? He may not believe in money, but Liam should still pay him."

"He is probably the kind who gives it all away."

"Yes," she said, still laughing. "And he is as ugly as a monkey too, poor thing."

Gideon, when applied to at dinner that evening, did not at first recall the name. "Ashby? Don't ask me— Yes, just a minute, there *was* an Ashby—the *Wiltshire* Ashbys. Good family, but if he's the one I'm thinking of, I can't recommend him. He was expelled from school, and it strikes me they locked him up later on for debt or libel or breach of the peace, or some damned political thing. No, I'm not keen to renew acquaintance. Nor, I imagine, is he."

We of course returned to the *Star*, my own interest claimed by the greater reality I found there than in Miss Mandelbaum's genteel petitions for the voting rights of middle-class spinsters;

Venetia because she had discovered a new game in the baiting of Robin Ashby, a game she did not always play with kindness and did not always win.

Dressed in her elaborate and costly best, a diamond on her hand, emeralds swinging in her ears, a feathered and beribboned hat perching among her curls, she amused herself by flaunting a deliberate and quite false extravagance.

"Come now, Robin Ashby, since you don't believe in money, what else is there to believe in?"

"Freedom, Mrs. Chard."

"Nonsense. No one is free. *You* are not free."

"As free as possible. I own nothing. I have a coat and a change of linen, a few other necessaries which will easily fit into a small bag. Nothing detains me—anywhere."

"Yes, and that sounds very grand, but you are one of the *Wiltshire* Ashbys—Mr. Ashby—my husband has told me so. It is easy to preach poverty when you have all that prestige and wealth behind you."

"I have no expectations from the Ashbys, Mrs. Chard. I long since cut myself adrift from all that."

"You can't be sure. Supposing they called your bluff and left you a fortune?"

"Then I should make the best possible use of it."

"You mean you'd give it away?"

He nodded and, suddenly disgusted with him, she rapped her parasol smartly against his desk.

"What nonsense! What you really mean is that you don't want the responsibility. Is it true you were in prison once?"

"Yes," he said as calmly as if she had asked him the time of day.

"And I suppose you are proud of it?"

"No."

"Well then, I expect you enjoyed it—because you thought it made a martyr of you."

"There was nothing about it to enjoy."

It had, of course, been a political matter, an inflammatory speech which had caused a riot in a cathedral town, six months of acute discomfort for Robin Ashby, who had suffered not only from degradation but from attacks of bronchitis and a severe fever which had nearly killed him.

"Serves him right," said Venetia when Liam explained this to us. "Insufferable creature that he is. Lord! Why do I talk to him?"

But talk to him she did, of freedom which she insisted to be impossible, of equality of opportunity which aroused her derision, of social justice which she declared to be a fool's dream, all these discussions taking place beneath the watchful eyes of Liam Adair and myself, who could see no threat in this shabby revolutionary, our idea of a crusader—and we both knew Venetia was ready for a crusade—being someone tall and bold and handsome like Liam himself.

"What an idiot he is—what a child!"

But when I decided to give a ball at the start of the winter and wondered if Robin Ashby should be invited, she flew at me in a quick burst of temper, caused not by her unreadiness to see him at Tarn Edge but by the embarrassment my invitation might cause him.

"Grace, have you no tact? You must know that he can have no evening clothes."

"Well, he is a Wiltshire Ashby and will know where such things may be obtained."

"Grace, he is not striking attitudes, you know. He means what he says. And why should we ask him to waste his time borrowing evening clothes, which would not fit, I daresay?"

But nevertheless he was an acquaintance, and a gentleman. He should, I decided, be given the opportunity to refuse. But the next time we visited the *Star,* Venetia, marching ahead of me, walked straight up to him and burst out: "Grace is having the dithers because she wants to invite you to her dance."

"And you do not."

"No. I don't."

For a fleeting moment there was something beneath the studious intensity of his face, his habitual concentration on the task in hand, which could have been hurt.

"Well then, since you do not wish to see me in your home, Mrs. Chard, there is no more to be said."

"Yes," she told him, her face, drained of its mischievous sparkle, looking very small beneath her dashing, high-brimmed hat. "You would not like my home, Robin Ashby. I think you would find it rather a poor place."

I had chosen to give a ball for no better reason than that the ballroom at Tarn Edge had not been used for its proper purpose for years. The time seemed opportune, for Blanche, who had produced her second son the year before with the same gracious ease as his brother, was at Listonby for the season, the Goldsmiths were once again in our area, staying with cousins in

Manchester who would be delighted to cross the Pennines. And since the Goldsmiths *were* coming, since the affair was not to be confined to our local industrialists and our local squires, it crossed Gideon's mind that a certain Monsieur Fauconnier of Lyons and a Mr. Ricardo of New York were both in London with their wives and might appreciate an opportunity to travel north.

"In fact," he said, coming into my breakfast parlour one morning and handing me a list of names and precise directions as to where their owners might be located, "you might care to consider these. Merely suggestions, of course, but if one is to give a ball one may as well make the most of it."

And I understood at a glance that his "suggestions" would involve me, not merely in a larger and more formal dance than I had intended, but in a considerable house-party, since the Fauconniers and the Ricardos, the Goldsmiths, the Brisbane Matthewsons and the Auckland Faringdons, could not be asked to stay at the Station Hotel.

There would be bedrooms which had not been used for years not merely to be "got ready" but to be made inviting, accommodation for foreign maidservants and foreign manners, trains to be met, gallons of hot water available at any hour of the day, the transformation of my home, for a day or so, into a luxurious, well-managed hotel.

It was a feat which Aunt Caroline had regularly performed for twenty-five years at Listonby, which she continued to perform at South Erin and at her elegant house in Mayfair. For me it was a challenge flung down by Gideon, and for his own good purposes, to which I eagerly responded, planning the whole affair, as Venetia said, like a military operation, immersing myself for days on end in railway timetables, dinner menus, breakfast menus, place settings, supplying Mrs. Winch with lists of everything I expected to find in each guest-bedroom when I came to inspect, lists of the dinner services I wished to be used, of the lace and damask table-linen I wished to be got ready, lists of who must be sent to meet which train and of the type of refreshment I wished to find awaiting each guest on arrival.

There would be a dinner-party before the dance, a shoot the following morning at Listonby for those who cared to sample the English sporting life, a tour of the Barforth mills for those who did not. There would be a house-party from Listonby—a small matter Gideon mentioned to me in passing—containing a few "politicals," no one *frightfully* important, of course, or so Gideon said, but one or two of them better placed than they might seem. And in view of Sir Dominic's budding career at Westminster, Gideon supposed I would have a quiet room ready with some decent brandy and a few good cigars in case anyone should want to have a quiet word.

"Yes, of course, Gideon."

"Good—and a card table or two, since these fellows don't usually dance. And by the way, I hear the Fauconnier son and daughter-in-law may be in London on the seventeenth. Would it be too much to write and extend a friendly hand?"

I wrote. Fauconnier *fils* accepted my verbal handshake gladly, assuring me that the journey north would in no way tire his very delicate wife. I ordered another room to be prepared, then two rooms when Gideon happened to mention that the young Madame Fauconnier's nerves were too fragile to permit the sharing of a bed.

"She drinks goat's milk too, for some reason," he said, and I went off at once to make arrangements for a goat.

I worked hard and long, to the exclusion of everything else. I got up at dawn with Madame Fauconnier's invalid diet in my head and sank exhausted into bed long past midnight with the violins I had hired from Manchester singing in my ears. And when the evening came, when the house was filled with light and fragrance and music, when the chrysanthemums I had pillaged from every available greenhouse were massed in my hall and on every step of my stairs, when my supper-table groaned with every kind of roasted fowl and game, with two dozen different kinds of savoury tart and two dozen different kinds of sweet, with ices and sorbets, soufflés and creams; when my champagne was chilled, my musicians in their places, my dinner guests mingling happily together and my ball guests eagerly arriving, *then* I became as taut as any fine-strung violin and would have been glad to send them all away again.

But such poor spirits could not last as I began to feel that the evening would be a success. There were partners in plenty for those who wished to dance, comfortable chairs for all who wished to sit, a convenient back staircase where a young lady could escape her chaperone. There was conversation for the serious, gossip for the frivolous, cards and fine wines, acquaintances to be made. There was Blanche, in gleaming blond satin, royal secrets and scandals whispering in the hem of her gown, and the Duchess of South Erin setting herself—on Gideon's behalf—to fascinate both Mr. Goldsmith and Mr. Ricardo. There was Sir

Dominic, who paid me the compliment of treating my home as if it belonged to him, looking worthy of a seat in any man's Cabinet. And if Mr. Disraeli himself was not present, there were among the Listonby party one or two who knew him well, somewhat to the disgust of the Sheldons, Rawnsleys, Fieldings and Mandelbaums, who were Gladstonians to a man.

I even remember the dress I wore, a fine apricot silk cut straight and tight with almost no bustle, draped at the back of my knees with lace frills and falling into a fluted train. I was bare-shouldered, my hair dressed very high, not by Sally, who, finding she was not pregnant, had left my service, but by a French maid Aunt Faith had lent me. I had seed pearls and apricot silk roses in my hair, pearl ear-rings, the diamond ring Gervase had given me four years ago and the sapphire my father had given me the previous Christmas. I thought I looked composed, not beautiful like Blanche nor striking like Venetia, but elegant enough to be interesting, forceful enough to be noticed in a crowd.

I remember Venetia in a green gown so vivid, cut so tight and so low that Gideon had raised a sardonic eyebrow at the sight of it; a guest as always in her own house and a very gay one that night, dancing, laughing, chattering, flirting, not with the younger Fauconnier, which might have served a purpose, but with a young lieutenant of Hussars, a young clergyman, the young squire of Winterton Park who was known to be just a step away from bankruptcy.

I remember her well. But most of all I remember Gervase and the exact moment when our relationship, which had been shredding away from me like mist for so long, finally evaporated, was dispersed as mist can be dispersed by a sudden wind, blown away, and gone.

He was not very much on my mind that evening, for I had a multitude of names, faces, last-minute details to remember, so many introductions to make, so many conversations which looked like flagging to bring to life again, so many wallflowers for whom partners must be found, so many tours of inspection to check that all was well, that no one would have cause, tomorrow, to feel neglected. And I remember—quite distinctly—my start of surprise when I saw Gervase in the supper room, not because he was with Diana Flood but because he was still in the house at all.

They were not touching, not even standing very close together. They were not flirting, not even talking very much. And it was their stillness and the stillness they had created around them which stuck me the first warning blow, for had I been a stranger entering the room I would have known, instinctively, that I must not speak to them, must not disturb them, must make no sound that might spoil their deep and blissful concentration on one another.

They did not notice me. But I saw her bold face grow timid, her eyes cast down, Gervase's eyes turning almost transparent with feeling as they had done long ago when he had cast his puzzled, despairing glances at me. I walked quickly away, upstairs, opened the first door I came to and sat in the dark until I could stop trembling, sickened and shocked with the certainty that what I had seen was no sexual caprice, no London socialite easing her boredom, no provincial actress earning her fee, but the giving and the acceptance of love.

How long he had been in love with her I didn't know. Nor could I tell how long it would last. But he loved her now, I was sure of it, and I was just coherent enough to be surprised that the pain should be so deep-rooted and so terrible. His promiscuity had been bearable—just—because it had been faceless and because I had grown accustomed to it. But Diana Flood's face was engraved on my mind, and how was I to accustom myself to that?

But one does not sit in a darkened room and shake when there is work that must be done, a house full of curious, not always kindly, eyes and plenty of spiteful tongues. One does not give way to private sorrow when one's services are urgently required by others. A woman worth her salt—thank God!—get on her feet and, having invited these guests in the first place, attends to their needs. She tidies her hair, walks down the stairs and smiles, and should anyone question the state of her health or her heart she answers "Very well," which is as much as anyone really desires to know. And when it was over and the carriages were already rolling away, the house-guests preparing for bed, I stood on the terrace, the empty ballroom behind me, the thin light of a winter morning already in the sky, unable to release the hurt I had clenched so tight, unable—for the rest of my life it seemed—to shed a tear.

Silence; in which to think of failure, of sterility. Silence; in which to contemplate the futility of all my efforts, the petty little tasks which I had welded together into a life. Silence; in which to confront myself with solitude. And then, very suddenly, Venetia appearing beside me, perhaps looking for silence too, one ear-ring missing, I noticed, and, incredibly, a cigar in her hand.

"Ah, yes," she said, holding it aloft with a flourish. "You might well stare, for everyone else did so. I have won fame tonight, Grace, as the first woman in Cullingford to smoke a cigar."

"Have you really?"

And she was too deep in her own disillusion to see that I did not care.

"Yes, really. Here on the terrace with a dozen people watching—with Gideon watching."

"Whatever for?"

"For freedom, Grace—because I remembered a remark some-one made to me about the petty restrictions with which women are shackled. Why—this person wanted to know—is it improper for a woman to smoke when all the men we know do so? Why?"

"I haven't a notion."

"Neither have I. Just a petty, futile shackle, I thought, and I decided to break it."

"And did you?"

"Of course not," she said, "of course not. Oh yes, I smoked a cigar all right and had a fine time shocking a few old ladies. A fine time—like the cursing and the cock-fighting—and what's the good of it? I'll tell you what I've achieved. I've made myself sick—that's all—like *they knew* I would—like Gideon *said* I would."

She threw the cigar down into the garden and went away, my voice too weary to say good-night, my head too weary even to turn and watch her go. Yet there were things still to be done, lamps and candles to be seen to, a final check that no gentleman— or no footman—had fallen asleep in some unlikely corner with a cigar burning in his hand. There were things to be done. Practical things, necessary things, safe things that would not shun me or hurt me. And crossing the ballroom and turning down the corridor beyond it, I saw Gideon at the smoking-room door, doing my work for me.

He had been, all evening, a careful but unobtrusive host, for he was not the owner of this house and he had borne that very much in mind. But he had been *there*, ready to step into any conversational breach, had danced a great deal and taken at least a dozen happy women, one by one, to supper. He had known—as I had known—the exact atmosphere of every grouping, had removed very adroitly a certain gentleman from the vicinity of a certain lady and introduced her to another gentleman whose attentions had proved more welcome. He had watched—as I had watched—had seen what was required and had supplied it. And now, being as full of brandy and champagne as anyone, he was still watchful, had remembered as his mother always remembered—that servants, if left to their own devices, will put off until morning the many things which he, and I, wished to be done tonight.

I had a word to say to Mrs. Winch about the arrangements for breakfast. Gideon wished to be assured that Chillingworth knew exactly who to call at that hour in the morning, and their eventual destinations. We settled everything to our liking and then, finding ourselves in the smoking-room, he drew up a chair close to the fire, handed me into it, poured out two glasses of brandy and held one out to me.

"You will rest better for this—for I believe you have gone beyond sleep."

"I believe I have."

"Then shall we drink to your success? It has been splendid, Grace."

"Thank you, Gideon."

"It is I who should thank you."

"Oh, no—"

Yet no one else had thanked me, no one else had cared whether I gave a ball or not. And now they had all gone off, happily or otherwise, to their beds, leaving me with the remains—and Gideon.

"I am so glad," I said hesitantly, for, after all, I had not done it for him, "so glad you enjoyed it—"

He raised his glass to me and smiled, his teeth flashing very white in his dark face, a wolf's smile I had often thought, although it seemed gentle enough now. "I did. And you did not. But a hostess never enjoys her own dances—at least so my mother tells me. She always took a brandy or two with my father—in the old days—when all was over."

Aunt Caroline? I had not thought her so human. And imagining her now, kicking off her shoes as I longed to do, holding out her glass to her husband, asking him "Matthew, did it go well?"; imagining him reassuring her—as Gideon had just reassured me—"It has been splendid, Caroline," I realized that this was his fantasy of how a marriage should be.

I had not believed him capable of fantasy. Now I recognized it, entered into it, for it had been my fantasy too, and in order to break the silence which was settling around us—dangerous because, astonishingly, it was so comfortable—I said quickly, "I hardly knew your father."

"Oh, he was a fine fellow. I suppose of the three of us Noel is the one most like him. I believe he and my mother did very well together."

Aunt Caroline? And once again I saw her through the fatigue and the brandy in my head, smiling at her Matthew as he refilled her glass.

"Come, darling, drink up—you have earned this."

"Oh Matthew, did you see?—did you notice?—heavens! I nearly died laughing when—"

"Yes, I saw it all."

The fantasy beckoned to me again and, blinking, I pushed it away, swallowed the last drop of the spirit and set down my glass.

"I am very tired now, Gideon."

"Yes, so you should be. Grace, would you accept a gift from me?"

"Why on earth should you wish to—?"

"To show my appreciation of all you have done. You have worked like a slave these past weeks, and although it was not on my account I have certainly benefited from it. It would please me enormously if you would take this. It is nothing of value—"

It was, in fact, quite beautiful, a bracelet of fine chains, each one a different shade of gold, coiled together into a delicate, intricate web sprinkled here and there with tiny amethysts. And it was exactly right. Not valuable enough for a husband to question it—and I did not really have a husband in any case—but so very tasteful, so different, that whenever I wore it some woman would exclaim "My dear, how exquisite. Where *did* you get it?" And every time that question was asked—had he been my lover—I would indulge myself by remembering.

He was not my lover. But he *could* be my lover. In this huge house, where we were thrown so much together, it would be possible—had he thought of that, did he want it? Had he understood—or had I—that the distance between us could be so easily crossed, should we ever wish to cross it? The thought struck out at me, held me for a moment in a kind of fascination, appalled me, and then—blessedly—became ridiculous, for this was Gideon Chard, the materialist, the opportunist, the fortune-hunter, who would not risk his share of the Barforth inheritance for a folly such as this.

"Gideon—how exquisite!"

"I felt sure you would like it."

Perhaps his father had always made his mother a gift on these occasions. In my fantasy it would have been so.

We walked together up the broad, richly carpeted stairs and then went our separate ways with a brief good-night. It was almost morning, and my bedroom seemed very muted and very cool, the winter sky behind the curtains letting in a pale grey light, Gervase lying on his back, his eyes closed, although I knew he was not asleep. I got in carefully beside him, leaving a chilly space between us, and lay there for a while watching the daybreak, listening to his shallow breathing, sensing his misery. What could I say to him? Nothing. How could I approach him? I could not. How could I bear it? I *would* bear it. I felt myself stiffen, a tremor starting somewhere inside me, a movement of distress, and then, breathing deeply, slowly, the rigidity of my body eased again. I had things to do. Work—that was how I would bear it. I had guests all day tomorrow, a luncheon, a dinner, a tour of the mills, a dozen farewells at the station. I would survive.

15

GIDEON WENT ABROAD THE FOLLOWING spring on a tour of Barforth interests in Germany, Austria, Italy, Belgium and France, in search of the personal contacts which the state of trade and his own instincts required, winning golden opinions, we heard, as a shrewd man of business and a gentleman, a combination very pleasing to Europe's commercial élite.

Venetia had not wished to accompany him. I do not think he had wished to take her. But—perhaps at her father's insistence—she set off in low spirits and returned with a great many new clothes and an air of dejection which did not augur well. They had been to Paris, to Rome, Vienna, Brussels, a dozen other famous cities. She had seen nothing, she said, but over-furnished drawing-rooms, grand hotels, expensive, identical women who were married to pompous men. She had seen nothing *real*, nothing particularly foreign, just Cullingford with a different accent, and worse than Cullingford, since she had not once been allowed out alone.

She had been bored to death, she told me, tolerated only as Gideon's wife and even then not always gladly.

"Oh, they all adore Gideon," she said. "He could have his pick of those foreign women and probably does. In fact I know he does. Well, good luck to him, for what difference can it make to me?"

She meant what she said. She had been grateful to him once but it had not escaped her notice that he had done very well for himself out of her folly, that he was successful and fulfilled, that he enjoyed his life, while she remained a frustrated, often desolate woman who had paid dearly for those two nights in Charles Heron's arms. The price was becoming too high and she had reached a point where she felt she owed Gideon no more gratitude and very little loyalty.

She spent the first days after her return at home doing her hair and changing her clothes, and when she did go out it was not to the *Star* but tamely to Fieldhead to take tea with Mrs. Agbrigg, to Elderleigh to visit Aunt Faith, to Miss Mandelbaum's where, after listening in moody silence as Miss Tighe explained the progress of the women's cause, she suddenly and very crisply announced, "You will not get your vote, Miss Tighe."

"I beg your pardon, Mrs. Chard."

"You will not get it, and I will tell you why. What notice do you imagine they take at Westminster of these genteel petitions of yours? None, you may be sure, expect to smile and shake their wise heads and say "These dear ladies are at their tricks again." You have no power, Miss Tighe, to make them pay heed to you. They know you hold your meetings here, around your tea-table, all nice and polite and proper, and what have they to fear from that? Some enterprising young politician may make a speech in your favour now and again to get himself noticed or to make his name as a 'progressive,' but once they *have* taken notice of him—once Mr. Gladstone or Mr. Disraeli takes him up—he will turn his mind to more profitable issues than yours. He will just put your petitions away and forget about them, and why not, since you have all the time in the world to write him another? No one who has privileges wishes to share them—I am not clever but that much I *am* certain about. The Duke of Wellington didn't want my grandfather to have a vote back in 1832. My grandfather didn't want his foreman or his shed manager to have it when their turn came in 1867. The shed managers don't want the agricultural labourers or the men who live in lodging-houses to have it now. And there are no more than a handful of men anywhere in the world who really want to give the vote to a woman. And if you did get it, Miss Tighe, then you certainly wouldn't want to share it with me. I should have to go around with a banner crying out 'Votes for *Married* Women. Give us the same rights as widows and spinsters.' And unless I can *demand* those rights—unless I have a weapon—then I won't get them."

"Oh dear!" said Miss Mandelbaum, and I have wondered if either she or Miss Tighe were ever aware that Venetia's sentiments were a direct quotation from Robin Ashby's latest contribution to the *Star*.

I don't know when she first saw him again nor how often they met thereafter, only that they did meet, for whenever she encountered him at the *Star* offices or elsewhere it often seemed to me that they were continuing, not starting, their conversation. Yet I said nothing, felt no particular alarm, did not in any case feel competent—having failed so abysmally myself—to advise her.

I believe I respected Robin Ashby in the sense that he was sincere in his aims and realistic about their chances of success. He was a clever, very separate man, compassionate towards the suffering masses but impatient of individuals and hard on himself, who would surely regard the intense personal commitment Venetia craved for as a burden, to be shunned like the property and possessions which in his youth had weighed him down. He might fall in love with causes, I thought, but hardly with a woman.

"I make no claims on anyone," he said, and surely that was the same as saying "I allow no one to make claims on me."

She was not enraptured by him as she had been by Charles Heron. Whatever existed between them caused her no outward joy, tending rather to sharpen her tongue and blacken her humour, making her touchy and unusually unkind.

"Grace, you amaze me—you used not to value yourself so low."

"I beg your pardon?"

"Oh, you know very well what I mean. Will you be content forever, just being polite?"

"I manage very well, Venetia."

"Lord! so you do. And you have your dignity, of course. I suppose you can warm yourself on that."

The Chards came early to Listonby that year, arriving for the August grouse, Dominic and Gideon spending long hours together charting their political and financial future, while Noel escorted Blanche on her country house calls, his face, which was a paler, better-tempered version of Dominic's, lit by her presence, indulgent of her whims and fancies, and a little amused by them but careful of her, *enjoying* her, his attitude not so much one of desire but of cherishing. He loved her, there was no doubt about it, everyone knew it and accepted it and found it quite delightful, taking their lead from her husband, who saw it as downright useful, particularly now that his Parliamentary duties were proving so greedy of his time.

The Listonby estate had always been large, the generosity of Aunt Caroline's father, Sir Joel Barforth, had increased it, and a property of this size required a capable and conscientious man at its head. Tenants were apt to encroach on manorial privileges when the squire was so often away; gamekeepers tended to rear birds for sale to city shopkeepers instead of preserving them for the guns of the squire's guests. There had been a shortage of grouse on Listonby Moor for the last two seasons; farmers had been shooting foxes, to the great annoyance of the Lawdale Hunt; while stewards, as everyone knew, were expert at falsifying accounts. Dominic, whose tastes and ambitions never left a penny to spare, believed he was being cheated, Gideon was too busy and a shade too grand these days to make a good second-in-command, and there was a move afoot that year to persuade Noel, whose military career had not greatly prospered, to resign his commission and take charge of affairs at home, a scheme enthusiastically endorsed by Blanche.

"Noel is so devoted to the land," she told us—and him—repeatedly. "The tenants adore him, and is it any wonder, for he has patience with them, as Dominic does not."

And one afternoon when she had refused, with a lovely drooping air of sadness, to listen when Noel mentioned that his regiment seemed likely to be posted abroad, and had then sent him off on some errand of her own, Venetia leaned towards her and said, very loud and clear, "Do you know something, Blanche? I wish with all my heart that Noel would rape you."

"My dear," Blanche replied in her best Marlborough House manner, "I am sorry to disappoint you, but he never will."

"Of course he will not, the poor devil. So why don't you do the *decent* thing, Blanche—the honest thing—and give yourself?"

"Because—Venetia dear," she said, smiling very serenely, "it is simply not necessary."

Venetia left us soon afterwards, having arranged—or so she said—to see her mother at Galton, and calmly pouring out more tea Blanche asked me thoughtfully, "Grace—is she having an affair?"

"I don't know. Are you having an affair?"

"With Noel? My dear, as I said just now, it is really not necessary."

"And if it became necessary?"

"Then I suppose one would have to think again. But about Venetia—if she should be having an affair, I do hope she will manage to conduct it—well—*suitably*. There is really no need for her to set the world on fire. Fortunately both you and I understand that."

So we did, for the Chards were very often apart, Blanche in London, Dominic on some political country-house visit. He went to Newmarket and she to Cowes, he holidayed *en garçon* each winter in Scotland, every summer in Baden, separations which encouraged his casual infidelities, her long basking in Noel's devotion. Their marriage retained a sound financial, legal and social base. She had given him two sons and they had done their duty by each other. Indeed, they considered themselves to be very definitely married, even though in real terms they did not live together.

And since Blanche neither expected nor wanted her husband to be faithful, she was not surprised by the conduct of mine, which could be no secret to her. Clearly, like herself, I had chosen the path of discretion, of compromise, the turning of a blind eye, which she considered a small price to pay for domestic harmony. She had her compensations in plenty; so, presumably, had I. And she seemed very glad—for my sake—to welcome me to this charmed circle of the worldly-wise.

I had my dignity, as Venetia had pointed out to me, and I had Tarn Edge. I had also a great fear of the future, which I managed more often than not to suppress to a bearable proportion. But the constant need for self-discipline often made me appear distant and cold, so that the younger maids were nervous in my presence, the menservants sullen. I became sharp-spoken and sharp-eyed, and having picked a quarrel with Miss Tighe and found it enjoyable, I went on, spasmodically, to quarrel with everyone except Gervase.

We said nothing to each other now beyond the bare civilities, knowing, I suppose, that if we began to talk it would have to be of Diana Flood. And since she had a conventional husband, he a virtuous wife, what could usefully be said? Major Compton Flood might tolerate a discreet flirtation, but he would not take kindly to an affair so intense, so passionate as to transform his wife's face with wonder whenever my husband entered the room. He would not sit idly by discussing the state of the nation and of the weather while my husband's eyes fastened themselves upon her, transparent in their desire and their longing. Care would be needed, for Major Compton Flood would know the way, and certainly had the right, to grievously punish an erring wife. And care was taken. Gervase went out with the Lawdale throughout the winter, but he came home often enough to put an end to any rumours that he and I were living apart, lying beside me sleepless and taut with misery; sick, I suppose, at the thought of his mistress in her husband's arms and the knowledge that his initial lack of judgement in preferring me to her had placed her there.

He was suffering, and although I was not saintly enough to pity him, I was well able to understand. He could have married her and had not done so. She could have been his, but his volatile emotions had played an atrocious trick on him, had convinced him that he needed an entirely different kind of woman, and he had let her go. Now, after straying through that wilderness of haphazard sensuality, he had fallen in love with her as desperately as he had once loved me, seeing in her the salvation I too had represented. And she belonged to Compton Flood. He was wretched, could neither eat nor sleep nor sit still for five minutes together, so that, having watched him prowl the confines of Tarn Edge like a caged animal, it was a relief to me when he rode away again.

He went to the mill too, more often than I had expected, partly to avoid trouble with his father, partly to be seen there so that Major Flood might be aware of no tell-tale changes in his way of life. But he did little more than hang about the mill-yard, seizing upon any excuse to break free, and I believe it was his father's acceptance of this turn of events which caused me finally to lose heart.

Mr. Nicholas Barforth, once again, had given up on his son. For a time he had hoped that marriage might bring about a change for the better, and would anchor him to the industrial side of his inheritance. But that hope had failed. And recognizing that he had set me an impossible task, my father-in-law did not blame me for that failure, choosing instead to make my life as comfortable as he could. After all, I could have made the house hideous with jealous scenes, could have lost my health and my nerves and publicly washed the whole laundry-room of soiled Barforth linen. Instead, I was mindful of my dignity and my duty—for what else is left to a failed wife but that?—and in gratitude Mr. Nicholas Barforth restrained his temper when Gervase was present and refrained from questioning me as to his whereabouts when he was not. I was a good girl. There was no scandal. And, as for the rest, we would just have to wait and see.

It was not the life I desired. A year and a half ago I would not have believed myself capable of bearing it. I bore it—just—at some times better than others and was infinitely relieved when my father-in-law, perhaps to ease my strain, sent Gervase abroad that summer.

I went—of all places—to Galton on the afternoon of his departure and lay on the summer grass, exhausted, greedy for rest, and spent ten days eating the new bread and the herb dumplings my mother-in-law set before me, sleeping in the sun and in the great bed where I had lost my child. I was an invalid again who could only be healed by quietness, by laying down— until he came home again—that sorry burden of pretence. And when I had energy enough to walk the leafy borders of the stream with Mrs. Barforth and her dogs, she talked to me about her brother, Peregrine Clevedon, of their happy childhood in the days when her world had been shielded by the Abbey stream, and by her love for this brown, stony land. But for most of the time we walked silently in the warm air, listening to the rippling of the water, a drowsy bee in the clover, birdsong, the busy life of the summer hedgerows and trees, two women who had failed at the great career of marriage—the *only* career—yet, being obliged to remain bound within it, had no choice but to adapt themselves, in their different ways, to that captivity.

She could have told me all I burned to know about Gervase. Would he force me, as her husband had forced her, to spend the rest of my life observing the conventions, safeguarding my reputation, conducting myself in such a manner that people would not talk about me and so *could* not talk about Diana Flood? Or might he lose his nerve one day, and his head, and throw her reputation and mine to the winds in a desperate bid for happiness? But I asked no questions, being too weary to grapple with the answers, while she, understanding my need for repose, told me no tales.

Oddly enough it was at Galton that I heard of Robin Ashby's imminent departure from Cullingford, Liam Adair riding over on purpose to tell me.

"Cullingford's not grim enough for him," he said, making light of it, although I knew he was uneasy. "He's going north to have a look at the Scottish mining villages. Somebody told him they still use women in the pits up there instead of ponies and he's off to put a stop to it."

"Did he resign, Liam, or did you discharge him?"

"Now why ever should I do a thing like that? He'll work all hours God sends, Sundays, high days and holidays—it's all the same to him. And he's clever. And cheap, too. Why should I want him to go?"

"Have you told Venetia?"

"I imagine he may have done that himself. Grace, it's the truth, you know, that I don't *want* him to go. But that's not to say it's a bad thing that he goes—if you see what I mean?"

I went home a day early but found Venetia perfectly composed.

"Have you heard about Robin Ashby?" she said. "Not that I ever expected him to stay in Cullingford. He could be comfortable here, you see, and that would never do. So he's going to work in a Scottish coalmine just to see how long it takes him to choke on the dust. Then he'll write about it and after that, who knows? I expect he'll be off to India to find himself a bed of nails."

We went to the *Star* the next morning to say goodbye and drink his health in Liam's champagne, Venetia once again in her extravagant feathered hat with its emerald buckle, a frilled parasol in her hand, a great deal of gold and emerald jewellery about her neck and wrists, marking her as the wife of a successful man.

"Goodbye, Robin Ashby," she said brusquely, "and good luck—unless you should be crushed to death in a rock fall, or choke—or starve—"

"Or be hanged."

"Yes—there's always that. I didn't like to mention it."

And I understood not only that they had been lovers, but that I had actually known it for a long time.

He left an hour later on the Leeds train and she came home dry-eyed to dress for a dinner-party her husband had asked me to arrange.

"I'm going to London in the morning," Gideon said, "and if it turns out that I have to bring Bordoni of Bordoni and McKinlon back with me, Grace, can you cope?"

He departed, returned, Mr. Bordoni being joined by a Mr. Chene, the one a most gregarious gentleman, the other something of a gourmet, both of them requiring to be lavishly entertained. I entertained them, aware, as I asked the questions they expected and made the answers they wished to hear, of Venetia watching me, her expression no longer indulgent or friendly as it had always been with me, but one of cool mockery, her pointed face, for the first time in her life, hard.

Messrs. Bordoni and Chene, after effusively kissing my hand, went away; and a morning or two later, at breakfast, Gideon looked up from his correspondence and said: "Damnation! I shall have to go down to Sheffield on the first train. And Grace, it looks very much as if I shall have to bring my trip to New York forward by a week or two. In fact next Friday would suit me, if you could have them get my things ready by then? And

Venetia had better come with me. From the tone of this letter I
think the Ricardos are expecting it."

"Yes, Gideon," Venetia said, getting up from the table, and
it seems to me that, in a manner of speaking, we never saw her
again.

There was no elopement this time, no note hidden in the folds
of a ball gown, no ecstasy. She walked calmly upstairs, packed a
small bag, ordered the carriage to take her to the station and—
while I was busying myself about the arrangements for her journey to New York—got on the train for Leeds. A dozen people
saw her on the platform at Cullingford, half of them saw her
walking towards the ticket office in Leeds and idly wondered
why Mrs. Gideon Chard should be travelling alone, without even
a maid. But she had the reputation of an unsteady woman—
Cullingford being unable to forget that sensational cigar—and no
one questioned her, although the booking-clerk did remember
afterwards that he sold her a ticket to Glasgow.

"I'll get up there by the next train," said Liam Adair, who
had been called in by me before the final pieces of the puzzle
became clear. But Mr. Nicholas Barforth shook his head.

"You'll do no such thing. It's not your place, Liam, nor
mine, to fetch her back. That's her husband's privilege and his
alone, if he chooses to take it. I'll be in my study, Grace, when
Gideon gets back from Sheffield. I expect you'll be glad to send
him straight in to me."

I sat in the drawing-room alone and utterly appalled as I had
done on the night they had rescued her from Charles Heron, the
double doors open so that I could not miss Gideon's arrival and
expose him to the risk of servants' gossip. The day had been fine,
but hearing the patter of rain on the window, sharp and cold as
summer rain can be, I shuddered, thinking of rain in the far
north, remembering the watchfulness and the scorn in Venetia's
face this last week or so, and grieving because in the end she had
turned against me. She had gone at the last because there had
been nothing in this house nor in her life here that she valued.
She had rejected us all, and I knew how cruelly I would miss
her.

Gideon came, received my message with raised eyebrows,
went into the study and remained there a long time—an hour and
a half, I think—before I heard his steps once again in the hall
and his voice curtly informing Chillingworth that he required his
carriage.

"Will you be dining, sir?"

"I will not."

"Very good, sir."

I got up and walked very carefully down the corridor and, tapping on the door, giving him time to compose himself should he require it, went inside, finding my father-in-law as I suppose I had expected him, sitting at his desk, cigar in hand, the butts of several others beside him, two glasses on a silver tray, the traditional comforts men offer themselves in times of stress.

"Ah, Grace—yes—you had better sit down."

"Thank you."

And, his movements a little heavier than usual, he stubbed out his cigar and lit another, refilled his glass and drank, reflectively and very deep.

"Well, Grace—you are entitled to know. What can I tell you?"

"Has Gideon gone after her?"

"No."

"But he will be going?"

"No, he will not."

"Then you will go—surely?"

"No, Grace."

"*Father-in-law.*"

He inhaled, narrowed his eyes against the smoke, closed them briefly as if the light hurt him, and shook his head.

"For what purpose, Grace?"

"To see that she is safe—at least that."

"I doubt if she would welcome the intrusion. And there are a great many mining villages in Scotland, Grace. How could I find the right one?"

"If you wanted to find it, you could."

He sighed, contemplated for what seemed an uncomfortable time the drift of cigar smoke, and then once again shook his head.

"You are remembering the episode of Charles Heron, Grace. I was her legal guardian then. Her husband is her guardian now. The decision is his. I intend to respect that decision and so will you. That is an order, my dear daughter-in-law—and believe me, it is the very least you can do for him."

"For Gideon?"

"Yes, for Gideon," and with the force of a whiplash his hand came smashing down on the table. "Damnation, Grace, what excuses can you find for her? I could find none. He has every

right in the world to call her a whore, every right—and not a
clever one either, by God, but an idiot, a lunatic. And what man
in his right mind would be willing to live with a mad whore?
Yes, Grace, she may *want* to come home some day, for she has
gone off with another lunatic, it seems, who will not look after
her, and I think we can safely take it that she cannot look after
herself. When that day comes I might have a few hundred
pounds a year to spare for her—I might—but what I cannot and
will not do is ask her husband to live with her again. Grace, in
his position—the position she has put him in—I would not live
with her. And let me make it very clear that for as long as
Gideon remains under this roof—and I see no reason at all why
he should not remain here—I expect him to be shown every
consideration by you and by everybody else—*everybody*, Grace.
I think you will understand me. And now, if you will excuse me,
I have a call to pay on my wife.''

Nothing could have persuaded me to stay in that empty house,
and had there been no carriage available I would have walked
down the hill to the town and found my own way to Gower
Street. But the victoria, as always, was at my disposal, Liam
Adair looking rather as if he had been waiting for me, his hat in
his hand, a travelling bag standing ready by the door.

''Liam, you are going to Glasgow after all, aren't you?''

''I am that. I don't work for Nick Barforth these days and if I
decide to go north, then it's no business of his.''

''They don't want her back, Liam.''

''Did you expect they would?''

I paused, frowned. ''Yes, I thought Gideon might *need* to.''

''Why? To stay at Barforths? By God, Grace, but you're an
innocent.'' And sitting down rather heavily he too reached for a
cigar.

''He doesn't need to do anything now, Grace, that he hasn't a
mind for. He's got Nick Barforth exactly where he wants him,
which only goes to prove, my girl, that they're two of a kind,
since nobody else has ever been able to put one over on old
Nick. But now Venetia—God love her—has played right into
Gideon's hands. He runs no risk now of being cut out of the
business. How could Uncle Nick ever do that to him when he's
the injured party, when Nick's daughter had given him such a
raw deal? And if Gideon goes on playing his cards aright—as he
will—he could even get Mr. Barforth to offer him something
fairly substantial as an inducement to stay. You'd do well to

warn your father to keep his eyes open, because if he *does* decide to pay Gideon some sort of compensation, it could be something that he'd have to take away from Gervase.''

"What compensation?''

"I know what I'd ask for. A limited liability company—Nicholas Barforth and Company Limited in the modern fashion instead of a private firm belonging to Nicholas Barforth Esquire. Mr. Barforth as chairman, of course, with a majority shareholding. Gideon Chard as managing director with a share or two. Gervase Barforth with a seat on the board and equal shares with Gideon, of course, at least to start with—I expect your father would make sure of that. But I can't see Gervase putting up with it for long. He'd sell out and go off to Galton, I suppose, which may not suit you, Grace. And if Gideon wants that company—which is the same as getting himself officially recognized as heir apparent— now's the time to make a push. If I can see that, then so can Gideon.''

But Gervase, I thought with a cold, shuddering sensation at the pit of my stomach, would probably go to Galton in any case. I was in danger of losing nothing that I could still call mine; and I had not come here to talk about myself.

"Will she be all right, Liam?" And it was this that I wanted to know.

"With Robin? Christ! I shouldn't think so. It depends what she's hoping for.''

"Did he even ask her to go with him?''

He smiled, remembering Robin Ashby, in spite of himself, with affection.

"No, no, that wouldn't be his way. He believes too much in freedom to make a request like that. She probably found him packing his bag one day and when he'd told her all about the Scottish miners he'd casually wonder if she might care to come and see for herself. And if not, then no hard feelings.''

"Dear God, Liam—does he even love her?''

"Do you know, Grace, I can't think of one single reason why he shouldn't.''

"And you knew?''

"Of course I knew. And if there was anything I could have done about it, then I'd be glad to hear of it—short of telling her husband—and even that crossed my mind. I expected it to run its course. I reckon I didn't realize she was so near the end of her tether. Well, she's gone on her crusade now, God help her—God bless her!''

"Liam, tell me the plain truth. What chance does she really have of any kind of happiness?"

He glanced at his watch again, took his coat from a peg behind the door, thinking carefully, trying perhaps, to rid himself of the hope that he might find her already disillusioned and willing, at last, to accept a compromise; to let Liam Adair love her since no one else would. But the memory of Venetia herself forced him to be honest.

"Just what was she leaving?" he said. "It may seem a lot to most people, but it was nothing to her because she didn't want it. She was sick of her life and of her husband long before Robin came. No—she won't regret anything she's left behind. And yes—he does love her. Yes—he is sincere in his aims. It's quite true that if he went home to Wiltshire they might not kill the fatted calf, but they'd give him a decent allowance so as not to be embarrassed by that threadbare coat. He won't take their money because he doesn't need it. I don't think he'd take it if Venetia needed it. He might not even notice she was in need. Money is excess baggage to him. It clouds his vision and makes it harder for him to see the truth. He's not a religious man—he calls that excess baggage too—but that bit about it being easier for a camel to pass through the eye of a needle than a rich man to enter the Kingdom of Heaven—that reminds me of him. He believes in that. I don't know what happens to men like him when they get old. Perhaps they never do."

I shivered, badly feeling the cold.

"Do you know where he is?"

"No. He didn't tell me and I didn't ask. I'll just go up there, in the general direction, and let it be known who I'm looking for, since a pair like that won't be anonymous. And if I make it worthwhile, somebody will let me know. If that's your carriage down there you'll be wanting to take me to the station."

We walked downstairs together, his large warm hand under my elbow, and drove in silence to the cobbled station yard.

"If you see her, will you tell her that I—that I am still the same—that she can rely on me—for whatever—?"

"Aye—if I see her."

And this sudden wavering of his confidence caused me such evident alarm that he put an arm around my shoulders in a companionable hug and kept it there, despite the astonishment of our stationmaster.

"All right, Grace, let's look on the black side. I reckon the worst that could happen is that I don't find her at all."

And looking down the track at the panting approach of the train, he smiled into the far distance and sighed.

"Aye, that's the worst."

"And the best?"

"Well—I reckon the best we can hope for is to find her living like a coalminer's wife. And I doubt either one of you can even imagine a kind of life like that."

16

MY FATHER APPEARED AT TARN Edge the following day and for several days thereafter, was instantly admitted to Mr. Barforth's study, to be joined at various intervals by Gideon, by the Barforth and Agbrigg lawyers, by Sir Dominic and the Duke of South Erin; by the males of the family gathered together in judgement upon one of our women, to condemn her sins and to reapportion her wealth.

Gervase came home, furious, hurt and spoiling for a fight, grieving for the loss of his sister yet unable to suppress a pang of malicious pleasure at seeing Gideon in the sorry position of a deceived husband. But the confrontation Gervase attempted to provoke was prevented by his father, by that solemn conclave of family lawyers, and by the dignity with which Gideon seemed determined to conduct himself. Gervase's belligerence giving way in an abrupt swing of mood to a contemptuous rejection of the proceedings and all who took part in them.

"To hell with it!" he said, slamming the study door behind him and very nearly pushing me aside when I tried to intercept him. "They're carving it all up very nicely in there. But don't worry, Grace. You've got your father to make sure they don't carve you up, too. And as for Venetia, I believe she's better off where she is."

I sat in the drawing-room again, not alone this time but with the other women who had strong interests in the negotiations taking place, with Aunt Caroline who insisted that Gideon's position must now be clarified, with Mrs. Agbrigg who did not intend to allow the Barforths to swallow Fieldhead, with Blanche who, to my everlasting gratitude and light surprise, was obviously saddened and alarmed for Venetia. Even my mother-in-law, who was so rarely seen in that house, kept vigil with us, looking, one supposed, for an opportunity of freeing Galton and herself from Barforth control, she and Aunt Caroline facing each other like a pair of spitting cats when, after several hours of polite whispering and several dozen cups of tea, the Duchess could no longer contain her indignation.

"It is my son who is the victim, Georgiana. And it is your daughter who has wantonly betrayed him."

"I suppose that is one way to look at it, Caroline. But it might also be said that your son had driven her away."

Opposing points of view which would never be reconciled, although they both did agree wholeheartedly that something must be done about it. In Aunt Caroline's view, Mr. Nicholas Barforth, her brother, must now make a legal and binding statement of his intentions with regard to Gideon's future. In the natural course of events Gideon had expected to inherit one half of Mr. Barforth's assets and holdings, but that inheritance had depended on his marriage to Venetia. Mr. Barforth's existing will, Aunt Caroline believed, covered the possibility of Venetia's death, but no provision had been made for her adultery. God alone knew what might happen to her now, and those family lawyers must stir themselves and devise some scheme which would make it impossible, no matter what the circumstances, for Robin Ashby to touch a penny that might even loosely be called Venetia's. In fact Mr. Barforth, however painful, must in his new will strike out the name of "Venetia" altogether and substitute "Gideon."

"Really?" said Mrs. Georgiana Barforth, for although she genuinely wished for no more than her widow's portion when her husband came to die, she was ready to do battle for her daughter. "Are you not being a little premature in your judgement, Caroline? It may seem unlikely at the moment, and you may not consider it even desirable, but it is surely not impossible that they might be reconciled. And before we cast my daughter once and for all into the pit, may I remind you of your Christian charity? I am not religious myself but I have seen you on your knees many a time, Caroline Chard, in the church at Listonby. And with all your preaching of morality and decency, it seems a pity you have not learned anything at all about compassion."

"I have never liked you, Georgiana Clevedon," said Aunt Caroline, her eyes blazing, to which my mother-in-law responded by tossing an aristocratic, auburn head.

"I shall lose no sleep over your opinions, Caroline, for I must tell you that when you married my cousin Matthew Chard you were so gauche and your views so narrow and middle-class that you provided amusement for the entire county. I suppose you entertain London just as thoroughly now that you have started to play the duchess.''

I believe they could have come to blows had not Mrs. Agbrigg inserted her persuasive, velvet voice between them, Blanche being far too amused by the possibility of their combat to intervene, while I quite simply did not care a rap. And when their grudging truce had been declared and I had sent yet again for more tea, it was not long before the study door opened and those sober, dignified gentlemen emerged to inform us of our various fates.

Mr. Barforth, certainly, had been subject to a great deal of pressure, but he was accustomed to that and I think all the Chards had really achieved was to hurry him a little in the direction he had already decided to go. There was to be a limited liability company, the previously separate mills of Lawcroft Fold, Low Cross and Nethercoats being welded together and given the commercial identity of Nicholas Barforth and Company Limited. Mr. Barforth, naturally, would hold the position of chairman and a hefty eighty per cent of the shares, while Gideon and Gervase would each occupy a seat on his board and divide the remaining twenty per cent shareholding between them, a concession which in itself made them independently wealthy men. But Mr. Barforth, for the time being—and he did not specify how long that time might be—would serve as his own managing director, and furthermore would retain the immensely profitable Law Valley Woolcombers and the Law Valley Dyers and Finishers as his own. And when this had been settled, not entirely to Chard satisfaction but a step at least in the way Gideon had determined to take, they turned their attention to Venetia.

Perhaps—I am not certain of this—but perhaps Mr. Barforth did not want to change his will, being accustomed to the fact of a married woman's property passing automatically to her husband who, when all was said and done, remained Gideon Chard whether she was sharing his roof or not. But it was pointed out to him by the lawyer representing the Chards that there was a growing inclination in the land for legal reform, that it might one day be possible for a married woman to inherit no matter what vast fortune in her own right, to administer it, spend it, give it or fritter it away without so much as asking leave of the poor husband, who would have no claim on it whatsoever. And when he had digested the implications of this, when heads had been shaken and they had all wondered at the state of a world where such things might come to pass—while Gideon stood silent, I suppose, looking if not disinterested then certainly not greedy—Mr. Barforth gave a curt nod.

"See to it, then."

And for the purposes of his last will and testament Venetia was no more. The bulk of his fortune—after due provision had been made for his wife—was to be safeguarded for his son and his son-in-law, while if his daughter was to be mentioned at all—and he made no promises either way about that—it would be in some codicil among the bequests made to his staff.

Aunt Caroline was jubilant. My mother-in-law asked for her hat and gloves and went away, although her distress over Venetia must have been to some extent offset by the new independence of Gervase.

"There'll be no profit to anybody in talking to me about this matter again," said my father-in-law and went out to dinner with Gideon at the Station Hotel, to discuss, in a more congenial atmosphere, the details of Gideon's trip to New York.

And there began a sad, slow year, a wasteland in my memory. There was gossip, of course, but no information was ever forthcoming, and Cullingford was obliged to content itself with the bare and eventually boring fact that Venetia Barforth—Mrs. Gideon Chard—was no longer in residence at Tarn Edge. But where she was, and with whom, Cullingford could not say. Probably she had absconded with a man, but there again it was also possible she had lost her flighty wits and been expensively confined somewhere, out of harm's way. How dreadful, they said, for her husband. But the romantic aura which settled on Gideon for a while was soon dispelled when he made it abundantly clear that he did not welcome sympathy. He went to America as planned, then to Germany and France, spent long days at the mills and two or three nights a week away from home, finding consolation, one supposed, in approved bachelor fashion, since no one expected him to live celibate.

I kept the house and waited, one day following another, faceless, lacking colour and flavour. Waited for something to crack the thin but nevertheless restricting ice which had overgrown my capacity to feel. Waited for something to move me nearer or further away from Gervase. Waited most of all for news of Venetia. I wanted to hear that she was well and happy, that her decision had been right for her. I wanted to hear that she had not been mistaken in herself, that Robin Ashby was truly the kindred spirit she had always craved, that his values really were hers, that this was indeed her crusade.

Our lives went on. I heard that Liam Adair had involved himself romantically with a widowed lady who might make a substantial investment in the *Star*, unless of course she should discover that he was equally involved with her niece, also widowed but ten years younger, who shared her home and had no money at all.

I heard, with a polite smile, that Colonel Compton Flood had gone with his regiment and his wife to India, and responded with the same smile—having gone far beyond hope—when I was told some months later that Mrs. Flood, unable to support the heat, had returned to Cullingford Manor. Her husband would join her in six months, a year. How very interesting, I said and was appalled to realize how little I could manage to care that she had come back to Gervase.

My waiting ended the following autumn on a day of high wind, a hurrying amber sky, when Liam came at last to see me, having just got off the train he said, hungry and thirsty—yes, muffins and gingerbread and hot, strong tea would go down a treat—his manner as jaunty as ever, his eyes tired.

"Have you an hour to spare for me, Grace?"

"Of course."

"Then ask them to bring a fresh pot of tea and tell them you're not at home. There's no chance of Gideon walking in, I suppose—or old Nick?"

"They're out of town, both of them. Is it Venetia?"

"It is."

And my whole body turned cold, so badly did I want her to be well, so completely did I doubt it.

I waited just a little longer until he drank his fourth cup of scalding tea and ate several quick slices of gingerbread, as if his hunger had been with him all day, all night in the train and he had only now become aware of it.

"Grace, can you get away for a day or two?"

"Yes."

"Without anybody knowing?"

"I could say I was going to Scarborough to my grandmother. Where will I be going?"

"Glasgow. And one way or another you've got to bring her back with you."

I heard the story little by little, first, as he sat still swallowing that scalding tea, the things he knew, the framework of facts with the substance left out; then, as we boarded the northern train, the things he had guessed, the conclusions he had drawn, the things he wanted to believe and the things he could not avoid believing.

He had first found her ten months ago, standing in a cottage doorway, thin and pale but with a kind of taut resolution about her that had reminded him of a young knight undergoing the exhausting but ecstatic process of initiation. She had been neither glad nor sorry to see him, had treated him politely but with her mind very obviously elsewhere, her interest in him entirely without depth, as if they had been twenty years apart and now discovered themselves to be strangers. His visit, he believed, had seemed irrelevant to her. He wondered if she would bother to mention it to Robin, or even remember it herself. She was living in a small mining town, in a rough community where violence was commonplace, yet she had smiled when he had asked her to promise that she would contact him in case of need. And having promised, she had smiled again, waiting politely for him to leave, so distant and somehow so pure that he had not dared to offer her the twenty guineas he had brought with him but had sent the money on to her later, and had never learned what she had done with it.

She had been, not happy exactly—not in the sense he understood it—but exalted, yes, that was the word—*exalted*. And although he wrote her several letters in the following months, he had received no answer, her silence confirming his impression that she was in need of nothing he could give.

But her situation had altered. She had called him and he had gone to her, not quite at once, since there were other demands on his time, but within the week, at the address she had given in Glasgow.

"Well, you'll see for yourself, Grace. It's a bad place, but that's not the worst of it. I reckon I was prepared for that."

The facts then—the points of which Liam was certain—were these. She had joined Robin Ashby in that pit-head cottage and had remained there until the local coal-baron, who was also their landlord, had discovered Robin's intentions, branded him a troublemaker and made it impossible for him to get work anywhere in the district. They had moved first to Glasgow, then Newcastle, Liverpool, back to Glasgow again, living by his itinerant journalism, which meant very meagerly, Liam thought. Shortly after their return to Glasgow, Robin had met a man—another thin, intense, exalted individual like himself—who had spent some time among the sweatshops in the East End of London where poor immigrants were herded into the tailoring trade like cattle, fifteen or twenty to a steamy, insanitary room, and forced to labour for considerably longer hours than the law allowed. Factory inspectors, this man alleged, could rarely gain admittance to these ''sweaters' dens''—in fact the reforms for which men like Robin and himself had fought so hard were not being carried out. It was the spark of another crusade.

By morning Robin Ashby had already made up his mind to travel south and no doubt expected Venetia to go with him. But he believed a woman should be an independent individual, entitled to think and decide for herself, not merely a possession who must automatically follow her man. They were comrades, partners, together because they wished to be together, not because the law or the Church or some intricate financial settlement insisted they should. And so—overestimating her strength or believing her to be as strong as she wished to be, overlooking the biological and social conditioning which had created her weakness—he asked her if she was ready for this new venture. She replied that, on the contrary, she had decided to return to her husband. And when he left, a few days later, she did not tell him that she was expecting his child.

I had never entered a common lodging-house before, but imagination had prepared me for the smell of damp and vermin, the peeling walls, the fouled staircase where those who had not even the price of a bed in such a place as this would huddle for warmth on winter nights. But at least—as Liam informed me— there were worse places, kennels not fit for dogs, where one did not rent a room but a *place* on a straw mattress thrown down on bare boards with a dozen others, men and women all together. And it was not until I had picked my way through the filth and litter of those stairs and entered a narrow, foetid corridor, that he said gruffly, ''You'll find her much changed. Some women bloom in pregnancy, others don't. As I say, you'll find her—different.''

She had asked him to bring me, and after a moment he left us alone together, Venetia sitting on the hard plank bed while I took the only chair. There was nothing else in the room but a low table, a high, uncurtained window, a cracked water jug, one small bag in a corner, and my own great astonishment at Venetia's calm. She was extremely thin, without any colour, her skin a dull chalk-white, her hair faded from its deep auburn to light brown, her dress, from which all the trimming had been removed, too big for her and not clean. She looked as I had sometimes felt, like a woman sitting an inch or two away from reality, no longer entirely in the world but conscious of its garishness and its clamour, too numb to feel pain but still able to recognize it; watching herself bleed, in fact, with a faint surprise, a certain cool pity.

Had she sent Robin away in a spirit of self-sacrifice? She shrugged her brittle shoulders and smiled. It may have seemed so to her at the time, but what else could she have done? Naturally, if he knew of her condition he would look after her, as he would care for anyone else he called comrade. She did not want that. Were she to write to him now and tell him the truth, then he would return, she knew. And if it became necessary, he would ask help from his family in Wiltshire and accept the terms on which they chose to give it. She knew that too, and refused to be the cause of his surrender.

They had never discussed the possibility of children. Neither Charles Heron nor Gideon had impregnated her and certainly Gideon had tried hard enough, she told me in her cool, toneless manner, since he had believed motherhood would steady her down. She had considered herself to be sterile. The mistake had been hers and now she must take the responsibility. She could not avoid becoming a mother. But she would not be the means of forcing Robin Ashby back into the conventional mould which had so nearly destroyed him. Her own female biology had trapped her. She would not allow it to trap him too. So she had thought to begin with, and for a little while she had felt herself to be quite heroic. But very soon she realized that there was no self-sacrifice—no heroics—involved at all. Her decision was the only possible one to take, which made it inevitable, easy, and absolutely right. "What happens to such men when they get old?" Liam had asked of Robin Ashby and had answered his own question. "Perhaps they never do." And a man whose own future was so limited, so soon to be burned out, perhaps, in its own fierce flame, could have no place in the future of a child.

She had never known freedom herself, merely an illusion of freedom in her younger days, and she accepted now that she never could be free. She was a woman, and as such could only escape from one captivity to another, not the least of these being her own unwelcome fertility. But she had desired freedom all her life, she desired it still, so intensely that she could not deny it to another. She had failed at everything else in her life but now—for the first and final time—she would succeed in this.

Yet there remained the question of the child, and she had had plenty of time these last weeks to contemplate the helplessness of her situation. She was acquainted now with the raw facts of poverty and knew that the moment her condition became apparent she would be turned out of her lodgings and into the street to wander and to beg—there being no work she was fit to do—and then to give birth and lose her child among the faceless infant multitudes of a workhouse.

Her intentions were very clear. She had no hopes and no desires for herself. Her own mind was, strangely enough, peaceful. But nevertheless she *was* pregnant, her child—in this masculine world—might well be a girl and she had seen—oh yes, she had seen at close quarters, the drudgery, the squalor, the exploitation of a working woman's life. She had herself been bred as an ornament for a man's pleasure and the propagation of his name, and had suffered for it. She had been imprisoned by trivialities until she had felt unable to breathe. But in the pit villages she had met old women who had been harnessed to coal-carts in their youth like brute beasts and forced to crawl down black underground passages where no beasts could be made to go. She had seen for herself other old women of nineteen with four or five infants trailing at their skirts and nothing in their futures but the prospect of four or five more. She had met cheerful young harlots in Glasgow of twelve or thirteen years' old, and then seen them again six months later, eaten alive by the harlot's disease. She had seen death by violence and by starvation, death by the desire for death which had caused a woman on the floor below to drown herself only last week, and, in the lodging-house before this, a girl—a child, in fact, no more than fourteen—to strangle her new born baby and then hang herself. And they had died partly from ignorance and poverty, mainly because they were women.

She had seen it. She knew. Women *were* weak, as everyone had always told her, not in their spirits but in these fertile, female bodies which continued year after year to give birth, and in these fertile, female emotions which caused them to love each unwanted child. Theirs was the crusade she had wanted to fight, but she was a woman too, her body draining itself to produce another life, and she believed the fight to be hopeless in any case. Once, a long time ago, she had wanted to have a child, had seen it as "half me and half some wonderful man." It was not so for the women of the pit villages and the workhouse hospitals, the mean streets of Cullingford, and she asked herself now what relevance such lofty ideals as the vote could have for them? What mattered was food and shelter, a blanket in winter, a few coppers to call a doctor to a difficult confinement and something put aside to pay for a funeral.

And if a woman must either be an idle ornament or a beast of burden, then she would rather condemn her own daughter to a life of frustration than of endless, brutalizing toil. I had money of my own, she knew, and Gervase did not interfere with my spending. Would I take the child when it was born and make the necessary arrangements? I could afford it, she said, raising her shoulders once again in a listless shrug, and if the child could be placed in some school, some establishment which would give it a measure of respectability, then she would be content. She had once scoffed at respectability, but she was tired now and she no longer scoffed at anything. She accepted her error. She had overstepped the limits of her femininity, of the role men like her father and Gideon had designed for women to play, and she knew now—had known for some time—that she could not win. *They* would always win—her father and Gideon, Charles Heron, the men who exploited women, the men who feared women, the men who desired women—and that being the case she wanted her daughter to be the kind of woman men desired, the kind of woman who did not threaten them and so did not require to be punished by them—a woman like Blanche.

She supposed I would be glad to help her and she would put herself entirely in my hands. She had discovered in herself these last few days a growing inability to concentrate, a buzzing in her ears and a loss of balance whenever she tried to fix her mind in positive thought.

I picked up her bag, wrapped her in her cloak, Liam paid what was owing to her landlady and together we took her to the station, both of us appalled by her weightlessness, her dreaminess, the way she drifted between us, passive and insubstantial as a curl of mist. I had no immediate plan beyond getting her to a warm, dry bed, a hot dinner, a doctor.

"Where?" said Liam, as we boarded the train for Leeds.

"I'll let you know."

And we were nearing the end of our journey before I told him to take her, as a temporary measure, to her mother at Galton.

She went with him, willing, it seemed, to be taken anywhere, while I found my way back to Tarn Edge, changed my clothes and thought—as Venetia did not appear to have done—of next October and the October after that, when she would have had her child and recovered at least something of her spirits. She was in a state of grief and shock, I knew, overwhelmed by a sense of failure, exactly as she had been on her forlorn return from Charles Heron. But she had overcome that, and she would overcome now. Her child would be born, her body freed of its obligations. Life would still be there, stretching ahead of her, to be lived, endured, enjoyed, and any arrangements I made for her now must take account of that. She no longer believed in the future, had given up all her desires, but the future existed and I had no intention of allowing her to produce her child as a cow drops her calf and then go drifting off again to certain disaster. I made up my mind that she must give birth to her baby in comfort, which was easy enough to contrive, but I was also determined that it would be no furtive, hole-in-the-corner confinement, no hurried whisking away of the child afterwards to some secret destination, never to be seen again.

She would love her child when she saw it, not because it was Robin Ashby's but because it was her own, and although I was not yet certain how to go about it, I was adamant that she and her baby would not only live together but would live in peace.

Left to himself, I did not think her father would stand in the way of anything I wished to do for her. My own father would support me. Aunt Faith would do her part. But Aunt Caroline would surely oppose the return of so disastrous a daughter-in-law, Sir Dominic would see no sense to it, now that Gideon had shown he could manage his affairs very profitably without her. And what might Gideon feel? But I could not think of Gideon in terms of feeling or sensation, could not even contemplate the possibility of his distress, preferring to regard him—certainly in this instance—as a survivor, a victor, an adversary. For he was Venetia's guardian and the decision would be his.

I ordered the victoria and drove to Nethercoats Mill, my carriage in the yard occasioning no comment, the clerk who showed me to Gideon's splendid, oak-panelled room being more concerned with the details of my dress—presumably in order to tell his wife—than with the nature of my business. I was, after all, the "young squire's wife," and so I walked boldly through the double doors, drew off a glove and smiled with far more composure than I was actually feeling as I saw how much I had taken Gideon by surprise. For we had kept very separate from one another while Venetia had been away—very separate, elaborately polite—and I could not expect the next half-hour or so to be easy.

His vast, polished table was in excellent order, nothing in evidence upon it but an embossed silver cigar-box, a silver-banded inkstand, a sheet of expensive parchment elaborately stamped and sealed, a contract, no doubt, worth many thousands of pounds, which he now replaced neatly in its folder. The room was fragrant with beeswax and tobacco, good quality wood and good quality leather, his panelled walls bearing a heavily framed picture apiece, dark landscapes borrowed, I thought, from Listonby. There were several highbacked leather chairs, a smaller writing-table, a wine cupboard which I knew—since I had placed his order for him—contained the finest of old brandy and cut crystal.

"Good afternoon, Gideon," I said, "or is it a little later than that?" And as he came round his desk to draw up my chair and to ask me if I had had a good journey from—where was it I had been visiting?—I wondered, with a terrible inclination towards nervous laughter, how best I might tell him that I had been to Scotland and brought him home a pregnant wife.

But one way or another it had to be said. The fact that I was here at all proved the matter to be serious, and once he had resumed his own seat I began to tell him as concisely as I could all that had occurred, my voice taking on the passionless tones Venetia herself had used, my eyes fixed on a corner of the cigar-box and his hand close beside it, square-palmed, and long-fingered, a scattering of black hairs disappearing inside an immaculate shirt-cuff, a beam of late sunshine slanting across his arm, glinting on his plain gold shirt-studs and the heavy gold ring with the Chard crest upon it.

I told him the "facts" as Liam had told them to me, then I told him what I had observed and what conclusions I had drawn, watching his arm stiffen as I did so, the beam of sunlight moving slowly away from him so that the room seemed to darken. And when I had finished he said, "How dare you come here and tell me this!" speaking not in anger, not in condemnation, but because he wanted to know.

"Someone else would have told you, Gideon."

"Ah yes, I see. You are merely saving me from the curious and the malicious."

"I am doing what I believe to be necessary—and right."

He snapped open the lid of the cigar-box, let it fall shut again, tapped his fingers irritably on the desk-top and then rapped out at me, "Quite so. And what am I to do about it, Grace? What 'right' am I to believe in? Are you suggesting I should play the Christian gentleman and take her back?"

"I could not make that suggestion."

"No," he said, throwing back his head so that I could see the tight clenching of the jaw muscles, the long dark glitter of the eyes, the brows drawn together into a scowl, his whole face a mask of suppressed anger and disgust. "No, I suppose you could not—not in words at any rate. But your attitude—your attitude, Grace, says it. And I ask you again how you dare?"

He got up, pushing back his chair, and stood at the window staring down at the mill-yard—the Barforth mill, the Barforth daughter—the line of his back still taut with anger, his fingers still tapping out their frustration against the window-sill, although gradually his wide shoulders seemed to haunch a little, the rhythm of his fingertips to assume a more measured pace.

"Very well, Grace," he said, making a half-turn towards me but remaining by the window. "What are you actually saying? Are you telling me that, since I married her in the first place to give my name to a child which never materialized—and for money—that now, when there *is* a child and I've made sure of the money, I should be willing to do the same? Is that it, Grace? If it is, then say so."

It was. And recognizing the need, I said it, word for word as he had expressed it himself, looking straight at him—because it would have been cowardly to have done otherwise—but not really seeing him.

"I am extremely sorry, Gideon. I am not insensitive to your position. I know—believe me, I *do* know—how very dreadful it must seem. But—"

"But what? My position has its inconveniences, but on the whole I have done very well out of it? Is that what you think, Grace?"

"I have said I am sorry, Gideon. And I think it only right to tell you that whatever you decide—or whatever anyone else decides—I shall not desert her. If no one else will look after her, I will find a way to do so."

"Should that surprise me? It does not. It is like you," he said, returning slowly to his desk and sitting down again, his brows still drawn together in a frown, but of concentration this time, his defences, which had been shaken by anger, now altogether intact.

"Has she expressed a wish to return to me?"

"I don't think it has even crossed her mind—either to come back or that you might agree to take her. She is here only because I brought her. She would have gone anywhere she was told to go. She is really—very unwell, Gideon. All she wants is to have her baby in safety and she has given no thought at all to what comes after."

"What seems strange to you about that? When did she ever make allowances for tomorrow morning? Have you spoken to her father?"

"No. But I am sure he would accept your decision—as he did when she went away."

"My decision not to follow her, you mean—to let her go and be damned? Yes, he accepted it. But did he *like* it?"

"One assumes so."

"Why? Because he formed a limited liability company as I'd been urging him to do for a long time? One should beware of assuming too much in one's dealings with Mr. Nicholas Barfoth, Grace. He did not give me the managing directorship which I felt I had earned and which I had been promised—merely a seat on the board, like Gervase. And the limited company does not include Law Valley Woolcombers, nor the dyeworks—both highly prosperous concerns over which I have no control whatsoever. Nor have I the faintest notion as to what his plans might be for their eventual disposal. So perhaps he was not altogether delighted by my readiness to let his daughter go. Perhaps he may have an Achilles' heel after all. Who would have thought it?"

I had nothing more to say. I had asked a man whose wife had left him because she disliked him to take her back now that she was pregnant by another man. What else could I say? He would make his own decision for his own reasons. I had simply placed the matter before him, and for the moment it was out of my hands. My bones were aching from the discomfort of the train, my stomach hollow and uneasy from scanty meals taken in dubious places. I was tired and from sheer weariness sank readily into the silence that fell between us, the sky darkening now towards evening, the mill-yard emptying and then filling again with shawl-clad figures as the night-shift came on; the screech of a hooter, doors banging, carts laden with wool-sacks grinding the cobbles, and Gideon Chard sitting at his desk, staring at his inkstand, his eyes unwavering in their concentration, thinking, planning, working it out.

"Thank you, Grace," he said, startling me. "I suppose you have been kind."

"I can hardly think so."

"Well, we will not argue about it. Let me see you to your carriage."

I put on my gloves, allowed him to take my arm as we walked downstairs and across the yard, his manner courteous and unhurried, although his glance was keen, checking, perhaps automatically, that everything was as it should be, letting it be seen that he was not the "young squire" like Gervase but the "young master."

"Take the top road," he told my coachman, "to avoid the wagons. And go steady. I shall not be home to dinner, Grace."

"Are you going to Galton?"

And in the twilight his smile seemed to flash out at me, his skin very dark, his teeth very white, a hungry, healthy man whose humour took me by surprise.

"We'll see about that," he said. "I reckon I'd do well to have a word with my chairman and managing director—our father-in-law—first of all. Well now, Grace—and wouldn't you?"

I returned to Tarn Edge and immersed myself gratefully in hot water, feeling bruised now in body and in spirit and totally unprepared for the slamming of my door, an hour later, as Gervase strode into my room. I had ordered a tray to be brought up to me, soup and bread and cheese, chocolate cake, a wholesome, almost nursery, supper which did not require me to move from my bedroom sofa; and neither his arrival nor his all too obvious temper could be welcome.

"You have been very busy, have you not?" he almost spat at me. "Yes, very busy—traipsing off to Scotland with Liam Adair and all the way back again with my sister—yes, *my* sister. I was at Galton this afternoon, which might have occurred to you had you given it any consideration. And what was I to feel when she arrived like that—with Liam? What the hell was I to make of it?"

"I just hope you didn't make a fuss."

"Christ! And if I did?"

"I just hope you didn't. She's been upset enough already."

"She's my sister," he said, coming to stand over me, his fury blanching and shaking him, my response to it being fierce and immediate since at last we had found a reason to abuse each other that had nothing to do with Diana Flood.

"She's my sister. Did you think of that? She's my sister and I have a right—damn it!—to help her."

I jumped to my feet, dislodging the tray as I did so, its contents scattering with a mighty clatter, no thought now in my careful housewife's mind of coffe stains on my rose-pink carpet, the soup bowl upended, the crumbs.

"She's your sister," I yelled at him, "and what does that mean? I'm your wife. That means nothing either. Just words—like company director, when you never direct anything. Like husband, when all you do is come home twice a week. Like brother, when—God dammit, Gervase Barforth, what help could she expect from you? Like son—"

"That's enough."

"Like son, when you live like a parasite on your father's money and lie to your mother. Yes, lie to her, Gervase, to keep her on that wretched estate so you can take your whores into the cloister—"

"That *is* enough."

"I'll decide that."

"I don't give a damn what you decide, Grace," he said, hating me. "And as for my whores, it strikes me you've never cared overmuch about that, so long as it meant I was leaving *you* alone."

It was enough then. Had I remained in that room I think I would have tried to kill him. I believe he felt the same. I walked out on to the landing and down the stairs. "Mrs. Barforth," my housekeeper said, intercepting me. "What has happened to your dress?"

"An accident with the supper tray! Please see to it."

And I walked past her and Chillingworth, not even acknowledging the discreet rapidity with which he opened the outer door for me, not caring what conclusions he might draw as I went out into the cold October air, and a blessed solitude.

17

IT WAS NOT REALLY VENETIA who came back to us, but I had great faith in the healing processes of time, in letting nature take its course, and did not despair.

I had play no further part in her restoration to the family fold and had been acquainted with only a bare outline of how it had taken place. The gentlemen, in fact, had assumed control and I had been sent, as so often before, into the drawing-room to wait. Gideon had spoken to his father-in-law. Mr. Barforth had then driven over to Galton and had returned very late that night. The following morning—a Sunday—he had called Gideon, and then Gervase, then Gideon once again, into his study where he had spoken to them at length, both separately and together. Mr. Barforth had next made his second journey to Galton Abbey, and Gideon, an hour later, had set out to join him. Gervase rode off, one knew better than to ask where. Mr. Barforth and Gideon returned for more discussions. Gideon rode off, not to Galton, I thought, but to Listonby to make his explanations to his mother, and a few minutes later my father-in-law sent for me.

"Grace—if you would see to the domestic arrangements. The room adjoining Gideon's might serve for the time being. And you might drop a hint to the servants that there's been a reconciliation in the offing these past three months and more, and they've been together a time or two to discuss it. You understand my meaning? Good girl—then you'll realize the importance of stressing that they have been *together*—secret meetings in hotels and the like, you'll know the score. She's been in the South of France, by the way, with my mother. People may not believe it, but if I say so, and you say so, and my mother says so, then I reckon it will suffice."

Gideon came back looking grim, having endured a gruelling interview with Aunt Caroline, who had never liked Venetia in the first place and would certainly never abide her now. We had dinner, and soon afterwards Venetia arrived with her mother, drank her coffee in the drawing-room and went up to bed, her luggage having been delayed, I told my housekeeper, by the vagaries of Continental trains.

"What a nuisance!" said Mrs. Winch, who did not believe a word of it. "Might it not be wise to wash and press some of her old things, since really, with foreign travel, one never knows?"

"Please see to it, Mrs. Winch."

The separate room, a lovely bay-windowed apartment adjoining Gideon's dressing-room, I did not attempt to explain and was thankful, when Mrs. Rawnsley and Miss Mandelbaum came to call, that if they had heard of it from their maids, who assuredly gossiped with ours, they would consider it a subject too delicate to mention. Nor did I try to conceal the fact that Venetia was a prodigal returned. Certainly—and in the strictest confidence—I was now ready to admit that she had absconded from her husband and her home. But Gideon had pursued her, which was exactly what one would have expected him to do, had shown himself masterful and persuasive, and now one must simply hope and pray for the best. The child—the result, it was implied, of his persuasions—had certainly influenced her decision to return, but all the world knew that children held a couple together, and one could only look upon it as a blessing. And because this was a more romantic version, a better story, than the truth, it was gradually accepted, while even those who continued to insist there had been a lover somewhere in the story were thinking of some Gallic or Latin charmer safely abandoned in the South of France, not of a pit village and Robin Ashby.

She was home again, that was all I cared for, and when, a month later, her father resigned his position as managing director and appointed Gideon in his stead, there was no conclusion I wished to draw.

"You see," said Venetia with her astonishing calm. "I have been sold for silver once again—or is it gold? A great deal of it, I imagine."

But there was no animosity in her voice and no humbleness either. She was not meek as she had been at the beginning of her marriage, nor grateful, nor anything else to which I could easily give a name. Neutral was the only word I found for her, the state of un-feeling which had enabled Sally Grimshaw's mother to accept her daughter's rape with a shrug. "It happens." Not apathy precisely, but an impenetrable resignation. "It happens."

And she seemed to be quietly, rather sweetly amused by women like myself who still believed that there was something to be done about it.

I don't know how much conversation Gideon had with her, if any at all, but since I lived with a husband to whom I rarely addressed a word, I could not be astonished at that. He had won his directorship, she had won respectability for her child. For the time being that would amply suffice. No entertaining was done at Tarn Edge that winter, Gideon making use of the Station Hotel, Mr. Barforth dining more often than not from a tray in his library. Christmas was bitter cold and almost friendless, Gervase at Galton, Gideon at Listonby, my father-in-law, as usual, at his mills, my father in Eastbourne with his wife. Only Blanche drove over to see us on Boxing Day, grieving a little because Noel, after all, had followed his regiment abroad to Africa of all places, where everyone knew the Boers, or the Zulus, or both, were spoiling for a fight. But one glance at Venetia's face caused her to forget both her sorrow and her curiosity as to whose child this actually was, a piece of information which not even Sir Dominic had been able to prise out of his brother.

"Venetia, you do not look well."

"I suppose I do not. You look very splendid, Blanche."

"I daresay. You will come to London, won't you, when this is over—you and Grace? It will take you out of yourself and will help me too, since I am worn out with worry for Noel—It is all right for him, having a fine time playing soldiers. He *knows* he is not wounded or dead. But I don't. And by the time I get a letter telling me he is not killed—well, heavens! by then he could be."

But as I walked outside with her to her carriage, she said quickly, "She's not well, is she? What beasts they are, all of them, Dominic saying straight out to Gideon that he hoped the Barforths had made it worth his while, and Gideon smirking and saying he wasn't complaining. And Aunt Caroline going on—and on—about how it had best be a girl, because a girl can be packed off with a dowry, whereas a boy would expect to inherit his fair share—and had he considered how best to protect the interests of his own children if he—and presumably Venetia—ever have any? And then I look at Venetia and it all seems so terrible. Oh dear! Noel would not have behaved like this. Would he, Grace? Noel would have been kind. Well, I shall just go and write to him and tell him never mind his regiment, he is needed at home."

Venetia was not well. Her ankles, from the very early days,

had swollen, her hands become so puffy that she could not wear her rings, and there had been recurring bouts of dizziness, a buzzing in her ears which increased her air of vagueness. Her abdomen became hugely distended, her arms and shoulders, her face, remaining very thin, so that instead of the bloom one often sees on expectant mothers, the whole of her health and strength, her substance, seemed to be draining away into that monstrous belly, and being absorbed by it.

By January she was too heavy and too uncertain of her balance to walk without difficulty and was forbidden to come unaided down the stairs. February sent her to bed and kept her there for three of its sleet-grey weeks, sleeping, waiting, smiling at the cradle with its spotted net draperies we had already placed in her room, and the minute garments of embroidered linen I had purchased ready-made in Leeds.

"I have never seen anyone so spent," her mother told me, "unless—dear God, I wish I had not thought of it! I have seen birds in cages like that, wild birds no longer trying to get out, which is the saddest of all. What did he do to her, Grace, to exhaust her so?"

"Nothing that he knew would harm her. I think he treated her as the kind of woman she wanted to be."

"Are there such women?"

"I hope so. But Venetia is not one of them. I think it was understanding that, that broke her heart."

She talked of course, sometimes a great deal but always of the distant past. She never spoke of Robin Ashby nor of Charles Heron but of herself as she had once been, that vivid, hopeful self she had believed in and to whom she now referred with affection and regret, sparkling madcap Venetia running from one Galton summer to another, completely unaware of the limitations of her sex, her class, which her family would so soon impose upon her. It had taken her a long time to understand that she could never be an explorer, a doctor, a lawyer, an architect, a *participator*, could not even ride a horse astride. And when she was asked to contort her body into a side-saddle and a corset, she had responded with that lovely ripple of laughter, only half-believing that anything so ridiculous could be true.

"Lord! Do you remember the trouble they had lacing me into those stays—me flat on my face on the carpet and Mary-Jane with her foot in the small of my back pulling away at those laces until I let out my breath and they snapped clean away? And what was the point to it when I was as flat as a pancake in any case and my waist only measured eighteen inches? Nobody could tell whether I was wearing stays or not—except that 'no respectable female ever goes out without them.' Lord, how I laughed at that!''

But the tight-fronted bustle skirts had obliged her to wear her corsets like the rest of us; she had given up riding not, she insisted, because of the side-saddle but because her sympathies in the hunting-field were increasingly with the fox. And the days were gone when she could simply shin up one of the ancient oaks at Galton and lie for hours stretched out like a cat among the branches, savouring her laughter.

She came downstairs at the end of February and sat in the drawing-room, her body so grotesquely swollen that it seemed impossible she had still two more months to endure. I engaged a nursemaid and a wet nurse on the doctor's recommendation, kept the cradle and the baby-linen aired, sent notes almost daily to Aunt Faith, whose assistance now I would have greatly welcomed.

"Two months," Venetia said. "Lord! I shall be a mountain by then."

But on the night of the fourteenth of March her pains began, she was assisted by Mrs. Winch, the nursemaid and myself to bed, the doctor, the husband, the mother, were all sent for, hot water was kept simmering at the ready, while I found myself brimming with a strange excitement, that feeling of childhood Christmas which can easily be accompanied by tears.

I had no real expectation of bearing a child myself. For a long time I had not wanted a child. Now—at this inopportune moment—I was consumed with the longing to hold my own child in my arms, to feel it tugging at my hand, needing me; and I was glad to be reminded that, for the time being, Venetia needed me more.

She was in labour the whole of that night, the next day and the night after. Not unusual, said the doctor, at a first confinement, although he conceded, when Mrs. Barforth pressed him, that her pains were close together and clearly very sharp. There was really nothing to do but wait.

"My dear lady," Dr. Blackwood said, venerable and easy and infinitely reassuring. "This is one little task which cannot be done without pain, you know."

"Yes, Dr. Blackwood, I do know—my memory retains this particular pain very well."

"Then perhaps, Mrs. Barforth, if we all remain very calm we will do her more good?"

Mrs. Barforth and I sat beside her, giving her such encouragement as we could, but by the morning of the sixteenth her pains were so rapid and so severe that she could scarcely draw breath between them, her cheeks had sunken into dark hollows, there were black rings around her eyes, she was exhausted, barely conscious, and the doctor had called in a colleague, a younger man with a less compassionate, more businesslike manner.

"Perhaps if you would leave us alone for a while," the new doctor said, and I went downstairs to confront the faces in the drawing-room, all of them—even Gideon's—showing evidence of lack of sleep, of strain, of the helplessness and the guilt men feel on such occasions.

"It is not going well, is it?" snapped Mr. Barforth, as if he held me to blame for it.

"They're giving her something now. I don't know—"

"Giving her something?" he shouted. "I should bloody well hope so! If this goes on much longer you can send that sanctimonious Blackwood down here to me, and I'll have something to give *him*."

"There are other doctors," said Gideon. "My mother would know the best. I'll get over to Listonby."

"I'll do it," said Gervase, leaping to his feet like an arrow, his face chalk-white and desperate. "You go to your mills, Gideon. Leave this to me."

I do not intend to dwell on the agony of childbirth. One has either given birth oneself and knows, or one has not, in which case it is useless and presumptuous either to describe it or to try to understand. She slept an hour or two that morning, whimpering in her drugged sleep, her face swallowed by black shadows, her nose standing out sharply against her hollowed cheeks, giving her head the appearance of a bird. And when her pains began again at noon with great violence and the child was still not born, the younger doctor declared that it had gone on long enough and that a forceps delivery should be tried; the old one decreed that nature was best left to go its own slow, sure way; and I had begun to be terrified.

I stood in the corridor outside her room, pressed against the wall while the two men of science expounded their theories to my mother-in-law.

"There is the danger of strain to the heart," said the younger man. "And, of course, one might also take the view that she has suffered enough."

"Indeed," Dr. Blackwood replied, his manner as avuncular as

ever. "But forceps, my dear fellow—yes, we might spare the mother a little pain that way, but these instruments of yours have been known to damage the skull of a child, you cannot deny it—and it would be wrong to conceal the possibility from these good people—wrong indeed."

"Do it," said my mother-in-law.

But the younger man raised his shoulders in the direction of Dr. Blackwood, whose case this was, while Dr. Blackwood shook his head and smiled his "favourite uncle's" smile.

"Dear lady, naturally you are moved by your daughter's agony, but she is young enough to bear it—in fact it is well known that these pains and the instinct of maternal devotion are most definitely bound together—most assuredly they go hand in hand. And neither your daughter nor her husband would thank us if any rash surgical intervention resulted in harm to her child. The child, madam. Above all, one must consider the child. Her husband may not care to take the risk of injuring what, after all, might well be his son and heir."

"Do it!" shrieked Mrs. Barforth.

"On whose authority?"

She turned, erect as a soldier on parade, and marched away down the corridor, returning some minutes after with her husband.

"You," said Mr. Barforth, indicating the young doctor with a jerk of his irate head. "Get in there and do what you can. And you, Blackwood, go with him and *assist*—if he needs you."

"The husband," Dr. Blackwood said smoothly, accustomed to childbed hysterics. "It is my policy to consult the husband in such cases."

"The husband," thundered Mr. Barforth, "will do as I tell him—and so will you."

They administered slow, blessed drops of chloroform, Mrs. Barforth kneeling at the bedside to hold her daughter's hands. "Darling," she said, "not long now—not long." And I caught Venetia's face in my eyes and my mind as the nurse ushered me from the room, that bird-skull surrounded by a wild tangle of auburn hair darkened by sweat, her lips flecked and bitten, immersed in pain as an ember immersed in fire, nothing left of her nature, her individuality, her civilization, just a female body engrossed in its labour.

I pressed myself once more against the wall, closed my eyes and listened to the sound of combat behind me, the footsteps, the haste, the sudden exclamations, the rapid instructions, a murmur of encouragement. And then, when I had stopped hoping for it, the thin wail of the new-born, releasing my tears, a whole flood of them running unchecked down my face in sheer thankfulness. I had lost track of time, could not have said with any certainty what day it was, much less the hour, but it was over. She could rest now, with her baby beside her in its spotted net cradle, could be pampered and spoiled, surrounded by sweets and flowers and gifts, as new mothers ought to be. And I was excited again, eager to tell her how clever she was and how brave, eager to say "How beautiful! What a darling! What a treasure!" so that I forgot both my anxiety and my fatigue.

"It's a girl," said Mrs. Barforth, staggering in the doorway like an old woman. "Go tell them."

But as I moved forward, wanting to see—wanting to touch— she shouted: "Grace—go and tell them," her slight body barring my way until something called her back into the room and she slammed the door violently shut, excluding me.

But her wish to protect me, for such it was, was unnecessary, for I would not have dared to enter that room. There was some horror inside, I knew it, and my immediate instinct was not to intrude upon it—in no way to draw myself to its attention—but to escape.

I heard the sound of sobbing through the wall, nursemaids who sob easily and my mother-in-law for whom it came hard, her voice raised in a sudden howl of grief and anger. "Go and tell them," she shouted. "Go and tell them you lost the mother but saved the child—and expect to be praised for it. GO!"

And it was Dr. Blackwood who obeyed her command and hurried downstairs. His younger colleague came next, still in shirt-sleeves, and then there were a great many comings and goings, the nurse, Mrs. Winch, both doctors again, Mrs. Barforth herself with a lacy bundle in her arms at which I no longer wished to look, and then the pretty net-draped cradle being taken away to another room by the wet nurse, leaving the room empty since Venetia had gone—when?—could it already be an hour ago?

I wandered to the landing, every joint aching, leaned against the banister rail beneath the great stained-glass window and looked down into the hall where the maids were standing in huddled conclave until Chillingworth appeared and with a flick or two of his agile wrists sent them all away. The drawing-room door was slightly ajar. I knew Mr. Barforth and Gideon, possibly Gervase, were standing within. I knew I should go down to them and could not. My duty was clear. Mrs. Barforth was fully occupied with her grandchild and could not be expected to do the many things which must be done. Somebody must stand firm, must speak to the servants, must offer comfort to those men down there who were surely—and differently—in need of it. And for the first time in my life I shirked utterly, *could* not, for if I should detect the faintest glimmer of relief in Gideon—for the child was a girl, the woman was dead, the money irrevocably his—I would want to kill him, and I had no strength left and little inclination to stand between him and Gervase. But perhaps most of all I could not cope with the grief of a man like Mr. Nicholas Barforth, who was unused to grief, did not wish to see him break, especially now when I was breaking myself.

And so I stayed at the head of the stairs leaning against the banister, my mind fastening upon such trivial details as the high wind and the clock in the hall which told me we had reached late afternoon. The sixteenth of March, I thought. We were twenty-four years old, Venetia and I, and soon I will be twenty-five. What does it matter? What's the good of it? I began to walk slowly downstairs—because what *did* it matter—and I have never known what miracle, at that moment, brought Aunt Faith into the house, what passing servant told her coachman as he waited for her outside the new shops in Millergate, what chain of gossip had carried the news so far, so that she bade him turn his horses and bring her to Tarn Edge.

She had not crossed this threshold for twenty years and for an instant I thought my need of her had transformed itself into an illusion.

"Grace," she said. "Is it true?"

"No." I told her. "Oh yes—yes it is," and flew into her arms. But the sound of the drawing-room door brought me alarm, for there had been a bitter quarrel between the Barforth brothers and even now I could not be sure my father-in-law would permit her to stay.

Nor, perhaps, could she.

"Nicholas?" she said, the question plain in her voice as he appeared in the doorway, his face looking as if it had been carved out of dusty granite.

"Faith." And for an instant he could scarcely believe it.

"Oh, Christ! Faith—" And she moved quickly towards him, as if she could sense the approach of his tears and wished to shield him, to throw a screen of concern around this man who had perhaps never wept in his life before. They went into the drawing-room together and shut the door.

I was left alone in the marbled hall with Gideon, and after standing in a frozen silence for a minute or two, I sat down on the chair by the bronze stag, knowing there was nothing in the world I could say to him. Tomorrow and for a long time hereafter he would be told by the well-intentioned and the sentimental, "Bear up, old fellow. At least you have your daughter to console you." But she was not his daughter. She could be no consolation, but no great encumbrance either. He was free now to take another rich wife and have sons of his own to inherit Venetia's money. And because, once again, his destiny had brought him out on the winning side, and because hate was easier, less complex, than grief and even soothed it a little, I sat for quite half an hour and hated him, accusing him and condemning him in my mind for everything. I had feared him, years ago, as a fortune-hunter when he had hesitated briefly between my wealth and Venetia's, and I had been so right—assuredly I had—to keep my distance. He had taken Venetia readily from Charles Heron's soiled hands and then, not content with the money alone—and notably discontented with the woman who came with it—he had tried to change her, as he had changed this entire household, to suit his precise requirements—*his* tastes, his desires, not hers, not ours. Fortune-hunter then, opportunist, seeing nothing but his own advantage; sensualist too, I supposed—yes, certainly that, although not with his wife. Widower now, of impeccable demeanour, looking not grief-stricken but saddened, very much moved beneath his patrician self-control. It was a sham, I was certain, and as I went on glaring at him, quite balefully I suppose, his eyebrows drew together into their black scowl and he came striding the step or two towards me.

"Well—and what have I done, Grace Barforth?"

"What do you mean?"

"You know very well. And you are not usually so squeamish when it comes to calling me a scoundrel. Come on, Grace—out with it—what are you thinking of me?"

"I am not thinking of you at all."

"Oh yes—yes, you are—and if the very worst you are thinking should be true, then tell me this, what have I done that your own father has not done—except that the Delaney woman was older, and faithful, and had stolen the money in the first place?"

But Aunt Faith intervened, appearing suddenly from the shadows, her gift of compassion enabling her to throw both arms around Gideon's unyielding neck and to tell him. "No one

would think it odd if you went to Listonby to be with your
mother.''

"Am I in the way, Aunt Faith?"

"No, darling. You are suffering and don't know how to show
it, like Nicholas. I am giving you the opportunity to hide.''

Suffering, I thought. Never. She's giving him the chance to go
and tell them he's free and that Aunt Caroline can advertise him
on the marriage-market again. And my heart felt like a stone.

"Grace," Aunt Faith said, "please come with me," and
slipping her hand into mine she took me upstairs, tears flowing
gently down her cheeks. I thought, for a moment, that she
wanted to see Venetia and started to tug my hand away from her,
knowing I could never enter that room again.

"No, dear," she said, and we went up another flight of stairs
to the nursery wing, which I suppose she remembered from her
own childhood when she had come here to play with Aunt
Caroline.

The nursemaid sprang instantly to her feet and dropped a
curtsy, beaming her relief that some older woman was here to
take the responsibility, for the child was very small, the wet
nurse a clumsy fool, and the poor dead lady's mother had been
put to bed now, on the doctor's orders, with a dose of laudanum
inside her strong enough to knock out a donkey.

"She'll not wake till morning, ma'am.''

"Good," said Aunt Faith. "I think we shall manage very
well, nurse, until then. Grace, dear, do come here and look at
this lovely little elf.''

It took me a long time, a dreadful time, to cross that room;
and when I did reach the cradle I could not bring myself to look
down but bent my head, at first, with closed eyes.

"Look, dear," she said, her voice telling me those tears were
still pouring from her eyes, and eventually, her hand on my rigid
shoulder stroking me, urging me, I obeyed and saw the tiny dark
head, eyelids already long-lashed peacefully closed, the shallow
but even breathing, the fingers of a minute hand delicately curled
in perfect innocence.

When I left the room my tears were flowing as freely as Aunt
Faith's, my head clearing sufficiently to admit the thought of
Gervase, a realization that my protective impulses towards him
were far from over. If I held out my hand to him now—for he
would need a hand—would he take it? Did I want him to need
me again? Could I need him now? Was this our final opportunity?
I heard his voice in the hall and ran, finding him face to face

with Gideon, the precarious balance between them almost visibly tilting in an atrocious direction. And having dreaded this confrontation for years, having held myself for so long in readiness to prevent it, I stood now aghast with some kind of fog in my mind, and watched it happen.

"What should I offer you, Gideon? Congratulations?"

And although I had had the same thought an hour ago, the terrible mockery in Gervase's voice chilled me.

"You can go to hell, Gervase."

"I shouldn't wonder. And where are *you* going, Gideon? To Listonby to tell them the good news?"

"Get out of my way."

"Oh—I reckon you'll make sure of that."

"I reckon I might."

And with an accompanying obscenity I had not heard before but easily understood, he put the flat of his hand on Gervase's chest and pushed hard.

I shook my head, cleared it, and somehow put myself between them, relying not on strength to keep them apart but on the fact that as boys they had been trained not to hit girls, that gentlemen did not strike ladies. And even then there was some more pushing and shoving, Gideon rock-hard, his eyes completely blank, Gervase like some kind of cold flame, my intervention merely making it harder for them to get at one another.

A scandalous, ridiculous performance in any circumstances, appalling in these. "Stop it!" I shrieked, becoming ridiculous too, striking out with my fists in all directions, this feminine violence which ordinarily would have amused them reducing their own to a point where insults began to seem more appropriate than blows.

"You didn't know what you had in her," hissed Gervase, shaking now with hatred and hurt. "Talk about pearls before swine—and you were the swine all right, Chard."

"I don't have to defend myself to an idle parasite—and a bloody alley-cat, like you."

"Then try defending yourself to a hanging judge—that's what I'd like to see."

"I told you, Gervase—get out of my way and out of my sight—*now*."

"And out of *your* house too, I reckon. Is that it, Gideon?"

There was no answer.

"I see," said Gervase. "Then listen here, Chard, and I'll tell you what you can do with this house, and those mills, and everything else that goes with them."

He told him, explicitly, obscenely, with a total and damning contempt. And when he had done—when he had entirely slaughtered the Barforth side of himself—I ran after him down the long, stone steps into the garden and caught him on the carriage-drive, walking fast towards the stable block.

"Gervase—oh Gervase, not like this—just a moment—"

But his nerve had snapped now, he was wild and very close to tears, and shook off my hand with a shudder as if it burned him or soiled him.

"Leave me alone."

And when I would not, he stood for a moment in front of me, took my shoulders in hands that hurt and shook me just once but very hard.

"You heard me, Grace. I told him what to do with the house and the mills and whatever else goes with them. That includes you, Grace. You ought to know that. *Now* will you leave me alone?"

I watched as he disappeared around the corner, and then turned and walked back to the house, each step taken as if through water, my skirt an impossible weight around my legs, the sensation one has in dreams of movement impeded by unseen hands, of running through a barrier of weariness and going nowhere.

Gideon was standing in the open doorway, the light behind him outlining the powerful set of his shoulders, the extent of his self-assurance and his authority; Gideon, controlled and immovable, the natural leader of the herd thriving on his power to drive his rivals away. Fortune-hunter no longer, since the fortune was assured, but the dominant male of the clan, the old man in the house behind him no longer desiring to challenge him, the young man who might have challenged him having proved unwilling and unequal.

"Let him be," he told me calmly, in no doubt that I—a woman of the clan—must obey him. "Let him go to earth for a while—it can do no harm. And you, Grace, come back inside."

18

SHE HAD MADE MANY MISTAKES in her life, which had, in the end, proved fatal to her. In her place I would not have been deceived by Charles Heron, and had I consented to a marriage of convenience I would have accepted its limitations far better than she had done. I would not have gone away with Robin Ashby, but had I done so I would have been less easily broken and quicker to mend. Being made of tougher, coarser stuff, I would have survived where finespun Venetia had not. Being less hopeful, I was less prone to disappointment. Being less honest, I was better able to compromise. But I expected no one, when my time came, to mourn me with the intensity so many of us mourned for her, no one to feel, as I now felt, that the world had grown cooler and dimmer, infinitely impoverished, for the sorry waste of her.

I had been unable at first to contemplate her funeral, but the mundane requirements of mourning had occupied my mind and I managed to stand at her graveside on that blustery March day without dwelling too closely on what the coffin contained. I had not looked at her, had refused all blandishments to try from those who assured me she was only "sleeping," that she looked "so very beautiful" when I knew she was dead and could find nothing beautiful in that.

I stood in stony immobility, irritated by the tears of Miss Mandelbaum and Mrs. Rawnsley, by the stately gesture with which Mrs. Sheldon lifted her veil and dabbed a wisp of cambric to her eyes, by the hushed and overblown condolences of Thomas Sheldon MP, who always attended the funerals of his richer constituents; irritated most of all by the vicar, a great favourite with Mrs. Agbrigg, who appeared to find it a matter for rejoicing that she had been too good for this world and was now a resident in a "better place."

The funeral was, of course, a major event, all five of the Barforth mills being closed for the day, so that the steep slope of Kirkgate leading to the parish church was lined six deep with Barforth employees craning their necks to watch the spectacle of upper-class Cullingford on parade; the black silk gowns beaded with jet, the hats with their black satin bows and black feathers; the women of the immediate family in knee-length mourning veils; the black-draped carriages and the black horses; the fun, I suppose, of identifying each party as it arrived, Aunt Caroline's coach with its ducal crest proving a firm favourite.

There were mourners, too, from far afield, coming to pay their respects not to Venetia, who was unknown to them, but to her husband, her father, her grandfather, Sir Joel Barforth, whose name lived on and whose widow was here today, standing for the first time in twenty-five years between her sons; Aunt Faith clinging to Sir Blaize's other arm, my mother-in-law standing up very straight and then suddenly leaning—for the first time in years—against her husband.

The widower stood among his own kin, maintaining a grave but otherwise impassive countenance, Aunt Caroline scarcely knowing what expression to adopt since she had not liked Venetia but was troubled by so young a death, Blanche looking tearful and out of sorts, Sir Dominic, who was probably very bored, looking every inch a baronet.

I stood with my own family and with a tightly controlled, not quite sober Liam Adair, my hand on my father's arm, glad even of Mrs. Agbrigg to shield me from Gervase, for I had not seen him since the night of Venetia's death and refused to demean myself by looking too closely at him when he appeared on the fringes of the crowd, his face as sickly and unreal as candlewax.

We walked away, all of us in the same direction, except Gervase who, remaining at the graveside a moment, went off down a path which would lead him nowhere but away from his family, and from me. We got into our carriages and drove back to Tarn Edge, where I served tea to the ladies, spirits to the gentlemen, conferred with Mrs. Winch about luncheon for those mourners who, having some distance to travel, might require it; functioned, in fact, like the machine I had become.

But the animosity to which I had become accustomed among my relations was absent today, Sir Blaize Barforth taking and holding his brother's hand for a long moment in the churchyard and thereafter staying closely at his side, while Aunt Caroline had no wish to pursue her feud with a woman who had lost her only daughter. They sat all together by the drawing-room fire when the guests had gone, the three children of Sir Joel Barforth, Blaize, Nicholas and Caroline, with their spouses and their mother, united if only imperfectly by distress, and talked quietly among themselves of neutral subjects, happier days.

"What is to become of the poor infant?" said Aunt Caroline, sensing a threat to Gideon, since this was not his child and already it was paining her to be obliged to pretend otherwise. But Mr. Barforth, never one to brook interference in his affairs, merely shook his head, and instead of informing her that the child, whatever else she might be, was *his* granddaughter, said wearily, "No need to fret, Caroline. There's enough to go round—more than enough, I reckon."

"I should hope so, Nicholas, considering the healthy state of the business my father left you. But I was not only referring to that. The child must be looked after, 'brought up'—Grace, dear, should you need advice at any time, I shall be very happy, for babies are not quite so simple as one supposes."

"Grace will manage all right," said my father-in-law, and there was an immediate chorus of family approval. "Of course she will." "Grace does everything so well." "How fortunate you are, Nicholas, to have her here—what a comfort to you— how very convenient!" "Grace is so fond of children."

Was I fond of children? What difference did it make? Here once again was a female task that must be performed. I was the obvious female person to perform it. It had occurred to no one that I might object, that I might have some other plan—some other hope or dream or desire—for my unique and unrepeatable life.

"I suppose you will be expecting to use the Chard christening gown," Aunt Caroline said to me with extreme reluctance a few days later, assuming already that I had taken on the authority, the responsibility of a mother.

"Of course she will," Blanche answered for me, being far less subservient to Aunt Caroline than she used to be. "I have brought it with me in the carriage. It was made for *giants*, Grace, I warn you, and you will have to stitch it around that little mite."

The christening was very painful. Blanche and I were the godmothers, still in our funeral black, Gideon, who should, I thought, have insisted on using the chapel at Listonby, looking just faintly embarrassed in this parish church of Cullingford, where he had married the wife who had left him and was now baptizing her child, not his. While Gervase, who was a blood relation and should have offered himself as godfather to his sister's daughter, was not there. Nevertheless the ceremony was performed, the duty done. We took an anonymous little creature wrapped in costly lace to church that day and brought home with us Miss Claire Chard, riding in the victoria with her Aunt Blanche—who had chosen her name—her Chard cousins, Matthew and Francis, and her Aunt Grace; the man who had agreed to call himself her father riding alongside with the man who would allow her to call him Uncle Dominic, while behind them, in his own carriage, there came the man with a sudden sprinkling of grey in his hair who was most decidedly her grandfather.

I had dinner that night with my father-in-law, the two of us alone in the high, panelled room among a splendour of crystal and silver, served as deferentially as if we had been at a banquet. The child was upstairs in her nursery, expensively tended. Gideon had taken the London train and would be back the day after tomorrow. Gervase was not there.

I left Mr. Barforth to his brandy and cigars and sat alone in the drawing-room, drinking my coffee and glancing with resignation at the pile of letters of condolence to which I must reply. This was my life. Gideon would return with his fine cambric shirts to be laundered, his well-cut coats to be pressed, and before long there would be his friends to entertain again, his recherché little dinners, his sophisticated appetites. I would visit my father on Sunday afternoons and go to London occasionally to see Blanche. I would argue mildly the tea-table issues of the women's cause as understood by Miss Mandelbaum and would be mildly irritated by the narrowness of Miss Tighe, the noble insistence of Mrs. Sheldon in considering herself not as a person in her own right but as Thomas Sheldon's wife. The child would grow. Gervase would not be there. Eventually Gideon would marry again, a woman whose wealth and solid family connections would make her a power at Tarn Edge. My father-in-law would not live forever. Where would Gervase be then?

"Grace, are you not well?" Mr. Barforth said, coming into the room and sitting down heavily in the chair opposite mine.

"Oh yes—quite well."

"Aye—so you would tell me even if you were in agony. Grace—there is something I ought to tell you."

"Yes?" But I was suddenly very tired, my eyelids aching for sleep, and could muster no curiosity.

"It concerns the Galton estate."

And even then, knowing how closely it must also concern Gervase, I could not stir myself to more than a faint interest.

"I have made the Abbey over to my wife, Grace, in such a manner that it is hers absolutely, to be disposed of at her wish, not mine. I wonder if you know what that means?"

"That you have set her free."

He smiled. "She may see it that way. But there is rather more to it than that."

"I know. It means she can give it to Gervase and that he, with the income from his ten per cent of your business, can live like his Uncle Peregrine, except that Gervase has turned thirty now and I believe Peregrine Clevedon never got so far."

"And you feel I've let you down?"

"Why should you concern yourself with me?"

"Don't talk like a fool, girl," he said brusquely. "It can't suit you to have that estate in your husband's hands. I knew that very well when I took my decision. My choice was between what suited you and what suited my wife, and I chose my wife. Something was owing to her. I paid—and since you may have to pay too—well, Grace, I rarely feel called upon to explain myself but I think you'd best listen to me for a minute or two. You haven't lived in my house all this time without knowing how matters stand between me and Georgiana. It might make things easier for you to know why. She married me for my money. That's no secret and it seemed fair enough at the time. I married her because I wanted her, and I suppose it wasn't all her fault that I got more than I bargained for. The fascination didn't last and I'm a poor loser—always have been. It struck me that I wasn't cut out for close relationships and so I made up my mind to keep to the things I was suited for—running the mills and making a profit. There's no reason to be ashamed of that. Well—I could have kicked that lad of mine into shape, I reckon, if I'd got myself involved with him. And when he didn't shape up on his own, I gave up too soon. I can train my managers and my son-in-law—by God, I can! The training I put them through is so damned hard that the job itself seems easy by comparison. But I can keep my distance, you see, from them and it would have brought me too close to Gervase. So—if you feel the need to blame somebody for the way he is, you can start by blaming me. You can call me a fool too, if you like, Grace—a damned fool. I kept my distance from Venetia, too. I denied myself all the things she could have been to me and what have I gained by it? It hasn't made losing her any easier—by Christ it hasn't!"

We sat for a moment in a strangling silence and then, gruffly, quite painfully, he demanded: "What else could I have done when she went off that first time? And I didn't drag her down the aisle to Gideon. Damnation! I even thought she'd put up more of a fight than she did, which was no fight at all, just "Yes, father—if you think that's best"—just that, no argument. And it *was* best. I had my own reasons for wanting him but I knew he'd look after her, do the right thing—I knew he *could* look after her, for he's got a head on his shoulders and an eye to the main chance—And what's wrong with that? So—when she didn't argue—it struck me that, at the bottom of her, she probably fancied him. He's a good-looking man—why shouldn't she have fancied him? What else could I have done?"

"I don't know."

"Then I'll tell you. I could have made more of an effort with my own wife in the first place, I reckon. If I'd handled my business like I've handled my marriage, I'd be a pauper now, Grace, and no mistake."

Once again we sat in a tense silence and then, leaning suddenly towards me, an undemonstrative man who resented the occasional necessity to demonstrate his feelings, he said angrily, "God dammit! Grace, you are valued here with us. You know that, don't you?"

"Yes, I know."

"I'm glad to hear it. See that you don't forget it. We need you here. In fact I'll go further and tell you straight that I don't know how we'd manage without you. This house is yours, Grace, for all practical purposes—entirely yours—and I shall allow no one to interfere with that, whoever they may be."

I let a few more days go by, coped with the small upheaval invariably occasioned by Gideon's return, and then chose a bright blue and white morning to drive over to Galton.

Mrs. Barforth was walking by the Abbey stream, two young retrievers splashing excitedly in the water, a black and white sheepdog puppy hesitating on the bank, one cautious paw extended to test the ripples; and I was glad to see no sign of Gervase.

"Grace dear—I was hoping to see you. I suppose you have heard my news?"

"About the estate? Yes. Do you feel differently, knowing it to be yours?"

She smiled, shaded her eyes against the sun to check the

progress of the young dogs who were chasing last autumn's leaves now on the opposite bank.

"Do you know," she said, "it is the oddest thing—I have lived years of my life for this moment, longed for it and taken every opportunity I could to bring it about. It seemed of the most desperate importance—truly the difference between life and death. Now I have it, and nothing seems really changed. I suppose I must have known deep down, all the time, that my husband would not really sell me up lock, stock and barrel as he used to threaten. Yes, that must be it. How very nice to know that, in a way, I have always trusted him."

She slipped her arm into mine and we walked across the ancient, unsteady little bridge, the gentle sheepdog at our heels, the two retrievers greeting us with boisterous rapture at the other side, leaping all muddy and eager against our skirts.

"What will you do now, mother-in-law?"

"Do? Must I do anything? Well—I might spread my wings and fly away. But I don't think so. Twenty years ago my husband thought I might fly to Julian Flood, which is why he clipped my wings and put salt on my tail—not from jealousy, you understand, but because he believed Julian would not be good for me."

"Would you have gone to him?"

"Oh yes," she said, smiling at the stony track ahead of her, seeing beyond it to a wealth of contented memory. "Yes. I would have gone to Julian had my husband allowed it. And I might even have been very happy. If I have a talent at all, it is for friendship. These storms of passion, you know, these truly gigantic desires—well, I fear they are a little outside my range. But I am very comfortable with friendship. And next to my brother Peregrine, Julian was the best friend I had. When Peregrine died, he often seemed my only friend. That was the ingredient I found lacking in my relationship with my husband. We were never friends."

She bent down to murmur a word of encouragement to the timid collie bitch and to restrain the gun dogs who had begun to root ferociously in the ground.

"Yes," she said and then, as if suddenly making up her mind, took a deep breath and muttered rapidly, wanting it to be over and done. "You have asked me what I mean to do. What do you mean to do, Grace? For I must tell you that, for the time being, I do not think Gervase will return to Tarn Edge. Nor do I think he will stay here, either."

"Where will he go, then?" And my voice was sharp, very cold, hurtful to my own ears.

"Dearest—I don't know—what can I say—?"

But her concern, her affection, her hand coming to rest gently on my arm, were all intolerable to me and I shrugged her away.

"You can tell me nothing I cannot see for myself, and indeed you should be obliged to tell me nothing at all, since Gervase ought to be here to say it for you. But I already know. He married me, as your husband married you, on an impulse that did not last. I believed he loved me, as you believed your husband loved you, and I relied on that. I feel cheated now, as you did. Can you blame me?"

"No. I do not blame you. I do not blame him either."

"Naturally you would say so."

"Why? Because I am his mother? And because I have always defended him? Grace, I do not defend him blindly and I am ready to accept my own share of the blame. When he was born and they first put him into my arms, I looked at him and saw my own son, a fine, red-headed Clevedon, and I forgot that his name was Barforth. And when he gave every sign of being a Clevedon, with no inclination for business and a downright aversion to that foul machinery of theirs, I encouraged him. I shielded him from discipline, told lies for him when he ran away from school, because it was a school for manufacturers, you see, not a school for gentlemen such as my brother and the Chards attended. When his father and I separated, his loyalty was all for me, such a little boy as he was then, saying he would always look after me—And I was always here, to hide him from school, from his father, from the mill. My only excuse is that I sincerely believed that the whole of his heart was here, at Galton."

"And is it not?"

"How can it be, Grace? He would not have married you had he been certain of his true inclinations. He had the mills within his grasp on your marriage, for my husband would have known how to tame Gideon had Gervase remained constant—had he continued to try. He did not remain constant. He let the mills go. He has Galton now, if he chooses to take it. I am not sure he will. Grace, if he felt the need of a breathing-space, a trip abroad, perhaps, alone, so that he could think, make a decision on his future—would you allow it?"

"Could I prevent it?"

She shook her head, her cheeks very flushed, her manner hesitant and embarrassed in a way which was unlike her.

"Oh, not physically or legally I suppose. I am simply asking if you could bring yourself to understand his need—oh dear, how very hard this is!"

"Yes, very hard and I imagine it will become harder still. I believe you are trying to tell me he has already decided to go abroad, and you are asking me not to make a fuss. Is that it?"

"My dear, I suppose it is."

"And he is running away from me as he used to run away from school, is he not? Well—is he not?"

"Oh dear, yes—yes, he is. Grace, it is so easy to view him as no more than a spoiled and worthless man but you saw far more than that in him once, and I cannot believe you to have been mistaken. We have asked too much of him, his father and I—pulled him in too many diverse directions, and now he *must* have time and solitude if his conflict is ever to be resolved. Failure—yes, of course he feels he has failed—at everything, not least as a husband. Enormous confusion—yes, of course. But Grace—my dear—I do not think he is running away from you, nor even from himself. He is trying to *find* himself. Please allow him to try."

And once again I saw her flush with embarrassment, sensed an uneasy movement of her mind, warning me that although her words were no less than the truth they were not the whole of it.

"He wishes to leave me, then—for good?"

"He has not said so. In his present state of mind he could not risk a decision of that magnitude."

"I see. And so I am to wait, am I—how long? Six months, a year or two? I am not to bother him—is that it?—until he feels able to make up his mind?"

We walked on for a while in silence, my anger extending my stride, quickening my pace and then gradually evaporating in its own futility. He had left me years ago and what was being asked of me now was perfectly in keeping with the conventions. Blanche and Dominic did not live together in any true sense. Certainly my parents-in-law did not. My own mother had withdrawn from her marriage by the gradual but complete process of making herself an invalid. It had not escaped my attention that ladies from such different walks of life as Mrs. Rawnsley of Cullingford and Mrs. Goldsmith of Berlin were content to live almost separately although under the same roof as their husbands. They had made an "arrangement" as I was now being asked to do, had retained the status, the protection, the *respectability* of marriage without the man himself. They had not made a fuss. They had obeyed the rules and had done their duty. And my own duty was clear. I had a position to keep up, a home to run, Venetia's child to raise. I had a life of my own. "One life," Venetia's voice whispered in my memory, from the days when she had believed her own life would be glorious and she had still trusted me. "This is the only life I'll ever have and my one chance to get it right." Was this my one chance too? Or had the choice been made for me long ago by my upbringing, bred into me by those generations of women behind me who had submitted to the limitations of their bodies and their easily aroused, easily exploited emotions; who had believed without question that their own claims on life must always be inferior to the claims of their children and of their men?

I was a decent woman and decent women made sacrifices. It was the basic instinct of womankind to protect the young. I possessed that instinct, and who would raise Venetia's child if I did not but a procession of governesses working not for love but for wages? And how could I explain myself to my father? "One life," Venetia whispered, "one only," and then, with sudden mockery: "But at least you will have your dignity."

We walked back down the hill and across the bridge, the air sparkling and clean, the dogs still playing around our feet, even the little collie exhilarated now by the scent of the new grass and the rich burden of the earth, forgetting her timidity at this promise of a fragrant springtime.

"You must see the kittens, Grace," and dutifully I went into her parlour to kneel by a cat-basket overflowing with minute tortoiseshell bodies, as dutifully drank my tea and ate the muffins she seemed anxious to serve me, aware, as I did so, that through her talk of cats and chickens and apple-preserves, she was acutely uneasy, badly troubled in her conscience.

I took my hat and gloves, and prepared to go outside again, my carriage at the door.

"Will Gervase agree to see me—here, if he cannot face Tarn Edge?"

"My dear, I believe it is *you* he cannot face."

"Ah—I thought he might *have* to see me, to tell me himself whatever it is that you—quite clearly—are holding back."

She bit her lip, her face flushing again a most uncharacteristic crimson, tears starting in her eyes.

"Oh dear, I could wish you less astute—"

"There is something else, then?"

"I am obliged to deny it."

"You mean you have been instructed to keep it from me. I shall find out, you know."

And for a long while she could not bring herself to speak but stood nervously clasping and unclasping her hands, her loyalty visibly and hurtfully torn, until finally she gave a deep sigh and raising her head gave me a look that held both determination and compassion.

"I should not tell you, Grace. There is no need for you to know."

"I am not a child to be kept in the dark."

"It will hurt you, Grace."

"I am hurt already. And if it is of such great importance, perhaps I have a right to know. If there are decisions to be made, then I think I *must* know."

"Very well. Diana Flood is to have a child five months from now, and since she and her husband have been apart for something more than a year . . . My dear—"

"Yes," I said, the high pitch of my voice taking me by surprise, my words rising straight up from a deep source of bitterness I had never before acknowledged. "Gervase, of course, is the father. Good. I am glad—yes, I am so glad—that he can do at least one thing that I cannot, that he can have children, whereas I must make do with other people's, with waifs and strays and orphans that are not wanted. Oh—pay no attention to me—none—"

I righted myself after a while, Mrs. Barforth standing quietly beside me, subduing her own feelings while I brought mine to heel and leashed them with a hard hand, seeing no profit to anyone in allowing them to escape again. And when I could, I asked her curtly, "What steps do they mean to take?"

"My dear, the usual ones—the sad things which are always done on such occasions. Julian will send her away somewhere to give birth in secret, for it is not the first time such a thing has occurred in his family, nor in mine, nor in the Chards either. It has all been done before, and *must* be done, for her husband will be Lord Sternmore when his uncle dies, and when there is a title to inherit a man must be very sure of his eldest son."

"You do realize that this is—*dreadful*?"

"Yes, I do."

"And Gervase?"

"He will accept financial responsibility, and then I imagine Diana will go off to India to brave the climate and her husband. The baby will be looked after and then, perhaps nine or ten years from now, I may offer a home to an orphan child, a distant relative, perhaps. Or Diana, even, may find it possible to offer that orphan a home, particularly if in the meantime she has supplied the colonel adequately with heirs. It appears—usually—to work well enough in the end.''

"And Diana Flood accepts this?''

"She does.''

"Why does she? You say Gervase will accept financial responsibility for the child. Has he not offered more than that? You tell me he wishes to go abroad. Has he not asked her to go with him?''

"I believe the offer was made—yes—yes, he did ask her to go abroad with him and live there as his wife. Yes, he did.''

"And she? Please tell me the truth.''

"Shall I? Yes, I see that it is only right. She seemed, at first, inclined to accept. But in the end—and after consultation with her family—she declined to place herself in so precarious—so very perilous—a situation. She has, after all, a great deal to lose. The Sternmore title is a very old one and although there is no great fortune to go with it, the land being somewhat encumbered, the house upon it is very noble—even rather famous. Lady Sternmore of Sternmore must always be a person of consequence. The adulterous wife of Colonel Flood living openly with her lover and their bastard child must be considered as one socially dead. And lovers, you know, do not always remain faithful. No one could guarantee her that—certainly not Gervase. He is in love with her now but it was pointed out to her that, not too long ago, he was in love with you. Forgive me, dear, but you asked me for the truth.''

"You are saying she is a conventional woman who will play the game. Gervase is not a conventional man.''

"In this case he is obliged to be.''

"And who else knows of 'this case' besides ourselves?''

"My husband. And your father. We felt it only right that he should be informed.''

"How scandalous that no one felt it right to inform me.''

"I have just informed you, Grace, and you have not thanked me for it.''

What had actually changed? I had known of the affair and had taken no action against it. I had already grown accustomed to the sterile existence of a woman separated from her husband. What had changed except that our separation, which had been known only to ourselves, was now to be acknowledged by a few others, by my father-in-law who had already reassured me as to my position at Tarn Edge, and by my father who would pretend he knew nothing of it to protect my feelings, just as I had tried to protect his. What difference? None at all except the hardening, or perhaps the recognition of a resolve to win for myself an identity, to put an end to this eternal legal childhood which added me to the sum total of a man who did not care for me. Perhaps that—and the dangerous, disturbing memory of Venetia.

She had looked at me sometimes, during her last few months, in an odd manner, her eyes clear and cool and pitying, picking out each one of the deceits by which I lived and shaking her head over them sadly but with a hint of amusement that said: "Poor Grace. She is just like the rest of them—she will endure any insult, any hardship, any wrong, so long as it *looks* right." But would it comfort me on my dying day to know I had obeyed the rules, had shown myself at all times to be a dutiful and reasonable woman?

"What has he done to her?" Mrs. Barforth had asked me, speaking of Robin Ashby and Venetia, and I had replied that he had treated her as the kind of woman she had wished to be.

"Are there such women, Grace?"

"I hope so."

Were there, indeed, women who did not simply allow things to happen to them—as we had been taught women should—but who took action on their own behalf, who *made* things happen in accordance with their own judgement and their own desires? Was I such a woman? Most fervently I hoped so.

There had been in my mind, in my conscience, a mountain to climb, an enormous, outrageous decision looming on my horizon, an impossible decision and a frightening one since I knew of no one who had ever taken it before me. Yet, as I drove back alone to Tarn Edge, it struck me that I was very calm—too calm—and at some point on that familiar journey the decision which should have crushed me and torn me apart and from which in the end I should have retreated, to slide meekly—almost gratefully—back into my feminine mould; that decision was somehow made without conflict, even without much awareness, an imperceptible passing from a state of desperate uncertainty to a state of being quite sure. Venetia had known, when she sent Robin Ashby away from her, that there had been no other course to take. I now understood and was comforted by the same complete assurance. There was nothing else I could do.

Chillingworth greeted me in the hall with some tale of

calling-cards, a note from Mr. Chard, some crisis in the nursery. I glanced at the cards and at the few words in Gideon's large, bold hand, warning me he would require an earlier dinner. I went to the nursery on the second floor and then came down again without going inside, afraid, perhaps, that Claire Chard, with her mother's fine sensibilities, would guess my intentions and accuse me of treachery.

I packed a small bag, no bigger than the one Venetia had taken when she went away, and leaving instructions for the week's menus and a few, quite false words of explanation with Mrs. Winch, had myself driven to Fieldhead, where I enquired of my father, in our cool, restrained Agbrigg fashion, how best I might obtain a divorce.

19

MY FATHER WAS A MAN of acute perception, of a brilliant and clear-sighted intelligence, accustomed throughout his life to the untangling of complex problems and situations. But even he, in his aloof manner, seemed stunned by my request and not at all disposed to treat it seriously.

"You have had a shock," he said. "Yes, I am acquainted with the circumstances in which your husband finds himself with regard to Mrs. Flood. And however deplorable it may be, I am bound to inform you that it is not unusual. Yes, you have certainly had a shock. I deeply regret it and can only suggest you remain here at Fieldhead for a day or so, to compose yourself."

And when I assured him that I was already very composed he added sharply. "Good heavens! Grace, it is a sorry business and I let my displeasure be felt when Nicholas Barforth came to tell me of it. But these things do happen, you know. Of course you know, and one must retain a sense of proportion. Perhaps it is the Floods one should pity the most, for either the woman must give away her child or the husband must tolerate a cuckoo in his nest—unpleasant for both, whatever they decide."

"I see, father. And all that is required of me is to forgive and forget?"

"Ah," he said, his long, pale eyes glinting with a wry humour. "You are a woman, my dear. Surely that is what women are made for?"

He let two days go by without another word and then on the third evening he called me again into his study, the same dark, panelled room where he had explained to me the terms of my marriage contract and had given me my mother's jewellery.

"Sit down, Grace." And for a few moments he barely glanced at me, occupying himself with the heavy, leather-bound volumes on his desk, his manner quietly efficient, thoroughly professional.

"You made a certain request to me the other evening. After thirty-six hours of reflection, I would like to know if you are of the same mind?"

"I am."

"You amaze me. Very well. No doubt when you have heard what I have to tell you then you will change it."

He had not practised the law for a very long time, had never in the whole of his experience handled a case of divorce and had therefore been obliged to return to his books. What did I know of my own rights in this matter? Nothing. He had thought as much and having made a thorough study—his intellect responding to the challenge after so long—he was in a position to inform me that, until some slight changes in the law a mere twenty years ago, I would in effect have had no rights at all. Divorces, of course, were granted before then, but only by the passage of a private bill through Parliament and almost exclusively as the result of a husband's complaint against his wife, the House of Lords in particular taking the view that a nobleman unlucky enough to have married an adulterous woman should be allowed to free himself from the entanglement so that he might remarry and provide himself with heirs.

In two hundred years, my father told me in his precise, neutral tone, only four women had been granted divorces against their husbands, a certain Mrs. Dawson having had all six of her petitions refused only so short a time ago as 1848, despite her conclusive proof that her husband had not only committed adultery but had beaten her with a horsewhip. The law, my father said, shrugging cool shoulders, had never regarded adultery on the part of a husband as being in any way so serious as adultery in a wife. And if one could not applaud the morality of such a view, my father thought one could bow to its logic, since a married man could be so easily tricked into believing himself the father of a bastard child who would inherit his property, while a married woman, who had no property in any case, could not.

But the high cost of the Parliamentary divorce had placed it far beyond the reach of all but the wealthiest in the land, and even among these few the fact that a woman who separated herself from her husband invariably lost sight of her children tended to make women submit more readily to the domestic yoke. And even for a woman who did not greatly care for her children, or who had none to lose, there remained the question of how and on what she might live. She could not take away with her any moneys she had possessed at the time of her marriage, since the very sacrament of marriage had made such possessions her husband's. She could not, by any act of separation, acquire a legal identity of her own, but remained so far as the courts were concerned an appendage of the man who had been her husband. She could not make a will, even if she had anything to bequeath, could not earn a living since there had never been any work for gentlewomen to do, and would have the greatest difficulty in denying her estranged husband's claim on anything she might herself inherit unless it had been settled on her separately in a most watertight manner. It was not unknown for a husband to live apart from his wife for twenty years and then to return, sell her valuables and her furniture, possess himself of her savings, and then to abscond again. Nor was it unknown for a man to remove his children from his wife's care and place them in the home of his mistress, the separated wife having no right of appeal against him and no hope of seeing her children again, unless he graciously allowed it.

However, in 1857 some few changes had been made, divorce being taken away from the ecclesiastical courts and the House of Parliament—a move bitterly opposed by Mr. Gladstone—and given a court of its own, these new proceedings being much simpler and cheaper, and having the decided advantage, from a feminine point of view, of restoring the divorced wife to the staus of a single woman.

Under this new form of divorce a woman could retain without encumbrance any money earned, inherited or otherwise acquired by her *after* the date on which her marriage had been dissolved. Her legal identity was now returned to her. She could enter into contracts and take legal action if they were broken, she could defend herself if necessary by suing anyone who slandered her or anyone who owed her money, matters which previously could only have been handled through her husband. She could even make her own will and leave her property where she chose. And, of course, it had for some time been possible, if the court thought fit, to grant the divorced wife access to her children, and in some cases even to award her custody of any infants under the age of seven years. Had I followed him so far, my father wished to know?

"Yes father. And how may this divorce be obtained?"

"I will tell you. In the case of a man it is amazingly simple. He has only to prove his wife's adultery and the thing is as good as done. A woman, however, is obliged to prove her husband's adultery coupled with another offence."

"What offence?"

"One of a number. I have them all listed here. One of them, no doubt, will serve to use against Gervase. In fact one of them *must* serve or you will have no case at all. Shall we proceed? Well then, has he been guilty of adultery coupled with incest— that is a physical relationship with a mother or a sister?"

"Good heavens! father, you know he has not."

"You are shocked, I see."

"I am revolted."

"Quite so. It is a revolting business, Grace, and if you go on with it you must be prepared for a great deal of unpleasantness. I would do you no service if I attempted to conceal it."

And taking up his pen he neatly and coolly crossed out the words "incestuous adultery" from his list.

"So much for that. Bigamy, I suppose, is not a possibility?"

"No father."

He raised an eyebrow, crossed out the words "bigamy with adultery" and gave a slight shrug.

"Sodomy, Grace. Do you know what that is? And bestiality?"

"*Father.*"

"My dear, I am not speaking to you as a father but as a legal adviser. I am interpreting the law as it stands, and I must ask you—as someone else could well ask you—if your husband has been guilty of adultery coupled with either of the above. And you would do well to restrain your quite natural repugnance and answer me calmly."

"Are there really men who do these things?"

"Grace, that is not a calm answer. *Of course* there are men who do these things. There are other men who despoil eight-year-old virgins, and women who offer their little daughters to be despoiled. We are talking of Gervase."

"No—no, of course he is not guilty of that. Is there nothing else?"

"Yes. There is rape, which I suppose we can dismiss—rape, need I add, not of yourself but of some other woman, since no man can be said to have raped his wife, who is not entitled to refuse him. And then there is adultery coupled with desertion—"

"Why, yes, that will do, surely, for his mother has told me he will not return to Tarn Edge and he has not asked me to join him anywhere else."

"—with desertion, Grace, that has lasted a minimum of two years."

"Oh, father—so long?"

"Yes, Grace."

But, having allowed me to suffer this acute disappointment for a moment or two, he neatly folded his list, placed it in a drawer and gave me his faint smile.

"However—"

"So there *is* something else to be done?"

"Yes, I do fear so. The adultery is well established, there can be no difficulty about that. Consequently, if you were to obtain a court order—or rather were I to obtain one on your behalf—instructing your husband to return to you and to restore to you your conjugal rights, and if he did not comply with the order within a period of six months, then divorce proceedings could be instituted against him."

"And would that order be difficult to obtain?"

"Apparently not. The difficulty—and I must warn you of this—is that your husband might obey it. For if he should return to Tarn Edge or invite you to live with him in any other home he may provide, then you will have no case against him. The adultery alone will not suffice and the desertion, my dear, could be made null and void at his choosing—any time he chose to make it so. You must keep that firmly in mind."

"I cannot think he will come back to me."

"My dear—and it pains me to say this—he may feel obliged to come back to you for Mrs. Flood's sake. He may see it as an act of gallantry towards her. I understand she wishes to conceal the affair and return to her husband. If you sue for divorce she can have no hope of that. And *your* husband might wish to spare her the social ruin it would entail—or pressure might be brought to bear on him to that effect. Have you considered that?"

I had not considered it. I considered it now and then shook my head, recognizing it as the first of many painful obstacles which would be put in my way. It was the first risk I was to encounter, the first occasion when I was required to choose between the interests of another person and my own. I would take the risk and I would choose myself.

"Father, I have made up my mind, you know. All I am asking you to do is legalize something which actually happened a long time ago. There is no marriage to dissolve. The marriage dissolved itself. It slipped away, little by little, and perhaps there never was very much of it to begin with. Gervase does not want me. I do not want him. There is no need for him to take any legal action to free himself. He can simply walk away, go wherever he chooses, live in the manner he thinks fit. I cannot. I am bound to him—shackled to him. He is not bound to me. And I will not—believe me, father, I will not continue to lead so false and futile a life. I am not afraid of the scandal. I would prefer to be the subject of Mrs. Rawnsley's gossip than the object of her pity.''

"Do not dismiss the Mrs. Rawnsleys of this world so lightly, Grace, for however trivial they may be when taken singly, when they come together they have great power."

"As I said, father—I am not afraid."

Once again he gave me his pale smile and carefully stacked his books away.

"Very well. We have established that you are not afraid and that you have made up your mind. Only one more question remains and I must insist that you answer it very carefully. How much of this, my dear, are you doing for yourself and how much for Venetia?"

I lowered my head for just a second and then raising it slowly met his eyes.

"You are very perceptive, father."

"Of course I am. I have an excellent mind, as you should know since you have been fortunate enough to inherit it."

"Fortunate? Do you think so? Surely it is better for a woman to be a little stupid and immensely good-natured. Surely that is best?"

"Easier, perhaps. But we are not concerned with ease. Nor are we concerned with avoiding the answers to awkward questions—at least, I hope we are not."

"No, father. I think Venetia would understand what I am doing and would want me to do it. She valued honesty and what broke her was being obliged to live a lie."

"No, Grace. What broke her was her discovery that she lacked the strength to live the truth."

I looked down again, my eyes filling with tears which, knowing his aversion to weeping, I hastily blinked away.

"Yes, father, I do know that. I believe I have that strength. And Venetia, you know, was not weak. There were times when she had great courage—greater than mine—although she could never sustain it. She felt more joy or sorrow than I feel, and consequently her disillusion went far deeper. What she lacked was resolution. I do not."

"I am well aware of that. I wish merely to be sure that you are fighting your own campaign, not hers. She was an enchanting young lady, I willingly concede it, but I cannot help thinking that her troubles were largely of her own making."

"No, father. She handled them badly, but she did not make them. No, no, please let me finish—I am not suggesting anyone treated her with deliberate cruelty or wished to do so. Her father and Gideon behaved as fathers and husbands are supposed to behave. They obeyed the rules society has laid down for men and women to follow—rules, like our laws, which were made by men and so *must* suit men rather better. Venetia was simply not the kind of woman society envisaged when those rules were made. Neither am I. For a long time I have been able to compromise. Venetia could neither conceal her unhappiness nor live with it. Her death has made me see the futility in living with mine. Father—I would say this to no one else—but I almost believe her elopement with Robin Ashby was a deliberate act of self-destruction. I almost believe she knew she could not survive it but chose to have something—just a year—that *mattered* to her."

I was trembling violently, and to my surprise he let his hand rest on my shoulder and pressed it just once, evenly and firmly.

"Very well. We shall proceed then—shall we?—with caution. And for your first move, my dear, I would like you to leave Cullingford for a week or two. Go to Scarborough to your grandmother or to my cottage at Grasmere, it makes no difference. Take long walks in the fresh air, consider your situation from every angle, and on your return you may instruct me again. I need not tell you, I suppose, that you must have no communication of any kind with Gervase, since the merest hint of collusion between you would entirely destroy your case. A husband and wife may not conspire together, my dear, to end their marriage, indeed they may not. If the case of Barforth v. Barforth ever sees the light of day, one Barforth must be shown as guilty, the other as entirely innocent, and there must be no hint or suspicion that you encouraged him in his guilt or in any way condoned it. These are criminal proceedings and must be treated as such. I trust you can be ready to leave tomorrow?"

I went to Grasmere, to test myself perhaps, since I had spent my happiest days with Gervase among these lakes and hills. But walking through the fine spring days as I had been instructed, I found myself thinking mainly of Venetia, acknowledging her as the source of my decision but not of my determination to follow it through. I would do the things she should have done. I would find the steadfastness of purpose she had lacked. I would be the woman she had dimly perceived in the mind of Robin Ashby, a woman strong enough to live the life of a man, to bear his responsibilities and thus lay claim to his privileges. I would be free, not to smoke a cigar or attend a cock-fight, but to think, decide, take charge of my life. I would carry my own burdens and choose my own pleasures. I would suffer the consequences of my errors and reap whatever reward I could on the occasions when I happened to be in the right.

I would be resolute. I *was* resolute, even on those treacherous evenings when the air was warm and scented with all the entice-ments of April, rendering me sleepless and forcing me to think of Gervase. He may well have deserved the blow I was preparing for him, but that did not make it easy to strike. And so I allowed my mind to proceed, as my father had said, with caution, no more than one step at a time. We had failed each other. My action now must hurt us both, but surely it would allow us in time to start afresh? Surely? But it did not seem the moment to dwell too closely on that.

My father wrote to me, setting out once again in grave lan-guage the procedure for divorce, its consequences, its dangers, neither forbidding me to proceed nor advising it, simply laying the facts before me in correct legal fashion. I replied that I had not changed my mind, and when I returned to Fieldhead three weeks later nothing had occurred to alter my decision.

"Very well," my father said, "I will apply to the courts for an order commanding your husband's return. And you, my dear, may sit here as quietly as you can and wait for the storm to break."

I expected unbridled anger from my father-in-law and when, on his first visit to Fieldhead, he sat for a while in Mrs. Agbrigg's hushed drawing-room, staring fixedly at her green and gold carpet, I interpreted his silence to mean the worst. But eventually he got up and stood on the hearthrug, his favourite vantage point, his back to the fire, his broad shoulders a little hollower than they used to be, not only the grey at his temples ageing him, and said in his abrupt, autocratic manner, "I suppose you realize that I could put a stop to all this—or at least your father and I together could put a stop to it. All we'd have to do, my girl, is to cut off your money—the allowance we've both been good enough to pay you all these years—and that would be the end of it. You'd be forced to come back to Tarn Edge then and play at being my son's wife whether you liked it or not, and whether he was even living there or not. That's the reason, I suppose, why thousands of women stay with husbands they don't care for and who don't care for them—for the sake of a roof and a blanket and a bite to eat. Now then—do you understand that?''

"Yes, I do."

"And if I was really set on it, young lady—if I really put my mind to it—I reckon I could persuade your father to clip your wings, since at the bottom of him he doesn't like the way matters are turning out any better than I do. He might be glad to see you back at Tarn Edge—glad of me to show him the way to get you there. Do you understand *that*?''

"Yes, I do."

"All right—just bear it in mind. And now I'll tell you what I *am* going to do. You brought money with you when you came to Tarn Edge and I'll see every penny paid back to you before you leave. There'll be no trouble about that.''

And because I knew he was thanking me for the effort I had made, expressing his affection in hard cash because that was the only way he could express it, I felt tears in my eyes.

"Thank you."

"Have you anything else to say to me—anything you'd like me to do?''

"Mr. Barforth—you do understand, don't you, about this court order? You do realize that I don't want Gervase to obey it?''

He smiled, sat down and shook his head, ruefully I thought, amused in spite of himself.

"There's no need for alarm, Grace. If you think I might drag him back to you by the scruff of his neck, then you can be at ease. I've got more sense than that. I reckon I've interfered in other people's marriages for the last time. He can sort himself out now, that son of mine, the best way he can.''

"Mr. Barforth, I wouldn't want you to punish him. I wouldn't want him to lose—I mean, to be made poor because of me. Really, I wouldn't.'' He lifted his dark, still handsome head and looked at me keenly.

"He has ten per cent of my business, Grace. He can live well on that.''

"And he couldn't lose it?''

"He could sell it, although the only customers he'd get would be me or Gideon. And you'll have to wait, like the rest of them, Grace, to find out what I mean to do with the Woolcombers and the Dyeworks and my eighty per cent of Barforth and Company.

Aye—I reckon you'll have to wait until the time comes to read my will.''

But he was not offended, and smiled when I replied, ''That will be soon enough.''

''I'll be off then, Grace. I just wanted you to know you'd be getting back your dowry.''

And I was acutely grateful that he had not mentioned tiny, helpless Claire, and his own deepening solitude.

Knowledge of my exact situation was reserved, of course, for a very few, but speculation as to the cause of my prolonged sojourn at Fieldhead grew quickly rife.

''My dear,'' Mrs. Sheldon murmured to me in her sedate manner, ''I cannot avoid the impression that something is troubling you, and there is a great deal of truth, you know, in the old saying that a trouble shared is a trouble halved.''

''I do not at all blame you for taking a holiday from Tarn Edge,'' Mrs. Rawnsley told me. ''Doing one's duty is well enough but I have often thought it scandalous how everything in that house is left to you. I would not wear myself out in their service, I can tell you, for it is not your house, after all, and not your child, and you will get small thanks for any of it when Mr. Gideon Chard brings home a new wife. I am entirely on your side, Grace dear—entirely in sympathy.''

While those ladies who were not sufficiently acquainted with me to hint or to pry came regularly to see Mrs. Agbrigg and to shower me with invitations to this and that which invariably contained the words ''and do, my dear, bring your husband.''

In these circumstances it was unwise of Sir Julian Flood to visit me at Fieldhead, the sight of his horse glimpsed through my window causing my stomach to lurch most painfully and my breathing to become far too rapid so that I had to walk downstairs very slowly to avoid the appearance of a woman badly flustered.

He was standing, as my father-in-law had done, on the hearthrug, a lean, dark, undeniably handsome man, the manorial lord of Cullingford whose family had dwelt here for three hundred years—when my family had been peasants or vagabonds or worse—and who now, although he was known to have gambled away what little money his spendthrift grandfather had left him— still had an air of distance about him, the disdain a man of high pedigree cannot always conceal in his dealings with his inferiors. Yet he was the man my mother-in-law had spoken of as her best friend, her salvation in the dark days after her brother had died, and I refused, in fact I could not afford, to be afraid of him.

"Mrs. Barforth. I trust you are well?"

"Quite well, thank you."

"And wondering what I'm doing here, I imagine. Although, really, there's not much cause for wonder."

"Sir Julian, I must tell you I think it improper of you to have come at all."

He laughed, his dark eyes brushing over me with the automatic appraisal he bestowed on horseflesh, womanflesh, particularly—and the suspicion caused me to flush with welcome indignation—women who had lost their caste or their reputations.

"Improper? Now that's not a word I'm much used to hearing, Mrs. Barforth. In my part of the world we tend to call it 'bad taste.' "

"You live ten miles away, Sir Julian."

"So I do, but it could be another world, m'dear, for all that—different manners, different values. I hope that we may manage to understand one another?"

"What is it you wish me to understand?"

"Well, I wish to put an end to this nonsense for one thing, m'dear. No need for it, you know. Shocking business—won't attempt to deny it—and nobody in the world could blame you for being peeved about it. But we can settle it in a civilized manner, surely?"

"Yes, of course. That is my intention."

His brows flew together in a frown, his face half suspicious, half ready to believe he had so easily got his way.

"You mean you've dropped this litigation?"

"I do not. I mean I intend to follow it through. *That* is the civilized solution."

He took a pace or two about the room, shooting at me from time to time a look of pure contempt, his nostrils dilating with it, his whole manner expressing regret that he had been born too late to settle this dispute, and any others, by having me flogged at the manorial cart-tail.

"I see. I see, Mrs. Barforth."

But eventually the realization that he could not evict me from my cottage nor refuse to renew the lease on my farm, that he had no real power over me at all, took the edge from his anger and he returned to the hearthrug, doing his best to calm himself, one hand restlessly clenching as if it missed the feel of a riding-whip.

"Civilized, is it, Mrs. Barforth, to drive a woman to her ruin? I wouldn't call that civilized."

"Neither would I."

"Then you'll be obliged to drop these proceedings, madam, unless you intend to make yourself responsible for the ruin of my niece. That's the plain truth, madam, and don't try to deny it."

A moment of silence, his anger snapping around me and something more than anger, for after all he had come to protect his own kin, his brother's daughter whom he had raised casually, perhaps, but as his own child, and no one could blame him for that. Silence, and then my own voice dropping cool words into it one by one, speaking slowly because I had dreaded this, and was not finding it easy.

"You are quite right that my petition for divorce will do harm to Mrs. Flood. I do not consider myself to blame for that."

"Who then?" he snarled, very nearly at the end of his tether.

"That is not for me to say."

There was another moment of silence, badly needed by us both, and then, remembering that he was here to defend his niece's reputation not to give himself the satisfaction of blackening mine, he overcame his temper and smiled.

"Come now, Mrs. Barforth, we will gain nothing by quarrelling. Have you really considered, I wonder, what this could mean to Diana? I don't excuse her, but you can't put her through this agony, you know. Public exposure of a very private matter—the newspapers having a field-day, the poor girl branded an outcast, which is what would happen to her afterwards. It could be the end of her, Mrs. Barforth, and I don't see how you could live easy with that on your conscience. And then there *is* her husband to be considered. He has his feelings, too, you know, and he at least has done you no harm. Very decent fellow, Compton Flood—absolutely first-rate—ambitious too, which would make it pretty well impossible for him to take her back after this sort of thing. With the best will in the world he'd be bound to feel that his career couldn't cope with the scandal."

"What do you suggest I should do then, Sir Julian?"

"Be charitable, m'dear—and sensible. I daresay you can't forgive, and I suppose women never forget. But be sensible. You know the fix Diana is in. Don't hound her, Mrs. Barforth. Let her have her child in peace and whatever arrangements are made for it afterwards—well, there's no reason why you should be troubled by them. That's the way these things are done, believe me. No need to go to extremes. And afterwards she'll be off to India to make her peace with her husband. No fuss, no mess, no proof, Mrs. Barforth—no scandal. That's the thing. Water under the bridge next year, or the year after. It's the only way."

"I almost wish I could agree with you."

"I beg your pardon?"

"I am sorry, Sir Julian. I fully realize the seriousness of Mrs. Flood's position. But I have my own position to consider and intend to do so. It seems to me a great pity that Mrs. Flood failed to realize the consequences of her actions before it was too late—or before those actions had taken place at all. I repeat I am sorry, but I do not hold myself in any way responsible."

He gave me a look of the most complete loathing and then, still restlessly flexing his hand, his lips drew apart in a grimace that was intended, but did not succeed, as a smile.

"So that's it. Vindictive, eh?—want your pound of flesh, do you? But I won't have it, Mrs. Barforth. I won't stand idly by and see you ruin a thoroughly delightful girl for your sanctimonious whim. I warn you, madam, this shopkeeper's morality is not to my liking and I shall not tolerate it."

I could have said, How dare you speak to me like that? I could have ordered him from the house, or I could have burst into tears. I believe I wanted to do all these things, but instead I remained quite still, hands folded, back very straight, rigid with my determination that I would not flinch. For, if this was the first abuse I had ever received, it could not be the last and I must school myself to meet it.

"Sir Julian, you may call me whatever names you choose, but the plain fact is that I have committed no offence against Mrs. Flood. When she became my husband's mistress she was surely aware of the risk she ran. She must have known what the consequences might be to herself and to Colonel Flood, and I do not feel called upon to bear those consequences for her. This divorce is of the utmost importance to me. It is the only possible course I can take in order to lead what I believe to be an honest life, and I will not sacrifice that for the sake of Colonel Flood's career nor Mrs. Flood's reputation. Would they put my interests before their own? Of course they would not, and neither would you. It is quite useless, Sir Julian, to bully me or intimidate me or to make me feel guilty, for I will not change my mind. I am prepared to take full responsibility for my own actions and Mrs. Flood must do the same."

He stood and glared at me for what must have been a full

minute, his mouth a thin line, his face taut with anger, although suddenly and quite shockingly there were tears in his eyes.

"This could kill her you know. Damnation, woman, can't you see that?"

And when I made no answer but continued to stand as tall and straight as I could, he clenched those nervous fingers into a fist, smashed it hard into the palm of his other hand, and rapped out: "Self-righteous bitch!"

"Good-day, Sir Julian."

"Not for you, madam—there'll be no 'good-day' for you, I promise it."

He took his thunderous departure and I sat down on the nearest seat, my legs trembling, my whole body, as it relaxed from its awful rigidity, full of little aches and pains, my mind far too distracted in those first moments to realize that this attack could only mean that Gervase had refused to put an end to the matter by coming back to me.

Beyond the window, the spring afternoon continued to sparkle, daffodils tossing their bold heads in the fresh breeze, new green on the trees and a hint of pink and white blossom; an impulsive, passionate season, more adapted to the making of light-hearted promises than the grim keeping of one's resolve. I heard a bee, the first of the year, new-born and boisterous on the window-sill, a voice in the hall saying something about tea, a deeper voice answering "Presently," and then Mrs. Agbrigg came into the room and sat down in the chair opposite mine, choosing her moment well, I thought, since I was still too exhausted by my confrontation with Sir Julian to engage successfully in another.

"Grace, I think it is time we had a word about your situation," she said, and I looked across at her, the dragon of my childhood, velvet-pawed now but still very powerful, and smiled.

"Yes. But you must not be afraid that I have come to seek permanent refuge here, you know. You will not be troubled with me forever, Mrs. Agbrigg, for it is my intention, when everything is settled, to live alone."

She returned my smile, her large, handsome face hardly creasing, folded her smooth hands, her rings catching the light in the way I remembered, the heavy gold cross still at her throat.

"Your father has explained all that to me and I have every confidence in your ability to keep your own house in order. It is the, shall we say *social*, aspect of the matter I would like to take up with you."

"My goodness, Mrs. Agbrigg—you mean Mrs. Rawnsley will

cross the street to avoid meeting me and Miss Mandelbaum may feel uneasy about asking me to tea?''

But she shook her sedate head with an unruffled, almost placid motion.

"No Grace, I do not mean that at all. I would not expect you to value the good opinion of Mrs. Rawnsley and Miss Mandelbaum since you have never been without it—as I have. Tell me, Grace, was Sir Julian very rough with you?''

"Yes.''

"In fact he spoke to you as no gentleman has ever spoken to you before?''

"Yes, he did.''

"I wonder if you know why? No, not entirely because of Mrs. Flood, but because you had placed yourself in a situation where he was no longer obliged to consider you a lady. Men have a keen nose for these things, my dear. And when a woman ceases to be a lady, she is just—well—just a woman and consequently fair game for anything a gentleman may have in mind. For a gentleman, you know, will do what he likes, or what he can, with a *woman*.''

I moved uncomfortably in my chair, surprised not only by her words but by the sincerity and the concern with which she expressed them.

"But Mrs. Agbrigg, why? I am not an adultress—I have done nothing to lose my reputation.''

"My dear, indeed you have. You have flouted convention, don't you see? You have shrugged off the authority of your male relations and are setting yourself up in an independent fashion— your own home, your own income, keeping your own carriage— while your husband and your father are still living. You are a threat to society, my dear, for what would happen if the rest of society's wives and daughters were to follow your example? Domestic chaos, dearest, and—which is a far more serious matter— *financial* chaos too. No, no, you cannot be allowed to live free and happy, for that would be an inducement, would it not, to other women. And so what can society do but shun you, impose a total ban on you, fill your life with as much insult and irritation as possible? My dear, they would find it easier to forgive you if you *had* committed adultery. And that apart, what man, meeting you in the years to come, will enquire into the exact circumstances of your divorce or even care about them? You will have a label, 'Divorced Woman,' that is all he will see. And what it will mean to him is 'Woman of Easy Virtue.' Once your divorce is granted—if it ever should be—no man who desires you will feel obliged to restrain himself from telling you so. You will be subject to the most positive advances, my child—to a degree of aggression which I doubt you capable of imagining."

"Mrs. Agbrigg—I believe you are afraid for me."

She sighed and unclasped her hands a little, looking fondly down at her rings.

"And of course that surprises you? You do not know me very well, Grace. I wore a label too, you see, from the start which said 'Wicked Stepmother' in bold letters, which was natural enough. You had made up your mind to dislike me and I saw no real harm in it. My maternal instinct is not strong. I wanted to be your father's wife, not the mother of his child, and beyond the physical comforts of good food and good shelter I had nothing to offer you. You had your Aunt Faith and your friends. I had your father and intended to keep him. You know that. But your Aunt Faith cannot tell you how it feels to be treated like a whore. I can. Will you listen to me?"

"Gladly."

"I made my first money, Grace, by satisfying the perverse appetites of a man who—well—let us say I was thirteen years old at the time and he was at least fifty years older than that. And if it shocks you that there are women—and children—who do these things for money, may I remind you that it is only men who do them for pleasure. When he died I found another 'protector,' which is an excellent description, since that is what a woman of my old profession most needs—protection. And not only from the lusts and hazards of her clients and of the streets but protection from the self-righteous, who are rarely charitable, and from the 'godly,' who more often than not have no imagination and not much compassion. I soon understood that the only real protection was respectability. I earned money. I learned to speak and dress like a lady. I tried, when my circumstances allowed it, to live a decent life among decent people. It always proved impossible. I was always 'exposed' and suitably punished. Eventually I came north and one night, at a music-hall in Leeds, I met Mr. Matthew Oldroyd of Fieldhead Mills, another old man of the type I was used to, although I was myself no longer thirteen nor even thirty. He brought me to Cullingford and set me up in the kind of little 'love-nest' I had inhabited often enough before—my last, I thought, considering my age and my competition, and so I was determined to make the most of it. I was warm and comfortable. I had gold rings and more than enough to eat. But the ladies of your town still drew their skirts aside, still looked down their noses as if I had sprayed myself with their own foul sewage water instead of the most expensive perfumes of France. Well, you will not find yourself in quite those circumstances, Grace, but once you step outside the charmed circle of respectability you will enter a jungle—believe me—where the hunters are very far from gentlemen.''

"But not all beasts, surely, Mrs. Agbrigg.''

"No,'' she said, looking into the far distance. "Not all. There was Tom Delaney, for instance—yes, there *was* a Mr. Delaney, who was my husband, if only in common law, until he died in prison, at twenty-five years old, of the fever. And Matthew Oldroyd was not a beast either, just old and sour and fool enough to marry me to spite his relations. And your father—dare I mention your father?''

I nodded, and for the first time since I had known her she leaned back in her chair, her large, handsome body arranging itself with less grace than comfort, a woman of a certain age who, having found a secure refuge, no longer felt the need to be young.

"I like your father,'' she said, a simple statement of which no one could have doubted the truth. "Indeed I do. I made up my mind from the start, when we were both employed by Matthew Oldroyd—your father as his lawyer and myself as his mistress—that I would get him one way or another.''

"And he?''

"Oh no—he was still half in love with—well, with a dream he once had, I suppose. But he found the reality—my reality—very comfortable. He wanted my money, of course, and I wanted the respectability I knew he would somehow contrive to give me. That was the bargain he thought we were striking and he expected nothing more, for his life had been meagre and at the start he was shy of taking. But I am very determined, Grace—as you are—and I made up my mind that if I'd survived what I *had* survived, if I'd kept body and soul together on fresh air and cold water sometimes, *and* made myself a fortune out of Matthew Oldroyd, then surely I could make my husband like me. He does. There now, I've got more than I deserved, but I came here to talk about you. Do you mean to go through with this, Grace?''

I nodded.

"I thought so. I don't like it, child, because it hurts your father. He doesn't know, you see, just how long it's been hurting you—as I know—and he's afraid you might not stay in Cullingford when it's done."

"I hadn't thought of it."

"Think of it now. Much easier, of course, to go away—a clean start where no one knows enough to tell tales. You could lose yourself in a big city, go abroad, buy a cottage in a country town and call yourself a widow."

"Yes—"

"It would ease his mind if I could give him the impression that you mean to stay here, where he can keep his eye on you."

"Yes," I said once again, and, smiling, she leaned forward and put her smooth, brown hand over mine.

"You see, Grace, there is no real freedom—not until the last person you care about is gone. I believe you were planning, were you not, on that fresh start?"

"I think so. I suppose a man would just up and go, wouldn't he—regardless of anyone else?"

"Not your father."

She stood up, having achieved her purpose as she always had, but I understood her now and it seemed right to me that she should go and lay my promise to remain in Cullingford at my father's feet as another gift of love—*her* love, she would make sure he realized, and not mine. And that seemed right to me too.

"Mrs. Agbrigg."

"My dear?"

"Is there a name I can call you? Mrs. Agbrigg no longer seems appropriate and I think we have gone rather beyond stepmamma."

"My name is Tessa," she said. "Why not? Call me that, dear, the next time Mrs. Rawnsley comes to tea, and when you see her pinched lips and her accusing eyes you will know that your apprenticeship in independence has begun."

20

"BUT WHAT IS IT ALL for?" Blanche asked in great perplexity. "I am broadminded enough I believe—good heavens! with the company I keep how could I be any other?—but I really cannot see the point of these extreme measures. Ask yourself, Grace, is it necessary? I will tell you plainly that it is not wise."

And when I merely smiled she gave an impatient little shrug and sighed.

"Ah well, if you are set on it you had better come back to London with me until it is over, for these old tabby cats up here will claw you to pieces once the news is out. Oh yes, they will, for they may have abused Gervase soundly so long as you were a poor, brave little woman who put up with his philandering. But once you are known to have turned against him they will all turn against you, for he is a *man* after all, and these dear ladies would rather have a wicked, attractive man any day of the week than a good woman. There is no need to worry about Aunt Caroline, if you should be worrying about her, for she is obliged to stay at South Erin, very likely for the whole season, to nurse the Duke's bronchitis. We shall have the house to ourselves."

It would be a quiet season, she said, since she was still officially in mourning for Venetia, but Blanche's idea of a mourning gown was a cascade of black lace frills which turned her shoulders to marble, her hair to silver; her notion of a "quiet season" involving her immediately in the complexities of calling-cards and invitation-cards with which, every morning, her hall-table was littered several inches deep.

Her friendship with the Prince of Wales which had launched her into society no longer occupied a great deal of her time, the Prince having turned his realistic eye on such ladies as the incomparable Sarah Bernhardt and Mrs. Langtry, that most enduring and enterprising of Jersey Lilies. But Blanche's reputation had been made, and every year now, from April to late July, she could make her selection of lunch-parties and afternoon teas, could be sure that her carriage, whenever it appeared in the Park, would occasion a great raising of tall silk hats and quizzing glasses, a great many curious and envious stares. She could make her selection, too, of grand formal dinners any night of the week or could dine out in a smart restaurant, dash along to the theatre afterwards with a supper-party to follow, and then go on to catch the last hour or two of Lady So-and-So's ball. She would certainly attend Ascot and Goodwood and the Henley Regatta, would go to Hurlingham from time to time to watch a polo match, would visit whatever art galleries and exhibitions were being visited that year, would fit in, somehow or other, a garden party, an afternoon concert, put in an hour's enthusiastic shopping, sit at least one night a week in Aunt Caroline's box at the opera, a programme of events which would keep her fully occupied from nine o'clock in the morning, when she breakfasted, to four o'clock the morning after, when she would be driven home in the clear summer daylight from a dance.

She saw little of Dominic, who had his own invitations and his seat in the House of Commons, which kept him busy, although not too strenuously, from February to August, all government conveniently closing down to accommodate the shooting of the early grouse and not reopening until very nearly the end of the hunting season. And in the spaces between his sporting and his political activities he maintained a friendly but very casual relationship with his wife.

No, Blanche admitted frankly in reply to my question, she would not say they actually lived together any more than Gervase and I had lived together this last year or two, but neither she nor Dominic felt inclined to make a drama of it. In Cullingford perhaps—and here she raised a pointed eyebrow—it may not have been so simple, but in London it was quite the thing and no one thought it worth a mention.

"You should spend more time in London, Grace."

"I have not the stamina, Blanche. The hours you keep would kill me."

"Nonsense. One easily gets accustomed to that. You know exactly what I mean. If you have this fancy to live alone, then take a house here for three-quarters of the year, while Gervase stays at Galton. The first year or two our good ladies might gossip but eventually they would find something else to gossip about—something they could prove—and would be delighted to see you whenever you came north, as they are always so delighted to see me. Grace—it would be *exactly* the same as divorce, except that you could keep your reputation."

"And I would still be married to Gervase."

"And what difference can that possibly make unless you should want to marry somebody else? You don't wish to do that, do you?"

"No."

"Then really, Grace—why make such a fuss? When one sees a chance to get the best of both worlds—to have one's freedom and still be married. Good lord! one doesn't just take it, one seizes it with both hands. Why ever not? Unless, of course—oh dear, Grace, I do hope you have not filled your head with notions of looking for a grand passion, like Venetia."

But there was a drop more passion in Blanche's own nature than she cared to admit, a certain very human anxiety and need for reassurance which sometimes succeeded in penetrating even the gilt and glitter of her "Season." In early January that year, five thousand British soldiers, Captain Noel St. John Chard among them, had marched into Zululand, supported by some eight thousand native troops, to confront, under the leadership of Viscount Chelmsford, the forty thousand warriors of the Zulu king Cetewayo. On the twenty-second of that month, Chelmsford having split his forces and ridden off with half his men looking for battle, ten thousand Zulu warriors fell upon the British camp at Isandhlwana, spearing all but fifty of our eighteen hundred British officers and men to death.

Noel Chard, it transpired, had not been at Isandhlwana, nor was he at Rorke's Drift where, that same day and the following night, a minute British garrison of eighty-five fighting men endured six ferocious Zulu attacks, losing only seventeen of their number. But as skirmish succeeded skirmish, as more British soldiers were hacked to death, here and there, by those fanatical Zulu spears, Blanche's fears for Noel grew, giving rise to sudden lapses of memory, sudden demands, through the bird-twitter of society's tea-tables, for news from Africa.

The Prince Imperial, the only son of the late, deposed Napoleon III of France and his Empress Eugenie, who had gone out as a volunteer, was killed that June in a Zulu ambush, a sad end for this young descendant of Bonaparte who had been popular in London, much liked by the Prince of Wales.

"How terrible!" said Blanche, speaking of the Prince Imperial, thinking of Noel Chard, who even now could be bleeding somewhere in the dust, the mud, on some foul bullock-cart, who could have been speared by a Zulu assegai or fallen victim to some filthy African disease.

"What a waste!" she said, "I don't even know what they hope to gain by it. If only he had stayed at Listonby as I told him."

On the fourth of July, Chelmsford, with a force of over five thousand men, caught Cetewayo at Ulundi and there, after hard fighting, slaughtered a sufficient number of spear-throwers to proclaim himself a victory in fitting retribution for the massacre of Isandhlwana. Cetewayo fled. The war was over.

"What of the casualties?" Blanche moaned, turning white when the news was brought to her with the morning's invitations. "And the dead? Are there no lists published as yet? Dominic must go and ask Disraeli, for surely the Prime Minister will know. And if he is listed as wounded, then Dominic had better go out there to fetch him home—or Gideon. What do you think?"

I couldn't be sure. Were her affections disturbing her or simply her conscience? But in either case once Dominic had made all possible enquiries there seemed nothing to do but wait, to continue the suddenly monotonous round of balls and dinners and drives in the Park. And it was there, some days later, during the hour before luncheon Blanche devoted to carriage exercise, that I saw Gideon Chard some way ahead of us, standing by a silk-lined victoria, in conversation with a lady.

He had, quite definitely, seen our approach—he could have done no other—yet neither he nor Blanche gave the slightest sign of recognition, Blanche, who had been planning to send him out to Zululand two days ago, looking through him now as if she had never set eyes on him before, while his expression remained polite but completely blank.

"Blanche, surely that is Gideon?"

"Don't stare," she whispered, and as the two carriages came abreast and we could both easily have touched him, she bowed to a passing acquaintance on the other side and adjusted the handle of her parasol.

"Really, Blanche—if he does not wish to speak to me—"

But she clicked her tongue with rare impatience and snapped her parasol tight shut.

"Don't be such a goose, Grace. It has nothing to do with us at all. You have been out in the world long enough by now, surely, to know that a gentleman does not embarrass a lady, nor a lady a gentleman, by acknowledging one another—no matter how well they are acquainted—when he is with his mistress. Good lord! Grace, I would have died if you had spoken to him—and so, I expect, would he. For goodness' sake do not look back—what are you thinking of?''

''Mistress? Already?''

She shrugged, pouted.

''Well, she may not be his mistress now. In fact she probably is not, for it must be all of three years since I first saw them together and these affairs do not often last so long as that. But come, Grace, you know the terms on which he stood with Venetia. One can hardly blame him. And Venetia would not have cared. She is an actress, or dancer, or some such thing and we could not be asked to meet her in any case.''

''So we did not see him?''

''We certainly did not. And we will not mention it when we do see him. I wonder when he arrived and why he is not staying with us? Perhaps he is, for we have been out since breakfast-time and Dominic would not necessarily mention it to me. I suppose they were both out on the town last night and slept until noon, for he does not look as if he has just got off the train in those clothes.''

I had not seen him since my departure from Tarn Edge and experienced now so powerful an aversion to sharing, even for one night, a roof with him that had it been possible I would have gone to a chance acquaintance, an hotel, anywhere to avoid him, I could not have said why. The fact that he had a mistress did not surprise me. Had it occurred to me to wonder, I would have assumed he had. Nor did I anticipate any interference from him in my own affairs. He had no right to interfere. I had no right to be disturbed by his visit to his brother. Yet I *was* disturbed. Irrationally, idiotically, I did not wish to see him or hear him, and was considerably put out on our return to see two silk hats in Blanche's hall, two pairs of gloves, two large, dark-skinned Chards, not one, lounging by the drawing-room fireplace, requiring fresh tea with *lemon*, for God's sake, not cream and sugar; is there nothing else, Blanche, for my brother to eat but these odd little rout cakes, and does that doorbell never stop ringing?

He had come, as we had supposed, for news of Noel, the Zulu war providing discussion enough for that uneasy tea-time hour, Sir Dominic taking his brother to dine at his club while Blanche attended an engagement of her own and I had my supper on a tray, my mind back in Cullingford among my familiar anxieties.

The court order requiring Gervase to return to me had been obtained. My father had written informing me of the date, the implications, what I must and must not do. Mrs. Agbrigg had written enquiring after my health and reporting on my father's, asking me to send her a special brand of clover honey from an address in Chelsea which, when taken with milk and cinnamon, would do wonders for his cough. Aunt Faith had written saying, "Darling—if this is what you want then God Bless you." My Grandmother Agbrigg had written from Scarborough supposing I had learned this kind of behaviour from Mrs. Agbrigg. Mrs. Barforth—did she still think of herself as my mother-in-law? —had written of her daily round at Galton, her joy in the fine weather, the progress of that timid collie puppy. Aunt Caroline had written to Blanche from South Erin, without once mentioning my name.

But no one had written or spoken to me a word about Gervase. I knew nothing of his whereabouts—except that he was not at Tarn Edge and did not seem to be at Galton—nothing of his plans, except that he would probably have made no plans; nothing of his fears, except that he would probably be afraid. I didn't know his reactions to the divorce itself, whether he wanted it, intended to contest it, or did not care. I didn't know if he still wished to go abroad, nor how much Diana Flood's decision not to accompany him had hurt him; whether, in fact, now that her ruin seemed unavoidable, she may even have changed her mind. I didn't know, at the start of every morning, if the day might bring him to Blanche's door demanding my return to our matrimonial home in compliance with the court order I had myself obtained. I didn't know what pressures Sir Julian Flood, or Diana Flood herself, may have put upon him to that end, nor how much—or how little—her desperation might move him.

The last time I had heard his voice he had ordered me to leave him alone. The last time I had seen him he had been standing like a wraith at Venetia's graveside with no more hope—it must have seemed to him—in his hollow, fretful life than she had found in hers. I couldn't help him. I knew it and I had been very careful, for a long time, not to love him. But he worried me— just that—a faint but ever-present anxiety hovering at the edge of my mind, leaving me in no doubt that it would have been far easier had I managed to hate him.

He worried me. Yet Gideon Chard worried me too, for reasons I seemed unable to bring to the surface of my mind, so that

I was far from pleased when, returning sooner than I had expected, he found me still in the drawing-room with the coffee-tray.

"They have left you alone, have they?" he said, although I believe he had expected to find me so.

"As you see. Is there any news of Noel?"

He shook his head.

"We know Chelmsford lost a hundred men and Noel does not seem to have been among them. The chances are he is perfectly fit and well, and has won medals and promotion—which pleases me enormously when one considers he is the least warlike of the three of us."

"Yes. But if you will excuse me, Gideon, I am rather tired."

Again he shook his head and smiled a little wryly but with a great deal of studied charm; the smile, I thought, of a man who wishes to persuade, or who has something to sell.

"I am sorry for that. I came back early on purpose to speak to you and would be grateful for just a moment—"

"I am really very tired—perhaps tomorrow?"

"I may not be here tomorrow."

"Then I am sorry but I must say good-night."

"No, Grace."

"I beg your pardon?"

"I have something to say to you. I intend to say it."

"Oh—do you catch the early train tomorrow?"

"My plans are uncertain. Sit down, Grace. Please."

"No—no—I simply wondered if you would take a package for me to Mrs. Agbrigg—something she asked me to buy for my father?"

"With pleasure—when we have had a word."

"I will let you have the parcel in the morning then, at breakfast—"

"*Grace.*"

And as I moved to the door, pushing the air away from me in my haste, he rapped out. "Grace, I will follow you upstairs if I must, which will do nothing either for your nerves or your reputation."

I paused, my hand on the doorknob, willing myself to turn it and walk up the stairs without looking back; willing myself to shrug off the claims he was about to make, the restraints he was about to impose, like the free spirit I wished to be I paused—for how dare he speak of *nerves*?—and hesitated, feeling, in fact, as nervous as I had ever done.

"Grace," he said, no hesitation anywhere within him. "Unless

you wish me to shout my questions through your bedroom door
for all to hear, you will remain in this room and you will tell me
why you are set on this folly.''

"You have no right to ask that question."

"I daresay. But I insist upon an answer and you should know
me well enough by now to realize that I will go on asking until
you give it to me."

I knew him. I knew him far too well. I walked back and stood
on the hearthrug before the empty summer grate in the favourite
vantage point of authority, the spot where he and Mr. Barforth
and my father and all the other masters of households and
fortunes and destinies were accustomed to stand, my hands
neatly folded, my back straight, the posture I had adopted for my
confrontation with Sir Julian Flood, telling myself—without
believing—that this confrontation could be no worse.

"By 'folly,' Gideon, I presume you mean my divorce. And
what I have to say to you on that score is quickly done, since it
does not concern you in the very least."

"You are quite wrong, believe me."

And now, forcing myself to look at him, I saw that the charm
was gone, leaving his face careful, serious, very determined.

"Grace, when all is said, and done, we have shared a roof
these past few years. I have come to value you very highly and
cannot keep silent when I see you embark on this course of
self-destruction. Whether you realize it or not, you have lived
very sheltered and somebody must tell you what the world is
like."

"There is no need for you to take the trouble, Gideon. Mrs.
Agbrigg and Sir Julian Flood have done it for you."

He made a movement that was both contemptuous and irritable,
dismissing Sir Julian as an older man and consequently out of
touch, Mrs. Agbrigg as a woman of dubious reputation herself,
who, being unreliable in her morals, could be trusted in nothing
else.

"I daresay—in fact I heard something of your interview with
Flood. But he has his own axe to grind."

"And you do not?"

"Yes, if you like—if concern for you can be called an axe,
then yes, I have one. I do not mean to stand idly by and see you
go to your ruin."

"Good heavens! Gideon, your knight-errantry does you credit,
but I do not expect to find myself entirely beyond the pale. I do
not intend to set up house with a lover, you know."

"You intend to live alone," he said, his jaw clenching as if the words made him very angry, "which is just as bad."

And his loss of temper where there should have been nothing warmer than a faint irritation, this smouldering anger when all that was required of him was to be mildly disappointed, alarmed me, for I did not feel very composed either, having far less inclination than usual to defend myself.

"There is no need for this, Grace," he said, speaking quickly while I still seemed disposed to listen. "What do you really have to gain by it? Yes—I know, I know—I have seen the difficulties you have had to face. I know what Gervase is, and what he does. I have seen your courage and feel no surprise that your patience is at an end. But why give up your home for his sake? And Tarn Edge *is* your home, Grace. If he could be persuaded to leave you alone—and he *could* be so persuaded—there is no reason why you should not continue to live there and enjoy the same respect, the same authority—the same *independence*, for who has ever attempted to restrain you? You are valued at Tarn Edge. Why cut yourself off from that? And for what? The pleasure of setting up in some poky place of your own and enduring the insults of those who—well, for want of a better word, those ladies who cannot hold a candle to you, and of those "gentlemen" who will come swarming like bees around clover. Surely, Grace—since you would be free of Gervase either way—what is the sense in deliberately exposing yourself to harassment and injury? I see no sense in it."

"Ah—and *I* see that you are not satisfied with the way they have been laundering your shirts since I went away."

He could very easily have thrown back his handsome head and laughed. I hoped rather earnestly that he would. But instead his heavy eyebrows flew together, his face not flushing but darkening with a rush of temper which would have gone ill with me had I been in his employ or had I been his wife. Yet when he spoke again his voice was low and even.

"Grace, since we are speaking plainly— I know there are times when you dislike me. I am not sure I merit it, not every time."

"Probably you do not."

"Very well. You believe I married for money. You are quite right, of course."

"Gideon, it has absolutely nothing to do with me—"

"*Grace*—will you leave off this constant side-stepping of every important issue, for God's sake! If I wish you to be concerned in it, then you are concerned, and I am entitled to defend myself. Yes—it was for money. But I wonder if you realize what small provision is made in families like mine for younger sons? We are all brought up to be princes, but in the end everything, the land, the title, such money as there is—everything—is for the eldest son, the heir. I don't quarrel with that. It is the only way an estate can be kept intact. If every son took his share there would soon be no great estates at all, important houses would fall into decay, and no man would have the means to support his title. I know that. Younger sons are obliged to do the best they can within the limits custom permits—and the one thing custom positively encourages is the making of a good marriage. Grace, I saw my way to the kind of life I desire by entering the mills, for my tastes are luxurious and exacting, I cannot deny it. And nothing—*nothing*—either in my upbringing or my education told me I was wrong to marry my employer's daughter.''

"Of course not.''

"Yet you have accused me, in thought, I know it, and now you will listen to my defence. Was I cruel to her? She believed I took her solely for the money, insisted on believing it, and it is perfectly correct that I would not have taken her without it. But the truth is that I found her attractive to begin with and if she had allowed it I would have— Damnation! Grace, you know exactly what I mean. You saw me today with that woman in the Park. You must know how little that sort of thing can matter—''

"Of course—just a woman for your convenience, at your convenience. What can it mean?''

"It means,'' he snapped, "a woman who gives me what I pay for and no more, and with whom I know exactly where I stand. Not an ideal arrangement, but businesslike—the best, from time to time, that one can manage—and which has the advantage of hurting no one.''

"Yes. I beg your pardon.''

"Will you agree, then, that my intentions were not wholly callous—that I may have had *some* fondness for her when we married, and that when I took her back I may have felt some pity? Do you think it was done entirely for the sake of that managing directorship?''

"Venetia thought so.''

"Yes. Venetia thought so. What does Grace think?''

"I think you asked for your promotion, or made it clear you would expect it.''

"Yes," he said unexpectedly, somewhat disarming me. "I did."

"Gideon."

"Why not? Mr. Nicholas Barforth, in my place, would have done the same. He knew what I wanted and how long I had waited for it. He also knew that I had earned it. When Venetia left me he gave only half of what he had promised—the limited company. When she came back I had no need to tell him I wanted the other half—to be managing director of it. He knew. I sat in his office and waited for his offer. And then I made sure it was exactly the offer I required before I took it. But he can't know—and you can't know, Grace—what I would have done if the offer had not been made."

"It can make no real difference now."

"Yes, it can, if I can gain your good opinion. And if not then—listen, Grace, if I am the reason you cannot return to Tarn Edge then *I* will leave, not you. A man can live anywhere, and I am away a great deal in any case."

"Yes Gideon—and for how long?"

And feeling suddenly hemmed-in with him in this large, high-ceilinged room, too close to him, impeded by him, although we were a yard apart, I knew I must end it as quickly as I could and walk cleanly and decisively away.

"I ask for how long because in fact once I was safely back at Tarn Edge and had rendered my divorce impossible, you would come back too."

"I would hope to do so—at your invitation—I admit it."

"And if I did not invite you, you would come back just the same."

He grinned, quite boyishly, my stomach lurching at the display of his charm in an altogether dreadful fashion.

"I imagine I might try that."

"I am sure of it. And I quite understand why. A house the size of Tarn Edge needs an efficient mistress, for even the best of housekeepers grow slack after a time. I suppose things are sliding already and my return would quickly put that right. I know, Gideon—there is a house to run and even a child to educate. I also know that sooner or later you will marry again. My presence at Tarn Edge would be less convenient to you then, and possibly most unwelcome to your new wife."

He came quite close to me, his feet on the hearthrug only an inch away from mine, the frilled hem of my skirt touching his polished evening shoe; his hand, on the mantelshelf behind my

head, allowing his body to lean forward, not touching me but
over me, my own awareness of his breathing, the movement of
pulse and muscle and vitality beneath his skin, the skin itself, a
great trouble to me; my own senses, which I had allowed to
grow sluggish, stirring now to curiosity and excitement, for
those senses, after all, were barely twenty-five years old and had
once been very strong.

"I will not marry again," he said.

"Nonsense!"

"*Grace*—I will not marry again and for a very good reason
which you should understand—which you *do* understand."

And leaning closer, his eyes seeming to bore into my skull as
if he meant to inject his meaning inside it, he repeated his words
over again, his face grim and hard with concentration, the force
of his will taking me prisoner so that my breathing came no
longer at my own pace but at his, my pulse catching the rhythm
of his pulse, quickening to meet it and match it and be absorbed
by it. Yes, I understood. And how could I be shocked by the
desire which had existed for so long, dormant yet terribly present,
in all our dealings with one another? All he was asking me to do
was call that desire by its proper name, to receive it, to *accept* it,
now that the obstacles to its fulfilment—my husband, his wife—no
longer stood quite so visibly in our way. He was asking me to do
what the very root of my body longed for and which only a
portion of my mind resisted. I was not ashamed of my body. I
was glad of the joy it had once brought me and could readily
admit how urgently I often craved that joy again. But if Gideon
was desire then he was also captivity, strong arms to enchant me
and bind me; demands that would obliterate my own demands;
needs that would soon swallow up my needs; an identity that
would overshadow mine. And I did not trust him.

His hand tightened on the mantelshelf, his face hardening still
further, not with anger but the sheer effort of his control.

"I should not speak to you now, I know it, and would have
said nothing, except that you leave me no choice. If you had
stayed at Tarn Edge as I expected, there would have been no
need for this. I could have bided my time—chosen a better
moment."

"Gideon—"

"Yes—and even now, when I am driven to speak, what can I
say that you will listen to? How can I make you understand the
necessity—that this is *right* for you, Grace? I am saying come

back to Tarn Edge, not to keep the house nor raise the child, but to make your life there.''

"With you?''

"Yes—in time. *Yes*. Grace, look at me—if you had not married him in such a rush I believe you would have married me. You ought to have married me, and I think you know it.''

"You did not ask me to marry you, Gideon.''

"I was given no opportunity to do so. Suddenly you became the property of Gervase Barforth—or so his father would have me believe—and I was warned off. And it has not been easy, Grace, believe me, these past years, living in that house with you, seeing the evidence, every day right beneath my eyes, of how perfectly we would have suited each other.''

"And now you want me to remain married to Gervase so that I can stay at Tarn Edge and continue to suit you perfectly—to be your mistress, in fact?''

"Yes,'' he said, bowing his head. "In time—I said in time. Put like that—and so soon—it can only shock you, I know. But I could hardly take the risk of keeping silent and allowing you to go on with your present plans. Grace, believe what I say. It would be right for us.''

I shook my head, compelled to deny it, and with great audacity—foolhardiness—force of habit, I couldn't tell, he put a hand on the nape of my neck, a large, warm hand as unlike Gervase's cool, narrow touch as it could possibly be, and let it stay there just long enough to be sure of his welcome before he began to stroke reassurance into my shoulders and the length and the small of my back, reminding my body—which had not forgotten—of hunger and pleasure, of the healthy need for a man's caresses.

"Yes, Grace, it is right. We know each other. You understand the life I lead and I understand the life you should be leading. I can give you that life. Gervase will be far away and will not trouble us. I want you, darling, and I think—I know—you want me.''

Of course I wanted him. I had stood years ago in the Long Gallery at Listonby and wanted him so much that it had terrified me and driven me to what had seemed the lesser peril of Gervase. I wanted him now and was no longer afraid of the physical consequences, indeed I was only too well aware of how glorious those consequences could be. I had only to take one step towards him and at once—tonight and in this house—he would possess me, claim me, take the whole course of my life into his capable, challenging hands. I could wake in the morning as his mistress, replete, perhaps, and purring like a satiated cat but entirely dependent on the duration of his desire, on how long and how much I could continue to please him. And what greater risk, what greater humiliation could there be for any woman than that?

I needed anger to combat that dreadful, wonderful melting of my limbs, disgust to subdue that quick, hungry stirring at the pit of my stomach. I needed a weapon. I found it, hurt myself a little against it, and then pointed its keen, cutting edge straight at him.

"Why don't you ask me to marry you now, Gideon?"

But perhaps he had expected this and had taken thought what to say.

"How can I do that?"

"After my divorce I believe you can?"

"If it were so easy I need not have spoken to you now. I could simply have waited and then, when the time was opportune, come a-courting in the proper manner. I should have enjoyed that, Grace. But a man may not marry his deceased wife's sister, that much I do know. What the law says in the case of a sister-in-law who is divorced from a deceased wife's brother, I don't profess to know. But it has an illegal ring to it, somehow. One would have to make very sure."

I needed scorn now to match my anger and disgust and, catching my breath—taking note of his smooth, easy manner, his confidence in his ability to persuade me—I found that too.

"I think such enquiries would be a waste of time in our case, Gideon, and had you thought otherwise you would have already made them."

"Come, darling—really, I had to seize my opportunity and could hardly equip myself with every detail—"

"Oh yes, you could—and did—for the truth is that you do not wish, whatever the law may say, to marry a divorced woman, do you?"

"Darling—"

"And I think you will never call me darling in public, Gideon, because—well, because your mother, the Duchess, would be likely to throw a fit at the very idea, and your brother, the baronet, would not like it. And moreover—and far more to the point—I think your own sense of good taste and expediency is rather revolted by it too."

"Grace—that is not kind."

"No. But true, I think, because—Listonby and Westminster apart—the Goldsmiths and the Fauconniers would not care to associate with me either. A divorced woman is a social embarrassment. I have been warned of that often enough, and that would not do for you, Gideon. After all, my skills as a hostess would be no good to you, would they, if no respectable— *useful* people could be persuaded to accept my invitations. But if I remained your sister-in-law, safely married to Gervase who would never be there, *then* I could be a social asset, I quite see that. And if at the same time I discreetly shared your bed, your friends would not mind that at all and—well, how very much more convenient to have a mistress waiting in one's own home than to be obliged to pursue one in the Park. I see that too. Yes, I could be of great use to you, Gideon, until your mother found you the earl's daughter or the merchant princess she has always dreamed of."

I saw the colour leave his face, felt his body harden and turn cold, and then, stepping away from me, he bowed, not, I thought, accepting defeat but disdaining to make any defence.

"I am sorry your opinion of me should be so ill," he said curtly. "If you would care to give me the parcel you spoke of, I will see that it is delivered to Fieldhead."

But there could be no question now of parcels for Fieldhead or anything else. If Gideon remained in this house tomorrow, then I would be obliged to leave it, for I could face him neither as the man I had insulted nor as the man I had desired and might—very probably—desire again. But I came donwstairs in the morning to find all changed, for news had been delivered in the night that Noel Chard had indeed been wounded at Ulundi, how seriously was not known. Blanche was in despair, had already sent a flurry of telegrams to her father in Cullingford who, she said, would have contacts, would know what to do; while both Dominic and Gideon were arranging to leave for Natal at once.

I remained in London with Blanche through a stifling August, a September that was wet in patches, hot and overcast in others, my own concerns overshadowed by her agonized waiting for telegrams, letters, casual, unfeeling gossip that prostrated her on her bed, struggling with the first passion of her hitherto passionless life, terrified as a child because, like a child, she believed it would go on hurting forever.

I gave what comfort I could, sat with her and shared her vigil, the Season being over now and all her acquaintances gone to their shooting-parties, their country estates, escaping her demands only rarely to walk alone in the empty autumn streets. And it was on one such solitary outing that I came face to face with Gervase.

It was not, of course, by chance, and seeing my shock and my inability to conceal it, he came hurrying forward, light and pale and thinner, I thought, than I remembered, the skin at his eye-corners crinkling as he smiled, his hat tilted at the rakish angle he always wore it, carrying himself with all the accustomed young man's dash and swagger but his face hollower somehow, and a little older.

"Grace, you look as if you had seen a ghost. Don't worry. I know the court order has nearly expired, but I have not come to comply with it and ruin your life all over again."

"They said we should not see each other."

"I know. But we shall not tell."

And for the first time in our lives the hand he put on my arm was firm and purposeful while mine was trembling, the strength of his will the greater, since I was too shaken to have any strength at all.

"One moment only, Grace. I am in London on other business and it seemed ridiculous to go away without seeing you, since there may not be another chance."

And to avoid the certainty of bursting into tears I could not ask him what he meant to do, could only question him by a glance, a movement of the hands, the whole of my mind overwhelmed not by pain but by a deep sadness. There was no bitterness left, no need to strike out, no sense of outrage, no sustaining anger. I felt like the parkland and the trees all about me, waterlogged, fog-bound, wet and weary.

"It seems I have a son," he told me, and through the mist which seemed to have settled around me I smiled weakly, knowing full well that I was here, wide awake, hearing this and believing it, yet feeling myself to be in a dream.

"Yes—and what now, Gervase?"

He shrugged, smiling too, his eye-corners creased again, those first marks of age sitting oddly on his boyish face, a mask he might suddenly remove and throw away.

"Well, I shall see Diana settled first, one way or the other. And then I shall go abroad if I can."

"Settled?"

"Yes. Compton Flood is to be Lord Sternmore any day now, and Diana is still rather keen on that. At first he said no, wouldn't hear of it. But the title has no money to go with it, you see, and at the moment he's having a good long think about that. If Diana goes abroad for a bit after you've done with her, to let the talk die down, and comes back a little richer, then he might forgive her. I expect he will. But if not she'll have to go abroad again, with me.''

"Gervase, are you still in love with her?"

"No. I'm not in love with anybody, Grace."

And feeling misty still and far away, I nodded and smiled.

"Do you understand why I'm going through with the divorce?"

"I do. Otherwise I would have come back to you, wouldn't I, like the court order said, and saved Diana. That's what they wanted me to do. I didn't—for what it's worth to you."

"It's worth a great deal. Where are you going?"

"Oh—sheep-shearing in Australia, perhaps—or herding cattle in America. It doesn't really matter. Not running, as I suppose you think. Searching might be nearer the mark. But why I'm here now is to put your mind at rest. I'll raise no sudden obstacles in your way, Grace. That's all.''

He took my hand and pressed it, the cool, light touch I knew, the sad smile I had not met before, my own sadness settling around me like a cloud, insubstantial but impenetrable, weighing me down.

"Goodbye, Grace—and good luck."

"Gervase—take care."

"Well, I don't know about that."

He walked away and the cloud was all over me, a soft barrier dimming my sight and my senses, making it impossible for me to cry out, since all sound must have died away in that thick, sorrowful air. And I walked back to Blanche's tall, tense house, tears dripping from my eyes like raindrops from those sodden trees, remembering that he had had no cloak, thinking of the dust and dangers of cattle stations, sheep stations, his eyes that betrayed lack of sleep, his fancies and his fears; his tendency to take cold.

21

AND SO IT WAS DONE. I entered a bare court-room in the company of lawyers whose main concern was for their fee, and placed before a judge who did not like me the better for it the evidence of servants and of a new-born child that my husband had committed adultery with the wife of Colonel Compton Flood—Lord Sternmore any day now. I proved conclusively that the guilty pair had lived openly together for some months at Cullingford Manor and before that had been seen in the most compromising of situations, quite regularly, by Mrs. Flood's maid. I proved that my husband had abandoned me and refused to return. I tore to pieces the reputation of the aforesaid Mrs. Flood, causing her to seek refuge abroad. I broke the heart of Colonel Compton Flood who, while the trial was in progress, finally became Lord Sternmore, leaving his uncle's death-bed a nobler and, if he chose to compromise, a richer man.

I forced my own husband to abandon his home, his inheritance and his mistress, to hide his disgraced head in rough colonial pastures, very likely never to return. I branded a tiny baby boy with the stigma of bastardy. Or so a certain section of the Press implied, finding more drama and consequently more sympathy in the plight of the disgraced but evidently warm-blooded Diana Flood than in the cold-hearted wife who had taken her revenge. Had I plunged a jealous knife into Mrs. Flood's heart perhaps I would have been more easily forgiven. But my vengeance had been cool, calculating and very mercenary, since far from making any sacrifices I had actually gained by it. A little womanly compassion, the newspapers thought, would not have gone amiss among so much self-righteousness; while certain among them suggested—in general terms—that when a husband went astray it might only be realistic to assume that he had his reasons.

The judge, in the moment of pronouncing the decree, could not conceal his distaste for it. The barrister who had represented me, although an old college friend of my father's, treated me with great caution, feeling, perhaps, that a woman who could divorce her husband might be capable of anything, while his clerks and the officers of the court stared at me speculatively, rudely, and did not always drop their eyes when I caught them at it, as they would have done had they still considered me a lady.

Our marriage had taken a whole day to perform, flowers and white horses, organ music, champagne, two hundred happy guests. A few caustic words accompanied by a bad-tempered sniff ended it. But I knew that our divorce had really taken place on a wet afternoon in Hyde Park when he had made no excuses, asked no pardon, but had simply said "Goodbye—good luck," and I had replied "Take care." He had brought me a gift that day, not of love, for I believed him when he said he loved no one, but of understanding, and I had wept—could still weep—with gratitude and with loss.

I walked from the court a single woman again, an adult with a legal identity of my own. Mrs. Grace Barforth now, no longer Mrs. Gervase. I went to bed, slept the rest of the day and the night, and the next morning came North again to Scarborough where my Grandmother Agbrigg, who had decided she was too old now either to understand or to criticize, was nevertheless deeply shocked when she noticed I had taken off my wedding ring.

"I am being honest, grandmamma."

"You are asking for trouble, my girl. There is a mark, plain for all to see, where the ring has been. And since no one will take you for a spinster, one must assume the worst. Since you insist on travelling alone you will oblige me by not removing your gloves on the train."

Blanche was appalled by my decision to remain in Cullingford.

"Darling, are you entirely mad? They wouldn't know what to do with you. There's simply nowhere to *put* a divorced woman in Cullingford. You'd do far better to get that little house in London we talked about—and it won't be easy even there."

But her mind, and Aunt Caroline's mind, the attention of most of the family was blessedly distracted from my affairs by the needs of Noel Chard, who, crippled by an assegai-thrust at the base of the spine, had seemed at first unlikely to walk again. He had been discovered by his brothers in exactly the fevered, squalid conditions Blanche had feared, plagued by flies and heat and overcrowding from which they had deftly extracted him,

bringing back a yellow, hollow-cheeked man who could have
been their father.

But the clean air of Listonby, the determination of Aunt
Caroline, the devotion of Blanche, who was herself embarrassed
by the extent of it, soon restored him. He would not walk again
without a limp or a stick, would no longer spend whole days in
the saddle, but he would remain now on the land where Blanche
could keep an eye on him, enabling Dominic to go about his
Parliamentary duties in peace. He would be at Listonby when
Blanche was at Listonby, which would be rather more often from
now on. He would come down to London when she needed him,
or would suddenly appear at South Erin during those duty visits
she found every year more tedious. He would be here to super-
vise her growing sons, to teach them to ride and shoot and know
their manners, as Dominic had no time to do. He would be here
to *talk* to her, to understand that there were days when she felt
less beautiful—less cheerful—than others.

"You see, Grace," she told me, "or at least you *should* see
how it is. If one can arrange one's affairs sensibly—if one can
get what one wants without hurting others—then why not bend a
little? Why be strictly honest and lose, when by just making it
look right— It did Venetia no good, being honest, you know, and
sometimes, Grace, I am quite afraid for you."

I stayed at Fieldhead for a while, accustoming myself slowly
to insolence, treading warily like an invalid after a long and
weakening disease, until the averted heads and pinched lips of
Cullingford's carriage trade no longer troubled me. I entered the
draper's shop in Millergate to find myself suddenly invisible as
Mrs. Rawnsley's glance passed straight through me. The first
time it was painful, then awkward, quite soon it meant as much
to me as she did, which was very little. I saw the timid Miss
Fielding risk a trampling to death by carriage horses as she
scuttled across the street to avoid me, and I stood in embarrassed
perplexity, since I too had reason to cross over. The first time I
remained on the opposite side of the street until she was out of
sight, greatly to my own inconvenience. The third or the fourth
time I strolled nonchalantly over to the shop I wanted, bade her a
good morning, made my purchase and went away. I accepted
Miss Mandelbaum's invitation to tea with surprise and gratitude,
yet found her so jittery with nerves, so overwhelmed by her own
daring and so fearful for her reputation that I did not go a second
time. I returned Mrs. Sheldon's bow, made when her carriage
was at a safe distance, in the knowledge that the distance would

be maintained until her husband had calculated the number of votes he might lose by permitting his wife to acknowledge me against the loss of favour at Fieldhead. I endured a short, sharp lecture from Miss Tighe who, caring for no one's opinion but her own, marched up to me in broad daylight and made me aware that, although I might now choose to consider myself a single woman, she did not, and hoped I would make no attempt to claim the voting rights which might one day be granted to the truly unwed.

But it hurt me immeasurably to be cut dead by Mrs. Winch, the housekeeper from Tarn Edge, when I happened to meet her in Market Square, although the butler, Chillingworth, was not ashamed to raise his hat to me and stood one Sunday morning for fifteen minutes beside my victoria, regretting both my departure and Mrs. Winch's now all too evident incompetence.

She did her best, of course, he didn't doubt it, but Mr. Chard was difficult and Mr. Barforth gloomy. Ah no, the child would make no difference, for yesterday morning they had sent the little mite to Listonby to be brought up with her cousins, Sir Dominic's boys, which seemed an excellent idea to Chillingworth. The nursemaid, it seemed, had got above herself, the wet nurse had twice had to be changed, Mrs. Winch had declared herself unequal to the responsibility and Listonby, where the nurseries were well-staffed, well-organized, well-supervised by Mr. Chard's mother, the Duchess, appeared a good and permanent solution to one and all. Unless, of course, Mrs. Nicholas Barforth should take it into her head to leave Galton Abbey after all these years and return to her rightful home, a suggestion much favoured in the servants' hall, since Mr. Barforth had been spending a fair amount of time at Galton lately, he and his wife having lost both their children in a manner of speaking, the daughter in the graveyard and the son gone to the devil, for ought they knew, in Australia, begging my pardon. A fair basis for reconciliation, thought the servants' hall, although, between ourselves, Mrs. Winch was already looking for another situation, and if Mr. Chard continued to make those scathing remarks about his dinner, no one expected Mrs. Kincaid to last long either. As for Chillingworth himself, yes, he would very likely stay on until they pensioned him off, and in any case, although I was sorely missed, his work was easier now. No mistress meant no visitors and he need hardly stir from his pantry in the afternoons. Mr. Barforth was rarely seen, while Mr. Chard could always get himself upstairs to bed whatever state he might be in, not at all like Mr. Gervase.

My hands were shaking as I drove away, my parasol unsteady against my shoulder, images inflicting themselves like small wounds upon my memory; the tiny, elf-face of Claire Chard who was not really a Chard at all, the child I had not wished to touch because I had known how easily love for her could have detained me at Tarn Edge; and then Gervase, who had been very much my child, wending his uncertain way upstairs in the small hours of the morning, humorous and somehow gentle in drink, the sharp edges blurred from his vision. I didn't know what had happened to his son. No one would be likely to tell me and I could not ask. My own miscarriage came back to me, not the fear or the pain but the sense of failure, for there had been no sign of pregnancy since then and could be none now. I felt defeated, sterile, and then—to complete the agony—I began to remember Gideon.

But I was not always so feeble. It was spring again, an excellent time to make changes, and having examined the state of my finances and found them healthy, I shocked Cullingford further by quitting my father's house, where it was felt I might have had the good taste to languish, and purchased a home of my own in Blenheim Crescent, a short, curved terrace of houses designed for those who aspired to gentility but could not quite afford the greater elegance of Blenheim Lane.

It was a narrow building with a long front garden, a flight of shallow steps to a door with a fluted, many coloured fanlight somewhat too grand for its surroundings. The hall was narrow too, accommodating a thin staircase which led to two large bedrooms on the first floor, three small ones above. I had a drawing-room with a dining-parlour behind it on the ground floor, a square, dark kitchen behind that, more steps, very steep this time, leading to a stone-flagged yard which offered me a view of houses very much like my own.

"Something of an ugly duckling, is it not?" Mrs. Agbrigg said, and so I set to work—badly needing employment—to create a swan. The dark and decidedly ugly kitchen was stripped of its bottle-green paintwork and repainted in cream and pale blue. I threw rugs in cheerful, possibly vulgar colours on the stone floor, placed a rocking-chair by the hearth, purchased a new stove, a brass fender, acquired a stray but rather disdainful cat. I took out the paltry little fireplace in the drawing-room and replaced it with cool, amber-veined marble, stood a porcelain clock in the centre of my mantelshelf, a Sèvres vase on either side. I hired a cook and a parlourmaid, a man to do the outside work and look after my carriage. I bought a carriage too, a brand-new, smart-as-paint victoria, although I allowed my father to provide the horses and see to their stabling.

I opened my first completely private and personal account at the bank, spending an hour with a considerably embarrassed Mr. Rawnsley, who, although well-versed in the financial requirements of widows and spinsters, had never been alone before with a divorcee.

I moved into my house, alone with three servants and a cat, closed my door, went to bed, got up the next morning, sat in my drawing-room, waited—saw the afternoon and the evening come on, ate my dinner, went back to bed—waited, between some hours of light sleep, for morning. Aunt Faith called, bringing flowers and reassurance, the promise that her house was always open to me and should I wish to accompany her to Venice next month I would be more than welcome.

There was a weekly letter from my Agbrigg grandmother urging me to find something useful to do, and from my Grand-mamma Elinor in France offering me asylum there where "nobody would know" and hinting that, whatever I might have heard to the contrary, I would soon find another man to marry me.

Gervase's parents surprised me by coming to see me together, Mr. Barforth looking older, although perhaps he was not ageing so much as mellowing, Mrs. Barforth covering the many things we could not speak of by her talk of good weather and good harvests, sunshine and fresh spring pastures. But, before coming to me, they had been to the churchyard to take flowers to Venetia, and her memory inhabited the air around them.

"If there's anything you want, Grace—" he said gruffly as they were leaving. "Anything I can get you?"

And when he had gone to fetch his hat, Mrs. Barforth pressed her cheek against mine and gave me what they both knew I most longed for.

"Gervase is in Mexico, darling. Don't ask me why, for I thought it was to be Australia, but no, Mexico. Good heavens! how very *far* that sounds. But he says he is well. Diana is still in Nice but Compton Flood—Lord Sternmore—is to call and see her on his way home from India, and Julian is very hopeful. Dearest, may I come and see you again?"

She came, sometimes alone, sometimes bringing that gentle, nervous sheepdog with her to the disgust of my imperious tabby cat. Mr. Barforth came too, usually at tea-time when he would eat large but absent-minded helpings of sugary foods and drink several cups of strong tea, a sure indication, I thought, that Tarn Edge no longer provided fruit cakes and gingerbread, no longer served scones hot from the oven and muffins freshly toasted and rich with syrup; an even surer indication that he was lonely.

My father came every day on some pretext or other, but these family visits occupied a mere fraction of my time and I could see no way of filling the rest. Cullingford society was closed to me and I did not care enough about it to attempt a breach in its ranks. Only one woman among my new neighbours would speak to me, for the very good reason that her husband was employed by my father at Fieldhead. I had expected all this and had prepared for it, yet now, when the decisions had been taken and the struggle was over, when each day opened out before me with nothing to distinguish it from the next, I was bound to ask myself, as Blanche had done: "What is it all *for*?"

What I required was work and there was none available. I had decorated and furnished my house and did not mean to spend my life obsessed with the need to be constantly changing my wallpaper for lack of better employment. Yet what else was there? Such few public appointments available to women specified, above all, that the women must be of good character, and I had lost my character altogether. I could not open a school, since no right-minded parent would entrust me with the instruction of the young. I could not sit on a school board nor on the administrative committee of the workhouse as Miss Tighe did. Indeed, I could not sit on any committee, charitable or otherwise, since no respectable woman would be willing to serve with me. I had no musical talent like Miss Mandelbaum, no interrupted artistic career like Mrs. Sheldon's which I could take up again, no particular religious faith like Miss Fielding's to which I could devote my time and ingenuity. What had it all been for?

I began to lose energy, to wonder about joining Aunt Faith in Venice, travelling as widely as I could and coming home just often enough to keep the promise I had made through Mrs. Agbrigg to my father. Running away, in fact, and it was Liam Adair who rescued me from my gloom, taking my house by storm one bright, windy morning, a dozen copies of the *Cullingford Star* under one arm, a bottle of champagne under the other, an enormous bouquet of white and purple lilac which he flung down on the hall table with his hat.

"Well, now—if you can bear a visit from a gentleman of the

Press after what some of my colleagues did to you. But you must admit that both the *Star* and Eustace Roundwood's *Courier & Review* left you alone—me because I love you dearly and Roundwood because he can't afford the wrong side of your father.''

And seeing the sharp, interested eyes of my maid as she closed the door behind him—for a man with flowers and wine and pretty speeches at ten o'clock in the morning was the kind of thing she had been hoping to see when she entered my service—I laughed, let him kiss my cheek, and invited him inside.

"Champagne, Liam—at this hour of the day?''

"Why not? When one visits an unusual woman one hardly expects to be fobbed off with tea. Miss Mandelbaum and Miss Tighe give me plenty of that.''

And for an hour I indulged myself with champagne and great bursts of laughter, as fallen women do, while he regaled me with the up-and-down fortunes of the *Star* and his own literary and amorous endeavours; the widow who had almost succeeded in marrying him; his exposure of bad housing in the neighbourhood of Gower Street, which had caused some irate landlord or other to put a brick through his windows again; his old landlady's daughter, who had taken it into her head to get into bed with him, which had necessitated yet another change of address; his concern at the rate of infant mortality in Cullingford's workhouse; the damnable little brats who raised havoc all day in Gower Street so that he was undecided whether to advocate shooting them or sending them to school; his new landlady who went to chapel three times every Sunday and looked like a martyred missionary, but who had started giving him some very odd glances lately from her eye-corners.

"Come and see us at the *Star*, Grace, and meet my new assistant. I can't think why you haven't been before.''

His new assistant, since the old one had been Robin Ashby, was the nearest he came to mentioning Venetia, my appearance at the *Star*, as he well knew, having been put off because I had not wished to be reminded of the happier days when she and I had gone there together. But his visit had warmed me, offered me a reason to get out my new victoria, to put on my new hat and gloves for something other than a visit to Fieldhead or an excursion among the stony stares of Millergate. I went, my mind on Venetia every inch of the way, my eyes misting over as Gower Street came into view, the unwashed, underfed urchins scuffling in the gutter, the stench of dung and garbage, those

boarded-up windows. But it was not my intention to forget
Venetia and I got down resolutely and quite calmly from my
carriage, walked briskly upstairs, past the aged printing-presses,
into the cluttered upper room, to be enclosed at once in a hearty,
just faintly alcoholic embrace.

"So you've come to look us over? I thought you would."

"Nothing seems changed."

"I don't know about that. I'm older—you're bonnier. There's
my new assistant—at any rate, *that*'s a change for the better.
I've been wanting to see the two of you together. Grace, this is
Mrs. Inman—Camille, this is Grace Barforth, my stepmother's
granddaughter, that we've spoken of."

"Mrs. Inman." And through my amazement that she should
be female at all—any kind of female—I realized I was holding
out my hand to one of the loveliest women I had ever seen.

She was, as I learned later, in her early thirties, a perfect oval
face, glossy black hair and a great deal of it in a huge coil high
on her head, eyes which should have been dark, too, but which
were an astonishing amethyst, long-lashed and altogether
entrancing. She was tall and very slender, plainly dressed but
extremely neat, a bunch of violets pinned on the lapel of a pale
blue bodice, a fall of white lace at the throat, a warm smile and a
firm handshake, a friendliness of manner which was one of her
greatest charms.

I sat down in the chair by her desk, fascinated, and we began
a conversation which lasted in fact for several days, my curiosity
about this woman who had once shared her life with a man who
sounded very much like Robin Ashby and who had not only
survived to tell the tale but could tell it with affection and
humour, proving insatiable. She was a missionary's daughter
who had spent her girlhood in the wild places of the world where
propriety—although her mother had made the effort—did not
seem to matter. Her parents had been killed, she did not say
how, and she had lived "here and there" for a while, finally
settling with a spinster aunt who, among other things, had
founded a shelter for wayward girls in the East End of London.
No one had ever really protected Camille as Venetia and I had
been protected. Her father had been too busy caring for his
heathen flock to concern himself with his daughter. Her mother
had trusted in God and hoped for the best. The spinster aunt had
put her to work, at an age when Venetia and I had been ignorant
of life's basic facts, among child prostitutes and the victims of
household rape. She had married at eighteen and gone adventur-

ing with her husband, a journalist ten years her senior who, like her father and Robin Ashby, had been more deeply touched by the sufferings of the masses than of the individual. But she was used to that. When her husband fell ill, she wrote his pieces for him. When he recovered, they continued to work together. When he died five years ago, she had gone on supporting herself as, for the six months of his final malady, she had supported them both.

She had a slender income of her own, barely enough to keep a roof over her head, and when Liam Adair, who had been a good friend for years both to herself and her husband, had offered her employment she had been glad of it. She did not live well, she was ready to admit, but she found life interesting. Sometimes very interesting indeed. No, she saw nothing alarming in walking about the city streets alone. She took a cab when she could afford it, which was seldom, but mostly she came and went as she pleased without too much hindrance. No one had ever told her she was frail and in need of care, and she had seen no advantages, therefore, in fragility. Her husband would have been irritated by it, her father would not even have noticed. Women, she had found, were very rarely frail in any case. As for herself, she was always busy. At the moment she was investigating housing conditions in a nearby street, selected at random, and Liam would publish her survey in weekly instalments in the *Star*.

"Why don't you lend a hand?" Liam said, leaning an arm along the back of my chair. "It's a job worth doing and, unlike Camille here, who costs me a fortune, I know you wouldn't expect any pay."

"Liam, you are still exploiting women."

"Yes—yes, I know. But these printing-presses of mine won't last forever, my darling, and neither will Grandmamma Elinor. Think it over. Camille could do with the help, and she'll tell you what a jewel I am to work with."

Camille Inman came to tea with me the following Sunday, stayed, at my urgent request, to dinner and told me, among a great many other things, that although Liam was assuredly no "jewel" she was not ashamed to be in his employ. The *Star* in his hands would make no one rich, but its readership was extending now from the few radical hot-heads who had previously purchased it to the more thoughtful members of all classes. There was no denying that, because of the *Star*, it was somewhat safer to eat Cullingford's bread than it used to be and she had great hopes for her survey of overcrowding in St. Mark's Fold.

She was no missionary like her father. She simply wished to
investigate and inform and would be content to leave the moralizing to others. Could she not tempt me to lend a hand? I would
need a strong stomach, of course, for she had known many a
well-intentioned and truly compassionate soul who had been
quite unable to cope with the *smell* of human poverty and
distress.

I drove to the *Star* the following morning dressed plainly,
without jewellery of any kind, as she had instructed, and together we took the ten-minute walk from Gower Street to St.
Mark's Fold, Camille once again with a bunch of violets pinned
to her lapel, her startling amethyst eyes expressing no shock, no
disgust, no anger, but remaining in all circumstances perfectly
serene and friendly.

A pleasant enough sounding place, St. Mark's Fold, reminis-
cent of some cloistered cathedral city, a green lawn and tapering
ecclesiastical spires. I had never heard the name before, although
I was Cullingford born, and discovered it to be a dank alleyway
among a hundred others just like it, a filthy cobweb of streets
built by Grandmamma Elinor's first husband, my Aycliffe
grandfather, around the Barforth mill at Low Cross. It consisted
of ten squat two-roomed houses on the right hand side of a
narrow, muddy street, with ten more built behind them, a further
twenty houses on the left-hand side constructed in the same
back-to-back fashion, the houses at the rear being reached by
passages that seemed no larger than arrow-slits cut into the walls.

And in these forty houses, with their total of eight rooms,
Camille expected to find between three and four hundred people
living, her calculations being difficult to make not from any
unwillingness on the part of the inhabitants to be counted but
because of their habit of taking in lodgers and throwing out
wayward daughters; and because only one in two of all infants
born here would be likely to reach the age of five. She had done
these surveys before, she told me, her composure unruffled.
She knew.

I was not to suppose that the whole of Cullingford's working
classes lived in such squalor. Far from it, for the Law Valley
produced a most enduring breed of men and women who, by
hard work and good management, and a kind of shrewd, down-
to-earth humour Camille found most appealing, organized their
affairs in a much better fashion. She knew many houses where
there was not much money but where the women were scrupu-
lously decent and the men hard-working and philosophical. She

had encountered in other houses a kind of realistic, almost sardonic nobility, a grudging respect between husband and wife, and a gruff-spoken affection, a family united against all comers, facing the insurmountable and somehow—without making too much of a fuss—surmounting it. But these were the ones who paid their rent on time and put something aside for a rainy day, who sent their children to school and who had the resilience, the nerve, the stamina, to pick *themselves* up whenever Life or Fate or the state of the textile trade knocked them down. I would meet very few of them in St. Mark's Fold.

It was slower work than I had expected, for we visited only five houses that day, Camille sitting herself down on whatever chair or packing-case or heap of shoddy seemed available, taking whatever stray urchin or stray dog or cat on to her lap that wished to go there, with no particular demonstration of affection, no grimace of pity, but as a matter of course, something quite natural. She had no money to give, no cast-off clothing, no basket of goodies, she made that clear from the beginning. There was no use asking her to pay a doctor's bill or find shoes for the children. She was hard pressed, often enough, to get her own shoes mended and could show the worn leather to prove it. But what she could do was tell other people, who might have something spare or who, better still, might tell the landlord it was high time he did something about those roof-tiles and those ugly damp patches. "Now then, Mrs. Ryan—Mrs. Backhouse—Mrs. O'Flynn—how many beds did you say you have?—and how many sleep in them?

Mrs. Ryan had one sagging double bed in her upper room where she slept with her husband and her three younger children, two girls and a boy. Her four elder children, "two of each," slept downstairs on the kind of mattresses I had seen at the home of Sally Grimshaw's mother. There was another daughter who "came and went" but had not been seen for six months and more now. Mrs. Ryan and her elder daughters worked sometimes at Low Cross Mill, sometimes elsewhere, for the girls, she said, were "flighty," prone to "answering back" the overlookers and spending their wages on themselves every Thursday night before she could get at them, while her boys could get no work and her husband was unfit for it, suffering so badly, as so many ageing mill-hands did, from bronchitis—the disease of smoke and damp and raw northern mornings—that he seemed unlikely to get through another winter. He had been a good man once, earning good wages as a wool-sorter at Low Cross which he had put straight into his wife's pocket, not across the bar counter. They had even managed to save a little, had got together some decent furniture, had been in a "fair way of carrying on." But the bad winter six years ago had finished him. He had lost his job at Low Cross for "breaking time" on those icy mornings when he had scarcely been able to breathe, and that had been the end of it. No job, no wages, and the doctor's bills had soon taken care of their savings. He could hardly drag himself to the end of the street now, her man, and had no interest any more in trying. Her boys and one of her girls were turning out troublesome—because, after all, they needed a man's hard hand sometimes and *he* wouldn't stir himself these days—the lads hanging about the streets all day, the girl loitering on her way home from the mill. No, the children never went to school. It was too far and in any case she had to be in her loom-gate at Low Cross by half-past five every morning and was not at home to get them out of bed and see them off. So far she had managed to pay her rent every week, although often enough it meant taking her decent shawl and her husband's boots to the pawn shop on a Tuesday morning and redeeming them on a Friday, as best she could. But if there should be any more doctor's bills this winter, then she might not do so well.

"Thank you," said Camille and as we went outside she sniffed the violets at her lapel and translated for me. "The eldest daughter, the one who 'comes and goes' is a prostitute, of course, and the other one who 'loiters' is serving her apprenticeship to the same trade. The boys she calls troublesome are starting to steal, there can be no doubt about that. They will go to prison sooner or later, I suppose, and their little brothers will be awfully proud of them. Oh yes—for in St. Mark's Fold, you see, it is thought quite bold and dashing to be in a House of Correction, and when they are released they will strut about like peacocks and take their pick of the girls—a fine old time until they are sent back again. Poor Mrs. Ryan, for it is poverty that does it, you know, and she can't help that—just as her husband can't help his bad chest. I wonder if she knows she will be better off when he is dead?"

Mrs. Backhouse did not get out of bed to greet us, having recently given birth to a child, a wailing little scrap wrapped in a corner of her blanket who looked no more likely to survive than the mother. She had no interest in us nor in herself, nor in the baby whose persistent crying she seemed not to notice. She had no man of her own and pregnancy had stopped her earnings. She was in arrears with her rent and when the landlord threw her out she would have no choice but the workhouse, where they would take her baby away from her in any case. So far as she was concerned it couldn't happen soon enough.

Mrs. O'Flynn had eleven children in her two rooms and four lodgers in her cellar. She kept a pig in her yard, which, she cheerfully admitted, did not please all her neighbours. She had been brought over from Ireland as a girl because the potato crop had failed and people were starving. They had been set ashore at Liverpool and had walked to Cullingford in slow stages, her parents and their six children pushing everything they possessed on a handcart, obliged to keep moving in order to avoid being picked up for vagrancy and shipped back to Ireland again. But her parents, being country-bred, had been unable to withstand the impact of the city. Cullingford's foul air and smoky skies had withered them quicker than the famine, their children being saved from the workhouse by the intervention of several large-hearted neighbours who had absorbed a child apiece into their own families on the principle that there is always room for one more. But these kind neighbours had long since moved away, taking Mrs. O'Flynn's brothers and sisters with them, she didn't know where, and would be unlikely to recognize them now in any case. She had given birth to her first child at fourteen or thereabouts—younger rather than older—and, like Sally Grimshaw's mother, had been pregnant more or less ever since. Her fertility was a nuisance, of course—certainly she could not comprehend how anyone could call it a blessing—but although she did not understand it, she accepted it, like menstruation, as one of the drawbacks of womanhood. She had kept her family decent because she was hard-handed and foul-mouthed when she had to be. Any man who molested a daughter of hers would have the mother to deal with and she had dragged her husband out of the ale-house by the scruff of his neck on many a Thursday night. She worked in the weaving-sheds at Law Cross and so did her girls as soon as they were ten years old. The only one among them to have lost her job had not dared face her mother and had run away from home. She had one son who had lost the use of his legs in an explosion at the local ironworks and yes, her husband was "chesty," so were all men, what of it? Women had babies, men who had worked in the mines or the mills and who smoked cheap tobacco coughed in the winter and were short winded in the summer time. The future? What did we mean by that? If she could get herself from Monday morning to Friday night and back again without coming a cropper, then she wouldn't complain.

"Four houses," Camille said, when we had interviewed a bustling cheerful Mrs. Clough, eighteen years old and two years married, her husband holding down a steady job, only one child in her cradle, her manner briskly assuring us that none of the misfortunes of these old women—her neighbours—could possibly happen to her.

"Four houses. Thirty-six more to go. Thank heavens Liam picked a short street!"

I accompanied her every day for a week after that, uncomfortable at first at being in the vicinity of Low Cross where I might possibly encounter my father-in-law, who would certainly enquire the nature of my business in this rough locality. But both the work and Camille's reaction to it absorbed me. No, she was not shocked by what she saw in St. Mark's Fold. It was not vice to blame, after all, but hardship, just people adapting themselves to poverty's rules as I had adapted to affluence. When there was no work and no hope of work the result was always the same. The boys stole and the girls took to street-walking. Her aunt in London had calculated years ago, when Camille herself had been a child, that there were upwards of six thousand brothels in the city alone and easily eighty thousand prostitutes, girls, in many cases, who were not so much wayward as extremely hungry. Naturally, even at her aunt's London shelter she had met girls who found nothing distasteful in offering their bodies for whatever such a body might fetch, finding the work less arduous and rather more profitable than the sweatshops of the tailoring trade. But mainly, she had found, a girl went on the streets because her choices were between that, the workhouse or starvation. And what, she wondered, in those circumstances would I myself have done?

Camille had encountered none of the great stars of the profession. Doubtless there were women who received pearls and diamonds and racehorses for their favours. In fact she knew quite well that there were. But they had never required the comforts of her aunt's soup and bread, nor her protection from an outraged, short-changed pimp. Camille's experience had been confined to girls like the daughters of Mrs. Ryan who, having grown up sharing a bed with several brothers, found promiscuity a natural extension of their family life; or the little fifteen-year-old mothers one could find ten a penny in Gower Street and who had to feed their babies somehow.

Doubtless there *were* brothels furnished with silk draperies and couches of rich velvet, at least she hoped so for the sake of one's friends who had had recourse to them. But she had seen nothing of the kind. The brothels she had visited had been dreary establishments, not much better than the house of Mrs. O'Flynn, where an old bawd offered for sale her own and her neighbours' daughters.

She had luncheon at my house the following Sunday, her glossy hair still dressed in its single massive coil which made her neck seem very supple and very long, her gown of light, forget-me-not blue with its high frilled collar bringing out the wonderful amethyst of her eyes. She had pinned flowers on her shoulder again, having no jewels, and her manner was easy and cheerful, her appreciation of my house and my possessions without envy. She was not, she confessed, cast in the domestic mould herself, tended to get her own cupboards and drawers in a frightful muddle, but how comfortable all this was, how enjoyable. We relaxed, became easy, almost frivolous, and were giggling like schoolgirls when the doorbell rang and my father-in-law appeared.

"Camille," I told her, feeling oddly flustered, "this is Mr. Nicholas Barforth. Mr. Barforth—Mrs. Inman."

"How do you do," she said and knowing of no reason why she should be intimidated by him she continued to chat of one thing and another, receiving from him the most monosyllabic replies. She smiled, talked on. He became quite forbidding, I thought, very much the master of the Barforth mills, a man of his class and his time who would instantly have assessed the cost per yard of the pretty but inexpensive fabric of her dress, the reason for that spray of tiny yellow flowers on her shoulder, the unusual freedom of her conversation, and would have judged her by that.

"I must be going," she said as the teacups were removed, shaking her head and making light of the distance when I offered to send her in my carriage. She would just put on her hat and could be safely at her own door by the time they had got out the horses. She was used to walking. There was no need to make a fuss. She was pleasant, amused, determined to have her way.

"How far?" snapped my father-in-law.

"Prince Albert Road, just down the hill."

"Yes—and across the centre of town and up the other side, on a Sunday when the streets are full of mill-hands drinking their wages. It won't do, you know."

"I beg your pardon."

"Now look here, young lady," he said, very exasperated, "you'll either take Grace's carriage or you'll take mine. In fact you'd better take mine, since its standing there ready and it's time I was off. I'll set you down on my way."

For a moment her eyes met his in a level stare and then her lovely oval face dimpled with mischievous laughter, her magnificent body bent itself forward into a swift, parlourmaid's curtsey.

"Certainly, Mr. Barforth, sir," she said.

"Good," he told her, smiling grimly but broadly. "Then you'd better put on your hat."

22

I ENCOUNTERED A WORLD I had never suspected but which had
been there all the time, running parallel with mine, Camille
Inman's world of tolerance and good humour, of undemonstrative,
unsentimental caring, of sound common sense; an atmosphere in
which Venetia would have blossomed and flourished. I had
started life as Miss Agbrigg, heiress of Fieldhead. I had become
Mrs. Gervase Barforth of Tarn Edge. The Cullingford I knew
now regarded me not as a divorced woman but as *the* divorced
woman, since Cullingford had no other. Camille and her acquaintances saw me as Grace who helped at the *Star*, an entirely
new and separate person to be assessed on her own merits or lack
of them, not on the bank balance of husband or father, nor the
immaculate condition of her linen cupboards and her reputation.

She took me, one evening, to the house of a Dr. and Mrs.
Stone, the younger of the two physicians, as it turned out, who
had attended Venetia. He did not remember me. I did not remind
him, being content to drink his wine, a rough, red vintage in
heavy glasses, and enjoy the conversation of a man who saw no
reason to treat me like a half-witted child. When Dr. Stone found
it necessary to refer to pregnancy he referred to it, no vague
suggestions of being "in an interesting condition" or "in the
family way" but pregnant—just that—an expression which had
not endeared him to Mrs. Rawnsley and her like who had great
admiration for those women who, rather than expose their naked
bodies to a male eye, preferred to suffer and eventually die in
chaste silence. If Dr. Stone felt obliged to mention legs or
breasts or buttocks he mentioned them, and consequently was
rarely consulted by those ladies—and we knew many—who did
not acknowledge possession of such things.

He was a square-shouldered, blunt-spoken man who had been
something of a radical in his younger days and—as he freely

admitted with a twinkle in his eye—had made himself very unpopular in his first practice by advocating the use of such contraceptive methods as were then available, among patients in a rough labouring area of Liverpool who had an abundance of nothing but children. He had seen, as one saw in St. Mark's Fold, the squalid overcrowding, the grinding poverty, the inability to feed even the mouths one already had, and he had thought, in his innocence, that the knowledge of how not to increase those mouths must be welcome. He had reckoned without the virtuous, the narrow-minded and, very often, the sterile, who saw these large, undernourished families as proof of the lustfulness and general inferiority of the poor. The remedy, for such people, was extremely simple. The sexual act was intended only for the procreation of children. A decent man fathered the number of children he could afford, and, when his limit had been reached, abandoned the act for ever. A couple who mistook its purpose and indulged in it for pleasure must accept the consequences of their over-breeding, must wallow in the mire they had themselves created. Dr. Stone, who by this time had made the acquaintance of a young schoolteacher and fallen deeply in love with her, had not agreed and had aroused so much ill-feeling by his recommendation of the contraceptive sheath—this device being normally used by gentlemen in their dealings with whores, not to protect the woman from maternity but themselves from venereal disease—that he had been obliged to leave Liverpool, taking his schoolteacher, now Mrs. Anna Stone, with him.

They had lived in London for a while, in the notorious Seven Dials district where they had first met Camille and her crusading aunt, and had come north some years ago, first to the fashionable spa town of Harrogate, where Dr. Stone's brusque manner had not succeeded, then to Cullingford to join Dr. Blackwood, who had been impressed by the younger man's qualifications and unaware until too late of his opinions. Dr. Blackwood, the senior and considerably more popular partner, lived in some elegance at the top of Blenheim Lane, where, despite the grubby out-thrusting of our growing town, it remained leafy, hushed, exclusive. Dr. Stone's house stood at its lower end, a yard or two from the point where residential Blenheim Lane deteriorated into commercial Millergate, bustling with shoppers, idlers, urchins, carts and carriages, clattering down the cobbles to Market Square, the raucous, often indecorous centre of our town.

Dr. Blackwood was a member of our town council, chaired several charitable committees, dined out a great deal. Dr. Stone had no time for committees and was suspicious of both organized charity and those who dispensed it. He had been asked to leave meetings many a time in his Liverpool days because of his impatience with those who expected a St. Mark's Fold mother to send her children to chapel every Sunday in starched white pinafores and expressed self-righteous disappointment when she did not. He had derided the maxim "cleanliness is next to godliness" in circumstances where soap was a luxury and hot water rarely available. He had suggested that the children of the ragged poor so rarely came to Sunday School because the children of the prosperous had been trained not to sit beside them, for fear of catching fleas; and he had fallen foul of the congregation. Now he tended to keep his own counsel or dispense it discreetly, and I had been a regular visitor for several weeks before Mrs. Stone showed me the hut in their back garden and explained its purpose.

Anna Stone was as quiet as her husband was explosive, a face as smooth as Camille's although it lacked Camille's beauty, having nothing remarkable about it but a pair of steady grey eyes. She was a competent woman who would stand firm, I thought, in a crisis, accustomed to the panic that often accompanies sickness, to hysterical men and women pounding at her door at midnight in search of medicines or miracles, or simply needing to be told that everything would be all right. She was assured, patient, gave herself slowly, and like Camille had never learned to rely on male protection, having been brought up by an older sister who, through two happy marriages and two widowhoods, had taken an active part in matters of education, woman suffrage and the "rescue," whenever possible, of girls from the city streets.

This "rescue" work was not uncommon, such notables as the very serious and very high-minded Liberal leader, Mr. Gladstone, having participated in it, somewhat to the disgust of Queen Victoria, it was said, who, disliking Mr. Gladstone personally, was inclined to think the worst. But the provision by Dr. and Mrs. Stone of a shelter in their garden, four narrow beds, an old table, a wash-stand with a metal jug, a mirror on a nail above it, pretty chintz curtains and a vase of garden flowers, seemed to me a sensible way of doing good.

Their aims were modest, their expectations of success extremely slight. They were not reformers in the sense that they hoped to make sweeping changes. They could, in fact, see little chance of lasting change at all. Conditions, for perhaps four-fifths of humanity, were very bad and seemed unlikely to get better. They were simply a practical couple who knew that sometimes a girl's whole life could take a disastrous turning because for a vital night or two she had nowhere to go. When they met such a girl they offered her an alternative, not much, of course, just a hard bed in that garden shelter, a decent breakfast, medical treatment if required, a little sound advice which usually was not regarded. Not much, and usually after a day or two, when the cuts and bruises were healed and the hunger-pains gone, when the miscarriage had been tidied up and the swelling in the groin seemed not to be syphilis, the girl was gone too. Usually—not always.

Mrs. Stone would not allow me inside the shelter to begin with, not wishing to give its occupants an impression, as she put it, of being monkeys at the zoo, and she entirely agreed with Camille that, although poverty was the usual and most powerful motive, there were girls who enjoyed this undoubtedly old-established profession and others who did extremely well out of it. I had myself seen Gideon Chard lounging beside the carriage of a woman whose favours would certainly not have come cheap. I had seen women gorgeously attired in satins and towering plumage strolling up and down the Haymarket when I had visited the theatre with Blanche, none of them among the first rank of courtesans, perhaps, like Gideon's, but well fed, cheerful, looking as if they had the means to pay their rent.

But Dr. and Mrs. Stone did not interest themselves in such as these. Nor were they concerned with the little girls of eight and nine years old who could be purchased easily in any of our cities, since such children were offered up by their mothers, more often than not, who would take care of them afterwards. And if it shocked me that there could be such mothers—as, of course, it must shock me—I should remember that these women, in many cases, had been compelled themselves, before the introduction of our various Factory Acts, to labour from the age of five for seventeen hours a day in woollen-mills, cotton-mills, coal-mines, had been deflowered by overlookers, foremen, workmates, their brothers, sometimes their fathers, in those hovels where they slept six or seven to a bed. To such women the loss of virginity for cash in an eight-year-old child could not seem so terrible as it did to me.

Terrible enough, of course. But sharing a practical disposition, Dr. and Mrs. Stone preferred to offer their assistance to the slightly older children, the girls of twelve and thirteen and fourteen one could find in abundance any day of the week at the railway stations of any city, girls from the country sent off to fend for themselves, particularly in these days of agricultural depression, because there was no room at home, or girls who had left home respectably to take up employment and had not given satisfaction, little nursemaids and kitchenmaids discharged without a reference for the crime, sometimes, of being too young to understand what was required of them, and with nowhere to go.

"Good" girls, of course, and usually quite innocent, unlike the urchins we bred in our cities. And Mrs. Stone was in a position to assure me that every train, in every city including our own, was met regularly by sharp-eyed, soft-tongued women who traded not in simple prostitution but the highly profitable marketing of virginity.

"Really?" I said and Mrs. Stone smiled, realizing I had believed virginity to be of importance mainly to husbands desirous of producing an heir they could be sure of. But no, for virginity, she told me, within her working memory had been valued as high as sixty or seventy pounds, a sum which had shrunk in recent times to a discreetly preferred five pound note, not for want of customers, she hastened to add, but because the commodity was now so much easier to come by and had lost the value of its rarity.

And why should it be so valuable in the first place? Well, of course, there *were* men who found the deflowering of virgins moving and mysterious, others who required it as an added titillation, but mainly it was seen as a sanitary precaution, a virgin being presumed free from venereal disease. There was no cure for syphilis, she told me, clearly wondering if I had heard the word before, and, as any doctor would tell me—or, at least, any doctor like Patrick Stone—there were times when it reached the proportions of an epidemic. It was a terrible, shameful way to die, but, men's needs being what they were, the risk continued to be taken, and since supply is created by demand she had met several women who had dealt for many years, and very lucratively, in virgins, procuring for some of their regular customers as many as two a week.

The girls were picked up, hungry and frightened, at the stations and in the public parks, persuaded, or in some cases given an entirely false impression of what would be required. Just a kiss and a cuddle, they would be told, a deceit which necessitated the used of rather isolated houses for such transactions, since when the truth dawned some girls would kick and scream, while others—suspected as likely troublemakers by the procuress—would have been so heavily dosed with laudanum in advance that they would have to be carried inside.

An evile trade, necessitating a rapid turn-over, since the same girl, obviously, could not be used twice. And when the damage was done she would be bundled back into a closed carriage, driven away from that very secret address and abandoned somewhere in an alien street, with perhaps a guinea from that purchase price of £5 in her hand. Sometimes the Stones would find her. Sometimes a more conventional brothel-keeper who did not deal in maidenheads would find her first. Often enough some man would pick her up and take her home with him for a night or two, which would lead, of course, to the brothel in the end. Sometimes, if she was badly torn or badly shocked, she would spend a longer time than usual in the Stones's garden, performing small tasks about the house, and even then the final reaction varied. Some girls would hang their heads in shame and creep tamely away, others would shrug their shoulders and realize they had now learned a trade. And so long as these disease-conscious gentlemen were willing to pay, neither Mrs. Stone nor my friend Camille could see an end to it.

I worked throughout the spring and summer almost obsessively, my enthusiasm and my indignation marking me, I knew, as an amateur, although Liam—professional to his fingertips—made full use of it, sending me, when the St. Mark's Fold survey was done—to equally appalling dens elsewhere in the city, thus proving the evil to be widespread. I listed the sordid details of every house in Commercial Close and the older, rat-infested Silsbridge Street, cowering a mile away from the splendid, Italianate façade of Nethercoats Mill; checked and cross-checked, with a novice's determination to get it exactly right, so eager to inform the world of these injustices which everyone in Cullingford, including myself, had always known and not wished to think about, that personal relationships—the stuff of which my life had hitherto been made—became slightly blurred, faintly unreal. And so it was that the sudden dreaminess of Camille escaped me, or, if it did not, then I had no time to think about it, and consequently missed the choicest scandal to hit Cullingford since my own, which had been going on right under my zealous nose.

"Do you know," she said to me one warm and, for me, extremely busy afternoon. "Mr. Nicholas Barforth is a very attractive man."

"My father-in-law? I suppose he must have been."

"But he still is, you may mark my words. That type of man improves with age. The ruthlessness mellows and the—well—the *attractiveness* remains. And he is not so old."

Of course she had been giving me a clue, worried—as Liam told me afterwards—that her unlikely yet obviously very satisfactory affair with my father-in-law might shock me; as indeed it did. Not for any reasons of morality but simply because he *was* my father-in-law, because she was beautiful, whimsical, adorable, and because I had rather hoped to see him reconciled to his wife.

It had happened very quickly, taking her so much by surprise that she had told no one, being herself barely able to believe it. They had met at my house and she had been a little irritated and very much amused at his insistence on taking her home in his carriage. They had measured each other, and although she acknowledged his attractions—power, shrewdness, toughness and wealth being a potent blend in any man—she knew they could have little in common and did not expect to get on with him. And they had not got on together. She had sat in his carriage for over an hour, outside her front door, while he poured disapproval—scorn almost—on the life she led, shredding her ideals to pieces while she, just as quickly, patched them up again. The horses had grown restless and he had simply driven off with her to the station, and since it had been nearly dinner-time by then and they had not eaten—well—they had gone to Leeds and dined, she couldn't—or wouldn't—say where, except that it had been extremely elegant and probably outrageously expensive.

They had met again twice that week and on the Friday she had gone with him to Scarborough—yes, so soon—how very shocking! —and had stayed with him until Sunday night, at a house right on the cliff-edge where they had—and here she swallowed and blushed, not from guilt, I thought, but from some quite blissful memory—where they had found themselves in harmony in every possible way. She had been seeing him since then as often as she could, which turned out to be very often, and yes, it was altogether a fit of madness, she would readily admit it, but the mere thought of him caused her to glow and tingle—how utterly insane, yet so *wonderful*, and to feel shivers down her spine— caused her to *long* for him, and she wasn't ashamed of it. She had been to Scarborough almost every weekend since then, surely I had noticed her unseemly haste, the way she had rushed to catch the train? And what of Mr. Barforth, my father-in-law—

whom to my amazement she now called Nicholas? Did he long, too?

"Don't be unkind," she said. "I know you can't believe it of him, but he does. He's beautiful, Grace. Perhaps you can't believe that either. But he is."

I could hardly bring myself to face him when next we met, not because I blamed him for desiring Camille—how could any man be blamed for that?—but because her blissful, sighing ecstasies had forced me to think of him not so much as an elderly relative but a potent, sensual male, and it embarrassed me. But, whatever his ultimate intentions might be, he made no secret that at present he could not have enough of Camille, and had called to see me solely for the pleasure of talking about her to someone who knew just how desirable she was.

"Why not?" said Liam Adair, finding me alone in the office the following Thursday morning. "So she's gone a day early this time, has she? Well, I didn't think the affair could get much hotter, but it seems I'm wrong. And why not? Every rich old man deserves a young woman to round off his life—or so most rich old men will tell you. Good luck to her."

"I rather thought that you and she—?"

"Ah well—I rather thought myself, at one time, that she and I— But no, she's met too many men like me, and at least Nick Barforth is *different*. I reckon we might send our congratulations to Gideon Chard, for if old Nick's in Scarborough every Friday to Monday—or every Thursday to Tuesday—with Camille, he'll hardly be troubling Gideon overmuch at the mills."

The story, as yet, was by no means common knowledge, Cullingford needing to be sure of its facts before spreading rumours about its most powerful resident, but I knew they must have been seen together, the gossip would be bound to start, and it would have been a kindness to go over to Galton in case my mother-in-law—his wife—had heard. But I delayed, shirked, fearing to be confronted by a too visible memory of Gervase, and in the end she came to me, bringing fern-scents and tree-scents in the folds of her plain green skirt, her hair spilling out of a hat she had crammed on her head at a rakish and very becoming angle.

"Now then, my dear," she said, sitting down and taking off her driving-gloves. "I know you are much occupied and very businesslike these days, so I shall not give you reason to accuse me of beating about the bush. I have come to enquire about this gorgeous Camille I have heard so much about. Yes, yes, don't look so astonished, Grace, for we are none of us children, and it is my husband himself who has told me. Now then, the fact that she *is* gorgeous I do not dispute. I can trust Nicky to be accurate about that. But what else is she, Grace? That is what I want to know, for to tell the truth, Nicky has been very disappointed in his women, including myself, and I should not like him to be disappointed again—not now when time is no longer quite so available. So tell me about this paragon."

I told her and she listened, her head on one side, concentrating hard, and when I had finished she nodded, brisk, assured, a woman who, against all the rules, appeared well content.

"Well, I did not expect to see him with a social reformer, which sounds a humourless breed, but you tell me she has a great deal of laughter—and generosity. Good. And she is quite besotted with him?"

"She is in an absolute trance."

"That is very good. I think he has always needed that."

"Mrs. Barforth, I rather thought that you and he—?"

And, as Liam had done when I asked him a similar question, she gave what amounted to a roguish smile.

"Yes, I could see you did, and I confess it crossed our minds. When Venetia died we realized how much we had wasted, and we were able to approach each other again, but not as lovers, darling. Yes, we *did* think about it, but the time had gone by for us and it would have been foolish to pretend. Yet Nicky has worried me lately—how strange, for I always thought him so self-sufficient and strong, so distant by his own choice, which of course he was. But since Venetia died I think he has been lonely. He never spent much time with her but I suppose he knew she was there—poor Nicky!—and because she was so frail in spirit he knew she might need him. He wouldn't admit it, and perhaps doesn't know why, but he has been lonely. I have been very far from that. And now that this wonderful thing has happened to him I find that I am glad. I confess to you—and only to you—that there was a moment when I *could* have felt quite otherwise, but no—on the whole I am glad."

"And you?"

"Yes, that is something else I have to tell you, and you may not be pleased with me. Please remember, dear, that men—and women—who can afford what they want do not *wait* for it at our age—Nicky's age and mine. Do you understand that, Grace?"

"I do."

"So—what my husband intends is to take his Camille off

quite permanently, to Scarborough, I suppose, which is where Blaize and Nicholas Barforth used to take their lady-friends in the old days. He is comfortable there and it is time he got away from the mills. If she will give up her freedom—give up *everything* for him—and if they are happy, then I—yes—I shall be happy too, not alone, of course, and not, my dear, in wedlock, for I am a woman of my own generation and divorce is far too extreme for us. But I shall be happy, just the same, with my dear friend Julian Flood—he in his house and I in mine, of course, but happy. Do I disappoint you?''

And when I did not answer she leaned forward and patted my hand, very brisk again, a vital and energetic lady with her mind made up.

"He is my friend, Grace. I realize he was rude to you but he was defending his own kin, which is what one would expect of him, and he was most distressed afterwards at the things he had said to you. He is loyal, you see, in the way I am loyal myself—and he is not so dangerous now as he used to be. Even the wildest of men settle with time and there is no denying that he has waited twenty years—not celibate, for course, but single— for my sake. He has denied himself the heir he should have had and which his ancestry demanded of him—all because of me. Nicky says he is the nearest I could ever come to my brother, Perry, and perhaps he is. But what is wrong with that? Perry was so close to me that it was difficult, sometimes, to tell ourselves apart, yet nothing took place between us that should not have taken place between a brother and sister. We simply belonged together, fitted together. Julian, of course, is not my brother. We can love each other differently, yet almost with the same belonging. It contents me, my dear. It is Nicky who needs the total devotion, the grand passion, not I. Be happy for me. And as for you, dear—well, to begin with, there is a place now vacant, is there not, at your so enterprising *Star*.

Liam's articles on St. Mark's Fold, Commercial Close and Silsbridge Street had appeared in consecutive weekly issues, liberally peppered with the facts I had supplied him, and had caused a great deal of angry murmuring, his judgement of callous landlords who expected men to live in worse conditions than pigs and callous millmasters whose wages were too low to permit them to live any better giving offence to some, satisfaction to others, fanning the resentment that had always smouldered very near the surface in Cullingford. Letters came pouring in thick and fast, indignant, self-righteous, abusive, offering threats or congratulations, provoking, when we printed the best of them, a controversy on social justice and responsibility that seemed to be raging fiercely enough to carry us through until Christmas. Letters began to arrive in direct reply to our readers' letters, arguments, we heard, began to flare up in common beer-houses and the saloon bars of our better hotels as to who was to blame, who ought to put it right. Who were the demon landlords of Silsbridge Street and St. Mark's Fold and Commercial Close in any case? Would the editor of the *Star* name them? The editor made no promises. One would have to buy next week's edition, and perhaps the week after, to find the answer to that.

"This is all very inflammatory," Mrs. Agbrigg said, "and very dangerous. Jonas, dear, do you own any property in that area?"

But Liam, I believed, was merely intent on selling his newspaper, for those guilty landlords could have been anyone, my Grandfather Aycliffe having built his workmen's houses in many areas of the town, throwing them up, in fact, and tacking them together in the interests of speed not durability; somewhere to put the mill-hands and fill the factories until something better came along. But that work-force, rushed in from anywhere when the new, power-driven machinery had sparked off the industrial boom, had doubled its size eight times since my grandfather's heyday, his terraced cottages—never substantial to begin with—sinking beneath the weight, their walls dripping damp, their floorboards rotten, their sanitary facilities so haphazard as to be virtually not there at all. Who owned them? Dozens of people, hundreds, Grandmamma Elinor very likely among them, with not a few held in trust for Aunt Faith, Aunt Prudence and myself, since one had solicitors, after all, to arrange the collection of one's rents and a lady was not expected to know exactly what she owned nor to concern herself with damp walls and doorless, overflowing privies.

Cullingford owned them. We were all their landlords, guilty because of our indifference.

"That's a very good line, Grace," Liam said. "I might use it presently. Now then, what about these peaky little bairns in the workhouse? Our Miss Tighe has got herself elected as a Poor Law Guardian again, so if you could make it in your way to have a word with her? She'd talk easier to you than to Camille—even if Camille could take an hour or two off from Paradise."

I saw Miss Tighe, who told me so firmly to mind my own business that the workhouse, the low, grey building which had

scowled down at me all my life from a patch of wasteland above
Sheepgate, began at last to cross the barrier between the things I
saw without observing and the matters which had lately begun to
prey on my mind. I visited Patrick and Anna Stone at least once
or twice a week. I accustomed myself to the smell of unwashed
humanity until it became bearable, then hardly noticeable, I
passed from the burning, crusading fervour which Venetia had
never lost, to an uneasy suspicion that I should give my money
away, and from there to a calm realization that it would do no
good. Charity, Anna Stone had said, was a crutch, a dependency
like alcohol or opium which, when removed, like any other
crutch would cause the addict to fall down. The answer, she
said, was education, the widening of opportunity, some sure and
just system in which men and women would be helped to help
themselves. She did not believe her theory to be possible, simply
right.

I was alone in the office one September day—Camille in
Scarborough, Liam heaven knew where—when a man dressed
with almost painful neatness came stepping into the room with
the air of one who feels certain of encountering something nasty
underfoot, his pinched expression and the curtness of his tone
making no concession to the fact that he was addressing a lady.

"Mr. Liam Adair?" he enquired.

"As you see—I am afraid not."

"May one enquire his whereabouts?"

"One may. But unfortunately I have not the faintest notion."

"Then would you be so good as to tell him—miss?—that Mr.
Gideon Chard requires to see him at his office at Nethercoats
Mill this afternoon at three o'clock?"

"I will tell him if I see him. But Mr. Chard might do better to
come here."

"Oh, no, Mr. Chard will not want to do that," Mr. Chard's
clerk told me, pained by my effrontery in suggesting that his
employer should risk his beautifully polished boots on this most
dubious of floors. "Three o'clock then. Good-day to you—miss?"

Liam's employees in those days, besides Camille and the men
who operated his ancient presses, consisted of an elderly, extremely scholarly man, Mr. Martin, and a young lad, Joss Davey,
learning the trade. And, as three o'clock came and went, then
four and five, I left messages with them for Liam and went
home, no longer inclined to make a fuss if the sauce on my fish
was not thick enough or if there should be a coffee stain on my
napkin, now that I had so much else to interest me.

I had no idea why Gideon should wish to see Liam. The arrogance of the summons had both amused and offended me, and I was sorry, I think, that Liam had not been there to inform that officious little clerk that if Mr. Gideon Chard—fine leather boots, silk waistcoat, curly brimmed beaver and all—wished to see him, then he knew where he could be found. But so little did it seem to concern me that I was taken completely unawares when, an hour or so after dinner, my doorbell sounded and Gideon walked into my drawing-room, three or four copies of the *Star* under his arm.

I had not seen him since the night last summer when he had asked me to be his mistress, but, like me, he had clearly decided to put that folly behind him, for there was nothing amorous in his manner now, his well-shod feet treading firmly, his eyes taking in without the slightest embarrassment every feature of the room, automatically assessing not merely the value of my furnishings and fittings but whether or not they were tasteful and well-chosen, and perfectly ready to inform me of it if they were not.

"Good-evening, Grace," he said calmly, apparently feeling no need to mention why for the past year we had avoided one another.

"Good-evening, Gideon."

"You are very comfortable here, by the look of it."

"Yes. I have been here now—oh, six months and more."

"Have you really? How time goes by! I believe you saw my clerk this afternoon?"

I nodded, not asking him to sit down since I preferred to remain standing myself, thus signifying that I expected his visit to be short. And understanding this, he too nodded and smiled.

"I take it then that Adair did not return?"

"As it happens he did not, but he may have been unable to see you in any case. He has a great many calls on his time."

He raised those strongly marked eyebrows in a movement of false surprise, anger only just beneath the surface of him, cool sarcasm above it, prepared to be as cutting as the circumstances— whatever they turned out to be—required. But this was the Gideon I knew—the adversary rather than the lover—and I had no intention of being intimidated by him.

"I am to make an appointment to see Liam Adair nowadays, am I?"

"I can think of no reason why you should not."

"I can think of several. However, you can probably tell me

what I wish to know, since you are so closely associated with him.''

And, his expression remaining perfectly calm, he let those rolled-up copies of the *Star* fall on to my table with a sharp, slapping sound of contempt.

''These articles about which there has been so much hot air expended—these surveys of St. Mark's Fold and Commercial Close and Silsbridge Street—can you tell me how these particular streets were chosen?''

''Yes. They were chosen at random, I believe.''

''Indeed? And by whom? By Liam Adair?''

''Yes, of course. Good heavens! Gideon, he had dozens and dozens of streets to choose from. One had merely to take a map and a pin.''

''Exactly,'' he said, his jaw set at a hard angle. ''Exactly, Grace. And so it would seem somewhat contrary to the law of averages, would it not, that with such a multitude of streets available his pin descended on the three which belong to Nicholas Barforth and Company Limited, and consequently—in a manner of speaking—to me?''

I heard the intake of my own breath, for, in my intense preoccupation with the tenants of those houses I had given no thought to this, did not really wish to consider the implications of it now, not with Gideon standing there, at any rate, his inquisitor's eyes fixed on my face, his mouth grim and sarcastic. But he had no intention of letting it go.

''We own a great deal of property, Grace,'' he said, ''most of it in very decent order. I presume you must be aware of that?''

''Yes, I am.''

''And is it not a fact that every mill in this town, in this valley—every mill and any mill—has a number of near-derelict cottages attached to it? *Every* mill, Grace, of which there are sixty or seventy in this town, including your father's business at Fieldhead. And not one millmaster implicated, among so many, but Gideon Chard. Could I be forgiven for suspecting that Liam Adair is not conducting this survey in the interests of humanity but as a personal vendetta against me?''

It was possible. I turned my head slightly away from him so that he should not see my growing realization that it was quite likely. The evil existed and needed to be remedied, Liam would not have lost sight of that, but if he could grind a very personal axe while he was about it, I rather thought that he would. It had been Gideon, after all, who had ousted Liam from the Barforth mills, Gideon who had married Venetia, Gideon who had gained, it seemed, from everyone else's loss. And Liam might easily have decided to exact a price. It was possible.

"I—I am sorry, Gideon. I can make no comment."

"Can you not? Your loyalty to your employer does you credit—if that is what he is to you?"

"I don't know what you mean by that, Gideon—or rather I don't choose to know. What I can tell you is that *I* was not aware of the connection between those streets. If it was done deliberately, then—yes—it was unfair and I shall tell Liam so. But those houses really are an abomination, Gideon, you know—we have been absolutely exact about that. And surely, if Liam is criticizing anyone, it could just as well be Mr. Nicholas Barforth as yourself?"

"I think not. I am in charge of affairs at Lawcroft and Nethercoats and Low Cross. Mine is the name Adair will use, which is just as it should be—I am not complaining about that. If one accepts the privileges, then one accepts the responsibility that goes with it. I simply wish to make him aware that I know I am being singled out and that I know why. I am able to defend myself—should the need arise—without assistance from my chairman or from anyone. Our father-in-law, in any case, is too occupied at the moment with his new woman to care—"

I swung round to him, ready to be angry now that he had given me a safe outlet.

"Camille Inman is a friend of mine, Gideon, and I am not prepared to hear her spoken of with disrespect."

He smiled, the sophisticated, disdainful smile of Blanche's London drawing-room, of Listonby and South Erin.

"My dear, I have the greatest possible respect for Mrs. Inman, who not only keeps my chairman thoroughly distracted but is decidedly one of the most gorgeous creatures—"

"So she is. But now you are talking about her as if she were a thoroughbred mare for sale at Appleton horse-fair. I cannot allow that either." He gave me no answer. I could think of nothing more to say. Silence came dangerously between us.

"Can I do nothing right for you, Grace?"

"It is not my place to judge what you do—or to be concerned—as it is not your place—"

And, hearing my voice trail off into a lamentable, tell-tale confusion, I was glad to hear the doorbell again, and then appalled when Liam came breezing into the room, his eyes—which had certainly recognized Gideon's carriage outside—resting on those rolled up copies of the *Star*, his mouth smiling its jaunty, Irish smile.

"Now then—and doesn't this turn out to be handy? I hear you were looking for me, Gideon?"

"So I was, Adair, and I reckon you'll know the reason why."

But still smiling, Liam walked past him and to my complete horror put one large, warm hand on the nape of my neck and kissed me, just a light brushing of his mouth against mine; the assured, almost casual greeting of a lover of long standing.

What happened then was over in a moment, never actually happened at all, since we drew back, all of us, from the brink of it.

"Now then, Gideon, what *was* it you wanted to see me about?"

"Information, Adair. But I have all I need to know."

"I'll see you out then."

And so he did—the man of the house escorting a casual caller, leaving me to grapple with the ferocity I had seen in Gideon's face, the murder I had felt in him, and, far worse than that, my own wild impulse to deny it, the urge I still felt to run out into the hall, to the gate, and call after him that it was not true.

Liam returned, smiling no longer, and I launched through the air towards him a fist that fell far short of its mark, my whole body trembling.

"How dare you use me like that, Liam Adair? How *dare* you?" And he pulled me firmly but gently into his arms and held me there until the trembling had ceased, giving me time to remember that Gideon Chard, by my own choice, was nothing to me.

I moved away from him when I could, calm now but sharp and bitter.

"There's no need to hold me any longer, Liam. If Gideon happened to look through the window, he's already seen us—and he's gone now."

"That wasn't the reason. And if it's bothering you how I knew he *would* be jealous, then—well—I don't suppose many other people know it. I'm sorry, Grace, but whenever the opportunity comes for me to scratch him a little beneath that aristocratic hide of his, I can't help taking it."

"You *did* choose those streets then, as part of a vendetta?"

"Is that what he called it? Very classy. You'll just have to bear in mind, Grace, that the survey needed to be done, that some good might come of it, like the adulterated flour and those workhouse brats. I think you ought to forgive me, Grace, because Camille has just given me her notice and the truth is I need you."

I walked to the window, stared out at the gathering dusk, putting myself carefully together, every piece snugly if a little painfully in its proper place, and then turned back to him.

"Yes, Liam. I'll take Camille's job, since I've been doing it for the past two months in any case, for the same wages you pay to her."

He laughed, jaunty and debonair again, nothing about him to suggest the merest whisper of passion or revenge.

"Now as to that, Grace, I was rather hoping—"

"That I would work for nothing? Of course you were. And of course I shall not. We're friends, Liam, although I sometimes wonder why, and distant relations. And I am not in need of money. But none of that gives you the right to ask me to work without pay. We'll be businesslike about it, shall we—and fair? I am ready to do Camille's work for Camille's wages, and in exchange for that I will be at my desk every morning at the hour you tell me and will stay until you permit me to leave. If you value my services, you must pay me for them, and I will earn far more than anything you are likely to give me. Agreed?"

He shook his head and grinned broadly.

"You're a hard woman, Grace Barforth."

"Yes, and you are not the first man to tell me so. But it is a hard world, is it not? Agreed?"

"Agreed," he said, and held out a hand which I clasped in firm, businesslike fashion.

"Tomorrow morning then, Grace, at eight o'clock."

"I shall not be late," I said, and those simple words transformed me. I was a dainty, useless little lady no longer, dispensing soup and milk-and-water charity to the poor. I was still shaken, still bruised a little in spirit. But I was employed.

23

CAMILLE GAVE UP HER LODGINGS in Prince Albert Road and went off to Scarborough, ecstatic as a young bride of seventeen. She was not a bride, of course, and might never be so again, but clearly and quite magnificently she did not care. All she wanted was to be with her Nicholas; she had cheerfully sacrificed her independence, her reputation, had given up everything to that end, and I was not the only one to be surprised at the speed with which he now abandoned his commercial empire to other hands, quickly adding his beloved Woolcombers and his dyeworks to the sum total of Nicholas Barforth and Company Limited, the better to concentrate on his love.

"How romantic," said Mrs. Agbrigg, smiling slightly. "I only hope he will retain the stamina—"

"How these men do make idiots of themselves!" declared my Grandmother Agbrigg, having made up her mind not to call on Camille unless she was married and possibly not even then, although her own house in Scarborough was only a mile or two away.

"What is she like?" Aunt Faith asked me, rather tremulously I thought. "Is she very lovely? *Dark*, you say? Is she really?"

"Shall we wish them happy?" enquired Uncle Blaize.

"Oh yes, darling," she told him, reaching for his hand. "As happy as we are—since no one could be happier than that."

"Well, it makes Gideon very powerful, I suppose," was Blanche's opinion, "and gives him a house of his own at last, since Uncle Nicholas can hardly be thinking of bringing the woman back to Tarn Edge. And now that Aunt Caroline is so busy getting Gideon married again it may turn out very well, for no second wife could possibly want to live with her husband's first wife's father."

But Aunt Caroline, although well pleased to see Gideon in

complete charge of the mills and in sole residence at Tarn Edge, was so incensed by her brother's behaviour that she made the journey to Scarborough to tell him so, installing herself at the Grand Hotel and sending him word—since she could not set foot in any house which contained a "loose woman"—to attend her there. He went, Camille told me, and entertained his sister to a lavish dinner, after which he advised her quite cordially that she would do well to leave him alone. But Aunt Caroline, from her suite at the Grand, had caught a glimpse of Camille strolling along the cliffs, the fresh and youthful appearance of my friend suggesting at once an additional and exceedingly unwelcome complication.

"That woman is young enough to bear children," she announced accusingly, as if we were all to blame. "And it would be most unfair to Gideon, at this stage, if Nicholas should get himself a son."

"My husband already has a son," said Mrs. Nicholas Barforth when this remark was conveyed to her.

But there was no news of Gervase.

I sat down at my desk every morning now at eight o'clock, a point of honour, although Liam quite often did not show his face until after ten; and I would work throughout the day and often enough into the night, talking to anyone about anything which might interest the readers of the *Star*. Had anyone asked me if I was happy I would not have welcomed the question. I was busy, which had always been a necessity to me, but in some ways I was still only playing at independence, and was uncomfortably aware of it. I earned Camille's wages but I had never tried to live on them, retaining my allowance from my father, the security of my capital in Mr. Rawnsley's bank, the lure of my inheritance. Not happy, then. Not even particularly content once the keen edge of my enthusiasm had blunted. But busy, willing to learn and interested in what the Stones and Liam Adair had to teach me. Busy and interested—and as an alternative to sitting in my house in Blenheim Crescent and wondering if Mrs. Rawnsley would ever call on me, it was good enough.

I was twenty-six and became twenty-seven, paring down my ideals as I did so, to make them functional rather than sentimental. I could not burn for long with a crusading fervour like Venetia's, being quick to see that even in the most ideal conditions many would never learn to stir themselves on their own behalf. Yet through the apathy of those without hope—those who had lost it and those who had been born with no capacity for it—I saw, often enough, courage working like yeast, fermenting to bring some hard-eyed, bright-eyed girl, some canny, curly-haired lad to the surface. There were lads in those streets around Low Cross who after their day-long stretch in the sheds would walk briskly home to wash off the engine grease at a cold-water tap and then, eating a slice of bread and dripping on the way, would spend their evenings in study at the Mechanics Institute; lads who, when brought to the notice of Gideon Chard or Nicholas Barforth or Jonas Agbrigg, pulled no humble forelock but looked the "gaffer" straight in the eye. There were girls who kept themselves decent not so much for virtue's sake but because they could see what haphazard pregnancy might lead to, tough-fibred girls, fiercely independent of mind and free of tongue, who when they became wives went clandestinely to Dr. Stone for the means to limit their fertility to a life-saving two or three, and kept their offspring—and their husbands—in order with a wry good humour and an iron hand.

These—as Camille had told me—were the survivors, lads like my Grandfather Agbrigg had been, girls such as I might have been myself. But there were others, like the aged, the sick, the feeble-minded—like the middle-class married woman—who could not speak out for themselves, thousands of them in a state of neglect or oppression, the recipients of cold charity or downright exploitation which I—like Venetia—could not ignore.

I paid rather less attention to my house and had trouble with my maids who, being respectable girls themselves, did not really approve of me and left my service as soon as they were able. I developed a crisp manner, a shell which concealed the occasional pinpricks of hurt I still felt from time to time, a brief but very sharp reminder that I had not succeeded as a woman, the restlessness—quite terrible sometimes—that overcame me when I saw the rich, slumbrous glow of Camille, the deep contentment of Aunt Faith, the perfect companionship of Anna and Patrick Stone, Mrs. Georgiana Barforth's vivid face as, with her close and loving friend, she set about the rebuilding of her life. I was at my desk every morning at eight o'clock. When I gave orders they were usually obeyed. I had friends and a few enemies, brief bouts of sorrow and sudden enjoyments. I was busy and interested. It was a life.

I did not meet Gideon Chard again and saw no point in thinking of him, although I did not always take my own advice. On the night he had asked me to live with him I had understood his motives, or so I believed, and told myself that I had hurt nothing but his pride. I preferred to think so, for I was used to his pride and could cope with it, as I was used to my own stubbornness which often made me unwilling to recognize the unease I sometimes felt at returning to my empty house each evening, a house where nothing awaited me but a cool, neutral order, each one of my tasteful possessions in its allotted place with no one to help me cherish them or break them, with no one to cherish or to break me.

And so, when this mood was on me, I did not return home, finding plenty to occupy me at the *Star*, plenty to interest and tax me at the Stones's garden shelter, where I met girls who had been truly crushed and broken in body and in spirit; and occasionally one who had fought back and would sit there, among her bandages, bright-eyed and pugnacious and ready, when the bones were set and the splints removed, to get up and fight again.

I liked such girls, recognized myself in them, although their willingness, sometimes their downright eagerness to return to the men who had maimed them truly appalled me.

"He's jealous, miss—that's all. Fair mad with it. He'd kill me before he'd lose me."

"If he killed you, he *would* have lost you."

But logic had no part of passion and the bruised little face would take on a certain smugness, the swollen lips curve into a superior smile, the undernourished body flex itself with a sensuality that I—presumably a spinster since I was not married and Silsbridge Street had never heard of divorce—could not be expected to understand.

"He loves me, miss—that's what it is."

And for the year or two that it would last, until poverty and childbearing wore it away, it was a very decided—and for me very disturbing—glory.

Blanche was very often at Listonby these days, since Dominic, having lost his seat in the Liberal landslide, had taken it into his head to travel abroad, to the wild places of the world where a man could shoot something more exotic and dangerous than grouse and pheasant, and where wives could not be included. Blanche gave him a farewell dinner, kissed him goodbye and came north to Listonby, her children, and to Noel.

"I believe I am a far more scandalous woman than you are," she told me, descending on my house in a dress the texture of sea-farm, roses of every shade of pink in her hat, "yet Mrs. Rawnsley almost fell out of her landau just now in her eagerness to greet me. I have always told you there was a right way and a wrong way, my darling."

"So you have allowed him to rape you at last, have you, Blanche?"

"My dear," she said, her serenity never for one moment wavering, "if I have—and I do not say so—then it is not a subject for conversation."

But on other matters she was more forthcoming and in a single afternoon I learned that Lord Sternmore had taken back his wife, the penitent and now very devoted Diana Flood, who was already expecting his child. I had news of Claire Chard, now two years old, the darling of the Listonby nurseries where she was in the process of being moulded—as Venetia had desired—into a perfect little copy of Blanche. What would happen to her when Gideon married again Blanche could not say, for neither the younger Mademoiselle Fauconnier nor a certain Miss Hortense Madeley-Brown, both apparently in the running, seemed very motherly to Blanche and would probably not wish to burden themselves with a first wife's child.

Did Gideon spend any time with Venetia's daughter? She shrugged. It was hard to tell. He came over to Listonby often enough, rode to hounds with Noel and stabled some excellent horses there for the purpose, better mounts than Noel could afford. He walked about the estate a great deal with his brother, or took out a gun, and in the evenings they would play cards together. He was *there* and how could one tell how much attention a man paid to a child? Dominic had always appeared totally oblivious of young Matthew and Francis, but would fall on them like a ton of bricks at the slightest hint of bad manners or if he caught one of them slouching in his saddle. In any case, the boys would be going away to school ere long, would be polished strangers when they came back again, and she would rather like a little girl about the house, to dress up and titivate, if Gideon did not object.

Tarn Edge was no place for children now in any case, since Mrs. Winch and Mrs. Kincaid had left and Chillingworth had been pensioned off—had I not heard?—and Gideon had got himself a French chef and a very suave butler, definitely a gentleman's gentleman in their place. Had I not heard? Goodness, had I no interest any more in what was going on around me—in the *news*?

My work with the *Star* prospered and my respect for Liam Adair with it, his easy, amorous disposition, the fact that he was unreliable both with money and with women, no longer blinding me to the generosity—more often than not—of his intentions. He was vain and promiscuous and thoroughly enjoyed his notoriety, yet on the whole his opinions were fair and honest, fearlessly expressed, unless they concerned Gideon Chard, in which case they would be heavily weighted with his memory of Venetia. He had wrung from the derelict housing of St. Mark's Fold every drop of gall that he could, managing, without naming Gideon, to make it very clear who was to blame, and since then every time a shuttle came out of a loom at Low Cross, Nethercoats of Lawcroft Fold, and struck a weaver with its pointed end, every time a woman's arm was broken by a picking-stick, every time a man was turned off for no better cause than he had not "suited" his overlooker, mention of it was made, discreetly but plainly, in the *Star*. Such accidents were common in all our factories, and far fewer than they used to be, now that we no longer employed children under the age of ten, but when a woman was struck by a flying shuttle at Neathercoats and lost an eye, the *Star* was as shocked as if such a thing had never been heard of before, while Liam had quite forgotten to mention that Barforths had paid the doctor's bills.

"Must you do this?" I asked, receiving in answer his jaunty, Irish smile.

"Well, Grace, look at it another way and you'll see I'm doing him a favour. What else has he got to worry about? And unless I keep goading him on a little, he'll get fat and complacent sitting in that big house all by himself, drinking his Napoleon brandy. He ought to thank me for it."

And I have not forgotten the glee in Liam's handsome, dark eyes when it was discovered that the whole area around St. Mark's Fold—or such of it as did not belong to Barforths already—was being purchased by them, and that the houses which came empty were not being let again.

"I'm on to something," he said, and so he was, a month of ferreting and foraging for news informing him that these mean streets, hemming in the thriving but cramped Low Cross Mill were to be demolished, the mill considerably enlarged and its work-force housed in new accommodation nearby.

"Liam—we said ourselves those houses were unfit to live in."

"Not all of them, Grace. St. Mark's is a pigsty, but there's St. Jude's. There's nothing wrong with St. Jude's. Good houses, good neighbours, people still living in the houses where they

were born and where their parents were born. They won't take
kindly to this, you know.''

"I know. I expect you'll make sure of that."

And so he did, explaining to St. Jude's Street and others like it
that their plight was no different to that of an agricultural labourer
turned out of his tied cottage—which was, in fact, quite true—to
suit the whim of the squire. New houses, indeed, were being
provided, but where were these houses to be? Nearby, said the
squire, but he had measured the distance from the saddle of his
thoroughbred gelding, or at the reins of his spanking, speedy
cabriolet. The *Star*, however, had walked those three miles from
the squire's new houses at Black Abbey Meadow to his mill at
Low Cross and had found them long, particularly on a raw
winter morning with the five o'clock hooter to beat, even longer
at the end of a day's hard labour, especially if one happened to
be very young or rather old, or a woman with infant children to
hurry home to. And if the residents of St. Jude's Street could
afford the rents of these new houses, which were bound to be
high, the *Star* heaved a sigh at the suspicion that the people of
St. Mark's Fold could not. Was it beyond the bounds of possibility that the people of St. Mark's Fold were no longer required at
Low Cross, being largely the unskilled, the weak, the ones who
coughed most in the winter and caused the most trouble, having
the most—let it be said aloud—of which to complain?

A larger mill meant more jobs, certainly, but not, it seemed,
for the tenants of St. Mark's Fold, and once their insanitary
hovels were gone, what remained for any of them but the
workhouse?

"Do you hope to stop him?" I enquired.

"Of course not. The mayor and half the corporation either
work for him or do business with him. Every magistrate in the
county is either related to him, dines with him, or would like an
invitation to Listonby. Our Member of Parliament will be careful
not to offend him and the *Courier & Review* can do nothing but
sing his praises. Of course I can't stop him. I am making
mischief, that is all.''

"Then be careful, Liam, for if you go too far he may sue
you.''

"I hope he may. But he is far more likely to knock me down,
which would sell me a great many newspapers, you must admit.
And I shall know how to pick myself up again.''

"Just take care.''

But he would heed no warning and as the area around Low

Cross began to simmer, its anxieties and the certainty of its doom made plainer with each new issue of the *Star*, I began myself to grow uneasy, waiting, I think, for that pompous little clerk to appear again, or a more official gentleman coming to tell Liam he had broken the law.

"You can't afford litigation, Liam. It's expensive. I ought to know."

"Then you'll lend me the money, Grace, won't you, my darling—out of the splendid wages I pay you? Unless he simplifies matters and has me set upon and murdered one night in an alley."

"If you go on like this he'll do something."

But I was not prepared for the afternoon that the office door was kicked open and Gideon himself strode into the room, every inch the squire whether he had intended it or not, from his immaculate leather boots to the crown of his shiny hat, driving whip in one hand, kid gloves in the other, nostrils wrinkling their distaste of these mean surroundings, and of the mean, sordid little people who inhabited them.

Liam, blessedly, was not there, just myself and the scholarly Mr. Martin, stooping over his desk, and glaring around him a moment Gideon allowed a pair of hard and angry eyes to rest on my face before he rapped out the parade ground command "Come with me."

"I beg your pardon?"

"Just *do* it."

I saw Mr. Martin, from the corner of my eye, raise a weary shoulder and glance at his watch reminding me that Liam was already overdue and could return at any time. I understood that Gideon would not go away until at least something of his demands had been satisfied—*could* not lose face by going away with nothing at all—and so I got my hat and my gloves, my mouth dry, terrified of meeting Liam on the stairs, and submitted—telling myself there was no alternative—when Gideon put a hand under my elbow and almost threw me into his carriage.

He drove very fast, the cabriolet swaying so alarmingly at each tight, narrow turning that I closed my eyes and pressed one hand against my stomach, fearing not only for life and limb but that I would lose the last remnants of my dignity by being sick. There was a final, terrible jolting, a rutted track, the smell of dust and earth, his body still snapping with anger as he drew in the reins not a moment too soon and shaved a heap of bricks with nothing to spare.

"Get down," and roughly he took my elbow again and set me down on the uneven ground of Black Abbey Meadow, where the foundations of his new dwellings were under way.

"Over there," he said, his hand in the small of my back pushing me towards a hut at the far end of the site, and kicking open the door with that expensive boot, thrusting me—there was no other word for it—inside towards a table littered with drawings and maps.

"Here it is," he said. "So just damn well look at it—every hovel I pull down I'll replace—every damnable, miserable one. And this is what I'll replace them with—five hundred cottages with dry cellars and good sculleries, gas and water, a stove and a boiler—will that do for you, eh? Some with two bedrooms and some with three, and not back to back either, but in separate rows with back passages wide enough to drive a cart through, so they can take out the night-soil and empty the privies. And you won't blush to hear me mention that, I know. One hundred and fifty pounds apiece they're costing me, and the overlookers' houses eighty pounds more because they've got a parlour sixteen feet by sixteen, four or five bedrooms and a nice little yard. How does that suit you? And I'm not asking more than ten shillings a week for any one of them—and as little as two shillings and ninepence. I'm building washhouses and bathhouses, and a school to keep the brats off the street while their mothers are at the mill. I'm building shops so they don't have to carry their potatoes and their bacon or whatever else they eat the three miles from town, except that it's not three miles and nowhere near. A mile and a quarter, or it will be when the new mill goes up, since I'm building out in this direction. Have you understood that?"

I nodded, but his temper was not yet done and, his hand descending like a clamp on my arm, he took me outside and marched me like a hostage up and down his building site, making no allowances for my thinly shod feet, nor the chill of the March day.

"This," he said, giving my arm a shake to be sure of my attention, "is where the school will stand. The baths over there. There are plenty of beer-houses already, not too far away, and I doubt anyone will object to walking a mile to them. And should religion be needed there is a chapel over there of some Noncomformist persuasion or other, and another just beyond it. I went over to Saltaire to see what Titus Salt had done—well, he's built himself a monument and a damned fine one—no beer or spirits of any kind to be sold in *his* village, no washing to be hung out across *his* streets. Well, I don't claim to be either a temperate or a religious man. I just want somewhere to put my workers, that's all.''

And for more than an hour, while the sky darkened and the wind grew colder, he fiercely propelled me over every inch of the ground, showing me and making sure I looked at his drains, the distance between his privies and his kitchen doors, the quality of his building materials, the substantial walled yard around his school so that the children would have somewhere to play without risking death every moment under somebody's horses.

"Not my idea," he said shortly. "My architect suggested it. I merey mention it because you'll be unlikely to read it in the *Star*.''

And when he considered I had seen enough—although it seemed to me I had seen everything twice over—he bundled me up into his carriage again, my feet so frozen it was hard to tell if they were scratched or bleeding, although I rather thought they ought to be, and drove me at the same killing speed to my door.

I did not ask him to come in. He simply came, slammed down his hat and gloves on my hall table, walked uninvited into my drawing-room and threw himself into a chair.

"I'm hungry," he said.

"What?"

"I'm hungry, which should surprise no one since it must be dinner-time. Have you forgotten how to treat your guests?''

Perhaps I found his effrontery amusing. That was the excuse I made. But, although I was in no mood to tell myself the truth just then, the truth was—as I was soon to discover that the whole tumultuous proceedings had exhilarated me. Of course I could have resisted him. Of course I could have got away from him. Instead I had allowed him to make off with me and had thoroughly enjoyed it. I had felt, and still felt, alert and eager, curious and adventurous, bold and rather better-looking than usual. What kind of a creature was I? What kind of a creature, indeed, could possibly set such store by independence and yet thrive on this bullying? Even now I had only to speak the word and he would leave. I knew it, and, somewhat more to the point, he knew that I knew.

But I had lain fallow for so long, involving myself in dramas which were not my own, that this personal flesh and blood confrontation was not to be missed. I might tell myself that I must settle this issue for St. Mark's Fold, but just then St.

Mark's Fold seemed very far away. Something real—whether it might be good for me or not—was actually happening to *me* —not to Camille nor to Blanche nor to some battered hopeful girl from Silsbridge Street—but to me, and I could not resist it.

And so I went tamely to enquire what might be found in my kitchen for this fastidious man to eat, knowing that the oxtail soup, the cutlets in mushroom sauce, the treacle tart my cook eventually produced could not hope to gain his favour.

"I gather you are less interested in *haute cuisine* than you used to be?" he said, examining the treacle tart with faint surprise before he covered its plebeian countenance with whipped cream.

"We cannot all of us afford a French chef, you know, Gideon."

"Ah—you have uncovered the secrets of my kitchen arrangements, have you? No doubt your employer finds you a useful source of tittle-tattle."

I ignored his rudeness, offered him port which he refused, although he would take brandy—assuming such a commonplace was to be had—and would drink it, with coffee, in the drawing-room as he had always done in the past when we had dined alone together. But in those days, with the well-peopled splendours of Tarn Edge about us, we had not really been alone. We were alone now, my drawing-room appearing suddenly very small and rather frail as he took possession of it, helping himself to the brandy I kept mainly for Patrick Stone and Liam Adair.

"You admit, then that although I am no philanthropist like Titus Salt, I am no ogre either?"

"Yes—I admit you are neither."

"And that I am building good houses?"

"You would hardly put your name to anything that was not of the highest quality, Gideon."

"Exactly. Then what are you complaining of?"

"Gideon—please understand that Liam, whatever personal rancour he may have against you, really does care about those people. You cannot accommodate all of them. It was never your intention to do so. These houses are being constructed solely for your work-force, you will not deny that."

"Certainly they are for my workers. We have agreed that I am no philanthropist. I do not feel called upon to make myself responsible for the sleeping arrangements of the whole town."

"Of course you do not—I realize that. I suppose our grandfathers did not feel responsible for the hand-loom weavers when the powerlooms came in—nor Mr. Nicholas Barforth, thirty years ago when his combing-machines made so many hundreds of hand-combers destitute. They were casualties of progress too, and of course we must progress."

"I am glad we agree on that."

"But those people in St. Mark's Fold are not your workers, Gideon—or very few of them. And even if you have any of your new houses to spare, they could not afford your rents. What is to become of them? I thought one could not sink much lower than St. Mark's Fold, but perhaps one can. There is the workhouse, of course—of which I know very little—but Liam seems to think death by starvation would be preferable to that. However rash he may be—however wrong-headed—he does care."

"Believe me," he said, clenching a hand and leaning towards me, "I don't give a damn for Liam Adair and his opinions. I feel no need to explain myself to him. I want *you* to know what I'm doing—that's all."

And leaning closer, he flexed his hand again and placed it deliberately on my knee, his presence completely filling the room, his touch penetrating the fabric of my dress, burning through to the skin and the bone and beyond it, to the pit of my stomach where I could feel a pulse-beat starting.

"*Gideon.*"

"Yes," he said. "Why else am I here? And I should have come a long time ago. I've wanted you for years, Grace—years—and I see no reason now to deny myself what other men—"

"There are no other men."

"I *saw* you—with Liam Adair—in this room. I saw you."

"You saw nothing."

"I saw him kiss you. I've never kissed you. Are you going to refuse me?"

"Of course!"

I fought him. I had to fight him. I struck out with hard fists at his head and shoulders, pounded them into his back as he caught me and dragged me forward against his chest; did everything, in fact but the one thing that *would* have stopped him, the simple calling out to my maid for help. His mouth hurt mine, his tongue parting my lips was an invasion, his teeth sinking into my tongue seemed to draw blood, his hands, taking in possession whatever they could, maddened me. I fought him and the plain truth is—oh yes, and I was well aware of it—that I was fighting not to make him stop but because the battle itself was exciting, splendid, a rich and rare feast in itself for my starved senses. And so I fought on until his hands and his mouth had already possessed so much of me that to deny him the rest seemed pointless—or so I convinced myself—my resistance petering out to a feeble, vanquished plea that the maid might come in.

He got up, leaving me winded in my chair, and I heard his voice saying calmly into the corridor, "Your mistress will not be needing you again tonight. You may retire," and then the sound of the key turning in the lock as he came back into the room.

He walked towards me, shrugging off his jacket, loosening his neck-tie, and then, kneeling down on the hearthrug, he carefully made up the fire and stirred it into a blaze.

"Dear Grace, I can't tell you how often lately, usually at this time of day, I've thought of you. Yes, when I've eaten my gourmet dinner, I've sat many a time with my brandy and wondered how you'd look naked, in the firelight. Come here to me now, Grace. I'll fetch you if necessary—but come to me."

I got up—entranced as I had seen Camille entranced—and sank to my knees on the rug beside him, wanting him so badly that it *was* unavoidable, my body telling me that he was air and water to me, my powers of logic—which knew better than that—being laughed to scorn by the unashamed urgency of my desire. I wanted him. Everything else was unimportant, unreal. No matter what he did to me, no matter what violence or shame he offered me, while that fire remained inside me—like the women of Silsbridge Street—I should want him still.

"Yes, you looked like this, Grace—a hundred times. You trembled too, and moaned how much you wanted me. Do it, Grace."

But for answer I kicked away the few garments which remained and fell against him, his chest as hard, his skin as supple and fragrant as *I* had imagined it, the clamouring inside me so urgent now that he felt it, laughed in triumphant excitement at it and then, without more ado, descended full upon me and inside me with great purpose.

"That's the first time—for possession," he said, but our excitement had not abated and we remained pressed close together in the firelight, a time of exploration, of long sweeping caresses that set me purring and glowing, offering my body to his eyes and to his hands, stretching myself against him, my own hands delighting in the firm, flat muscle of him and the hard angles, my nostrils luxuriating in his odours, my mouth tasting his skin until desire came again and, in this new frenzy, I wanted not merely to be possessed but to be swallowed whole and alive, unable to give enough to take enough until fulfilment thudded through me, retreated and came again as intense as before, causing me to bite my lips and cry aloud.

We slept then, my head on his shoulder, waking, when the fire burned low, to the chill of the March night. And when I shivered he got up, pulled me to my feet, and smiled.

"I want you again," he said, "but in your bed this time"; and so we went upstairs to my virginal bedchamber which, once again, he filled and transformed so that it was his room, his bed, as I was his woman.

The excitement was less this time, the possession deeper. There was more leisure, more caressing, an arousal not only of the senses, his mouth brushing with closed lips over my face, my fingertips tracing the heavy arch of his eyebrows, the high-bridged line of his nose, the length of his firm, full lips which kissed my exploring hand playfully, gently, then my wrist and the inside of my arm, the sensitive angles of neck and shoulder and thigh. There was no haste, no urge to devour this time, a joining together that seemed to happen of itself, quite naturally, my body flowing into his happily; opening itself readily and with a simple, wholehearted joy, to pleasure.

He lay for a moment on his back staring at the wall and then, decisively, he said, "I'll marry you if I can. It may not be legal because your marriage and mine made us close kin. But if it *is* legal I'll marry you. And if not then, I'll take you back to Tarn Edge and be damned! You don't mind if I smoke, do you?"

And having made his decision—having decided when and where to "take" me—he smoked his cigar and fell asleep abruptly, both of us having good reasons for exhaustion, although I lay beside him very far from rest, watching the sky lighten to a cool dawn behind my curtains, passing from a state of bitter conflict—not with him but with myself—to an attitude of stubborn but grievous resolve.

I wanted him. The fire in my limbs had subsided now and still I wanted him. I had wanted him long before I had wanted Gervase, had been so overwhelmed by him that even complex, unstable Gervase had seemed safe by comparison. And so it had proved, for although Gervase's light-weight, auburn body had delighted me, it had never possessed me as Gideon's had just done; had given me pleasure which had rippled over me and left me free, not the pleasure I had just known, which could weld me irrevocably and quite slavishly to the man who had created it.

I had wanted Gideon and feared him. I wanted him now and I still feared him. I could go to Tarn Edge and be the woman he

wanted, the woman I had been before. But did that woman still
exist? And if she did not, then could I recreate her? Did I even
like that obsessive housekeeper, that efficient hostess, with all
her brilliant, irrelevant skills? But she was the woman Gideon
wanted and yes—if I desired it—I could bring her to life again,
could place myself entirely under his protection—sacrificing my
independence as Camille had done—and, little by little, could be
completely possessed by him, for I knew he was the stronger and
had always known it. I knew he would expect me to want only
what he wanted, act only as he acted, think only as he thought,
not from any conscious need to dominate me but because, like
his mother, he sincerely believed only his own way to be right.
He would possess me, absorb me, that was why I feared him,
but what frightened me most was the part of myself that even
now, in this cool dawn of logic and common sense—of survival—
would have submitted joyfully to that possession, asking nothing
in return for the whole of my ingenuity, my will, my brain, every
drop of my energy and my time but the pleasure of moaning and
sighing in his arms every night.

I wanted him and feared him. For an hour, while he slept, I
hovered precariously balanced between the two, wanting him so
keenly at one moment that the submerging of my identity in his
seemed a small price to pay, terrified the next moment and
furious with myself when I remembered the implications of that
price, the captivity I had struggled so hard to escape and to
which now I was so mindlessly eager to return. And unlike
Gervase, Gideon would hold me fast whether he continued to
desire me or not. Once I was his, once I had committed myself,
then his I would remain.

I wanted him. It was all that mattered and if the time ever
came when I found myself neglected—as Gervase had neglected
me—then at least I would have lived through who knew how
many years of bliss. I wanted him as Venetia had wanted Robin
Ashby and, like her, was prepared to offer myself, if necessary,
as a sacrifice. But, as dawn came slanting through the window,
my fear was greater, the risk too terrible and the price too high.
We were too alike. I would resist too bitterly and, in the end, I
would not be possessed, I would be broken. Fear prevailed—
that, and the acute, heart-rending memory of Venetia. I could
not do it.

He woke and, finding me sitting on the edge of the bed,
leaned over and kissed the base of my spine, his hands very

warm and very sure as they travelled the length of my back and reached my shoulders.

"*My* bed next time, Grace, on my satin sheets," he whispered against my skin which responded exactly as it should have done, and as he had intended, with the frisson that anticipates pleasure.

"Ah—you have satin sheets now, do you?"

"I do. I have every conceivable luxury that money can buy. I indulge every whim, give way to every extravagance—you should know that, my darling."

"I am not a luxurious woman, Gideon."

"But you are—you are. You are a rare woman—altogether unique—and what has more value than rarity? What would the *Mona Lisa* be worth if there were a dozen? I find everything I want in you, which makes you very luxurious indeed."

"And the things I want?"

"You shall have them, better and more of each one than you imagined. You'll want me gone, I suppose, before the maid comes in?"

"Yes."

"Then I'll go. I'll obey the conventions for now, at any rate. Remember—I'll marry you, Grace, if I can."

"That's very good of you, Gideon."

But my tone did nothing to dispell his easy, tolerant humour, the content of a man who is well satisfied both with himself and with his woman, and pulling me against him he began to kiss the nape of my neck and my ear.

"Don't play the independent female with me, Grace Barforth. We know better than that now, don't we?"

So we did. I leaned back against him, surrendering to his hands, the warmth and strength of his body and his will, letting his odours wash over me, indulging myself just once again, just once— But he was not inclined to be amorous, for morning was fast approaching, he had many things to attend to and must go home, change his clothes and shave before showing his face at the mill.

"I have appointments until half-past ten," he told me, dressing quickly, knowing exactly what he wanted from those appointments and how to get it. "And then I'll drive down to see my lawyer and find out if, and how soon, we can be married. I'll be back here at half-past eleven or thereabouts."

And already my time was his time. He would come back at half-past eleven if he could, but if not, if other matters should delay him, then I must wait cheerfully, sweetly, since what activity of mine could possibly compare in importance to his?

"I shall not be here at half-past eleven, Gideon. I have my own employment to go to, remember."

But instead of the impatience I had expected, he remained warm and indulgent, not in the least inclined to take me seriously.

"Lord! as to that, just send Adair a note saying you've made other arrangements. He doesn't pay you, does he?"

"He certainly does."

"Really? But never mind, I doubt he'll expect you to work your notice. Just send a note, that's all."

"I can't do that, Gideon."

"Of course you can."

And defeated by his good humour I swiftly changed direction.

"Gideon, I don't want to go back to Tarn Edge."

"Yes, you do—to begin with, at any rate. There's nothing wrong with Tarn Edge that *you* couldn't put right. Nobody may want to visit us for a while but we can eat our little dinners together, drink our brandy in the firelight—make love on those satin sheets of mine. And when I can afford it I'll build you a palace. I'll buy a couple of hundred acres one of these days and put a house the size of Listonby on it. You could play hostess to the county then and you'd like that. You'd be splendid—first-rate, my darling—you'd do it as well as my mother and a damned sight better than Blanche. And whatever you may think, they'd scramble for your invitations, once they'd got used to the idea of us, because propriety is all very well but it's money that counts—the right sort of money—and I've got that money now. I can *afford* to please myself now, Grace—I can afford the life I want and the woman I want to go with it."

"Gideon, I can't—"

But, without waiting to know what it was I could not do, he slid his hands under my shoulders and bent over me.

"Darling, there's no reason to worry. There'll be talk, I know, and what of it? My mother won't like it, and Dominic won't be pleased, I know that too—and yes, all that influenced me before, when I spoke to you in London, I admit it. I don't give a damn now. My shoulders are broad enough and my position in this town secure enough. I can look after you, Grace."

"I can look after myself."

"There's simply no need for that now. And where's the fun in it, my darling, anyway?"

"But, Gideon—"

"Just leave everything to me."

I began to say no, there was more to consider, and he kissed the words away. I implored him to listen, to understand, and cradling me in his arms he told me not to be afraid, that he would allow no malicious tongues to hurt me. I tried again, tearfully, to resist, and, smiling, he replied that my bare shoulders, in this first light, were so enticing that he wondered if he might sacrifice another half-hour and come back to bed. He shrugged off his clothes again and made love to me, convincing me that I couldn't live without this raging joy, that if I *did* leave him and he came to find me, he would only have to put a hand on me and I would follow him anywhere.

"Now just what is it that is worrying you?" he whispered into my hair. But lying in his arms in those vulnerable moments after pleasure, all that worried me was how to stay there as long as possible, how to be there again just as soon as ever I could.

I stood in my window and watched him drive away, knowing, since I could not withstand his presence, that I must not allow him to come back again. I remained, my cheek pressed against the glass, for a long time and then, stony with resolution, went downstairs to my writing-desk and penned the most difficult letter of my life.

"Dear Gideon—You want me to be the woman I was before. I could not even if I wanted to, for I am no longer that woman."

But this was not enough, these were the words he had kissed from my mouth an hour ago and so, with a heavy, aching hand I wrote: "As you supposed, I am already somewhat committed to another man and in the cold light of day I find myself unwilling to give up a relationship of such long standing and which suits my present way of life so exactly."

I signed my name, folded the paper, handed it to my maid who, bustling into the room, was surprised to see me up and dressed.

"Lord, ma'am, you fair startled me!'

"Yes. Have this delivered to Mr. Gideon Chard at Nethercoats Mill at once. And tell Richards to hurry since I shall need the carriage at half-past seven to take me to Gower Street."

It was the letter of a cool and promiscuous woman, the kind of letter polite society expected a woman of my sort to write, and I did not think he would answer it. For I had raised the one objection he could neither demolish nor forgive. I had told him I preferred Liam Adair.

I waited until my coachman had set off, walked stiffly upstairs, speaking to my maid as I did so about the badly polished mirror in the hall. I went into my room, fell face down on the bed in a storm of weeping that lasted until I feared it could not stop, and although eventually I got up and dried my eyes, put on my hat and went to Gower Street, and although no one else was aware of it, I knew that I was ill for days—and days—thereafter.

24

I TURNED GRATEFULLY TO WORK as one turns, in great thirst, to water, and found it in plenty, for the circulation of the *Star* was growing, our advertising revenue with it, enabling us quite soon to put out two weekly editions instead of one, to take on more staff, more enthusiasm, and eventually perhaps to replace those ailing presses which had seen service in my Grandfather Aycliffe's day. But, in that far off time when Aunt Faith and my mother had been young, the stamp duty on newspapers which had made them too expensive for the working man to buy had been less of a hardship than it seemed, very few of those working men being able to read. Now, in these enlightened times of Mechanics Institutes and public libraries, when the Act of 1870 had decreed there should be a school within walking distance of every child and the Act of 1880 had just, with the heartfelt approval of the *Star*, made school attendance compulsory, a few hours a week, for all children between the ages of five and ten, literacy was spreading, the craftsmen, the artisans, the workmen at whom the *Star* was aimed being able to purchase it now with the same nonchalance as Gideon Chard purchased his *Times*, his *Yorkshire Post*, his *Cullingford Courier & Review*.

I worked, all day and every day, not only at the amassing of sordid or sensational facts, the uncovering of human dramas and injustices, but the small doings of a small community which enjoyed hearing about itself. I sat in draughty church halls on hard wooden benches and listened to interminable lectures on "improving," artistic, or scientific subjects. I drank weak tea in those same halls when some fund-raising activity was in progress, admiring both the examples of fine needlework which were for sale and the charity for which their proceeds were destined. I watched amateur theatricals, operas, dancing displays, remembering to note the name of every single player and the number of

flounces on the organizers' dresses. I attended weddings, not of
Blenheim Lane or Elderleigh, but of skilled workmen, weaving-
overlookers, shopkeepers, schoolmasters, clerks, publicans; and
their funerals, finding an appropriate mention for each one. And
on the evenings when the *Star* could not detain me I went to the
Stones and talked to women whose basic need for food and
shelter should have made my own needs seem irrelevant—or, for
an hour or two, more bearable.

I left my house by half-past seven every morning and was
rarely home before midnight to a supper of cold meat, bread and
cheese, some kind of cold pudding on a tray. I lost weight and
colour and a great deal of sleep, and suffered for a short while
after my letter to Gideon from a strange imbalance of mind, a
feeling half dread and half desire that I had conceived his child.
Three painful weeks convinced me otherwise and even then, my
reactions remaining considerably off-key, I wept first for the
sheer, blessed relief of it, and then wept again at my own
continued sterility.

I acquired a professional manner, pleasant yet cool, a woman
not easily pleased and who did not care to please everyone. I
wore plain but stylishly cut gowns in good quality fabrics and
dark colours which made me taller and thinner, did my hair in a
low chignon since I had no time now for ringlets, although I did
not abandon a certain musky perfume which had its uses in
Silsbridge Street. I was acutely miserable for some part of every
day, then less so, for the decision to part from Gideon had been
mine and, having taken it, it would have been senseless to waste
my cherished independence grieving for him. He lingered in a
raw place at the back of my mind, a guarded area quick to bleed
when one prodded it but bearable if left alone. I knew now that
his feeling for me went deeper than convenience and that had I
married him before making my dangerous acquaintance with
freedom we would now be living happily together. But I had
married Gervase. Gideon had married wonderful, maddening,
enchanting Venetia and had not been enchanted. It was too late.
I knew it and the fact that he had neither answered my letter nor
thrown it in my face proved that he knew it too. I began to busy
myself with the affairs of the workhouse, falling foul once again
of Miss Tighe, for whom I was now a competent adversary.

"There is nothing wrong with the administration of the Poor
Law," she told me.

"Not for those who administer it," I replied, "although one
has yet to learn the opinion of those it is supposed to benefit."

And I concentrated throughout the next few months on gathering those opinions together and repeating them, with my own reactions to them, in the pages of the *Star*.

I had never—as Miss Tighe reminded me—seen the inside of Cullingford's workhouse and while she remained on the Board of Guardians would be unlikely to do so. But it took little imagination to picture the bare, whitewashed wards, the narrow wooden beds like coffins all in a row, the conviction that in this bleak place Charity was not only cold but cruel. And I found many who had been obliged to suffer that Charity to agree with me.

This system of Poor Relief had come into being in my grandparents' day, based on the assumption that, except in the case of the old, the infirm or the juvenile, poverty was invariably the result of laziness, lustfulness or strong drink. And consequently a committee of frock-coated, silk-hatted gentlemen had decreed that outdoor assistance on the old parochial system be abolished and that those who could not maintain themselves must be maintained in workhouses—"Bastilles" their inmates called them—where the conditions were so harsh that the able-bodied would do anything—presumably even go to work—in order to avoid them.

The diet was of the most meagre, little more, it seemed, than water-porridge, dumplings and thin gruel, the paupers being obliged to eat all their meals in total silence and to pay for them with their labour, the men being set to stone-breaking, bone-grinding, the picking of oakum, the women to housework and coarse, monotonous sewing. There was, in all workhouses, the strictest segregation of the sexes, husbands and wives being separated on entry and allowed no contact with each other, a precaution thought necessary by the Poor Law Commissioners to prevent the breeding of infants who would be a further drain on the rates, although this same rule was applied to old couples, long past child-bearing age, who had lived together for fifty or sixty years and were often much distressed at being so roughly torn apart.

In fact old couples thus separated quite often died soon after. Infants removed from their mothers and placed in the children's ward as soon as they were weaned tended to do the same. And since no account had been taken by those original Commissioners of the fluctuating state of trade, the fact that a man thrown out of work by bad weather and bad conditions could, if given a little something to tide him over, soon find employment again when things picked up, many were forced into the Bastilles who need never have been there at all.

One heard of mothers who were not told of a child's death until after the funeral, of men in their seventies forced to hard labour; of unruly children punished by being locked in the mortuary for a night or two with corpses for company. One heard of overseers who sexually abused young girls and young boys, of strange outbreaks of disease, and other deaths which, being unexplained, were presumably suicide. One did not, I must add, hear of these things in Cullingford where our Board of Guardians, at the direction of Miss Tighe, was most vigilant, making regular inspections of the wards, employing a qualified teacher for the children who, in their natural habitat, would have received little or no education at all; ensuring medical attention for men and women who had never in their lives possessed the wherewithal to pay a doctor's fee.

But there were abuses of a more subtle nature and it had come to Liam's attention that the superintendent was a very sleek little man, rather better dressed than he should have been when one considered his wages; that the matron had a cool air of competence which had pleased Miss Tighe but a greedy mouth and crafty eyes, quite capable, Liam thought, of further watering down that eternal porridge, of reducing the five ounces of meat allowed each adult pauper four times a week to four ounces, the twelve daily ounces of bread to ten, and thus, with the dreadful patience of a spider, building a profit.

The workhouses, of course—as Miss Tighe was quick to point out—were not prisons, only infirmity, extreme old age or extreme youth obliging anyone to stay there. But since entry to the Bastille meant the breaking up of homes and families, the sale of furniture and pots and pans, of anything one had that would fetch a copper or two, the meagre treasures of a lifetime all gone to purchase that wooden bed, that bowl of gruel, it was not easy, once incarcerated, to get out again. We all knew that in the area around St. Mark's Fold there were old husbands and wives who preferred to starve or to freeze *together*, rather than apply for the workhouse test; young women who would go to the brothel before the Bastille; we knew of the desperate young man, quite recently, in Simon Street, who, crippled in some accident for which no one felt the need to pay him compensation, had watched his furniture sold, his wife and small children led away, and then hanged himself. I had, to my shame and distress, heard an old woman pleading with her daughter: "Just hold a pillow to my face, Lizzie, when I'm asleep, so I'll not wake again. It's kinder." But Lizzie had eight or nine children of her own, a husband who was violent in drink, pains in her chest and dizziness in her head, the fretful cough and wasted cheeks of the consumptive.

"They'll look after you, ma. I can hardly look after myself. And I'll get you out when I can."

"It's a pernicious system," Liam decreed. "I think I'll make a little mischief again."

But when the *Star* printed a sketch of an unnamed but easily identifiable Bastille, portraying the superintendent as a fat tabby cat, the matron as a weasel, the inmates as tiny skeletons of mice, Miss Tighe, who would not visit the *Star* and could not set foot in the lodgings of so notorious a bachelor as Liam Adair, brought her complaints to me.

"Good-morning, *Mrs.* Barforth," she icily greeted me, a martial light in her eye. "I have one thing to say to you. I have here Miss Mandelbaum's copy of the *Star*, since I do not take it myself. It will have to stop."

"The *Star*, Miss Tighe?"

"Preferably. But I am referring to these attacks not only on the workhouse, which I believe to be the most efficiently managed in this union or any other, but on its employees, Mr. Cross and Mrs. Tyrell—for that is what they are, Mrs. Barforth, just employees. I would have thought such attacks to have been beneath even so dubious a publication as your own."

"I will convey your opinions to my editor, Miss Tighe."

"I daresay. And while you are about it you would do well to note my further opinion that while your editor, as you call him, is moralizing about the Poor Law and hinting that my superintendent is somehow making his fortune out of it, he turns an entirely blind eye to the scandalous conduct of his friends, Dr. and Mrs. Stone."

I was, for a moment, astonished.

"I know of no scandal concerning the Stones."

"Do you not? Then regretfully, Mrs. Barforth, I must tell you that you cannot be speaking the truth. Come now, my house is directly opposite theirs in Blenheim Lane, Miss Mandelbaum's a few doors above, and we have *seen*, Mrs. Barforth, the use to which they put their garden shelter—it is the talk of the neighbourhood. Can you deny that Dr. Stone, if indeed he *is* a doctor at all, goes on the prowl at night and brings home—well,

I shall not say the word—*persons* of the lowest character, dis-eased minds and diseased bodies too, I shouldn't wonder—''

"Miss Tighe, you must know as well as I do that Dr. Stone's purposes are the very opposite of immoral."

"I know no such thing. What I do know is the evidence of my own eyes. I have seen that man set off alone and return accompa-nied by some creature who quickly disappears with him into that shed. I have heard cries and screams on many occasions, and the unmistakable sounds of drunkenness. I have seen girls who had no business to be in Blenheim Lane and would never have come there had he not brought them, running out of his gate and past my windows in a state of terror. And I have asked myself what it is that could terrify *them*. What is going on in that garden, Mrs. Barforth? Is it a shelter for vagrant women, as he declares, or is it a bordello to accommodate the perversities of his friends?''

"How *dare* you, Miss Tighe—especially when you know it to be entirely untrue?''

"Are you accusing me of lying, Mrs. Barforth. How dare *you*?''

"This is all nonsense, Miss Tighe."

"Really? Then the whole of Blenheim Lane is nonsensical, for I am not the only one to watch and complain—not the only one by a long way.''

"Dried up old stick," Liam said, grinning broadly when I reported the interview. "She enjoys it. There's nothing she can do.''

Yet I was uneasy and mentioned the matter that evening, hesitantly, to Anna Stone.

"Poor Patrick!" she said calmly smiling. "They broke our windows in Liverpool and threw stones at his horse. He is quite accustomed to it. But the really sad thing, you know, is that if Martha Tighe would only broaden her views a little she could be most useful. She really believes that her workhouse is humane and orderly—certainly it is clean. And if it is ever proved to her that Liam's suspicions are true, then that superintendent and that gimlet-eyed matron will have a very angry Miss Tighe to deal with. There was a girl here last week who lost her baby in Miss Tighe's Bastille. There is an allowance of two pints of beer a day given to nursing mothers until their infants are weaned, not only for the extra liquid to make the milk but because the hops and malt are strengthening. It was never given, although one assumes it was charged for. The girl lost her milk, other forms of feeding did not succeed, and the child died. Well, perhaps it would have

died anyway, for the mother was very undernourished, somewhat beyond the remedy of two pints of beer, nor was she too
badly grieved by her loss, for a baby would have been an
encumbrance to her and would have obliged her to stay longer in
the Bastille. She went off quite cheerfully, knowing just how to
get another baby whenever she wanted one. But Miss Tighe, had
she known the truth, would have been very grieved indeed."

I returned home preoccupied as always by the extent of
Anna Stone's tolerance, to find two notes awaiting me, one from
Mrs. Barforth, the other from Aunt Faith, both telling me that
Gervase had returned to Galton.

"Will you be dining, ma'am?" the maid asked, and for an
instant I could barely understand the sense of her question, much
less answer it. Would I be dining? I had not the faintest notion.
But there was something I must do, although exactly what it was
eluded me. I must hurry. But where? And why? I must make
arrangements. But for what purpose?

"Yes, Jenny. I will be dining."

But even then, seated at my plainly set table, eating the kind
of food servants choose when left to themselves by a mistress
who does not care—the kind of food which would have revolted
Gideon—I could not lose the feeling that there was something I
had neglected or forgotten, something to which I absolutely must
attend.

"He is looking well," Aunt Faith told me the following
Sunday. "Very well indeed. I was at Galton on Wednesday and
he had walked in quite unannounced, half an hour before me.
Georgiana was in ecstasies of course, for she had feared never to
get him back again. Well, he is here, very bronzed and healthy,
and I believe on Friday he went over to Scarborough to see his
father. My dear, if he means to stay you must be prepared to
meet him."

A letter from Camille reached me on the Monday morning.

"Grace, I was terrified, for if he had come to accuse me of
blighting his mother's life what could I have answered? What he
actually said was: 'I believe you have become, more or less, my
wicked stepmamma?' We laughed and *I* could have wept with
relief. 'I suppose you have come a-begging?' Nicholas said to
him, which sounds ungracious except that it was said with a
twinkle in his eye and that unwilling little smile, as if he didn't
really mean to smile at all. We dined very pleasantly, Gervase
telling us his traveller's tales, which made me laugh until I ached
and even made Nicholas grunt once or twice in the way he has

when he is actually very amused but doesn't want to show it. He says he wishes to settle at Galton and farm the land and I suppose there is some suggestion that if he sticks to his plan Nicholas will buy him more land in compensation for the fortune he could have been making in the business. I certainly hope so. He is much quieter than I supposed. And of course we talked a great deal of you."

I waited, still prone to that sudden need for haste when nothing required it, until another letter was delivered to me, and holding it in a carefully steady hand it seemed incredible that I had never seen Gervase's handwriting before. It was pointed and slanting, rather fine, suggesting that, since we certainly would meet, it might be easier for both to meet by arrangement rather than chance, and in the privacy of Galton, without danger of observation by any Mrs. Rawnsley, any Miss Tighe. Did I agree? I did. He wrote again appointing a day and an hour he hoped would suit me. It suited me. I informed my coachman, begged a day off from Liam, and found that my mind had wandered rather foolishly to the subject of hats, a certain blue velvet confection veiled with spotted net and topped with a pile of blue satin roses which I had glimpsed in Millergate only a day ago.

I bought it that evening on my way home from the *Star*, knowing as it went into its box that it would not do, that it was a hat for high days and holidays, for garden-parties and fashionable churches, fashionable promenades; a hat for the life that used to be mine.

In the end I put on a smart but not extravagant cream straw with a black velvet ribbon, a cream silk dress draped up to show an underskirt patterned in cream and black and hemmed by a black fringe, a cream parasol with a black handle, cream silk gloves and cream kid shoes. And as we drove away from town, up Blenheim Lane, past Lawcroft Fold and Tarn Edge, past Aunt Faith's suburban Elderleigh to the narrow crossroads which led one way to Listonby, the other to Galton, I was pestered by a fly-swarm of senseless anxieties, the probable muddiness of the Abbey grounds that would spoil my shoes, the specks of soot which could ruin my silk gloves, a conviction that I was too smart—or not smart enough—which occupied my mind and helped me not to admit that what really ailed me was cowardice.

It was early June, the sky a soft, light blue streaked here and there with gauzy cloud, the hillsides around Galton fragrant with new grass, the hedges dotted with unexpected flowers. The house looked empty as I approached, the river which almost encircled it sparkling and hurrying in the sun, the massive oaks just coming into leaf, since spring had been late and cool, a tender, delicate green running riot now on those venerable branches.

I busied myself a moment with gloves and parasol, the cream velvet reticule embroidered in black which I had picked up from my toilet table without checking what it contained. I should, most assuredly, have brought an extra handkerchief. Had I done so? I opened the reticule, saw that I had, closed it with a snap, and there he was, waiting to help me down from the carriage, looking—and that first impression remained with me ever after—quieter than before, as Camille had said; not a quietness of speech or movement, but *quietness* for all that, an absence of restlessness which, for a moment, since restlessness had been the deepest shade of his nature, made him almost a stranger.

"Grace, I am glad you could come."

"Yes. How are you?"

"I am extremely well. You are looking very smart."

And to ease our way carefully through those first vulnerable moments we employed the device of etiquette, making the enquiries one can make with such perfect safety as to the state of the weather and of the Listonby road, the convenience of living in Blenheim Crescent so near to town, the extent of his journeyings, how long it had taken him to get there, and how long to get back again. I took off my gloves, smiled at him, asked my courteous questions, made my courteous replies, so that a listener would have taken us for casual acquaintances who were suffering no particular strain.

The stone-flagged hall was cool and dim as it had always been, the family portraits so dark that, after the strong sunlight, it was hard to distinguish one Clevedon from another. There was no fire today, branches of purple lilac standing on the hearth in great copper jars, the long table, more scarred and battered even than I remembered it, set with wide copper bowls full of blossom, their perfume blending pleasantly with the scent of beeswax, the dusty odours of old wood and stone.

"What can I give you, Grace? Tea—or a glass of wine?"

"Is your mother not here?"

"No, she has gone down to Leicestershire with Sir Julian, I believe."

"You don't mind, then—about Camille and Sir Julian?"

"No. I don't mind. And Venetia would have been glad.

Grace, will you take some refreshment now or shall we walk a
little first? The ground has dried up wonderfully already after
yesterday's rain.''

We went outside again, walking towards the stream, the old
wooden bridge, the stepping-stones leading across the water to a
gentle green hillside, a dog I had not noticed getting up from the
chimney corner and padding after us, the black and white collie,
so nervous last year, who now kept correctly and closely to heel.

I had not yet discovered just what had so changed in him for
in appearance he was remarkably the same. His auburn hair had
faded, perhaps, or been bleached lighter by the sun, certainly his
skin was browner than I had ever seen it, the cobwebbing of
lines around his eyes much deeper, the eyes themselves keener
somehow, as if they had grown accustomed to scanning horizons
far wider than one found at Galton, or in Cullingford.

''What a lovely day!'' he said and took a deep breath, inhaling
the moist green land, the heavy earth, the hint of moorland on
the brow of the hill, the warm air bringing the fragrance of
small, pastel-tinted flowers, newborn oak leaves, no tropical
flaring of violent colour but the slow and gentle unfolding of an
English June.

''How very lovely!''

''You missed Galton then, Gervase?''

''Yes—happily I did.''

''And now you are going to live here and look after the
estate?''

''I am. And if you are wondering why I could not have taken
that decision years ago and spared myself—and you—all this
trouble, then that is why I asked you here today. To explain
myself and to tell you that I am sorry.''

We had reached the bridge, the dog still closely to heel,
looking up at Gervase enquiringly, wagging a hopeful tail.

''Yes,'' he said, ''go''; and daintily, almost cautiously as a
cat, she went down the river-bank to take a well-mannered drink,
looking back at him from time to time to make sure he was still
there.

''That dog was not so well behaved when last I saw her.''

''No, my mother never manages to train her dogs. However,
this one appears to be my dog now. Grace—I went away to find
out what it was I *would* miss, and had it turned out to be nothing
I would not have come back. In the end it was Galton. It struck
me that I really was a Clevedon and that what had caused the

trouble before was that I was trying to be the wrong Clevedon. Do you understand?''

I nodded, my mind releasing the memory of his taut, white face years ago as he had forced his horse over a fence beyond its stamina and his nerve, and his shame afterwards at the distress Perry Clevedon could never so much as imagined. And suddenly I felt, not love, not even affection but *akin* to him—closely akin.

"I understand. I think you would have been afraid of that Clevedon.''

"My dear, that Clevedon—Peregrine Clevedon—*was* frightening. Unfortunately from my early childhood I thought it absolutely necessary to be like him. I have only one clear memory of him. My mother had taken me and the Chard boys out with the Lawdale, when we were all six and seven years old, the Chards on reliable ponies because Aunt Caroline was nervous about them breaking their necks, and me on a brute about sixteen hands high because I was a Clevedon and wasn't supposed to bother about trifles like that. No hanging back and keeping out of the way for me, as Aunt Caroline had told her boys to do. I had to *keep up* like my mother and my uncle had kept up at my age—they weren't asking me to do anything they hadn't found easy and enjoyable themselves—and, of course, because I was scared, I couldn't. I did take a tumble that day, head first into a ditch, and at first I thought they hadn't noticed and would just leave me lying there—damned uncomfortable and freezing cold, of course, but at least I wouldn't have to go on sitting that terrible horse. Then Uncle Perry came at me at the gallop, heaved me out of the ditch by the scruff of the neck and threw me at my mother—what seemed to me a mile away. And she just tossed her head and laughed, because they'd both had plenty of rough treatment when they were cubs and taken no harm. I remember how very splendid they both looked. Poor Uncle Perry! His horse reared up and fell over backwards on top of him that same afternoon, and neither of them got up again. They buried him over there, in the Abbey churchyard, and my mother brought me here after the funeral and explained that the land and the house would be mine now. The trust that would have been Perry's when old Mr. Gervase Clevedon died would now come to me, the family traditions, the holding of the land for future generations, the responsibility of making sure there would be a future generation. And every time I went into the village or round the farms some sentimental old woman would start telling me I was the 'image' of Master Peregrine.''

"And so you simply thought you had to *be* Peregrine, and do the things he used to do."

"So I did, which would have been bad enough even if I'd had the nerve, as well as the face, for it. But unfortunately there was somebody else I was expected to be, was there not? A second Perry Clevedon at Galton. Another Joel Barforth at Tarn Edge. I loved my mother the best and so I tried harder for her, but there were times when I couldn't have said what scared me most, riding one of Peregrine's wild horses or standing in those weaving-sheds and in the counting-house knowing I was supposed to understand those machines and those columns of figures and give orders to men who *did* understand. And it wasn't merely a question of courage. It was the sense of failure that really troubled me. I stood between two splendid inheritances and was not fit for either. Consequently what was I fit for? Not a great deal, perhaps. It has taken me all these years to find out and I have hurt you and some others in the process."

"You said when I arrived that you wished to apologize. For what? For marrying me?"

"Dear Grace, how could any man be sorry for that?"

"Yes—well, that is the *right* answer, of course. Now tell me the truth."

"That I regret marrying you? For your sake I must regret it. I treated you abominably. I was like a wilful child constantly seeing how far he could go, except that I was playing adult—and very cruel—games."

I sighed, remembering.

"Yes, I know. You thought I could make everything right for you—as if I had some kind of magic formula. And when I hadn't—and couldn't—you were angry with me. You resented me, I think."

"Yes. And when your magic failed me I turned to Diana, thinking she could do the same. I had formed the habit of clinging to strong women, you see. My mother—then you. The failure was entirely mine and I reacted as I always did, by running away. Not far, just into other women's beds to start with. I believed, for quite a long time, that those casual affairs were as much as I was capable of."

"Until Diana."

"Yes," he said quietly. "Until Diana. I was in love with her, and it turned sour like everything else I had attempted. I was so full of self-disgust when I went away that I hardly expected to survive it. After all, how could I possibly survive without my father's bank account to draw on, or my mother to provide me with a bolt-hole? Or without you to blame for all my shortcomings? I found that I could. And for a while the blessed relief of being with total strangers who had never heard of Perry Clevedon or Joel Barforth—of Galton or Tarn Edge—was the most marvellous experience of my life. For a while all I wanted to do was relax into it. For a while. Then I stood still and found that, after all, I could look at myself squarely and coolly and live with what I saw. I hadn't been cut out to run the mills. My mother was right about that. And my father would have accepted it—as he's accepted it now—if I'd been able to show him something else I wanted to do. But I was never sure. I needed first to discover that I really was a Clevedon, but of an entirely different breed to Peregrine.''

He smiled once again into that far distance, quietly, easily, the hectic rhythms of his nature slowing, it seemed, and mellowing, no longer driven by his old, fast-burning uncertainties but at the gentle pace of the seasons.

''If you came here with Venetia, Grace, when you were children, then you must have met my great-grandfather, the old squire? He was a man who occupied the one place in the world which suited him best. He had never been rich, because a life of service in keeping with the Clevedon code is no way to make a fortune, but he understood the land, as my mother understands it—as Peregrine did not—and he understood the needs of those who farm it and graze their beasts on it. I don't know if he could bring down eighty grouse with eighty shots like Peregrine—certainly I can't—but he looked after his fields and his moor and he looked after his people. That is the kind of Clevedon I am. Not in the least exciting like Peregrine but—amazingly—quite solid and rather sound. Who ever would have thought it?''

We turned to retrace our steps, smiling and easy with each other, the dog, aware of Gervase's slightest movement instantly leaving her game in the water to follow after him, and then, recognizing the path he must take, frisking ahead of us into the cloister, our quickest way back to the house.

''How peaceful it is,'' he said, breathing in once again the scents of his heartland, the perpetual dusty twilight of this strange corridor where nuns had once walked with bowed head and folded hands. Yet I had never been at peace here, and quickening my step had almost reached the far end—the strong uncomplicated daylight of every day—when I heard someone call out, a quick burst of laughter, and a child, presumably escaping from the house and with his nursemaid in hot pursuit behind him, came toddling towards us.

I stood quite still for a moment because I was unable to move, watching the sturdy little legs, the self-important step of a child already three years old, the eager, explorer's hands outstretched, expecting to encounter nothing in the whole world but affection and pleasure, as mine had done at that age.

"This is my son," said Gervase quietly.

"Yes, of course," and I bent down as any other woman would have done and reached forward to welcome him as anyone— certainly the child himself—would have expected me to do. He looked like no one in particular, light brown hair in soft, loose curls, a rounded, rosy face, light eyes which could have been green but which reminded me far more of two bright little buttons than of Gervase or Venetia, or Diana Flood. There was nothing there of the sharp-etched, auburn profile, the birdlike delicacy which could have disturbed me—which *my* child might have had—yet to my complete horror I knew that I could not touch him, that even if he stumbled I could not put out a hand to prevent his fall.

I straightened up swiftly and turned my face to the wall, tears spilling from the corners of my eyes, utterly ashamed, while Gervase retrieved the little boy, gave him back to his nurse, and then put a cool, steady arm around my shoulders.

"Grace, I am so sorry. I should have warned you."

"Heavens! I can't think why I am being so stupid."

"Can't you? When you lost your own child here, in this house—our child? I grieved for him too. I couldn't tell you then. May I tell you now?"

"No. Tell me about *him*—the child you have. Please. It's better."

He gave me a moment to dry my eyes and then, understanding that I could not bear to speak of my own loss, he shrugged and smiled.

"Very well. He is called Peregrine, I fear. My mother's choice, of course, and since it seemed, at the time, that she would be left to bring him up, one could not complain."

"I thought he had gone abroad with Diana."

"No. Diana did not wish to grow accustomed to him, for she knew Compton Flood would never take him. Had he been a girl possibly, but with a title in the offing a boy was always out of the question. She understood that and once she had made up her mind to be Lady Sternmore she planned accordingly. She wanted that title badly and now she has another son. My mother was to have had this one, but, like the sheepdog, I seem to have acquired him. Will you take that glass of wine now?''

I took, in the end, rather more than a glass, sitting at the scarred oak table beneath the portrait of Peregrine Clevedon, Gervase, who still looked so like him, lounging beside the hearth telling me once again his traveller's tales, easing our way from the past, where love had been difficult and had not succeeded, to a future that might offer us friendship.

''I must go.''

''Must you really? May I come and see you in Blenheim Crescent and scandalize your neighbours?''

''Please do.'' And I knew I would be very disappointed if he did not.

He had changed, and as I drove away, my head pleasantly confused by his excellent wine, I knew that I had no need ever again to feel anxiety or guilt on his behalf, no need to worry on sharp, raw nights if he had found a place to lay his head, no need to concern myself with his tensions, since he was not tense, nor with his nervous rages, since he was neither nervous nor angry. He had changed far more than I—had done better, perhaps, than I had done, at picking up his pieces. Who ever would have thought it? And I could not deny that this assured and steady Gervase Clevedon intrigued me.

25

THESE FRESH OUTBREAKS OF SCANDAL in the Barforth family, rather
surprisingly made my own social position no easier. Mr. Nicholas Barforth, defying all conventions, had gone off to live in
open and apparently most enjoyable sin with a woman half his
age. But Mr. Nicholas Barforth had always been a law unto
himself. Mrs. Georgiana Barforth was known to be, if not
precisely living, then spending far too much of her time with Sir
Julian Flood. But Mrs. Barforth had simply transferred her affections from one gentleman of distinction to another, a procedure
which Cullingford might abhor but was well able to understand.
And it was I, who had not abandoned my husband for a lover but
for a solitary and unseemly independence, who remained
Cullingford's true disgrace; the woman who had betrayed her sex
and her class by shunning the charitable duties and the unsalaried
employments appropriate to a lady and selling her services, like
a common housemaid, for money.

And I suppose it was only natural when, the better to account
for my perversity, it was whispered that I must surely be the
mistress of Liam Adair.

"They flatter me," Liam said. "And they tempt me too—I'll
not deny it."

But Liam, whatever else he lacked, could find temptations—
and mistresses—in plenty and had more than that to occupy his
mind just then. There was the eternal problem of finance, or the
lack of it, the printing-presses which he still could not afford to
replace, the salaries—including mine—which had to be paid, the
advertisers who could not always be convinced they were getting
value for money. But more pressing than that was the problem of
the demolition of the streets around Low Cross, and, as the first
hammers began to fall, Liam was quickly aware that he had
unleashed rather more than he had, I think, intended.

I knew that the houses in St Mark's Fold had not been fit to live in. I knew that those who can help themselves must be allowed and encouraged to do so. I knew that progress in all its forms has always displaced and often destroyed the weak, the sick, the unnecessary, and that enough of them had survived each fresh catastrophe to implant its memory in their children. The power-looms introduced into this valley by Joel Barforth had thrown a whole generation of hand-loom weavers out of work. The combing-machines, brought in twenty years later by Nicholas Barforth, his son, had made the occupation of hand-comber a thing of the past, causing some to starve and thousands to emigrate. I knew that Gideon Chard, who could not comprehend poverty in any case, did not expect and was not expected to make himself responsible for the hundreds who had been living in debt and near destitution in St. Mark's Fold.

Millmasters built houses, as landowners built farm cottages, for the simple reason that they required workers who in turn required somewhere to live. That was the extent of the obligation, and if the farm labourer or the mill-hand turned out to be idle or ill-tempered, fell ill or in some other way failed to give satisfaction, then he was turned out of his job and the cottage that went with it. Everybody in Cullingford understood that and few were prepared to dispute it, taking the view that, when employment and accommodation were tied together, a man with any sense at all took good care of both, and in the case of accident or sickness or a slump in trade, well, these were hazards which all working men must face and, however much one might sympathize in some cases, no one could expect a landlord to find alternative accommodation for his tenants. Cullingford's landlords did not expect it. The *Courier & Review* did not expect it either. By far the greater part of Cullingford stood solidly behind Gideon Chard in his plans for expansion and improvement, well aware that he was about to dispossess only those tenants who had been undesirable in any case, those who would take no care of their squalid cottages even if they were allowed to remain in them, and who, quite often, could not pay their rent.

Eviction notices for rent arrears which should have been issued months ago had been held in abeyance pending demolition, thus giving the families in question a far greater respite than they had been entitled to. Gideon had made a charitable gesture which had not, in fact, cost him a great deal and, for the rest, he paid his taxes, a part of which maintained the Poor Law which in its turn maintained the poor. He had been taught, as I had—as we all had—that poverty was a sin that brought its own punishment, and I knew there were those in St. Mark's Fold who were idle by nature and would always remain so. But I had seen courage and intelligence and humanity there too, and the seeds of it, which would not come to flower in the workhouse. And I had no thought in my mind of attacking Gideon when I tried to share my horror of that grim establishment with the readers of the *Star*.

I hated the Poor Law with all my heart. Liam hated the Poor Law and Gideon, and although we told St. Mark's Fold clearly that it had society to blame for its desperate condition—those Poor Law Commissioners who believed they could cure poverty by making it too unpleasant to endure—there were times when Liam could not resist apportioning a hefty share of that blame to the new squire of Low Cross.

"You should stop this, Liam," I warned him.

"Yes," he said, "I know I should."

But society was an abstract concept somewhat beyond the grasp of St. Mark's Fold. The Poor Law Commissioners were very far away. Gideon Chard was there, visible and tangible, riding every day to the mill on his glossy chestnut mare, immaculate in tall hat and perfectly tailored coat and trousers—different ones each morning—which fitted him without a wrinkle. And the night after St. Mark's Fold was finally reduced to a heap of smoking rubble, the mill at Low Cross was attacked by a gang of youths, resulting in broken glass and broken heads, a watchman knocked unconscious, a lad of sixteen severely mauled by a Low Cross dog; and a tremendous increase, throughout the whole area, of bitterness.

We condemned the attack in the *Star* as unnecessary, foolhardy, but some days later an old woman from St. Mark's Fold who, after a lifetime at the loom had been obliged to sell the few sad little possessions she had saved and enter the Bastille, hanged herself there. A month after that, a young family who had gone on the tramp to avoid the workhouse test, and who had been considerably undernourished to start with, were found dead, presumably of starvation, in a derelict barn. Liam condemned that too. The attacks continued.

Additional dogs and men with sticks and possibly shot-guns were stationed in the mill-yard, but boys in their teens are agile and far too brave and almost nightly one would climb a wall and throw a stone which, with luck, would result in nothing more serious than broken glass. And when enough of them had been bitten, and a few had been rounded up and despatched to the

House of Correction, attention was diverted to Black Abbey Meadow where damage was done and building materials stolen, with the result that houses for which tenants were waiting could not be finished on time.

"You should tell them to stop this, Liam, before one of them gets killed. They might just listen to you."

"Yes," he said. "I know."

But he did nothing, and in the end the person who could have been killed was the squire of Low Cross himself, when half a dozen youths who had been painting obscene slogans on the mill wall early one morning decided to wait for him, presumably to observe his reactions, and then, when he appeared, took it into their heads to throw lighted paper at his horse.

I was not there to see what happened, but many were, and I heard how the thoroughbred animal quivered, reared up in panic and then, as fire came at it from all directions, went completely out of control, the very devil, they told me, screaming and snorting and trying to do murder with those thrashing hooves, with another devil on top of it, cursing, spitting blue flame, until the pair of them went crashing to the cobbles and only the human devil got up again.

He must certainly have been winded and bruised, and there had been blood on his cheek and on his hand, staining an immaculate shirt-cuff, greatly—I well knew—to his displeasure. But the horse, the only completely innocent party in the whole affair, had broken its knees, for which death was the only remedy. The wiser, or the softer-hearted of the lads, ran away. The fiercer, or the more foolhardy, waited while a gun was fetched from the mill—why, Liam was to ask later, had a gun been there in the first place?—and watched as Gideon, without any visible tremor, put it to the animal's head and fired the one merciful shot and then, whipping round to face his assailants, caught two particularly skinny little urchins and thrashed them with his riding-whip until they bled.

"Don't print it," I told Liam. "You *shouldn't* print it."

"I know," he said, but the next day the *Star* carried not only the words but the picture of the deed, a millmaster at least eight feet in height, dripping gold chains and fobs and rings, with two bleeding children cowering at his feet.

"You forgot to include the horse, Liam."

"Yes, I should not have forgotten that. There are some who used to live in St. Mark's Fold who'd be glad of the carcass to eat. Are you very angry with me, Grace?"

"I'm trying not to be."

But a day or so later, after months of painstaking detection,
some bribery and bullying and not a little risk to himself from
the burlier characters in the story, he was finally able to supply
the evidence that the workhouse master, Mr. Cross, had indeed
been falsifying his accounts, and gave Miss Tighe and her Board
the choice of dismissing him forthwith or facing a scandal. Not,
I suppose, that the scandal would have been very great, Mr.
Cross's habit of serving meat only twice a week instead of on
alternate days—and very suspicious meat at that—not likely to
shock those, and there were many, who wondered why paupers
should eat meat at all. But Miss Tighe's reputation as a shrewd
woman of impeccable judgement was at stake, and she so abhorred any kind of fraud or theft that she almost chose scandal
for the pleasure of sending Mr. Cross to jail. Her Borad, for the
first time, defied her by deciding otherwise. The guilty man and
his matron were sent packing, a comfortable couple selected in
their stead, largely at the recommendation of certain voices on
the Board of Guardians which had not been heeded in Miss
Tighe's heyday. Miss Tighe retained her position, but her authority was no longer quite the same, and we knew she would blame
Liam for that.

"You are not quite so angry with me now, are you, Grace?"

"No. But have a care for Miss Tighe. She will harm you if
she can."

"I daresay she will. But you know me by now, Grace.
There's always some woman coming after me, wanting to harm
me in one way or another. I reckon you'll stand by me when the
time comes."

The summer was intense and overcast that year, heavy yellow
skies, airless nights, a perpetual taste and smell of dust as one by
one the streets around Low Cross disappeared, reducing the area
in which I spent my working days to a wasteland. Gower Street
itself remained intact but half of Simon Street was gone. Colourful
if by no means aptly named Saint Street, with its pawnshops and
lodging-houses and brothels, was a memory by August, and
unrest generally was so rife that, even in the streets where
property had not been condemned, people were on the move,
packing up as fast as they could and leaving as if from a
besieged city, unable to be certain of what Gideon Chard might
buy up and knock down next.

The new factory buildings were already growing outwards, the
same handsome, Italianate façade as Nethercoats, containing—

because Gideon was in charge of it—everything of the very latest and best.

"Yes," Gervase said on his first visit to me in Blenheim Crescent, "I came by Low Cross and I can only be delighted to see that Gideon is increasing our fortune so grandly. *His* fortune rather more than mine, these days, I imagine."

"I know nothing about that."

"Well, I don't know all the ins and outs of it myself, for I believe he has a sideline or two that perhaps even father is not aware of. But I have no cause to complain. Do you remember the meadow where we used to jump the young horses? I have put cows in it now. Why don't you come and see?"

"Why on earth should I want to look at a field of cows?"

"To watch them pleasantly grazing on the place where you first saw me cry."

"I'll come."

I went, and we had a long, warm afternoon together strolling the leafy little pathways around Galton in the sunshine. I went again, walking farther afield this time, even daring to risk myself on the stepping-stones bridging an admittedly very narrow and very shallow stream. And when I was safely across he found me a seat in a grassy hollow and, stretched out beside me, spent a lazy hour telling me the names of the grasses and the delicate wild flowers, of the trees and the birds which he could identify, to my surprise, by their song.

"Wherever did you learn all these clever things?"

"Grandfather Clevedon taught me when I was a boy. I never mentioned it before because—"

"Because you thought it wasn't the kind of thing Uncle Perry would have been likely to mention. But he must have known all about it too."

"I suppose he did."

"Then what a bore he must have been, with nothing but his fast horses and his fast women."

"Ah—so I bored you, did I?"

"Oh no. Almost everything else, but not that."

I met Noel Chard on that second visit, waiting near the new cow pasture as we came back to the house, his resemblance to Dominic and Gideon diminished now not only by the assegai-thrust he had received at Ulundi, which still caused him to limp slightly, particularly in damp weather, but by the same weather-wise earthbound calm I had noticed in Gervase.

"Blanche wouldn't care for cows so near the house," he said,

merely stating a fact without the slightest hint of criticism, being
a man, these days, who could recognize the nucleus of a prize
herd when he saw it.

"Grace wouldn't mind," said Gervase and indeed, although I
had never consciously thought of cows before, the sound of their
lowing, coming with the scented breeze through the window as
we drank our afternoon wine, had a gentle monotony that was
not unpleasing.

Whenever Blanche was at Listonby, which was almost all the
time since Dominic went abroad, we met the first Sunday of
every month in the parish churchyard to take flowers to Venetia.
And that first hot August afternoon, having arranged the wonderful roses Blanche had brought from Listonby to our satisfaction,
Blanche ran her fingers along the marble of the elaborate head-
stone and murmured, talking to me but actually telling Venetia,
"My husband has written to say he is thoroughly bored with
Africa. But don't worry, for I am in no danger of seeing him
again. He thinks he may go after tigers in India next. He believes
a man may really live like a lord in India and consequently is
bound to stay there."

"I suppose he must come home sometime, Blanche."

"I suppose he must. But I am relying on India to call him
back again—all those tigers to shoot and elephants to ride and
beautiful brown girls in plenty, I expect, who are very willing.
He is a perfectly happy man."

"And Noel?"

She smiled, gave what for her was almost an ecstatic sigh and
suddenly pressed her living, blushing cheek against the cold
tombstone.

"What else could I do, Grace? He had loved me for such a
long time and I—oh yes, I admit it—I made sure he kept on
loving me. I stopped him from loving other people, didn't I? Of
course I did! Which is why Venetia said she wished he'd rape me,
which *of course* he never would. I started to wish the same
myself, so that I could make the excuse—only to myself—that
he forced me and that afterwards I'd thought, oh well, what's
done is done, and allowed it to continue."

"How like you, Blanche!"

"Yes. That is exactly what Noel said when I told him. And
that very same night—quite a long time ago now, as a matter of
fact. It was not rape, of course, although according to the law it
seems to be incest. Well, what Dominic did to me on our
wedding-night and for a year or two thereafter seemed more like

rape to me than this—and as for the incest, I sometimes try to worry about it, without much success.''

She remained for a moment, her cheek against the stone, her face as finely chiselled and serene as a porcelain angel, her pale hair pure silver in the sunshine: beautiful, surprisingly competent Blanche who had always meant to have everything her own way and who now that she had it was quite hesitantly asking our approval—mine and Venetia's.

''Well, I only wish Venetia had realized that, in our dishonest fashion, we are all three of us very happy. I can't help thinking she would expect me to bring it all out into the open, as she did—and as you did.''

''Blanche, I only decided what was right for me. You are the only person who knows what is right for you. Don't allow anyone to persuade you otherwise.''

''Oh, Grace, do you really think so?''

''I do, since you are ready to take the responsibility for your choices, and are hurting no one else.''

We rearranged the flowers once or twice again as we usually did and then drove off quietly to take tea with Aunt Faith, an essential part of our pilgrimage, finding, as we approached Elderleigh, that there was already a carriage on her drive.

''Oh lord!'' said Blanche disgustedly, ''it is Aunt Caroline. Yes—I did forget to mention it—she has come up again from South Erin to plague the life out of me and has brought a house-party with her. I expect she has driven over to show Gideon's new fiancée to mother.''

''Oh—'' And then, because whether Blanche knew it or not, my silence was very strained, my breath gone clean away, I said with a blessed coolness, ''I did not know Gideon was engaged.''

''Well, perhaps he is not, but his mother is certainly very keen on it and the girl is willing. It is an excellent match, but of course there can be no need to tell you that. She is thoroughly tedious but very rich and, I must admit, rather beautiful. Gideon came over to dinner last night and spent quite an hour with her alone in the Long Gallery, so I imagine we may expect the announcement at any time.''

They were sitting in the garden screened from the sun by Aunt Faith's wide-spreading chestnut trees before a table set with a lace cloth and the expected tea-time apparatus of silver tea-kettle and sugar-tongs, wafer thin cucumber sandwiches on flowery china plates, scones and chocolate cake; Aunt Faith, like Blanche, in a gown of soft white silk, Aunt Caroline in a robust shade of magenta; another white dress at which I only glanced as I walked slowly across the lawn.

Chairs were awaiting us, and Aunt Faith welcomed us into them, talking easily, ignoring the awkwardness she knew was coming, presenting Miss Hortense Madeley-Brown to me with the simple explanation that she had come with Aunt Caroline, until the Duchess herself, who had not forgiven me for introducing Camille to her brother and had piled up other grievances against me since then, announced crisply: "Well, Grace, I had not expected to see you here today, since Blanche does not acquaint me with all her plans, and I find it most awkward. My son Gideon is to join us presently to escort us to Tarn Edge and I am not sure he should be asked to meet you."

"I beg your pardon," I said, not quite so sharp-spoken as I might have been, since, for a shocked moment, I thought she was implying knowledge of our tempestuous, night-long affair. But of course it was my connection with the *Star* that troubled her and which, as she quickly informed me, raised doubts in her mind as to the suitability—even to herself—of my company.

"Caroline," said Aunt Faith smoothly, since in her view this was simply "Caroline being Caroline," "that is very harsh."

"I believe it to be just. Forgive me, Hortense dear, for speaking of these matters in your presence. I regard you quite as one of the family already, from whom no secrets should be kept. And, like all families, we do have our little difficulties. Grace can hardly deny that she has been disloyal—"

"I most certainly *can* deny it."

She smiled at me with the same total self-assurance which exasperated me so thoroughly in Gideon.

"Nonsense, my dear, of course you cannot. Is it not disloyalty to ally yourself with a man who has deliberately slandered my son—your own second cousin—a man who has whipped up so much ill feeling that my son might have lost his life only the other day as a result of it? If that is not disloyalty, then the world must really be changing."

I did not wish to lose my temper, partly for Aunt Faith's sake, partly because I considered it essential to be composed when Gideon came, and so I answered rather quietly, "Aunt Caroline, it is a very complex situation and I am truly sorry about the accident to Gideon's horse. But Liam Adair is not my ally. He is my employer. I am not responsible for his opinions and, after all, he too is a member of my family."

''Good heavens!'' she said, diverted, as I had intended, into matters of genealogy. ''He is no such thing.''

''Indeed he is,'' Aunt Faith said quickly, understanding my motive.

''Faith, he is no such thing. Her grandmother married his father, and what sort of a relationship is that? But on our side of the family, her mother was your sister and my first cousin. She married my brother's son, although the least said about that the better—''

''Do you really think so?'' murmured wicked Blanche. ''For my part I find Gervase much improved. I am sure Grace does too.''

''And what would Grace know about Gervase?'' Aunt Caroline snapped, her eyes, bright with the dawning of a new suspicion, flashing from one politely smiling face to another. ''You surely haven't been *seeing* him, have you, Grace?''

And although she was both deeply mortified and deeply shocked—for how could I be so shameless and what effect might it have on Gideon's inheritance?—at least it distracted her sufficiently from Liam to enable us all to drink our tea, while I took my first uninterrupted stare at Miss Madeley-Brown.

She was, indeed, the kind of girl who, in her first appearance in London's drawing-rooms is acclaimed a ''beauty,'' a tall, in fact a very tall girl with fine, broad shoulders, a bosom which even now, in the seventeenth or eighteenth year of her age, was magnificent, a lovely if rather vacant face and a haughty manner, coils of bright gold hair doing exactly as they had been bid beneath an expensive, much beribboned hat.

''You will be pleased with Tarn Edge,'' Aunt Caroline told her. ''It is not a palace, of course, but for a town house, and for this part of the world, I do not think one could do better. My father built it for my mother and I must confess it has been sadly neglected since she left it. My brother's wife, Mrs. Nicholas Barforth, took no care of it, my niece Venetia even less, and now, although my son has made many improvements since Mr. Barforth retired to the sea, it is sadly in need of a woman's touch. I know it will please you.''

Hortense Madeley-Brown smiled, a dazzling exposure of strong, pearl-white teeth which did not waver for one moment when Blanche, who had raised pained eyebrows over Aunt Caroline's deliberate failure to mention my own meticulous housekeeping, now lazily enquired: ''I dare say it will. But tell me, Aunt

Caroline—for I am often puzzled by it—to whom does Tarn
Edge actually belong?''

She received no answer, Aunt Caroline detecting a bee somewhere in the branches above her head; Aunt Faith quickly handing round more chocolate cake, which Miss Madeley-Brown,
with the keen appetite of youth and something not too much
under six feet of thoroughbred blood and bone, began placidly to
consume.

She would look superb, I thought, on horseback, her riding-
habit cut so tight that her maid would be required to stitch her
into it every morning. She would be a luxurious adornment to
any man's table, that creamy bosom half-revealed in the
candlelight. Those pale, slender limbs of hers—I could not
dismiss the image, no matter how hard I tried—would look more
than enticing on the satin sheets Gideon now used to cover his
bed. She was the kind of girl I had expected him to choose when
Venetia died, the kind his mother had always wanted for him,
rich, conventional, not too bright, who would obey him and
please him, produce for him a pair of healthy, uncomplicated
sons; a girl who would bring out the worst side of him and stifle
the rest. Vapid creature, I thought, sitting there sipping her tea
with nothing in her head but how pretty she looked, a bosom like
a Renaissance Venus and a brain no bigger than a pea—how
could he demean himself by wanting a girl like that?

I must not think of it. I drank my tea too quickly and too hot,
burning my tongue in my determination not to think of it. It
made no sense. I had given him up and in order to do so
effectively had hurt him and made him despise me. Now, because of the increasing bitterness between him and Liam Adair,
he must despise me even more. I had known quite well I must
face him sooner or later. The time had come. And if it was to be
made more painful by the presence of his mother and his recently
acquired fiancée, then I would have to grit my teeth a little
harder and bear it. What else could I do? Certainly it was not the
moment to begin examining my own feelings towards him, and
as Blanche—more perceptive than she used to be—drawled:
''Here comes Gideon now,'' I arranged myself carefully and
decided to model my own behaviour on his, whatever it turned
out to be.

If he had really wanted me as much as he had said he did just
six months ago—*if*—and if I had hurt him as much as I had
intended, then the situation might have been difficult for him
too, although nothing in his manner, trained first by Lady Chard

and then by the rigours of a particularly harsh public school, betrayed it.

"Aunt Faith," he said easily, kissing her cheek with the degree of affection exactly appropriate to a nephew. "Have I kept you waiting? I do apologize."

"No. You are just in time," Aunt Caroline answered instead, squeezing the hand he held out to her across the table in vigorous welcome. Blanche received no more than a nod from him, a smile and an almost imperceptible wink, a familiar, friendly greeting quite suitable for the woman who, as he must know quite well, was making both his brothers happy. And then: "Hortense. How are you?" he said very quietly, the whisper of the accomplished successful lover who can create a moment of intimacy while still permitting others to hear. And taking her hand he kissed it lightly but so near the wrist—bringing his head too close, in fact, to that splendid bosom—for casual gallantry.

"I am very well," she told him, which so far was the longest sentence I had heard her speak.

And it was not until Aunt Faith, fearing he did not mean to speak to me at all and hoping to cover the gap, had placed a teacup in his hand; and even then not until he had slowly helped himself to milk and sugar, stirred his tea, replaced the spoon in his saucer, that he glanced in my direction, nodded curtly, and said, "Grace."

"Good-afternoon, Gideon."

"Do you know," Aunt Faith said brightly, "I believe it is the warmest afternoon we have had this summer."

"Oh, I don't think so, mother," murmured Blanche. "Last Sunday was scorching and the one before it. What do you think, Hortense?"

"Oh, absolutely," she said, "scorching—quite."

And thus we settled it.

He took his golden young Amazon strolling in the rose-garden soon afterwards—the same roses, I supposed, which Venetia used to admire with Charles Heron—and no sooner were they out of sight than Aunt Caroline leaned towards me and said crisply, "Well then, Grace, I was not prepared to speak of this matter in Hortense's hearing, since it would concern her very closely, but I suppose you are in a better position than most to have some inkling of my brother's intentions. Does he intend to remain in Scarborough, which is quite bad enough, or is he so lost to reason as to contemplate setting that woman up at Tarn Edge?"

And turning to Aunt Faith she made a wide gesture, half anger, half distress. "You understand me, Faith, I am sure of it. Here is my poor Gideon, after all he has done—the work, the responsibility—and all he has suffered—yes, here he is without even a home to call his own. Tarn Edge, as you well know, belongs to Nicholas and I cannot tell you how much I regret making over my share in it to him when my father's property was divided. Yes, I know, I was paid handsomely, or so I thought at the time, but those few paltry thousands—I forget how many—would be no compensation at all for seeing that woman in the house my son has *earned*. Yes, Faith, earned—not only by his labour, and he has laboured very hard, but by the insult he has endured there. The Madeley-Browns are great people, Faith—this is the best marriage I could have made for him—and he must have somewhere decent, somewhere fitting, to take his bride. And you, Grace, I cannot tell you how deeply it shocks me to learn you have been in contact with Gervase. He has been over to Scarborough too, I hear, making up to that creature, so one must assume his travels have taught him on which side his bread is buttered. He has just bought three hundred acres of Winterton land adjoining his own, my son Noel tells me, and since I have not heard that he has sold any Barforth shares to pay for it—and my son Gideon would be sure to know—one may safely assume that the money was a gift from my besotted brother Nicholas. Certainly the world *is* changing."

For Aunt Caroline it was and for that reason I found it easier to be patient, accepting her scolding as I would not have done in the days of her social glories. But her husband, the Duke, had declined rapidly this last year or two, and when he passed away his land, his title, his property, would pass with him, placing Aunt Caroline in the same dilemma from which on her first husband's death she had extricated herself. A new duke would take possession of South Erin the very day the old one was carried out of it, bringing a new duchess to preside at his table, giving Aunt Caroline nothing to do but hand over her keys and the family jewels and take her leave.

She would have been surprised to know how well I understood her bitterness. She was a strong-willed, intelligent, forceful woman who had nevertheless accepted one of the roles traditionally assigned to her sex and had played it brilliantly and to the full. She had devoted herself entirely to the ambitions, interests, property of others, living her life not through her own achievements but at second-hand through theirs, and was now beginning to find that one by one those who had depended on her to create an atmosphere in which they *could* achieve were in their different fashions leaving her.

She had raised Listonby from the dust to create a splendid home for her husband and a fitting inheritance for her eldest son, had surrounded herself for years with influential, possibly quite boring men, who might one day make a Cabinet Minister, a Prime Minister, of Dominic, only to find that he preferred tiger shoots and polo games and—and she surely knew this—brown-skinned women. And then there was Noel, who should have been a general by now—*she* would have been a general by now in his place—content to roam about the farms with none of the dash and swagger she had bred into him, refusing, for all her coaxing, to restore the Listonby Hunt Ball because it would be "too much" for Blanche. Only Gideon remained and I knew how fiercely she would defend him against all comers, against Camille who, apart from the luxuries which would be lavished upon her, might further complicate the Barforth inheritance by producing a bastard but much-loved son; against the existing son, Gervase, who might worm his way back into his father's favour; against that son's former wife who, if she became his wife again, might claim Tarn Edge and more besides.

I understood and so, following Aunt Faith's example, I drank tea, smiled, made sympathetic noises or indignant ones as required, said, "Really?" "How very provoking," while Blanche, sitting between us, fell gracefully but deeply asleep.

"Wake up," said Aunt Caroline, prodding her with the handle of her parasol. "Gideon is coming back and Hortense would be very surprised to find you in that condition. They are very well-connected, Faith. She has one uncle a bishop, another who is very high up at the Treasury, and one who has some kind of a place at Court. How very gratifying to find a girl with all that money who has breeding too, and who is young enough to be *adaptable*—who will allow herself to be moulded, for she has a most pliant disposition. Gideon will have not one moment of anxiety with her. Hortense, dear, did you enjoy your stroll?"

Hortense agreed that she had enjoyed her stroll, Aunt Caroline beaming at her fondly, her good spirits entirely restored as she contemplated this rare find, this biddable, beautiful girl who—unlike her other daughters-in-law—would run her home and raise her children as Aunt Caroline told her, who would even be glad of her advice.

"We must be off now, Faith," she said, drawing on her

gloves. "For we are to make quite a little tour with Gideon—the estate at Black Abbey Meadow, the mill of Low Cross and the new property beyond—"

"New property?" said Blanche, asking the question which burned the tip of my tongue. But for once Aunt Caroline was not being astute or malicious or inquisitive, simply talkative in the manner of ageing aunts, and looked vaguely for assistance to Gideon.

"Why, yes—there has been some more property investment. Where did you say it was, dear?"

But he was not at first inclined to be very precise.

"It seemed advisable," he said, smiling beyond his mother at Miss Madeley-Brown, who seemed intent on examining the lace flounces on her sleeve, "in view of recent difficulties, one wished to be certain of one's hold in the neighbourhood, should one wish to expand again or to house an additional work-force. And so as certain properties became available, it seemed pointless to let them go elsewhere."

I looked pointedly at Blanche and, knowing as well as I that he was up to something, she asked obediently: "Which properties, Gideon?"

"Oh—whatever came to hand, here and there around Low Cross—and Gower Street. A buyer's market certainly, at the moment. In fact I have seen nothing like it. If one judged by the willingness of landlords to sell, one might think the hordes of Genghis Khan were encamped about a mile away—that or the Black Death. One can have just about any house one wants at the moment, for a very decent price, around Low Cross—and Gower Street."

But I had endured long enough and taking up my gloves to give my hands an occupation, I said with a calm *I* at least thought creditable, "What is it you have bought in Gower Street, Gideon?"

And I did not need his voice, merely his faint, malicious smile and the glint of satisfaction in his eyes to tell me it was the offices of the *Star*.

26

"SO HE IS OUR NEW landlord, is he?" said Liam. "Well, well, I suppose we must look for a hefty increase in our rent."

It came heftier than we had supposed, and we knew there would be worse to follow.

"Well, I reckon there's just about one thing left for me to do," said Liam. "I'll give him a run for his money. But while I'm about it you might look around, Grace, and find us another address before he puts me and my old presses into the street."

But rehousing the *Star*, as Liam—and Gideon—had foreseen, was no easy task, for the healthier buildings in Sheepgate and Kirkgate and the new business premises which were raising their handsome heads these days, from Market Square to the fringes of Blenheim Lane, were either beyond Liam's price range or their owners—quite often friends of Miss Tighe—did not view our tenancy with favour. While in the poorer quarters of the town everything I inspected was too small or too squalid, a verminous tenement in Leopold Street where the rotting floors could not have supported our presses, a slightly less flea-bitten address a street away but directly alongside a slaughter-house where the stench of death and panic, the squealing of sheep as their legs were broken to render them easier for butchery, was unacceptable; in fact, nothing at all.

"You'd best have a word with our advertisers," Liam told me, "in case they've heard rumours—which wouldn't surprise me." And so, in my smart blue velvet hat, wearing enough jewellery to inspire confidence, I made the rounds of the small business men and tradesmen whose services we publicized, playing Miss Agbrigg of Fieldhead Mills to those who might respond to it, flirting discreetly with some others, calling a spade, in some quarters, a plain shovel; assuring one and all that, whatever they may have heard to the contrary, Cullingford's *Star* would continue to shine. Nevertheless, a certain amount of business was not renewed and it seemed certain we would soon be obliged to retrace our steps to a single edition a week.

"I'd best be off to Cannes for a word with Grandmamma Elinor," said Liam. "That is, Grace, if you can manage a week or two without me—and if you can lend me the fare?"

"I could save you the journey altogether, Liam, and pay your rent."

"So you could. And when I'm desperate enough no doubt I'll ask you. But I reckon I can manage till then."

"As you like. But at least you can forget about my salary for the time being."

"Now that's very sporting of you, Grace," he said, easy and debonair as always, although I couldn't miss the occasional weariness in his face "But considering the pittance I pay you— well, you may as well have it as not, for I know what it means to you. In fact, while there's still something left, how about me taking you to the theatre in Leeds tonight, and then to supper?"

We saw a melodrama, as I recall, from the splendours of a stagebox, his arm resting on the back of my chair more from force of habit, I thought, than real interest, his eyes on my *décolletage* from time to time as we ate our discreet and very expensive supper largely because that was the correct way to behave in a private supper-room. He even enquired in a round-about but extremely good-humoured fashion if I would care to spend the night and expressed a pleasing degree of equally good-humoured disappointment when I decided it would not be wise.

"They say you are my mistress already, you know."

"So they do. But you have mistresses enough, Liam. I think you have more need, just now, of a friend."

"And I think you may be right. We'll drink to it."

We drank deep, returning to Cullingford on the last train, at a scandalous hour when no decent woman should have been abroad.

"Of course you'll not let me in?" he said as we reached my door.

"Of course not." But I had no objection to the kiss he lightly planted on the corner of my mouth, and went inside still smiling at his assurance that if Miss Tighe happened to be awake—and it could surprise no one to learn that she *never* slept—and if she happened to be standing on a footstool at her back landing window, she would, with a certain acrobatic skill, be able to see us in an embrace about which she would draw her own conclusions.

A pleasant evening, a happy time, but, as the summer progressed, each day hotter and more malodorous than the next, the game of baiting Low Cross Mill continued nightly, any tenement lad who could break a window or steal a few bricks, who could show off the tooth marks of a Barforth dog, a cut lip or a black eye received from a hard-handed navvy, being declared king of his own particular muck-heap the next morning.

"They wear their scars like medals," said Liam, who would have done the same at their age. But this constant raiding of the newly cleared site was a serious nuisance to the building contractors, who needed to take advantage of the good weather to complete their schedule. If the walls were not up and the roof not on by October, then Mr. Chard would be out of temper and everybody else out of pocket. The tenement lads decreed that the roof would *not* be on by October. The building workers, with their bonuses at stake, decided otherwise. Threats were made and ugly scenes ensued, one of them in the street directly below my office window when a gang of navvies, strapping Irishmen for the most part, encountered an equal number of our local breed, smaller and perhaps not quite so fierce but wiry and cooler, more reasoned, so that the battle was evenly matched and most unsightly.

"Appalling," thundered the *Courier & Review.* "Unfortunate," said the *Star,* without adding for whom, and I suppose it was not to be wondered at when some days later our office was not so much entered as invaded by a man, well-dressed yet somehow not a "gentleman," huge not only in girth and muscle but in the anger that was mottling his heavy cheeks and his thick, bull-neck, who, even before a word was spoken, had curved his big-knuckled hands into fists.

"Tom Mulvaney," he said, considering this sufficient explanation, since we would be sure to know that the firm of Charlesworth and Mulvaney had won the much-coveted contract for the building of the new houses at Black Abbey Meadow and the new mill at Low Cross. And, after making his announcement, Mr. Mulvaney remaining at his vantage point in the doorway, glanced swiftly around the room, assessing the fighting strength against him and seeing just old Mr. Martin, sorting through the morning telegrams, the boy, Davey, the printers on the floor below, who were as elderly as their presses, myself and Liam.

"Good morning," Liam said without getting up, very sensibly keeping his desk between himself and this very obviously superior adversary. "And what can I do for Mr. Mulvaney?"

"Call off your rat-pack, Adair."

"Which particular rat-pack did you have in mind?"

The desk was reached in two long strides, an iron fist smashed down upon it, oversetting the inkstand and the water jug. Liam always kept there, the pool of ink and water doing a small violence of its own among his papers.

"*Mr.* Mulvaney," he said, and leaning back in his chair clicked his tongue reproachfully, an act of provocation which brought me to my feet, my presence as a woman, which might appeal to Mr. Mulvaney's sense of decency, the only support I could offer.

I was not sure just how old Liam was. There was no grey in his hair, no apparent lessening of vitality, certainly no sign of the sobriety men are assumed to acquire with age. But he was older than Gervase and Gideon, had seemed a man to me when I had still been at school, and could not, I thought, be much short of forty, while this murderous, mountainous Tom Mulvaney might at a guess be twenty-nine. I doubted if Liam could withstand him. I saw that Liam doubted it too, and I did not wish to see him try.

"Call off your bloody rat-pack, Adair."

"I have no rat-pack, Mulvaney."

"This is the last warning you'll get."

"You're threatening me, then? Would you care to be more explicit? And would you watch your languaage, old fellow, in front of a lady?"

"I see no lady," snarled Tom Mulvaney, darting me a glance as vicious as any he had bestowed on Liam, and, having been drawn to his attention, I came forward to the side of the desk, unable to stand between them but positioning myself so that he would have to push me aside to get at Liam.

"Then I must bring one to your notice," I said, my voice emerging very cool although in fact I was quite terrified. But Liam, for all his possible forty years, could not consent to shelter behind a woman, and as he got to his feet, exposing himself to attack for his pride's sake in a manner I found most exasperating, there was an ugly moment when I felt myself to be physically holding them apart as once—in another world it seemed—I had stood between Gideon and Gervase.

I had lost my head that night. I must not do so now. "Mr. Mulvaney," I told him, "you may not see a lady but I am sure I see a gentleman. And certainly you have a grievance—"

"A grievance? Is that what you call it? As fast as we put the windows in at Black Abbey those louts of his have them out again. And who pays? Not Chard, who can afford it. *I* pay. And if it goes on then I'm telling you—"

He was right, entirely right, and I told him so, repeating at such length and with such conviction how right he was that at last his killing rage turned sullen, smouldered a while and then hardened to a point where he would be more likely to sue for damages than extract blood for them.

"You think you're a clever woman, don't you, Mrs. Barforth? I've heard about you."

"She *is* a clever woman," said Laim.

"Aye. Maybe so. But I'm not much taken by cleverness in women. And I warn you, Adair, if this goes on, then the next time we meet she'll not talk me out of a thing."

"There's no need to wait, Mulvaney. I'll meet you any time you like."

But Tom Mulvaney, in his full green prime, could recognize an older man's bravado when he heard it, and making a gesture of contempt I had seen often enough by now in Gower Street, he turned and went down the stairs, a victor who condescends— until it suits him to do otherwise—to leave the field.

"My goodness, gracious me!" said Mr. Martin returning to his telegrams.

"You can't do anything about it now, can you, Liam?" I said, feeling suddenly very weak about the knees.

"Of course I can't. But I reckon that bog-trotter in his Sunday suit could do something about me any time he had a mind. So it looks as though you'll have to guard me, Grace, day *and* night, my darling—I can see no help for it."

Was he afraid?

"Of course," said Anna Stone later that evening, adding with her habitual gravity: "There can be no courage without fear."

"Which means," said the Doctor, with a twinkle in his eye, "that if one measures on that scale then Liam is probably a very courageous man indeed."

But the Stones themselves had come increasingly under attack, a campaign of hostility being waged against them which, although admittedly genteel, was nevertheless as virulent in its way as anything likely to be devised by Tom Mulvaney. It was no new thing in their experience. In Liverpool, people had risen against them as once they might have risen against a coven of witches and warlocks, and made it physically unwise for them to remain in the city. Cullingford's hostility, taking its character, I thought, from Miss Tighe, was a more silent matter, no vicious stoning of the culprits to the town gates, but an ostracism, a withdrawal of all those who considered themselves decent, which was designed to smother them out. Mrs. Stone found herself ignored in the better shops of Millergate, all of them patronized by Miss Tighe, who had far more money to spend. Dr. Stone found the more lucrative side of his practice dwindling away, no respectable woman liking to openly consult a man who was known to advocate contraception in case there might be talk that he was advocating it for her; few gentlemen caring—with Miss Tighe's drawing-room windows directly across the way—to risk their reputations at a house where such dubious characters were known to frequent the back garden.

The Stones reacted in their separate fashions, Anna Stone becoming more preoccupied, more intense than ever, the Doctor whistling a great deal as he went about his business, continuing to prescribe as he thought fit and to bring home with him such waifs and strays as he believed might best profit from his attention, arriving one September night with a young woman who had a child of two or three years old fastened to her side by a shawl.

There had been heavy rain, an early autumn cloudburst so violent that within moments the gutters had been overflowing, the streets transformed to muddy, narrow streams, everyone, rich and poor alike, soaked instantly to the skin. And running for shelter, Dr. Stone had found the woman half-collapsed in a doorway, willing—despite her obviously weak condition and the child strapped to her hip—to go anywhere with him, for any purpose, and for as much or as little as he might care to pay.

She was very thin and dirty when he brought her into the garden shelter, the child knotted so tightly in the sodden shawl that we were eventually obliged to cut him loose, this bondage being necessary, we understood, to prevent him from crawling away, down some squalid alley or through the mire of some cheap lodging-house while his mother slept. And occupied with hot water and hot broth, soap and towels, milk and bread for the whimpering child, I did not immediately recognize this gaunt, suspicious, flint-eyed woman as cheerful Sally Grimshaw who had once been my personal maid.

She had recognized me at once, of course, but had not particularly cared to make herself known to me. If she had fallen on hard times, so had thousands of others, and she could see no point in discussing it, since talk, although cheap, made things no better. But, with a plateful of beef broth inside her and her child washed and wrapped in clean, warm blankets, she shrugged her shoulders and, in the spirit of one who is paying for her supper, allowed me to question her.

She had left my house because she had been uncomfortable there, with people who knew her circumstances. She had been raped, true enough, but she had lost her virtue just the same, or so everyone had told her, and there were plenty of others who had said, behind her back but loud enough for her to hear, that rape was impossible and all it meant was that she had not fought hard enough. At any rate, she *knew* more than she ought to know, whether one called it rape or seduction, sin or folly, and the others knew she knew. The maids kept on asking her questions, the menservants—or some of them—tried to take advantage, because what was done was done, and what more had she to lose by doing it again? She had moved on to get away from her reputation, but it had followed her on the below-stairs grapevine and eventually—well—if you give a dog a bad name, sooner or later it will probably earn it. There had been a baker's boy who had coaxed her into folly for a week or two, succeeding mainly because she had been very lonely. And then, in her last place, she had fallen in love with the butler, a man of dignity and authority, older than herself, who had first taught her to enjoy her body and had then impregnated it.

The mistress had dismissed her the moment her condition was discovered—very early, since speed was to her lover's advantage—and he had stood nearby, impassive and slightly disdainful, while she was turned off without a reference. She had worshipped him and even then had seen no sense in implicating him so that he would have lost his job too. He had told her from the start that he could not marry her, but she had not really believed him, had thought he was testing the strength of her feelings, which had been—she admitted it—powerfully strong. And she knew he had been considerably annoyed with her, had called her a little fool, a damned nuisance, when she had turned down his offer to pay for an abortion, refusing to be mutilated for his convenience by some old woman with a knitting needle. No, she had made no appeal to the law, for no court in the land would award her more than two shillings and sixpence a week for the support of a bastard child, and in any case her lover needed only to bring other men before the judge—the menservants directly in his employ—to swear they had had her too and the case would be dismissed.

He had made only one other approach to her. He had found a

woman who specialized in these things who was ready to adopt the child, no questions asked, as soon as it was born, for a cash payment of ten pounds, which he—to be rid of the obligation once and for all—was prepared to supply. But knowing what this meant, that these baby-farmers would keep a child in misery for a year or two and then let it die, handsomely insured, or, failing that, would sell a girl to a brothel-keeper, a boy to a gang of thieves, she had again refused. She would manage, one way or another, on her own and had expected it to be hard. Domestic service being no longer possible, she had gone to work, first as a trouser-hand at a sweatshop in Leeds, stitching all day and into the night, until her fingers were raw and her eyes smarted with strain, for as little—when she had paid for her thread and her share of the lighting—as three shillings and sixpence a week. And since it was impossible to live on those wages, much less put something by for the few days after her confinement when she would earn nothing at all, she had taken the only course that had seemed available

It was not unusual, she said, in the sweated trades for girls who had neither parents nor a man to support them, to supplement their incomes by some part-time street-walking. And Sally was not unusual. She had gone out for the first time with a friend, another trouser-hand, and thereafter alone, transacting her business in dark corners and back alleys since she could not take men back to her lodgings. But she had earned just enough, before her pregnancy became too cumbersome, to enable her to stay in those lodgings—such as they were—while her baby was born.

Had she felt disgust or shame at her new trade? She could not afford disgust, and whose was the shame? She had stood many a time with her back to a wall and marvelled at the filth men were ready to pay for. And if they despised her for supplying it, then she had nothing but the most complete contempt for them. And as for the moralizers, the churches, the police, the law, if they really wanted to sweep the streets clean, they should discourage the demand, surely, not the merchandise? And as for the respectable ladies who drew aside their skirts and averted their eyes when she passed, she would be interested to know how many of them had ever been hungry or unable to find an honest penny to buy milk for a child?

She had gone out again after her baby was born, too soon, and had suffered an illness which had nearly killed them both. But she had made up her mind not to die, had not died, and had taken up with a man soon after, a former, very minor champion of the illegal bare-knuckle prize-ring, an unstable character—even Sally admitted it—but the kind of companion her trade required. They had looked after each other, the woman contributing her earnings, the man the protection of his muscle, but he had been caught at a race-meeting relieving a gentleman of his wallet and had been given twelve months' hard labour.

It had not been an easy year for Sally. The very week of his sentence she had been badly beaten by a customer, an occupational hazard to which the loss of her man exposed her, and had recovered slowly. She had lost her regulars, then her lodgings, and had been reduced once again to doing business in back passages, coal-sheds, a man's jacket on the hard ground, and to living where she could, in constant danger of being picked up as a vagrant. She had taken refuge for a while in a navvy camp, a law unto itself, and had been travelling recently with a tinker who after a quarrel had dumped her in Leicestershire. She had been on the tramp since then, making her way north again since her man was soon to be released and she had agreed to meet him in Leeds. He would not have a penny piece in his pocket and neither had she, and she did not expect his stint at the treadmill, on prison rations, to have sweetened his temper; but two, she found, were better than one. He had lost an eye, she'd heard, in a prison brawl, which in a way could be counted a blessing since it meant that his thieving days were over. What future did she see for herself and her son? Future? She lifted her head from her mug of hot, sweet tea and gave me a look of frank contempt. Future? She had not thought me so simple-minded as that.

"You could come and work for me again, Sally?"

"I doubt it, ma'am. Your other servants would walk out of the door in a body the moment I came in."

"I daresay. But I have a very small house these days and do no entertaining. You could manage it yourself, Sally, with a girl to do the rough."

"And my boy?"

"I am seldom at home and there is no reason why he should inconvenience me. It's a future."

"Yes," she said, no more; but when I returned the next day intending to take her with me, she had gone, had left very early that morning, her child knotted to her side, refusing to take anything but a packet of bread and cheese to sustain her until she got to Leeds, some time that night.

"Why?" I asked, and Anna Stone sighed and shook her head, her husband clicked his tongue, irritable with pity.

"It has gone too far with her, I suppose," he said. "When a woman suffers some gross physical deformity from an accident which was no fault of her own, she will usually hide her face, partly to spare decent people the pain or the embarrassment of looking at it, and partly because she does not wish to be seen. Perhaps your Sally feels much the same. And after all, with this man of hers—she has no need for any kind of embarrassment. He is vicious and inadequate and has lost an eye. She had no reason to feel inferior to *him*. Poor woman! It could happen to anyone."

It could have happened to Venetia. I went home, haunted afresh by the memory of her slight figure in that dingy, rented room, unable to face the hopelessness of her situation and so retreating from it, gathering just enough of herself together to do what was necessary for the child. And I had done nothing for that child, could do nothing now but send expensive, impersonal trinkets to Listonby at Christmastime and make occasional, rather guilty enquiries of Blanche. But what I could do, for what it was worth—and I was uncertain as to its exact value—was to write a thinly disguised account of Sally Grimshaw which Liam included, with my signature, in the following Friday's *Star*.

I made no judgements. I did not even question the wisdom of the law which, considering a bastard child to be a fitting punishment for the sin of sexual depravity, regarded that punishment to be an entirely female matter, according maintenance settlements that would have been insufficient to feed a sparrow. I did not ask why one partner in a crime should go unscathed while the other paid the penalty for two. I merely stated that it was so. I did not ask who was responsible for this woman's downfall, whether it was her attacker or her seducer, the mistress who had coolly dismissed her, knowing full well the misery that awaited her; whether it was the owner of the sweatshop who had not paid her a living wage, or the narrowness of a society which allowed only half its members—the male half—to possess realistic emotions and desires which in the other, female half were condemned as vice and lust. I did not ask, but the answers came thick and fast, letters of abuse some of them, others of mild reproach, suggesting to me that such things should not really be spoken of and certainly not by a lady. But there were other letters bristling with honest indignation, a few with compassion, a few more declaring stoutly that Sally Grimshaw was a victim of circumstances beyond her control but not beyond ours, and asking what could be done.

"We'll have some more of this," said Liam, and I had only to visit the Stones two or three evenings a week to find all the material he required, managing at the same time to show the work of Patrick and Anna Stone in an entirely different light.

I did not wish to moralize, having met too many self-indulgent moralizers far too fascinated by their own "goodness" to be of use to anyone. I did not wish to force my opinions on others, nor even to persuade, being myself suspicious of persuasion and hostile to force. I wished simply to speak my mind, and, if nothing else, my controversial opinions helped to sell a great many copies of the *Star*.

"Keep it up," said Liam, "and we may just pull through this little contretemps." But that was the day before we received yet another increase in our rent, intended to remind us that, when all was said and done, power lay only with those whose standing was highest at Mr. Rawnsley's bank.

"Liam, will you allow me—?"

"No," he said, very sharply for him. "No, Grace, I'll not borrow your money. I thought I could do it when the time came, believe me—I fully intended to do it. You were a kind of insurance, I suppose, at the back of my mind—always there and always willing. But now—well—no, Grace. I won't borrow your money. It turns out that I'm too fond of you—quite a bit too fond of you—for that."

27

"IT MAKES NO REAL DIFFERENCE," Camille told me, speaking of her uncertain status. "Nicholas would marry me if he could, because then he could give me things and leave me things without interference from Duchess Caroline. But what exists between us could be made no deeper by a legal document. I wish you would fall in love, Grace."

"No, thank you. Is that all you can think of now, Camille?"

"Do you know, I believe it is. It leaves me no room for anything else. One day you will see."

"I very much doubt it. I don't think I would care to build my life entirely around another person. Yes, I know women are supposed to give themselves completely in love and marriage, and I have seen some women dissolve themselves in their menfolk with obvious fulfilment. You, for instance, and Aunt Faith. It is certainly what Venetia *wanted* to do, and it would probably have saved her life had she succeeded. It seems dangerous to me. Perhaps it is not in my nature."

But Camille dismissed my objections with the smile of a woman who no longer uses the word "perhaps"—a woman who *knows*.

"I used to think that too, and I did not dissolve myself in my husband, you may be very sure. We were colleagues and companions, which was pleasant enough, and we thought it daring and very progressive to tell everyone we were no more than fond of each other. And 'fond' was very nice, you know. Life was busy and various, quite complicated sometimes, and full of concerns and necessities, battles to fight and problems to solve—like your life, I suppose. Now there is Nicholas. I wonder, sometimes, what all the rest was really about."

"Camille, you are not so blinded as all that."

"I am."

I did not entirely believe her, but no one, after two minutes in her company, could have been unaware of her bliss. Her house, set high and very lonely on the cliffs looking down on the Spa and, across the grey sweep of the bay, offering a view of the steep little town and its ancient castle, was not large, a square box merely of four rooms downstairs and four rooms up, but set in a shady, high-walled garden and furnished with a blend of luxury and cosiness that was essentially Camille.

"A perfect little love-nest," my Grandmother Agbrigg described it, although she had never been inside and in any case her experience of such establishments could only have been slight. Yet so it was, over-abundant in its splendours, the typical retreat of an elderly millionaire and a penniless woman, who apart from youth and beauty had also, surprisingly, brought him love.

Nor was she shy of expressing it whenever the mood overcame her.

"I adore you, Nicholas," she would tell him, leaning through the evening firelight or suddenly taking his arm and squeezing it during an afterooon stroll, a declaration made as naturally as a remark about the weather.

"Excellent!" he would answer gruffly. "See that it continues."

"Oh, it will, for it does you so much good. Your sister thinks I shall very likely kill you, but in fact I have never seen you look so well. And I have not heard you cough once all winter, not even when you have been obliged to go to Cullingford."

But his visits to Cullingford grew fewer and fewer, Gideon being called to Scarborough instead at regular intervals to give an account of himself, occasions which Camille found difficult, for although he was always charming and even treated her sometimes with the same teasing gallantry she found very acceptable in Gervase, he was nevertheless Aunt Caroline's son and she felt certain he shared his mother's belief that her involvement with Nicholas Barforth was solely for money.

"He kisses my hand sometimes," she told me, "and admires my dress, and he has a look at my shoulders while he is about it, and I know he is thinking what a clever little minx I am to have got myself so many diamonds and furs and a snug little place in Nicholas's will, but that when the time comes I had better watch out, for he will not let me have everything my way. Well, when *that* time comes I shall be too stricken to care or even to notice how they carve up the mills. They will have no trouble with *me*. How dreadful, Grace! Gervase never makes me feel like that, although I believe Duchess Caroline has accused him of worming his way into my favour. Heavens! I never expected to see the day when my 'favour' counted for anything, although Gervase certainly has it and I am not ashamed to say so. What absolute hell these families are, for, as Nicholas says, there is plenty to go round and all we ask in return is that they leave us in peace.''

Yet, despite her understandable reluctance, she entertained Gideon and Miss Madeley-Brown to a celebraton dinner shortly after their engagement was officially announced, Gideon considering it politic to introduce his chairman and his bride, although Aunt Caroline—who had brought Miss Madeley-Brown to Scarborough under her chaperonage—remained adamantly at the Grand Hotel.

"She is very splendid to look at," Camille told me, "and has a diamond solitaire quite as big as mine. She sat and watched it sparkle in the candlelight for most of the evening, being too refined, I suppose, for conversation. Certainly she thought herself a cut above me. When I took her into the drawing-room after dinner I was not at all sure what I would do with her, for I knew our gentlemen would stay a full hour over their port and cigars. But I had no need to worry. She looked at her ring again and arranged the flounces of her skirt and was perfectly content. She rides—that much I *did* discover—and Nicholas says she will be very accommodating in bed and what more can a Chard want in a wife than that? Caroline would not come here to dine, of course, but I am afraid Nicholas forced her to take tea with me at the Grand—told her absolutely straight that unless she did he would not even *discuss* Tarn Edge, which just goes to show what money can really do. Oh dear, that dreadful house! I wish Nicholas would just give it to them as a wedding present and have done, for I shall never live in it.''

But Tarn Edge was a valuable property not to be parted with lightly, and further complicated by the fact that if half of it might reasonably have been expected to pass to Venetia—and consequently to Gideon—the other half might equally well be considered as belonging to Gervase. Aunt Caroline made another journey to Scarborough, alone this time, abandoning her husband on his sickbed at South Erin in her determination to do her duty by the son who most resembled her. Gideon was to make a splendid marriage and needed a suitable home for his bride. He had lived at Tarn Edge now for nine years, had maintained and staffed it at his own expense this last year or two. Rent free? How dare her brother suggest such a thing. Or if he did suggest it, then perhaps he might like to consider his granddaughter, Claire Chard—who was no granddaughter of hers—and who had been maintained, rent-free, at Listonby virtually since her birth. Mr. Barforth did not wish to consider that. He did not wish to remind Aunt Caroline that her son's entry into the Barforth mills—bringing nothing with him but his ambitions—and his eventual shareholding had depended entirely on his marriage, in full knowledge of the circumstances and ramifications, to Venetia. He did not wish to remind her of any of these things, although he forced himself to do so.

For a moment brother and sister faced each other across a gulf which seemed likely to widen into a final breach, and then, because in their way they were fond of each other, they backed down, Aunt Caroline hastily, Mr. Barforth deliberately, having led her, I suppose, to the point he had intended. There might be a measure of right on her side, he conceded. Gideon had worked very hard and certainly his efficiency had made Mr. Barforth's own life much easier this last year or two. Yes indeed, it was a great relief to see the business in the hands of a man whose commercial acumen he could trust. But, looked at another way, where would that man be today without Nicholas Barforth? A country parsonage, perhaps? Some minor administrative appointment in India? And Mr. Barforth wished to make it very clear that, if Gideon Chard ever became the owner of Tarn Edge, it would be because such an arrangement was pleasing to Mr. Barforth, not on account of any pressure whatsoever from either his sister, his managing director or even from Camille. Mr. Barforth, as always, would decide for himself and when he had reached a decision he would let his sister, his managing director and any other interested party know.

A valuable house, then, full of valuable furnishings, silver, pictures, porcelain, built fifty years ago by Sir Joel Barforth to astonish the Law Valley with its grandeur. If Gideon wanted it, no doubt he could afford to buy it, since he drew healthy dividends every year, was the possessor of a princely salary and engaged in various profitable little trading ventures of his own from time to time of which his uncle—and his managing director—was supposed to be unaware. All circumstances considered, perhaps the best thing would be to have a proper valuation, after which Mr. Barforth could name his price, half the market value perhaps, which he would then most likely pay over to Gervase. That way Gideon would be getting Venetia's half of the house for nothing, which seemed fair enough. Mr. Barforth had felt

obliged to provide a home for his daughter and for his son, but
hardly for his son-in-law's second wife. And if the dowry was as
handsome as one had been led to believe, then Gideon would be
in easy street in any case.

"How absolutely splendid!" remarked Gervase when I next
visited Galton to inspect the progress of his prize Friesians. "I
shall invest my share in land, of course. And then I shall buy our
lovely Camille a rather ostentatious gift to convince Aunt Caroline more than ever that we have been conspiring against her.
Perhaps we could go somewhere rather expensive, you and I,
and choose it together?"

"To convince Aunt Caroline of *our* conspiracy?"

"No, Grace dear, for the simple pleasure of your company."

"I have no time for shopping trips, Gervase. I am not the
squire of Galton with nothing to do but plant my crops and then
wait for them to grow. I must be at my desk every morning,
Monday to Saturday, at eight o'clock."

"Who says you must, Grace?"

"I do."

It was a rule I strictly kept, arriving so early sometimes that I
was greeted only by the foraging of a hungry mouse or, on one
occasion, by a rat grooming himself serenely on my desk-top. I
was becoming a strange woman, Miss Tighe said so, and I was
to annoy her further that winter by a renewed interest in the
women's cause. I had already stated on several occasions in the
Star that women caught up on the treadmill of the factories and
overburdened by large families could not be expected to care one
way or another about the franchise, an opinion with which Miss
Tighe definitely agreed, since she did not mean them to have it
in any case, sticking to her belief that government, having been
created to serve the interests of property, automatically excluded
all those who, for whatever reason, did not possess it. Married
women did not possess it, and I became aware that winter of the
proposals for a new Act which, it seemed to me, would alter the
entire concept of matrimony.

Former legislation—now over ten years old—had made no
real difference, simply giving a married woman the right to keep
her own earnings, which in most cases would be nothing at all or
would be eaten up every pay-day by the demands of hungry
children and a persistent landlord. But this new Act made the
revolutionary and thrilling proposal that any women who married
after the date of its passing should be allowed not only to keep,
but to administer without the interference of a trustee, the money

she brought with her; while as a concession to husbands who had long since spent or invested their wives' dowries, women already married might claim similar rights over any money acquired by them in the future.

It excited me and I transferred my excitement to the *Star*. What hope for fortune-hunters now? Doubtless the breed would continue to exist but at least, after the passing of the Act, they would be obliged to behave themselves, for the fortune they married would no longer be *their* fortune but would remain attached to the woman who came along with it. Never again would a man be able to spend his wife's money on himself and his mistress and leave her to starve. Perhaps few men had ever gone so far as that. One would be quite enough. But now, surely—if this new Act ever reached the Statute Book—a husband and wife would be able to look at each other differently? Surely the removal of total female dependence and total male dominion must imply that there was space for two individuals in a marriage, that it was no longer a question of master and servant but of two responsible and—if possible—loving adults? And moreover, if the vote was about property and married women were about to hold on to theirs, what objection could Miss Tighe and her party raise against their claiming the vote, on equal terms with those widows and spinsters so dear to Miss Tighe's heart? None, I declared and went on declaring it until Liam, harassed by yet another increase of rent, no nearer to finding new premises and increasingly uncomfortable in the old, requested me to devote at least part of my time to other things, such as a wedding in the family of one of our principal advertisers, who had little interest in votes for women.

I attended that wedding on a chill December Saturday and spent the evening cheerlessly writing all the flattering, tedious details of white silk and orange blossoms, describing the extreme elegance of the mother of the bride, the dignity and substance of the father, a saddler whose patronage was not only desirable but necessary to the *Star*. And when it was done—when I had tried to see the bride as a lamb going to the slaughter and had been forced to admit she had looked extremely happy about it—I wrote a letter to Camille putting off her invitation for Christmas, since I knew Gervase would be in Scarborough then and I was reluctant—by fits and starts—to grow any closer to him.

There was a keen frost that Saturday, a long, cold Sunday to follow, a high wind the next morning that woke me earlier than usual and sent me—since I had nowhere else to go—to the *Star*.

I expected the office to be unwelcoming and empty, Monday morning never finding Liam at his best, and I was mildly surprised—no more—to see his horse among the crowd which seemed to be gathering around our door. What of it? Liam might well have been at the office all night, not necessarily alone, and when was there not a crowd of idlers in Gower Street?

"Oh good lord, Richards!" I said to my coachman's indifferent back. "I believe someone has put out our windows again."

"Yes, madam," he said, probably not in the least surprised, helping me down and then, quickly withdrawing his valuable horses and his own superior person from too close contact with the mob, leaving me on the pavement to contemplate the gaping holes where the windows and the window-frames had been, and the havoc inside.

I cannot remember, in those first moments, any feeling whatsoever. I simply walked through the crowd and went inside, through the space where the door had been torn off its hinges and into the ground-floor rooms which had contained our printing-presses. There was nothing there now that I recognized, just a litter of wood and metal, the junk of a scrap dealer's yard, and I understood that this was how the first power-looms had looked when the Luddite hammermen had worked over them. The whole of some millmaster's investment gone in a single, violent night, the *Star* lying in inky, rusty fragments about my feet, and Liam—who had no insurance, no capital, no credit—standing among the ruin, haggard and unshaven yet managing to smile.

"I reckon I can give you the day off today, Grace. You'd be better at home in this cold."

I picked my way across the debris to his side, my skirt catching and then tearing on something that had once formed an essential part of our livelihood—something else, sharp-edged and probably very rusty cutting into my shoe—and stood close to him, closeness being necessary, I found, in the face of such total disaster, the proximity of a sympathetic body offering more than the empty indignation of words. He was ruined and he knew it. He had no need of me to tell him so. A senseless and brutal thing had been done to him—a foul thing—for which no one but himself would ever pay the price. He knew that, too. And when I could speak it was simply a name.

"Tom Mulvaney?"

"Well, I doubt Miss Tighe to be capable of it, so yes, I reckon it was Tom Mulvaney. He got his roof on but he was late, and I hear Cousin Gideon cut up rough about the bonus. So

yes—Tom Mulvaney—with or without instructions from Gideon
Chard we shall never know.''

I put my hand on his arm again and pressed it, seeing no point
in telling him that Gideon would have been most unlikely to
involve himself in this massacre, not from any moral scruple or
lingering kindness of heart but because he had no need of such
crudity. He had only to sit in his luxuriously appointed office at
Nethercoats or in the splendid boardroom at Lawcroft Fold, had
only to despatch, at regular intervals, those notices of increased
rents, in order to bleed Liam dry; a procedure, I thought, which
would suit Gideon's nature far better than this. But if it eased
Liam now to blame Gideon, or anyone else, then I would not
quarrel with it.

"When did it happen?"

"Sometime in the night. They sent a lad to fetch me about two
o'clock this morning, but it was over then, of course—"

"Liam, that was six hours ago."

"So it was."

"And you've been here all the time since then?"

"I reckon so. I sat and looked at it for a while, and thought
about it. It's much the same upstairs. No machines to smash, of
course, and the furniture wasn't worth much, so they tore the
floorboards up and knocked a few holes in the walls. It's a
wreck, Grace.''

The staircase was a mess of fallen plaster and splintered wood,
hatchets, it seemed, having been used to attack the roughcast
walls, while the upper room was a battleground, the door thrown
down, desks and chairs overset and shredded as if for firewood,
the partition wall between office and storeroom knocked clean
through, broken glass and builders' rubble underfoot, papers—
papers—churned and scattered everywhere, and, in case there
might be anything we could salvage, soaked in whitewash and
green paint—the colour they had been using at Low Cross—which
had been thrown down by the bucketful and left, most foully, to
congel.

Total devastation which must have taken several large and
noisy men at least an hour to perpetrate. No one had intervened.
No one, thank God, had sent for Liam until it was over. Now, as
the shock abated, it seemed that something, however futile, had
to be done and so, without making any visible headway, we
began to go through those soiled and scattered papers, a task so
very much akin to emptying the North Sea with a ladle that I
knew it would either break my heart or make me very angry.

And so, kneeling there among the sodden litter, in the bitter cold of that December day, I grew very angry indeed.

We sent the boy for bread and cheese and beer at noon and worked on, sorting, discarding, achieving nothing, while on the floor below us the helpers Liam had recruited from the street were sweeping up the corpses of his printing-presses, to carry them away by the barrowload and bury them in the nearest midden.

"There goes the *Star*," he said, raising the brandy flask he always carried with him as the unkempt cortège trundled by. And by this time, still on my knees on that loathsome floor, I was crying with the sorrow of true bereavement and my terrible fury. I had needed the *Star*. I loved her, and I wanted blood for her now.

"What are you going to do, Liam?"

He remained silent for a moment, staring after those funereal barrows, and then, raising his flask again, he took a rapid swallow.

"That's not a question you should be asking me now, Grace. Give me until tomorrow."

"Mr. Liam Adair?" we heard a dry little voice calling, and through the gaping doorway came stepping a painfully neat, self-important figure I recognized, a clerk from Nethercoats Mill, hastily taking a handkerchief and pressing it to his nose and mouth with the gesture of one who enters a plague spot.

"Mr. Liam Adair?"

"Who wants him?"

"Mr. Gideon Chard presents his compliments—"

"Does he, by God?"

"—and asks me to deliver this letter, sir."

A long brown envelope changed hands, the pompous little man smirked, seemed disposed to linger and then, catching a hint of his peril in Liam's eye, moved hastily away.

"Will there be an answer, sir?"

"Get out of here." And the simple command was followed by so explicit an obscenity that the precise little gentleman turned tail and fled.

I gave him a moment to read and then went to stand beside him again, my skirt, smeared with paint and damp, filthy patches, feeling heavy against my legs.

"What is it now, Liam?"

He folded the letter, replaced it carefully in its envelope, his hands steady, his face grey.

"Aye, what now? News travels fast in Cullingford, it seems.

Mr. Chard has heard of my misfortune and wonders when it would be convenient for someone to call and assess the damage to *his* property."

"Liam!"

"Yes—damage to his floorboards and his walls, his doors and windows, for which, naturally, I am liable."

"How much?"

He shook his head as if to clear it and blinked hard.

"God knows! More than I can afford, at any rate, which wouldn't make it very much. Enough to bankrupt me, I shouldn't wonder, which would mean I couldn't carry on this—or any other business—again. Enough to silence me once and for all, should Gideon decide to take legal proceedings against me. And I'm not in much doubt about that, Grace, my darling. Are you?"

His eyes closed again, just for a moment age touching every feature, until his sudden grin sent the years, but not all the greyness, away.

"I'll have to make a run for it, I reckon. The world's wide enough. How about coming with me, Grace? I wouldn't be the first man who went out to the colonies to escape his creditors and came back a millionaire."

"There's Grandmamma Elinor."

"So there is, except that I've got nothing for her to invest in, and whatever else I am, I'm no beggar. I wouldn't feel right about taking her money now, Grace, and I hope you know better than to offer me yours. I think we've done all we can for today. Go home now, my darling, you look done in."

"Come with me."

"Later. I'll call and see you this evening, a little after dinner maybe. Right now I'm going to do the only rational thing I can think of. No—no—there's no need for alarm. I'm not considering blowing Chard's brains out, nor my own. I just want to get quietly drunk. It won't solve anything, I know, but—whether you approve of it or not—it won't hurt."

I watched him walk down the stairs and pause for a word or two with the men who were still sweeping the lower floor, take another swig from his flask, and then go out into the street. I had never been so angry in my life, had not even realized anger could be so burdensome and so painful. I went out into the street myself, speaking to no one, went home and kicked off my soiled clothes, refusing to answer the foolish girl mouthing at me questions to which she knew the answers.

"Lord! ma'am, whatever have you been doing? Paint, ma'am—and the state of your shoes—it won't come off—"

"Burn them—everything. Now shut up and get me my hot water."

I washed, dressed, brushed my hair and did it up again, that load of anger still pressing hard against my chest.

"Tell Richards to bring the carriage round again."

"But he's just taken it away."

"Should that be of any interest to me?"

He brought it back again and I got into it, feeling as if I was made of granite. I had hoped, by the delay of changing my clothes and making myself presentable, to reduce my anger to manageable proportions. I had not done so, and since one way or another I would have to unleash it before it suffocated me, I was going now, not tomorrow morning as I had first intended, to see Gideon. I still did not suspect him of ordering the attack on Liam's presses, but I wanted to ascertain the extent and the nature of his complicity, whether his letter had been the result of a malicious impulse or part of a cruel plan. And what else did I want? To save the *Star* if I could and to strike a blow for Liam, to keep him from bankruptcy and out of jail in some way that did not oblige him to borrow money he could never repay from his female relations? Certainly I wanted that. But there was something else, at the very root of my nature, which I wanted too.

I had desired Gideon as I had desired no other man, to a point where it had become difficult for me to desire other men. One day, if I ever found the courage to face the truth, I might well find that I had been very much in love with him and unable to love anyone else because of him. But that day had not yet dawned and since he was committed to marry Hortense Madeley-Brown and I was committed to independence—and since neither one of us would be likely to deviate from those commitments—it would be easier for my peace of mind if I could think ill of him. I wanted to eliminate the slightest possibility that I might ever again—for no matter how fleeting a moment—long for him. I wanted to greet his wedding morning with a detached amusement—dear God, not another wedding!—to report in the *Star* on the astonishing beauty of his bride, the splendour of her jewellry, which *would* be very splendid, and then casually to remark: "Vacant little fool—pompous opportunist—they deserve each other." I wanted him to mean nothing to me, and to achieve that blessed state of indifference I would have to hate him first. I would have to hurt him again and give him the opportunity to hurt me.

I knew his habits. In the morning and the early part of the afternoon he was difficult to trace, dividing his time among the four other factories in his care, but in the days when I had had charge of his social engagements, his travelling schedules, his recherché dinners, a note sent to Nethercoats at this hour had usually reached him. I was kept waiting, as I had expected to be, sitting with several curious strangers in the ante-room through which he passed twice, a flurry of clerks about him, without even glancing at me.

"Mr. Freeman, if you'd care to go in now, sir?" the clerk said, the same smirking little man who had twice delivered messages to Gower Street. Mr. Freeman went in and half an hour later came out again. A Mr. Porter did the same. I was still very angry.

"Now then, who's next?" said the clerk. I was alone, and without answering him I got up and walked into Gideon's room unannounced, letting the heavy door swing shut behind me.

I had last come here—was it almost five years ago—to ask him to take back his wife who was pregnant by another man. It had been painful then. It would be painful now and for both of us. I was determined to make sure of that.

"Good-afternoon, Gideon."

"Yes?" he said, curtly, dismissively, the tone of a man too busy for any woman's arguments, since he is always in the right in any case. And I understood that he was very angry too.

"You have not asked me to sit down."

"I beg your pardon. I merely thought the length of your visit unlikely to warrant it."

"Are you asking me to leave unheard? I should be inclined to take that for a sign of defeat you know—or of a troublesome conscience."

"Then you have the advantage of me, Grace, for I have not the faintest notion as to what you mean."

I sat down, carefully arranging the folds of my skirt in the manner of Miss Madeley-Brown, took off my gloves and placed them, with my muff and reticule, on his immaculate desk-top, a gesture calculated to annoy. For I had come to engage him in battle and it was essential now to strike hard, to strike first if I could, and after that to stand firm against the returning blow.

"It occurred to me, Gideon, that your letter came very promptly."

"And you see some significance in that?"

"I am not sure. Perhaps you can enlighten me."

He leaned slightly towards me, assured and sardonic, a man in his own territory, abominably at ease.

"My dear, you have worked for the gutter press until it has affected your judgement. Can you seriously imagine I would hire a gang of drunken navvies to break into my own property and smash a few machines which would have fallen apart ere long in any case? It would make a good headline in the *Star*, I admit—except that the *Star* is no longer with us, it seems."

"You have missed my point, Gideon."

"Then do please correct me."

"I shall. It is my opinion that you did hire those navvies. Not as Luddites, of course, but as building workers on your sites at Black Abbey and Low Cross. And if you cannot keep your employees in order, it is my further opinion that you have no claim against Liam Adair or anyone else for the havoc they create."

He leaned forward again, a great deal of incredulous amusement, even a very faint, very grudging respect in his face. But then, perhaps, he too remembered the purpose of my last visit here and all tolerance was gone.

"Unfortunately the law does not share your opinions. You might advise Adair to cast a glance at the terms of his lease. I understand the damage was very extensive."

"Yes. I understand it would be in the interests of anyone who did not entirely approve of Liam Adair if the damage should be very extensive indeed. So—by that reckoning—Tom Mulvaney has done a very good job for you."

"How very ably you defend your—well—what shall we call him?—your friend?"

"Yes, you may call him my friend. And the reason I defend him is called loyalty."

"Whatever one calls it, my dear, it will not suffice. I did not order his machines broken, as even he must know. But just the same he is quite finished now. I would have arranged it differently, but one way is quite as good as another."

"I am not so sure he is finished."

"Oh, yes. He may extricate himself from the worst of it with the help of some foolish woman or other. But he knows now how vulnerable he is and he will not be quite so brave, you can be very sure, if he ever acquires a platform again. I must offer you my commiserations, I suppose, on your loss of employment. You will no doubt find some other way of passing your time.''

"You have intended to close down the *Star* for some time, have you not, Gideon?''

"Naturally.''

"I see nothing natural about it.''

"You were not the subject of Adair's slanders.''

"There was more to the *Star* than the slandering of Gideon Chard—my dear Gideon Chard.''

"Yes, tales of whores and thieves and child-molestation— titillation for perverse appetites—vice made available and interesting to the general reader by the pen of a lady—''

"How *dare* you say that to me?''

"I dare say anything I like to you. If you choose to lead a man's life, then you must take the rough with the smooth. One feels obliged, often enough, to curb one's tongue when dealing with a lady. One expects a man to be *man* enough to handle the truth.''

"Very well,'' I said. "Yes—very well.''

For it was this I had come for. He was hurting me, goading me, giving me every reason I needed to strike him a foul blow. It was just as it should be.

"You call it a man's life, Gideon, because I earn my living?''

"You do not earn your living. Your living comes to you from your father. You are supported by a man as women are and should be. The pittance you *earn*, as you call it, would not pay your own servants' wages.''

But I had expected this, for in his place it was the line of attack I would myself have used; and I was prepared for it.

"I take nothing from Fieldhead to which I am not entitled, Gideon. My allowance comes from money left in trust for me by my mother. And you are in no position, you know, to dispute my right to that, since so much of your own good fortune has been willed to you by a woman.''

It was done. I had struck hard and foul, and it should have been enough. But that heavy, angry boulder was still there in my chest, pressed tight against my lungs. The remnants of what I had once felt for him had not been wrung out of mé yet. I would have to strike again.

"Bitch!'' he said very quietly, rather pleasantly, as if it pleased him to call me so. I understood that it did please him, that he wished to abuse me as much as I desired to be abused. His need was exactly the same as my need, his aim identical to mine. We were playing the same game by the same rules, and if we were harsh enough and hateful enough we might succeed in making the next half-hour too painful to remember, and in consequence would have good reason never to think of each other again.

"So we are to exchange insults are we, Gideon?"

"Why not? I imagine Grace Barforth of the *Star* might know a filthy name or two."

"She might. However, all I really want to say to you is that I find your conduct towards Liam Adair astonishing."

"*My* conduct? Would I have done better to break his neck?"

"I think you would have done better to remember this famous public school training we hear so much about. I thought it contrary to the code of a gentleman to strike someone in a weaker position than himself, or to hit a man when he was already down?"

"Very clever, Grace. But a gentleman does not allow himself to be stabbed in the back. And when he deals with a scoundrel he deals accordingly. Adair began this."

"He had his reasons."

"Yes. He was in love with my wife."

"She was a lovable woman."

"I don't deny it. And I was the brute, in his opinion—and I suppose in yours—who did not deserve her?"

"You did not understand her."

"Did she understand me? I am not so hard to please."

"I know. You take the view that women should be seen and not heard—like children—which is easy enough for a woman who has nothing to say."

"I take the view that women should be women—"

"Ah yes—gentle and sensitive and clinging—"

"I see nothing wrong with that. Women who *are* women seem to thrive on it."

"Domestic drudges."

"Domestic angels, cherished and respected in their own homes, as any woman would be, if she could—"

"One does not respect a dressed-up doll who might open her mouth occasionally to say 'Just as you wish dear, how very clever of you, dear.' "

"One might prefer her to a woman who talks too much and to no good purpose, to prove what?—that she cannot face a woman's responsibilities and is only playing at taking a man's."

"So I am irresponsible, am I? Well—of course I am. For I

refused to devote my life to the care of your shirt-cuffs and the temperature of your bathwater, did I not? How terrible!''

"I shall survive it. I may even consider myself well out of it."

"I do hope so, Gideon, for let me ask you this. What makes you—or any man—imagine he has the right to a servant of my calibre? What makes you think yourself entitled to the lifelong obedience of a woman—another human being—who has a brain every bit as good as yours and whose talents may be different from your talents but just as valuable?"

"Because I pay for it," he snarled, a very dangerous man now.

"Pay for it?" I snarled back at him, feeling dangerous, if a little dizzy, too. "The devil you do! You take it. You have made laws that allow you to do as you please."

"I?"

"Yes—and the rest of you—and you have been able to do it because you have the physical strength and you do not bear children."

"Ah yes—I have read something to that effect in the *Star*."

"Then pay heed to it. You admire gentleness and sensibility in women because it flatters you and because it is easy to use against us."

"Easy? Perhaps. But expensive too, you know, for the very gentlest of women, in my experience, are never averse to life's little luxuries. And one needs a generous man, my dear, for that—any gentle woman will tell you so."

"I daresay. And what about the women you employ in your mills because they will work for lower wages than the men and are easier to handle? And why are they easier to handle?"

"I feel sure you are about to tell me."

"I am. Because you—and the rest—have informed yourselves in advance as to the nature of motherhood and you know a mother will put up with anything, for as little as you are inclined to pay her for it, so long as her children can be fed."

"Forgive me for mentioning it, but I seem to have read something about that too—one is obliged to conclude in the *Star*."

"If you wish to make me lose my temper, then you have succeeded very well, you know. There is no need to continue, Gideon."

"Ah—but I suppose one can hardly hope that *you* have done?"

"Assuredly not. You call those women who accept your pathetic wages weak and foolish. You ought to call them victims of exploitation. You make laws to prevent your wives from owning property so that they are obliged to depend on you and obey their marriage vows. And I wonder—if you are really so lovable and wise—why you need the power of the law to make your women honour and obey you? You talk about women who *are* women and you know nothing about it. You just want a silly sheep to bleat at you and breed for you, and that—my dear Gideon—is not a woman. It may, of course, be called Madeley-Brown, but what sort of a brood-mare is that?''

His hand shot out and fastened around my wrist—his attack now as crude and brutal and childish as mine—dragging me forward so that the desk bit hard into my legs.

''That is quite enough.''

''When I say so.''

''When *I* say.''

''You have no authority over me, Gideon Chard.''

''And want none.''

''I am delighted to hear it.''

''In fact I will tell you what it is that I do want. I want a woman called Hortense Madeley-Brown, who is beautiful and much younger than you are—''

''Oh, fresh from her schoolroom, Gideon—that is very clear—''

''—who satisfies me most perfectly in all of my appetites—''

''I hope you may satisfy hers—for they seem hearty to me.''

''—who will give me beautiful children and plenty of them, being of an age and a disposition for maternity—*that*, Grace Barforth, is the sum total of my desires.''

''Then let go of me.''

''When it pleases me—for I have the physical strength, as you pointed out just now, and do not bear children. But then, neither do you.''

I tried very hard to hit him with my free hand, this being no time at all for dignity, but he caught it and held me fast, exultant now that he had located my most vulnerable spot—the one wound that did not seem likely ever to heal—and had used it so ruthlessly against me. Perhaps I had expected him in the final instance to be merciful. I had been wrong. I must show no mercy either.

''You had better wait nine months after your marraige, Gideon, before you taunt me with my sterility, for we may be in the same boat together since I know of no child you could *honestly* lay claim to.''

And although the words meant very little, were on the same

infantile, foolish level as the rest of it, their intention to insult and to maim, to probe and reopen the very rawest of wounds, was enough.

"One day, Grace," he said, his voice only a whisper, "one day—if I could contrive it—I would like to see you helpless and penniless and—"

"And what Gideon? Pregnant and *manageable*—like Venetia?" It was done.

"Get out!" he said, dropping my wrists as if suddenly he was aware of their contamination. "Get out! *Now*." And it was part threat, part plea, for he could no longer bear to be in the same room with me. It was done.

There had been no victory and no defeat, not really a battle. I had performed an amputation, had destroyed one unreliable, troublesome part of myself for the benefit of the whole. It had been essential. "Get out!" he said, and he was right—quite right. I must go now and quickly, so that I might heal myself cleanly, and fast.

28

I WENT THROUGH THE OUTER office quite blindly and then, turning right instead of left, going up instead of down—I am not certain—missed my direction, the sound of machinery, the rancid smell of raw wool, warning me I was approaching the weaving-sheds when I should have been leaving them behind.

"Can I help you, ma'am?" And a puzzled junior clerk escorted me back to the imposing main staircase, the marbled and panelled walls, and then to my carriage.

"Where to, ma'am?" Richards asked me and I could not tell him.

"Home ma'am?"

No, not home. Not yet. I told him to take the road to Elderleigh and then, when the town was far behind me, I got down and entered a little wood, just an acre of naked, winter trees, leaves silvered and crunchy with frost underfoot, a pink December sky feathered with white cloud, approaching twilight. I felt the cold and welcomed it, drawing it into my lungs, its sharpness awakening me to other sensations. I had been a stranger to violence but I understood something of it now. There were lads in Gower Street who would batter each other until they bled, who would get up no matter how many times they were knocked down, no matter how tough or how numerous the opposition, and come back for more. I understood now that while the killing rage lasted they felt no pain, did not care how much damage was done to them so long as they could continue to damage their adversary. But when the rage had cooled, when the lad finally crawled away to count his wounds, he would find them to be many and grievous.

Face to face with Gideon I had felt no pain. I felt it now, accepted it, allowed it to run its course, took hold of it when it became manageable, parcelled and tied it and stored it away. I felt the cold again, a damp icy blast reminding me that women who live alone with only indifferent servants to care for them cannot afford to fall ill.

"Home now, Richards." And throughout the journey I thought carefully and deeply about the *Star* and Liam.

He came to see me quite late that evening, freshly shaved and presentable despite the odour of whisky and tobacco he brought with him.

"Have you dined?"

"I seem to remember that I have."

"Then it was probably a long time ago and more likely to have been liquid than solid."

I ordered him a supper tray, cold beef and pickles, custard tarts, a great deal of sweet tea which he accepted with a grin.

"What's this? A good meal for a condemned man?"

"You'll survive."

"I'm honestly beginning to doubt it."

"I shouldn't if I were you. You're far too old to go back to sheep-shearing in Australia."

He ate his supper, asked for more tea, finished his second pot and then smiled across at me, tired—bone-weary by the look of him—but determined, somehow or other, to live up to his reputation as a carefree, come-day-go-day Liam Adair.

"Do you want to tell me where you went to this afternoon, Grace?"

"No, since you obviously know. Did you get very drunk?"

"It sufficed. Listen, Grace—it's not the money. I can lay hands on enough to settle the damages bill—my grand relatives won't want to see me in court for debt. But—well, as far as the rest of it goes, I reckon this has taken the heart out of me."

"Nonsense. You mean you've lost your nerve. Gideon Chard said you would."

"Now, Grace—"

"Yes, Liam, *you* declared this war on Gideon and we both know why. You were wrong and we know that too. I think you'd have been glad to put a stop to it a long time ago, if you could. You couldn't. So now you'll just have to put up with the consequences. He's beaten you because he has more money than you. He didn't get Mulvaney to smash your machines. He'd have had much more fun starving you out. You know you can't fight money, Liam—nobody can—unless you've got money to do it with."

"So I'm a damned fool—I'll be the first to admit it."

"And I'll be the second. But I can forgive you that. What I don't want to do is lose the *Star*. It's worth more than your fued with Gideon Chard—to me and to plenty of others. So you'll just have to get back on your feet and build it up again."

He sat for a while looking down and then slowly—heavily for him—shook his head.

"I know what you're leading up to and it's no good. I'll not borrow money from you, Grace."

"I'm not about to lend. But I might invest."

"In me? I couldn't advise it."

"No, not in you. In myself and you together."

He frowned, started to say something; but the time had come for me to be businesslike—brusque if necessary—and I quelled his objections with a gesture I copied exactly from Gideon.

"I've given it a great deal of thought, Liam, and this is what I propose. I am not the wealthiest woman of your acquaintance, but I have some capital and a fairly decent allowance. Put another way, I have a great deal more than it would take to get the *Star* in production again—unless, of course, you object to an equal partnership with a woman?"

"Not if I had anything to contribute."

"Oh, for heaven's sake! Liam, why must you be so feeble? You know quite well that it can't be done without you. The *Star* was nothing when you took it over. All money could have done then would have been to make it another *Courier & Review*. But you put your signature on it and made it something—not perfect, of course, but perfection is hardly human, after all, and whatever else the *Star* lacks it does have humanity. Do you want to lose it?"

"No, Grace—by God, I don't!"

"Very well. We have established what you want. What *I* want is to earn my living—really earn it. I can't do it without risk, and I can't do it if I remain an employee. My money and your expertise might serve us both. But I warn you, if you take me as your partner I will *be* a partner. I will do my share of the work and take my share of the responsibility—that goes without saying; but I will make my share of the decisions, too. If I take the risk, then I am entitled to the authority. What do you think?"

"I think you are a fine and lovely lady, Grace Barforth."

"I daresay. But do we have a bargain?"

His hand reached out and took my arm just below the elbow in a hard, unsteady grip, his emotion very evident and very burdensome to him, weighing heavily on his tongue.

"I believe we do."

And it was a bargain I did not intend to regret, the final seal on my liberty and which had the additional merit of convincing anyone who wished—or needed—to think ill of me that I *was*, indeed and almost in broad daylight, the mistress of Liam Adair.

New premises became quickly available once it had been established that we could pay the rent, and having selected a square, solid three-storey building at the top end of Sheepgate, I saw no reason to disabuse the landlord of his notion that we had the power of Fieldhead Mills behind us. Our partnership became a legal reality amidst the disapproval of my father's lawyers, who also believed him to be supporting yet another expensive and decidedly improper whim of his wayward daughter. Liam saw to the installation of the new presses. I equipped and furnished the offices with the meticulous attention I had once bestowed on the kitchens and larders of Tarn Edge. We interviewed staff, took decisions, not always with immediate agreement on our policies, and it became quickly apparent that Liam was the true journalist, the investigator, the innovator, the schemer, while I was the organizer of his creativity, the coordinator of his efforts and the efforts of our employees, the woman of business. I was harder than Liam and found it easier to refuse, to dismiss, to discard excuses. But it was his personality, his flair which moulded the *Star*, and each one of us recognizing the contribution of the other, we worked well together.

I set out at once to win back our advertisers and to pursue others, with a fair degree of success. I sought to increase our circulation by broadening the appeal of what we had to offer, delegating, each morning, our town's humdrum social and cultural events to young reporters who, however bored they may have been by Temperance Meetings and Philosophical Societies soon learned the folly of neglecting my requirements. I invited our readers' opinions on the issues of the day and printed them with the signatures prominently displayed, recognizing any controversy, from the annexation of the Transvaal to the correct preparation of a suet pudding, as the stuff of which our profits were made. And, with my mind on suet puddings one day and the amazing ignorance of even basic cookery I had often encountered in the streets around Low Cross, I organized a group of sensible, thrifty women to supply me with cheap and simple recipes which could be prepared at the open fire and the narrow coal-oven of a small kitchen range.

I went on to include as a regular feature the daily happenings

of an imaginary Gower Street family, a vehicle for general
sanitary precautions and the recognition of the symptoms of
various children's ailments which I put together with the help of
Patrick Stone. And for readers of a different order I supplied
such details of the London and Paris fashions as were passed on
to me by Blanche; discovered herbal 'remedies' for beautifying
the hair and the skin which need not be called by that disreputable word "cosmetics"; suggested dinner-party menus that were
within the reach of any young married couple with five hundred
pounds a year, a maid of all work and a cook, and, to whet the
appetite and stimulate the ambitions of such couples, some other
menus which would have required a fully staffed kitchen and the
expertise of Gideon Chard's French chef.

We followed the progress of Gladstone's new Liberal Government very carefully, assuming that the Conservative influence on
the Queen had been lessened by the death of Disraeli almost a
year ago, that colourful gentleman having refused a visit from
his grieving monarch as he lay dying because he thought she
would be all too likely to ask him to take a message to her
departed husband, Prince Albert. We applauded Gladstone's bill
to allow Dissenters to bury their dead in parish churchyards, and
supported his move to abolish punishment by flogging in the
Army, although, of course, no one suggested that this leniency
should be extended to our public schools. There had been trouble
in the Transvaal, where the Boers, whose territory had been
added to the sum total of the British Empire by Disraeli in the
face of strong Liberal opposition, rather thought that Gladstone
might give it back again, his failure to do so resulting in the
slaughter of British soldiers at Majuba Hill. There was trouble
brewing in Egypt, where a certain Colonel Arabi seemed intent
on spreading the notion that Egypt should belong only to
Egyptians, thus threatening our prized passage to India. There
was, as always, trouble and tragedy, murder and bitter misunderstanding in Ireland, culminating in the imprisonment of the Irish
leader Parnell and in the stabbing to death of the Irish Secretary,
Lord Frederick Cavendish and his Under-Secretary, Mr. Frederick Burke, in Dublin's Phoenix Park.

In March that year an attempt was made to assassinate Queen
Victoria—the seventh, so far, since her coronation—when a Mr.
Roderick McLean, known to be but half-witted, took a shot at
her carriage as it stood outside Windsor Station, and was in-
stantly set upon and overpowered by two schoolboys from Eton;
Her Majesty faring much better than the Tsar of Russia, who had

been virtually blown to pieces by a bomb the year before, leaving as his successor his son Alexander III, who was the brother-in-law of the Prince of Wales.

There was a royal wedding, the Queen's haemophiliac son Prince Leopold marrying Princess Helen of Waldeck and being created Duke of Albany for the occasion, although his mother continued to call him "Prince Leopold," since in her imperial opinion "*anyone*" could be a duke.

In Cullingford, trade remained stable; those who set themselves out to make profits usually made them, and those who did not were considered to be unenterprising rather than unfortunate. The wool merchant, Mr. Jacob Mandelbaum, went into retirement, handing his business over to his son and setting off, in the company of his sister, Miss Rebecca Mandelbaum, on a series of extensive foreign travels. Miss Tighe became an active member of the Temperance Society and acquired a paid companion and a pedigree cat. The Cullingford Bicycle Club and the Cullingford Photographic Society were formed, the names of their founder members recorded for posterity in the *Star*. The new mill at Low Cross was completed that summer, a splendid six-storey building five hundred feet long and seventy-five feet high, covering fourteen acres of what had once been Simon Street and Saint Street, and in which four thousand people would produce an estimated thirty thousand yards of cloth each day. The main weaving-shed was over eight thousand square yards and would hold over a thousand looms. There was a reservoir with a capacity of five hundred thousand gallons of rain-water, every drop of which would be needed for the scouring of Low Cross woll. The opening celebrations would include a banquet at which, among other delicacies, a baron of beef weighing two hundred and fifty pounds and eighty hindquarters would be served to the upper two thousand or so Barforth employees, the Lord-Lieutenant of the West Riding, our Mayor and Corporation, members of Parliament and magistrates, the Duke and Duchess of South Erin, the board of directors of Nicholas Barforth and Company Limited and their wives and families, and such other guests as those directors chose to invite.

And if this was not enough—and for my part I thought it was more than enough—it was suggested by no less a person than Lady Verity Barforth herself that as a further tribute to the memory of her husband, Sir Joel, the banquet be followed by a general exodus of upper and middle Barforth management to

Scarborough, where they and their wives might be offered a day at the sea and a night at the Grand Hotel.

"The dear old lady is trying to patch things up between her sons," Camille told me, having arrived somewhat unexpectedly at my door while Mr. Barforth went on to Low Cross to confer with Gideon. "The idea is for Blaize and Faith to come too, and certainly Nicholas has no objections to it. Indeed, I shall be glad of Faith, for she has been very sweet to me, and if I am to contend with the South Erins and the Chards *and* the Madeley-Browns, I shall need every friend I can get. Would you prefer to stay with us, Grace, or with your Grandmother Agbrigg?"

"Camille, I shall not be there at all."

"Ah well," she said, "that is what you think, and no doubt what you intend, but you will give in, my dear, there is no doubt about it, for Nicholas, who is chairman of the company, and Gervase, who is still a director, are both determined to have you."

"I daresay, but—"

"But nothing, darling, for there is too much against you. Lady Verity has expressed a wish to have *all* her family about her, and since she is old and getting rather frail one can hardly refuse her that. She wants Nicholas and Blaize and Faith and, very kindly, she also wants me. She wants Caroline and her duke; Grand-mamma Elinor is coming from France; your Grandmother Agbrigg is already here. I daresay she would also like to have Georgiana and I should not mind—except that it would probably kill Caroline. And of the younger generation there is to be Blanche, Gervase, Noel—and Grace."

"And Gideon."

"Ah yes, but one can hardly think of him as part of the younger generation, since he is organizing the whole proceedings with what Nicholas calls a typical fit of Chard grandeur. There is to be a special train, a dinner and a ball on the Saturday night, heaven alone knows what else, and you cannot abandon me to the tender mercies of Duchess Caroline, who would certainly like to murder me. Oh yes, she would, for Nicholas has issued warning that unless *everyone* is very kind to me he will very likely cancel the whole celebration and evict Gideon from Tarn Edge. Now Grace, you cannot leave me to face Duchess Caroline alone after that."

"Somebody must cover all this high life for the *Star*," Liam told me, "and *I* can't do it, Grace."

"What are you going to wear?" asked Blanche. "White for me, I think, although I will check first with mamma, for she is fond of white, too, and there is no need to encourage people to tell us how alike we are. The Madeley-Brown will cut a dash, of course, with that quite stupendous diamond Gideon has given her, and I have no intention of being put in the shade. I think, between us, Grace, we can make short work of her. So—white for the journey and the luncheon and the walking about the promenade they are sure to make us do, and for the dance I really wondered about black, cut very low since my shoulders are still worth looking at—and pearls. Yes—that's exactly right. Now what about you, Grace? Something the Madeley-Brown will remember."

"You will naturally want to stay with me," my Grandmother Agbrigg wrote from Scarborough. "I shall have your room ready."

"Please come," Gervase wrote on the corner of my official card of invitation.

"I can't think of any reason why you shouldn't," said Liam. "Can you?"

There was no reason I would admit and that evening I forced myself to take out my "London" clothes and selected an ice-blue taffeta walking-dress that would exactly suit a warm July day, a pale blue velvet parasol with white lace edging, the blue velvet hat with the blue satin roses and the spotted net veil I had bought for my first visit to Gervase. I had an evening gown I had never worn, cream tulle over pale gold silk, and another, worn only once, a cream satin skirt embroidered here and there with a single crimson rosebud, a crimson velvet bodice with tiny puffed sleeves. Either one would take me creditably to the Grand Hotel. And in my jewellery box, in the lower drawer that I never opened, I had a diamond too, given to me by Gervase, and the bracelet of fine gold chains scattered with tiny amethysts from Gideon.

But that bracelet and that ring were a world away and I must make it my business to see that they stayed there. I would go to Scarborough in fitting fashion, as the guest of my former husband, and as Grace Barforth of the *Star*.

29

THE BANQUET AT LOW CROSS was held on the second and warmest Friday in July, all the Barforth mills, including the one belonging to Sir Blaize, being closed for the occasion; and the following morning early we boarded that special train to Scarborough, to the accompaniment of Cullingford's brass band and the good wishes of her Mayor and Corporation. The journey, which I made in the company of Gervase, Noel and Blanche, was unexacting, even rather pleasant—the train being amply provisioned, in accordance with Gideon's grandeur, with hampers of cold chicken, little savoury delicacies and champagne—until we reached our marine destination, where my Agbrigg grandparents, another brass band, and—by express command of Mr. Nicholas Barforth—Camille, were waiting to greet us.

Camille had not made the journey to Cullingford for the opening of the mill, fearing, she said, to give Duchess Caroline an apoplexy, but as her august lover got down from the first compartment she came forward to greet him with the composure of an empress, a performance she had been rehearsing for weeks in front of her mirror and which, for all her good intentions, lasted but a moment, melting clean away in her gladness to have him home again; a show of emotion which wrinkled the nostrils and quite visibly curdled the sensibilities of Aunt Caroline. Yet because Mr. Nicholas Barforth required it, and because his was the power, the authority, the title-deed of Tarn Edge, she forced her mouth to smile, her tongue to pronounce a stiff but audible. "How do you do, Mrs. Inman," choosing, as she had always done, to sacrifice her own beliefs, her own pride, very nearly her own moral values, in the best interests of her sons.

We were driven to the Grand Hotel in solemn procession, Sir Blaize and Mr. Nicholas Barforth in the first carriage with their mother and their sister, Aunt Caroline, the Duke of South Erin being now so frail that it was thought unlikely he would ever make the journey north again. Camille and Aunt Faith came next with my dainty little Grandmamma Elinor, who had been Sir Joel Barforth's sister and was worldly enough to appreciate that a mistress could be every bit as valuable and powerful as a wife; while behind them came Sir Joel's other sister, my Grandmother Agbrigg, my grandfather, who had been Sir Joel's mill-manager and Cullingford's first mayor, followed by my father and my very good friend, his wife. The next carriage should have carried Gideon, Miss Madeley-Brown and Gervase, but finding large and determined *Mrs*. Madeley-Brown occupying her own place and half of the one reserved for him, he gracefully withdrew and got in with Noel, Blanche and myself and a delightfully frilled and beribboned little doll called Claire Chard who had just been retrieved from her nurse. And so we set off, the Barforth managers and their well-dressed, self-conscious wives coming behind us, their quick, keen glances leaving us in no doubt as to how much we, the Barforth women, were on display. We were served a light but delicious luncheon, the menu certainly chosen by Gideon, who I knew would have come over to the Grand several times in person to make his requirements known, although the rather casual arrangement of the small tables which allowed us to seat ourselves was not to the taste of his mother, Aunt Caroline, who clearly felt that even at so informal a meal as this some distinction should be made between her son, who was the managing director of this company, the man responsible for the continuing prosperity which we had come to celebrate, and her brother's son, a director in name only, accompanied by his former wife who, in Aunt Caroline's further opinion, should have had sufficient good taste not to come at all.

"I trust we shall be more formally arranged at dinner," she said, intending to be heard, her sharp eyes rapidly calculating that the table occupied by Gervase—and, to her intense indignation, by me—was at least six inches nearer to Mr. Nicholas Barforth than the table where Gideon had calmly seated himself with his golden young financée.

"Poor Aunt Caroline!" murmured Gervase. "She believes the most arduous task I perform in a twelvemonth is to go down to Nethercoats on the due date to collect my dividend."

"But you are always there, I suppose—on the due date?"

"Ah yes, with not a moment to spare. But let me remind you, Grace, of the hard life of a working farmer. Noel here will confirm it."

"My son's position is most awkward," I heard Aunt Caroline explaining to Mrs. Madeley-Brown, "for when father and son are present he feels unable to put himself forward."

Nevertheless, when the meal had reached its coffee and brandy stage and neither father nor son seemed inclined to make a move, Gideon got up and went from table to table speaking an appropriate word to every manager and his wife, the length of time he devoted to each one being regulated by the fine social instincts of Listonby, so that all were satisfied. He spent a longer moment with my Agbrigg grandparents, paying his respects to my rough-grained but mayoral grandfather with a warm double handclasp, exchanging a brief but pleasant word with my father, a slight inclination of the head and a smile conveying a different sort of respect entirely for my father's wife.

He kissed Lady Verity Barforth, his grandmother, on her hand and her cheek, and seeing that Grandmamma Elinor, with her notorious fondness for tall, dark, youngish gentlemen, expected the same treatment he kissed her too. He took Camille's hand and held it long enough to prove himself a man of the world who could well understand—could even envy—his employer's obsession with this luscious woman. He whispered something in Aunt Faith's ear that made her smile, chatted with Uncle Blaize and Mr. Nicholas Barforth pleasantly but without the slightest hint of subservience to these two powerful men of affairs, letting it be seen that, although he respected their opinions—which had made them several fortunes apiece—he had opinions, and perhaps fresher ones, of his own.

He came to our table too, slapping his brother Noel companionably on the shoulder, ruffling the hair of pretty four-year-old Claire Chard who after all was supposed to be his daughter and who tugged at his sleeve with more familiarity than I had expected her to show.

"How goes it, Gervase?"

"Not bad—not bad at all."

"You're managing to rear your young stock, then?"

"So I am."

He sat down, took brandy, discussed stirks and heifers with Noel and Gervase, told Claire to be a good girl, told Blanche she was looking beautiful. He stood up, lingered a while longer with his hand on the back of Noel's chair, describing the arrangements for the rest of the day. He ruffled Claire's curls again, made some remark to a passing waiter, walked away. And he had not spoken one single word to me.

At Lady Verity's request there were to be photographs after luncheon, a camera having been already set up on the terrace, and knowing how awkward this might be—for Aunt Caroline was not the only one to feel surprised at the sight of Gervase's hand on my arm—I would have made my escape, as Camille swiftly made hers, had not my Grandmother Agbrigg detained me with an imperious command to "Come here, my girl, and sit beside *me*," and an equally imperious request that I should put an end to the rumours about my involvement with Liam Adair.

"You would do well to go back to France with Elinor," she told me. "In fact I have had a word with her and she is more than willing to take you. I have had a word with your father about it, too, which may surprise you—the first word I have had with him in many a long year—and he gave me his gracious permission to put my suggestion to you for your consideration. Now what sort of an answer is that?"

But luckily she was called away by that other imperious lady, Aunt Caroline, to have her portrait taken, the first group consisting of the older generation, Sir Joel Barforth's wife, Lady Verity, and his two sisters who were both my grandmothers; just one male survivor of those harsher, elder days, hollow-chested, hollow-cheeked Mayor Agbrigg, the pauper brat brought up to Cullingford in a consignment of a hundred half-starved little factory slaves, who, from such meagre beginnings, had outlived both of Grand-mamma Elinor's husbands, my refined grandparent, Mr. Morgan Aycliffe and the charming Mr. Daniel Adair; and Sir Joel Barforth himself.

Lady Verity was next positioned between her two sons, then alone with her daughter, then all four of them together. Her eldest son's wife, Aunt Faith, was next added, a perfectly proper procedure until Lady Verity, her sweet and knowing smile passing from her daughter Caroline to her son Nicholas, said very clearly, "If this is to be for daughters-in-law, then surely we should include Camille, who is my daughter-in-law in everything that matters. Yes, certainly we must have Camille. My other daughter-in-law, dear Georgiana, who could not be present, would say the same."

"Mother!" Aunt Caroline muttered, much shocked, hoping the Madeley-Browns had not grasped the significance of this, trusting she could plead her mother's age and long sojourn in France if they had. But Camille was sent for, placed between Mr. Nicholas Barforth and his brother, Uncle Blaize, Aunt Faith

greeting her warmly, Aunt Caroline obliged—as she so often
was obliged these days—to make the best of it.

Lady Verity's grandchildren were then required to come forward,
or such of them as were available, Noel, Gideon, Gervase,
Blanche in her cascade of lace-edged white frills with a flower-
garden of pinks and apricots and mauves in her hat, biting her lip
as she remembered Venetia—as I remembered Venetia—and
then frowning, biting her lip even harder when Aunt Caroline, not
thinking of Venetia at all but simply wishing to compensate
herself for the effrontery of Camille, called out "Hortense dear,
do come and pose for this—here, between Noel and Gideon,
with Blanche on Gideon's other side—and Gervase, oh—at the
other side of Noel, I suppose. Yes, Hortense, do come—you
don't mind, mamma, I know, since after all she will be your
granddaughter quite soon now. And since Dominic cannot be
here—simply could not get away—we are one short."

Miss Madeley-Brown got up, parting her lips in her wide,
brilliant smile and came forward, quite splendid in a yellow
gown that might have been painted on to her full-breasted,
long-limbed figure, her shoulders as broad, her back as strongly
arched as an Amazon queen. Her hair, beneath the chrysanthe-
mum colours of her hat, looked like spun gold, she had swinging
drops of topaz on her ears, that huge diamond on her hand, no
idea at all of the hornets' nest into which she was so obediently
and so elegantly stepping.

"Blanche!" Aunt Caroline said sharply, expecting no defiance
from this quarter. "Move over to make room for Hortense."

"I thought this was to be grandchildren only, Aunt Caroline—
that's what you said a moment ago."

"Blanche, don't make a fuss!" Aunt Caroline gave warning.

"Oh, I am not in the least inclined to do that. I am just trying
to be helpful, Aunt Caroline—just trying to get it right—and
since we are rather more than *one* grandchild short, I suppose
Claire is the best person to take the place of the other one we are
missing. Claire darling, do come over here—yes, nurse, just
give her ringlets a little shake and straighten that ribbon. Oh,
good. Now then, Aunt Caroline, where would you like little
Claire Chard to stand?"

She stood, in the end, beside her Uncle Noel, having found
his presence the most reassuring, her rosy little cheek pressed
against the hip he had damaged at Ulundi, Blanche still most
uncharacteristically scowling, Gideon looking as if he had noticed
nothing amiss, Miss Madeley-Brown, who really had not noticed

anything, smiling until she was told to stop, Gervase, who had been pushed into the background by Aunt Caroline and then dragged forward again by Blanche, appearing much amused. Yet Venetia had been his much-loved sister and it was no doubt in tribute to her memory that when the photograph was taken he shook his head and told Aunt Caroline: "We have still not got it right, you know, for we did not include Grace."

"Oh, Grace—come on," said Blanche.

"Good heavens!" said Aunt Caoline.

"Who is Grace?" Miss Madeley-Brown's fixed smile seemed to enquire.

"Of course we must have a picture of Grace," Lady Verity agreed, settling the matter. "I was just about to say so."

"Grace," said Gervase, holding out a hand to me, and so we were captured for posterity, Blanche and Noel side by side now, with Venetia's child happily between them, Miss Madeley-Brown with her hand on Gideon's arm, her diamond showing to advantage against his coat-sleeve, Gervase holding me by the elbow, his fine-etched profile quizzical, my face looking puzzled and by no means at its best, only my hat, I thought, doing me credit beside the stupendous Madeley-Brown.

We escaped soon after—Blanche, Noel, Gervase and I—to stroll along the cliffs, enjoying the salt breezes and the bright sunshine, in surprisingly easy harmony, Gervase still holding my arm, Blanche and Noel, with Claire skipping between them, behaving openly now not as a pair of lovers but as the married couple they felt themselves to be. We sat for a while on a shady wooden seat, Blanche, who was careful of her complexion, making full use of her parasol, while the men took Claire to look at the sea, Uncle Noel and Uncle Gervase taking it in turns to carry her shoulder high, stopping every now and then to explain the sand and the shells, the busy population of a rock-pool, a sail hurrying across the horizon, the purposes of the noisy, greedy gulls.

"I shall never let her go back to Gideon, you know," Blanche told me, her eyes on the dark, sturdy, serious child who bore so little resemblance to Venetia.

"I didn't know you were so fond of children, Blanche."

"Well, and neither did I—but, oh heavens! I may as well confess it, I cannot stop myself from pretending she is mine and Noel's—can't you see that? The boys belong entirely to Dominic and are as remote from me now as he is. When they come home from school we are no more than polite to each other, and Matthew is already talking of spending his next long vacation in

India. So she is the nearest I can ever come to having Noel's child—I take good care of that. Why not, Grace? Nobody else wants her. The Madeley-Brown will set about breeding, one can see that, as soon as he consents to ask her—which will be as soon as he has finished his negotiations for Tarn Edge—and Claire will not be welcome in *her* household then.''

We met Gideon and Miss Madeley-Brown on our way back, Blanche having no need at all to bristle like a mother cat, since no one threatened her kitten, Miss Madeley-Brown merely glancing at the child, perched on Noel's shoulder and saying ''Was it fun on the beach, little girl?'' a remark designed to draw Gideon's attention, Blanche thought, to the sand on Claire's shoes and the hem of her dress, which prompted him, although not without humour, to warn his brother: ''You'll ruin your coat, Noel.''

''Oh—we farming men don't pay much heed to things like that,'' Gervase murmured wickedly.

''Luckily he has another,'' declared Blanche, in a great huff. ''But come along, Noel, that child must have her tea and be put to bed. Come along, for nurse is waiting.''

And once again Gideon had not addressed a word to me.

I wore the dress with the crimson velvet bodice and the cream satin skirt that evening, largely because Blanche told me it was elegant and unusual and cut low enough to give Aunt Caroline the vapours.

''And you have rather a lovely bosom, Grace—which is most unexpected since the rest of you has got so thin. And if you take your hair a little higher and lift it off your forehead just there, your eyes—which are quite big enough anyway—will look simply enormous. Have you nothing better than that gold chain to put around your neck? Oh Grace—you had heaps of jewellery once.''

''Yes—that was once. I have put it all away. I don't wear it anymore.''

''Well, I am sorry, but that gold chain will not do. It should be rubies, of course—big ones surrounded by pearls and set in antique gold. Your friend Camille has just the thing. But since Aunt Caroline would be sure to recognize it and draw all the wrong conclusions, you had better borrow from me instead. Luckily I have my black velvet ribbon with me and it has enough pearls stitched on it to make a decent show. It will look well enough.''

It did, or so Gervase told me as he took me in to dinner, it having been found convenient, for the purposes of the seating arrangements, to restore to me for the duration of the evening my position as his wife, an arrangement which, astonishingly enough, appeared to offend no one but my watchful Aunt Caroline. And so I sat beside him, allowed him to unfold my napkin and place it on my knee, to touch my hand as he gave me my menu, to lean over me, breathe on me, to remind me—as several people present wished me to be reminded—how easy it would be, how *restful*, to turn back to him, to restore myself truly and finally to this family which had never really meant to relinquish me.

We had a lengthy, complicated meal, a great many toasts and speeches, both Gideon and Gervase saying a few accomplished words, Mr. Nicholas Barforth making a dignified reply, Sir Blaize Barforth, who had been something of a ladies' man in his day, raising his glass to his female relations with a witty salutation. It was all very pleasant and very civilized, extremely well done, each lady now being invited to open the little trinket box beside her plate amidst squeals of delight, gold lockets of very adequate value being provided for the managers' wives while each Barforth lady received a pendant of heavy gold set with her birth-stone, a diamond for Miss Madeley-Brown, I noticed, a pearl for Blanche, a ruby for me, the very thing my outfit required.

Gervase fastened the clasp for me, adjusted the jewel to a correct central position on its chain, the back of his hand brushing the tops of my breasts as he did so, the precious metal very cold against my skin when he took his hand away.

"Uncle Nicholas—thank you—how lovely!" trilled Blanche, who knew the market price of pearls and was very pleased with the size of this one.

"You'd best thank Gideon," he told her, "for it was his idea, and he took the trouble to find out what month you were born."

"Thank you, Gideon," she said and, as everyone was getting up now in preparation for the dancing, she went up to him and, being rather tipsy by then, stood on tiptoe and gave him a reasonably flirtatious kiss.

"Yes—thank you, Gideon," smiled Camille, an amethyst sparkling around her throat, kissing him too, without any need for tiptoe. Aunt Faith, his grandmother, my grandmother, followed suit. Miss Madeley-Brown, no doubt, would thank him later and privately. Only my thanks remained to be said and there was no doubt at all that I would have to move forward, to attract his attention, to say "Thank you, Gideon"; and if he

snubbed me or brushed me aside, I would have to carry it off
somehow or other and pretend to anyone who had noticed—to
Gervase who *would* notice—that it was solely on account of the
Star.

I walked forward. He did not appear to see me coming, but
started to turn away. I put out a hand to touch his sleeve and
withdrew it as sharply as if the fabric had scorched me, and for a
moment, as he looked down at me with no expression, almost no
recognition on his dark face, I did not think my voice could
penetrate the sudden, quite total dryness of my throat and my
tongue.

"Thank you, Gideon."

He nodded sharply, gave me a smile that was a brief parting of
the lips, obeying his training as a gentleman far more than his
inclination, which would have been—I thought—to order me
from his premises, his sight, his hearing, from the quota of air he
wished to breathe. And I understood, with horror and a futile
quite terrible distress, that his silence was intended neither to
punish nor humiliate me, but had come about quite simply
because he could not bear to speak.

I went into the ballroom where the Barforth men were dancing
with their lovely ladies, Mr. Nicholas Barforth with Camille in
her floating amethyst gauze, Noel with Blanche in her sensational and very daring black lace, Uncle Blaize and Aunt Faith,
who had chosen her favourite blonde silk, Hortense Madeley-
Brown in gold satin and not too much of it at that, going twice
round the floor with Gideon and then sitting placidly beside her
mother and Aunt Caroline while he did his duty by his managers'
wives. I danced with Gervase, my hand going gratefully into his,
my body taking shelter in his arms, for I was shaken and
disarmed, most unusually defenceless, and no longer cared what
speculation our being so much together might arouse, no longer
cared what I should or should not do when he was the only
person I *could* be with just then, the only person who could
accept my silence—and my suffering—without question, the
only one who could give me time to gather myself together. Yet
when that much was achieved, I had been in his arms for rather a
long time, admittedly in full view of most of our relations, but
nevertheless in an embrace that was not polite but familiar and
affectionate—*companionable*—and which, if allowed to continue,
could give rise to a companionable desire.

"If we were meeting for the first time," he said, "I would be
quite thrilled with you by now, do you know that?"

"Then it is perhaps as well we are not meeting for the first time."

"Well—and if we were, I wonder how much you would object to me? I *am* the father of a bastard child, but the enlightened and liberated Grace Barforth of the *Star* should be able to forgive me for that."

"Gervase, I do—in fact I never really blamed you."

"I am not speaking of the past, Grace. I am telling you of my life *now*, as I would have to tell you if we had just become acquainted. The boy and the estate are an essential part of what I am. They make up the sum total of me. I can present myself to you now as a whole man—which I could not do before. I am not altogether displeased with that man. If we had just met tonight I would be doing my best to make you like him too."

"With a very fair chance of success."

"Why, thank you, Grace. Had I known, long ago, that you had it in you to like a very ordinary farmer with a quite moderate estate and a delightful but probably—in anybody else's eyes—a very ordinary son, then I wonder—"

"Don't wonder. Everything would have been just the same."

"Unless, of course, I had shown any real aptitude for business, in which case you would have been the hostess here tonight— and far better at it, I must say, than the luscious Madeley-Brown."

"It does no good to wonder about that either."

"Then I wonder if you would care to drink some more champagne with me? That seems a reasonable occupation for those who *were* married—and *are* not."

We drank rather more than I had intended, his new occupation having in no way lessened his taste for fine wines, and returning to the ballroom an hour later, seeing Hortense Madeley-Brown seated beside Aunt Caroline, too placid and too pleased with herself to know she was being neglected, I asked him: "What do you really think of her, Gervase?"

"Miss Madeley-Brown? Well—I would very much enjoy a night or two in her bed, for her physique is awe-inspiring, there is no use in denying it. One would being with the feeling of paying homage, almost, at a shrine of Aphrodite, which would make—if nothing else—a delicious aperitif."

"Gervase, that is not the language of a working farmer."

"No. But I was a wild young man, if you remember."

"I remember."

"No longer, Grace—believe me. Not dull, I hope, but quite dependable, if you can credit it."

"Perhaps I can. Gervase—what do you think of me?"

He took my hand, companionably, and, not caring who saw us, brushed a closed and friendly mouth against my cheek.

"I like you, Grace. I think one can build on that."

And so one could. All day I had been surrounded by the faces and figures and attitudes which had peopled my childhood, formed me and moulded me and had never for one moment lost hope of my return. Warm affection awaited me here on a dozen faces; and one man who hated me. The affection was like the thin vapours of an autumn morning glimpsed in the distance. The hatred was real to me.

I left, some time after midnight, with my Agbrigg grandparents, Gervase escorting us gallantly to their house half a mile away.

"I do not pretend to understand this," my grandmother told me when he had strolled off along the cliff-top. "I presume he wants you to return to him as his wife, since I can think of nothing else he has a right to want from you."

"I think he might want that—yes."

"Well then, I have no right to interfere—your father has assured me of that—but it would seem—*suitable*—would it not?"

"I suppose it would. But it will not break his heart, you know, if I refuse him. I think he would quite like me to say yes, but he will not really mind if I say no."

"Good gracious! I have never heard such coolness."

"Not coolness, grandmamma, just good sense. He is so remarkably self-sufficient, you see—whoever would have thought it? He likes me but he doesn't need me. Well—at least *that* has turned out all right. Grandmamma, you will not be pleased with me, but I am going back to Cullingford on the early train tomorrow."

"Ah—and do you imagine there is somebody in Cullingford who needs you?"

"I simply think it is where I belong."

"Hannah," my grandfather said sharply, "leave the lass alone. She knows what she's doing."

But I could not share his confidence, for I was not leaving Scarborough for any high-minded principles of self-sufficiency, independence, who needed me or did not need me. I was running away from Gideon.

30

My GRANDFATHER TOOK ME TO the station the next morning, found me a compartment—in accordance with my grandmother's instructions—in which two elderly ladies were already seated, and asked me no questions. I had left a note in his care for Camille and one for Blanche, explaining that "pressure of business" had required my early return, and although neither one of them would believe me I did not really care for that.

"That is not a good train," my grandfather said. "You will have to change at Leeds and there might be a long wait. Now take care, lass—" And it was as I began to reassure him of my ability to travel alone, my understanding of the dangers of rape and kidnap to a life of sexual slavery in a warmer clime— although I did not use these words—that Gideon Chard came striding along the platform, a leather document case under one arm, a newspaper under the other, and, raising his hat to me with an automatic gesture, got into a compartment as far away from mine as he could.

"Now what the devil—?" my grandfather began, for no matter how deep a grudge Gideon might bear the *Star* it was discourteous, it was ungentlemanly, it was downright peculiar of any man to refuse his company and his protection on this hazardous Scarborough to Cullingford line to any lady of his acquaintance— unheard of, if she happened to be a relation.

"Grace, lass, what *is* all this?" But doors were slamming now, the train getting ready to pull out of the station, I was already on board, and there was nothing to do but stand at the window and wave to him, and then, feeling considerably shaken, to sit down and defend myself against the curiosity of my two elderly travelling companions by closing my eyes.

I had thought, in that first numbing moment of recognition, that he had come to meet the train, not travel on it, and I spent the first thirty or forty miles telling myself the many reasons he might have for doing so. The festivities, as such, were over now. A special train would be waiting that afternoon to convey his employees back to Cullingford, suitably provisioned with those luxurious little hampers of chicken and champagne, but few if any of the Barforths would be on it.

Uncle Blaize and Aunt Faith were to stay in Scarborough for the rest of the week and perhaps another with Lady Verity, who wished to bask for as long as possible in the renewed friendship of her sons. Blanche and Noel would not be leaving until Wednesday, perhaps longer if the weather should hold, and Gervase had declared himself in no hurry to get away. I had not been informed of Aunt Caroline's plans but it seemed unlikely that she would neglect this opportunity of persuading her brother to finalize the transfer of Tarn Edge to Gideon and might well stay at the Grand with Miss Madeley-Brown in tow until she had. And in that case it was not surprising that Gideon, who would have appointments tomorrow morning, should wish to avoid the special train, preferring to travel alone with his newspaper and his documents than in the effusive company of his managers' wives.

He could not have known I would be here. I had not known myself until last night and had told no one. He had been as shocked to see me as I was on seeing him, yet what real difference could it make? I would not have stayed in Scarborough even had I known he meant to leave it. What I needed was to return to my own home, my own atmosphere, my own life, and his presence, although awkward, could not hinder me in that. Yet throughout that hot, tedious journey I spoke not a word to those kind, well-meaning ladies, who whenever I closed my eyes began at once to tell each other how ill I looked, how pale; and by the time we arrived in Leeds I could not deny that I was feeling wretched indeed.

That station was busy enough, I suppose, and people who wish to avoid each other can usually manage to do so. I remained in my compartment until he had passed the window, walked slowly down the platform, giving him time to get far away with his long strides, and went at once to the waiting-room reserved for ladies. A half-hour passed—a dreadful half-hour—before I got up and went to find the Cullingford train, hoping that he was staying in Leeds or going to London, anywhere, since the small station-yard at Cullingford would be difficult; but he was there, as far down the platform as he could get, irritably pacing, irritably smoking—he was there—and it was then, in that moment of distraction, that something struck hard against the backs of my knees, and aware of wheels and shouts and, oddly, the shapes of boxes, cages, canvas, I realized to my complete horror that I was falling down.

I know what happened only because other people were there to tell me so, a great many of them, it seemed, in those first dizzy moments of returning consciousness, bending over me and arguing quite ferociously with one another as to whether the porter who had run into me with that trolley of bags and baggage had been drunk or just malicious, or whether *I* had been drunk or deaf or just plain slow-witted not to have got myself out of his way. But although I had certainly not been drunk a moment ago, I felt very drunk now, helpless and incapable and bewildered, and very willing to abandon myself to Gideon when he parted the crowd, helped me to my feet and then, when I found I could not stand erect, picked me up and carried me somewhere or other—did it matter where?—to remove my shoe and give orders that something was to be done about my ankle, which was swelling.

A capable-looking woman bathed my foot in cold water and applied a bandage, while I drank the brandy Gideon had sent for—all of it, every drop—although it made my head no clearer. And realizing dimly but with a weak inclination for laughter that he had obliged them to hold up the train, I allowed him, with complete docility, to lift me into the compartment of his choice and to place me exactly to his liking, my back supported by the pillows he had by some means acquired.

I was suffering, perhaps, from a slight concussion, certainly from a sprained ankle and a drop more brandy than I was used to at this hour of the day, and as the train began to ease its way out of the station—Gideon, no doubt, having told the driver to go slow and be damned to anybody who might be in a hurry—I began to wonder why I did not feel more ashamed.

"Heavens, Gideon, what a ridiculous thing!"

"Accidents happen."

"Oh—my bag—"

"There, in the corner."

"Yes—oh lord, where *is* my hat?" For I had just realized it was not on my head.

"Ruined, I'm afraid. The railway company will buy you another."

"Oh—*damnation*!"

"What is it now?"

"I don't know—I just feel so—"

"Don't feel anything. Just be glad you were not alone."

I drifted then, partly because it was easier to drift placidly, docilely, spinelessly, easier just for a little while to leave everything to him, to let him decide—since he so much enjoyed deciding—than to gather my cloudy wits together and decide for myself. And when I recovered sufficiently not merely to wonder where I was but to care what I was doing there, we were approaching Cullingford.

"Will there be anyone to meet you, Grace?"

"No. I am not expected until tomorrow."

"Then I will take you—"; and I allowed myself, like a dreaming child, to be "taken" in his carriage to a destination he did not name but which I knew, quite soon, must be Tarn Edge.

The butler, whose extreme elegance had long been the talk of Cullingford, greeted us without the faintest hint of surprise, as if he was accustomed to see his employer arriving home every day of the week with a bareheaded, bedraggled and probably slightly tipsy woman in his arms.

"Sandwiches and coffee in the drawing-room, Sherston, and a bottle of Chablis if you have one chilled."

"Certainly, sir."

"And Mrs. Barforth, I imagine, will first wish to attend to her dress."

"Certainly—at once, sir."

Two parlourmaids and a housekeeper with the bearing of a dowager duchess assisted me to a dressing-room, brought me hot water and warm towels, combs and brushes, and then returned me, no longer quite so bemused although still dangerously passive, to the armchair their master indicated. The drawing-room was cool and fragrant, a haven from the heat and dust of the long day, roses and carnations standing in very professional arrangements in silver-rimmed bowls of exquisitely cut crystal I had not seen before. Two nymphs in white biscuit porcelain, a foot high, were poised in graceful flight at each side of the hearth, more nymphs in costly groupings by Sèvres on the mantelshelf above them, the mirror I remembered replaced now by the portrait of a dark-eyed, curly-haired lady clad in the scanty muslin draperies of the Regency, unmistakably a Chard.

The sandwiches, when they came, were of smoked salmon very daintily garnished, the wine ice cold in its long, fluted glasses, delighting my tongue and rising at once to join the pleasant confusion in my brain.

"Well, I wanted you weak and helpless, Grace," he said, raising his glass to me. "And now I have you."

"Yes." Not for long, of course, but for the moment I had, not surrendered precisely, but certainly ceased to struggle. My grandfather's fears for me had all been realized. I had exposed myself to the risks of travelling alone and a man had kidnapped me. Astonishingly, I laughed.

"What is so amusing?"

I told him, and received a slow, almost unwilling smile.

"Unfortunately it is not so simple."

"Unfortunately?"

"Yes, Grace. If I took you away and locked you up and made love to you often enough, you would eventually stop trying to escape and then you would stop wanting to—or so the theory goes. I can't do that."

"Would you even want to?"

"Oh yes. There was a time when I might just have succeeded. My misfortune has been that I wanted you to come as a willing captive. I have not been able to achieve that."

"Oh Gideon—*Gideon*—"

Never in all the years I had known him had I seen him look so weary. Never in the whole of my life had I felt such a desire to reach out, in body and in spirit, to another person. Never before had I lost sight of my own needs, my own futile, fussy dignity, my own most precious common sense, very nearly my own identity, in my need to give whatever I could give—whatever he would take. And it seemed to me advisable that this impulse of quite overwhelming devotion should not last long either.

"I thought I had made you hate me, Gideon."

"You did. I understood why and played the same game. I have hated you very well—by fits and starts."

"Yesterday you couldn't bring yourself to speak to me."

"I do not forget it."

"That is why I took the early train today. I was running away from you."

"Is there anything new in that? You have been running away from me, have you not, ever since—"

"Ever since I was eighteen and you came to have a look at Fieldhead as if you might buy it and me with it—or so I thought—and made yourself pleasant to my father's wife instead of arranging to meet me at the bottom of the garden and trying to

kiss me, and telling me—telling me—lord, why am I prattling on
so?''

"Telling you that I loved you? But I didn't love you then,
Grace. That happened later—would have happened no matter
what the circumstances. But before I say another word—since I
retain my pride in these matters, or such of it as you have left
me—I must know that you have loved me too.''

"Yes. Yes, of course I have.''

"That will not suffice me, Grace. If you came upstairs with
me now and gave yourself to me in the most slavish fashion I
could devise, it would not suffice me.''

"How, then?''

"You have taken every opportunity you could to hurt me and
humiliate me, have you not?''

"Yes—I am afraid so.''

"Now make atonement for it. You are a clever woman. You
will find a way.''

"Will it serve a purpose?''

"At this stage I don't much care for that. You are very
accomplished when it comes to wounding me. I think you must
now show me your skill as a healer. I need that much from you,
Grace.

"Yes.''

I had been asked only the night before if there was anyone in
Cullingford who needed me and I had not expected it to be
Gideon, yet now, although I could never have spoken the words
and would be very likely, I believed, to deny them tomorrow,
my thought urged him: "Yes, need me and go on needing me.
Need me so that I am filled to my capacity with it and strained
even beyond the limits of my need for you. Ask more of me than
I can possibly give and see—just *watch*—how I shall find the
means to give it.'' This was the consuming emotion Venetia had
felt for Robin Ashby, the crusade of which I had not believed
myself to be capable. I loved him. *Naturally*, I loved him. I had
lived in the shadow of it for years. The only difference now was
that I wanted to tell him so.

"It was fear,'' I said slowly. "A physical fear to begin with
because I desired you—quite acutely—and didn't understand it.
How could I? Young girls of eighteen are not supposed to
understand desire. They are not even supposed to feel it. And I
am not going to take all the blame, Gideon, for you were older
and you were not a virgin. You could have understood and
helped me get over it—couldn't you?''

"No," he said, smiling slowly, sadly almost, as if at a very distant memory. "I was behaving as I had been told a gentleman ought to behave, you see—with a virgin. I was a little older, and had a little more experience, yes, but not enough—believe me—to know that I'd have done better to drag you off somewhere by the hair. That kind of knowledge came much later. And even then, Grace, when you were eighteen, there was more to your fear of me than that. My dear—I *know* you didn't trust me in those days and I know why, but you are going to *tell* me."

"Yes. I knew you needed a rich wife and I understood that. I had money and I had been told, at an early age, that men would want to marry me for it. I understood that too. My father had educated me to believe that marriages should be made with a cool head. I couldn't name my feeling for you at that time but it was not cool, and we have all seen the pathetic spectacle a woman makes when she has married for love but has been married only for her money. That was my fear and you did nothing to alleviate it. Your marriage to Venetia suggested to me that I had been right."

"You had married Gervase by then, Grace. I certainly did not jilt you."

"And you were not in love with me then either, were you—not really?"

He shook his head, still sadly, I thought, and slowly, a movement—like every movement he had made since entering this room—which was full of regret.

"I fear not. If I had really fallen in love with you when you were eighteen and ripe for the plucking, then you would have known about it, my darling, for I would have been far less gentlemanly, with far greater success—But even so you were the reason I hesitated as long as I did in marrying Venetia. I didn't want to share a house with you. I wasn't sure why. I simply thought it would not be wise. Quite soon—too soon—the house, *this* house, in fact, would have been unbearable to me without you. Those were not easy days for me, Grace. I had a trade to learn, prejudice and hostility to overcome on both sides, for my own people thought me sadly *déclassé*, and any one of the managers we had then would have put a knife in my back given half a chance—and it's a weary business when a man has to guard his back all day and every day. You were the only person who understood the effort I was making, except Nicholas Barforth, for whom no effort could ever be enough, and even he failed to realize just how damned distasteful I found those sheds—this town—any town—to begin with. I didn't *want* to be a manufacturer, Grace. I simply wanted to be rich. If I could have made my money in land or on the high seas or in any other clean and clever fashion, then I'd hardly have condemned myself to twelve hours a day shut up in those mills. I think you understood that too. I think, in my place, you would have done the same."

"I understood. And I admired you enormously for it."

"Admiration? Is that all you had for me?"

"Possibly not. But it was all I was prepared to admit, and I am very stubborn. You were married, Gideon, and I loved your wife like a sister."

"I know," he said, his smile once again heavy with regret. "I know. Oddly enough, so did I. Oh yes, you may look startled and surprised, but it is the plain truth. That is exactly what I felt for her, the exasperated kind of affection I would have given to a sister, and which in her case was sadly inappropriate. When she left me for Robin Ashby I made no attempt to get her back. Well, I was not slow to spot my own advantage, I never am. But the truth is that I wished her well. If it was what she wanted, then I had no mind to spoil it for her. I thought her reckless to the point of madness, but I hoped just the same that she might succeed."

"Gideon—I am so glad you told me that."

"Yes, I thought it might please you. What I am about to say now will not suit you so well. Venetia was gone, with my blessing, although she didn't know it. I knew how Gervase was situated with Diana Flood. I can't be certain how much Nicholas Barforth suspected but he watched me like a hawk those first few months, and so I had to keep away from you. But you were the woman I wanted and I was going to have you, my dear, as soon as ever I could. We were going to live together in the way we actually *had* been living together for several years, except that when the dance was over and the dinner guests had gone we were going to walk up those stairs hand in hand and get into the same bed. I was going to take you abroad with me, bully you and rely on you, spoil you and make sure you spoiled me. I was going to *have* you, Grace—and then suddenly there you were, asking me to take Venetia back. Once again my sense of timing had been at fault."

"I would have asked you to take her back, Gideon, even if we had already been lovers."

"My dear, I know. There is nothing I want to say about her death. But, yes, as you guessed, I was appalled when I heard of your intention to divorce Gervase—appalled and furious, and quite determined to put a stop to it. Your assessment of my motives, that night in London was quite correct. The social stigma of divorce was more than I could stomach, especially when I could see no need for it. One way or another I was going to make you abandon it and come back here with me, where I was certain you belonged. No one raises any objection to Noel and Blanche. Why should anyone have objected to us? I would have been faithful to you, you know—far more scrupulous in my behaviour than if you had really been my wife, just like Noel has to be. A man assumes his wife will forgive him. In most cases she has very little choice in the matter. But he is obliged to tread rather more warily with a mistress, who can make up her own mind. I believe Grace Barforth of the *Star* may have said something like that. Will you admit that I could have made you happy?"

"Yes, perfectly happy—once. The life you planned for me was everything I desired and would have given me complete fulfilment—once. By the time it became possible I had moved on—forwards or backwards I don't always know—but *moved*, anyway."

He came very swiftly to sit on the edge of my chair and leaned over me, sliding one hand beneath my shoulder-blades, gathering me up in an act of possession into which my body nestled with gratitude and content.

"Grace, listen carefully, for I cannot think I shall ever say this to you again. This is all I know how to give—this house and the luxury inside it, the gracious way of life we could make for each other here. This is what I have worked to achieve and to maintain, and I shall achieve much more—much more. I can afford, by my own efforts, to surround you with ease and beauty. I can offer you protection and security. I can provide for you. These are the things I understand—the things I have always believed women wanted. Will you take them, Grace?"

I leaned forward, my head against his shoulder, my arms around him, holding him like a woman drowning, for this was our final chance and we both knew that, once again. Time had cheated us, had forced us along parallel but separate roads, at varying rates of progress, so that we could glimpse and hope and strive but never really meet.

"What must I give you in return?"

"Yourself."

"Which is everything I have. You would not give me

everything, Gideon. Would you allow me to continue my association with the *Star*.''

''Of course not.'' But it was spoken sadly, no rancour, no disgust, no jealousy, just a simple statement of self-knowledge and regret. He *could* not.

''And would you allow me to continue my work with Anna and Patrick Stone?''

''No.''

''Would you receive them here?''

''Grudgingly.''

''Would you expect me to break off with them entirely?''

''Yes, I would expect that. I would try not to enforce it, but if you delayed then I probably would enforce it.''

''Oh, Gideon—''

''Yes, I know,'' he said, his mouth against my hair. ''You see how very carefully I have thought it over, for I am indeed a calculating man. But in this case I am as much a prisoner of my own nature as you are. I cannot rid myself of the belief that if you loved me you would willingly give up your friends and associates for my sake. I know you will not agree, but I cannot feel I am asking too much, or even anything very much at all. I am asking you to be my wife and I am entitled, surely, to my notions of what a wife should be? I am ready to be your husband, which also entails a measure of sacrifice, for if you take me there is every likelihood that my mother—of whom I am very fond and who is getting no younger—will never speak to me again.''

I had no wish to move from the shelter of his arms, would have been grateful, I think, if he had forced me to stay there. But I had asked for freedom of choice. He had given it to me. And I knew by now that the liberty for which I had struggled and on which I would not relinquish my hold could be a cruel burden indeed.

''I love you, Gideon.''

''I wonder what good that is going to do me?''

''Very little, I suppose, unless you can accept me just as I am.''

''Yes, I knew you would say that. I am prepared for it. Go on.''

''And what good will it do?''

''None, I suppose, for you cannot accept me as I am either. But say it.''

''Gideon—you once told me I did not earn my living, that I

had rejected a woman's responsibilities and was not fit to take a man's.''

"I remember.''

"Now I *do* earn my living, or at least now I can see the way to earn it. I can see where my living is and I have the ability—I know I have—to go out and fetch it in. I have taken the risk. I have done the work and continue to do it, whether I feel inclined for it or not; and I spare myself nothing. I may send home my clerk if he has a bad cough or a bad headache, but I do not go home myself, no matter how unwell I might feel, until the work is done. And I want you to respect me for that, Gideon, not for my dinner-parties and my dances, which are only life's frills, after all, and come nowhere near its substance. You could not fill your life with menu cards and invitation cards and small-talk, you know you could not. Neither can I. I want you to believe in my ability, Gideon, and to value it, instead of trying to dismiss it like a child's toy. You have told me of your own early days here in the mills and how difficult it was for you to gain acceptance because they thought your accent too refined and your hands too clean—because you were not a Cullingford man. Can you imagine what it has been like for me—a woman—to gain even a hearing? I have to work ten times harder than a man, I can tell you, just to convince some people that I am actually working at all. And even now I waste hours a day sometimes—hours I cannot spare—with men who are too small-minded to take me seriously, and with women whose peace of mind I seem to threaten. I am ambitious—which is considered unwomanly—and I am not ashamed of it. Whatever I promise I perform, and since women have a reputation for light-mindedness and are generally supposed to break their promises rather freely I have to be very certain of keeping mine, not only to the letter but on time. And in any case I prefer to call these promises 'commitments' which cannot be casually abandoned. You would not abandon yours. I have employed men who have wives and children to feed, and I am responsible for that. I cannot put those families in jeopardy. Neither could you. Could you?''

"I could not.''

"And if I can respect that in you—and find it pleasing—then why can you not respect it in me. I love you, Gideon. If you had married me when I was eighteen I would have been your adoring wife ever after and would never have cast a glance beyond you. For years I wanted exactly the life you wanted, and if we had become lovers before I left Tarn Edge, then—yes—I am sure I would have been here still, with no sense of frustration or regret. I would have made your life my life—would have considered you to *be* my life—and the sad thing is that I would have been happy. I cannot do that now, however much a part of me may still want to—and a part of me does want to—*I* know that I cannot. I am ready to share your life but not to live it at second-hand. I want you to share my life but not to live it for me, not to absorb it into your own or to deny that it even exists. The last time I came to your office I said terrible things to you—it makes me shiver when I remember them—but there was some truth there. I believe men and women should be equal if they are fit to be equal, and I think I am fit to equal you, Gideon, to complement you, to live with you independently but in harmony, to trust you and to deserve your trust—to live together as two *people* who love each other. It should be possible, Gideon—oh, really it should.''

"Yes," he said, his face almost hollow now with fatigue and strain. "I know. And it pains me—I can't tell you how much—to realize that I cannot—"

He got up and went to stand by the fireplace, my body turning cold without him, but before I could follow or call him back to me the door opened and his butler informed him: "The carriage, sir."

"Thank you, Sherston."

The man withdrew, and across the spreading, splintering gulf between us Gideon said, "I ordered the carriage to be ready in an hour. I had no hope, you see, and I thought an hour would be long enough. I took the liberty, too, of sending a message to your house, warning them of your arrival and of the accident to your foot, and they will have all ready for you—even your friend Dr. Stone to attend you."

"Gideon—"

"No more. At least, just this, although I have no right to say it—absolutely none at all. I would not like to see you married to Liam Adair. It has nothing to do with his treatment of me— nothing—"

"I am not going to marry him. There has never been any question of that."

He nodded curtly, his head bowed, half turned away from me, my own face wet, I suddenly realized, with tears, although I could not recall the moment they had begun. Nor could I force any kind of voice at all through my tight throat to ask him when or if or how he could bear to marry Hortense Madeley-Brown.

But he heard my thought and gave what looked like a dismissive, impatient shrug.

"I have gone rather far along that road now to be able to withdraw with honour. You may think her vain and slow, but in fact she is very young and shy and has a good heart. She will—she will *do*. Excuse me, I must say a word to Sherston—"

He did not come back. The butler and two impassive underlings assisted me to the carriage, the housekeeper getting in beside me and giving a masterly performance, all the way to Blenheim Crescent, of a woman who has not the slightest idea that her companion is crying. They helped me down, took me inside, bowed, made some impecable murmurings, and went away.

"What ails you?" said Patrick Stone, not referring to my swollen ankle.

"God knows!"

But I knew. And this time, no matter what anyone told me, I did not expect to recover.

31

I WAS *BUSY*. THAT WAS the only thing I thought about and spoke about. I was frantically, permanently busy.

The Duke of South Erin died that summer, thus further delaying Gideon's wedding and somehow, when the mourning period was over, the engagement was over too, Miss Madeley-Brown or more likely her mother having got wind of a better offer and feeling she had waited for the Chards long enough.

"Poor Gideon has been jilted," Blanche told me, "for the Madeley-Brown has got herself a baronet."

But I had nothing to say about that.

He went abroad soon afterwards, to stay with the Fauconniers in Lyons, the Goldsmiths in Berlin, undoubtedly, Blanche thought, to have another look at the younger Mademoiselle Fauconnier, to cast an appraising eye at a supposedly very promising Goldsmith niece.

"And he had better be quick about it," she declared, "or he will have Aunt Caroline moving herself into Tarn Edge now that the new duchess has moved her out of South Erin."

I had nothing to say about that either.

I was busy. I had so much to do. I had my bright new *Star*, my plans—endless plans—to make it brighter, my desk, my decisions, my authority. *My Star*, increasingly mine, as Liam, who had always preferred a battle to a victory, began somehow to keep his distance.

"There's nothing wrong, Grace," he told me in answer to my sharp enquiry. "Nothing at all. It's just that I'm an odd sort of character, and to tell the truth there are times when I miss the life we had in Gower Street."

"You mean this is all too easy now—too civilized?"

"Is that what I mean? You could be right. You usually are. Yes—I've often thought I'd like to climb a mountain, one hell of a big one, just to prove I could. But the chances are I'd be wondering what the devil to do with myself when I got to the top. I reckon the mountain next-door, or the one next-door to that, might look very good to me.''

But if he preferred to remain Liam Adair of the Gower Street *Star*, I could only respect him for that. And if Monday mornings rarely saw him in the office these days and he took frequent, unexplained trips away, then it suited me just then to be over-burdened, to have more work than I could possibly do and then, by a total concentration of energy and will, to do it, so that I had no time to think of other things.

"My dear, you are losing weight," both Anna Stone and Tessa Delaney told me. I had not noticed it and when I did I had no time to care.

"Dearest, we never see you," gently complained Auth Faith. "Could you not come to tea on Sunday?"

Of course I could not. Good heavens! Sunday was a working day like any other, the only day when I could really sit down and plan my schedules and the schedules I imposed on others for the week ahead. I would have no time for tea.

I suffered a severe chill that November from which I recovered slowly and, succumbing to the combined pressure of my father, Patrick Stone and Camille, I agreed to spend a week in Scarborough. And, having agreed, instantly regretted it, for Mr. Martin was getting too old, Liam too careless, the rest of them had too little experience and too little sense, and I believed their chances of getting along without me to be very slight. Liam took me to the station, laughed at me, kissed me, saw to the bestowal of my luggage and myself in a compartment where—and I knew how poor a safeguard this could be—another lady was already sitting. I wore a sealskin coat with a grey fur trim, a huge fur muff, a dashing Russian hat. I felt cool and purposeful and pleasant. I looked poised, I thought, and expensive, which, in my case and unlike my travelling companion, did not mark me as the wife of a rich man but as a successful woman. I was my own person, in charge of my own life and responsible for the welfare of others. And on the whole, despite an occasional tightness in my chest, a weakness in my legs—the remains of my influenza—I was pleased with myself.

I received a rapturous welcome from Camille, the usual gruff affection from Nicholas Barforth, who entertained us to a spectacular dinner that evening at the Grand, not quite managing to conceal his surprise, which gave way to wry amusement, when he understood I had not known Gervase would be there.

"Did I forget to mention it?" Camille murmured. "Yes, of course I did. I am a disreputable woman, after all, and one can expect no better of me. But since you are both here, then—well— here you both are. You must simply force yourself, Grace, to enjoy it."

Force was by no means necessary. Dinner was exceedingly pleasant, Camille vibrant as always with her happiness, Mr. Barforth entertaining us royally but waiting, just the same, to be alone with her, Gervase smiling his quiet assurance at me as if he knew why I required it. And as the evening drew to its close I did require it, for by my own choice, the complexities of my nature and of my past, I had rejected my own chance of tasting Camille's bliss and did not always care to be reminded of it.

"Nicholas," she said, "it is late—"; the same words, the same spoken caress Mrs. Agbrigg had used to my father and which had threaded themselves so uncomfortably throughout my childhood. But now I understood the joy they offered, the physical harmony I had briefly experienced, and the more complete harmony of the spirit which had always eluded me. And abruptly I was calm and poised no longer, but seemed—among the most substantial glitter of the Grand Hotel—to be falling into a void, a fading away of reality, so that I stood like a wraith, invisible and insubstantial, on the fringes of Camille's humanity, aware of her emotion, her joy, her deep personal fulfilment, the very heat of her body, without being able to touch her; feeling nothing distinctly but a chill air blowing, not around me but through me. And I was horrified.

I managed to walk outside, glad of my expensive fur coat and my dashing Cossack hat to anchor me to the ground, since there seemed nothing heavy enough inside me to withstand the high sea-wind.

"Home now," said Camille, since there was nowhere else in the world she wished to go.

"Grace and I would like to take a walk," Gervase told her easily. "The night is so fine and the stars quite exceptional."

And once their carriage had gone, I collapsed against him as we stood in the shadow of the hotel and burst into tears, not with the ugly, convulsive sobbing of pain but the fast-flowing, unrestrained weeping that brings relief.

"Is this for the past, Grace?"

"I think it must be."

"And for our child?"

"Gervase, I can't speak of that—really, I can't speak of it—"

"I think you must, for it has been inside you too long. Let it go, love—let it go."

And until it was over and I had dried my cheeks and adjusted my hat, and we had strolled away hand in hand along the cliff-path, he had nothing more to say.

"Are you strong enough now, Grace, I wonder?"

"For what?"

"My confession?"

"Lord! I don't think so."

"But I am going to make it. Listen to me, darling—if I could have crossed the room to you that day at Galton instead of hovering in the doorway, and knelt at your bedside—as I wanted to do—and held you and cried a little and asked you to forgive me—because I did blame myself—If I could have done those things, you would have forgiven me, that terrible silence would never have fallen between us, and you would still be my wife—"

"Gervase, you are always telling me what might have been."

"I think I am trying to make amends. I am happy, Grace, and I see that you are not. I am *satisfied*—thoroughly satisfied—with the life I lead, because every facet of my nature is involved in it. I feel that I am using myself to capacity, and it is a rather marvellous feeling. Forgive me, Grace, but it strikes me that you are concentrating all your energies on one side of yourself— which is a most interesting and provocative side, a very challenging side, I admit. But there is another side to you which you seem to have put into some kind of cold storage, my darling. And that saddens me."

"Really?"

"Yes, Mrs. Barforth—really. And there is no point, you know, in taking that brisk tone with me, for I am a gentleman of independent means and not in the least inclined to tremble before the proprietor of the *Star*."

"I suppose you are telling me I need a lover."

"Possibly you do. But what I really wish to say is that if I have hurt you so badly that you are too afraid to risk yourself again, then I must find some way of healing where I have harmed."

"You are taking a great deal upon yourself, Gervase."

"I would take *you*, altogether, if you would have me."

I came to an abrupt halt, finding myself somehow face to face with the cliff wall, a sharp salt wind across my back, my answer coming as naturally and easily as my tears.

"It would not be fair to you, Gervase. If you were in love with me, then perhaps you might be ready to put up with me, but since you are not—"

"Am I not?"

"No. You like me, and I like you, probably better than anyone. But it would take a very grand passion to shift you so much as an inch from your way of life—or me from mine—and you are not a man for grand passions, Gervase."

He smiled and kissed me, very lightly, on the mouth.

"No, thank God! Venetia was the Barforth for grand passions—and Nicholas, as it turns out. I am entirely a Clevedon in matters of the emotions, with my mother's fondness for friendship and—hopefully—something of her talent for it. She is divinely happy with her good friend Julian, you know. Do I not tempt you?"

"From time to time—but not to be mistress of Galton."

He laughed, kissed me again, we laughed together.

"Very well. I accept your refusal. And at the risk of sounding decidedly unromantic I will even confess that I expected it. But I wanted to ask you so that you would know there was an alternative—that you could if you would—"

"I am very glad you did ask me, Gervase."

I was calm again, or calm enough to contemplate our return to Camille's warm and welcoming home, the sight and sound of her joy and the reasons for it, calm enough to endure both her bliss and my own rejection of it—calm enough. And when I came downstairs to breakfast the next morning Gervase had gone.

I stayed the whole week as I had promised, restraining myself from sending more than half a dozen telegrams to Cullingford, marooned in Camille's snug little parlour by the weather which had turned steel grey and intensely cold.

"Let us sit by the fire and keep warm," she said. "That's the great thing." But I had not chosen to live safe and warm, and could not be dissuaded from setting off for Cullingford the following Sunday, despite a heavy fall of snow.

It was from the start a terrible journey, the train bitter cold and sluggish, the changes, first at York and then at Leeds, chilling me to the point of numbness, the Cullingford train departing from Leeds an hour late and then proceeding to exhaust and alarm me by its shuddering, unexplained halts among desolate snowfields, freezing rock-hard as night descended, to receive another burden of snow. The sky, which had been overcast and menacing all day, darkened entirely, robbing me of any sense of time or direction, the world and its ills and injustices reduced ere long to my own physical discomfort, my total isolation, since my compartment had emptied a very long time ago and no one since Leeds had been rash enough to get on board this train.

There would, of course, be no one at the station to meet me—supposing I ever reached it—for no one would expect me to travel on such a day, and if my coachman had stirred himself so far, he would by now have gone home again. There would be no other vehicles available, and unless the roads were blocked with drifting snow, which seemed quite likely, I would have to send the station boy with a note to Blenheim Crescent and spend another freezing, tedious hour in the waiting-room until someone came. And if the roads *were* blocked, then—with the resolution of a woman who has chosen to live alone—I would have to grit my teeth, wrap myself a little tighter in my sealskin coat, and walk.

It was a dark and dangerous night when I reached Cullingford, the snow falling in fine, slanting lines, driven by the wind, the stationmaster, who had not really expected the train to arrive, cross and confused, taking charge of my luggage, but waving me away towards the yard where, miraculously, through the gloom, I saw a solitary carriage waiting. Liam I thought, for who else would dare risk himself and his horses for me in this storm? And hurrying forward, grateful and glad, I was defenceless when Gideon said curtly, "Get in."

"I beg your pardon?"

"Get in. Get in. I've been waiting here since God knows when and I'm frozen to the marrow. Get in. Don't stand and argue."

Where to? I didn't ask him and there was nothing more he seemed inclined to say, his concentration and his skill being required in full measure to handle the reins, for the snow was very deep, Cullingford's steep cobbled streets very treacherous, and I was always passive, it seemed, whenever he chose to kidnap me, or to rescue me. I closed my eyes and went with him, as I had done when he had marched me around his building site at Black Abbey Meadow, when he had carried me to the Leeds train and then to Tarn Edge; as I would have done in my far away girlhood if he had then understood his need to master me. I went with him, not for long, not too far, but pleasurably, almost slavishly, for this was my very secret, my very precious fantasy, my sole indulgence, and would last no longer this time, I supposed, than the others.

Where to? My own front door, my own servants waiting—was I surprised, or disappointed about that?—and then, as we stood in the hall, his face tight and strangely guarded, he said curtly but somehow without anger—with something in his voice I did not recognize, "When you have changed your shoes and whatever else you wish to do, I would appreciate a word."

There was a good fire in the drawing-room, and seeing him installed before it, a brandy glass in his hand, I flew upstairs and down again, seriously incommoded—there is no use in denying it—by the persistent thumping of my heart, that gave rise to a breathlessness I could not hope to conceal.

"Gideon, I must thank you—"

"Must you? There is no need."

"But there is—and I am sure you are wet through. I only hope you will not take cold."

"I shouldn't think so," he said, his faint air of surprise indicating that the Chards did not take cold so easily, if at all. But in fact he looked extremely chilled and I was full of concern for him.

"Well—do have some more brandy, just the same."

"Thank you. I will. Grace—there is something I must tell you."

"Yes?"

But as I waited dry-mouthed, preparing myself to face some new injury—my heart not for a moment abating its giddy, quite painful thumping—he said nothing, set down his glass, picked it up again, refilled it but did not drink, the movements, so very unusual in him, of a man who could not bring himself to speak his mind.

"I knew this would be difficult, but really—indeed it is very hard, Grace, very awkward—"

And looking at him keenly, almost with disbelief, I said, "Gideon—I do believe that you are *nervous*."

"I believe I am—very nervous."

"Lord—what have you done?"

"I have put myself in a damnably difficult situation—and a very delicate one. I have only myself to blame."

"Is it very serious?"

"I fear so. I have staked, perhaps not everything, but a very great deal, on one card, which is not at all my habit. And the truth is I hardly know which way to turn."

But he had turned to me.

"How can I help you, Gideon?"

"Are you sure you want to help me?"

"For goodness sake! Of course I am. It involves money, I suppose?"

"Money is concerned in it—yes."

"And since you do things on such a grand scale, I suppose it must be a great deal more than I have available. I shall have to try and raise the difference from my father."

He picked up his glass again and drank the spirit straight down this time, his head turned away from me so that I could see only his heavy Chard profile and could not read his expression.

"Grace—have I understood aright? Have you just offered me what amounts to everything you have and as much as you can borrow?"

So I had. And what was astonishing about that? It had seemed the most natural thing in the world.

"Well, I shall not go hungry, you know. And I have the very greatest confidence in your ability to pay me back."

"And if I do not?"

"Then you will have a very good reason. And I shall still not go hungry."

"My dear—that is not a businesslike answer. One does not accept these 'good reasons' for the non-payment of a debt in business."

"No. But had it been a simple matter of business you would have gone to Mr. Rawnsley's bank."

"Quite so. And you have not yet asked me why."

"Then tell me."

"I think I am afraid to tell you."

"Gideon—tell me. Nothing could be so bad as that, and if it is, we shall just have to look harder for a solution. If it is failure, and you are afraid of failure, then I can understand, because so am I. And if you have been unscrupulous, then at least I shall not be surprised about it."

"And if I have cheated?"

"Yes. You may have cheated. But I do not think you have done anything mean."

He swung round towards the fire, remained a moment with his back to me, and then turned to face me again.

"Very well. I am entirely in your hands, Grace. I have made Liam Adair an offer—a very substantial offer—for his half of the *Star*. He would be glad to accept it but will not proceed—and

neither will I—unless we have your full agreement. Now then—
you may pronounce my sentence."

I felt so many things, so acutely, all of them crowding me and
filling me, each separate feeling clamouring to be heard above
the others, that I was—most uncharacteristically—speechless, could
do nothing but stare at him, almost deafened now by my thunderous heartbeat, and by so many other things inside me which
seemed to be stirring, rising to the surface, preparing to take
flight. I was about to lose my head, I knew it, to be deliriously
happy or to agonize with despair, to do something huge, something stupendous, some magnificent, gigantic thing which would
alter the whole course of my existence, and I needed just a
moment more of that breathless quiet before it came.

"Adair really wants my offer, Grace," he repeated belligerently,
striding forward and putting hard hands on my shoulders. "I did
nothing to force him or intimidate him. In fact I behaved so well
I amazed him—and me. He wants to go off and find himself
another Gower Street somewhere—he says you know that."

"Yes."

"He says you practically run the place without him now
anyway."

"Yes. I do."

"Then come out of your trance, for God's sake, and listen.
You said you were ready to share your life with me. If I buy into
the *Star*, then I can share it. Grace—I know nothing about
running a newspaper and care even less. I haven't the very
slightest intention of interfering in what you print or don't print,
whose battles you fight, what you condemn—all that is entirely
up to you. All I want is a link between us that people—ordinary
people—can understand, something to salvage my pride, I suppose,
and satisfy the conventions, because I *am* a conventional man
most of the time, and it would be easier for me this way.
Rawnsley and Mandelbaum and Goldsmith would assume *I* was
supporting you—indulging your whim—instead of your father.
And why should you refuse me a harmless compromise when
the people you care about would know different—and when
there's always a chance that, given time, I might be able to
accept it and admit it? I understood you, Grace, when you talked
about two people who loved each other living together in harmony but retaining their separate identities. I understood all
right, but I could see no way to make it work. It needed a link, a
key—something *else*, something I couldn't name, to bind us,
however loosely together. I have it now. It's not ideal but I can

see the way to make it work. Grace, for God's sake, don't just stare at me. Say something, if only to damn me to hell—''

"Yes, Gideon."

"*Grace*. Everything I said to you that day at Tarn Edge is still true. I would prefer you to give all this up and devote yourself to me if I thought there was a chance of it. You may call me jealous, insecure—anything you like—but if I could choose, then I'd choose that—by God, I would!''

"Yes, Gideon.''

"And everything you said is still valid too. It won't always be easy. I'll try, Grace. That's the progress I've made—I'm willing to try and I shall expect you to try damned hard too. And if you say 'yes Gideon' to me once again I may take it very much amiss. Do we have a bargain?''

"How clever you are, Gideon!''

"Yes. But do we have a bargain?''

"In fact you are quite brilliant.''

"I won't deny it.''

"Don't ever deny it, for I mean to tell everybody. You have absolutely overwhelmed me.''

"Ah yes—and for how long? Let me tell you this, Grace Barforth. You have talked a great deal about clever women and how only a strong man is able to cope with one. Very well, I am a strong man and I will readily admit you to be a clever woman. Let us see, shall we, just how you will cope with me?''

"Let us see how we cope with each other—shall we?''

Bemused and tremulous, I put my arms around him, so unaccustomed to this pure joy that it easily took control of me, my whole being luxuriating in it like a sudden burst of sunshine, my spirit altogether triumphant, desiring only to sing his praises, my fear all gone, so that for the first time in my life I was truly at liberty.

"You will take me as your partner then, Grace?''

"Yes, I will.''

"And your lover?''

"Oh yes.''

"And your husband, in due season?''

"Yes. I will even say please to that.''

"And you will trust me?''

"I will.''

"And obey me?''

"Whenever it seems right to me—which may be rather more often than you suppose. Will you obey me?''

"Ah well—it is a little early, I think, for that. Should it ever seem right to me, then I will give it my consideration."

"I suppose that is something."

"It is a very great deal."

"But you will trust me, will you not?"

"That I will. And should I ever be facing bankruptcy, as I led you to believe a few moments ago, then I shall know exactly who to turn to."

"Gideon—how did you know I would come home tonight? You had waited a long time at the station and you were not at all surprised to see me. Yet it would have been more natural—surely—considering the weather, to have stayed in Scarborough. How did you know?"

He lifted me just an inch or two from the ground and we sat down together on the sofa, cosily installed before my good fire, our arms about each other, my heart almost bursting now with the release of that other side of myself which I had so carefully encased in ice.

"How did I know? Because, my darling, I knew you would have 'commitments' tomorrow, and that no matter what the weather or the inconvenience you would wish to be at your desk by eight o'clock—as I shall be at mine."

"Gideon—I think that is probably the most beautiful thing you have ever said to me."

"Ah yes—except that I have flattered you a little too much, of course, since I am usually at my desk by seven."

"How convenient! I can take you to Low Cross in my carriage, can I not, and have plenty of time to go on from there to Sheepgate—in the morning."

He had indeed found a way for us, not an easy one, but what did that matter to us when we both knew that difficulties existed to be surmounted, problems to be solved, mountains to be climbed and then, when one reached their summits, not to be abandoned but cultivated, guarded, nourished. And we would do all these things together, two very individual people who loved each other. It was the only direction in which either of us could go. It was our beginning.